# WHAT SHE WANTS

Cathy Kelly is the author of four other novels – *Never Too Late*, *She's the One*, *Woman to Woman* and *Someone Like You*, all of which were No. 1 bestsellers in Ireland as well as reaching the *Sunday Times* Top Ten. *Someone Like You* was the Parker RNA Romantic Novel of the Year. Cathy Kelly is also a journalist. She lives in Wicklow with her partner and their dog and is currently working on her sixth novel, to be published by HarperCollins in 2002.

For more information about Cathy Kelly, visit her website at www.Cathy-Kelly.com.

# WHAT SHE WANTS

## CATHY KELLY

HarperCollins*Publishers*

This novel is entirely a work of fiction. The names,
characters and incidents portrayed in it are the work of the
author's imagination. Any resemblance to actual persons,
living or dead, events or localities is entirely coincidental.

HarperCollins*Publishers*
77–85 Fulham Palace Road,
Hammersmith, London W6 8JB

www.fireandwater.com

Published by HarperCollins*Publishers* 2001
1 3 5 7 9 8 6 4 2

ISBN 0 00 226174 X

Set in Sabon
Typeset by Rowland Phototypesetting Ltd,
Bury St Edmunds, Suffolk

Printed in Great Britain by
Clays Ltd, St Ives plc

To Francis and Lucy,
with much love.

# ACKNOWLEDGEMENTS

People always want to know if you put real people in books. And the answer, for most writers, is no. But I've found that readers come up to me later and say 'you know that TV reporter woman in the last book, the vindictive, horrible cow with the platinum hair and the lisp? Well, we all know she's meant to be so and so . . .'

This is the sort of comment that makes me go pale with fear. There's no point babbling that you didn't mean it to sound like any particular person. Nobody will believe you. You live in fear of meeting a TV reporter with platinum hair, a lisp and a strong right hook. Which is why I decided to write a book where I could make up things left, right and centre. Just in case anyone in a village in Kerry got upset with the carry-on in the village in my book, I invented my own village.

The other problem with writing fiction is that you do a teeny bit of research and then go off and invent things merrily. This is a problem when the people who've given you the benefit of their experience actually read your book and say, shocked, 'something like that would never happen!'

So apologies to all my friends in Sony Music Ireland in case there's a bit that makes them go pale. I'm sorry, but I just made lots of things up! And thanks to Hugh Murray and to Angela for the detective work.

Writing books involves lots of people and I'm lucky in that I work with some of the nicest book people ever. Thanks to my dear friend and agent Ali Gunn and all at Curtis Brown, especially Carol Jackson, Diana Mackay and Doug Kean. A huge thanks to my editor, Rachel Hore, for her kind words and encouragement. Thanks to Jennifer Parr for making editing such fun, thanks to Fiona McIntosh for all her hard work, unfailing good humour and kindness, thanks to everyone at HarperCollins UK for their incredible efforts, especially Nick Sayers, Adrian Bourne, Victoria Barnsley, Maxine Hitchcock, Anne O'Brien, Jane Harris, Martin Palmer, Moira Reilly, Tony Purdue, Lee Motley, Venetia Butterfield, Phyllis Acolatse, Tilly Ware, Esther Taylor, Leeza Morley, and especially all the sales team who do the really hard work. Thanks also to Tony, Dave and Barry for making the M25 fun, thanks to the RNA for giving me the thrill of winning the Parker RNA Romantic Novel of the Year award (I'm using my gorgeous pens to sign contracts and big cheques for handbags).

Thanks to everyone at HarperCollins Australia for all their support, especially Christine Farmer, Karen-Maree Griffiths and Sarah Ward. Thanks to marvellous Deborah Schneider, and my American family at Dutton, especially Carole Baron, Laurie Chittenden, Seta Bedrossian, Stephanie Bowe and Lisa Johnson.

Thanks to the wonderful people in Gummerus, Empiria, The House of Books, Emece, Bertelsmann, Kadokawa Shoten and Norsk Ukeblad for all their hard work on my behalf.

Thanks to my writer friends who write, phone and send cheering e-mails. Thanks for that go to Kate Thompson, Marian Keyes, Sheila O'Flanagan, Patricia Scanlan, Jenny Colgan and Martina Devlin. Thanks to dear friends like Sarah, Lisa, Susan, Esther, Joanne, Yvonne and LisaMarie for all their support. Thanks to Stella and John O'Connell for dinner parties that would be entire novels on their own! Thanks to my Powerscourt friends, especially Angela and Eddie, thanks to Siobhan O'Reilly for the ballet on the ball lessons, also hi Damyen and Bev!

Thanks and love must go to my family for always being so supportive. Thanks Mum, Francis, Lucy, Anne and Dave. A big hello to Laura, Naomi, Emer and Robert.

Thanks to darling Tasmin who keeps me from turning into a couch potato, and thanks and much love to John for everything.

Finally, a huge thank you so much to the people who read my books. And to all the lovely people who write nice messages on my web site. You have no idea how cheering it is to log on and find people have said kind things. Hope you enjoy this one.

# WHAT
# SHE WANTS

# PROLOGUE

As yet another noisy Cork and Kerry tour bus crunched gears over the hump-backed bridge, belching out diesel fumes, Mary-Kate Donlan closed the door of her chemist shop and locked it. If any Redlion inhabitant wanted either lipstick or flu remedies in their lunch break, they could go without. Ever since her assistant Otis had been on holiday, all she'd managed for her lunch for the past few weeks was a bit of a sandwich munched between customers and she was fed up with it. Today she'd arranged to meet her niece, Delphine, for a leisurely lunch and a chat.

Wrapping her coat around her, she hurried down the village to the Widow Maguire's, a pretty stone pub with window boxes, traditional music sessions twice a week and the best pub food for miles. She ran across the main street, a slim middle-aged woman with plain bobbed hair and not a speck of make-up on her shrewd, inquisitive face. She hurried past 'Lucille's: Fashions For All Occasions' with just a brief glance in the window. Lucille's fashions were always a little on the eccentric side. This week, the window sported plenty of knobbly knitwear in jewel colours, along with one magnificent cruise wear rig out that would probably look fine in the South of France but was a little skimpy for Kerry in October.

She slowed down when she spotted Emmet from the convenience shop ahead of her. A crotchety old bandit with a fondness for porter, Emmet would talk the hind legs off a donkey and made for a very

CATHY KELLY

irritating luncheon companion on account of his tendency to wax
lyrical about the rare ould times as he sank his lunchtime two pints.
When Emmet had nipped into the pub, Mary-Kate speeded up again.
He'd have met some other poor soul by the time she got there, so
she was safe.

'Hello Lara,' she greeted a tall red-haired woman in a stylish
trouser suit who was just climbing out of the sleek silver Mercedes
she'd parked outside the pub.

'Hi,' said Lara warmly. 'How's business?'

'Mad. The place is full of hypochondriacs. I should have bought
shares in a drug company.'

They both laughed. 'How are things going for you?' Mary-Kate
asked.

'Marvellous,' Lara said. 'Just sold the old O'Brien place.'

'Shanrock Castle?' asked Mary-Kate, impressed. A crumbling
castle set in fifty acres of weed-infested parkland, only someone
very rich could have afforded to buy it because they'd need to spend
two fortunes renovating it. 'Another rock star I suppose?' The dis-
trict surrounding Redlion boasted four rock stars, at least six
novelists and one eccentric classical composer. The rock stars all
lived sedate lives while the crazy parties took place at the classical
composer's home. Helicopters bearing Hollywood producers were
always landing on his helipad, trying to get him to write music for
their blockbusters.

'No, an actress this time. I can't name names but she's one of those
who keeps her Oscar in the toilet.'

Mary-Kate grinned. 'They all say that. I'm meeting Delphine for
a sandwich. Do you want to join us?'

Lara said yes just as a battered beetle pulled up and a voluptuous
red-head in a purple velvet coat emerged.

'Hi, girls,' Delphine Ryan greeted her aunt, Mary-Kate, with a kiss
and hugged her old school friend. 'I haven't set eyes on you for ages,
Lara. What's the gossip?'

In the Widows, they discussed everything from the price of property
to the appalling state of the roads.

'There's a pot hole on the Blackglen road the size of a swimming

2

pool and I spend my life avoiding it,' Lara complained. 'If I destroy a wheel on the Merc going into it, I'm going to sue the council.'

'I love the Blackglen Road,' sighed Delphine. 'There's a beautiful old period house out there that Eugene and I would have loved to buy, but it was way beyond our price range. It was fabulous, lovely old fireplaces and a big, sprawling garden with a bit of wood at the back.'

'You mean Kilnagoshell House, the old B & B,' Lara said. 'I sold it six months ago. A woman from Dublin bought it, a widow actually. Virginia Connell is her name and she's lovely. Lonely too, I daresay. You should call out and see her, Mary-Kate.'

'If she doesn't want to meet people, that's her business,' Mary-Kate said wisely. 'It would be wrong to intrude. When she needs people, we'll be here.'

Lara finished her sandwich.

'Must fly, girls. I've got to value the sweetest little cottage on the Killarney Road this afternoon.'

'Not old Gearóid's place?' inquired Mary-Kate. 'Are they selling it or what?'

'Or what, I think,' Lara said. 'Apparently the house will belong to Gearóid's nephew from Britain once they've got probate. God love him,' Lara added with a shudder. 'Gearóid left it in a terrible state. Then, I've got a viewing at the Richardsons' farmhouse. It's a pity they're leaving the village, they're nice people.'

'I should go too,' Delphine said, getting to her feet. 'I've a facial peel, two manicures and a bikini waxing this afternoon. Bye Mary-Kate.' She kissed her aunt goodbye fondly.

'I am going to finish my coffee in peace,' Mary-Kate smiled up at them, her grey eyes warm. 'Age must have its compensations. Take care, girls.'

The two younger women walked outside.

'It's a lovely day, isn't it?' said Lara as they stood for a moment enjoying the pale October sun. 'When the sun shines, Redlion is magical. I think the Richardsons are mad for leaving. I don't know why anyone would ever want to sell up and leave.'

'I know what you mean,' Delphine said, gazing fondly up the

winding main street where pastel-coloured houses appeared to doze lazily in the sunlight. 'It's got a healing, comforting sense to it or does that sound crazy?'

'Not at all,' Lara said ruefully. 'I was on ten cups of coffee, one Prozac and at least half a bottle of wine a day when I lived in Dublin. Since I came home, I've discovered the calm side of myself.'

'Lara Stanley calm!' teased Delphine. 'That'll be the day.'

Lara grinned. 'Calmer, then,' she said. 'But it is down to this place. It is special. You know, when I left my job in Dublin, all my colleagues thought I was mad burying myself back in the country. "Dullsville" they called it. And I told them there's nothing dull about Redlion.'

'We could do with a bit of dull,' Delphine pointed out. 'Too much happens round here. There's going to be another one of those political think tanks in the hotel next week and the place will be swarming with media and politicians desperate to get their faces in the paper. And Mrs Rock Star up the road was in having her nails done yesterday and she told me they're having a huge party for the album launch in November.'

'All go as usual,' Lara said. 'So much for the quiet life in the country. Still, I don't want to tell the people in the city what it's really like here or else they'd all up sticks and move down.'

Delphine laughed. 'And we want to keep Redlion a secret, don't we?'

# CHAPTER ONE

Hope Parker let the shopping bags sit in a heap at her feet as she stood in front of the cookery books section. Her eyes flicked past *Perfect Cakes*, *The Definitive Chinese Cookbook*, *Catering for Parties* and *Easy Meals*. A recipe book full of easy meals was not what she was looking for. They were all she ever cooked in the first place. No, she wanted a comprehensive and simple cooking book, something big, fat and informative and full of explanations of what a bain marie really was and precisely what you did with yeast and did you have to have an airing cupboard handy when you cooked with it? That was all she wanted: a book that would finally explain how to cook something that didn't involve chicken pieces and a can of ready-to-go tomato sauce.

Her gaze moved past a massive advanced French cooking manual and she leaned closer to the shelves, trying to ignore the bookshop's lunchtime rush. Then she spotted it, a fat tome with bright gold writing on the spine: *Cooking for Cowards: Become the Queen of Your Kitchen.*

Queen of her kitchen? Yes, that was exactly what Hope wanted. No more ready-made lasagne and frozen solid stuffed chicken dinners in tinfoil. But lots of home-cooked meals that would have Matt beaming from ear to ear, no longer able to tease that he never put on weight because she couldn't cook.

Hope pulled it free from the other books and stared at the cover, hoping there was no mention of the word 'advanced'. There wasn't. Instead, there was a picture of an ordinary looking woman standing smiling behind a veritable feast of glistening, delicious food.

Hope flicked inside and found an introduction that was funny, easy to understand, and made no mention of buying complicated utensils before you started. She couldn't afford to buy lots of new pots and pans and strange things for chopping up herbs.

'Cooking really is easy,' cooed the introduction. 'If you're one of those people who've never had the chance to learn, then let me show you how, the easy way.'

There was no implication that you had to be a twenty-something newly-married to be buying this book, no implication that thirty-seven-year-old women should be ashamed of themselves to be purchasing a cookery bible that included a section on 'how to buy meat'.

Hope never bought meat from the butchers'. She never knew what to ask for or even what you'd do with rack of lamb if you got it. She bought her meat ready packed from the supermarket where nobody could look down on you for not knowing what a gigot was.

'There's no need to be scared of buying meat,' continued the introduction, as if the writer had read Hope's mind. 'It's easy once you know how.'

Sold. Hope collected her shopping, paid for the book and hurried up to Jolly's department store, already lost in the fantasy of being a superb cook. Imagine the dinner parties they could have: Matt wouldn't have to entertain important advertising clients on his expense account in Bath's elegant restaurants any more. Instead, he could bring them home, and she, dressed in something elegant but sexy, would waft out of the kitchen with the scent of crème brulée clinging to her while jaded businessmen gobbled up melt-in-the-mouth things in delicately flavoured gravy, asking her why she'd decided to work in a building society instead of starting up her own restaurant?

And Toby and Millie would love it. Well, when they were older, they would. They'd think that home-made chutney and made-from-scratch mayonnaise were the norm and would smugly tell their school-

mates that their mother was the 'best cook in the world, so there!'
Hope remembered this type of culinary boasting from her own school-
days. But she and her sister, Sam, had always stayed out of the 'whose
mother is the best cook' arguments, knowing that whatever could be
said about their aunt Ruth, that she was an excellent cook wasn't
one of them. Hope wondered, as she often did, if her mother had
been any good at cooking? Aunt Ruth had never talked about things
like that. Maybe Mum had been a wonderful cook. It might even be
genetic: all Hope had to do was move beyond instant chicken sauces
to discover that she was the next Escoffier.

In Jolly's, she got sidetracked in the women's department. She
couldn't resist stopping a moment to finger the pretty floral skirt,
running her fingers wistfully over the soft cotton with the delicate
sprigged pattern of roses. In the middle of all the new season's dark
wintry clothes, the rail of prettily patterned skirts had stood out like
a wildflower meadow in a landscape of muddy ploughed fields.

Feeling the plastic grocery bags threatening to cut off the circulation to her left hand, Hope unhooked them from her wrist before
indulging in a proper examination of the garment. The background
colour was the pale blue of delicate Wedgwood with tiny lilac flowers
mingling with tiny raspberry pink ones. Hope sighed wistfully. This
wasn't a skirt, it was a lifestyle. A lifestyle where the wearer lived in
a pretty cottage with lovely, well-behaved children, cats, maybe a
rabbit or two, and an adoring husband who appreciated her. This
woman sewed her own cushion covers, knew how to dry lavender
and could bottle fruits and vegetables instead of buying them from
the supermarket. She didn't need a safety pin to hold the top of her
skirt together and she never raised her voice at the children in the
morning when an entire carton of milk was spilled all over the said
children's clothes, necessitating a complete change. No. This woman
wore floral perfumes that came in old-fashioned bottles, never got
angry with her children and wafted around with a basket as she
bought organic vegetables that still had bits of earth clinging to them.
People would say things like 'Isn't she lovely? Wonderful mother,
fantastic cook, have you tried her apple crumble? And she still manages to work . . .'

Yeah right. And pigs might fly. Hope patted the skirt one last time and picked up her shopping. She wasn't Mrs Floral Skirt and she never would be. She was Mrs Tracksuit Bottom, whose two children were quite accustomed to her roaring 'Stop that right now or I'll kill you!' She never wafted anywhere – difficult when you had a spare tyre and stocky legs – and she never talked to the neighbours long enough for them to have an opinion of her. Apart from the woman two doors up who let her dog do its business in Hope's garden, resulting in an un-neighbourly stand-off one morning. And as for sewing cushion covers she still hadn't managed to sew the button back on her work skirt and it had been held up with a safety pin for months. Although the good part of that was that the safety pin was of the big nappy variety and was more comfy than the constricting button had been. Thinking of work, she'd be terribly late back if she didn't get a move on.

She shook her head as if to rid it of the remnants of the idyllic floral skirt fantasy and, collecting up her shopping, hurried into the men's department and over to the ties. It took ages to find one she thought Matt would like: an expensive buttermilk yellow silk with a discreet pattern. Hope held the tie up against every shirt on the display; it looked lovely against the blue shirts and went particularly well with an azure striped one. She groaned in indecision.

Matt didn't go in for blue shirts much. The grey tie was more versatile, definitely, and cheaper, but Matt loved expensive things. He'd adored that ugly key ring his boss had given him one Christmas, purely because of the designer logo stamped into the leather. She held both ties up and squinted at them, dithering as usual.

OK, the yellow it had to be. So, it cost more than the coat she was wearing, but what the hell.

The woman behind the counter daintily placed the tie in a box. Perfectly coifed, she had lovely cared-for nails, Hope noticed, and her lipstick looked faultlessly applied; as if she'd just that minute rushed out from primping in the ladies'. Hope was conscious of the fact that her own windswept fair hair was dragged back in a pony tail and her morning lipstick a thing of distant memory.

Sales assistants invariably made her feel like an unkempt road warrior. She remembered a time when she herself was always beautifully groomed, those far off days before the children, when giving herself a French manicure had been a prerequisite on Sunday evenings. These days, she spent Sunday evenings sweating over the ironing board, worrying about the week ahead and trying to match socks from the enormous laundry pile.

'Is it a present?' inquired the sales woman, her tone implying that there was no way someone like Hope would be coughing up for such an expensive tie otherwise.

'Yes,' said Hope, stifling a wicked urge to say, no, it was for her, she dressed up in men's clothes at the weekends and, actually, was looking for a partner to go with her on a Harley-Davidson-Lesbian Day Out on Sunday.

Instead, she arranged her face into a polite expression. Being honest, there was no way she'd pay that much money for a tie otherwise. Even if as a fortieth birthday present, it was still ridiculously expensive. The only consolation was that Matt would love it. It would go with the very sophisticated new suit he'd just bought and with his image, also highly sophisticated. The only unsophisticated part of the Matt Parker experience was Hope herself. Was that the problem? she thought with a pang of unease.

Matt hadn't been himself lately. Usually he was one of life's optimists, happy, upbeat. But for the past few months, he'd been listless and moody around the house, only content if they were doing something; filling their time off with endless activities. He didn't seem happy to sit and blob around on those rare occasions when the children weren't murdering each other. Edgy, that was it. Matt was edgy, and in her dark, terrified moments, Hope was scared that it was something to do with their marriage. Or her.

'Shall I gift-wrap it?'

'No, I like wrapping things myself,' Hope confessed. Anyway, getting the shop to wrap things was always a waste of time, she'd discovered, as she could never resist trying to open a bit of the wrapping paper when she got home so she could admire the gift. Invariably, the paper got ripped when she was trying to shove whatever it was back in, so why bother?

She added the tie to her selection of plastic bags and left the shop hurriedly.

Hope rounded the corner at Union Street and collided with a gaggle of tourists oohing and ahhing over the city's elegant sandstone Georgian buildings. It was a beautiful place to live but after five years there, Hope was guiltily aware that she took Bath's beauty rather for granted. For the first six months, she'd walked around with her neck craned, but now, she raced along like all the other residents, almost immune to the city and constantly cursing the tourists who straggled across the streets like wayward schoolchildren. She pushed open the glass door into Witherspoon's Building Society, conscious of the fact that it was now twenty to three and she should have been back at half past two.

Mr Campbell, manager and assiduous time-keeper, was also conscious of the time.

'You're ten minutes late, Mrs Parker,' he said mildly.

Hope gave him a flustered look, which wasn't hard after her dash down Union Street. 'I'm so sorry, Mr Campbell,' she said breathily. 'It's my husband's fortieth birthday and I was buying him a present . . .'

'Never mind,' Mr Campbell said soothingly. 'Don't let it happen in future.'

She rushed into the staff room, stowed her shopping in her locker, wriggled out of her navy woollen coat and hurried back to her counter.

'How can you get away with being late and not get the face eaten off you by that tyrant?' demanded Yvonne. Yvonne had worked at Witherspoon's for five years, the same length of time as Hope, and complained she was still treated like a delinquent probationary by the manager.

'Because I have an innocent face,' replied Hope, managing to smile all the while at Mr Campbell, 'and you look like a minx.'

Yvonne was placated, as Hope knew she could be. Yvonne liked the idea of looking minxy. And she was so good humoured that she never took offence; not like Betsey, Hope's other good friend. Betsey took offence at everything and would have demanded to know what Hope had meant by calling her a minx.

Hope knew that she'd never look like a minx in a million years. Minxes did not have fawn-coloured curly hair with lots of wispy tendrils that you could do absolutely nothing with, nor did they have rounded comforting faces with large, almost surprised hazel eyes, and small delicate mouths like shy girls from 18th century French paintings.

Matt had once told her that he'd fallen in love with her 'other worldliness'. 'As if you've got lost from a historical mini-series and have stepped out of your gown to appear in the twenty-first century,' he'd said lovingly. Matt was given to saying wildly romantic, unusual things. He was wasted in advertising, she thought fondly.

All five counters were frantically busy for the next half an hour, with huge groups of time-pressed tourists arriving to change their traveller's cheques into hard currency, all frantic to get some cash so they could buy huge quantities of Bath Abbey tea towels, T-shirts with the Abbey printed on them and decorated mugs before they were due back on the coach.

Finally, there was a brief lull in custom. Hope sat back in her chair, feeling drained and wondered how she'd last till her four o'clock tea break.

'What did you buy for Matt?' asked Yvonne, sneaking a forbidden packet of toffees across to Hope. Eating was forbidden behind the counter but Hope reckoned her blood sugar needed a top-up.

'A tie, a bottle of that wine he likes and some aftershave,' she said as she surreptitiously unwrapped a toffee.

'That's nice,' mumbled Yvonne, her mouth full.

They chewed in silence for a while and Hope began to mentally plan her evening, the highlight of which was to be Matt's special birthday dinner. Just the two of them, assuming that Millie didn't kick up a fuss and refuse to go to bed. She was only four but she already ruled the Parker household with a chubby little iron hand in a velvet glove. Two-year-old Toby was such a contrast to his older sister. He was so quiet that Hope worried about him being at the day nursery every day. She knew Millie was well able to stand up to anyone who'd look sideways at her but would she stand up for Toby? You heard so much about children bullying other kids and Hope

11

would kill any child who'd hurt her beloved Toby. With his pale, sweet face and watchful eyes, he reminded her of herself as a child. She prayed he'd grow up to be stronger and more forceful, like his father.

'Presents for men are so difficult,' sighed Yvonne. 'I love the idea of those women who say things like "I'm wearing your present." You know she's wearing some basque or suspenders and stockings and that's his present. I might try that with Freddie.'

'Lovely,' said Hope automatically, a bit embarrassed to be getting so much detail about Yvonne's sex life. Yvonne was twenty-nine, Welsh, and very open about everything, in direct contrast to Hope. Hope liked to keep her personal life personal, although it was difficult when you worked with someone as inquisitive as Yvonne, who was quite capable of asking questions like what would Hope do if Matt ever had an affair or had Hope ever used a Dutch cap.

'Er, no,' Hope had said, going pink, on that particular occasion. Aunt Ruth had not brought her up to be chatty about sex and things like that. When she'd had her first period, Aunt Ruth had said nothing but had given her a book on girls growing up. Well, she'd actually shoved it into Hope's hand and gone off abruptly to her bridge class. The subject had never been referred to again. Hope was fascinated when she read those 'how to keep your sex life alive' articles in women's magazines, although she'd never have dreamed of trying any of it out with Matt.

'You should give Matt that sort of present tonight,' Yvonne nudged her.

'What sort of present?'

Yvonne lowered her voice because Mr Campbell had come out of his office and was standing near the photocopier. 'Wear something sexy and tell Matt it's the final bit of his present.'

'Honestly, Yvonne,' whispered Hope, 'you've a one-track mind.'

'Yeah, one track and it's a dirt track,' giggled Yvonne, flicking back a bit of jet-black poker-straight hair.

Three customers arrived all at once and Hope managed to put Yvonne's suggestion out of her mind. It wasn't that she was contemplating wearing sexy underwear and surprising Matt. She was uncomfortably aware of the fact that Matt would probably be much happier with a new tie and a decent bottle of wine.

Two hours later, she'd braved the traffic going out of the city towards Bristol and was turning into Maltings Lane. One of the more modern streets in Bath, it was a winding road of pretty houses built in the fifties with honey-coloured Cotswold stone. Because the houses were small and reasonably priced, the street was full of young, professional couples with small children, two cars and no time for doing their handkerchief-sized gardens.

When they'd moved in five years ago, Hope had had great plans for becoming a gardening expert and had bought a gardening encyclopaedia along with a book dedicated to creating a haven from a small suburban plot. These books were currently jammed into the bookcase on the landing, alongside the home decorating book she'd got in a jumble sale. Hope rarely even looked at their patch with its overgrown sliver of lawn and weed-encrusted rockery where four stunted conifers sat huddled together in tight misery and refused to grow taller than six inches. Hope didn't look at the garden tonight either: she was too late even for her usual guilt-laden 'I wish I had time to do something with the garden this weekend'.

Marta would be furious if she picked the kids up after six fifteen. Marta ran Your Little Treasures, the nursery where Toby and Millie spent every week day. The nursery was so well-run and well-staffed that Hope couldn't afford to voice the opinion that Marta herself was a bad-tempered bitch when it came to dealing with her charges' parents. There was such fierce competition for places in YLT that she daren't risk antagonizing her. If Hope's children left the nursery, there would be thirty families queuing up to fill their places. 'Marta is definitely short for martinet,' joked Matt every time Hope came home on the verge of tears because of a dressing down from Marta for being late. Matt didn't understand how Hope hated those confrontations.

The nursery closed at six fifteen and any parent who arrived a second later was treated to a lecture of the 'if you think I'm going to be taken advantage of, you've got another think coming' variety.

Hope couldn't imagine a single person who'd dare take advantage of Marta. Pity.

She unpacked the shopping from the Metro's boot. Next door's cat sat plaintively on Hope's doorstep, sheltering from the icy late September wind and generally giving the impression that he was a candidate for an animal shelter despite being so fat that he no longer fitted through his cat flap and had to be let in through the windows. Hope dragged the shopping to the door, hoping that a few hours in the locker at work hadn't made the milk go off.

'You can't come in, Fatso,' Hope told the cat, trying to open the door and insinuate herself inside without letting him in. She managed it, dumped the shopping on the kitchen floor and looked at her watch.

Six o'clock on the nail. She wasn't going to be late. Relieved, she shoved the milk into the fridge and raced out of the house.

She hurried round the corner to the nursery which was, as usual, surrounded by double-parked cars, weary parents and cross toddlers. Hope had found it was easier to walk there instead of spending ten minutes trying to park.

'Hello,' she said with false cheeriness to Marta, who stood like a rottweiler at the door, grimly working out whom to bite and whom to suck up to. 'Cool isn't it?'

'It is nearly October,' Marta snapped, gypsy earrings rattling furiously.

Hope grinned inanely and then hated herself for it. If only she had the guts to tell Marta where she could stuff her sarcastic remarks. Not for the first time, Hope indulged in her favourite daydream; where she and Matt had won the lottery, thereby allowing her to give up work and devote herself to the children full time. In her fantasy dream world, being a full time mum included help from a cleaning lady, an ironing lady and someone to trail round the supermarket doing the grocery shopping. It also meant being able to tell Marta to take a running jump because Hope wouldn't need the nursery any more. She'd look after her children herself, thank you very much. She'd be able to spend hours every day with them, doing finger painting, making up stories and doing things with cooking chocolate and Rice Krispies when the children could help stir the mixture without her shuddering at the thought of cleaning bits of cereal and slivers of chocolate off the kitchen floor for hours afterwards. She'd get to serve wonderful home-cooked food instead of making do with convenience stuff, she'd learn needlecraft and the garden would be a riot of beautifully tended plants. Bliss.

In the main section of the nursery, a bright cheery room decorated in warm colours and with plenty of toddler-sized furniture, Millie and Toby were waiting for her, clad in their padded coats and looking like baby Eskimos. Dark-haired Millie, as impatient as her father, had an outraged expression on her rosy-cheeked face. Her brown eyes flashed at the indignity of being made to wait in a restricting coat when she could have been in the play corner wreaking havoc with the bouncy cubes. Toby, pale like his mother, stood quietly with his hat in his hand. When he spotted Hope, a great smile opened up his chubby little face.

'Mummy, 'got a star,' he said delightedly.

'No you didn't,' said Millie indignantly. Even at four, she had a perfect command of the English language. 'I got a star.'

Toby's face fell.

'Millie,' said her mother reprovingly. 'Be nice to your little brother.'

'He's a baby,' sniffed Millie, wrinkling up her snub nose.

'He's your brother,' Hope said. 'You have to look after him, not be unkind to him.'

Millie took Toby's fat little hand in hers and looked up at her mother expecting praise.

Despite herself, Hope grinned. Millie was as bright as a button.

She said goodbye to Marta, who was hovering with intent outside the door, jangling her keys like a warder.

Holding hands, the family walked slowly home: Millie chattering away happily, Toby silent. It was the same every evening. Toby was very quiet for about half an hour, then, as if he'd been frozen and finally thawed out in the warmth of his own, safe home, he began to talk and laugh, playing with his favourite toy, currently a violently purple plastic train with endless carriages that were always getting lost under the furniture. It worried Hope. She was afraid that he

15

hated the nursery, yet she was just as afraid of asking him in case he clung to her and begged her not to send him every morning.

One of the women at work had gone through two horrific months of her small daughter doing just that, sobbing her little heart out every day, begging her mother to 'stay, Mummy, stay, please!' until she was hiccuping with anguish.

The mothers with young children had all sat in silent guilt when they heard that story in the canteen.

'I hate leaving my son,' a single mother from accounting had said tonelessly.

'Men just don't feel it the same way,' added an investment advisor who was also a mother-of-three.

They had all nodded miserably, united in agreement.

After that, Hope had spent weeks anxiously scanning Toby's face every morning for signs that he was about to cry. If he did, she knew she'd have told the building society to stuff their job and told Matt they'd have to manage the mortgage some other way, because she couldn't bear to go out to work when her darling little boy was sobbing his little heart out for her. But Toby never cried. He went off every morning, snug in his anorak, big eyes wide when Hope gave him a tight hug goodbye with Marta watching over them.

'He's just a quiet little boy,' Clare, one of the teachers, had reassured her when Hope had voiced her fears, 'but he enjoys himself, honestly, Hope, he does. He loves playing with the Plasticine and he loves story time. We all know he's a shy little fellow so we really look after him, don't worry. Millie is totally different, isn't she?'

Yes, Hope had agreed, Millie was totally different. Boisterous and confident compared to her little brother. They reminded Hope of herself and Sam when they'd been kids: Hope had been the quiet, placating sister, while Sam, three years older, had been strong, opinionated and sure of herself.

Tonight, Millie wasn't inside the hall door before she was off into the playroom to collect her dolls, bossing them around, telling them to drink their milk and no being naughty or there'd be trouble. She sounded a lot like Marta bossing the parents around. Hope got down on her knees to undo Toby's coat.

'Did you have a nice day, sweetie?' she asked softly, helping him wriggle out before pulling him close for a big cuddle. Toby nodded his head. Hope planted a kiss on his soft, fair head, breathing in the lovely toddler scent of him. He smelled of classroom, baby shampoo and fabric conditioner.

'Mummy loves you, Toby, do you know that? Loads and loads of love. Bigger than the sea.'

He smiled at her and patted her cheek with one fat little hand.

'Mummy has to make a special birthday dinner for Daddy but I think we have to play first, don't you?'

Toby nodded again.

'Shall we have a story? What one would you like me to read? You pick.'

The three of them sat on the big oatmeal sofa, cuddled up companionably, as Hope read Toby's favourite story about *The Bear With The Magical Paw*. Millie always started by saying it was a baby's story, not for big girls like herself, but by the end of the first page she was engrossed, chewing her bottom lip anxiously and listening to the bear's adventures. Hope followed the magical bear with *The Little Mermaid*, which was Millie's favourite. She slept in Disney *Little Mermaid* pyjamas and her bedroom was a shrine to Mermaid merchandising.

After twenty minutes when she knew she should have been starting Matt's birthday dinner, Hope finished the story and began to make dinner for the kids. They were fed tea at the nursery at around half four but Hope never considered a few sandwiches enough for them. Children needed hot food in her book. As the children played, Hope prepared chicken breasts and vegetables, thinking that if she was Mrs Floral Skirt, she'd be giving them organic carrot purée made from her own carrots with delicious home-made lasagne or something equally made-from-scratch.

Mind you, Millie hated home-made food and was passionate about fish fingers and tinned spaghetti shaped like cartoon characters so there wouldn't have been any hope of her eating anything organic.

Hope thought proudly of her new cookbook still in its plastic bag in the hall. Soon, she'd be making fabulous meals that everyone would love. She undid the cling film covering the steaks. The instructions looked simple enough but steak was so difficult, so easy to ruin and cook until it tasted like old leather. She'd have loved it if they were going out to dinner instead but Matt's colleague and best friend, Dan, was organizing a birthday dinner on Thursday, in three days' time, and that was going to be his party. The agency had netted a huge new account and it was going to be a joint celebration. Hope knew it would be childish to say that she'd prefer a private birthday dinner with just the two of them. After all, Matt was a much more social animal than she was and he loved the idea of a big bash where he could charm them all and get told he was the cleverest ad man ever. Hope always felt a bit left out at these fabulous advertising parties. Even though, as a working mother with two small children, she was the Holy Grail for advertisers, they weren't nearly as interested in her when she was physically present as they were when she was represented as the target market on a graph in the office.

She'd better buy a dress for the party, she reminded herself. Adam, Matt's boss, had a new glamorous wife, Jasmine (Matt had, in an unguarded moment, described her as 'better than any of the women on *Baywatch*'), so Hope planned to doll herself up to the nines for the occasion.

Thinking of the party to come, she dished up dinner for the children and brought it and a cup of tea for herself to the table.

'Dinner! Toby and Millie,' she called.

The dinner routine involved Toby and Millie sitting opposite each other at the small kitchen table so that Millie couldn't reach Toby's mug of milk and spill it. Their mother sat at the end, refereeing. Millie, as usual, played with her food and demanded fish fingers in between sending bits of carrot skidding across the table. Toby loved his food and ate quickly, his Winnie the Pooh plastic fork scooping up bits of cut-up chicken rapidly. He drank his milk and ate his entire dinner while Millie bounced Barbie backwards and forwards in front of her plate, singing tunelessly and ignoring her meal.

'Millie!' remonstrated Hope as Barbie kicked a bit of chicken onto the floor. 'Eat up or I'm going to have to feed you.'

She whisked Barbie from Millie's hand and the little girl immediately started to roar. More bits of chicken hit the deck.

'Millie! That's so naughty,' said Hope, trying to rein in her temper and wishing she didn't feel so tired and cross. So much for quality time with the kids.

At this point, Millie wriggled off her chair and pushed herself away from the table, jerking it and spilling her mother's cup of tea.

'Millie!' shouted Hope as scalding tea landed on her uniform skirt, which she knew she should have changed as soon as she got home.

'I always know I'm in the right house when I hear screaming as soon as I get home,' said Matt caustically, appearing at the kitchen door looking immaculate and out of place in the small kitchen which was always untidy.

Hope ground her teeth. This wasn't the homecoming she had planned for his birthday. Candlelight, the scent of a succulent dinner and herself perfumed and in grape velvet had been the plan. Instead, the scene was chaos and herself a frazzled, frizzled mess scented only with perspiration from running round the shops at lunchtime. Children and romantic, grown-up dinners were mutually exclusive, there was no doubt about it.

Millie stopped wailing instantly and ran to her father, throwing her rounded baby arms around his knees and burying her face in his grey wool trousers.

'Daddy,' she cooed delightedly, as if she hadn't just been flinging her dinner around the room like a mischievous elf moments before.

He picked her up and cuddled her, the two dark heads close together, one clustered with long curls, the other a short crop with spreading grey at the sides. Matt was tall, rangy and lean, with the sort of dark, deep set eyes that set female pulses racing and a solid, firm jaw that had stubborn written all over it. The scattering of discreet grey in his new, very short haircut suited him, transforming his handsome good looks into something more mature and sexier. Even after seven years together, the sight of him all dressed up with his eyes crinkling into a smile and that strong mouth curving upwards slowly, could set Hope's heart racing. The terrible thing was, she didn't think that his pulse still raced when he saw her.

'Are you in trouble with Mummy?' Matt asked.

Millie managed a strangled sob. 'Yes,' she said sadly.

'She wouldn't eat her dinner, she was throwing it everywhere and she's just spilled my tea,' Hope said, knowing she sounded shrewish but unable to help it.

'Never mind,' Matt said easily without even looking at his wife. 'It's only a bit of tea, you can wash it.'

Still cuddling Millie, he ruffled Toby's hair and walked into the living room, his big body cradling Millie easily. Toby clambered off his seat and ran after him. In seconds, the sounds of giggling and laughter could be heard.

Hope looked glumly down at her cream uniform blouse which was now stained with splashes of tea. One corner had escaped from her skirt and hung out untidily. Very chic. Ignoring the tea things, she went upstairs and stripped off her uniform. She'd have to sponge the skirt because she only had two and the hem was down on the other one. In her part of the wardrobe, she found the grape velvet two-piece and pulled it on. She brushed her hair, put on her pearl earrings and spritzed herself with eau de cologne, all without looking in the mirror. It was only to apply her lipstick that she sat at the small dressing table and adjusted the oval mirror so she could see herself.

She was old fashioned looking, she knew. Not the showily beautiful and spirited leading lady of romantic novels: instead, she was the quiet, sober Austen heroine with expressive, anxious grey eyes. Empire line dresses would have suited her perfectly because she could have shown off her generous bosom and hidden the slightly thick waist and sturdy legs. She looked her best in soft, muted colours that complemented the thick-lashed, eloquent eyes. Her grape outfit fitted the bill, while the dark navy and maroon of her uniform clothes made her look dull and middle-aged.

Now she put lipstick on and pinned her hair up. Piled up, it showed off her slender neck. Finished, she touched the small silver and enamel pill box on the dressing table for luck. It had been her mother's and touching it for luck was as much a part of Hope's day as brushing her teeth after meals. She didn't remember her mother so the box with its orchid illustration was special, the only thing she'd got left really. Sam had a matching box only hers had a picture of a pansy on it.

The pillboxes were among the only things they had of their mother's. She and their father had been killed when the girls were small, when they'd been driving home from a night out and their car had been hit by a drunk driver. Their father had been killed outright but their mother had lived long enough to be taken to hospital and died soon after. Not that Sam or Hope remembered much about it and Aunt Ruth, left to bring them up in her austere house in Windsor, had been very keen on 'not dwelling on things' and had disposed of most of their parents' personal belongings. Consequently, they had very few mementoes of Camille and Sandy Smith. Except that Millie was named for her grandmother. Dear naughty little Millie.

Hope smiled and wondered what she'd leave her children to remember her by if she died suddenly: a dirty dishcloth or a basketful of ironing probably.

Downstairs, Matt was watching CNN with the children sitting either side of him, both utterly content. Hope stood behind the sofa and planted a kiss on his head.

'Sorry I was a grump when you came in,' she said softly. 'Let's get this pair to bed and I'll make you a lovely birthday dinner.'

'Daddy, you have to read me a story,' said Millie querulously, knowing that the treat being discussed didn't involve her.

'I will, honey,' Matt said absent-mindedly, still watching the news.

'A long story,' Millie said, satisfied. 'Really long, about trolls and fairies . . .' She shuddered deliciously.

'No trolls,' Hope said automatically. 'You'll have nightmares.'

'I won't,' insisted Millie.

'No trolls,' said her mother firmly.

Matt did his bedtime story duty and when he came downstairs, the steaks were sizzling deliciously under the grill and Hope was wrestling with a recipe for herb and garlic butter she'd found in a women's magazine. Fresh herbs, honestly. Who could be bothering with fresh herbs when they cost so much in the shops and went limp and tasteless after two days.

'Smells good,' Matt said, returning to his seat in the sitting room.

He flicked around with the remote and found the sports channel. Through the double doors between the sitting room and the kitchen, Hope could see him put his feet up on the coffee table. He'd changed from his suit into his oldest jeans and a faded sweatshirt she could have sworn she'd thrown out. She shrugged. It was his birthday, he could wear what he wanted to.

She took in the bottle of special birthday wine, eager for praise. 'Will you open it?' she asked, producing the madly expensive cork-screw that Matt had seen in a restaurant and had insisted on sending off for.

'Yeah,' he said absently, still watching the TV. He opened the bottle and he handed it back to her. When she'd poured two glasses and assured herself that the steak was getting along fine without her, she returned, gave Matt his glass and curled up beside him on the sofa.

'Nice day?' she asked.

Matt grunted in return.

Hope tried again. She was absolutely determined they were going to have a lovely coupley evening in for his birthday. She adored nights like this. She and Matt having a companionable dinner together and their beloved children asleep upstairs – that was what happy families were all about. She knew it, she insisted on it.

But Matt was having none of it. He watched the television intently, his lean body sunk back against the sofa cushions, his handsome face in profile with his eyes hooded as he concentrated.

After a few more of Hope's attempts at conversation, he sighed and asked when dinner was.

'Now, soon,' Hope said, jumping off the sofa and heading back into the kitchen.

She lit the candles on the kitchen table, repositioned the burgundy linen napkins someone had given them when they'd got married and dished up the second dinner of the day.

Instinctively, Matt appeared as soon as his plate landed on the matching burgundy linen mat. He dug in hungrily.

'This is lovely, isn't it?' Hope said.

'Mm,' grunted Matt, one eye still on the television which was visible from his seat at the table. News had been replaced by the monotonous roar of motor racing.

He cut his steak into small pieces so he could fork it up without missing a bit of the action.

'Is everything all right?' Hope asked.

'Yeah, it's lovely. Nice bit of steak,' he replied.

'I didn't mean the steak.'

Matt sighed and took his eye off the TV for a brief moment. 'Hope, do we have to have one of these "is everything OK?" conversations tonight? I'm tired, I've had a hard day and I'd like to relax if that's not too much to ask.'

Her eyes brimmed.

'Sure, fine.'

The commentator's voice droned on and Hope ate her meal mechanically, not tasting anything, worrying.

There was something wrong, she knew it. Had known it for weeks. Matt wasn't happy and she was sure it was nothing to do with his job. It had to be personal, something about him and her, something terrible.

He'd been depressed since his favourite uncle had died in Ireland two months ago, and at first, Hope had thought Matt was feeling guilty because he hadn't seen Gearóid for years. Matt's family were terrible for keeping in touch and when they'd first been married, Hope, who'd expected to be welcomed into the bosom of a real family at long last, had been astonished to find that the Parker family had only one trait in common: apathy about family get-togethers. His parents were remarkably self-sufficient people who'd had Matt, their only child, late in life and clearly weren't pleased at the intrusion of a small child into their busy lives. Now that he was an adult with a wife, they appeared to think they'd done their bit. Hope found it impossible to understand this, but was grateful that, despite his upbringing, Matt was so passionate about her and the children.

Sam wisely said it was clear that Matt was determined to live his life very differently from the way his austere and cold family lived. 'He's insecure about people loving him and he needs you. That's why he's so controlling,' Sam had added, with a rare touch of harshness.

Hope just wished *she* was sure her husband needed her. If she was sure of that, she wouldn't be so nervous about asking him what was wrong. Was it Gearóid's death? He'd been incredibly fond of the eccentric uncle he used to spend summers with as a child.

But when she'd tried to comfort him about Gearóid, Matt had snapped at her, so perhaps it wasn't that. What was it, then?

She knew she should be quiet, that it was fatal to probe at this unknown awfulness, because once she'd probed, she'd know and she wouldn't be able to bury her head in the sand and pretend everything was OK. But she had to probe.

'Don't tell me it's nothing,' she said quickly. 'I know you're not happy, Matt.'

'OK, you're right, you're right,' he snapped, slamming down his fork. 'I'm not happy. You win first prize for noticing.'

'I just want to help,' Hope said in a small voice.

'I'm just . . . oh,' he threw his hands in the air, 'I don't know. I'm a bit down, that's all. Unfulfilled, pissed off, depressed, I don't know what you call it.'

She stared at him mutely, not knowing what was coming next.

'Don't say it's a mid-life crisis,' he added harshly. 'That's what bloody Dan said. Said I'd be running off with a seventeen-year-old soon.'

Hope flinched.

'He was only joking,' Matt said, seeing her face. 'Who'd want me?' he added in a voice resonant with bitterness. 'I mean, I'm forty and what have I done? Nothing. Worked my butt off for years for what? A decent car and the chance of a good pension. I haven't *done* anything, not anything I'm proud of.'

'You've got Millie and Toby,' Hope said weakly, not wanting to add '. . . and me,' in case Matt didn't feel as if she was much of an asset.

'I know, I know, it's a . . . male thing.' Matt seemed lost for words, possibly for the first time in his life. He couldn't appear to say what he meant. Or perhaps he knew exactly what he wanted to say but wanted her to figure it out. He was leaving, that had to be it.

Hope waited, guts clenching in painful spasm. This was it: Matt was leaving. People left all the time. Her mother and father had left before she'd had a chance to know them, just when she needed them. All right, they'd died, so that was different. But Hope had been expecting Matt to leave almost from the moment she'd fallen in love with him. History repeating itself. There had to be a price for winning such a handsome man – you could never be sure of him, never keep him. All the fears Hope had successfully kept to herself over the years were coming to the surface.

Matt was watching her across the table. He knew her background, knew her horror of being abandoned. 'It's alright,' he said sharply, almost harshly. 'I'm not going to leave.'

The tears Hope had been successfully holding off now flowed unchecked. She knew he was lying: it was obvious. There was someone else, he wanted to leave her and it was just a matter of time. He'd merely decided not to dump her on his birthday.

'I'm going through a bad time and I'm trying to deal with it,' Matt said. 'I'm better if you leave me to it.'

'But I can't,' whispered Hope. 'I love you so much, and I can't bear it if you feel upset. I mean . . .' she pushed aside her plate, her appetite gone, 'I'd do anything to make it all right.' She was too scared to ask him if there was someone else. Too afraid that he'd tell her the truth.

'You can't make it all right,' Matt said bluntly. 'I'm the one suffering the mid-life crisis, not you. You can't magic it away so we can play happy families. Life isn't like that. Now can we just have our dinner and try and have a relaxed evening? Please,' he added more gently. 'I don't feel up to talking about it.'

Hope nodded. She poked her steak around the plate, trying to pretend she was hungry. Matt went back to eating and watching the television.

She watched him surreptitiously, her nerves in tatters, wishing she wasn't so needy and pathetically hungry for love that she'd take any excuse. She didn't believe a word of it. Matt was lying. If only she were stronger, she'd demand the truth. Someone like Sam would have sent the entire dinner flying and demanded an explanation. She'd have yelled that he wasn't moving from his seat until he told her exactly what was wrong and cut all the crap about how he was better off dealing with it on his own. Hope knew how Sam would handle this situation, because Sam's responses were programmed into her brain. You didn't grow up practically joined at the hip to your older sister without knowing everything about her. But that didn't mean you could apply her no-holds-barred type of reaction to your own life. Sadly no.

Hope, hating confrontation and loving Matt almost obsessively, was content to know nothing if that was what Matt wanted.

Matt finished his meal and smiled at his wife. 'That was lovely,' he said kindly. 'Let's forget about everything and watch a video. I stopped at the shop on the way home.'

'I can give you your presents,' Hope said, eager to leave the desolate place she was currently in. If they had a nice evening after all, it meant their marriage was OK. Didn't it?

Matt was up early the next morning. An early meeting, he said as he threw back the duvet at half six instead of the usual seven. Hope, head heavy after a practically sleepless night of worrying, couldn't move. She was exhausted, her head throbbed with tiredness and her eyes felt piggy, as if someone had injected them with some type of swelling agent. She knew she should get up and talk to Matt – anything to convince herself that it was all okay – but she was too tired.

The speediest dresser in the world, Matt was showered, shaved and ready in twenty minutes. Wearing the black Armani suit with a white shirt and his new tie, an outfit that made him look like he was auditioning for an Italian James Bond, he stopped by the bed to pick up his watch from the bedside table. Hope sat up on the pillow and rubbed frantically at her sleep-filled eyes.

'Bye darling,' she bleated. 'Love you.' She hoped he'd kiss her goodbye but instead he smiled briefly and busied himself with his watch strap.

'Bye, I'll see you this evening,' he said and he was gone, without kissing her.

Hope remembered a time when they'd been so in love that some mornings Matt had ripped off his suit and got back into bed with her to make mad passionate love, not caring that he'd be late for work. She bit her lip miserably. The seven year itch wasn't just an itch: it was a damn outbreak of eczema.

Her only consolation was that he had looked tired too and clearly hadn't slept well. Whether it was because he longed to make it up, or whether he'd been mentally going over the various ways of informing her their marriage was over, she couldn't tell.

As usual, Millie was naughtier than usual because she sensed that Hope was tired and cross. Millie may have *looked* like an angelic child model from the Pears soap adverts, but there was definitely a vein of sheer mischief running through her body that belied her sweet face. Hope knew from experience that whenever Millie was looking particularly innocent, with her full bottom lip jutting out and her dark eyes round with naïveté, she'd undoubtedly done something very naughty. Like the time she put the plug in the upstairs bathroom sink and set the taps running full blast until water poured down the stairs. The carpet had been ruined.

This morning, she belted downstairs and started to make cakes out of tomato ketchup, mayonnaise, broken up biscuits and breakfast cereal, squelching out an entire bottle of ketchup with the subsequent splodges getting all over the kitchen floor, while Hope was upstairs getting Toby ready.

'Millie,' was all Hope could say when she got downstairs with Toby to find an ocean of Millie's ketchup cake covering the table, a good deal of the floor and most of Millie's lime green fluffy jumper, clean on half an hour ago. Even worse, it was a jumper that had to be handwashed and spent much of its life at the bottom of the laundry basket with the other handwash items until Hope had the time to tackle them.

'You're a very naughty girl; you're all messy and I'll have to clean this up. Go upstairs immediately and take off that jumper. We're going to be late.'

'Shit,' said Millie mutinously.

Hope's jaw clanged so low she could hear the joint creak.

'What?' she gasped, appalled. Where could Millie have learned that?

Even Millie seemed to realize that this was a very, very bad thing to say.

She scampered upstairs like a greyhound. Hope stepped over the ketchup cake blindly and switched on the kettle. Very strong coffee was the only answer. She had a husband who wanted to leave her and a delinquent four-year-old daughter who had apparently picked up the worst swear words in the world at the nursery which Hope had to shell out most of her salary to pay for. Wonderful.

> *Hi Sam, how's the new job? Is everyone friendly?*
> Stupid question, Hope decided, deleting it. People were friendly to newcomers in offices but not to new bosses.
> *We're all great and looking forward to Matt's birthday dinner. I did plan to buy a dress but decided against it. If only I could fit into your designer outfits. Next time you have a wardrobe clear out, send a plastic bin liner of stuff down to me and I'll diet!*
> *Talk soon,*
> *Love Hope.*

By the Thursday night of Matt's birthday dinner, Hope had lost two pounds with the stress of it all. Normally, that would have thrilled her, but when her weight loss was connected with the fact that Matt had been almost monosyllabic since his birthday, it wasn't a cause for celebration.

Over the last couple of days, Matt had been very quiet and had stayed very late at the office on two evenings, ostensibly to get some work done on an important campaign they were presenting on Monday.

Hope was convinced he was going to see *her* and had resisted the temptation to follow him in the Metro. But it was impossible to play private detective with two small children in tow. Hope could just picture Millie announcing loudly over breakfast the next day: 'Daddy, we saw you and a strange lady and Mummy cried and said a rude word.'

Even more telling, he'd been looking over some papers in their bedroom and had quickly stuffed them back in his briefcase when Hope walked in unexpectedly. Distraught, Hope had walked out again. They had to have been divorce papers. What else would he want to hide?

She longed to confide in someone, but whom? Sam had never approved of Matt and would probably arrive in fury from London with a top lawyer in tow and order Hope to screw everything she could out of Matt in the divorce settlement. Betsey, her closest friend, was married to Matt's friend and colleague, Dan, so there was no way she could tell Betsey of her fears. In fact, she was scared that if she said anything to Betsey, the other woman would take her hand pityingly and say yes, she'd been dying to tell Hope that Matt had someone else. She had other friends but they were mainly couples that she and Matt went out with, friends of both of them, in other words, so unsuitable for spilling the beans to.

How could she phone up Angelica and Simon and say that no, the Parkers wouldn't be coming for dinner in three weeks' time and had they heard anything about Matt and some bimbo?

So Hope did what she'd been doing all her life: she bottled it up inside herself and lay wide-eyed in bed at night, listening to Matt's even breathing beside her and wondering what the hell she was going to do with the rest of her lonely life without him.

The restaurant was buzzing with a glam Thursday night crowd but even so, other diners looked up when the Judd's Advertising crew were escorted to their table. Most of the eyes were on Jasmine Judd, new wife to the boss, a radiant, satin-skinned blonde who was spilling out of a dusky pink sequined dress and made Hope feel more than a little inadequate in the safe jersey number that had looked sophisti-cated and modern at home but had been transformed into several-seasons-out-of-fashion in this elegant setting. She never got clothes right, she sighed. But then, Hope was beginning to feel as if she never got *anything* right.

If the male diners were all open-mouthed at the sight of Jasmine swaying on her high heels, the female diners were able to feast their eyes on Matt, who was looking particularly good in a fawn-coloured suit that made him look even more matinee idol than ever. His hair suited him in the cropped style; it made his deep set eyes look darker than usual and showed up the firm, he-man jaw that made lots of the women in Maltings Lane wave at him too energetically when he was out cutting the grass in his shorts and T-shirt.

He certainly looked after himself, fitting in three nights a week in the gym come what may. Hope now knew he wasn't keeping himself fit for her. But at least he was wearing his birthday tie.

'George Clooney eat your heart out,' Yvonne had joked the first time she'd clapped eyes on Matt at the annual building society barbecue.

Hope knew this was high praise indeed but hadn't liked to tell her that Matt considered gorgeous George to be common and modelled himself more on Cary Grant. If his temples weren't already greying in a distinguished manner à la Cary, Hope wondered if Matt might start bleaching them himself.

Many times in their marriage, she'd wondered how she'd ever managed to end up with Matt. Quite a few other women wondered that too, she felt, judging by the calculating gazes she got from them at parties. Hope never realized that the calculating gazes held plenty of envy for her. Convinced she was frumpy and dull, she had no idea of her own attractiveness. To her, beauty meant the glossy sophistication and superb bone structure of people like Jasmine. It couldn't possibly mean a sweet, kind face or big anxious eyes or a soft mouth that constantly twitched up at the corners into the most bewitching smile.

Nor did Hope realize that while Matt might sometimes look briefly on the stunning creatures who flirted with him, he needed a yielding, gentle woman like Hope as his partner. The strong, glamorous women who eyed him up boldly, simply reminded him of his strong, glamorous mother, a woman who wore signature red lipstick, kept her dark hair in a sleek bob and flirted with all and sundry. Hope, who was scared of her mother-in-law and always felt deeply inadequate beside her, never realized that one of the reasons Matt loved her so dearly was because she was the direct opposite of his mother.

Hope walked behind Matt to the table, miserably thinking that maybe she should announce that her delectable husband was back on the market. She'd be flattened in the rush, that was for sure. Matt was a nine on a one-to-ten scale of attractiveness while she'd been maybe a five when they'd married. In her black dress with her hair refusing to behave and a pre-menstrual spot emerging like a beacon on her chin despite all the concealer plastered on it, Hope currently felt as if she was a two. Compared to Jasmine, she was in minus figures.

She stared at Jasmine jealously. Was *she* the one? No, Hope decided. Matt was a career man first and foremost. Having an affair with the boss's wife was career suicide.

A long table against one wall was reserved for the party of ten. Dan had organized the dinner party and was now telling everyone where to sit. As the others obediently went to their seats, Hope's prospects of a red-wine fuelled evening where her mind would be taken off her troubles vanished. Dan told her to sit in the centre with her back to the wall and she realized she was going to spend the evening hemmed in by people she didn't like.

Lucky Matt had Betsey, the flamboyant journalist who was married to Dan, on one side. Betsey was one of Hope's closest friends, although she was a teeny bit self-obsessed and tended to swing all conversations back to herself. Hope would have loved to have been able to sit beside Betsey and confide in her: she was almost desperate enough to do so.

On Matt's other side, he had Jasmine. Both women were chattering away happily to the birthday boy. Hope, on the other hand, was stuck with the art director's husband, an eternal student with a goatee and dirty finger nails, who could bore for in the Olympics on the subject of the changing face of industrial architecture. Hope didn't give a damn about industrial architecture and could see nothing interesting in Victorian glassworks.

On her other side was Adam Judd, the agency boss, who never had anything to say to her and who was now avidly watching his luscious wife, Jasmine, flirting with Matt.

Across the table, Dan smiled at Hope. She automatically smiled back, thinking 'you pig, you've stuck me with the most difficult people at the table.' Sam would have said something sarcastic to him: Hope knew she'd never dare.

Dan immediately turned to his neighbour, the agency's commercials director, a quiet woman named Elizabeth.

Soon, she was laughing too.

Hope sighed and took another big slug of wine. She wasn't a heavy drinker but the thought flitted through her mind that perhaps tonight was the night to get plastered and confront Matt. She'd never have the nerve unless she was drunk . . .

Then again, Matt would go ballistic if she got drunk and made a fool of herself. These people were Matt's colleagues, she must make an effort. But it wasn't easy. Tortured by thoughts of Matt's infidelity and watching all the women at their table like a hawk, in case *she* was one of them, Hope was not enjoying herself. The silence at her side of the table was deafening, made all the more obvious by the machine gun rattle of conversation on the other side. Adam ate like he was starving, only speaking when he wanted butter, pepper for his smoked salmon, or the bottle of wine passed down his end. Hope gave up trying when her third stab at conversation ('Are you and Jasmine going anywhere nice on holiday?') was deflected with a grunted 'no'. Adam looked grim at the notion, as if he wasn't letting Jasmine go anywhere she'd be able to stun passing men with the sight of her in a sliver of uplift bikini.

Peter, the student, was eager to discuss his thesis whenever Hope turned in his direction.

'I'd really like to develop the idea into a book,' he was saying grandly in between hoovering up goats' cheese salad, 'but bizarrely, I can't get anyone interested.'

Hope had tuned out by now but nodded and said 'Really? How interesting.' She wished she was more like Sam who could invest the words 'how interesting' with an iciness that would freeze the Pacific Ocean and immediately make the other person realize they were the exact opposite of interesting.

'Funding is the problem, control of funding,' Peter said, tapping his bony nose mysteriously. 'It's impossible to get funding for the really worthwhile projects like mine,' he added pompously.

'It is outrageous that so many commercial books get published when worthy, unsaleable books like yours don't,' Hope said gravely.

Peter blinked at her, unsure whether she was serious or not. But Hope's face was the picture of earnestness.

'Well, yes,' he drivelled on, satisfied that Matt Parker's quiet little wife couldn't possibly have been mocking him. 'You see, if you let me explain my theories . . .'

In desperation, Hope turned to find that Adam was now talking business to Sadie, the art director. Sadie's eyes caught Hope's briefly but as Adam was talking, Hope couldn't interrupt. Adam ignored Hope completely. Just like Matt, she thought bitterly. He'd barely looked at her during the first course, concentrating on making everyone else laugh and have a great time.

'You can see the problem,' Peter continued as she turned back to him.

'Of course,' Hope said, wondering why the hell she'd been looking forward to an evening out when it was proving as thrilling as having her blackheads squeezed. She'd thought it might be more enjoyable than enduring another silent evening of telly-watching at home. But at least at home, her mind was taken off its problems thanks to prime time viewing.

'More wine, Hope?' asked her husband from the other side of the table, seeing no-one else had bothered to refill her glass.

She nodded glumly.

Matt's long fingers reached across the table and touched hers. He winked at her and mouthed 'thank you'. Thank you for being bored senseless on my behalf, she hoped he meant. She smiled weakly back with relief. He did love her, he did. She knew Matt well enough to know he was trying to make up. Even if there was somebody else, she could weather it as long as Matt loved her. Hope gave his fingers a final squeeze.

It wasn't too much of an effort to be nice to Matt's colleagues and their spouses. It was the least she could do. She only had to put up with Peter once or twice a year.

*　　*　　*

33

Long fingers twirling the stem of his wine glass, Matt watched Hope doing her best to be charming to boring Peter Scott. She was great at that sort of thing, he thought fondly. You could always rely on Hope to do the polite, decent thing no matter what. Nobody else in their right mind would let Peter start off on his 'my thesis' saga but Hope was too kind to stop him. That was her problem: she was too kind. She let people walk all over her.

He didn't know why she'd worn that clingy dress. Tight stuff didn't suit her. His wife had an other-worldly air that made her look nice in flowy stuff, long dresses, that type of thing. Not like Jasmine. You had to hand it to Adam, he knew how to pick them. There wasn't a man here who hadn't thought for one brief, erotic moment of what the new Mrs Judd would look like without that sparkly dress. Probably cost more than all the dresses in Hope's wardrobe put together. Anyway, Hope would never wear such a thing. That dress was a statement: Look at me, it said. That wasn't Hope's scene at all. She was much more of a background person, happy to be out of the spotlight.

It was a pity she didn't realize how gorgeous she was. He was always telling her but she just didn't get it. He'd seen scores of men eyeing her up over the years and Hope never, ever noticed them. When people looked at her, she checked to see if she had her skirt tucked up into her knickers or had gone out in her slippers.

'Great night, isn't it?' Dan said, leaning over and touching Matt on the shoulder.

'Yeah, fantastic night,' Matt said automatically.

It was a great night. He had his colleagues here, cheering him for his birthday, and his boss who'd just brought him into the boardroom that day to say he was giving Matt a raise. Two lovely kids, a nice wife . . . everything a man could want. Only he wanted more.

Matt stared into the middle distance and thought about how his perfect, wonderful life was choking him. He'd had a crazy and impulsive idea about how to fix it, well, how to fix *some* of it, but how did he break it to Hope? He didn't know where to start. Confiding in Jasmine had helped a bit.

She'd promised to put a good word in for him with Adam if he ever actually made the break. Telling Adam would be a doddle compared to telling Hope.

By the time people were staring happily into their liqueurs, Hope had finally managed to move seats and was now between Jasmine and Dan.

Jasmine was very nice, Hope decided, convinced now that there was nothing between her and Matt. She could see how other women would feel threatened by her: that amazing figure, tiny waist and gravity-defying boobs, not to mention a sweet face with huge blue eyes. But she was funny, unaffected and not at all the predatory bimbo that Betsey had initially dubbed her. Well, she wasn't predatory, anyway.

'Your husband's wonderful,' Jasmine said in between sips of sambuca. 'I was telling him how I wanted to write a book and he said "snap!" The last person I said it to told me not to bother my head with books when I could be on the cover of one.' Jasmine looked vexed at this.

'Matt said *what*?' Hope asked, curious and hurt at the same time. How had Matt discussed this with Jasmine and not with her?

'I daresay it's a pipe dream,' suggested Jasmine. 'It is for me too. But Matt writes for his job, he's got a better chance than most. I'm thinking of doing a creative writing course, myself. I know it's tough. Like selling records. I went out with a musician once and he was obsessed with record sales.' She laughed ruefully. 'Oh, speaking of music, Matt was telling me about your older sister and this great job she's just got in the record company. I love the sound of that. What's she like? Very clever and high powered, I suppose?'

'The opposite of me, you mean,' said Hope automatically. And it was true . . . Sam was a human dynamo, all fire and energy. Now she was running a label at Titus Records. Hope still wasn't exactly sure what the new job entailed because Sam had only been there a week and their e-mails had been short, but it was demanding, that was for sure. Sam couldn't bear to be free of pressure. She'd worked herself into the ground for five years as marketing director of another huge record label and now, when Hope thought her sister should be slowing down a bit and perhaps thinking about settling down, Sam had moved companies to another, bigger job.

Jasmine was back on the subject of writing: 'Matt told me about his plan to take a year out and live in the country. I know it's only an idea and you've nothing settled yet but I think you should go for it. It'll be easier for him to write with no distractions. Harder to see your sister, mind you, if you were to move abroad. Matt was telling me your parents died when you were kids and that you've only got one sister.'

Hope's heart missed a beat. 'What are you on about?' she asked, feeling a queasy sensation in the pit of her stomach, a sensation that had nothing to do with drinking too much.

'It's fine, really,' Jasmine assured her in a stage whisper. 'You don't have to pretend you don't know. I won't say a word to Adam about it, I promised Matt I wouldn't. I'm sure that Adam will go ballistic when he discovers Matt wants to take a year's sabbatical but you have to pursue your dreams, don't you.' She got misty-eyed. 'I'd love to move somewhere remote to write but I'd hate to be away from twenty-four hour shops. Won't you mind?'

Hope recovered her composure. This was not the moment to say the notion of Matt taking a year out was news to her. She tried to look resigned instead of astonished. 'Who knows what'll happen,' she shrugged. 'The whole idea is very much aspirational right now. We love Bath and . . .'

'Jasmine, time to go,' announced Adam suddenly, looming behind his wife and putting proprietorial hands on her slim, golden shoulders.

With Jasmine and Adam gone, the party deflated. Betsey insisted to Dan she was tired and had to go home.

'We should go too,' said Elizabeth, reaching under the table for her handbag.

With the wisdom born of being slightly drunk, Hope realized that her husband's colleagues weren't so close to him as he thought. Their eagerness to party only lasted as long as the boss's presence. When Adam was gone, so was the party spirit. But Matt didn't seem to mind and waved everyone off with great bonhomie.

In the taxi, Hope sat quietly as they drove out on the Bristol road. Matt lay back against the seat with his eyes closed, his face expressionless now they were alone. As houses sped by, Hope worked out what she was going to say when they got home. It went against the grain to start an argument in the back of a taxi with the driver listening to every word.

The pieces of the puzzle had fallen painfully into place thanks to the artless Jasmine. Matt was dreaming up an enormous career change and Hope and the kids didn't figure in his plans. Would she stay on in the house in Bath or move to London to be near Sam, Hope wondered in shock. She'd move, definitely, she couldn't stay in the house where they'd been so happy. Correction; where *she'd* been so happy. Matt obviously hadn't been happy or he wouldn't want to leave it and her.

The children had been little lambs and the chocolate biscuits had been great, Elaine, the babysitter, said when they got home.

'Good,' said Hope absently, getting out her purse. Her hands were shaking, like an alcoholic's before the first drink of the day. 'Matt will walk you home.'

'It's only across the road,' protested Elaine.

'Better safe than sorry,' Hope said. 'It's half twelve, you know. Time for the deviants of the world to emerge.'

'In Maltings Lane?' asked Elaine incredulously.

When Matt came back, Hope was sitting waiting for him at the kitchen table. Her hands were still shaking, so she put them on her lap and clasped them tightly together as if she was praying. Perhaps if she had prayed, none of this would have happened, she thought wildly.

'I thought you'd be on your way to bed by now,' Matt remarked, pouring himself a glass of milk. It was the longest statement he'd made in about a week.

'Jasmine said a very strange thing to me tonight,' Hope said evenly. 'She said you were taking a sabbatical to live in the country to write a book – not this country was the implication. I just wondered when you were going to tell me of this plan and if I and the children were actually included.'

'Ah.' Matt sat down with her. 'Too much red wine is a terrible thing.'

'You mean Jasmine misunderstood?' Hope could barely get the words out.

'Not exactly,' Matt said slowly. 'I'm afraid I got a bit carried away and said too much.'

'So it's true.' Her legs began to shake too with fear.

'Hope,' Matt wasn't sure how to start but he knew he had to. Telling Jasmine had been a decision fuelled by too much wine but it had been a relief to talk about it with someone other than Dan. It was time to tell Hope. 'It's been a dream of mine for years and you know me, respectable family man, I'd never do anything wild or out of the ordinary, anything that would jeopardize our future but now I've got the chance and I thought, why not take a year out. I know that Adam would keep my job open for me – he'd have to, I'm the best he's got,' he added, proud of the fact.

'But what about me and the kids?' asked Hope, eyes wet and filled with terror. Was Matt drunk? Didn't he care about them at all?

'I mean all of us going away. You, me and the kids for a year. To Ireland; Kerry, in fact. Uncle Gearóid's solicitor phoned me on Monday about the old house. I know it's sudden but it's like the answer to my prayers. I've been so down, Hope, so depressed and then he phones to say the house is officially mine. I haven't been able to think of anything else all week.'

Hope's whole body was shaking now; she could barely take in what he was saying because her mind was so befuddled with fear and anxiety.

Gearóid had been a poet who, over forty years before, had left his home in the UK for a small town named Redlion in Kerry, where he lived a bohemian life with gusto. Hope had never met him because he'd refused to leave his beloved adopted country to come to their wedding but he'd always sounded like a mad old rogue who pickled his liver and wrote bad poetry that nobody had ever wanted to publish. He'd even changed his name from Gerald to the Irish and unpronounceable Gearóid, which Hope still found impossible to say, no matter how many times Matt said it phonetically: '*Gar*, like garage, and *oid* like haemorrhoid.'

Matt had spent a few summers in Redlion as a child and still talked mistily about what a wonderful place Kerry was. But as Gearóid became more eccentric with age, he refused to travel to stay with Matt, who, in turn, never seemed to have the time to visit his ageing uncle. When he died, he left Matt everything; partly because he didn't have any children of his own and partly, according to his solicitor, to annoy the other distant relatives who'd been hanging around like vultures hoping for a piece of property in a popular tourist destination in south-western Ireland. 'Everything' turned out to be a run-down house the solicitor imagined wouldn't fetch much. Hope had assumed that Matt would simply sell the house. They could certainly do with the money.

'Probate's finally been sorted out,' Matt explained. 'The house is mine. And yours, of course. There's a bit of land but only an acre or so. It all seemed much bigger when I was a kid. I thought he had loads of land. Anyway,' he paused, 'this is my idea. I've told you about the writers' community there that Gearóid helped start up in the Sixties?'

Hope nodded, still looking shell-shocked, although Matt didn't notice because he was fired up with the enthusiasm of telling her his plan.

'It's spooky because this is so coincidental,' Matt went on eagerly, 'but last week I read an interview with the novelist, Stephen Dane – you know the guy, he writes those literary thrillers. Anyway, he's just sold a book to Hollywood. We're talking millions, Hope. And in the middle of the interview, he mentioned that he wrote his first novel in Kerry, in Redlion, actually, in the writer's centre. Don't you see, it's got to be a sign.

'We'd both take a year out and go and live in Gearóid's house. I'd write a novel. I've got one in me, I know it. Imagine it, Hope,' Matt said, his eyes alight with enthusiasm, desperate to transmit his excitement to her and unaware of what she'd been thinking since his birthday, 'we could be with the children all day. I could get some part time copy writing work and we'd live cheaply enough. We could rent out this place for a year and cover the mortgage. We wouldn't lose out. This is our big chance.'

And it was, Matt was convinced of it. He'd slay the demons that lived in his head and told him he'd never amount to anything but a bitter old ad man. And he'd get the chance to live another life, even if only for a brief time.

Hope stared at him, hardly daring to believe that it wasn't the death knell she'd been expecting. Matt wasn't leaving her; he wanted her and the children with him. She leaned her hands on the table. Her sleeve immediately stuck in the sticky patch left behind from Millie's morning yoghurt.

'Why couldn't you tell me?' she said, her voice unsteady. 'I didn't know you felt this way.'

'I'm sorry I kept it to myself. It's embarrassing to talk about your dreams like that, Hope, but I want to write and I'm never going to do it here, not with a full-time job, not in this house. You need a creative atmosphere. It would be fantastic for us as a family. Having the house there in Redlion takes all the hassle out of it. It's perfect.'

'Why didn't you tell me any of this on your birthday?' she said helplessly. 'I knew there was something wrong, I asked you what it was then and you wouldn't tell me! I thought you were having an affair.'

It was Matt's turn to look astonished.

'An affair! Whatever gave you that idea?' he said incredulously.

'Everything,' Hope said. 'You told me there was something wrong but that I couldn't fix it. And you didn't kiss me or touch me and I was just so sure . . .'

Her voice broke off and Matt sat down at the table and took her hands in his.

'Darling Hope, what a crazy idea. I was killing myself wondering whether I could do this to you. All I could think of was that you'd hate it, that it was such a huge step to go abroad for a year. I kept telling myself it was a stupid idea, that I shouldn't do it but I've been talking to Dan about it and . . .'

'Dan!' Hope felt a spark of fury that while she'd been dying inside at the thought of Matt leaving her, he could have saved her a lot of anguish if only he'd told her the truth. Meanwhile, he'd actually been asking other people's opinions on a move that affected her more than anyone else. 'Is there anyone you haven't discussed this with, apart from me, of course?' She ripped a tissue from the box on the table and rubbed violently at the yoghurt marks on the table.

'I need you to understand, Hope,' Matt said quietly.

Hope thought she understood all right: Matt had made another unilateral decision about their lives. There had been the time a mere month after their marriage when he said he'd accepted a job with the ad agency in Bath even though they'd both decided to travel round the world for a year. (Well, the trip around the world had been his idea initially, but she'd agreed to it, had bought the rucksack and got the typhoid injection.)

Or the time he'd agreed to rent a holiday cottage in France with Dan and Betsey, without even discussing it with Hope. And what had she said on each occasion? Had she roared: 'It's my life too, Matt. I don't agree with your plans so you'll have to unmake them?' No. Anger and neediness had fought and neediness had won. Too scared at starting a battle with the one she loved, Hope had smothered her upset and said: 'Of course, that's a good idea. Let's do it.'

Sam had been furious with her: 'How dare he bloody give up your year travelling for some crappy job without talking it over with you first!' she'd raged.

'Marriage is about give and take,' Hope had countered.

'What percentage applies to each person?' Sam had demanded. 'You give ninety-five per cent and he takes ninety-five per cent? Is that the way it breaks down?'

'You don't know anything about marriage,' Hope had replied, stung by the unfairness of her sister's comments into saying something sharper than she'd ever normally say to Sam.

Her sister was quiet for a moment. 'Neither do you, sis,' Sam remarked sadly.

Unspoken between them was the knowledge that happy families was a game they hadn't grown up with. Brought up by their strict, middle-aged maiden aunt who thought that children should be seen and not heard, their vision of happy families came from watching *Little House On The Prairie.*

'Penny for them?' Matt put an arm around her shoulders. She leaned her head against it. He was so demonstrative with her, a fact which had thrilled her when they'd first met. Matt linked his arm through hers from the first date, squeezed her fingers affectionately just for the hell of it. Hope, brought up in austerity where hugs were for Christmas, had loved his touchy-feely-ness. After six years of marriage, he had been as affectionate as ever. They had slept spooned together and on the odd occasions Matt was away working, Hope found it impossible to get any sleep without the sensation of his body next to hers. Until the past painful few months.

Hope remembered the sheer fear of thinking their marriage was over. She adored Matt, she couldn't live without him. Now, relief that he still loved her too was flooding through her limbs, filling her with the sweet sense of release that all her worst nightmares weren't coming true.

'I wish you wouldn't make decisions without consulting me,' she said, head still resting against his arm.

As if sensing that the worst was over, Matt stroked her hair with his other hand. 'I *am* consulting you,' he said.

'Only after you've talked about it with other people, including Jasmine.' She was still hurt that he'd talked about something so personal to a woman he barely knew. Jasmine had learned all the facts while Hope, whose life it involved, was still ignorant of them. Despite her relief, that still rankled. 'We can't have a very good marriage if you never discuss the big issues with me, Matt. Why couldn't you tell me what you were thinking in the beginning? I couldn't begin to tell you how awful it's been for me, knowing there was something wrong but not what.' She didn't want to mention her affair fears again. It sounded so stupid now she knew the truth.

'It was only an idea then . . .'

'That was when you should have talked it over with me, then. What am I? Your wife or your landlady?'

Matt moved his arm away. 'I thought you'd jump at the idea. You're forever going on about how you never get to spend time with

Toby and Millie, how they'll grow up thinking Your Little Treasures is their real home and we're the night-time babysitters. And you hate your job.'

'Sometimes I do but that doesn't mean I want to stop doing it,' Hope protested. 'AndI doubt very much if I could get a sabbatical; I'm hardly a top flight executive they can't do without. So you're asking me to dump a good job. And all our friends are here,' she added, 'not the mention the children's friends. Toby's only just settled properly into the nursery and I have to drag him out again.'

'It's only for a year, not forever. Unless of course, I get a good publishing deal . . .' Matt's face lit up at his daydream but Hope was even more horrified. Perhaps the move *would* be forever . . .

'What if I don't agree to it?' she asked.

Feeling a bit guilty about blackmailing her, Matt launched his final, lethal weapon. 'Don't be angry, love. Think of what it could mean to us. We could bring the children up as a real family, in a real community environment. Not with both of us working so hard that we're too tired to get involved with the outside world. Wouldn't you love to live in the country and be a part of the children's lives?'

Hope wavered. Family: that was her Achilles' heel. Aunt Ruth had been the most unmaternal person on the planet and Hope had longed for a family atmosphere like something out of a Disney movie. Picnics with homemade sandwiches, walks along the sea shore, great excitement hanging up stockings over the fireplace at Christmas. She and Sam hadn't experienced any of that, which made her all the more keen to give it to her children.

'We could look after the kids ourselves, not work each other into the ground,' Matt said fervently, warming to his theme. 'Think of it, fresh air, no pollution, good food . . .'

'Bath is hardly covered with industrial smog,' she pointed out.

'I know, but this would be different.'

'What about our families? We'd be so far away from everyone.'

'I never see my lot anyway – you know we're not close – and Sam can fly over and see us in Ireland. They all can, it's not a million miles away. Besides, my parents haven't been to Bath since the Christmas before last, they'll hardly miss us.'

Hope knew what he meant. Matt's parents were chilly and reserved, and not too interested in spending time with their only son and his family. Since his father had retired, his parents had spent much of their time travelling, saying that they had neither the time nor the money to travel when they were younger.

'Sam jets off all over the world for work,' Matt added, 'it'll be easy for her to hop on a plane and visit us. The trip would be an hour and a half, max.'

Hope thought about it. Imagine being able to take care of the children, giving them quality time, learning tapestry, sitting in a rural garden with butterflies dipping in and out of the flowers, birds singing and not a sound of cars roaring up and down the motorways.

Hope thought of the floral skirt she'd admired in Jolly's and her plans to become the queen of her kitchen.

And she and Matt would become closer than ever. After nearly a week of fear when she'd thought her marriage was over, she desperately wanted to work on it, to make sure they stayed together. She took a deep breath.

'OK, let's investigate it. But stop making plans without asking me, will you?'

'I promise.' Matt buried his face in her neck, the same way Toby did. And in a rush of warmth she felt her objections melt away.

# CHAPTER TWO

That same Thursday, Sam Smith sat in her office and put her head on her desk for one wonderful minute. Not on the desk, exactly: the bleached maple was hidden by layers of paper, mostly marketing reports, spreadsheets of expenses and letters she had yet to read. She had to clear it all before seven o'clock that evening, an impossibility since her assistant, Lydia, was off with flu. Sam's own throat ached and a dull throbbing behind her eyes convinced her that she was next in line to get it. Only she simply couldn't afford to take any time off. She had a gig tonight, one that would go on until the wee small hours, and an eight-thirty meeting the following morning, followed by a three-hour budget meeting. Illness, like tiredness, was not an option. Not when you were barely two weeks into the job, a job people would kill their grannies for.

Sam rubbed her eyes, not caring for once whether she'd smudge her mascara and give herself racoon eyes. Why did she have to feel ill now? Everything had been going swimmingly for the last eight working days. She loved Titus Records, adored her new job as managing director of the LGBK label, got hugely excited at the idea of developing people's careers and making them international stars. It was a huge step up from being director of marketing at Plutonious Records. Despite the long hours she'd been working, she'd gone home every night buzzing with an inner electricity at the thrill of the job she'd been fighting for every day of the past fifteen years.

But Lydia had been snuffling and sneezing all day Wednesday and had given Sam her germs. Lydia, a carefree twenty-five-year-old, could afford to take a few days' sick leave. Sam, teetering on the abyss of forty and the most recently hired executive with a lot to prove, couldn't. Illness in female execs was viewed with as much disfavour as working mothers racing home from important meetings to take care of toddlers with high temperatures. At least Sam, childless by choice, didn't have to worry about the latter.

The telltale click of her door handle alerted her to the fact that someone was about to enter the office. Immediately, she jerked upright, flicked back her glossy dark blonde hair, and opened her eyes wide to banish the exhaustion from them.

The door opened abruptly to reveal Steve Parris. Sam mustered up her best, most professional smile. When the company chairman himself deigned to arrive at your office at half-past five on a Thursday evening, it was your duty to look alert, on top of things and enthusiastic. Not half-dead with flu symptoms.

Sam shoved her seat back and got to her feet in one fluid movement. 'Steve, what can I do for you?' she said, hoping to infuse her words with the correct amount of deference. In her two weeks at LGBK, the biggest label at Titus Records, she'd divined that Steve Parris, no matter how much he slapped workers on the back and went about with his hail-fellow-well-met routine, was a control freak who needed subservience the same way other people needed oxygen. Short and skinny, he was still a formidable presence in his black Prada suit. People who underestimated Steve because he was so physically unprepossessing rarely made the same mistake twice.

With his shock of hair, heavy eyebrows and disconcerting habit of smoking a cigar the size of a nuclear weapon all along the no-smoking corridors of Titus, Steve was the sort of man who made people nervous. Sam was no exception.

She was no coward but she knew Steve didn't like her. He'd wanted a man for the job. The Titus European President, who was Steve's superior, had wanted Sam. Steve had given in but he wasn't happy about the decision.

'Just dropped by,' he said now, small black eyes constantly moving over Sam, her messy desk and the office, which was still only half-furnished. Sam had dumped the previous incumbent's furniture, an act designed to show people that she was the new broom.

Sam smiled at him as warmly as she could manage. Steve never 'just dropped by'.

'You're going to see Density tonight,' he said, half-question, half-statement . . .

That was it, Sam realized. Density, the band Steve himself had signed at huge expense, and who had just finished recording their first album, were performing in a small club in Soho. Sam, as head of the label they were signed to, would be very involved with their future, so it would be interesting to see them live for the first time. A future that would mean big trouble for Steve and Sam if they didn't make it. He was in her office to make sure that she was giving his protégés every help, so that their album would be a mega success and he'd get the kudos for signing them. If it wasn't, someone's head would roll and Sam would bet her enamelled golly badge that it wouldn't be Steve's.

For the first time, Sam felt the strain of being the boss. Suddenly she wondered why she hadn't stuck with her enjoyable first job all those years ago in the film distributors where the biggest stress was looking after some neurotic movie star on a promotional tour who wanted Earl Grey tea and lemon in a motorway café where the only serious menu choice was what sauce you got with your deep fried chicken. But no, she'd wanted power and a fabulous career and had left the film industry to spend fifteen frantic years in the music business. Fifteen years of hard slog to end up with Steve Parris growling at her every day. Had it been ambition or masochism? It was the flu talking, she thought, angry with herself for such weakness.

'I'm really looking forward to seeing Density live,' she said now. 'I love the parts of the album I've heard.'

Steve's beetle eyebrows bristled and the small black eyes got smaller and meaner.

'You mean you haven't heard it all before?' he barked.

'I've heard most of the tracks but they're remixing three. The producer is going to send the final version tomorrow,' Sam said, trying to remain cool.

'Jeez, you should have heard it before tonight. It's out in a month. I'll see you at the gig tonight and we'll talk about the album tomorrow,' he said, slamming the door shut on his way out.

Sam sank back into her chair and automatically put one finger to her mouth to nibble the nail. Shit, shit, shit.

She shuffled her papers again and then made up her mind. An executive decision. After all, she was a bloody executive, so she could make a decision. She was flu-ey, she had a gig to go to and she really needed to change her clothes if she wasn't to look like a complete dork at the gig. The change of clothes she'd meant to bring was still sitting in the hall of the flat where she'd left it this morning. Wearing a suit, even if it was a pretty slick grey one with a discreet DKNY label, she'd stand out like an elderly sore thumb amidst crowds of combat-trousered trendies with Kangol hats and trainers. Bugger the paperwork: she was going home to mainline anti-flu products and to change her clothes. She locked her door and walked past the glass offices, and past the open-plan section of the fifth floor, LGBK's centre of operations. Luckily, Steve's office was on the seventh floor, with all the Titus presidents, vice presidents, and other assorted control freaks. She hoped nobody was looking at her, sure she had a guilty look on her face that said 'Going Home Early'.

But even though she didn't know it, as she strode along the glass corridor, people *were* looking; people just looked at Sam Smith. Not that she was beautiful or supermodel-tall or startling in any movie star way. But because energy emanated from her like electricity and because she moved like a dynamo.

At five foot six, Hope was two inches taller, physically bigger, and yet when the sisters were together, Sam was the one people noticed.

While her sister was a mixture of pale shades, with fragile colouring and a rounded, welcoming face, Sam was the opposite: all strong colours and strong features. Sam's hair, mouse at birth, was long and a gleaming dark blonde. She had it blow-dried at a salon most lunchtimes and it fell in severe, gleaming straightness to her shoulder blades. It was a classy look, one which she'd deliberately chosen so that people would look at her and instantly know she was a player: a somebody. Her face was oval with a strong chin, a long straight nose and slanting eyebrows that showed up intensely coloured tawny brown eyes. Her skin was darker than Hope's, almost olive. In the summer, she could pass for an Italian because she went a rich, golden brown. At school, people never believed she and Hope were sisters. Only their mouths were similar: they shared the same soft plump lips, a feature which made Hope look unsure and innocent and which gave Sam the look of a woman who'd had collagen injections. To counteract this model-girl plumpness, Sam drew her lipliner inside her natural lip line and only ever wore pale lipstick so as not to draw attention to her mouth. Hope's mouth was vulnerable and slightly sexy, both looks Sam was keen to avoid. As far as Sam was concerned, once you let your hard-as-nails façade down, you were finished in business.

Slim, due to hyperactivity rather than because of any time spent in a gym, Sam looked like the perfect career woman in her tailored grey trouser suit, with a sleek nylon mac, mobile phone and briefcase as accessories. Straight out of *Cosmopolitan*'s career woman pages, except that at thirty-nine she was a fair bit older than the Cosmo babes. The vibes she gave off said 'unapproachable' and that suited her just fine.

'If you were seaside rock, you'd have a line through you saying "tough cookie",' joked her best friend, Jay, on those nights when they shared dinner together in the local Indian restaurant they both loved.

Sam always laughed when Jay said that but lately it didn't sound as funny as it used to. Jay was a willowy Atlanta woman she'd met in college, part of a small group of people who were Sam's closest friends. Jay who wore bohemian chic clothes, worked in a bookshop and was only interested in her job as a means to pay the bills. She admired Sam's single mindedness but said the career fast track wasn't for her. Tonight, Sam didn't feel as if it was for her, either.

On the packed underground train, she clung to the side of a seat as they hurtled along. Sam hated it when the train was full. She got off at Holland Park, bought some anti-flu capsules in the chemist, and trudged through sleeting rain to the flat, one of four in a huge, white-fronted converted house in an expensive, tree-lined street.

The place looked as if it had been burgled, which was pretty much the way she'd left it that morning. A huge pile of ironing lay on one corner of the dining room table; the previous few days' papers were scattered on the rest of it and the coat she'd been wearing yesterday was thrown on the sofa. Usually chronically tidy, she hated mess with a vengeance. And when the flat was messy, the cool, clean lines of the all-white rooms looked all wrong.

Since starting her new job at Titus, Sam had been working horrifically long hours and the housework had fallen by the wayside. Her cleaner had left a month before and Sam hadn't managed to find a new one. The flat wasn't enormous or anything, but doing any housework at the end of a murderously hard week was the last thing she had energy for. The flat was a two-bedroom, financially crippling, investment in a posh bit of London and the living room cum dining room was the only decent-sized room in the entire place. The kitchen was so small that two people really needed to know each other intimately if they wanted to spend any amount of time in it together, while the bathroom was minuscule and without one of Sam's favourite amenities: a bath. Showers were functional, she'd always thought, but a bath was luxury. Still, with her mega new salary, she'd be able to move soon, to somewhere bigger, more opulent and with a bathroom where you couldn't stand in the centre of the floor and touch both walls with your outstretched hands.

She couldn't face the effort of sticking anything in the microwave, so she spread a few crackers with cream cheese, poured herself a vodka and red bull to give herself energy and took the first dose of her anti-flu medicine.

In the bedroom, she sat down at the computer and connected to Outlook Express.

> *Hi Hope, she wrote. How's it going with you, love? I'm a total grump today because I'm feeling fluey and work is a nightmare. Sorry, shouldn't be bothering you with this but I've got to tell somebody. Going mad. It must be my age. I am running out of the ability to talk crap to people, which is worrying in this business. Talking crap is how I got hired in the first place. (Only*

*kidding.) Plus, I've got to go to a gig tonight and the
band in question make the sort of music that Toby and
Millie might make if you left them alone in a room with
two guitars, an effects pedal and a drum kit. Just as well
there's paracetamol in the flu stuff I've taken. Talk more
at the weekend,*
    *Sam xx*

She had a speedy shower to rinse off the sweaty flu feeling and
dressed quickly in black nylon trousers, a small orange T-shirt and
a long black leather coat that clung to her like it had been tailored
to her body. The stuff in the bag in the hall would be creased and
would have had to be ironed again. Wearing crumpled clothes was
not her style. Draining her vodka, she was out the door only an hour
after arriving.

'I hope you're not going to have any wild parties this week,' yelled
a reedy male voice from the landing above hers. 'I've got guests and
they couldn't sleep last night with the noise.'

Sam resisted the impulse to answer back. There was no point. Mad
Malcolm, as the rest of the residents called him, was oblivious to
reality. He lived on the top floor flat and spent his life accusing the
other residents of having orgiastic late-night parties and disturbing
him, which was utterly untrue. The most noise Sam had ever made
since moving into her flat a year ago had been the night she'd dropped
a saucepan of hot pasta sauce and it had splashed onto her leg,
making her yelp in pain. Used to getting up at dawn to be at her
desk by seven thirty, her idea of a late night at home was being in
bed at half eleven watching the late movie. The people who lived
downstairs were similarly quiet and it was only Mad Malc himself,
who had wooden floors, bad taste in music and a constantly barking
Pekinese, who disturbed the peace. Neighbours. As if she didn't have
enough on her plate without a nutter living above her.

The club was hot, sweaty and already full of Density fans when she
got there. Her name was on the guest list and she slipped past the
queue near the backstage area.

Backstage, long-haired roadies humped equipment around, biceps glinting with sweat in the hothouse club environment. They ignored her completely. Sam had no idea where she was going and had no intention of asking.

She blindly followed a winding corridor and found herself in a big cool room where tables, plastic chairs and two kegs of beer were positioned. Two record company people were sitting in a corner, drinking beer from cans and chatting to a skinny young bloke with a shaved head.

She didn't know the Titus people very well yet but at least she recognized these two. Darius was a handsome, upper-class sort of boy in his late twenties from Artists and Repertoire, commonly known as A & R. Normally young, musical and deeply hip people, A & R staff trawled clubs and venues spotting talent. They worked on the road and were rarely in their offices before half ten, arriving with tired eyes and demo CDs people had pressed on them the night before. A & R people sometimes resented people like Sam, whom they saw as 'suits' who screwed up their wonderful signings and who refused to sign up avant garde stuff the A & R people were passionate about. Sam had heard that Darius was brilliant at his job and had a fantastic ear for music; vital in a job which involved working closely with bands, songwriters and producers.

The other Titus person was a publicity woman whom Lydia had said was nicknamed Cher because she looked exactly like the American singer as a thirty-year-old and loved wearing Seventies hippie clothes to emphasize the effect. Sam couldn't for the life of her remember Cher's real name.

'Hi guys,' she said, pulling a chair up. 'You been in to see the band yet?'

'They don't like seeing people before a gig,' said Cher severely. 'Except Steve,' she added reverently, as if Steve Parris was God. Steve certainly thought so, Sam thought ruefully.

'Is Steve here yet?' she asked, knowing she'd have to stand beside him during the gig.

'No, he's delayed,' said Darius. 'Would you like a cigarette?' he added politely, proffering a pack.

Sam momentarily wished she still smoked. Everyone else was dragging deeply on full-strength cigarettes. At least it gave you something to do.

'Given up,' she said. 'But thanks.'

What she could have killed for was a cup of tea to soothe her throat. There was a huge hot water urn in one corner complete with teabags, plastic cups and sugar but in this beer 'n' fags atmosphere, Sam felt it would mark her for ever as a dorky 'suit' if she had tea now.

After fifteen minutes of chat, the support band went on and the room cleared while everyone went to stand backstage and look at them. The noise was terrible. Like the sound of two wrestlers having a fight in a saucepan factory. Sam managed to look interested for two songs, then sloped back to the hospitality room and made herself a cup of tea. Who gave a damn who saw her. She wasn't a kid who had to pretend to be cool, she was probably fifteen years older than most of the people backstage and if she wanted tea, then she was going to have tea. Age had to have some compensations.

When the support band were mercifully finished, she rejoined the others at the side of the stage and waited for Density. Finally, after ten minutes of screaming and clapping from the fans, they appeared, none of them looking over the age of twenty-one, all lanky young guys with weird haircuts, mad clothes and strange piercings. Their music wasn't her scene but she could sense the raw intensity of it. She only hoped that the people who bought CDs agreed with her.

Steve appeared, deep in conversation with the band's manager, so Sam was able to just nod hello to them. She'd have to speak to them both later and say how wonderful the band had been, but for now, she wanted to listen and not have to make polite small talk.

After half an hour, she decided to go down into the club itself and watch the band from the audience's point of view. She liked doing that: seeing how the fans reacted was one of the essential litmus tests for a band. Seeing if people bought their album was the other, more important one.

Telling the backstage bouncers that she'd be back, Sam slipped out into the crowd and was hit immediately by the scent of young bodies, sweat mingling with perfume and the tang of dope. She stood at the back and breathed in a waft of what smelled like l'Air du Temps.

The smell of floral perfume at gigs always astonished her. There she was, surrounded by gyrating young bodies, a mass of humanity in leather jackets, hipster trousers and death-defying heels with hard young eyes staring at her arrogantly. Then she smelled the fresh scents of their perfume rising in the heat: floral bouquets from their mums' dressing tables mixing with the fresh scent of carefully applied deodorant, innocence meets sexy. Suddenly they weren't tough little cookies any more, but vulnerable young girls anxious before they went out, hopeful that they were wearing the right clothes, yelling that 'Honestly, Dad . . .' they wouldn't be home late as they blasted themselves with a spritz of something suitable for a wood nymph.

They were all so young really; trying hard to be grown up. And she felt so old. Sam rubbed her temples tiredly. What was wrong with her? She'd been feeling so old and worn out all day: too old to be standing at a heavy rock gig trying to get it. She didn't want to get it any more, she didn't want to have to stand in a smoky club and tap her foot to some incomprehensible beat.

She wanted to be sitting at home, drinking a nice glass of red wine, perhaps listening to some mellow Nina Simone and feeling relaxed.

Sam closed her eyes and gave herself a mental pinch. Get a grip! she told herself. You're a working woman, so work. She went looking for Steve to tell him he'd signed the band of the century.

The following morning, the flu hit her like a ten-tonne truck. She woke at half past five, bathed in a cold sweat with her head aching and her throat the consistency of rough gravel. Moaning as she dragged herself out of bed, Sam stumbled into the kitchen and boiled the kettle. Hot lemon and honey might help. So much for the anti-flu stuff she'd gulped down the night before.

Enveloped in her big navy towelling dressing gown, she slumped in front of the television with her hot lemon and flicked through the channels.

'Useless rubbish,' she muttered as she discovered that the breakfast television shows hadn't started yet and the only alternative was Open University or news. After half an hour watching a programme about mountain gorillas, Sam still felt physically sick but mentally much improved. She never read anything any more apart from marketing reports and *Music Week*, and her daily culture came in the bio yoghurt she tried to eat most mornings. She really must learn more stuff. It was terrible to be uninformed, capable only of discussing sales, royalties, budgets and the marketing spend per unit of the latest hot CD. She dimly remembered a time, fifteen years ago, when she went to museums and galleries; when she had a bit of a life.

She went into the bathroom and showered, determined to make herself feel ready for work. Calling in sick so early in the new job was not a possibility, no matter how swollen and painful her head felt. Then, wrapped in her dressing gown again, she slumped down in front of breakfast TV. Just another little rest and she'd be ready to leave the house. Seven ten, Sam's normal time for leaving for work, came and went and she still felt as if her head was the size of a basketball.

She'd call a taxi instead of going by train. She was sick, she had to cosset herself.

The taxi driver finally arrived at half eight and turned out to be one of the cheeky Cockneys so beloved of tourists and so hated by anyone with the flu and a thumping headache.

'. . . so you see, they nicked him for having six people in the cab even though they were all one family. Ridiculous, it is. You can't break up a family who're looking for a cab, even though the rules say you can only carry five passengers. Mad, that's what I'd call it . . .'

Sam sat in the back and made heroic efforts with her Clinique base. However, being mere base and not miraculous make-up straight from the Jim Henson creature shop, it couldn't hide her blotchy, feverish skin, or make her look anything other than a sick, 39-year-old woman who hadn't slept well. To compensate, she made her eyes up heavily, hoping they'd distract from the rest of her.

'. . . so I says to him, don't go busting me, mate. I'm just doing my job . . .' said the taxi driver.

She got into work at ten past nine to find a chirpy Lydia behind her desk.

'You look rough,' Lydia said.

Sam glared at her and wondered where she'd gone wrong in the choice of this particular assistant. Normally, her assistants would never volunteer such personal opinions. She must be getting soft in her old age. The only consolation was that Lydia was proving to be very efficient, despite her breezy, carefree demeanour.

'Thank you for that, Lydia,' Sam replied, 'and thank you for giving me your flu.'

'You poor love,' Lydia was sympathetic. 'It was a bad dose. Do you want me to get you tea or some tablets?'

'Tea would be nice,' Sam said tiredly. 'Any calls?'

'Yeah, Steve Parris's assistant's assistant, wondering where you were because you'd missed the half eight meeting.'

'Shit!' Too late, Sam remembered the all-important breakfast meeting. She was forty minutes late, unforgivable. Well, unforgivable when the person you were meeting was Steve. Her mind sprinted through several plausible excuses but the only real one was a no-no. She'd already heard that Steve was phobic about illness. He'd have the entire office fumigated if he thought anyone in it was ill. Not for the rest of the staff's benefit, mind: for his own.

Lying was the only option. She phoned his assistant and lied that she'd been sure the meeting was for half nine. 'It's my fault,' she said apologetically, 'my assistant was away and I mistakenly scribbled it in the wrong line of my appointments book.' She dutifully wrote 'Important meeting with S Parris – NNB' on the half-nine line of her book just in case Steve appeared and asked for proof. She wouldn't put it past him.

'The meeting's over and Steve isn't happy,' said his assistant in nervous tones.

Steve was never bloody happy, Sam groaned. He'd been born bad tempered. After knowing him for two weeks, she knew this to be true.

'Oh gosh, I'm so sorry. What do you think I should do to make it up to him?' she asked sweetly, knowing that if anybody knew how to handle Steve, it was the poor woman who had to put up with him all day.

'Grovel,' was her advice.

Grovelling didn't work. Steve roared into her office just before lunch, evicting the two publicity people who'd been discussing a forthcoming album release with Sam. He hadn't waited until they'd fled before he'd started shouting abuse at her. Sam sat calmly, then apologized for her mistake.

'But,' she said, naked steel in her voice, 'coming into my office and screaming at me is not the answer. That isn't the way I run my office and it's not the way I expect to be treated, Steve. I am not some junior you can intimidate.' Her tawny eyes were as hard as nails. She glared at him.

Faced with resistance, Steve backed down. 'Yeah, I guess I get a little riled occasionally.'

Sam smiled glacially, wishing he'd lose the American accent. He was from Liverpool.

'I'm glad we understand each other,' she said, then, knowing that it was time for her to kowtow a bit, added with a large dollop of fake enthusiasm: 'and I loved Density last night. They were incredible on stage, they just blew me away. They were one hell of a find.'

Steve smiled smugly. 'It was a good gig, wasn't it?'

'We're going to make a fortune with them,' Sam added.

Steve practically swelled with pride.

He was so pathetically easy to manipulate. Was it because he wasn't used to women standing up to him? Most of the female staff were so many levels below him that when he barked at them to make him a coffee, he almost expected them to hop. A woman who gave as good as she got unnerved him. Perhaps that was why Steve had been so keen to hire a man and not Sam. She sighed silently. This job would kill her if she had to go up against Steve Parris every day.

It was a frantic Friday. Sam managed to eat half a sandwich at her desk before she had to attend the weekly marketing meeting. Then, she had to work on paperwork, talk to someone in production about a glitch in an album cover and return all her phone calls and internal e-mails. Lydia went at six and so did most of the rest of the staff but Sam stayed at her desk until half seven, wearily returning e-mails. The pain of her sore throat and throbbing headache were almost eclipsed by her exhaustion. On her way out, she popped into the loo and grimaced at her reflection. She looked like death microwaved up, all pale and pasty.

The security guard nodded as Sam left. Outside, it was dark and raining, typical October weather in London. It was hard to remember that only a month ago there'd been a week of Indian summer sunshine. Feeling miserable, Sam trudged along to the Underground, stopping only to buy some milk and a couple of lemons for her lemon and honey tea.

She got a seat on the train and sank into it gratefully. Around her, people were visibly relaxed, happy that the week was over. A crowd of young women all dressed up to the nines stood like colourful birds of paradise just inside the train doors, too fired up to bother sitting down even though some were wearing ankle-breaking stilettos. Sam leaned back in her seat and watched them laughing and chatting. She remembered being like that once, young and thrilled to be going out. Full of joie de vivre and enthusiasm for life. Now, the only thing she felt full of was flu remedy. What was *wrong* with her? It wasn't just being sick; it was something more. But what? At home, she boiled the kettle and made herself some lemon tea before heading to her bedroom to change clothes. On the off chance that Hope might have sent her an e-mail, she switched on the computer while she drank her tea. Hope *had* been in touch. Sam grinned. Why was it that she loved the words: 'you've got mail' when she was at home and hated them in the office? Probably because the home mails were nice, friendly ones and the office ones were generally staccato demands to get statistics, information and updates *now*!

> *Hi Sam,*
> *You sound terrible, you poor thing. I bet you're not looking after yourself at all. I know you: all work and no play. And never feel you can't moan to me about work and stuff. That's what sisters are for. Matt says*

*thank you for your card. He had a dinner party that was
more corporate hospitality than wild fortieth birthday
party. But I do have one piece of news. Matt and I are
thinking of moving to Ireland for a year. I know it
sounds a bit sudden but we've been thinking about it for
ages and now seems like a good time.*

*He thinks he can go on sabbatical and it's not as if
I'm exactly on the fast-track to promotion in
Witherspoon's. It's still only a plan right now so I'll tell
you more when I know more. It's a bit of a long story.
See you soon, love, Hope.*

Sam stared at the screen, stunned. Move to Ireland? Matt taking
a sabbatical and Hope giving up her job? Weird wasn't the word
for it.

Hope always discussed things with Sam; it was so strange of her
not to have even mentioned this startling new plan, unless . . . unless.
Sam's eyes narrowed. Bloody Matt. This was some damn fool plot
of his, she'd swear to it. As ever, Hope was going along with it. Sam
quickly checked out the train times to Bath on Saturday mornings,
then phoned her sister. Flu or no flu, Hope needed sense talked into
her and face to face was the only way to do it.

They stowed Sam's small weekend bag in the boot of the Metro with
the groceries, Hope marvelling that her sister could always look so
immaculate and yet bring so little with her. To look half-way decent
when she travelled, Hope needed a giant suitcase and would still
forget something vital. Though very pale, Sam looked Vogue-fresh
with just a small, squashy bag. Her flu had improved miraculously,
probably due to the quantity of anti-flu capsules she'd been con-
suming.

'Let's go for a coffee in town before heading out,' suggested Sam
to her sister, pleased that, for once, Hope hadn't brought the kids,
which gave them the opportunity to have a private chat about the
madcap idea of moving away for a year. In fact, Hope hadn't told
the children their beloved aunt was coming so she could have some

time alone with her sister. If Millie had heard the news, she'd have thrown a complete tantrum wanting to go along too. Hope had also told Matt she preferred to pick up Sam alone: Matt wouldn't have been able to resist arguing with Sam if she criticized his precious plan.

'Is this quiet cup of coffee on our own so that you can give me the "are you insane?" lecture without Matt butting in?' inquired Hope with a faint twitch to her mouth. She wasn't stupid. Her sister wasn't given to last-minute visits and you didn't need to be a nuclear physicist to figure out why she was here now.

'Yes Sherlock, that was precisely the plan,' admitted Sam, grinning. 'I'm shocked that you saw through me that quickly. I must be losing my touch. I can remember the far off days when we were small and I could make you do anything I wanted purely by using the correct tone of voice.'

'I remember that too,' Hope remarked, 'and I have moved on a bit.'

'Only a bit,' Sam retorted. 'Matt certainly manages to make you do exactly what he wants.'

Hope locked the car. 'How about we have a cease-fire on the question of our trip, at least until we've got a cup of coffee in our hands.'

'Done.'

It was only half ten in the morning: a crisp early October day with a watery sun low in the sky. They strolled past the cathedral, vast and majestic in the sunlight.

'This is such a beautiful city,' Sam sighed. 'I never seem to get the chance to spend any time here, just wandering around like a proper tourist.'

Hordes of tourists meandered through the streets, some excitedly wielding high-tech cameras and taking endless photos, others looking weary, as if the tour bus had just dumped them there and they were feeling the strain of a whistle-stop tour of the hot spots of Britain.

Hope and Matt had done all the touristy things when they'd moved there first. They'd sipped the sulphuric water in the Pump Room. 'Disgusting,' gasped Hope, wishing she could spit it out. 'A bit like tonic water,' said Matt, reflectively. They'd toured the Roman baths and listened to stories about when the city was Aqua Sulis, the Roman stronghold with lots of gracious villas complete with proper under-floor heating. Matt's favourite part of the tour had been the Roman sites, while Hope's romantic soul loved the Georgian history of Bath. As a teenager, she'd secretly adored the Georgette Heyer romances where Bath often featured as the fashionable watering hole for wealthy aristocrats. She was fascinated by the Assembly rooms where both Jane Austen and Georgette Heyer's heroines had swirled around in Empire line dresses; she loved the Museum of Costume and she liked nothing better than idling around the pretty, curving streets with their yellow sandstone colonnaded buildings, imagining ladies stepping from carriages and sedans into the houses.

The sisters walked past a trio of classical buskers playing something that Sam instantly identified as Mozart. Two years as product man-ager of a classical label had taught her a lot, and she no longer immediately thought of the *Lone Ranger* theme music when she heard the first strains of the 'William Tell Overture'.

'It is lovely here, isn't it?' said Hope, who practically never came into Bath to do anything other than rush into work or rush into some shop or other. Simply coming in to wander around aimlessly was sheer heaven.

Sam insisted on going into Sally Lunn's cake shop, a spot where Hope insisted that true Bathites would never set foot.

'It'd be like you walking round London's Piccadilly Circus with your mouth open in awe or having your picture taken right outside Buckingham Palace,' she said as Sam dragged her into the cosy, tourist-filled spot where the scent of the unique Sally Lunn buns rose into the air. 'My reputation for being cool and trendy will be ruined. Locals don't "do" Bath!'

'Don't be a spoilsport,' said Sam, suddenly aware that she'd eaten practically nothing for the past few days because of her flu. She could murder one of those Sally Lunns covered in salmon. 'Next time you come to London, I promise I'll get my picture taken with a Beefeater. Deal?'

'And in Madame Tussaud's and outside Harrods too?'

'You drive a hard bargain,' Sam sighed. 'I'll even buy a "My friend went to London and all she brought me was this lousy T-shirt" T-shirt, OK?'

Sam ate her Sally Lunn and had the left over half of Hope's too. Hope was currently on what she called her 'half' diet: she got to eat half of anything she fancied. Half her dinner, half a biscuit, etc. It was very difficult.

Sam chatted as she ate, being funny about work, how she'd missed an important meeting and how her social life was suffering as a result of the new job.

'Mad Malcolm upstairs accused me of having a party,' she said, licking crumbs from her fingers. 'Honestly, I'm in the office so much, there's as much chance of me having a wild party as there is of Steve Parris developing a nice personality.'

'That bad?' Hope asked, knowing that her sister used humour and funny stories to hide how she really felt.

For a moment, Sam's eyes were opaque. 'We're not here to talk about me,' she said quickly.

'Pardon me,' said Hope. 'As you've come all this way to deliver a lecture to me on living my life, at least let me get my two penn'orth in about your life.'

'I don't have a life, I have a career. There's a difference,' Sam said sourly.

Hope leaned forward over the little table in a 'spill the beans' manner.

'It's this flu,' Sam said quickly, sorry she'd revealed so much. 'I've been feeling a bit low lately, I don't know why. I've had two 24-hour bugs since September, although it's one way of keeping my weight down. I keep getting the most awful periods that put me out of commission for two days each time, and to cap it all, Steve Parris, my new boss, is a complete asshole, excuse my language, but he is. I'm going to have to keep proving myself until I'm a hundred, which feels like it'll be any day now.'

Hope reached over and squeezed her sister's hand.

'Sam, you should go to the doctor and have a check up. That's three bouts of illness in nearly two months, it's not good. And the periods . . . you need to get it checked out. I bet you're anaemic, heavy periods can do that. You need a tonic or something.'

'Don't mind me, I'm grumpy today. There's nothing wrong with me. I'm strong as an ox,' Sam said. She managed to laugh convincingly: 'Too much sex and not enough sleep, probably,' which was a lie. She couldn't remember the last time she'd had sex. Well, she could; she and Karl had been in Paris. That was the last time, the last bittersweet time.

'You're seeing someone?' asked Hope delightedly.

It was time to change the subject. 'I'll tell you about my love life another time,' hedged Sam, who didn't want to have to admit that her last relationship had ended two years ago. Career women appeared to scare men off faster than saying you had herpes. 'So, what are you going to do in Ireland? I know Matt has it all worked out but he hasn't thought about you.'

'He has,' protested Hope. 'I've wanted to spend more time with the children for ages. You've no idea how soul-destroying it is to send them into that nursery every morning when I'm going into work to smile at total strangers, knowing Toby's doing new things every day and I'm missing it. Somebody else saw him walk for the first time.' That memory still haunted her.

'Fair point,' Sam conceded. 'But you like going out to work, it's part of your life too. How will you cope in a strange country with no work mates, perhaps no nursery nearby and no old friends to rely on when you're miserable?'

Hope had no real answer to this.

'What about at night, what about going to the theatre, or the movies, or to the latest restaurant?' Sam continued.

'Oh come on, Sam, let's be real here,' interrupted Hope. 'This is me you're talking to. I'm a woman with two small children, not some socialite who spends her life in the Gucci shop wondering what dress to wear to the movie premiere. I can't remember when I last went to the theatre. We saw *Miss Saigon* in London with you that time and I haven't been since. And as for films, by the time we get the kids in bed, I'm too tired to think about going to see a film. I prefer to get videos.'

'Oh well, that's OK, then,' Sam said fiercely. 'You'll settle in fine as long as there's a video shop in this village at the back end of nowhere.'

She knew she sounded cruel but she had to say it. Hope wasn't one of life's outward people. Well, she was chatty and bubbly when she was with Sam, but with other people she was one of the quietest women imaginable. Hope was the woman who liked sitting in corners at parties, watching others instead of joining in. Some people would thrive in a new country, relishing the opportunity to meet new friends and become part of a thriving community. Hope was not such a person.

'You've never been the sort to join in,' Sam pointed out. 'You're not into amateur dramatics or joining the choir or becoming the stalwart of the parents' association. That's fine and dandy when you've got a job and you live on a housing estate beside a hundred other families, but not when you're in the middle of nowhere and you're not working.'

There, she'd said it.

Hope didn't react for a moment. 'I can learn,' she said finally. 'Anyhow, I'm going to be with Matt and the children, that's what I'm doing this for.'

'But what about *you*?' Sam said earnestly.

'It *is* for me,' Hope repeated. 'Haven't you been listening, Sam? It's for them, for me, for all of us.'

She'd have loved to have told Sam about how terrified she'd been when she thought Matt was having an affair but Sam was brittle and sharp today. Hope was convinced her sister would briskly tell her that gratitude because her husband *wasn't* cheating on her was no reason for upping sticks to live in another country.

Sam would have loved to have told Hope that she was feeling miserable, middle-aged and somehow unfulfilled despite her fabulous new job. But Hope had enough problems of her own to cope with without hearing Sam's. Ever since Hope's wedding day, Sam had been convinced that Matt was trouble. He made all the decisions and he was far too good looking to be trusted. But then, Sam never trusted any man.

Millie threw herself delightedly at Auntie Sam as soon as they arrived home.

'Auntie Sam!' she squealed, before realizing that there had been more to her mother's trip than buying groceries. Her bottom lip wobbled ominously.

'Auntie Sam wanted to surprise you, darling,' Hope said brightly.

'A nice surprise, I hope,' Sam said gravely. 'Won't you say hello to me?' she said to Toby.

He gave her a small hug and showed her his toy train. 'Look Auntie Ham.' He never could say Sam.

'Hello,' said Matt guardedly, appearing from the kitchen.

'Hello you,' she replied, just as guardedly.

If Sam and Matt did not get on, it wasn't because they were so different. It was because they were so alike. Both were strong-minded, a bit bossy and capable of being jealous. Neither seemed happy about the presence of anyone else important in Hope's life. Their rivalry was a source of anxiety for Hope, although neither Sam nor Matt seemed bothered by it.

'So what brings you here, or can I guess?' Matt said sarcastically.

Hope glared at him. 'Sam's only here until tomorrow lunchtime so let's have a nice weekend, shall we?' she said in the voice she used when she was trying to get Millie to eat broccoli.

It wasn't the best weekend ever. Sam was furious with Matt because of what she thought of as his 'crazy plan'. Matt was furious with Sam for daring to put a spanner in the works and on Saturday night when he and Hope were getting ready for bed, he said he hated the way her sister barged in and tried to tell people what to do.

'She's the most bossy woman I've ever met in my life,' he snapped, walking round their bedroom somehow managing not to look ridiculous in socks and a shirt.

As Sam had said practically the same thing about Matt only hours before, Hope just gritted her teeth and prayed that she'd be able to survive the rest of the weekend. Normally she loved it when Sam visited. They spent lots of time on their own, going for walks and talking. But after that first morning, Matt seemed to be there all the time, as if he didn't want to give Sam the opportunity to put her sister off the trip to Ireland. He nagged Hope about Sam who, in turn, nagged Hope about Matt.

Like piggy in the middle, Hope felt weighed down by their disapproval and broke out her secret supply of dark chocolate soft centres to comfort herself. She couldn't bear to upset either darling Sam or her beloved Matt, so she did her best to stay out of it and spent her time saying 'more tea anyone?' or 'look at what Millie's up to,' in a cheery manner every time the other pair began to argue.

They were all relieved when Sunday afternoon came and Hope drove Sam to get the train.

'I'm sorry we were all a bit tense over the weekend,' Sam said as they stood in the station.

'Don't be silly, it was great,' lied Hope, who hated acknowledging that things were ever less than perfect.

'Will you try and get to London to see me before you go?'

'I hope so.' Hope's eyes filled with tears. 'And we can have a proper visit.'

They hugged each other and then Sam turned and walked away, elegant in her shearling coat and buttermilk cashmere wrap, her pale hair gleaming as she walked. She waved as she got on the train.

Hope fought a losing battle not to cry as she watched her sister disappear into the carriage. She wished she saw Sam more often; she wished Sam and Matt didn't fight so much; she wished . . . she didn't know what she wished any more.

On the train back, Sam thought about Karl. She tried not to think about him these days. Karl. Even his name sent a shiver of remembered pleasure rippling through her. She'd met him at a sales conference in Brussels and they'd hit it off immediately. In fact, a lot of the record company women had liked the idea of hitting it off with the tall, blond Swede but he'd had eyes only for Sam.

They'd delicately side-stepped around each other for the entire week, talking about their respective jobs (Karl was with the international office and travelled a lot) and sitting beside each other at dinner, but nothing more. It was only afterwards, when Karl arrived in London for two months, that they began to see each other properly. He had the use of a company apartment in the Barbican but he spent most of his free time with Sam, curled up in her bed in the old mansion flat she lived in then. They did things like Häagen-Dazs couples did in adverts: feeding each other take away food in bed, drinking wine while dressed in knickers and T-shirts, lounging around with the newspapers and watching old movies on late night TV.

In spite of his cool, measured demeanour, Karl had been impetuous and deeply romantic at heart. He saw their future together and begged Sam to follow him to Paris where he was going to be based for at least two years.

Something in Sam had recoiled at the idea.

Give up her job to follow Karl, to be his girlfriend, his companion, a hanger on instead of a mover and a shaker? No way. He'd pleaded with her, pointed out that with her skills and experience she'd get a job in a shot, a better job, perhaps. But Sam was having none of it. She wasn't going to be anybody's accessory, their significant other instead of a person in her own right. She'd always wanted to stand on her own two feet and she wasn't about to change the habit of a lifetime.

It had taken a week of arguments before Karl had realized she meant what she said. That had been two years ago. Last she'd heard, he'd married a French woman who worked in the couture business. Now there was a job with little possibility for relocation. Let him try and move *her* to his next posting.

A woman with a toddler got on the train and sat opposite Sam, the woman pale and make-up less, the toddler rosy cheeked and up to mischief.

'Sit Lily, don't mess, please,' begged the mother. 'It's only for half a hour. We'll get into trouble with Mr Train Driver if we don't behave.'

She produced several books for Lily to read.

'Juice!' demanded Lily loudly, clearly not bothered by idle threats about Mr Train Driver. To prove her point, she shoved the books out of her way and stared big-eyed at Sam.

She was just like Millie, Sam thought with amusement, utterly sure of herself and determined to get what she wanted. How had poor insecure Hope ever produced such a confident child?

The woman extracted a carton of juice from a huge shoulder bag, the same sort of bag Hope always seemed to drag around with her, Sam noticed. Mothers were all lop-sided from schlepping round giant shoulder bags that contained everything from toddler outfits to entire meals with plenty of toys, books and bumper boxes of baby wipes thrown in for good measure.

Sam looked out of the window and tried not to notice Lily staring at her while sucking on her juice straw. The more Sam gazed out of the window, the more Lily leaned towards her, standing up on the seat beside her mother and leaning over the table until she was lying on it. Her big eyes were fixed on Sam, willing this new grown up person to look at her, intent on being noticed.

'Lily!' warned her mother.

Lily moved back a fraction and stopped sucking on her straw. She inadvertently squeezed the carton and an arc of juice sailed up in the air like a fountain and then down onto Sam's beige shearling coat.

'I'm so sorry,' said the child's mother with a deep weariness.

Sam, thinking of Hope dragging Millie and Toby around, desperately hoping they wouldn't cover other people with orange juice or smears of chocolate, shook her head. 'It's fine,' she said. 'It needed to be cleaned anyway.'

The woman shot her a look of such gratitude that Sam was pleased she'd been polite. Once, she'd have snapped about people not being able to control their children in public. It must be age creeping up on her. She was getting mellow now that she was on the brink of forty.

Forty. She shuddered. It sounded so old. Karl would never fall for her if she met him now, she thought ruefully. It was odd thinking about him: he never crossed her mind most of the time. She didn't miss him per se, just the experience of being with somebody. *That* was nice; cuddling up in bed with a man, having someone to share the day with, someone to occasionally buy coffee or milk when she forgot.

She liked that side of things but not all the other hassle that went with it. All that crap they were forever talking about in women's magazines or at women-only dinners: maintaining relationships, worrying about whether he felt happy or not, trying to keep the spice in your sex life . . . sheer hell. Sam couldn't see why women were supposed to do all the hard work. Men carried on doing whatever they felt like while women did questionnaires to see if He was happy or if He would stray or if He needed to talk more. Why the hell bother? Sam thought. Let Him worry about Himself, she wouldn't.

What she needed was a virtual boyfriend: a sophisticated robot who could cuddle her, make love to her and ask her about her day at work, and who shut up when she was tired and who never said things like 'I've been thinking about our future and I want to take up this job offer in Mars . . .'

She grinned to herself. How weird that nobody had ever thought of it before. A virtual boyfriend would be perfect for millions of women. No emotional hassle but all the physical advantages.

Lily smiled engagingly at her.

Sam smiled back. 'Sweet, isn't she?' she said.

'When she's asleep,' Lily's mother said with feeling.

Back in London, Sam picked up some groceries from the nearest shop and cooked herself some vegetable pasta with organic pesto sauce. Stir-frying vegetables, boiling pasta and adding a sauce and some parmesan shavings was the nearest thing to cooking that Sam ever got.

She piled it all onto a large white plate and sat down at the table with her favourite Nina Simone CD playing softly in the background and the Sunday papers spread out in front of her. But strangely, she didn't feel hungry. Normally, she adored pasta and hoovered up anything with pesto sauce on it but tonight her appetite had deserted her.

After a while, she gave up and shoved the almost untouched plate away from her. If she wasn't hungry, it was her body's way of telling her she didn't need any more food. Anyway, after two days with Hope shovelling down Sally Lunns, she could hardly expect to be hungry.

On Monday before lunch, Steve held a top level meeting where the subject was company cutbacks. Ten senior executives sat around the glossy boardroom table and focussed on their departments. All present looked outwardly unconcerned but quivered inside their designer jeans and hoped they personally weren't for the high jump. All except Sam. She was fed up with quivering at things Steve Parris or anybody else said. She'd had a hellish morning and didn't care a fiddler's toss if she was fired at that precise moment, not least because she'd just signed a three-year contract. She'd spent the entire morning on the phone to Density's manager who was explaining all the things that his charges *wouldn't* do to promote their album. So far, the 'wouldn't do' list included talking to any interviewer who hadn't been at one of their live gigs and doing any breakfast television or any other media the band described as '. . . facile and cretinous . . .'. They didn't want to pose for any photos on the basis that they liked the publicity ones and couldn't go through all that hassle again of having make-up applied and having to look moody for hours. And they were not, absolutely not, letting any tabloid journalist near them.

Sam had tried pointing out that this little list would make the record company's job extremely difficult but the manager was having none of it.

'Steve Parris said we could have what we wanted,' he hissed down the phone. 'This is what we want.' With that, he hung up.

Because she didn't want any blood spilled just yet in relation to Density, Sam hadn't rung him back and threatened the manager with a do-it-yourself vasectomy. But she was tempted to. Now she sat at the meeting and caught a sympathetic glance from the publicity director, who had heard all about Density's can't-do list. In Sam's first weeks at Titus, the LGBK publicity director, a tall black American woman named Karen Storin, had been the friendliest of all her new colleagues.

'Welcome to Steve's elite club,' Karen had joked quietly the first time they'd met.

'Elite club?' inquired Sam.

'The women execs club,' Karen explained. 'Steve's not big on female empowerment.'

'You mean I'm here because I'm a woman and you're here because you're a black woman?' Sam joked.

Karen grinned. 'We're here *in spite* of those facts – and because we're damn good.'

Sam knew there was another reason she was there: because the European President had put his foot down.

'OK?' Sam asked Karen now, hiding a smile because they'd just had a variation of this conversation minutes before on the way to the meeting, safe in the knowledge that they could talk freely before they reached the boardroom where Steve's earwigging second-in-command would be listening. Karen was handling Density's publicity schedule and was encountering the same problems Sam had.

'Everything's under control. The schedule for Density is working out just fine,' Karen said gravely, which was a million miles away from what she'd said originally.

Then, she'd been in a rage. 'I've just been on the phone to their manager and I have never dealt with anyone like him in my life. If I didn't know he was working with them, I'd swear he was trying to sabotage them. They refuse to do anything I ask. Do they want the album to flop?' she'd hissed at Sam.

'How about you?' she said now to Sam across the board room table.

Sam smiled: 'Utterly under control too,' she said deadpan, as if moments before she hadn't told Karen that the Density manager was ruining her entire week. Maintaining the façade that everything in your label was hunky dory was vitally important when you worked under Steve Parris.

The great man himself arrived bringing with him the noxious smell of a cigar. Sam quite liked cigar smoke, having once been a twenty-Dunhills-a-day woman, but she objected to the fact that Steve ignored all the office signs and smoked anywhere he liked. Everyone else who smoked had to rush downstairs to the street so that at coffee break time, the pavement outside the Titus office was jam packed with hollow-cheeked people inhaling furiously to make up for the previous, stressful, nicotine-free hours.

Steve threw himself into a leather chair, shoved it back from the table and put his leather-booted feet on the blotter his assistant had neatly laid out in front of him. 'So what's happenin', gang?' he asked.

Sam could hear a growl deep inside her body. Where did he think he was? A biker's club with a bottle of beer in front of him? He was such a weedy little shit. She hated him.

'Great, just great, Steve,' said Zak, the Titus A & R director, who probably *did* think they were in a biker club with beer in front of them. Too much cocaine in the eighties, Sam had been told. If he hadn't been one of Steve's personal pals, he wouldn't have been in the job.

'Cutbacks and reorganization,' Steve intoned gravely. 'We have to lose at least ten senior people to go along with the global restructuring.' Everyone stared at him, stricken. Ten jobs. Ten senior level jobs. That meant ten people in their building, people who worked for them, people they liked. People *they* would have to sack. Sam felt the by-now familiar clenching sensation deep in her insides, a painful knotting spasm that she'd half-diagnosed as irritable bowel syndrome. What else could it be? And she felt nauseous too. She still wasn't over her flu, that had to be it. She hadn't been able to touch her wholemeal toast this morning and she'd felt so exhausted, it had taken three strong mugs of coffee to get her out the front door.

'The staffing levels in Europe are way too high and we've got to cut back,' Steve said. 'The international office say we're top heavy with staff and this is the only way. Making our powerbase smaller is going to streamline the whole organisation, stop us getting lazy.'

'Have you identified any particular departments or is it going to be across the board?' Sam was amazed to discover that she'd spoken.

Steve cleared his throat. 'Your label is going to be badly hit,' he said. 'The ratio is way off compared to the American offices. You need to cut four people.'

Sam felt sicker.

'We've got four hundred people working for us in this country, so it's not that big a percentage,' cut in Steve's favourite yes-man, a smooth guy from finance.

'But it's a big deal,' snapped the company's head of legal, a dynamic dark-haired man named Curtis. 'We're talking about your colleagues, not worker ants. What about my department?' he asked Steve.

Steve was nervous of Curtis, Sam had noticed. Probably afraid to browbeat a man who knew employment law backwards and could draw up a constructive dismissal suit in ten minutes on the back of an envelope. 'You're fine, nobody from your department,' he said now.

The meeting lasted another twenty-five minutes with Steve giving them the party line on how this was to be dealt with, both within the company and publicly. The trade papers would have a field day speculating on the company's bottom line if the cutbacks were explained incorrectly. Personnel had already identified the people who were first on the list: they'd inform each department head at a private meeting. Sam's was scheduled for an hour and a half later.

As they all left the boardroom and walked to the lift, nobody spoke. Suddenly she couldn't face standing in the claustrophobic lift. She needed some air. Turning away from the lift, she hurried to the stairs and practically ran down four flights to the street. Curtis was there already, lighting up a cigarette.

'Can I scab a cigarette from you?' Sam asked, hating herself for having one after all these years.

'I didn't know you did,' Curtis remarked, handing her the pack.

'I don't. Not any more. That was a bit rough, wasn't it?'

He nodded silently.

'I don't know how I'm going to sack four people. Sorry, "lose four members of staff to keep us in line with company guidelines,"' Sam said bitterly. 'I haven't been here long enough to make any judgements on the staff and yet, now I'm going to be the bitch from hell and get rid of some of them. That'll be great for morale. And Steve looks as if he doesn't give a shit about them. He almost smiled when he said I had to lose four people. I swear he hates me.'

Curtis smiled slowly. 'Steve doesn't like *anybody*,' he said. 'Understand that and you're going to be fine, although it's no secret that you're not on his Top Ten list because he wanted someone else to get the job.'

Sam rolled her eyes. 'Tell me about it.'

'I've known Steve for ten years and he's always been the same,' Curtis added. 'He's good at his job, though. This company was

73

screwed up when he took over. He's hell to work with but he gets the job done.'

'He enjoys making people sweat,' Sam sighed. 'He deliberately told us there was a redundancy meeting this morning but never said who was going to be made redundant so that everyone would be nervous.' She didn't mention that since she'd just signed a three-year contract, she'd known that she, personally, wouldn't be on the list. Just her staff.

'Psychology,' Curtis shrugged. 'Steve's plan is that by the time he tells you that you have to fire four people, you're so pleased that your name isn't on the list, you agree to it like a shot. Steve rules by fear. He likes terror and arguments among the staff: divide and conquer are his management rules. That's the way he learned and he thinks it's the only way things work. He's terrified that if he ever tries to be nice, he'll be taken over in a bloody coup.'

Nauseated after her forbidden cigarette, Sam went back to her office feeling nervous. She shouldn't have said anything to Curtis about Steve Parris. That was stupid, unprofessional behaviour. She hadn't been at Titus long enough to understand where allegiances lay and was only guessing that Curtis and Steve didn't get on. They could be bosom buddies behind it all. She really was losing her marbles when it came to how to behave in the corporate jungle. What was happening to her? It must be the after effects of the flu. She'd better get some perk-you-up supplement in the chemist.

At three o'clock, Sam steeled herself to enter the lions' den. Steve and the personnel director were sitting in front of a list of names and the personnel director launched into the list of people Sam was to make redundant even before she'd sat down.

Sam listened calmly, hiding her distaste. One of the women on the list had just made it public that she was four months' pregnant. A young guy in publicity Sam had been very impressed with had just bought an apartment and had signed up for a huge mortgage. Sam's insides did their clenching routine.

What could she say? Nothing. She was a boss now, she had to make tough decisions and implement them if necessary. Four people from her department had to go and if she balked at it, all she'd be doing was undermining her own position. The personnel guy kept talking and Sam listened, feeling wooden.

When he was finished, she coolly pointed out that there was a pregnant woman among the names. 'You should check whether she could sue us for getting rid of her at this time,' Sam said unemotionally, as if she was talking about squashing a spider instead of discussing another person's life.

Steve laughed from behind his vast desk. 'I told you Sam Smith would be able to sack her entire department and it wouldn't bother her in the slightest,' he said triumphantly to the personnel guy. 'We did good the day we hired you, Sam. We needed somebody who understands the game. Not some dumb cow who's going to sob her eyes out whenever she has to sack people.'

Sam blinked. She remembered back to her final interview, the one where Steve had delicately – well, as delicately as someone as bull-headed as Steve could manage – tried to find out her views on kids. They couldn't ask outright, of course. Asking a woman if she planned to have children, and was therefore looking for maternity entitlements and leaving them with six months of a problem, was illegal. Sam had always understood this interview difficulty and had made it plain to prospective employers that she was not one of those biological-clock-about-to-go-off women. It was an advantage and she used it. Always had.

She remembered giving Steve and the other board members her steely look as she had said 'I'm not the mumsy type.'

They'd all breathed a sigh of relief, and Steve had given her a matey look.

'Tough as old boots,' he said now, looking as if, under other circumstances, he'd pat her shoulder in a friendly manner. But Sam wasn't the demonstrative type. Shoulder patting, double kissing and all that stupid, fake affectionate stuff drove her mad. She shook hands. Why pretend to be best pals with people you didn't know? It was hypocritical.

'That's what I like about you, Sam. You don't take any prisoners. That's what they say and it's true. I like that in my team. Sacking people isn't easy but we've all had to do it.'

Steve waved his cigar, leaving a trail of smoke. Sam was dismissed.

She went back to her office thinking of the irony of Steve saying there was anything about her he liked. Yeah, right.

She also wondered what else people said about her. *Tough as old boots. You don't take any prisoners.* Hell, she sounded like a hoary old sergeant major at a boot camp who scared the hell out of the rookies and who could drink rotgut with the best of them. *Smith is tough as old boots but boy, can she do the job. There's a heart in there somewhere, if you can find it. Not bad looking but too tough for any man . . . Women like her always end up on their own.*

Being tough had seemed like a good idea when she was twenty or thirty and desperate to prove herself in the corporate jungle but now, with forty facing her like the north face of the Eiger, she wasn't so sure. Tough but able to carry off a trendy designer dress was one thing. Tough but wrinkled like an old chicken was another thing entirely. How would she come across at sixty-five when she was tougher, older and with a hard little face grooved into a lifetime of wrinkles?

At that moment, she thought of Aunt Ruth. Ruth Smith, civil servant and scourge of those beneath her in the planning department, had not been the maternal type either and having two small children unceremoniously dumped on her hadn't changed that. She'd continued to live her life exactly the same way as before her brother and his wife had been killed. To cap it all, Ruth had never even looked motherly: she'd looked like an eccentric maiden aunt from a novel.

Sam could remember the boys across the road teasing herself and Hope about their mad aunt.

'She's a witch, she is, eye of bat and leg of toad!' they'd chant nastily at the girls.

Secretly, the girls had to admit that their aunt bore more than a passing resemblance to a witch, mainly because she insisted on wearing her hair in an antediluvian bun and fancied herself in pince nez spectacles which did nothing for her pinched, narrow face.

Sam felt weary. She'd always had a difficult relationship with her aunt, and swore she'd never be anything like her. And here she was turning into a carbon copy. Aunt Ruth would probably have run Titus Records with a rod of iron and made it the most successful record company ever.

There was a giant skip outside the house next door when Sam arrived home that night. The builders had finally moved in. Sam glared at the rather run down building which was the next in the terrace. For the two years she'd lived in her flat, she'd been irritated by the dilapidated state of the adjoining house which was owned by a dotty old lady who clearly had no time for painters, window cleaners or gardeners. When she'd died, the house had been put up for sale and all the neighbours watched the property pages with interest, dying to know how much it would go for so they could figure out how much their own places were worth.

It had taken ages, but when the sold sign was finally pasted on, all breathed a sigh of relief. Except now, Sam thought grimly, there would be building work going on for ever as the new owners ripped it apart. Kango hammers thumping at dawn and scaffolding positioned so that builders could peer curiously through her windows, not giving her a moment's peace. Feeling put upon and miserable, Sam stomped up the stairs.

'Stop making noise,' roared Mad Malcolm reedily from the top landing.

Sam growled deep in her throat and just managed to stop herself telling him what orifice he could stick his head into.

Inside the sanctuary of her own apartment, she dropped her briefcase wearily, shed her coat and sat down on the big pale couch in front of the fireplace. Determined to ignore the fact that the place was a mess, she switched on the television and watched the end of the evening news. But when it was over, she couldn't relax. It was no good, she had to tidy up. Compulsive tidiness, Karl had teased her when she'd start changing the sheets on the bed while he was still in it.

Pulling on an absolutely ancient pair of jeans and a threadbare old grey jumper, Sam planned the clean out. The bedroom to start, she decided, tying her hair up into a ponytail.

It took two and a half hours to clean every area of the apartment to her satisfaction. By the time she was finished, the kitchen was restored to its sparkling, pristine perfection and the sitting room was once again a restful, Zen-like spot with all clear, white surfaces free of old newspapers, magazines and scribbled yellow post-it notes about work. The four big modern oils that hung on the warm cream walls stared down at a tranquil, clutter-free room furnished cleanly with big white couches, a low pale wooden coffee table and a muted cream rug on the pale floorboards. The grouping of fat creamy church candles on the fireplace was dust free and perfectly aligned, while the blond driftwood carving on the windowsill had been dusted to within an inch of its life. Even the big Indian silver elephant that stood in the corner beside her towering ficus plant gleamed. Sam knew that not everybody liked the clutter-free look but she adored it. She liked the order and the sense of calm that it brought.

Hope hated it.

'You've no . . . stuff, no knick knacks,' Hope had said the first time she'd seen the apartment in all its spartan modern glory. 'It's all too perfect for me,' she'd added, eyes sweeping over heavy cream brocade curtains that would be speckled with grubby fingerprints if Millie and Toby were ever let run riot there.

Seeing the place through Hope's eyes, Sam had to agree. Hope would have had tonnes of junk on every occasional table, instead of simply placing a lamp or a piece of sculpture there.

When they'd been kids, they'd shared a bedroom and Hope's side had been a riot of cuddly toys, empty boxes kept because they were pretty, bits of tangled up jewellery and hand-sewn lavender sachets for her clothes, most of which were hung on her chair.

Sam's side had the only colour co-ordinated wardrobe in their school. Graded from white to black, Sam's clothes hung in a regimented line that awed Hope just to look at it.

Tidying her wardrobe properly would have to wait tonight, she decided, as she finished the bedroom. It annoyed her when the wardrobe was messy with the greys infiltrating the rail of blacks and skirts hanging with the trousers, but she'd do that tomorrow.

In the kitchen, she put away her cleaning equipment and put some cheese on a couple of water crackers. She poured herself a glass of crisp Sancerre and sat down on the couch again, this time content. As the strains of Mozart echoed softly around the apartment, Sam finally felt herself relax. She willed herself to forget about work and the job losses.

Then, the noise started. It was strange, because at first she wasn't sure where it was coming from. Surely not upstairs? Even Mad Malcolm wasn't mad enough to be playing loud rock music at ten o'clock at night. And then the penny dropped. Next door. Still clutching her glass of wine, Sam stared out the front window at the adjoining house and saw two young women lugging a crate of beer up the path. Standing beside the window, the music seemed louder. A taxi pulled up and disgorged more people, all happy and clearly party-bound, judging by the number of off-licence bags they were carrying. Sam felt the veins in her head throb. This was not wild party land. This was a wildly expensive neighbourhood where the notion of a wild party was one where the caterers served too much Bollinger or where guests tripped on their Manolos while staggering out to the chauffeur-driven Mercedes.

Whoever had bought the house couldn't, wouldn't, dream of ruining the discreet peace of Holland Park with a party? Or if they thought they could, they'd soon discover the error of their ways, Sam snarled.

Just as abruptly as it had started, the music stopped and Sam felt some of the anger leave her body. Good. Some other resident had complained; therefore she didn't have to go in and do so. In her current mood of pent-up tension, who knew what she'd have said. The police would have been called sooner rather than later.

She curled up on the couch again, sipping her wine and letting the Mozart soothe her.

With a loud bass thump, the music next door cranked up even louder this time, sounding as if Black Sabbath had turned up and were playing a live gig.

As the music reached a crescendo, so did Sam's temper. Downing half her wine in one gulp, she grabbed her keys, slid her feet into the espadrilles she used as slippers and rampaged downstairs and out into the street.

'Oh no, a party,' sighed one of the nice couple from the basement flat, who were just coming in after an evening out. 'Have you rung the police, Sam?' he asked.

'No,' snarled Sam. 'But phone for an ambulance because whoever's having this party will need it when I'm finished with them.'

With giant strides, she raced up to the other door and pushed. It wasn't locked and opened easily. From here, the music was eardrum-splitting. The house, which was just a shell with stripped walls and bare, elderly floorboards, had excellent acoustics. Sound reverberated through it. Sam stepped over a rolled up rug and a crate of beer. The place was a disgusting mess. She could just imagine the thought process of whoever had bought it: have the party now, before the wallpaper was up and the carpets down. Or rather, Sam thought grimly, the spoiled teenage children of whoever had bought the house had thought it was a good idea to have the party now and their stupid parents had agreed, not caring about their new neighbours. Big mistake.

In a huge airy room, fairy lights were strung from the high ceiling and a gang of people stood around, smoking furiously and drinking beer from bottles. The scent of marijuana was heady. Nobody took any notice of Sam. In her jeans, she fitted right in. All she needed was a beer and she'd have looked like the rest of them, except for the fact that she had to be up at six a.m. and needed to get some rest, Sam thought furiously as she searched through the throng for her quarry.

The noise was coming from another room. Sam pushed through into what was obviously the nerve centre of the party. It was barely recognizable as a kitchen because most of the units had been ripped out by builders but there was still an island unit piled high with bottles of booze, six packs of Coke and a half eaten loaf of tomato bread. Sam ignored the people in the kitchen and headed for the dining room.

There, behind a bespectacled youth with a pile of CDs, she found it. The stereo system.

'Is there anything you want me to play?' yelled the disc jockey eagerly.

'Yes,' hissed Sam. 'Cards.'

With one expert movement, she wrenched the plug from the socket and all was quiet.

'Why did you do that?' asked the DJ in shock.

Everyone stared at Sam, bottles of beer held at half mast. They saw a small, slim woman with a blonde ponytail who wore ragged jeans and worn espadrilles and had what looked like newspaper smudges on one cheek. 'I live next door and I don't want to listen to this sort of crap late at night, do you understand?' she yelled, not in the least perturbed to have at least twenty curious thirty-somethings staring at her. Sam had bawled people out in public before.

'Sorry . . .' said the DJ politely. 'We just thought it wouldn't matter because nobody was living here yet . . .'

'Nobody may have been living here but there are eight people living in the house next door, an adjoining house,' Sam pointed out, 'where you can hear every bass thump.'

'So you thought you'd come in here and pull the plug instead of calmly asking us to turn the volume down, did you?' said an amused, low voice.

Wearing jeans that were astonishingly more torn and faded than hers, jeans that clung to a long, lean body, and a white creased shirt with most of the buttons undone to reveal a hard, muscled chest, was a man who made Sam's breath suddenly catch.

He wasn't handsome and he wasn't a mere twenty-something either. His face was too long, his eyes too narrow and his nose was too hooked to be model material, yet he was somehow the most incredible looking man she'd ever seen. Around her age, she guessed. Sam, who spent hours looking at pictures of male singers who sent other women into paroxysms of joy and left her utterly unmoved, could only stare.

If he could sing, she'd bet her bonus she could sell millions of albums with his face and body on the cover. Even if he couldn't sing, come to that. Still smiling, the corners of that fabulous mobile mouth twisted up into an ironic little smile, he ambled towards her. The tawny rumpled hair and the barely buttoned shirt made it look as if he'd just dragged himself out of some bed or other. Narrowed, treacly eyes surveyed her lazily as though he was eyeing her up with the intention of dragging her back to bed with him.

Sam objected to being surveyed. She was not some bimbo: she was a managing director, a woman who made subordinates flatten themselves against the walls in fear when she was angry. She drew herself up to her full five foot four inches and prepared for battle.

'I live next door –' she began fiercely in her killer boardroom voice.

'Do you?' he interrupted, still unhurried and unperturbed. 'Is it a nice neighbourhood?'

He stopped right in front of her. Even though he was barefoot, he still towered above her. Sam hated that. It was why she liked wearing perilously high shoes for important meetings so only the tallest people ever got to look down on her.

'It used to be,' she hissed. Talk about invading her personal space, his body was only a few inches away from hers. Normally, she'd have slayed him with an icy word but feeling strangely vulnerable out of her normal habitat, Sam took a step back. The wall was behind her, she couldn't go any further. Retreating was a mistake in business, it was now too. She stuck her chin out defiantly and the hand clenching the stereo plug tightened.

'Is this your house?' she said, trying to stay fearsome in the face of this Adonis invasion.

He ignored the question. 'You have something of mine,' he said, his voice almost a drawl. He reached long arms around her, and for a second Sam's breath stilled. He wouldn't, he couldn't. The charismatic, mocking face was close to hers as he reached down and she felt her stomach contract. His mouth was laughing and it was getting close to hers, so close she could feel the heat of his breath and smell a sharp citrusy tang from his warm body. Without knowing why, she closed her eyes. Then she felt the plug being pulled from her hand.

'Mine, I think,' said the man. With one graceful movement, he reached down, brushing against her leg, and plugged the stereo in again. He flicked a switch and loud music pumped into the room.

'You bastard!' screeched Sam, shocked and embarrassed. 'You

absolute bastard.' She had to really yell now to make sure he heard her. 'How dare you . . .'

'I think you're the one who dared,' he said, faintly amused. 'If you wanted us to turn the noise down, you should have asked me. I wouldn't have refused you.'

Impotent rage surged through her and for one terrible moment, Sam forgot all about good business, about how revenge was a dish best served cold and how any corporate raider needed a cool, calm mind.

He was using his physical presence to intimidate her and she reacted in the age-old, instinctive way of a woman confronted by a larger predator. She kicked him. In the shin as hard as she could, the blunt end of her espadrille connecting with hard bone and sinew.

'Ouch!' His yelp of pain could only be heard by her as the current song was at a eardrum-splitting decibel level.

That got rid of the mocking smile. Sam smirked. It had hurt her toe too, mind you, but now was no time to think of her own personal pain. Those years of ballet meant she had tough little feet.

'Who the hell do you think you are shoving your face in my personal space, you asshole!'

At that precise moment, the DJ unaccountably turned the music down. Sam's roar reached the entire room and provoked some giggles.

What the hell was the sound down for? Sam wondered blindly before she spotted the one soberly-dressed person in the premises.

The policeman stood in the doorway and hovering behind were the couple from the basement apartment in Sam's building, who were watching the proceedings anxiously.

'We've had a complaint about a party and loud noise,' said the policeman in a calm voice.

Sam shot her opponent a triumphant look and was enraged when, instead of looking worried or ashamed, he smiled lazily back at her.

'Yes officer, I'm afraid we turned the music up a bit high, I'm sorry,' he said and led the way into the kitchen.

Sam sniffed and held her head high as she marched out of the house and back into her own, followed by her downstairs neighbours.

That bloody man. How dare he make so much noise. How dare he humiliate her like that. And her foot hurt . . . ouch.

'Are you OK, Sam?' asked the wife from downstairs as Sam hobbled up the stairs.

'Fine,' she said breezily.

In the hall mirror, she caught sight of her face. She looked as if she'd been slapped. Both cheeks were as rosy as bramley apples. As she thought of the scene next door, her cheeks blazed some more in sheer embarrassment. She grabbed the wine from the fridge and poured more into the glass. You moron. Imagine turning into some cretinous, violent bimbo just because some he-man sticks his hairy chest in your face?

Anyway, you're hardly a bimbo, she groaned inwardly. You're staring into the abyss of forty.

Sam took a large gulp of wine. How could she have let herself down like that? She should have fixed him with a steely glare and told him exactly what forces of the law she'd use to make him stop his horrible party. When she'd suitably reprimanded herself, Sam went to bed. But sleep evaded her.

It was like being fifteen again, fifteen and horribly embarrassed because the boy in chemistry class had overheard her saying she fancied him like mad. Even twenty-four years later, that memory could still make her burn with shame. Now she'd done it again.

Finally, Sam got up and took one of the sleeping tablets she kept for emergencies. This certainly qualified. She slept eventually but her hot fevered dreams were full of a tall, laughing man in a soft, loose white shirt, a man who laughed at her for behaving like a petulant, hormonal fifteen year old.

When Sam left for work the next morning, she waited to check her mobile for messages until she was outside. She wanted to be doing *something* when she passed the house next door, she didn't want to be vulnerable and on her own in case she met him.

'You have no messages,' taunted the impersonal voice on her phone almost before she'd got to the front gate. Instead of hanging up, Sam was forced to listen to all her old, undeleted messages in order to keep up the pretence of being a busy, high-octane career woman who wasn't interested in men. Suddenly she noticed the dilapidated house's front door swinging open. Quickly averting her eyes in case she saw him again, she began talking into the phone.

'I'll be there soon, we'll have the meeting if you've got all the documents lined up from New York,' she blathered. A taxi sailed up the road and Sam stuck out her hand to hail it.

'Bye, talk soon,' called a female voice behind her.

Sam automatically turned to see a beautiful dark-haired girl leaving the house, smiling at the man in denims and bare feet who was holding the door. Bare chested too, Sam noticed with a jolt, and blowing kisses at the girl who looked around twenty-two at most, a stunning doe-eyed twenty-two who'd clearly stayed away from home all night if the silvery dress she was wearing under a big, man's coat was anything to go by.

'Take care,' the man said in that caressing voice, but he was looking mockingly at Sam who stood there, mobile in hand and her mouth open.

'Do you want a taxi or not, love?' demanded the taxi driver.

'Oh, er yes,' stammered Sam, pulling open the door and half falling in, with her raincoat trailing after her.

'Late night?' inquired the driver with a smirk.

'No,' hissed Sam, reasserting herself. 'Covent Garden please.'

What an asshole, she thought. Loud parties, having flings with women half his age. I mean, that girl was twenty and he has to be late thirties at least. Bloody playboy. Probably some trust fund moron who'd never had a job in his life but lived off inherited cash. Sam stared grimly out the cab window and simmered. She hated men like that.

# CHAPTER THREE

'I can't believe you're moving in a little over two weeks. I can see it now,' sighed Betsey dreamily. 'A summery little cottage in a beech glade, with a thatched roof and pretty sun-bleached rooms, gorgeous home grown food and quaint little pubs where you can sit outside and eat oysters and watch the world go by with the Riverdance music in the background.'

Hope glared at her over a plate of fisherman's pie. 'It'll be November, not summer.'

'I think that's Hollywood's version of rural Ireland,' laughed Dan from his position beside three-year-old Opal where he was attempting to clean up the mess she'd made squelching the insides out of several packets of brown sauce. Despite his efforts, Opal managed to fling a few opened packets on the floor before he could tidy them all away.

'No,' joined in Matt, 'it's the tour operator's version of Ireland when they're trying to sell you a time share. You know, Dan, maidens at the crossroads, sheep in the middle of the road and a friendly local with no teeth, a pipe and a tweed cap welded to his head waving at you!'

'Haven't we made an ad like that already?' Dan asked.

'Don't think so. But we will, we will. I love the originality of advertising,' Matt joked.

Matt, Betsey and Dan all laughed merrily. Hope stabbed her fish pie. Hilarious. Trust them all to make a joke about it all. It was her *life* they were talking about, not a location shoot for a bloody commercial. She was the one who'd be transported into another country, away from her friends and Sam, so that Matt could live the advertising man's dream. His dream, her sacrifice. A fortnight after her sister's visit, her delight that her marriage wasn't over had disappeared to be replaced by a gnawing fear of the unknown. Matt and Millie were thrilled with the idea of moving; Toby was thrilled because he was going up in an aeroplane; Hope was terrified.

'It's going to be great, love, isn't it?' Matt said, noticing the tautness around his wife's jaw. 'You'll love Kerry, I promise you.' He was about to reach over and hug her, but Millie, sitting between them, catapulted her plate of chips all over the table.

All four children started giggling.

Hope sighed, grabbed a handful of kitchen towels out of her bulging, ever-present toddler bag, and began cleaning up.

Sunday was family day in the local pubs and that meant a war zone of small children rampaging up and down the premises while their exhausted parents rocked irate babies in their pushchairs and mashed up food for toddlers who were straitjacketed into high chairs, in between trying to shovel some pub grub down their own throats.

Hope, Matt, Betsey and Dan had often shared Sunday lunch together but the birth of Millie, Toby, Ruby and Opal meant lunch no longer took the form of a civilized clinking of wine glasses over sea bass fillets in elegant restaurants. Now, Sunday lunch was a grab-while-you-can bean fest in whichever local child-friendly establishment wasn't jammed by twelve thirty.

Today, they were in the Three Carpenters, a huge pub with an adventure playground outside. This was very useful for exhausting small children but it was raining today, so the kids had turned the inside of the pub into an adventure playground.

There was always *one* family, Hope thought crossly, who let their kids run riot and didn't move a muscle to stop them. Millie and Toby weren't saints but she wouldn't dream of letting them behave like those brats who were now trying to dismantle a high chair in the corner after spending at least half an hour ripping up beer mats.

'Seriously though,' said Betsey, waving at the harassed young waitress in the hope of getting more wine, 'I've always had a yen to live in the country. There's something about the whole rustic life that appeals to me.'

'Betsey, honey,' Dan said affectionately, 'you couldn't survive without the buzz of traffic, a shop that sells the perfect cappuccino around the corner and your monthly waxing or whatever it is you do in that wildly expensive beautician's emporium.'

Not to mention a hairdresser to transform her hair from brown to a glossy chestnut every six weeks, thought Hope with unusual bitchiness.

Betsey, with her perfectly styled short hair, tiny personal-trainer-honed body and predilection for weekly massages, was a high maintenance woman. Hope, who got her bikini line waxed when she went on beach holidays and who'd had one massage in her life when the girls in the building society had bought her a voucher as a birthday treat, felt like a no-maintenance woman.

'Anti-ageing facials not waxing,' Betsey said unperturbed. 'You make me sound like a yeti. Anyway, I have sugaring done these days. It's much better.'

The talk turned to business, with Matt and Dan discussing work before Betsey made them all laugh by telling them about an interview she'd done with a TV comedienne.

Hope half-listened because she was keeping an eye on the four children. The two men and Betsey seemed to think that as long as none of the children were actually choking to death, they were fine.

Beside Hope, Toby was half asleep in his high chair. Opal and Millie were, for once, playing together, and even Ruby, a four-year-old terror with her father's innocent gaze and her mother's devil-may-care attitude to life, was busy investigating something under the table. For once, Hope didn't feel like checking what it was. Ruby was Betsey's daughter: let her sort it out. Hope was fed up of being the designated babysitter at these get-togethers.

She ate the rest of her lunch, half-listened to the chat going on around her, and wished she felt more cheerful.

It was two weeks since Matt's bombshell and he'd made startling progress for someone who'd spent a year promising to do something about bleeding the air from the bathroom radiator. He'd got Adam Judd to, reluctantly, give him a year's sabbatical, although the sporty company Audi had to go back. The only caveat was that Matt had to promise to help on certain campaigns if necessary and he'd be paid on a contract basis, which suited Matt fine.

He'd also found an estate agent who assured them there'd be no problem letting the house for a year; he'd checked out transporting their belongings to Ireland; had told his uncle's solicitor that he'd be flying over to take possession of the house shortly. In short, Matt was on a high, joyous that he'd made the move and was now on his way to making a long-cherished dream come true. Hope felt the way she had three days after Millie had been born: depressed and liable to burst into tears at the slightest provocation. When she'd mentioned the fact that Millie should be starting primary school the following September, Matt had merely nodded and said they'd be back. Probably.

*Probably*? thought Hope weakly.

It was after two when Dan went to get the bill and Matt went to the gents. Betsey turned to Hope.

'You're a bit down in the dumps,' she said. 'Is it the move to Ireland?'

Hope nodded, not wanting to say too much in front of the kids. Little pitchers had big ears.

'It's such a big step,' Hope whispered to Betsey now. 'I feel as if I'm being swept along on a tidal wave and I can't stop it, do you know what I mean? It's frightening. A new country, new people, a new home and I won't have a job there. Matt knows what he's doing but I don't.' She stopped miserably. She didn't want to say too much but she was sure Betsey would understand. Betsey knew Matt and knew how much Hope adored him, but she'd surely see Hope's side of things and would know how scary it felt to be swept along on somebody else's dream. 'I mean, imagine if you were expected to give up your job to travel with Dan? That would be tough.'

'It's a bit different, isn't it?' Betsey said. 'It's taken me a long time to get where I am on the magazine. I mean, I could work anywhere in the world, obviously, but I've got a great career here.'

'And I'm only working in the building society,' Hope said acidly. She was still steeling herself to hand in her notice. Mr Campbell would not be impressed.

'Don't be so touchy. I didn't mean that at all but our situations are rather different after all. You've got to learn not to be so uptight about everything, Hope,' she added. 'Go with the flow.' She waved one hand languidly. 'Treat it as an adventure. You'll have a ball. I'd adore a year off to have fun, play in the country and get out of the rat race.'

Hope looked Betsey straight in the eyes but Betsey had finished draining her wine glass and was looking around for her handbag. Had the other woman heard one word she'd said? She'd hoped for female bonding over how she was going to deal with this enormous upheaval in her life and instead, she'd been treated to Betsey's views on how much *she'd* have liked a year in the country. And been told in no uncertain terms that Betsey did not consider working in the building society to be a career on a par with the fabulous world of magazine journalism.

'Ruby, what are you doing under there? Is that my handbag?' Betsey said sharply. A heavily-made up Ruby emerged from under the table, her face plastered with Clarins base, vampish dark Chanel eyeshadow and plenty of Paloma Picasso red lipstick. Betsey only used the very best cosmetics.

Her mother gasped with rage and pulled her neat little Prada handbag from Ruby's red-lipsticked grasp. The bag was smeared with base and lipstick and had obviously been sitting in a pool of brown sauce left by Opal's earlier game.

'It's ruined,' Betsey shrieked. 'Three hundred pounds worth of handbag ruined!'

Hope patted her arm. 'Oh well,' she said benignly, 'you've got to go with the flow when you've got kids, haven't you, Betsey?'

Matt sang along to the children's tape they played on the drive home. Millie and Toby sang along too, making Hope feel like old prune-face in the passenger seat because she wasn't deliriously happy too.

'Dan told me he's dead jealous about what we're doing,' Matt confided as they pulled up outside their house.

'Why doesn't he give up his job for a year, then?' Hope demanded. 'Betsey wouldn't stand for it, that's why. She'd have heart failure if Dan suggested upping sticks for a year in the country.'

'Betsey was very enthusiastic,' Matt pointed out helpfully. 'What was it she said: she loved rustic things.'

'Betsey doesn't know the first thing about living in the country and would hate it,' Hope hissed. 'Her idea of rustic is jam pots with gingham covers on them. She thinks the country will be like Bath with livestock and handsome farmers in Range Rovers thrown in.'

Matt annoyed Hope by laughing heartily. 'Oh darling, you're so funny sometimes,' he said. 'You're the one who should be in advertising and not me.'

Proving that she wasn't quite as thick-skinned as a rhinoceros, Betsey phoned Hope at work the next day and apologized for upsetting her.

'I'd hate you to think I didn't value your career. I didn't mean to imply that my career was worth more than yours,' Betsey said, while Mr Campbell, Hope's boss, looked on disapprovingly. Personal phone calls were a no-no unless the person at the other end was about to drop dead and was phoning with details of where they'd hidden their last will and testament. Despite having his own office, Mr Campbell never received any personal phone calls. Yvonne and Denise, the other woman who worked on the counter, had decided that he was secretly gay and too scared to come out publicly, so he ruthlessly instructed his lovers not to phone.

Hope thought it was because Mr Campbell was very keen on rules and regulations and wouldn't dream of asking his staff to follow a dictum he wouldn't follow himself.

'I think we should meet for lunch,' Betsey was saying, blithely oblivious to the fact that Hope couldn't really talk. 'I'm working from home today and I've got my eye on these fabulous kitten heels in that new shoe shop near Pulteney Bridge and I feel today's the day to splash out. Do you fancy a trip up there?'

'Betsey, I can't talk at work,' whispered Hope anxiously.

Betsey commuted to London a couple of times a week to work in an office where making personal phone calls was part and parcel of the day. She didn't understand Hope's office environment.

'Outside Accessorise at one, then?' said Betsey.

'Yes,' Hope answered. Anything to get her off the phone before Mr Campbell self-combusted with disapproval.

The morning flew past, giving her little time to think. So it was only when Hope was belting out of the office door buttoning her coat, that she realized she wasn't in the mood to go shopping for extravagant shoes. And that she wasn't really in the mood for Betsey either.

She liked Betsey, had considered her her best friend, really, but there were days when she wondered was their friendship one of those which existed purely because their husbands were best friends and therefore, the four of them spent a lot of time together. After that infamous holiday in France which Dan and Matt had arranged one day at work without asking, she and Betsey had been great pals. Mind you, Hope thought, it hadn't bothered Betsey to go on holiday with someone she barely knew. Quite happy to relax from noon on with a bottle of Burgundy and a paperback while the children splashed about in the toddlers' pool, Betsey was very laid back about holiday companions. Hope always felt that nothing much upset her, except when somebody else got a better assignment in the women's magazine she wrote for. She was great fun and an amusing friend. But, Hope wondered, with Dan and Matt out of the picture, would she and Betsey ever meet up to have lunch or to trail around the shops together? Was Betsey really her best friend, either?

No, she decided an hour later as she sprinted back to the office, trying to eat a Mars bar simultaneously because they hadn't had time for lunch.

'Did you buy anything?' asked Yvonne as Hope slid into her seat behind the counter at one minute past two.

Hope shook her head. 'Betsey was on a shoe shop trawl. We trekked round four shops and ended up buying the ones she'd tried on in the first shop. Pale blue leather and very dainty. Plus, we didn't have time for a sandwich so I've just eaten a Mars bar,' she added guiltily.

'She's a selfish cow, that Betsey,' Yvonne remarked. 'When she meets you for lunch, she knows she can swan off home and have lunch whenever she wants to but you daren't have so much as a bag of crisps here.'

'She just didn't think,' protested Hope, used to standing up for Betsey because Yvonne didn't like her. They'd met once and it had been handbags at dawn. With her black curtain of hair and dancing green eyes, Yvonne was far too vampish for Betsey's tastes. Plus, she was younger than Betsey. Yvonne hadn't taken to Betsey much either, because she had a better job than Yvonne and kept boasting about it. Proof positive that trying to link up friends from different parts of your life didn't work.

'She just doesn't care,' Yvonne retorted. 'She's out for one person and that person is her. I bet you a tenner she'll be the first one who'll put her name down for a free holiday in Ireland with you. You wait and see, Madam Betsey will turn up with hubbie and kids, stay for a week and not lift a finger except to ask for more drink and another blanket for her bed.'

The thought had crossed Hope's mind.

'Well, if she's so keen on the country, maybe we can do a swap and she can stay in the cottage while I live in her place back here,' Hope remarked.

Yvonne shot her an inquisitive look.

'You don't want to go, do you?'

'That obvious, huh?' Hope stopped trying to look merry and let her face reveal how she felt: utterly depressed.

Yvonne's bosom welled up with indignation like an enraged bull-frog. 'Why didn't you tell me? You can't go, Hope,' she said, 'not if you don't want to. You'd be mad.'

A cluster of tourists, just disgorged from a tour bus, swarmed into the building society before Hope could answer.

Hope, Yvonne and Denise expertly changed travellers' cheques for the hordes and engaged in a bit of friendly chatter. When they'd all cleared out, one of Hope's favourite customers, a sweet little old lady who wore a fox collar wrapped around her neck come rain, hail or shine, arrived to discuss how much money she should take out of her account to go on holiday.

'Where are you going?' Hope asked Mrs Payton.

The old lady's dark eyes sparkled under her felt hat. 'The Greek Islands,' she said. 'I'm going with a friend. I haven't been there since the Fifties. We're going to do the Oracle at Delphi first. Can't wait.'

My god, I'm turning into a boring old cow, Hope told herself as she processed Mrs Payton's savings book. This woman is eighty if she's a day and she's all fired up about a trip to Greece, while I'm only thirty-seven and I'm whinging about going the short trip to Ireland.

When she was gone, Yvonne was busy with some teenage boys, and then a stream of people kept coming into the office, all with complicated business. It was nearly closing time before they had a chance to talk. Denise was making tea in the cubby hole kitchen behind the photocopier because they'd been too busy to have their afternoon tea break.

'Don't go,' said Yvonne.

'It's not that easy.' Hope was fed up with the whole subject.

'It is,' asserted Yvonne. 'Can you imagine what you'll feel like when you're there if you're this depressed now? You'll be down the doctor looking for tablets for your nerves like a shot.'

Hope laughed. 'I think I need tablets for my nerves as it is,' she joked.

Yvonne didn't laugh. 'Yeah and you'll be on double strength ones when you're dying of depression next month. Think about it, you'll be away from your friends, your sister, everyone. It's not fair to expect you to go along with this.' Yvonne scowled. 'Men can be right bastards, you know.'

'It *is* only for a year,' Hope said.

'Hope, you're the sort of person who wouldn't expect someone to sit through a two-hour film you'd like in case *they* didn't enjoy it. You never ask anyone for anything. Matt's asked you to do this huge thing and you don't want to go but you don't want to say no either. There's a fine line between keeping the peace and getting walked on, as my mother would say. And what are you going to do? You love working, even here, you'll go out of your head with no job. Matt's asking too much.'

Hope took her tea from Denise and thought of what Yvonne would say if she knew that Matt hadn't really *asked* her anything: he'd told her, wheedled a bit, and had assumed she'd go along with it. She was so happy that he wasn't having an affair, she'd said yes quicker than a hooker touting for business on a rainy night.

Yvonne would levitate with temper if she knew the truth. 'My Freddie wouldn't dream of doing anything like that,' she'd say, and it was true. Freddie had to work hard to keep Yvonne. She was not the sort of person who got walked on. As far as Yvonne was concerned, if anyone was going to do any trampling over anyone else, she'd do it, thank you very much.

'It's what everyone dreams of, Yvonne,' protested Hope. 'Giving up the rat race to live in the country, spend quality time with the children and not work.'

'Yeah right,' said Yvonne grimly. 'You and your winning the lottery dream. Except if you won the lottery and bought some palatial mansion down the road, you might not be working but you'd have the cash to do whatever you wanted and you'd be able to afford to have someone look after the kids if you wanted to get the chauffeur to drive you into town. You haven't won the lottery, but I reckon Matt has.'

For the rest of the afternoon, Hope thought about leaving Witherspoon's. She did love her job, Yvonne was right. She didn't want to be some high flying executive like Sam but she enjoyed working, enjoyed having her own money and her independence, and liked meeting new people. Of course she adored the children, but surely she wasn't a bad mother to want to combine loving them *with* a job?

Right on cue, the heavens opened as Hope ran, raincoatless, to her car after work. It was only a five-minute walk but by the time she wrenched the door of the Metro open and flung her handbag onto the passenger seat, she was soaked.

Shivering despite having the heater on at full blast, she drove home in worse than usual traffic. Yvonne didn't understand. Yvonne was a blunt person who said what she thought. Hope was exactly the opposite. She longed for some way of telling Matt she didn't want to leave Bath, but without the inevitable confrontation. Ideally, she wanted him intuitively to work out what she wanted, the way men did in films, and then agree that it was all a mad idea and that they should stay at home. No hassle, no arguments.

Only it wasn't working out like that. Matt appeared to be taking her stoic silence for a thoughtfulness, as if she was busy mentally working out what the family would need to take. Why didn't he see that she was upset? How could he be so blind?

The clock on the dashboard said it was six fifteen when Hope pulled up outside Your Little Treasures, not caring that she was double parked. Head down against the rain, she ran up the path to the glossy pillar box red door.

Marta was standing sentry in the small hallway, looking less Rottweiler-like than usual on account of her upswept hairstyle and a very un-Marta-like lacy dress. She was obviously going out for the evening.

'You're late,' she snapped as Hope reached her.

The build-up of misery over the past few days came to a triumphant head in Hope's mind. 'So sue me,' she snapped back with unheard of venom.

Marta took a step back at this unprecedented attack from the meek and mild Mrs Parker.

'As long as it's just this once,' she muttered, giving Hope a wide berth.

Matt couldn't remember when he'd felt this fired up over anything. Not the local television ads they'd won off a top London ad agency, not the excitement he'd felt when Hope had first become pregnant. Nothing had ever given him the buzz that this new adventure was giving him.

He arrived home with a bouquet of flowers for Hope and a bottle of rosé wine. She loved rosé. She was a bit unsure about the whole trip, but that was just Hope. Dear Hope, he loved her despite her nervousness about things and her fear of the unknown. She'd love Kerry when she got there.

Matt remembered when he was nine, and his parents, to whom

he'd been an unexpected interruption in their marriage and careers, had shipped him off to Uncle Gearóid's. At first, he'd hated the idea of leaving his home to travel to Ireland, but after that first summer, he'd wanted to go every year.

There was something magical about Redlion. Maybe it was the fact that Gearóid didn't believe in rules so there was none of that palaver about being in by a certain time or eating three meals a day, but Matt had loved it.

Meals were whenever Gearóid took it upon himself to open a tin of beans and nobody batted an eyelid when the nine-year-old Matt was brought into the local pub (shop at the front and small snug at the back) to have his first taste of porter. They'd gone on fishing expeditions, on wild adventures to the Beara Peninsula, where Gearóid had practically gone into a coma after a drinking session with a fellow writer in a small hillside dwelling that Matt's mother would have disapproved of no end. Matt had grown up with a mistily romantic memory of sitting on cracked leather stools in the dim, stained snug, listening to farmers talking of their herds and the trials of bovine mastitis, while Gearóid and his cronies rambled on about novels and poems, their plans for being the next Yeats, and how they'd got a consignment of good quality poteen and maybe after the next round they'd take a ramble back to Curlew Cottage for a wee dram.

Gearóid, with his wild woolly hair, long beard and fondness for brown corduroy suits he got directly from Dublin, had been an idol to his nephew. He lived outside the system, he told Matt proudly, which was why he'd left his home in Surrey to travel to Kerry and become a writer. Taking the Irish version of his real name had been part of the fun. The one-time Gerry had become Gearóid, more Irish than the Irish, a man who could sing old Irish songs for hours on end and knew the location of every stone circle in Munster. Gearóid supplemented his income by giving tours to the hordes of tourists who came to Kerry searching for their roots, but, as he got older, his fondness for the jar meant he was quite likely to turn on them and tell them they were all a pack of feckers and should feck off back wherever they came from.

To his shame, Matt hadn't visited for over four years and he'd felt terrible about the fact that when Gearóid had died, he'd been in the middle of a vital campaign and hadn't been able to make it to Redlion for the funeral. He'd make it up to Gearóid, he promised, by becoming a writer. Turning his back on Bath and his career, albeit only for a year, was his tribute to his maverick uncle.

# CHAPTER FOUR

Virginia Connell stood in the garage of her new home in Redlion, looked at Bill's golf clubs and smiled wistfully. She'd hated those bloody things all their married life. Well, maybe not hated but certainly felt irritated by them. Every weekend, come rain or shine, Bill had played golf. A brilliant man, he never managed to remember anniversaries, parties and dates she'd put in his diary months before, but thanks to some male instinct, he never forgot an arrangement to play golf.

They'd never really argued about it. Virginia had been very self-sufficient; you had to be when you had three small children and a husband who worked away from home a lot, she always said briskly. When Bill forgot a date she'd made with him, she'd wag a reproving finger and tell him she'd reschedule when he had an opening in his diary. He'd grin, kiss her and promise they'd go somewhere really exciting, which they never did, naturally. Steak and chips in the local had been a treat. Virginia hadn't minded. She loved Bill and he loved her in return. That was all there was to it. What did posh dinner dates matter when there was much more to life? She much preferred their quiet evenings in the local dunking chips into garlic mayonnaise to those high-powered affairs where Bill's business partners insisted on bringing the entire company, plus wives, out to four-star restaurants. Virginia hated those nights where the conversation was brittle, every subject was a potential minefield and where the only fun was watching which of Bill's partners could pretend to know most about wine.

The food was just as good in the pub and when she and Bill were alone together, they could relax and be themselves.

Over the years, Bill did his best to get her to learn golf. She laughed and said he was only suggesting it so they'd see each other in the golf club instead of blearily in the kitchen in the morning over coffee.

Virginia gently pulled the suede cover from his driver, stroking the polished club head and remembering how delighted he'd been when he bought it.

'This is space age technology,' he'd said gravely that glorious Saturday morning in April more than eighteen months ago, before going on to explain how he'd had a nine degree driver before but this one was eleven and a half.

'And that's better?' Virginia had teased as she made them both tea.

'It's about the degree of loft . . .' Bill had begun to explain before he noticed her grinning. 'What am I explaining it to you for, you philistine,' he laughed. '*Some* wives take an interest in their husband's game.'

'Yes, and *some* husbands get home occasionally,' she retorted. 'I'm thinking of having an affair if you don't get home tonight before eight. Would you mind?'

Bill pretended to consider this, angling his grey head to one side and screwing up his brown eyes. 'Could you have an affair with the golf pro?' he suggested. 'Then I might get preferential rates on lessons.'

'No problem, darling,' Virginia smiled. 'Biscuit?'

He didn't get home before eight that night. He didn't get home at all. He'd crashed the car on the twenty-minute drive home and the only thing to remain unscathed were his clubs, safely in the boot.

The front of the car was destroyed, as was her darling Bill. But he'd never felt the pain of the crash: he'd died from a massive heart attack, they told her. As if that made it better.

The police thought she'd like the clubs. Virginia threw them into the garage with fury because she needed to hurt *something*. She was in such horrific, numbing white pain that something or someone else must suffer. Bill's precious clubs seemed like the only obvious candidates.

The boys, Dominic, Laurence and Jamie, all in their 20s now, had been wonderful, towers of strength through it all. They'd arranged the funeral because Virginia hadn't been able to. For the first time in her life, the eminently capable and sensible Virginia Connell fell to pieces. She could barely make a cup of tea; she, who was known for her exquisite baking and fantastic Beef Wellington so tender you could cut it with a spoon. People phoned with shocked, murmured condolences and she barely heard them. Once, she left someone hanging on the other end of the phone while she went into the kitchen to try and boil the kettle. She hadn't managed that either: boiling the kettle and managing to put a teabag in a cup was beyond her. Choosing what to wear in the morning was a momentous task. Remembering to brush her teeth was impossible.

She stopped bothering with her hair and it hung in dank grey curls around a drawn face that was the same shade of grey. Laurence had insisted on driving her to the hairdresser one day, three months after Bill's death, shocked when he'd seen how terrible she looked.

'I can't go in,' she said simply, sitting in the car outside the hairdresser in Clontarf with Laurence wringing his hands beside her. 'What's the point?'

To add to her misery, a month after Bill's death, their beloved Spaniel, Oscar, had been run over. Without even Oscar's warm, velvety body to comfort her as he laid on the bedspread and licked her hands lovingly, Virginia felt there was no point to the world at all.

Time was a great healer, Virginia remembered her mother saying. She didn't agree precisely. Time didn't heal, it numbed. Like a good anaesthetic, it made the pain more bearable but it never went away.

She'd never balanced the bank statements or talked to the insurance people about the car or the house contents. Bill had handled all that. When the letters surrounding his death began to flood in through the letter box, Virginia realized just how much Bill had done. She'd often teased him that he was a lucky man coming home to a clean, tidy house where there was always food in the fridge, ironed shirts in the wardrobe and plenty of toothpaste in the bathroom. Now, Virginia realized that he'd been just as busy on her behalf as she had on his. She'd never even seen a final demand bill for electricity or handled a single query from their accountant. Now, she had to open all the mail and deal with it herself, inexpertly and bitterly. Bitter because Bill shouldn't have been gone in the first place. The phone was nearly cut off in those first six months because Virginia had taken to sweeping the mountains of post into a drawer, refusing to look at any of it. She couldn't cope with the kindly meant letters of condolences and she didn't want to cope with the stilted letters from the bank, the insurance people and the lawyers. There was so much to do when someone died. She could barely believe it. The awful irony was that Bill had left her a wealthy widow thanks to a huge insurance policy. He'd looked after her even in death. But money couldn't compensate for the pain and the trauma that went with sudden death.

Bereaved people were suddenly supposed to lay aside their grief and deal with employers, the tax office, government departments, an endless list. It was cruel, cruel and unnecessary. She wouldn't do it. A horrified Laurence had gone through it all one day, six months after his father's death, when he'd discovered what she'd been doing.

'Mum,' he said wearily as he sat in Bill's big recliner chair surrounded by opened envelopes and official looking letters, 'you can't go on like this.'

Virginia had shrugged listlessly. 'Why not? It doesn't matter any more. Nothing matters. And anyway,' her eyes had a spark of life in them momentarily, a spark of fury, 'what else can they do to me? Your father is dead. That's the worst that can happen. Do you think I care a damn if they lock me up because I haven't declared that I'm not entitled to a married person's tax allowance any more?'

After a year of not bothering, Virginia had made scones on the morning of her husband's first anniversary. Her sons were coming to Clontarf for the day and she didn't have anything in the house. The boys ate the scones with thankful smiles on their faces, grateful that their mother was finally coming out of the tunnel she'd been in. Virginia was astonished how easily she slipped back into her role of gracious hostess. On the outside, at least.

She wondered if it had been she who'd died, how would Bill have coped? Would he have spent a year in mourning, worn down by grief and unable to take an interest in anything? Their first grandchild had been born just eight months ago, an adorable poppet named Alison who had her parents – Virginia's eldest son, Dominic, and his wife, Sally – in thrall. Virginia had been godmother and managed to get through the christening service dry-eyed, despite crying inside at the thought of how happy she'd have been if only Bill had been with her.

'He *is* with you, Ma,' Laurence, the sensitive one, insisted. 'Dad's still here, watching over you.'

But he wasn't with her. That was the hard thing. Virginia didn't bother telling Laurence that his words of comfort did no good, he wouldn't have understood. She'd gone to church all her life and yet now, when she needed it most, the very idea of God and the afterlife had deserted her. There was no sense of Bill anywhere except in her memory. She couldn't feel him in the room with her, she took no comfort in going to church and talking to him. He was gone. It was over, that was it. And that really was the most awful part of her grief.

That was why she'd sold the house in Dublin six months ago and swapped the suburban calm of Pier Avenue for a rambling old house in Kerry. The boys had been upset at first, Laurence had said she couldn't run away. But Virginia had told them she wasn't running away: she just needed to start again, in Kerry, where she and their father had come from all those years ago and to where they'd always had this distant dream of returning.

They'd both been farmers' children, madly keen to get away. Kerry had seemed like the back end of nowhere when they were young. In their fifties, though, Bill and Virginia had thought they might like to retire back to where they'd come from, a place that didn't seem anywhere near as dull and quiet to them now as it had when they were younger.

They'd never been sure whether they'd go back to their homelands near Tralee where only a couple of relatives now lived, or whether they'd start again somewhere else in the county. Somewhere without second cousins once removed living down the road.

Bill's death made the decision for Virginia. She would sell the house and move to Kerry but far away from Tralee. She couldn't face living near where they'd grown up, places redolent of their courtship and awash with memories of the first time they'd met at a dance in a small parish hall. No, that would be too painful. When she saw the advert for Kilnagoshell House in Redlion, a long way from Tralee and yet still in Kerry, her mind was made up. In May, fourteen months after being brutally thrust into widowhood, Virginia had up sticks and moved to the small Kerry village where she knew nobody and where, she hoped, nobody knew her.

The rambling old house was in a good state of repair but could have done with some decoration as the previous owners were very keen on flock wallpaper and swirly, sea-sickness carpets. The wash hand basins installed in the bedrooms for the B & B guests didn't suit the grand old house but Virginia had done nothing to restore its beauty so far. She felt weary enough from simply moving in. She didn't have the energy to decorate or even remove the numbers on the bedroom doors. Besides, she had the rest of her life to do it, she thought sadly.

The boys were still getting used to the idea. Relief, Virginia felt, was a part of it. They had felt guilty with their interesting lives in London (Dominic and his wife, Sally) and Dublin (Jamie and Laurence) while their mother grieved in her suburban semi. She knew that Jamie and Laurence had shared a rota whereby each tried to visit her every couple of days, keeping in contact by phone the rest of the time to make sure she hadn't downed a packet of sleeping pills in misery. Now she was hundreds of miles away, the duty visits would have to stop, which would be better for all concerned.

She'd meant to give away most of Bill's possessions when she moved, but she'd found herself unable to throw out his clothes. And thinking of the pleasure they'd given him, she hadn't thrown out his precious clubs.

Now she held Bill's driver in her hands and tried to remember the all-important grip. Was it too late to take up golf at the age of fifty-eight? Bill would have loved her to. Maybe he could see her, was grinning with that irrepressible twinkling grin of his to see her holding his clubs in that professional manner. She liked the idea of Bill grinning wherever he was.

The bell rang. Virginia raised her eyes to heaven. Tourists, she'd lay a bet on it. Kilnagoshell House had been a noted bed and breakfast establishment in the past and people with fond memories of it kept turning up on the doorstep, smiling and wondering if she had a double with bath for two nights and 'do you still make that lovely black pudding for breakfast?'

When she'd moved into the house four months ago, she'd smiled apologetically in return, saying 'sorry, no, it's not a B & B any more.'

Now, she felt like throwing burning tar out the top windows and yelling 'leave me alone!' every time a fresh influx of visitors arrived with their five-year-old B & B guidebooks and hopeful expressions on their faces. It was beyond her why the owners had sold up in the first place. Judging from the amount of walk-in custom they were getting, even in October, they could have run a hundred-bed hotel and still be busy.

She put the driver carefully back in the golf bag and walked round to the front door where a gleaming people carrier was parked. Four people were standing on the gravel.

One man was stretching aching limbs and another was hauling bulging suitcases from the vehicle. A small, dark-skinned woman was peering at a guide book, reading out bits in heavily-accented English, while a taller woman looked over her shoulder.

'Can I help you?' inquired Virginia.

'Excuse me for not phoning,' said the woman with the guide book. Italians, Virginia thought, judging by that lyrical accent with its exotic rolling consonants. 'We hope you have rooms we can rent tonight.'

'I'm afraid this isn't a bed and breakfast any more,' Virginia said apologetically polite in spite of herself.

The foursome looked crestfallen.

'We have been driving for so long,' said one of the men tiredly.

'There is another place you can stay in the village,' Virginia offered and went on to tell them about Mrs Egan's De Luxe B & B down the road, just the other side of Redlion. No, it wasn't in the guide books but if they needed somewhere in the locality, Mrs Egan would definitely have rooms.

She felt sorry to be turning them away; they looked exhausted and she was no longer sure if it was fair to direct people to Mrs Egan's premises. She'd met Mrs Egan in the butcher's and hadn't liked either the way she ordered the cheapest rashers for her breakfasts, or the way she snapped at the butcher himself, a friendly giant of a man who didn't deserve to be given out to because he'd forgotten to put aside a leg of lamb for her.

From what the constant stream of visitors said to her about Kilna-goshell, Virginia felt it had been a welcoming place where nothing was too much trouble and where the owners wouldn't have dreamed of giving guests fatty, cheap rashers for their breakfast.

The foursome wearily packed up their belongings and waved at her as she watched them drive away. Virginia waved back, thinking that she mustn't look quite as decrepit as she felt if these people wanted to stay with her. In her mind, she was still light years away from the tall, handsome Virginia Connell who'd always been perfectly dressed, not a silvery grey hair out of place as she helped out in the local Oxfam shop. That Virginia was the old one. The replacement was darker, sadder, with hollows under her hazel eyes and pain etched on every inch of her fine-boned face. She didn't bother any more setting her thick hair in the gentle waves that managed to look so elegant: she tied it back in a taut knot. But that would have to change. She'd lived as a recluse for long enough and if she was to put a tentative foot back into the real world, she needed to look normal instead of like some loopy old dear with Miss Havisham tendencies.

She closed the garage and went inside to the kitchen to pull on her walking shoes and old waxed jacket. The waxy smell always reminded her of Oscar. He'd been such a darling little dog, a soft fawn coloured Spaniel with velvety ears and a melancholy expression that made him look like a dog from a chocolate box. Every weekday of his life at half eight in the morning, Virginia had taken Oscar for his walk and when the weather was wet, she'd worn this very waxed jacket. Oscar had only to see it to go berserk, circling her feet with delight, barking and bouncing deliriously. The jacket still smelled of him. Virginia still tortured herself with the thought that if only she'd kept walking him after Bill's death, Oscar might have still been alive.

It was her fault, all her fault. With enough exercise, Oscar wouldn't have been so keen to escape the garden and run out onto the main road. She was glad that her local vet had offered to bury his silky little body in their plot in the mountains, otherwise he'd have been buried in the garden in Pier Avenue and she hated to think of the new owners digging him up in some garden revamp and dumping him.

'Get another dog, Mum,' Laurence had advised. 'You and Dad always had dogs, you need one. It'll be company for you; go on, you really should.'

But Virginia wouldn't dream of it. A dog was something to care for and she was far too afraid of losing anything else to commit to any new responsibilities. As it was, she was possessed of a great fear that something would take the boys, Sally or baby Alison away from her. A fat tear fell onto the jacket's worn corduroy collar. Virginia wiped her eyes fiercely. She wouldn't cry, she wouldn't. She'd go for her walk and try and forget Oscar.

She walked briskly down the avenue, past the beech trees with their glorious russet leaves. The last glow of autumn was still everywhere; trees and bushes holding onto their golden leaves, the single copper beech still a fiery bronze in the middle of the silver birches. In another month, the landscape would have changed totally, Virginia knew, with banks of leaves underfoot and every tree stark and bare against the hills. But for now, it was magnificent. She crunched through a stretch of road strewn with chestnuts. The boys had loved chestnuts, she thought fondly, picking one up and rubbing it until it gleamed like mahogany.

Onto the main road, she marched firmly towards Redlion. Her house was a mile from the village and she'd decided that she should walk there and back every day, if only to buy a newspaper. It was all too easy to bury yourself and see nobody.

She liked Redlion: it was quaint and somehow untouched. The winding main street, called, for convenience, Main Street, probably looked much the way it had fifty years ago, with small terraced houses on either side interrupted only by shops and pubs. There were three pubs, rather a lot for a small town, tourists were always saying in surprise. Virginia knew from experience that visitors were fascinated by the number of pubs in Irish towns. She remembered a friend of Bill's from London being astonished by that. They'd taken him on a short trip down to Kilkenny and he'd kept remarking on the fact that they'd driven through several tiny hamlets that consisted of a scattering of houses, but which still managed to support two pubs.

'How do they stay in business?' he'd asked Bill in bewilderment.

Bill had laughed his warm, deep laugh and told his friend that he was in Ireland now and the usual rules didn't apply. 'There are different sorts of pubs for different people,' Bill explained. 'The old farmers might use one because it hadn't changed since they were lads, and the younger people might go for another one with music and bar food. Real ould pubs only serve drink and cigarettes, you see. At the first sign of music, bar food or young women in short skirts, the ould fellas would take their custom elsewhere.'

Madigans in Redlion was a real ould pub in Bill's definition of the word, Virginia thought. With its red and white lettering over the door and an elderly Guinness sign hanging outside, it looked like the pubs of her childhood.

On her walks, she'd often seen men in heavy boots, farm clothes and old caps ambling in for a quick lunchtime pick-me-up of porter. Her father, who'd been a farmer, had been fond of the odd lunchtime drink himself and she reckoned he'd have liked Madigans, which was the sort of place where you could happily go in with your trousers held up with baler twine and nobody would pay you the slightest bit of attention. The only part of the experience that required utter and complete attention was the pouring of the pint, which could take ten minutes of the barman's loving art, meaning that wise drinkers ordered the next pint a good fifteen minutes before they'd need it, giving it that much needed time to settle.

The Widows, on the other hand, was a modern phenomenon complete with a bar food menu as exotic as you'd find anywhere. It had traditional music nights, quaint Oirish interior decor straight out of

*The Quiet Man*, and a proprietor who understood that money in the pub business was trying to please all the people all the time. Virginia had been in there a couple of times and had marvelled at the modern take on an old-fashioned idea.

Virginia had never walked as far as the third pub, which was right at the other end of the village over the humpbacked bridge. That would be her mission today, Virginia resolved: to walk right through the village. It would make it a longer walk, certainly three miles all told.

She passed the painted sign that told her Redlion was twinned with a French town she'd never heard of. Redlion wasn't at its best in the lashing rain but on a clear autumn day, the village was pretty and somehow timeless. Virginia walked past the chemist with its big side entrance for animal foodstuffs, past a row of whitewashed houses with a brightly painted blue one in the middle, and along past Lucille's, a fashion emporium with a window display that changed weekly and was always wildly glamorous. This week, Lucille was showing off low-cut tops and mohair sweaters with an animal print theme. The centrepiece was a fake fur coat in dramatic leopard print with a matching Russian style hat. Virginia resolved to watch out for the ensemble at Mass. She wasn't quite sure who actually bought any of Lucille's extravagant outfits, but she knew she'd recognize anyone who did at fifty paces.

She walked on, keeping her eyes trained firmly on the distance in case she met anyone on her side of the street. People were very friendly, always smiling and saying hello, but she didn't want to get dragged into friendships, and answering a simple 'isn't it a grand day?' could be disastrous. Replying would mean a full-blown conversation and she didn't want to talk to people, she wanted to be left alone.

It wasn't hard today. The village was quiet. At this time of year, the tourists were few and far between. But Virginia knew that once Easter came, the place would be crammed with people stopping at the Widows for a plate of smoked salmon and a blast of traditional music. They clambered out of cars and buses in droves to admire the painted houses and the quaint arts and crafts shop which did a roaring trade in hand-knitted sweaters, bits of lace, plaques with Irish family names on them, and odd pottery bits and bobs made by the hippies who lived in a commune far up the mountains. The hippies were tolerated, Virginia knew thanks to overhearing a conversation in the post office, because they kept themselves to themselves.

But the hard-working local people with businesses were always nervous of a whole tribe of crusty travellers arriving and setting up messy shop in a field somewhere and ruining the successful business of tourism.

Virginia had seen one of the hippie women once: tired-looking with yellow dreadlocks, tattoos on her arms and a child glued to each hip. Close by, a business-suited young woman marched out of the estate agent's and climbed into her Mercedes sports car, rushing and ignoring everything around her. Both would have looked out of place in the Kerry of Virginia's youth.

Today, Virginia had the place pretty much to herself, apart from a couple of women standing outside the butcher's with their striped plastic bags, having a chat now that they'd bought the dinner. As she walked, her hip twinged a bit. Why you got arthritis in one hip and not the other, Virginia didn't know, but that was no excuse for not getting her daily walk. She walked firmly on. She was nearly half way there after all.

The phone was ringing furiously when she got back and she raced into the hall, still in her leaf-covered walking boots.

'Mum,' said the chirpy voice of her daughter-in-law Sally in London, 'how *are* you?'

'Fine, Sally,' Virginia answered, pleased to hear from the only member of her family who didn't say hello with the expectation that Virginia would burst immediately into depressed tears. 'How are you lot? Is Alison still ruling the roost with Dominic wrapped round her little finger?'

Sally groaned. 'Don't ask. He ruins her. She'll have a bike, a pony and a toy motorbike before she's two if Dominic has anything to do with it.'

They chatted away for a few minutes, talking about how Jamie had been in London and had come round to dinner one night with his new girlfriend, 'very pretty and clever. Dominic kept teasing that she was much too clever for him.'

Virginia smiled a little wistfully. That was what she missed: being a proper part of her sons' lives, being there to meet new girlfriends and give her opinion on them. Laurence, who was a dentist, had told her about Barbara, the fabulous dental nurse he'd only just met and how Virginia would love her to bits, but the three of them hadn't managed to meet up yet. Still, she mustn't dwell on things. She'd chosen a new life because it was a break from the pain of the past. What was the point in whingeing about parts of the old life that she missed?

They talked about Alison's sleeping pattern or rather, her non-sleeping pattern; how tired Sally was from looking after her *and* working from home; and how much she and Dominic were looking forward to their skiing holiday in Austria over Christmas.

'Virginia,' Sally said suddenly, sounding anxious. 'We won't go to Austria if you'd like us to come to you, you know that. I don't want you to think that we wouldn't want to come to you. We'll cancel Austria and hop on the ferry . . .'

'Don't be ridiculous,' Virginia interrupted. 'I wouldn't dream of it. You need a proper holiday as a family, not one where you're forced to visit me. I've told you I'm spending Christmas here this year and you're all to stop feeling guilty about it.'

Virginia thought of a fridge magnet she'd seen: 'my mother is a travel agent for guilt trips.' She'd laughed heartily at the idea because it had been a fair description of her own mother.

Therefore, Virginia had been determined never to lay guilt trips on her three boys. Even in the darkest days after Bill's death, she'd refused to let herself beg for their help. Laurence had stayed with her for a week but then she'd sent him back to his apartment in Swords.

'I'm the mother and you're the child,' she'd told him firmly. 'It's not your job to mind me. I've got to get on with it myself.'

By the same token, Dominic and Sally deserved to spend Christmas any way they liked without worrying about her. Besides, she felt even more wretched than ever when the kids were tiptoeing around her. The joy of having them to stay was overwhelmed with the sense that Bill should be there too, which was just too painful.

At least when she was on her own she could deal with her grief on the bad days. If that meant spending the entire day crying with her face as red and raw as beetroot, then she was free to do just that. When there were other people around, pride made her stifle the tears.

Virginia changed the subject. 'I've just come back from a long walk and I'm looking forward to having a hot bath and curling up with my new book.' This wasn't entirely true. Virginia hoped that a hot bath would ease her aches but she couldn't cope with reading any more. Her favourite novels just made her cry at their memories of happier times. She managed the newspaper and that was it. Even the crossword reminded her of Bill asking for help with eight across.

'It's great that you're walking again,' said Sally. 'Is your hip bothering you much?'

'Not at all,' lied Virginia. 'There are some very pretty walks around here. The village is lovely. You'll have to come and stay. In the summer,' she added rapidly, in case she sounded all needy again.

'We can come . . .' Sally began.

'Sally love, I need this time alone,' Virginia interrupted. 'I really do. Please make Dominic see that, you know I can't tell him myself.'

'I know. He only wants to help,' Sally said quietly. 'We all do.'

Virginia shrugged. 'Nobody can help me but myself.'

# CHAPTER FIVE

Nicole Turner looked as if she was working – for once. Her dark head was bent over her desk and there was no tell-tale grin on her impish face which would have been a sure sign that she was telling jokes with her next-door neighbour, the equally feckless Sharon Wilson.

From her position at the top of the room, Ms Sinclair, claims department supervisor, narrowed her eyes as she looked at the bane of her life. Nicole Turner could look demure and hardworking even when she was secretly planning some prank that would cause uproar in the busiest department of the London headquarters of Copperplate Insurance. Like that time she'd rigged the big clock behind Ms Sinclair's desk so it was half an hour early, meaning that everyone left for lunch at half twelve instead of one.

Naturally, Nicole had switched the clock back during lunchtime, so that when everyone arrived back at two, they'd actually had an hour and a half for lunch. In Ms Sinclair's eyes, this was a sacking offence but she had no proof that Nicole was responsible so nothing could be done. And the section head pointed out that Nicole's work was always excellent, so there were no grounds for firing her.

You had to watch her all the time, Ms Sinclair decided darkly. It was a task she relished.

At her desk at the back of the room, Sharon Wilson's phone rang and she picked it up.

'Hello, claims department,' she trilled.

'Is that old bitch still watching me like a hawk?' asked Nicole, who was less than three feet away but who knew that clerical staff talking without actually being attached to their phones were in for a big black mark from Ms Sinclair.

Sharon peeked up the room. 'Yes. Actually, she's really staring at you now.'

'Shit.'

Out of the corner of her eye, Sharon could see Nicole stand up and search through some files on her desk, her brow furrowed as if she'd been asked a sticky question by a customer and needed to check it out. Nicole located the big Copperplate Insurance manual and sighed theatrically as though her greatest wish in the entire world had been granted because she'd found the manual. She flicked through the pages and stopped in the middle.

'Ms Wilson,' she said now in her best placate-the-customer voice, 'I'm afraid we won't be able to cover your claim for the deer running out onto the road and flattening your Mini Cooper . . .'

Sharon giggled and had to hide behind her computer so nobody could see her.

'You see, Ms Wilson, we happen to know that you were down the Three Crowns public house on the night in question and had seventeen pints of best bitter, before you climbed into the driver's seat and drove home, with your boyfriend in the seat behind you attempting to remove your brassiere; a feat not recommended in the Rules of the Road handbook. Therefore, we feel unable to cough up the twenty-seven thousand pounds you feel entitled to. We will be, however, paying for plastic surgery for the deer, alright?'

Sharon giggled some more.

'Seriously.' Nicole had switched into her normal voice although to any onlooker, her expression was as grave as if she was on company business. 'I've just got an e-mail from my pal Bacardi King. One of his friends is getting married and the stag party's in the Red Parrot tonight and if you're interested, we can go.'

'To a stag party on a Thursday?' said Sharon dubiously.

Nicole allowed herself to smile. 'Ms Sin-Free-Zone-Clair isn't in tomorrow so we can be as hungover as skunks and nobody will mind. And all Bacardi's female friends are going. Having men only at stags is very old fashioned.'

'OK,' said Sharon, who adored Nicole and who felt that in the three years she'd worked with her, her own social life had improved no end. Nicole hung up and returned to her e-mail.

> *'Hi B-King, love to hit Red Parrot with u. Is dressing up part of plan? Haven't dressed up since I went to hallowe'en night party as a mummy – all rolled up in loo roll taken from the last pub. The bouncers in the night-club didn't see the funny side of it, for some reason. Said I could be charged with robbing loo paper! No sense of humour. See u at 8.*
> *Nicole.*

Thursdays were perfect for going out. Her gran came over on a Thursday, so Nicole didn't have to worry about who was going to be babysitting five-year-old Pammy.

At six o'clock on the nail, Nicole got up from her desk, dragged her backpack from underneath it and stalked off to the loos on her gravity-defying knee-high boots, regardless of the fierce glares from Ms Sinclair.

Sharon watched her friend enviously. Nicole just didn't care about what people thought. Nicole never got embarrassed when she went to buy her round and found she didn't have enough cash, and she'd just laughed the day they'd been running for the bus and she fell into a puddle of water, with at least thirty people watching. Sharon would have been puce with embarrassment. Nicole groaned good humouredly because the entire front of her skintight jeans were damp.

'I'll look like I wet myself,' she said, 'and we haven't even had a drink yet!'

At five past six, having delayed for a few minutes because that way, it looked as if she was so engrossed in her work that she hadn't noticed the time, Sharon gave her desk a cursory bit of tidying and rushed to the loos. Nicole was there, having a forbidden cigarette before she put on the minuscule amount of make-up she wore.

That was another reason to be jealous of her best friend, Sharon thought with a resigned sigh as she compared their reflections in the mirror. Nicole was so beautiful. Her café au lait skin glowed no matter how exhausted she was, and the tigerish amber eyes with their feline tilt at the outer edges dominated her triangular little face. Her concession to make-up was lots of glossy lipstick because her mouth, inherited from her mother instead of from her Indian father, was on the small side.

Her hair was her one vanity: she spent a fortune on conditioning treatments and shine products and it hung in a long, glossy curtain down her back. Even her body obeyed her. Tall, and slender as a reed, she had fantastic legs that looked scarily long in the black PVC mini-skirt she'd just changed into.

But Nicole was just about the best friend in the entire universe, which meant you couldn't be jealous of her.

'Want a fag?' Nicole asked now in her husky voice.

Sharon took one, lit it and went into a cubicle to pee. They weren't supposed to smoke in the loos but if Nicole could do it, so could she.

'Are you up for karaoke tonight?' Nicole said, pulling off her cream work jumper and wriggling into a small pink T-shirt with glittery stars emblazoned all over the front.

From behind the toilet door, Sharon groaned. 'You know I can't sing and I'm not making a fool of myself in front of all those guys at the stag night.'

'Oh come on,' Nicole begged. She needed someone to get up and sing with her or she'd feel stupid doing it. She hated show offs. Nicole adored singing and had been exercising her raw husky voice in private since she'd been a child. She often wrote her own songs but it was only for fun. Singing publicly was another matter. There was nothing worse than people who thought they were Kiri Te Kanawa getting up at family parties and sounding like a collection of drunken crows. Nicole couldn't bear that. But since, at the age of fifteen, she'd sneaked into the local pub for an illegal drink and discovered karaoke, she'd loved it. While the other people she partied with thought that the sing-a-long part of an evening was just drunken fun, for Nicole, it was the best bit. She adored singing to Tina Turner and Whitney Houston tracks and loved having her pals waving their beer bottles up at her happily as they hummed along and cheered. But you had to get someone to get up there with you in the first place, Nicole felt. Otherwise you looked like a stupid show off.

'Ready?' she asked Sharon.

'Just a minute,' said Sharon, struggling with mascara that promised lashes like Cindy Crawford's.

'Right. I'll phone my mum,' Nicole replied. Using the office phone saved her from spending too much on the mobile.

She slipped back into the office where Miss Sinclair was still at her desk tidying up. Nicole immediately crouched down and crept along behind the desks until she reached her own. She took the phone down and wriggled into the space underneath where she'd be safe from detection. Sinclair would kill her for using the phone for personal purposes. At least during office hours, you could always pretend you were on a work call. It was annoying that Sinclair hated her so much. It wasn't that Nicole didn't work hard: she did. But Sinclair didn't understand that Nicole could finish her work more quickly than most people in the department, and then she got bored. She couldn't help the practical jokes, they helped pass the time.

Her mother answered on the first ring. 'Hello love,' she said to Nicole's whispered hello.

'Hi Mum,' hissed Nicole.

'I can't hear you,' said Sandra Turner in her soft, breathy voice. 'Speak up love.'

'I can't,' hissed Nicole. 'I'm at work.'

'Oh yes,' said Sandra vaguely. There was a pause.

There were always pauses in conversations with Nicole's mother.

'I'm going out for a bit tonight, Mum. That's OK, isn't it. I know you've got Bingo but Gran's coming over for a few hours, isn't she?'

'I suppose. She didn't phone.'

Another pause.

'Shall I check if she's coming over, Mum?' Nicole volunteered. 'We can't leave Pammy on her own and she hates bingo.'

'OK. You do that. Oh, the doorbell. I'll get it.'

Nicole heard the phone drop and then her grandmother's voice with the strong accent that was a strange hybrid of Cockney and Irish even after fifty years in London. A few minutes passed before her mother picked up the phone again. 'Your gran's here so I'm going out. See you later.'

She hung up before Nicole even had a chance to speak to her grandmother to ask what time she was staying until. Slowly, Nicole put down the receiver. She was glad her grandmother was there: it gave her a chance to have a night out without worrying about Pammy. She needed someone looking after her and sometimes, even though Nicole hated to admit it, her mother wasn't up to it.

She crept back the same route to the office door where Sharon was waiting for her, all done up now and reeking of Eternity.

'Let's hit the pub, babes,' Nicole said brightly.


The Red Parrot in Camden was not Dickie Vernon's idea of a nice venue. It was a young people's pub for a start, full of computer games, with lots of different coloured condoms in the dispenser in the loos and very loud karaoke. But in his job as a talent scout, Dickie had been in lots of headache-inducing places. Not that he ever said he was a talent scout. No, he was a manager, or so he told people to impress them. It was a great pity that his greatest find, the golden-voiced Missy McLoughlin, hadn't had the balls for the music business. She was something else that girl. If she'd made it, he'd have been home and dry for life. Fifteen per cent of millions, he'd been sure of it. No more sitting around horrible old clubs looking for the next Celine Dion. The independent record label had been so interested until he'd got greedy and asked for more money. He wouldn't make that mistake again. When they backed off at his increasingly outrageous demands, Missy's nerve had failed her and she was now the proud mother of a toddler, lived in an Aberdeen semi and sang at weddings and funerals.

Dickie was back to managing the Val Brothers, a barber shop quartet, and taking care of the affairs of a country and western girl singer whose only resemblance to the successful Nashville ladies was her big, blonde hair. Anyone listening to her murdering 'Jolene' would immediately start looking for cotton wool for their ears. Still, she looked the part and that was half the battle, wasn't it?

His trip to the Red Parrot was to meet up with a small record shop owner who was going to introduce him to a teenage rock band who were all still at school. The record shop guy was late and Dickie, bored rigid now he'd done the crossword in the *Daily Star*, was sinking whiskies. The karaoke machine was switched on and two drunk rugby playing types were howling their way through 'Purple Haze'. Jimi Hendrix would turn in his grave, Dickie thought.

It was definitely a stag party. There were around thirty lads, all plastered, and one with a blow up rubber doll on his lap. The stag himself, stupid git. Dickie looked away and ordered another whisky. It was half nine, he'd give the record shop owner another half an hour and he was gone.

He blanked out the dreadful singing from the stag night people who were performing one dreadful rendition after another. A curvaceous brunette wearing spray-on jeans and a clingy red top sat at the table next to his. Dickie admired the way her small waist made her bum look curvier. She turned round and smiled at him. Dickie smiled back, giving her the full works, gleaming capped teeth and the Jack the lad cheeky grin that had been working since he was fifteen, a good twenty-five years before. The brunette winked at him.

He might stay a bit longer after all.

The strains of the old Al Green hit, 'Let's Stay Together', drifted out from the karaoke machine and Dickie didn't notice. He was considering asking the brunette if she wanted a drink when the vocals started. Two voices were singing, one flat and terrible, the other husky and rich. The husky voice penetrated the room, soaring above the music.

Dickie stared, the brunette forgotten. There, on the Red Parrot dais, stood a tall dark-skinned girl belting out this incredible noise. She was young, maybe twenty. But that voice: throaty and full of age, experience and sex. She sang like a world-weary divorcée who'd had it up to here with drink, drugs and men. Life in the very fast lane. If he hadn't seen her for himself, Dickie would have sworn blind the singer was at least forty and a chain smoker with tired, hard eyes. Her voice resonated with experience, sex, excitement and power.

And incredibly, it was coming from a young, slim girl with an unlined little face that reminded him of a cat's, slanting eyes and a profile like an Indian princess. Watching that tiny little face transported as she sang, Dickie felt the hairs stand up on the back of his neck. He'd found her. His star. His ticket out of here.

'I haven't seen you here before,' said the brunette flirtatiously.

'Wouldn't be seen dead here normally,' Dickie said flatly and went back to watching Nicole Turner. The brunette flounced off.

When the song ended, the audience applauded loudly and Nicole and Sharon bowed happily.

'Sing another one,' roared Bacardi King.

'You sing on your own, Nicole,' urged Sharon. 'You're so much better than me.'

'No,' insisted Nicole. 'You've got to stay.'

Normally, the sound of 'The Power of Love' at a karaoke session promised the sort of drunken howling that put you in mind of dogs at the full moon but not the way Nicole sang it. Dickie smiled beatifically as her lovely voice reached every high note, swelling where the song demanded it and fading down to gentleness at exactly the right moments. He watched her, mesmerized. He *had* to talk to her.

She was perfect, made to be a star. But he'd had too much to drink and probably looked more than a little worse for wear. He'd just hit the men's loos for a minute and make himself respectable, then he'd approach her. After all, who'd believe he was a top-flight manager if he looked seedy and pissed. It would only take a minute.

Nicole flopped onto a seat and fanned herself with the cocktail menu. She felt exhilarated and tired. Now that the fun of the evening was over, she thought she might go home. Duty called, the way it always did. It was half ten and Gran liked to be in her own bed by eleven, come what may. Who knew if Mum was home yet.

The stag night boys were playing a drunken party game that involved discussing your wildest dreams.

Nicole was beside the groom-to-be, who was now wearing a

pirate's hat and eye patch. The blow up doll was sitting on his other side and had a pair of black lacy knickers on her head. The stag put an arm around Nicole and grinned drunkenly at her. With her little cat's face glowing from the lights and her eyes glittering from her singing triumph, she looked stunning.

'What would you really want if you could have anything in the whole world?' he said, pulling Nicole closer to him and breathing in the scent of her hot, slender body, a musky scent mingled with Sharon's Eternity.

Nicole smiled wryly. She knew what he was thinking: the stag wasn't ready for the night to end yet. He was getting married in two days and yearned for one last wild fling to finish off his days of bachelorhood. Nicole was mildly amused that he'd even dreamed that she'd be up for it. He absolutely wasn't her type and he was roaringly drunk. What a plonker.

'Go on,' he crooned, obviously thinking he was onto a good thing. 'What would you like?'

'I'd love a place of my own,' she said suddenly. 'My own flat where I could come and go as I liked and didn't need to be there for anyone, total freedom.'

'Wayhay!' roared the groom. 'I've got my own place and we could go back there now, I've got drink and everything . . .'

'That's not what I meant, you toe rag,' Nicole said, calmly emptying the remains of her beer all over him. She'd had enough to drink.

He squealed with horror and Nicole daintily leaped up from the seat beside him, blew him a kiss and then tapped Sharon on the arm. 'I'm outta here,' she said, ignoring the furiously mouthing groom.

Dickie Vernon came out of the men's room, looking much more together, much more like a successful manager of incredible talent. Thank God they still sold those mini toothbrush and toothpaste combos in toilet dispensers. Slicking back his dark hair, he made his way over to the stag party and looked around for the young, dark girl. But she was gone.

Nicole locked the front door and pulled over the curtain that kept the draught from blowing straight up the stairs. 12a Belton Gardens was a great place for draughts. Sometimes, the winter wind whistled from the front door right through the flat and out the back door again, making the kitchen and the narrow hall no-go areas. Nicole had tried draught excluder but it kept falling off so she'd bought a big curtain for over the front door instead. If only her mother would remember to draw it.

She walked into the small cosy sitting room where her mother was sitting on the old flowery couch wrapped up in a tartan blanket and watching a late night film. A mug of tea sat in front of her and she had a bowl of popcorn on her lap.

'Hello love,' she said, not taking her eyes off the screen.

'Hi Mum,' Nicole said, sitting on the faded pink armchair beside the fire. Her mother's collection of china pigs glared down at her from the mantelpiece, alongside several scented candles which Nicole was always in mortal terror would set the place alight.

Her mother kept chewing popcorn. Nicole picked up the TV guide to see what was on. It was a 1970s Goldie Hawn film. Her mother loved Goldie Hawn. With her baby-soft blonde hair and sweet, faded smile, she liked to think she looked like Goldie too. Only in Sandra's case, the kookiness wasn't an act. Sandra Turner was kind, terribly naive and possessed of a vague dizziness that made her utterly unsuited to dealing with normal life. She felt helpless around domestic problems or money matters, hated confrontation of any kind and was addicted to the herbal tablets she took for her nerves. Men, especially, adored her helpless female act, until they discovered it wasn't an act.

If Nicole didn't do the grocery shopping and make sure that the bills were paid on time, the small Turner family would never have survived. Not that Nicole ever complained. Fiercely protective of her lovely, dizzy mother, she wouldn't let anyone say a word against her. There may have been just the three of them but they were still a family and Nicole dared anyone to say otherwise. She knew that it had been hard for her mother to rear her on her own and that many men over the years had steered clear of dating a single mother. Sandra's one chance at happiness had been with Pammy's father. He'd been a nice man, Nicole remembered. But it had somehow gone wrong and the Turner girls were on their own again.

The film cut to a commercial break and Sandra Turner came to life.

'Have a nice evening, love?' she asked, turning to her daughter.

'Lovely, Mum. How about you? Did you win?'

Her mother's face scrunched up into an irresistible grin: '£100, love!' she said jubilantly. 'I'm going to get my hair permed and buy new shoes. They've got lovely ones down the market, just like Versace but they're not the real thing.'

'Good for you, Mum,' Nicole cheered, mentally chocking up some more overtime. They were late paying the electricity bill.

She watched a bit of Goldie and then decided to go to bed.

'I'm knackered, Mum,' she said, leaning over to give her mother a kiss. 'I suppose Gran's asleep in my bed?'

Her mother bit her lip, like a small child asking forgiveness. 'I was a bit late and you know she hates getting a cab home after eleven. You can sleep with me,' she added eagerly.

Nicole checked the kitchen to make sure everything was switched off then climbed the stairs. She passed her own tiny bedroom and went into Pammy's. Barbie predominated. There wasn't any bit of Barbie equipment that Nicole hadn't bought her little half-sister. Quiet as a mouse, she peered down at her fondly. In sleep, Pammy looked even more angelic than she did awake. Her tousled white-blonde hair stuck up at all angles and her soft, babyish cheeks were plump and innocent. She was only five and Nicole completely adored her. She thought guiltily back to what she'd said to the drunken groom in the pub: yes, she'd love a place of her own, somewhere she could be utterly on her own and not responsible for any other human being. But she'd miss little Pammy so much. And her mum. No matter what her gran said about Sandra being a few sandwiches short of a picnic, she was a good mum and she did her best. She was Nicole's responsibility and that was that.

Pammy woke Nicole up at half six by climbing into the small double bed and bouncing up and down. Sandra moved just enough to pull the duvet closer around her neck.

'Nicole, wake up!' sang Pammy before she started trying to tickle her big sister under the arms.

'C'mere, brat,' she growled in her best tiger voice and pulled Pammy's small, squirming body under the covers where she began to tickle her, much more successfully.

'Lemme go! Lemme go!' squealed Pammy delightedly as she tried to wriggle away.

'No, the tiger has got you!' growled Nicole. 'Grrr, grrrr, I love yummy little girls in the morning . . . I'm hungry, grrrr . . .'

After a bit more growling, she let Pammy go and then swung her legs out of the bed, shivering in the coolness of the bedroom. She pulled on her mother's dressing gown and went downstairs with Pammy to get her breakfast.

By seven forty-five, they were both fed, dressed and ready to leave the house. Nicole took a speedy cup of tea up to her grandmother.

'Thanks love,' said Reenie Turner, sitting up in Nicole's bed. 'You're a good girl.'

'Sorry I didn't see you last night, Gran,' Nicole said. 'But I'll see you on Sunday. Don't forget to wake Mum before you go. She's due at work by ten today.'

She ignored her grandmother's snort of disapproval. Despite being mother and daughter Sandra and Reenie Turner were like chalk and cheese. Keeping the peace between them was a full time job. Reenie disapproved of Sandra's part-time job as a manicurist and the way that Nicole took care of Pammy as though she were her mother. And Sandra hated Reenie's comments about her occasional men friends.

'Once in a blue moon I meet a nice man for a drink, once in a blue moon, that's all. Just because I've got kids doesn't mean I have to live like a nun, you know,' she'd snap.

'Fat chance of that,' Reenie would sniff unfairly.

Nicole hated her grandmother criticizing Sandra. For all that her mother was dizzy, she'd worked hard to bring her and Pammy up and hadn't so much as dated a man when Nicole was a kid. It was only when Nicole was a bit of a teenage tearaway that Sandra had met Pammy's father.

Pammy danced along the wet footpath with Nicole, singing tunelessly to herself. She'd settled incredibly well at St Matthews, for which Nicole was grateful. Apart from the first day when her lower lip had wobbled when Nicole finally left her in the capable hands of Miss Vishnu, she'd run happily into school ever since. Miss Vishnu was very young and sweet and the children appeared to love her.

Once Pammy was dispatched into school with her Pokemon lunchbox, Nicole had to rush to the bus stop to catch the five to eight. She had to stand for nine stops but finally got a seat on the top deck where she could sit and listen to her CD Walkman as West London rolled by.

She enjoyed those moments to herself on the bus or tube, even if she was surrounded by people. There was still a solitariness to it that she liked: listening to music and not having to talk to anybody.

Copperplate buzzed with the usual Friday morning excitement of 'only a few more hours and it's the weekend!' In the canteen, plans were being made for lunchtime shopping expeditions for new clothes and discussions were going on about what everyone was doing that night. Top Shop had a sale and there was great enthusiasm for butterfly tops like one Jennifer Lopez wore which were reduced to twenty quid.

Nicole bought a cup of tea and sat in the smoking section of the canteen. She flicked through a paper that someone had left on the seat beside her, scanning the news rapidly before reaching the horoscopes. Leos were in for a good day, she read. *Be prepared for breathtaking news to hit you. How you react could be very important but remember not to do anything rash.*

Breathtaking news could mean she got the sack, Nicole thought, lighting up another fag even though she didn't really want it. Sharon appeared at the canteen door, face lit up with excitement.

'You'll never guess!' she yelled at Nicole as she ran over to the table.

'We've been given a day off?' Nicole suggested. 'Ms Sinclair Bitch has been run over by a truck? You're engaged to Leonardo DiCaprio?'

Sharon slid into the seat beside her friend and passed a small, rather grubby card over to her. 'Better than that,' she smirked.

'Dickie Vernon, manager,' Nicole read. 'What's this mean?'

Sharon beamed. 'He heard you sing last night in the Parrot. He's a top class band manager. He told me about some huge band he managed but I can't remember which one. Anyway, he wants you!' Sharon could barely contain herself. 'He thinks you've a wonderful voice and you could be a pop star! Imagine it.'

Nicole laughed. 'This is mad, this is. Just have a look at my horoscope. It says I better not do anything rash.'

'Rash?' demanded Sharon looking up from what the day foretold for Geminis. 'They'll never let you on *Top of the Pops* with a rash.'

Nicole had never felt so nervous in her whole life. Her hands were actually shaking as she peeled the cellophane from the cigarette packet. She'd better get a grip or she'd sound like one of those dolls who stutter 'Mama' when their string is pulled. Taking a huge drag of Rothmans, she let the nicotine enter her system and give her the hit. The drug did its thing. Great. She sagged a little in her new high leather boots and leaned against the wall as her body relaxed. Then she jerked away: this place was such a dump. Who knew when it had last been cleaned. You'd probably get rabies from just leaning against the scummy wall.

From the way Dickie had spoken about the small recording studio owned by a friend, Nicole had been under the impression that she was practically going to Abbey Road. Instead, she was in a dingy old premises in Guildford with a warren of rooms and a studio that looked as if it hadn't been used since the sixties. And the equipment looked even older, like stuff from the *Antiques Roadshow*.

The man who owned it seemed nice enough, though: a skinny old guy who wasn't exactly threatening, which was good. Nicole had been a bit nervous about going there on her own with Dickie.

'What if they're rapists who just use this "you could be a singer" line to get you on your own?' Sharon had protested. 'I'll go with you; you need moral support.'

But Nicole had insisted she went to the studio on her own. 'If we both take a sickie on Tuesday, Sinclair is going to figure something's going on. She's not that stupid,' Nicole pointed out. 'I'll be fine. I'll take my army penknife just in case.'

'I thought the actual knife fell off,' Sharon said suspiciously.

'I'll stab them to death with the bottle-opener bit,' Nicole retorted.

She had the penknife in her bag but she didn't think she was going to need it. Dickie may have looked like a total sleazezoid but he seemed genuinely only interested in her singing ability.

'You shouldn't be smoking,' he'd said, scandalized, the first time he'd seen Nicole light up, the seventh of her twenty a day.

'Who the hell are you? My bleedin' mother?' she demanded.

'It's bad for your voice. No top singer would ever smoke,' Dickie said.

Tough bananas, Nicole thought, stubbing out one cigarette and extracting another from the packet. She needed to smoke. She'd never be able to sing otherwise. She had the words and music to one Whitney Houston song ready not that she could read music, but it looked good.

Dickie came back into the studio. 'Everything's ready to go,' he said breezily. 'Just one more thing.' He casually held a piece of paper out to Nicole. 'You just need to sign this, love. To make it all legal and formal, you know.' He held out a pen with the other hand.

The corner of Nicole's mouth twitched. Did this guy really think she was that dumb? Just because she'd taken a chance by going to a studio with him, he couldn't honestly think she would blindly sign a bit of paper that would undoubtedly give him rights over her and her unborn children for the rest of her life?

She gave him her Bambi look, the one where she widened her eyes and blinked slowly, as if blinking quickly was too much of a mental strain. 'Sign this?' she repeated.

Dickie nodded, more confident now.

'I don't know,' Nicole said, still in Bambi mode.

'It's legal stuff, nothing to worry about,' Dickie urged.

Nicole took the paper and skimmed over it. What did Dickie think she did at Copperplate Insurance: make the tea? She may have been on the bottom rung of the office ladder but she still spent enough time dealing with insurance claims to know about the law. Plus, she could probably work out percentages more quickly than Dickie could and fifty per cent was a bit steep in her opinion. All at once, she decided that it had been a mistake to come here. If she wanted to be a singer, she'd have to approach it another way. She folded the piece of paper up and stuck it in her handbag, while Dickie stared at her open-mouthed.

'Wha . . . ?' he started to say.

'I'd never sign anything without getting a lawyer to look at it,' Nicole said with an impish grin. 'And I think that asking someone to sign something without explaining what they're signing, is described as "sharp practice".'

She waved at the skinny guy behind the glass plate. 'Thanks but no thanks.'

'You can't do this!' roared Dickie as the penny dropped. 'You can't walk out like this. I've invested time and money in you, I've talked you up.'

Nicole gave him a wry look and headed for the door.

'I've got people interested in you, you stupid little black bitch,' he shouted.

That did it. He'd been fine until he'd called her that. How dare he? She was proud of her Indian heritage and her colour, not that she knew much about India really, but she was proud of it anyway. Rage coursing in every vein, Nicole whirled round. She wanted to hit him but pride stopped her. *He* could behave like scum from the gutter but she wouldn't.

'When I'm famous, Dickie, I hope you'll remember that you could have been a part of it.' She gazed at him superciliously. 'Except you got too greedy. And I *will* be famous, I promise you.' With that, she left, her long silky hair flying as she strode out of the building.

She would be famous. She knew it in her bones. Dickie had done one good thing for her: he'd shown her that she wanted to make it as a singer. She'd been hiding from it for years but he'd helped her see that she could do it – and that she wanted to. She owed him that. Maybe she'd send him a ticket for her first gig.

Sharon was furious. 'The scumbag,' she raged. 'I knew he was trouble. I'll go round and kill him meself. No, I'll get my *brother* to do it.'

'Don't waste your time,' Nicole said. 'No, what I need you to do is help me with some research. I need to make a demo tape and I want to know where I can do it cheaply. Secondly, I've got to find out who to send it to. Put your thinking cap on, Shazz. Between the pair of us, we must know somebody who can help.'

Sharon's second cousin's flatmate knew a studio engineer who wouldn't mind a bit of moonlighting as a one-off. He knew who to send demos to but warned Sharon that record companies got zillions of tapes every year. 'They probably file them in the black plastic filing cabinet,' he said.

Nicole shrugged. 'I'll take that chance.'

The cheapest studio time for recording sessions was in the middle of the night, so at two a.m. two weeks later, Nicole, Sharon and Sharon's second cousin, Elaine, lined up in Si-borg Studios. The engineer had drummed up four musicians to play along with her and, to hide her nerves, Nicole whispered to Sharon that the musicians mustn't be much good if they were prepared to play in the middle of the night for damn all money. The money was from Nicole's building society account and she still felt anxious every time she thought of spending it on something so ephemeral.

'Shut up,' hissed Tommy, the engineer, 'or they'll all go home. They're not that desperate.'

Embarrassed, Nicole lit up. Nobody looked askance at her. At Si-borg, it was the people who didn't smoke who looked out of place. The musicians, engineer and even the receptionist all puffed madly so the entire premises was fuggy with smoke and the walls were stained a cloudy vanilla thanks to years of late-night Marlboro sessions.

The first hour was hell for Nicole. Used to launching into a song as soon as the karaoke machine played it or singing her own compositions alone in her bedroom, she found it impossible to stop and start as the real musicians warmed up by snapping strings, getting riffs wrong and grumbling about unfamiliar songs.

'What's wrong with them?' she whispered to Tommy as they took a break, mindful of keeping her voice down in case the musicians walked out.

'Whitney Houston and Sade are not their thing,' he grinned. 'If you wanted to launch into something by the Manic Street Preachers, these would be your men.'

'Charming.' Nicole stomped off to the loo. She leaned her head against the mirror and closed her eyes wearily. This wasn't working out as planned. She'd taken Tommy's advice and had gone for covering other people's songs instead of her own ones because he said her voice was the main thing and the demo would have greater impact that way.

She'd been so excited at the thought of working with real musicians and had had visions of herself belting out flawless hit after hit with everyone in the studio watching her in admiration.

Instead, all she had was a sore throat from the combination of singing and smoking too much, and she really wished she hadn't worn those ultra tight pink snakeskin jeans and high-heeled boots. She felt bloated because she was pre-menstrual and the waistband of the jeans was cutting into her flesh like cheese wire. Why was she doing this? She must have been mad. Just because she could hold a note didn't make her Mariah Carey. Would it be awful if she told them all to go home because she couldn't keep going?

'Nicole!' said Sharon, dancing into the grimy loo clutching a can of beer and a roll-up that Nicole would swear was filled with more than just tobacco. 'Isn't it exciting? God, they love you. I just overheard the bass player telling Tommy that you had a fantastic voice and wondering if you needed a band?'

Nicole stood up straight and blinked tiredly. The harsh fluorescent light hurt her eyes: they were red-rimmed with tiredness, no matter how much kohl she'd painted around them.

'They said what?'

'That you're marvellous! That you've got "star quality",' Sharon said happily. 'Well, I could have told them that but it's good that they think so, don't you think?' She prattled away about the bass player and how he'd said that Nicole was 'mega'.

Nicole half listened and stared at her reflection in the mirror. Underneath the tired face and the weary eyes, there was a certain radiance. She smiled and the radiance shone out at her, bypassing the tiredness instantly. Star quality, huh?

'Have you got any of that bright red lipstick on you, Sharon?' she asked. 'I left my bag downstairs and I look like death warmed up.'

Sharon rummaged around in a handbag the size of Santa's toy sack and found the lipstick in question.

With a slightly shaking hand, Nicole applied a thick buttery layer. On her dark little face with her eyes glowing like jet, the rich crimson looked incredible. Sexy and mysterious at the same time. Nicole pouted theatrically at herself. 'Let's go get 'em,' she said with a huge grin.

# CHAPTER SIX

Millie's roars could be heard in three counties at least.

'Don't want to be in the car!' she bellowed, her small face screwed up with anger and rage.

'Neither do I,' muttered Hope tight-lipped as she negotiated the hire car along the winding road, oblivious to the wind and rain swept scenery they were passing by. When the plane had banked before it arrived in Kerry's airport, Hope had done her best to peer out the window and see what sort of fabled, emerald isle she was landing on, but Toby had chosen that moment to grizzle miserably at the jerking motion of the aircraft, so she'd dragged her eyes away from the slightly bleak looking patchwork fields and comforted him. Now the rain was lashing down, giving the whole place a dismal air that was at odds with Matt's description of it.

'I remember sitting with Gearóid on the steps in the sun, him with a bottle of Guinness, the sound of the bees droning around us and the smell of hay being cut in the fields nearby. Everything was rich greens and soft golds . . .'

They must both have been drinking Guinness, Hope reflected, because there was nothing sunny or golden about the modern version of Kerry, even allowing for the fact that it was a blisteringly cold November day. Any bees buzzing around would have been drowned in the downpour.

This was not what she'd hoped for. Definitely not.

'It's going to be fabulous,' Dan had said enthusiastically at the Parkers' leaving do in the Three Carpenters two days before Matt's departure. 'The way Matt has described Ireland to me makes it sound magical.'

'We all envy you so much,' said a swaying Betsey, who'd come from a publicity launch in London for a new perfume and was half-plastered on free champagne, not to mention reeking of free scent. 'You'll have a blast.'

Hope, still exhausted from the stress of packing up the house and the misery of having to hand in her notice in the building society, sincerely hoped she would, although she felt that a week in a health farm was probably what she needed to relax her.

'You will keep in touch, won't you?' begged Yvonne, who was unexpectedly tearful at the thought of Hope leaving. 'I'll miss you, you know.'

Hope hugged her. ''Course I will. I'll be back in no time at all. And you can come and visit us. Matt tells me it's a beautiful place.'

He'd talked longingly of sitting on the coast on the Beara Peninsula looking over the rugged Atlantic, listening to the sound of the curlews as you created perfect prose. And he'd told her how Redlion nestled in a valley that protected it from the cruel winds that blew in off the sea. 'Idyllic' had been his word for it.

It didn't seem very idyllic at the moment, though. Hope began to think that the original idea of Matt driving her Metro via the ferry to Ireland ten days earlier to get the cottage shipshape hadn't been such a good idea. Travelling with the children was always a nightmare and she could have done with some help. It would also have been nice to have some reassurance that it didn't rain all the time and that this downpour was unusual she hoped.

But Matt had insisted that someone had to do some work on the cottage because the lawyer had mentioned it was a bit 'uncared for.' And he'd also been keen to meet the artistic community people he'd been corresponding with, in relation to working in their centre, as soon as possible.

Hope tried to concentrate on the road, which wasn't easy with Millie yelling. Their progress since landing had been slow to say the least. Just when Hope was panicking about being stranded without their luggage, her five suitcases had finally turned up. Battling through the small but incredibly crowded airport with two fractious children, she'd picked up the sturdy four-wheel drive vehicle she'd booked in advance and had just managed to hump all their cases into it without giving herself a hernia when Millie decided to throw a tantrum.

A visit to the ladies, bribery involving biscuits and juice, and the purchase of a cuddly bear in an Aran sweater had all been useless. Millie had decided she was not in a good mood, wailing so hysterically that a cluster of little old ladies disembarking from a coach at the airport doors had looked at Hope as if she was wearing a sign saying 'unfit mother.'

True to form, Millie had yelled and cried at full blast for the last hour as her harassed mother read the map, worked out where she was going and made it out past the lunchtime rush in Killarney. Trying not to mow down pedestrians had been the biggest problem. People in Killarney just seemed to walk out in front of the car, not caring that she was a few feet away from them in a deadly piece of all-terrain vehicle with bull bars on the front. Did they look right and left before crossing the road? No, they just threw themselves blithely into the traffic, hopping over puddles and treating the passing cars like nuisances. The Irish were all mad, she decided darkly. She wished Matt had been able to collect them but as the Metro had burst a gasket and was currently languishing in the local garage, it made more sense to rent a car because they'd need transport until the Metro was fixed.

Toby sat quietly in the back, strapped in carefully. Millie, feeling liberated because the car seats were coming later, kept trying to remove her seat belt until Hope had to stop the car and attach her even more firmly. Outraged at being unable to move so freely, Millie decided to roar even more.

Finally, Hope could stand it no longer. The rain had practically stopped and they all needed a bit of fresh air. A few miles outside Killarney, she stopped the car by a gate at the side of the road, got out and unhooked the children.

It was windy and there was still a fine mist of rain that dampened the children's hair immediately, but Millie didn't care. Delighted to be free, she bounced over to the big rusty gate, surprising the herd of muddy black and white cows huddled next to the ditch.

'Cows,' she said as happily as if she'd just discovered a herd of rare beasts.

Toby clung to his mother nervously. He wasn't keen on big animals and when he'd been taken to the zoo, he'd sobbed at the sight of the elephants. Millie, on the other hand, had had to be restrained from clambering up the monkey enclosure, waving her ice cream enticingly.

'It's all right, darling,' Hope said now, hoisting Toby onto her hip and carrying him to the gate. 'They're friendly.'

As if to disprove this point, one of the cows lurched towards the gate in investigative mode.

Millie squealed with delight and Toby hid his face in Hope's shoulder, shuddering with fear.

'Mummy, will we have cows?' demanded Millie excitedly.

Hope had absolutely no idea. If cows were included in the property, Matt hadn't mentioned them. His memory of Uncle Gearóid's had included a quaint cottage covered with old fashioned roses and an expanse of wild looking garden out the front. He'd been a bit woolly on the other details although the lawyer's letter had mentioned four bedrooms, a kitchen with a genuine iron range and a bathroom with an antique claw foot bath. It all *sounded* lovely, but then, so did novels about the Middle Ages where nobody mentioned the pain of not having dentists and how women routinely died in agonizing childbirth. Hope thought about her lovely, only-just-paid-for modern freezer and the shower in their house in Bath where you'd swear you were being stabbed with millions of exquisite tiny needles when you turned it on at full blast. She didn't hold out much hope for a quaint cottage having such a marvellous plumbing innovation. But then, who knew? Uncle Gearóid could have been a modern sort of man with a passion for Bang and Olufsen stereos, giant kitchen equipment with icemakers, and a jacuzzi. The unknown was exciting, Matt had said before he left.

However, on the phone since then, he'd sounded a bit dreamy and short on facts about things like plumbing and installing two phone lines for the e-mail so he could correspond with the office. Men liked the unknown, women didn't, Hope decided.

'It's so unspoiled,' he'd said the night before over a crackly phone line. 'You're going to love it.'

Mind you, he'd thought she was going to love the black lace thong underwear he'd purchased for her birthday on a trip to Bristol. Sam had insisted that if you wore thongs for two weeks, you never went back to normal knickers again. Hope had given up after two days.

Still, they had the house in Bath. If the rural writing retreat proved too rural, she could always up sticks and bring the children home. So, they had rented it out for a year but Hope was sure she'd find a way round that. That's what lawyers were for.

'Come on,' she said now in bright Mummy-speak. 'Back to the car, we've got a bit longer to go and then you can explore our new home!'

The children clambered back into the car and Hope strapped them in, thankful they'd fallen for her faux enthusiasm. Back on the road, she admired the scenery and tried to pretend that it didn't look very bleak. Beautiful, certainly, with those majestic purple mountains looming in the horizon and a faint mist covering them like icing sugar rained down by some heavenly cook. Everywhere was astonishingly green in the rain but a tad desolate. Not really like the idyllic, sun-drenched place she'd seen in the *Discover Ireland* travel book.

So far, Hope couldn't imagine the sun ever shining in this remote part of the world. She liked visiting romantically desolate spots for cosy weekends, enjoying going for a walk in the woods as long as there was a glorious hotel complete with log fire in the bar when they got back so they could roast their wet socks, giggle over a couple of hot ports and plan what to wear for dinner.

Real life desolation all the time was a different proposition. The scenery around her looked so ... well, untamed. The countryside around Bath was green too, but it seemed more laid out and more normal. Here, the fields were all sizes with stone walls and briar hedges going off in all directions. The drivers were all mad too: she'd nearly been forced off the road by some little old man in a van who could barely see over the dashboard and at least six flashy new cars had overtaken her in exasperation on dangerous bits of road, obviously furious to be behind a hire car going at a respectable forty miles an hour.

At a tiny crossroads with no signpost at all, she consulted her map again. If it was to be believed, she had to take the right turn, follow the road for a few miles and then she'd come to a town. She drove carefully until she came to the first signs of habitation.

'Quaint, untouched,' had been Matt's verdict on Redlion, the small town where their house was situated.

'Really quaint,' Hope thought grimly as she drove into it a few minutes later.

She had to turn off before she got to the main street, therefore not seeing all of the place, but on first viewing with the rain pelting down in a sheet, Matt's quaint town was anything but. What she could see consisted of a winding line of terraced houses, one battered pub, a tiny post office, a convenience shop with security bars that looked capable of stopping a tank, and a caravan park with its signpost hanging drunkenly from one corner. Thinking she must be in the wrong place, because this could hardly be the pretty place Matt had described, she came to a hump backed bridge. An elderly green water pump over the bridge signalled that she was, indeed, in Redlion. Matt had mentioned both the bridge and the pump and according to him, she had to take the next left which was a winding road that led away from the town to her new home. It was official, she decided: she was now in The Back Of Beyond.

With an increasing sense of doom, Hope drove down a narrow lane with a grass spine in the middle and big puddles of mud either side. She felt the same way she'd felt when she and Sam had gone to big school for the first time: a little bit excited at the thought of being a big girl, a bit more excited about her school uniform with the dark blue jumper, and absolutely terrified at the thought of all those other girls with their normal families who'd think that she and Sam were weird having no parents and only a mad old aunt to pick them up from school.

She rounded a corner, past a giant monkey puzzle tree that bent out over the lane, and then she saw it. Her new home.

If the outskirts of Redlion had been given a grievous battering with the ugly stick, Curlew Cottage had escaped. Gloriously pretty, it sat snugly in a wilderness of hedges and beech trees and looked as if it been drawn by an illustrator who was trying to imagine a home for the Seven Dwarves. From the small windows with their latticed shutters to the fat wooden door with black iron fittings, it was adorable. The pretty climbing rose that Matt had waxed lyrical about had been cut back and, as it was December, there would have been no flowers clustering round the door anyway, but that was the only negative thing she could see. It was a bit run down but what would you expect from an elderly man living here on his own for years?

Hope sighed with relief. At that exact moment, an unseen cockerel loudly proclaimed that this was his territory and that they better back off. Toby shrieked with fear and Millie shrieked with delight.

'Let me out Mummy,' she roared, desperate to explore.

The cockerel crowed again.

An attack hen, Hope decided, feeling her sense of humour return.

The rain had stopped, so she let the kids out, warning them to stay close. Toby didn't need any telling and clung to her trouser legs. Millie, on the other hand, raced off after the cockerel.

'Come back!' yelled Hope nervously with her city-mother mentality. 'Right now!'

Millie wavered long enough for her mother to grab her anorak hood. With Millie reined in and wriggling crossly and Toby sucking his thumb nervously, they made their way to the front door.

'Where's Daddy?' Millie said with interest.

Good question, Hope thought. She'd hoped he'd be waiting for them, ready to run out, throw his arms around his family and say he'd missed them desperately for the past ten days. She'd been watching too much TV, she reckoned. Husbands only ran out in thrilled delight on made-for-TV movies or romantic dramas. They never did it in real life except when they were famished and you'd just been at the shops buying food.

She knocked at the front door. No reply. After a moment, she turned the handle and the door creaked open a fraction. Should they go in or not? She dithered until an ominous rumble in the sky signalled an end to the brief interlude of dry weather.

Rain started pelting down again like a tropical storm. 'Gosh, isn't this exciting,' Hope said gaily to the children as she pushed the door fully open.

Inside, the adorable cottage scenario went awry. The first thing to hit Hope was the cold. Still warm from the steamed-up atmosphere of the car, the cool November air had barely registered with her at first. Now, standing inside the cottage she was struck by an arctic sensation. Stone floors, stone walls and no visible source of heat made for a combination of bone-chilling damp and cold. In fact, everything in the cottage looked damp and cold. Instead of the hand-crafted wooden furniture, lovingly made frilled curtains and air of sparkling cleanliness she'd prayed for, she was faced with a big bare room with no curtains at all. The only furniture was a coffee table and two elderly tweedy armchairs with disturbing dark, oily patches on the cushions.

Hope held the children's hands more tightly as she gazed around her in horror. This wasn't fit to live in: it hadn't been painted for years and was completely filthy. The cobwebs that festooned the ceiling were the least of her worries. Matt had made the entire family emigrate and their new home wasn't a cosy cottage but a dishevelled shed. She wanted to cry. Her thoughts were broken by the sound of a car engine and a slamming door.

'Millie, Toby! Sorry I'm late, love. Just got caught up with the gang!' Matt rushed into the room, hair plastered down on his forehead, wearing an unfamiliar sludge brown jacket, mud splattered corduroys, Wellington boots and a welcoming expression.

He gave Hope a brief warm kiss and then picked a child up in each arm, hugging them to him.

'Did you miss Daddy?' he demanded.

'Yes,' said Millie huskily, burying her little head lovingly in his shoulder. 'Lots and lots and this big.' She demonstrated how much she'd missed him by holding her arms wide.

Hope didn't want to break up this cosy family thing. She felt like the bitch from Hell about to remind Snow White that it might not be a good idea to shack up with seven small men who were looking for a cheap housekeeper, but it had to be done. Besides which, Matt hadn't thrown his arms around *her*.

'Matt,' she said in her everything-in-the-garden-is-rosy voice so as not to alarm the children, 'we need to talk about the cottage.'

'Isn't it lovely,' he said. 'So naïf.'

'What?' she said, rosy garden voice disappearing to be replaced by sour-milk voice.

'You know, unspoiled,' he said artlessly.

'How about unclean, unpainted and utterly unsuitable for two small children,' she snapped back at him, tiredness and a general feeling of being unloved making her cross. 'Not to mention freezing. We'll all get hypothermia if we live here. This is a dump. I don't suppose you were roughing it here?'

'Well, no, I was at Finula's and I know we have a lot to do here and I'm sorry I haven't really got started but I thought we could manage for a few days with those portable stoves and then get some work done on Monday . . .'

'Matt, you mean you haven't told Hope the place wasn't ready yet?' said a low, throaty female voice. 'How bold of you. Slap, slap.'

They both turned to face the newcomer. Tall, rotund and exuding rural friendliness, she was forty-something and wore a selection of flapping garments that all appeared to be patterned by the hand of Laura Ashley. Hope identified pyjama-style trousers, a voluminous shirt and a rakishly-angled hat, all flowery and pink. A big tartan shawl completed the outfit.

'Hope, meet Finula Headley-Ryan, the leading light of the artistic community in Redlion and the lady who's been so kind about getting me into the writers' centre at short notice.'

'Tsk, tsk,' said Finula, clearly delighted with this description but pretending she wasn't. 'I'm only an old dauber, hardly an artist at all.'

She sailed over to Hope and held out a freckled hand, weighed down with elaborate old gold rings. The glamorous effect was slightly ruined by chipped scarlet nail varnish that revealed yellowing nails underneath.

'I'm sure you're not so pleased to meet anyone when this house is like the wreck of the Hesperus,' she said in that low, thrilling voice. 'Matt, you are a melt for not telling the poor girl that the place isn't habitable. Think of the shock she got when she thought this was her new home in all its freezing glory. What are you like?'

'Well, I wanted Hope to come and I knew she'd hardly be keen if I told her what was left to do' he said, giving Finula the benefit of his handsomest smile. 'Anyway, Hope,' he added, slightly wheedling, 'I'll get the workmen to start on Monday.'

'Obviously, the children can't stay here,' Hope said, her shock at the state of her new home overcoming her dislike of getting personal in front of strangers. 'We'll have to stay in a hotel.'

'Nonsense,' Finula declared. 'You'll stay with me. The only hotel round here is five-star and would cost a bomb. We'd love to have you. A couple of days and we'll have this house spick and span. It's not at all fit for children.' She leaned over and rubbed Millie's cheek.

Instead of scowling the way she usually did when someone she didn't know touched her, Millie dimpled up at Finula.

'Little dote, isn't she?' sighed Finula. 'My Cormac is twelve now, too big for cuddles but they're lovely at that age.'

Thinking of Millie's waking-the-dead tantrums on the journey from the airport, Hope managed a weak smile and said yes, lovely.

'Now, follow me,' Finula ordered.

Within minutes, she'd bundled Hope and the children into her car, a battered green station wagon that had been side-swiped so often there were only stripes of green paint on the doors.

'Matt can take your car,' Finula said, crunching gears as she drove over a few bushes doing a five-point turn. 'My house is down an awful pot-holed bothreen and you'd be tortured following me.'

The inside of the car was as messy as the outside, with a filthy pair of Wellington boots on the back seat and several smelly water-proof coats, exuding a scent of mud and wet dog, crumpled up on the floor.

Hope sat in silence as they drove at high speed along a narrow road. She was suddenly exhausted after her journey and so angry with Matt for expecting her to live in such squalor that she was incapable of making polite conversation. Finula, however, kept up a stream of talk that, luckily, required no response.

'There are seventeen of us in the community who live here full time. Mainly artists but we've got three novelists and two poets. I'm sure you've heard of Maire Nic Chinneide.'

Before Hope had time to nod dishonestly at this, Finula was off again.

'Amazing poet, so lyrical. Her poems about the traffic on the Killarney Road would bring a tear to your eye. Anyway, as I was saying, as well as the full timers who live in the area, at least two hundred artists and writers come during the year, and we have a wonderful time. I've been here ten years and I feel like part of the furniture. Myself and Ciaran – Ciaran's a novelist by the way – came from Dublin originally. I wouldn't go back for all the tea in China. There are no twenty-four-hour shops here or high rise buildings: it's heaven.'

Hope, longing for a twenty-four-hour shop and a couple of high rise buildings, said nothing.

Finula described the entire artistic community, how often they met in the Creativity Centre (every day, as far as Hope could make out) and what sort of wonderful entertainment was available (weekly dinners during the high season and two creativity workshops during the year when the place sounded as if it was over-run with would-be writers and painters.) Matt had explained all this to Hope previously but when he'd said how it worked, it hadn't sounded like some demented religious commune. Feeling more and more anxious, Hope wondered if there were other women with small children.

'The locals don't bother with us much, they think we're all mad artistic types,' Finula tittered.

Hope privately thought that Finula relished being a mad artistic type. Compared to Finula's flamboyant floral rig out, Hope felt like a mouse in her serviceable navy chinos, navy wool polo neck and beige casual jacket. Would she have to start wearing loads of mascara, plenty of shawls and her Liberty nightie to fit in?

'I'm sure Matt has told you all about us,' Finula said, swerving rapidly as she made a right hand turn into a beautifully-kept driveway.

'Not really,' Hope hedged, vowing never to get in a car with Finula ever again.

They pulled up outside a big homely farmhouse set amid a forest of pine trees. Unlike the cottage, this was beautifully maintained, with big planters full of dwarf conifers in a regimented line beside the porch and ornamental wagon wheels set along a veranda. A swing seat took pride of place on the left of the veranda, complete with stripy canopy. The entire premises would not have looked out of place in a Doris Day movie.

'Let's get you all in and get some food into the little ones,' Finula bossed.

Finula's home was everything Hope wanted in a rural retreat. Rambling yet cosy, with plenty of squashy sofas, Turkish rugs on the stone floors and lots of pictures, ornaments and books to enliven the place. Her kitchen was the sort of place that highly successful television cooks always seemed to have: a triumph of golden wood complete with an Aga, butcher's block and bulbous copper saucepans hanging from the ceiling. Hope had always wanted one of those saucepan-hanging things.

'I know it's a shock when you up sticks and move to the country for the first time,' Finula said when Hope and the children were installed at the huge wooden kitchen table, the children with home-made yoghurts and home-made apple juice, Hope with a big glass of red wine – thankfully not home made.

'But it's so good for the children. You can have a chance to bring them up the right way here, to teach them about life and nature, to feed them natural, organic foods and to be with them all the time. It's a quality of life you can't get in the big city. No rapists, murderers or burglars.'

Hope took a slug of wine and mused on how the locals had managed to keep murderers, rapists and burglars out: with an electric fence, perhaps?

'Of course, personally, I think those degenerate hippie people up the road aren't to be trusted,' Finula added nastily, 'but we've had no trouble with them yet. Matt's been telling me how you've

143

longed to spend time with the children, that you were tired of the rat race.'

Hope wished Matt hadn't been quite so free with his confidences. Finula already seemed to know everything about her. She idly wondered if he'd mentioned her pre-menstrual tension or that time he'd had shingles and been off sex for a month, just to give a rounded psychological picture of them as a couple.

'Wait till you've had the thrill of growing your own vegetables,' Finula sighed.

Now did not seem like the time to mention that Hope only liked her vegetables fresh from the supermarket counter and that the last thing she'd grown was a peace lily given to her when Toby was born. It was long since on a tip somewhere, withered because she'd forgotten to water it.

'And hens, you'd love hens,' Finula said. 'Old Gearóid had a lovely hen house out the back and you'd be mad not to get hens. Think of it,' Finula's eyes went misty, 'your own free range eggs. You have to watch the foxes, mind,' she added, waving a finger to illustrate how dangerous foxes were. 'Matt really needs a gun, you know. For the foxes, although I doubt if he'd get a licence for one.'

'I can't imagine Matt shooting anything,' Hope ventured.

'Well, he's great at fishing so I assumed he could shoot as well.'

Hope stared at her. 'Fishing? I didn't know he could fish.'

'There's no point hiding your light under a bushel here!' Finula wagged a finger. 'He's wonderful fisherman. He didn't let on at first, but we soon got it out of him. There are no secrets in Redlion. I'm sure you're very into organic food as well. I wouldn't dream of having anything else in the house. And as for convenience foods, tsk!' Finula's snort indicated what she thought of convenience food. 'Shop bought meals and tins of food, they rot your insides, believe me.'

It occurred to Hope that she'd have to visit the village shop under cover of darkness if she was to purchase things like fish fingers, Lean Cuisines and the tinned spaghetti the kids adored. Then again, maybe the village shop didn't *have* things like fish fingers or tinned spaghetti. Maybe it only sold tofu, yak's milk and bean sprouts. And not a single packet of crisps and Hula Hoops. Suddenly, she yearned for a delicious packet of Hula Hoops, full of non-organic preservatives and things Finula would disapprove of. Gorgeous.

Finula was still talking. Did she ever shut up? 'Cormac has done so well since he came here. We spend quality time together. You don't get that when you work outside the home,' she said beadily.

Hope wanted to stand up for working outside the home. Millions of women have to work, they have no choice, she wanted to say. And many more want to work, they want a career. That doesn't mean their children suffer. But she said nothing. Matt had obviously painted her as an earth mother who couldn't wait to give up her job, so there was no point. She hardly knew this woman after all and they were her guests. So Hope smiled her polite smile and wished she was at home in her own kitchen in Bath, doing the ironing. Yes, that would be a suitable swap. A mound of ironing as big as a house would make up for being in this mad woman's kitchen feeling her life spiralling out of control.

At that moment, Matt arrived and to Hope's utter surprise, started to make himself a cup of tea, seemingly completely at home in Finula's kitchen. 'Ciaran and I put the cases in the two back bedrooms,' he said. 'Finula's been putting me up since I got here. Isn't she wonderful?' he said to Hope, patting her arm affectionately.

'Yes,' said Hope, tight-lipped.

Tired from their journey, Toby and Millie miraculously went to bed without a fuss. Hope would have loved to have thrown herself onto the double bed in hers and Matt's room and joined them in the land of Nod, but she knew she had to have dinner with the others.

Ciaran, who turned out to be a short, bald and spectacled man looking a million miles away from his description as an arty type who wrote historical novels, was making his special beef in Guinness, the family's favourite recipe.

'You'll adore it,' said Finula throatily to Hope. 'Oh my dear, do meet my lovely little Cormac.'

Cormac was a big, sullen lad who was anything but lovely. He wolfed down his meal almost before the rest of them had picked up their forks and immediately shoved his seat back from the table and left.

'Homework,' said Ciaran.

Bad manners thought Hope.

It was a strange evening. Over dinner, Hope watched her husband laugh, joke and tell stories about the advertising rat race and how he was glad to be out of it. There was no trace of the focussed, ambitious ad man who lived and breathed for his job and who read the advertising magazine, *Campaign*, as if it were the Bible.

She also watched Finula gaze raptly at the handsome happy face like a dog drooling for a marrow bone. Matt seemed utterly unaware of Finula's admiration.

'I love this place,' he said, squeezing Hope's hand. 'It makes me feel alive.'

Hope squeezed back. It was wonderful to see Matt happy again and to feel that there was new life in the marriage. It *was* only for a year after all.

The local people were, according to Ciaran and Finula, all very boring. Having overheard herself being described as boring more than once, Hope felt a glimmer of pity for the locals.

'I *have* tried, believe me,' Finula said querulously after her sixth glass of wine. 'I've tried to get them involved in the community. We had that Thai evening in June and invited everyone to come. I even got a Tai Chi teacher to come in for a demonstration, I thought it would be lovely to start local classes. But no.' She sniffed. 'Only a few came and they were out the front door like a shot as soon as Su Lin started the demonstration. Although my tiger prawns went down well. They're all only interested in business and the prices of property. Honestly, we came here to get away from all that. And the women are always on about this Macramé club they have going. I ask you, macramé. That went out in the seventies.'

'Not everyone's into stuff like Tai Chi,' volunteered Hope. 'I mean, I'm not. I love aerobics though. I hope there's a class round here, otherwise I'll balloon. I could certainly do with a few sessions of tums and bums.'

She looked up from her meringue with blackberry coulis to see Finula staring at her in shock.

'Aerobics,' said Finula as though she was speaking of tertiary syphilis, 'is hardly the same as Tai Chi.'

'I know, I know,' said Hope, backtracking, 'but that's what I like. Everyone likes different things. You can't make people interested in Tai Chi if they're not . . .'

She felt Matt's hand gripping her thigh under the table. 'Hope, love,' he said, 'that's the point of the community. It's not just about letting a group of artists work in a supportive atmosphere, it's about fostering culture in Kerry. Teaching people that there's more to life than existing in the humdrum working world.'

He sounded so earnest when he spoke that Hope wondered if her real husband had been body snatched and replaced with this look-alike. And no wonder the locals weren't keen on the artistic gang. It was a bit rich to turn up in an area and basically accuse everyone of being culturally illiterate.

'I understand,' she said gravely.

In the end, Matt drank so much of Finula and Ciaran's lovely wine that he got plastered and by the time they climbed into the comfortable big bed, Hope knew there was no point in raising the state of Curlew Cottage again, and adding that she'd be on the first plane back to Bristol if he didn't take immediate action to make it habitable.

The next morning Hope got up at seven with her energetic offspring and went downstairs to make them breakfast. Her reserved soul didn't like the idea of pottering around in someone else's kitchen. There was no sign of Finula or Ciaran. Sleeping off massive hangovers, she supposed. Being artistic seemed to mean sinking an awful lot of booze.

Coco Pops were the current favourite breakfast with Millie. But true to her beliefs, Finula didn't have a single packet of manufactured cereal anywhere. Not even cornflakes, which were practically a health food in Hope's book. There was just a big jar of home-made muesli that looked for all the world like mouse droppings.

'Want Coco Pops,' whined Millie after a few minutes' waiting. Toby sat quietly as usual, turning the pages of his *Silly Pig Finds A Friend* picture book.

'I can't find any,' Hope said. She opened another cupboard and bingo: no Coco Pops but lots of lovely home made bread.

They breakfasted on toast and jam, with milk for the children and coffee for Hope.

Afterwards, she wrapped them all up in anoraks and Wellingtons and they set off to explore. If the previous day had been dismal and wet, this was the perfect example of a glorious winter day. Crisp and cool, with a bright wintry sun shining low in the sky, dusting the landscape with piercing light. It was beautiful. Today, the hills in the background looked picturesque instead of brooding and Hope could pick out a myriad of colours in the landscape instead of yesterday's dull, rainy grey. She could see warm peat browns, soft umbers and rich plums. The stone walls that criss-crossed the land were a flinty grey and there were traces of green everywhere, from the gleam of dewy grass to the faded verdigris of moss clinging to the walls. It would be a wonderful place if you were a painter. She breathed deeply, letting the sharp country air permeate her lungs. In the distance, she could see two cottages and one two-storey farmhouse but for at least a mile on either side of Finula's house there was nothing. Incredible, she thought. This really was the country.

'Let's go for an adventure,' she said. 'We might find some animals.'

Toby looked unsure. 'Mummy will pick you up if you're scared,' Hope told him gently, 'but we've got to get used to cows and things. Maybe we'll find some baby cows.'

She had no idea if this was possible. Did cows have calves in winter? Or maybe they had them at Easter. Or was that lambs she was thinking of? Who knew. The countryside was very mysterious.

The ground crunched as they walked down the drive and out onto a lane bordered by a low stone wall. Holding both the children's hands, Hope walked slowly, admiring the stark leafless trees, bent and gnarled as they clung low to the ground.

The ground was mucky after the previous day's rain and she stepped around puddles delicately, while Millie struggled to jump in them.

A car drove past and the driver raised a hand in greeting. When the driver of the second car waved, she decided that the local people were simply friendly and waved to everyone. The next vehicle was a tractor with a grizzled old farmer sitting on it.

'Let's all wave,' said Hope enthusiastically.

'Helloooo!' they all yelled.

The farmer kept both hands on the steering wheel and looked at them as if they were mad.

They found a herd of cows clustered around a trough of hay, all up to their hocks in mud. Millie was fascinated as to why they were all so dirty.

'Mud, darling,' Hope said.

'Oooh look!' Millie yelled as one beige coloured cow lifted her tail and let forth a stream of manure. 'Cow pooh pooh, Mummy! Cow pooh pooh! Can we smell it?'

Back at the house, Finula was up and already organizing.

'PJ Rice will be down at the cottage at eleven and he'll discuss what work you need done,' she told Hope bossily.

'Is he a contractor?' Hope asked, extracting Millie from her Wellington boots and hoping that she didn't have cow pooh on them.

'He does a bit of everything,' Finula said.

'Surely we need a separate plumber and heating man . . .' Hope began.

'Nonsense. We'll all muck in with the painting and as for heating, sure Gearoid had a great range that'll heat the entire cottage. All it takes is to get it cleaned out and a bit of a knack to keep it running.'

'We saw cow pooh pooh, Daddy,' squealed Millie happily as her father appeared, clutching a glass fizzing with soluble painkillers.

Hope had had her suspicions about PJ, but after three days of back-breaking work from all parties, the cottage was looking better. *Homes and Gardens* wouldn't be desperate to photograph it for their latest issue, but at least Curlew Cottage was fit for human occupation.

PJ had installed a new shower in the bathroom and the pipes in the kitchen no longer rattled ominously when you turned the taps on. The big cream range was going and indeed, it did heat the whole cottage, although it gobbled up fuel at an horrific rate.

Matt had rented a sander and the floors upstairs were soon smooth and pale gold. The downstairs flooring was icy stone slabs and Hope vowed to buy nice rugs for them as soon as she got a chance. PJ's two colleagues, a couple of hard working teenage lads, painted the entire inside of the cottage with white paint because Matt said it would be a good idea to lighten the place up as the windows were so small. However, as the two painters painted any dirt and dust into the walls at the same time, Hope soon learned that she had to scrub and clean each room before they started. The bathroom was the biggest nightmare because under the infamous claw footed bath was a thriving and wriggling community of bugs.

'Clock beetles,' PJ remarked laconically as several jet black insects scurried out from under the bath, frantically running in different directions. 'They're lucky, you know.'

'Not in this house,' Hope said with feeling.

Worn out and with reddened hands from plunging them into buckets of soapy water, Hope insisted that Matt deal with the wild life in the bathroom.

'I hate creepy crawlies,' she shivered, handing him the soapy cloth and the bucket, 'even lucky ones.'

On Thursday, Matt bought three beds and a second-hand couch in Killarney, along with a fridge freezer and washing machine. All were to be delivered on Friday. The few bits of furniture they'd had shipped from Bath were due to arrive at the same time.

'What about a cooker?' asked Hope suddenly, realizing that there was one vital omission from Matt's shopping list.

'We can cook on the range,' Matt shrugged. 'Anyway, I'm too broke now to buy anything else. Paying PJ and paying for this lot cost a bomb.'

Hope bit back the retort that it had been his idea to come here in the first place and if he hadn't thought they could afford it, they shouldn't have come. He wasn't going to have to cook on the horrible old range, that would be her job.

She stormed off to their bedroom. So much for the wonderful revitalization of their marriage.

By Friday evening, five days after their arrival, the family were finally installed in their new home. Matt's computer was set up in the tiny box room, ready for the consultancy work he was going to do part-time for Judd's, and the kids' rooms were as perfect as they could be under the circumstances, full of their toys and pictures, if a little barren.

Their own bedroom was a bit of a mess with just an old rail for hanging clothes and two upturned boxes as bedside tables. Everything was still a long way from her vision of country life with the cosy cottage, Hope thought. Instead, she'd found herself in what looked like a barren holiday cottage where the owners had never really made themselves at home.

'It's a bit sparse,' she said, looking around the sitting room with its meagre furniture and no pictures on the walls.

'Yeah, I remember Gearóid having lots of oil paintings, stuff his friends had painted. I suppose he had to sell them in the end. Money was always tight with him. I thought he was brilliant but he never had much success with his poems.'

'How many books did he have published?'

'Three and they're out of print now,' Matt said sadly. 'Poor Gearóid. He *was* talented. Still, let's not get maudlin. We'll be so happy here.' He hugged her. 'Thank you for this, Hope. I know it's been strange for you this week, but it'll be fantastic for us all from now on. We need this, I need this.'

He kissed her tenderly, the way he'd kissed her on their wedding day: as if he didn't believe it was all for real. For the first time in ages, Hope felt her insides contract. She hadn't felt even vaguely sexy all week. It was the strain of sorting things out. But she felt a definite frisson now. It was wonderful the way he could do that to her. They loved each other, she knew, they'd survive anything.

'Let's go to bed early tonight,' Matt murmured.

As he pottered around in his study, Hope walked through the cottage thoughtfully. She had plans for it. She'd drape throws over things, the way Finula did to such effect. The modern silver frames with their wedding photos and pictures of the children looked somewhat wrong too. Perhaps she could learn how to make curtains. It couldn't be too hard, it was a challenge. Hadn't women always travelled to strange destinations to be with their menfolk. They had followed armies in centuries gone by, enduring enormous deprivations just to be with the ones they loved. They had in Jane Austen's time, Hope reflected trying to feel suitably noble. If they could do it, she could.

She fried some of Finula's homemade sausages and free range eggs for dinner. It was the only thing she could think of to cook as she had no idea how to deal with the range. It could take twenty minutes to boil the kettle on it – Lord knew how many years it would take to cook a chicken casserole.

After dinner, she sat in front of the range with a cup of cocoa and watched Matt fiddling around with the television trying to pick up a signal. There was no noise outside, no sound of other people or car doors slamming or horns blaring. Nothing. Just the silence of the countryside.

Used to the madcap atmosphere of Ciaran and Finula's where people arrived at all hours, unannounced and wandering into the kitchen to make themselves tea, it felt strange to be on their own again.

Finula had been very kind but she was so overbearing, as if she wanted to lay claim to the newcomers as her own possessions. Matt couldn't see it and felt that any criticism of his new friend was a sign of ingratitude after all she'd done for them. Well, they wouldn't see that much of Finula from now on, would they?

Matt cursed under his breath as the snowstorm effect on the television got worse instead of better. He'd been fiddling with the damn thing for half an hour and so far, all he'd managed to locate was an Irish language television channel, which was going to be bugger all use to them. Maybe they had sub-titles for the films: that was going to be the best they could do at this rate.

'We could always watch with the sound turned down and make up our own dialogue,' he joked, turning round to Hope. But she was deeply asleep, squashed into a corner of the uncomfortable old brown sofa with a cushion wedged against her head. Matt watched her for a moment, smiling at the way her fair hair was all fluffed up around her face, lots of little curls running wild because she probably hadn't run a comb through it since that morning. She hadn't bothered with make up either and her long, thick eyelashes rested palely against her flushed cheeks. She looked very vulnerable in sleep, her rounded face defenceless against the world, her gentle coral mouth moving as she dreamed. She certainly didn't look like a thirty-six-year-old mother-of-two. More like a naive, trusting twenty-something. Naive, that was certainly Hope, Matt thought with a twinge of guilt. Despite his fierce belief that this was a good move for them all, he couldn't help feeling selfish for bringing her here. Dear Hope loved her routine, the comfort of the familiar. A creature of habit, she was nervous of the unknown and yet he'd transplanted her from her own world into a strange place where she knew nobody.

He knew she'd follow him to the ends of the earth and that was why she was here: because she loved him utterly.

And he was here for purely selfish reasons. Sure, he'd managed things so that he'd have a job to go back to in Bath, and their mortgage there was taken care of by letting the house out. So the family wouldn't lose out financially. But the reason they were here was because of *his* dream, not theirs. He wanted the peace to write and he'd brought them all here because of that.

Hope would forfeit every dream in her life just to make sure her beloved family were happy and content. And he'd forfeit all their contentment so that *he* could be happy. Matt thrust that thought out of his mind. Redlion was a beautiful place. He loved it here, he felt connected to it on some deep, emotional level. He'd had such wonderful holidays here as a child. Hope would learn to love it too. He'd work his backside off to make his book a success, then they'd have real financial security for the rest of their lives. He could do it: he was sure of it. Whenever he thought about the book, he felt a fresh burst of excitement.

He'd started it in a rush of ideas, racing to get his thoughts on paper, eager to tell the story of a man on the verge of a breakdown who takes off around the world to escape his misery but ends up in a parallel universe where he's living fifty years in the past. In his fantasies, Matt imagined literary magazines reviewing his novel with words like 'lyrical', 'exquisitely written' and 'a breathtaking new talent.'

It wasn't going to be easy, he knew, but life wasn't easy, was it? He'd write a wonderful book with the drive and determination he was well known for. He'd work deep into the night every night if necessary but there was no way he would fail. He dismissed the idea. After all, he smiled to himself, his drive and brilliance had worked magic for Judds, making them the hottest agency in the area. He could do that again, for himself this time. When had he ever failed at anything?

'You're the new people from old Gearóid's place,' said the elderly man behind the counter at the convenience shop when Hope went in to buy groceries for her newly painted cupboards.

'Er yes,' said Hope, a bit startled. It was the day after they'd moved into the cottage and this was her first time in the village. How did he know who she was?

'Lovely house, say it's a bit wild on the inside. He wasn't the full shilling, old Gearóid. Them hens had the run of the place, inside and out.'

'Really,' Hope said politely as she dawdled in front of the eggs. She wanted to buy free range but they were more expensive and she'd better economize until she knew how their finances were going to pan out. The hire car had gone back and they were stuck with her Metro, which had been fixed at great expense.

'Would you be thinking of getting hens yourself?' the old man inquired sweetly.

'Well, I don't know . . .' Hope hesitated, disarmed by his twinkling faded blue eyes in a warm old face. Finula had suggested she got some, she just hadn't felt ready for livestock just yet.

'They're very easy to look after. Just throw in a bit of feed and sure, you've got your own eggs. You could even sell the eggs and make a few bob. The tourists are mad for eggs in the summer. And the winter,' he added hastily. 'I know just the man you should see.'

The six baby chicks tweeted maniacally all the way back into Redlion. Muffled thumps from the big cardboard box in the back of the car made it sound as if they were clambering hysterically over each other, falling off and landing painfully on each other's fragile yellow feet. Slowing down, Hope peered in the back. The chicks *were* clambering hysterically all over each other and were making desperate, upset baby noises at being separated from their mother. Oh God, what had she done, Hope wailed out loud. Matt would kill her. It had sounded like a brilliant idea for saving money when Emmet, the man from the shop, had explained it.

All she'd need now was a feeding trough, some hen meal and maybe to put a light bulb over the box to keep them warm at night. The chemist was also the animal foodstuffs provider, Emmet's brother, Paddy said happily as he waved her off, her cheque in his hands. It seemed a lot of money for six little birds but Paddy insisted they were pedigree.

The kind-looking woman in the chemist, who introduced herself as Mary-Kate and who, like Emmet, seemed already to know who Hope was, was sceptical: 'Pedigree, my backside. That old rogue Emmet Slattery sold you his brother's runts. Nobody else would buy them at this time of the year. It's too cold to have them outside for months unless you put central heating into the hen house. You'll have them killed with pure temper long before you've got an egg to your name. What are they?' she relented. 'Speckled or Rhode Island Reds?'

'I have absolutely no idea,' Hope said. They both peered into the cardboard box in the car.

Mary-Kate's hard face softened at the antics of the tiny balls of yellow fluff.

'I love chicks but they're not always easy,' she sighed.

'I thought they were no trouble at all,' Hope said anxiously. 'Finula said they weren't. So did Paddy.'

'Finula Headley-Ryan has killed more pullets than the chicken factory,' snorted Mary-Kate. 'Don't mind her. She thinks farming is so easy a child could do it but she hasn't a clue. She's a city girl born and bred and until she landed here, the only time she'd ever seen a hen was in an illustration over the frozen chickens in the supermarket. And as for that pair of old bandits, Paddy and Emmet, I wouldn't listen to a word they said. Come on in. I'll make you a cup of coffee and tell you what to do with your hens.'

Smiling guiltily at the thought that the spectacularly efficient Finula wasn't as brilliant at everything as she thought, Hope opened a window in the car for the chicks and followed Mary-Kate, not thinking that it was unusual to be asked in for coffee when you were shopping. This was Redlion: everything was different here. Talking to total strangers seemed bizarrely normal.

Mary-Kate's office at the back of the chemist was a cosy nook complete with a comfortably worn couch, portable television and a sophisticated looking Italian coffee machine. Three darling kittens played in the corner, taking turns to mangle a knitted mouse. While Mary-Kate began the complicated business of brewing coffee, Hope sat down and watched her hostess. She was tall, thin and on the wrong side of forty. Soberly dressed in a grey dress with her brown hair cut in a neat, shining bob, she was as far removed from the flamboyant Finula as it was possible to be. She also had an intense, clear gaze. 'What you see is what you get,' said Mary-Kate's honest expression.

'Are you settling in?' she asked.

'Well, it's a bit difficult,' Hope said, wanting to be loyal to Matt. 'The house is a bit of a mess and I have to admit that it wasn't my idea to come here,' she amazed herself by revealing.

'I'm not surprised the house is a mess. Your husband's uncle was a complete nut,' Mary-Kate remarked, handing Hope a cup of coffee. 'He used to say he couldn't get married because he was too eccentric for any woman to live with. The truth was he lived like a pig. I had to throw him out of the shop on many occasions because he'd put the other customers off with the smell of him.'

Hope laughed. 'So far, everyone I've met has claimed he was a misunderstood genius who deserves a statue erected for him.'

'Genius doesn't mean you can't wash your clothes,' said Mary-Kate, proffering biscuits. 'If they erect a statue to old Gearóid, I hope it'll have a scratch 'n' sniff bit to get the whole effect.'

They talked about the trials of doing up old, damp cottages and how terrible the weather was, managing to consume two more cups of coffee while doing it. Hope found it an incredible relief to talk to someone who wasn't discussing culture, with a capital C, organic food or making your own compost heap. At home, she'd have never let her reserve down in such a manner but Mary-Kate was very easy to talk to.

'Do most people round here grow their own food and kill their own animals?' Hope asked cautiously.

'Are you crazy?' asked Mary-Kate, stunned. 'There's a Dunnes supermarket five miles away and there's Tescos in Killarney. The butcher's shop is beside the pub. It's closed now because it's being refitted but he'll be open again in two weeks. I'd much prefer to buy my food in the shop than grow it myself. Stay out of Emmet Slattery's if you don't want to be fleeced. I have a shampoo in the chemist that costs two pounds and I caught him selling the very same one for three! He's a crook, rob his grandmother for a shilling.'

Hope grinned. 'I sort of thought everyone made their own bread and jam and everything.'

'Only if you're stone mad, you do,' Mary-Kate said. 'Hope, this is the 21st century. What are supermarkets for?'

'Well, Finula said . . .'

'God preserve us from that woman! We're modern people who just happen to live in a rural community, not a remote tribe fresh from the pages of *National Geographic*. We've got running water, you know. Not to mention the internet and digital television. Yes, there are plenty of farmers around but they specialize: beef or dairy herds. That's a hard enough job without growing everything themselves into the bargain. I'm a pharmacist, for God's sake. I'm not going to spend half a day killing, plucking and cleaning out a chicken for my dinner when I know I can wander into the butcher's and buy a lovely chicken breast for myself for a few quid with no bother.'

'My sentiments exactly,' Hope said, relieved. 'I was beginning to think that buying food from the shop was a sort of local no-no.'

The shop bell pinged.

Mary-Kate got to her feet. 'Farming is a tough business,' she said soberly. 'Lots of the people round here grew up on farms but it's hard to make a living out of it nowadays. People had to give up the land and got jobs in industry or tourism. Half the village work in the computer factory in Killarney, the other half are involved in tourism up in the hotel, the Manoir Rouge Leon. Without both of those, this would be a ghost town. People don't have the time or the patience for growing anything but a few vegetables and geraniums. It's great if they can grow the odd bit of rhubarb and a neighbour of mine goes to great lengths to grow strawberries but that's the height of it. The only people who are obsessed with being self-sufficient are the likes of the Headley-Ryans who think they're better than the rest of us because they play at farming. If they get a bad crop of potatoes, they can go into town and buy them. A real, cash-strapped farmer can't afford to do that.' Mary-Kate sniffed disapprovingly. 'You can hear that poor cow of theirs wailing for miles around some mornings because they can't get themselves out of the bed to milk her. That's what farming is about – hard graft and dedication. Not poncing around talking about it.'

Matt was pacing around the kitchen when Hope got home while Toby and Millie were squabbling loudly in living room.

'You were gone *hours*,' Matt said accusingly. 'I was meant to be up at the centre at eleven.' (He insisted that he if he was to work properly, he had to treat writing like any other job. 'The plan is to go in every day and write for five or six hours. It's a silent zone, nobody talks except in the kitchen.')

'And what's that?' he pointed to the box of baby chicks.

'Hens,' said Hope.

'For eating?' he said incredulously, peering into the box where the chicks were chirping at their usual high-speed level.

'For eggs, stupid. Finula told me we should get hens. I thought you'd approve.' She didn't want to say that she thought she might have bitten off more than she could chew.

'Oh well, if Finula said it, she's probably right,' Matt shrugged.

'Tell me, what time do Finula and Ciaran milk their cow in the morning?' Hope asked suddenly.

'You're not thinking of getting a cow, I hope?'

'No, no, just wondering, that's all.'

Matt kissed her goodbye. 'Sorry I was cross. I was worried because you were gone so long. You're certainly settling into this country living bit very well,' he added with a smile.

'Six chicks do not make me a lady farmer,' joked Hope.

The chicks provided great amusement for the children for the first hour while Hope set up their home in the small hall off the back door. Bedded down in a huge cardboard movers' box with a bigger one outside and a filling of old newspapers for insulation, the chicks chirped happily, basking under the light of two old desk lamps to keep them warm. Soft hay and newspapers made a cosy nest in one half of the box and in the other, Hope placed their shiny feeding container filled with grain and some water. A covering of chicken wire on the top of the box kept prying little fingers out and when Hope sternly pointed out that the baby chicks were not playthings, Millie got into a huff and scrambled upstairs to pull all her clothes out of the big wooden chest Hope had brought from home. Tidying it up took half an hour and then it was still only a quarter to four.

Hope stared out the window. The sky was already growing heavier, a combination of swollen rain clouds and the onset of evening. It looked gloomy and depressing. Just like she felt. She looked into the small back garden. You could barely see the outline of the wall that circled it. Hope had always liked the idea of a walled garden: a sheltered spot where you could laze in the summer in the midst of fruit trees and fragrant flowers, pottering around with a small trowel, digging up the odd weed, then relaxing back onto a charming deck chair to read your book and sip your glass of wine. Gearoid had obviously not felt the same. His walled garden was the jungle variety, full of six-foot-high weeds and brambles no sane person would want to walk past. You'd need to be on mind-altering drugs to want to sit in it and drink wine and the only way to clear it had to be by mechanical digger. She wondered what time Matt would be home at. Soon, she hoped.

Two days later, Matt came home early and took the children for a walk while Hope took advantage of their absence to have a lukewarm bath – the plumbing still needed tweaking. Then, wearing her dressing gown and socks to keep warm, she sat down at the computer to e-mail Sam. She longed to begin by writing how depressed she was and how her picture of bucolic life was vastly different from the reality. But she couldn't. Sam had warned her against the move in the first place. She couldn't tell Sam how absolutely correct she'd been. Not yet.

*Hi Sam. Greetings from Kerry.* That sounded suitably breezy, didn't it? *How are you? We're all fine.* No, that sounded too false. She erased the word 'fine' and wrote *tired but happy. The cottage needed a good bit of work done but we stayed with this wonderful – family nearby while it was being tidied up.* Not that the Headley-Ryans were that wonderful – Finula drove Hope mad – but saying that would sound as if she was already in need of Prozac. *Let me describe our new home to you: Curlew Cottage is about a mile outside this little village. You drive down a winding track and come to the sweetest cottage which is definitely covered with rambling roses in the summer. It's like something from the kids' storybooks. Inside, we've got genuine old wooden beams and amazing latticed windows.*

Which are hell to clean, Hope thought grimly, remembering the hours she'd spent scrubbing at the tiny panes.

*There's this incredible old stove, they call it a range, in the kitchen-cum-sitting room and it's very cosy. We've even got a walled garden, although it needs some work and this local woman we stayed with suggests clearing it to grow vegetables.* That sounded good. No need to mention that when Matt had remarked that Finula had suggested growing vegetables, Hope had looked at him incredulously and said that *he* could clean out the jungle if he was that keen on home-grown parsnips.

*The bathroom is amazing* – now that the earwigs, beetles and other assorted creepy crawlies were gone, it *was* amazing – *with this huge old claw-footed roll top*

*bath. The kids love it here.* At least that was true.
Neither Toby nor Millie appeared to miss all their pals
from Your Little Treasures, but that was probably only
because everything was so new to them. Give them time
and Hope was sure they'd start wanting company of
their own age. She'd have to investigate a local
playgroup or somewhere so they could play with other
children. And so she could kick-start her own life. She
hadn't thought she'd miss work so much. It wasn't
about having a pay packet at the end of the week: it was
about independence and the camaraderie of working
with other women. The more she thought about it, the
more Hope was determined to find some part-time job
locally.

If she was honest, she felt a faint tinge of resentment
towards Matt that it hadn't occurred to him that she
might be missing her job.

*We haven't made many friends yet because we've
been so busy but Finula – the woman we stayed with –
assures us there's a vibrant social scene. Matt is settled
into the creative centre and he goes there every day to
write. So far, so good! Write back soon,*
   *love Hope.*

The rain pelted down all Monday afternoon.

'Mummy, I'm bored!' wailed Millie, pulling at Hope's trousers.
'Want to do something!'

Mummy's bored too, thought Hope. This was not the charming
rural idyll she'd imagined. Instead of a pretty cottage where she could
sit snuggled up with the children and spend quality time with them,
she was stuck in a remote cottage with the television not working
and none of the creature comforts of home. There was only so much
finger painting you could do. The cottage was a lot cosier than it had
been when they'd first moved in because Hope had been working
hard to brighten it up with little homely touches, but it still needed
more work.

They were at least a mile from the village, nobody ever came down the lane to visit them, which was unsurprising since they didn't know anybody yet, and the nearest big town was miles away. Matt was gone off to work in the centre. Lucky him, thought Hope grimly, as Toby and Millie began screaming at each other over a pop-up book.

She stuck it out for another twenty minutes when, noticing that the rain was easing off, inspiration struck.

'Let's go for a walk and visit some kittens,' she said.

'Yeah!' said Millie enthusiastically.

Matt had taken the car, so Hope kitted out the children in their winter woollies and anoraks, complete with Wellington boots, hats and gloves. When they looked suitably like arctic explorers, she pulled on her own coat and boots and off they set. It was still drizzling a bit but it was good to be out. At first, Toby was happy to sit in the buggy. Then he decided that he wanted to walk, which meant a complicated hand-holding arrangement as Hope had to hold both children's hands as well as dragging the buggy along.

Then, Toby decided that he wanted to be carried. 'Please Mummy,' he said tearfully.

'Me too!' wailed Millie as Hope struggled along with Toby on one hip. 'I can't darling, you're too big,' Hope panted.

'Want to be carried. Put Toby down. Carry me!!!'

Feeling like a Himalayan baggage carrier, Hope hefted her children in strict rotation for ten minutes each before she became exhausted.

'You'll have to walk, Millie,' she said as she put a protesting Toby in his buggy.

With both children wailing, she arrived in the village, silently cursing the fact that they only had one car. The Metro was hers too, although Matt had taken it over as if it was his. It wasn't her fault he'd had to give up the company car.

The village was prettier when you walked through it. Whizzing past in the car, Hope hadn't noticed the small window boxes outside the post office, how quaint the small, pastel coloured houses actually were or how lovely the old stone of the Widow Maguire's pub was. On first sight, in the heavy rain, everything had appeared dull but in the soft mist of a faint drizzle, she could see that it wasn't just Curlew Cottage that had a fairy tale air about it.

The children stopped grizzling long enough for her to look at the signs outside the pub door. 'Entertainment every weekend, fiddlers welcome,' said one sign. Another was a menu listing a range of gorgeous-sounding bar food with plenty of the sort of things that Finula would approve of: goat's cheese tart, spinach and ricotta ravioli, crab cakes, Guinness pie. Hope's mouth watered just looking at it. There wasn't a pig's trotter in sight. Maybe she and Matt could come there some evening if they could arrange a babysitter.

Toby started to grumble again so they trudged on towards the chemist shop. The children would love the kittens and she could tell Mary-Kate that the chicks were settled in.

Taking the children into anywhere as exciting as a chemist's was dangerous on the grounds that colourful little bottles of nail varnish, small pots of creams and exciting packets of plasters were enticing for little fingers. Toby was remarkably adept at grabbing things from the safety of his buggy and opening them before Hope had even realized he'd taken them. With this in mind, she bypassed the front door. Mary-Kate's little office door was shut, so Hope knocked.

Mary-Kate appeared instantly with not a gleaming brown hair out of place.

'Are these special visitors for me?' she inquired, bending down and greeting Toby and Millie as if they were grown-ups. 'How do you do,' she said gravely, shaking Millie's hand.

It was exactly the right thing to do. Millie beamed at her and Toby smiled shyly.

'What is your name, madam?' Mary-Kate asked, still grave.

'Millie,' Millie said, dimpling up at her.

'And this gentleman?'

'Toby, my little brother. He's only three,' Millie said disdainfully.

'I thought they might like to see your kittens,' Hope said. 'I hoped you wouldn't mind.'

'What a grand idea. Would you like to come in and play with three lovely little kittens?'

It was an offer they couldn't refuse.

Miraculously turning into model children, Toby and Millie played happily with the three tabby kittens while Mary-Kate and Hope had coffee.

'I only dropped in to say thanks for the advice the other day,' Hope said apologetically.

'It's lovely to see you,' Mary-Kate said kindly. 'It must get very lonely on your own if you're not used to it.'

'Not at all,' said Hope stoically. 'I love it.'

'Well, isn't that great then,' Mary-Kate replied.

# CHAPTER SEVEN

Virginia spent the first two hours of the train journey from Dublin to Killarney jammed into her seat with a large man beside her, a large man who took up more than his share of space and whose bulk meant she was squashed uncomfortably against the window. The arthritis in her left hip was growling at the position she was forced into and Virginia thought longingly of the anti-inflammatory tablets she had in the bathroom cabinet at home. It wasn't the express train and the journey seemed to take forever. She'd finished reading the newspaper and as she hadn't been able to concentrate on novels since Bill's death, she had brought nothing else to read. Wintry rain lashed the train windows which then steamed up with the passengers' hot breath, obscuring the view.

When the tea trolley arrived and the tea man asked her what she wanted, her large neighbour rudely demanded a cup of tea and a chocolate muffin before Virginia had a chance to reply. Immune to passenger battles over the last plastic ham and cheese sandwich, the tea trolley man said nothing and handed over the chocolate muffin before asking Virginia again what she'd like.

'Just a cup of tea, thank you,' she said tightly. It had been a terrible day and she could have done without this fresh nuisance. No, that was the wrong word, she thought, her heart fierce with pain and anger. The horrible man beside her wasn't a nuisance, he was worse: a pig with no manners who deserved to be shouted at or shoved off the train for being so rude. If Bill was there, he'd have done it. She felt hot tears well up in her eyes. Bill would have looked after her but Bill was gone, forever. He'd left her. Abandoned her and she had to look after herself forever more. *It wasn't fair.*

Suddenly, she realized that the brown-haired middle-aged woman sitting opposite had handed her a paper cup of tea, complete with little sachets of sugar and milk.

'Oh, thank you,' muttered Virginia, aware that she'd forgotten where she was in her misery. It happened all the time: she became lost in her private grief and time seemed to stand still, while life rushed on around her. She hated that. It made her feel like an idiot, a feeble old woman.

The tea man handed the woman opposite a cup of coffee and some change and Virginia realized that the woman had paid for Virginia's tea as well as her own drink.

'Forgive me,' Virginia said quickly, 'I'm sorry, let me pay you . . .'

'It's fine,' the woman said softly. She was quiet and refined looking, maybe in her late forties, with dark hair and a kind, make-up free face. 'It was only a few pence and after all, you hardly have enough room in that seat to get your money out of your pocket.' She gave the man beside Virginia a hard, slightly ironic glance and he moved away from Virginia, suddenly giving her lots more room. The woman kept up with her intense gaze and the man moved some more.

In spite of her misery, Virginia smiled.

The woman smiled back and lowered her eyes to her crossword.

A lot of passengers got off at Limerick, including the big man.

Virginia sighed with relief, finally able to spread out and put her packages on the seat beside her.

'Some people have no manners,' said the woman opposite.

'You're right about that,' Virginia replied. 'Thank you. I should have asked him for more room,' she added, 'but there are some days when you don't have the energy to demand things. And this has really been one of those days.' She didn't know why she was saying this. But it had been so awful in the accountant's office, signing more documents. Sorting out the tax implications of Bill's insurance policies was mystifying and endless. Every time the accountant lowered his voice and asked Virginia if she was 'coping . . .' she wanted to hit him with her handbag and scream 'NO! I'm not bloody coping. As if you care!'

'I'm Mary-Kate Donlan,' the woman said, holding out a hand.

'Virginia Connell.' They shook hands formally as if they were at a party instead of rattling along on the Killarney train.

'How about another cup of tea?' Mary-Kate suggested. 'The trolley doesn't come round again but I can get us tea and a biscuit from the buffet car.'

'Let me get it,' Virginia said, getting to her feet. 'Do you want tea or coffee?'

Mary-Kate shuddered. 'I never drink tea because I love coffee but that last cup was like drinking boiled socks. It'll have to be tea, thanks.'

When Virginia had returned from the buffet car, they drank their hot tea and chatted idly, Mary-Kate making Virginia laugh as she recounted her search for a posh dress for a wedding she was going to soon.

'Not that I'd go to Dublin for a dress, mind,' Mary-Kate pointed out, 'but I was there anyway and I thought I'd try it.'

Virginia grinned. Her new friend's sober and slightly old-fashioned navy cardigan and white silky blouse made it obvious that she wasn't the sort of woman who took many high-fashion shopping trips. Virginia herself had always loved clothes, not that she'd bothered buying anything recently. But she still had some beautiful pieces in her wardrobe. Today she was wearing a burgundy high necked dress in a soft knitted silk with a matching long flowing cardigan made of knobbly burgundy chenille wool. An Irish designer piece, Bill had bought it for her fifty-sixth birthday. He'd admired her tall, slim figure in it and said he loved the way the rich colour showed up her silvery blonde hair so well.

'You don't think it's too young for me?' she'd said, scrunching up her patrician nose as she looked at herself in the changing room mirror.

'You *are* young,' Bill had said, swatting her rear lovingly.

Mary-Kate was talking about her shopping experience.

'I went into this boutique and I ask you, the prices! Three hundred pounds for this filmy scrap of a chiffon thing you'd run up yourself on the sewing machine. And it wasn't exactly practical either. You'd freeze your bosoms off in it, I can tell you. Well,' she looked down at her narrow, flat chest, 'not that I have any to freeze off.'

Virginia went off into peals of laughter and Mary-Kate joined her.

'You can tell I'm not the Vogue type,' Mary-Kate laughed. 'They kept trying to put me in these mother of the bride rig outs, all pastel blues and pinks with matronly skirts and discreet camisoles.'

'*Are* you the mother of the bride?' Virginia asked.

'Lord no. I've no children and was never married. I'm just your average maiden aunt.' She looked at Virginia mischievously. 'Can't you tell? I'd say I have it written all over me.'

Virginia thought that if Mary-Kate had one thing written all over her it was that she was both shrewd and funny. Her grey eyes glittered with fun and if her dress, undyed bobbed hair and general demeanour were those of a quiet, maiden aunt, two minutes in her company would soon put paid to that idea.

'So did you buy anything in the end?'

'No.' Her companion looked glum. 'I have to have something new for this wedding because if I turn up in my usual grey suit, the real mother of the bride will be raging with me for not making an effort. I suppose I'll have to take my life in my hands and venture into my local shop, Lucille's. They don't stock anything normal in there. I'll either come out in lycra tiger skin or see-through black with a skirt up round the cheeks of my backside. She's a very persuasive woman, Lucille. You know it looks terrible on you but she somehow manages to convince you that it's you.'

'You're from Redlion!' Virginia exclaimed. 'Me too. I pass Lucille's every day and I love her window. It's . . .'

'I know,' Mary-Kate interrupted. 'Fake fur leopard at the moment. I have thought of buying the matching little Russian hat but it might frighten people out of the chemist.'

'You run the chemist?' Virginia said. 'That's amazing. I walk past your premises every day. I live out on the Blackglen Road in Kilnagoshell House and I go into town every day. I've only been in your shop a couple of times, though.'

'Have you lived in Kilnagoshell House long?' asked Mary-Kate, who knew perfectly well how long Virginia had lived there but who didn't want to say so. It was obvious that Virginia knew nobody in the town and therefore had made a conscious decision not to do so. She'd probably hate to feel that Mary-Kate had known who she was all along, even though in a village like Redlion, it was impossible to remain anonymous.

'Over seven months. I've been a bit reclusive, I'm afraid. My husband died last year you see and I moved to Kerry afterwards. I wasn't up to socializing.'

She could feel tears surging up and swallowed hard to get rid of the lump in her throat.

'I'm so sorry,' Mary-Kate said with warmth. 'It's hard to ease yourself back in the real world after something like that.'

'Today, I had to see his accountant and it was awful,' Virginia said bleakly. 'Every time he mentioned Bill, I felt like crying. It was like having a long nail hammered into my head again and again. Each time I think the pain's getting better, someone else hammers away and it's just as bad as it was in the beginning. I don't know why I'm telling you all this,' she added apologetically. 'I don't even know you.'

'Sympathy of strangers can be the best kind,' Mary-Kate remarked. 'Strangers have no agenda, no desire to meddle and no way of telling what's true and what's not true.'

Virginia looked at her curiously. It seemed as if she knew what she was talking about.

'Strangers never tell you to get a grip and get on with your life,' Mary-Kate continued.

'Strangers don't tell you to buck up because Bill wouldn't have wanted you to waste away,' Virginia added with some rancour.

Mary-Kate grinned.

'It's amazing,' Virginia went on, 'people who were really only acquaintances and who wouldn't have had a clue what Bill was really like are the first ones to tell you what he would and wouldn't want now that he's dead. On the day before the funeral, Bill's second cousin phoned to tell me which reading we should have at the ceremony, *'because Bill always liked it'*. What rubbish. They never saw each other.' She'd been furious at the intrusion. 'People like that couldn't have bought him so much as a jumper when he was alive and now that he's dead, they can figure out exactly what he'd be thinking. God,' she added, 'you're sure you're not a psychiatrist? You're doing a great job of letting me get it all out and you're only nodding your head and saying 'mmn' at the right moments.'

'Did I mention the forty pounds an hour charge?' Mary-Kate dead-panned.

Virginia told her new friend about her three sons, her darling little grand-daughter and dear sweet Sally, who was the kindest daughter-in-law you could meet.

Mary-Kate explained that she'd grown up in Redlion where her father was the chemist but had longed to escape the small town. She'd qualified as a pharmacist herself in Dublin and worked there for fifteen years until her father died. She'd taken over the family business ten years ago.

'There are times when I love Redlion; there's great truth in the adage that the place of your birth has a certain hold over you,' she said. 'But there are other days when I long for the anonymity of Dublin. In Redlion, everyone knows everyone else's business.'

'Did you never have the chance to marry?' Virginia asked, then immediately felt sorry for it. 'I'm sorry, that just slipped out. It was a very personal question and you've just been talking about nosy neighbours.'

'No, it's fine. Sure, I've been asking you things. There *was* a man but it didn't work out.' Mary-Kate shrugged and gently changed the subject. 'As you don't know many people in the village, I'll have to introduce you around. You really must meet Delphine,' she added.

Virginia noticed the sudden change of subject but didn't comment.

'Delphine's my niece and she's wonderful. You'd love her. She's a beautician at the Manoir Rouge Leon up the road and she's a lovely girl. A bit eccentric, you see, which is why she and I get on so well. Delphine can go into Lucille's boutique and actually buy things there that suit her.'

They both giggled at this thought. Delphine must be very unusual, Virginia reflected.

'We go out every couple of weeks, sometimes to the cinema,' Mary-Kate said, 'sometimes for a meal. I'd love you to come along and meet her.'

'I'd like that,' Virginia found herself agreeing.

The train shuddered to a stop in Killarney and both women collected up their belongings. Virginia's hip ached and she thought again of her anti-inflammatory tablets. It would definitely be an early night tonight after a hot, soothing bath.

'Can I offer you a lift?' Mary-Kate asked.

'No thanks, I'm driving too.'

'Well, here's my phone number,' Mary-Kate said, handing Virginia a piece of paper. 'Phone me when you feel like company.'

As Virginia walked to her car, clutching her woolly cardigan close around her to ward off the icy wind, she smiled to herself. It was nice to feel she had a new friend.

Hope listened to the steady thrum of the rain falling on the corrugated roof of the outhouses and wondered if she could ring Dr McKevitt's surgery, plead an emergency, and be sent a crate of Prozac immediately. Or Valium. Or some other mood-altering drug to make her feel happy.

They'd been in Redlion an entire month, it was now an icy December, and she didn't think she'd ever been as miserable in her life. Every morning, an increasingly grumpy Matt headed off to the creative centre with his laptop and didn't return until at least six. She had no idea how much he'd written since they'd arrived because whenever she asked him about it, Matt snapped her head off and muttered that 'creativity can't be rushed.'

So now, she asked nothing and wondered if Mrs Shakespeare had to put up with this sort of behaviour. But even if Matt was bad tempered, he was at least adult company, someone who could converse about things other than the chicks' pooh and the latest episode of *Tweenies*.

Once Matt was gone, the day stretched ahead of her blankly, with nothing to fill it except Toby and Millie's latest craze, which was making endless Christmas decorations out of bits of coloured paper. They now had enough glittery garlands to cover four cottages. The only other diversion was the inevitable rainy walk through the mud into Redlion. She adored the children and, in theory at least, loved the idea of being able to spend quality time with them but the problem was, the quality dimmed when there was so much quantity. Except for the weekends when Matt mucked in, she was the only person looking after Toby and Millie and no matter how much she loved them, being sole carer in an isolated little cottage with no other grown up help meant they spent every moment together. Hope simply never had a moment to herself even to read a magazine or blow-dry her hair properly.

Even having a bath in the evening when the children were supposedly in bed was impossible as Millie was so demanding she'd clamber out of bed and insist on getting into the bath too. The simple fact was that the children were bored, too and needed the company of other kids but there didn't seem to be any young families nearby.

Hope thought longingly of Your Little Treasures and regretted ever giving out stink about the sergeant-majorish Marta. She'd have done anything to get the children into a local playgroup but when she'd investigated, there wasn't a place to be had for miles around and wouldn't be until late January when Hunnybunnikins on the far side of the village would have room. Roll on January. Then, of course, Hope would face the question of exactly what she'd do while the children were at playgroup. Redlion didn't even have a bank and she didn't fancy trekking into Killarney to work, assuming she'd even be eligible for a job here. She wasn't qualified for anything else apart from bank work, so what else could she do?

Another nine months and they'd be gone. Nine whole months. She sighed.

Now it was Monday and another week loomed ahead of her, empty except for her by-now daily trips into Redlion for the shopping. If she hadn't had Sam to talk to by e-mail and Mary-Kate to talk to in person every day, she'd have gone completely mad. Visiting Mary-Kate constituted her entire social life as she never set eyes on anyone else. Finula kept inviting them to her house for dinner but on the one occasion they'd gone, Finula had been so patronizing to her that Hope hadn't wanted to go again. Matt went on his own after that which frequently left Hope alone in the evenings.

Mary-Kate had twice invited her out with her female friends but Hope had refused both times, partly because Matt hated her going out without him and partly because she didn't want to feel like a burden on anyone. It was one thing to go into the chemist every day for something, it was another entirely to impose on a group of old friends going out at night. Sweet Mary-Kate never pushed her, unlike Sam who was getting increasingly pushy via-e-mail.

*'Your life is revolving around Matt's,'* Sam wrote. Hope could almost hear her sister's voice rising in anger as she read her words. *'He has set himself up with a new life and he expects you to kow tow and have the dinner on the table when he gets home. Tell him it's not on!!!'*

Sam was right, Hope decided firmly. She needed to do something about her life. She needed to get out and meet people and get a job. She even daydreamed about the old days in the building society where there was a constant stream of conversation. But first, she'd better clean out the chickens' box.

The raising of the chicks was going remarkably well. She found that she liked looking after them and decided that, when they were old enough to live outside in the hen house, she'd get more chicks. The thought of having her own eggs made her feel smugly self-sufficient and she was determined to get the back garden cleared so she could grow vegetables. And maybe herbs, she decided. Basil and rosemary that would scent the entire garden deliciously. Unlike the chicks' box, which did not smell delicious.

Nobody had mentioned that chicken shit smelled, she reflected as she stood at the hidey hole by the back door and peered into the box. Finula's chicks lived in her roomy scullery, Matt had informed her, so the Headley-Ryans never had to put up with the pong. And smell it did.

'Oooh yucky!' declared Millie holding her nose ostentatiously.

'I thought you liked chicken pooh,' Hope laughed. 'You're always talking about it.'

Millie giggled endearingly.

Both children liked the chicks' coop being cleaned out because it was the only time they got to play with the chicks. Well, the only time officially. Hope was forever finding Millie standing on tiptoes and trying to squeeze one fat little hand under the wire into the coop to catch a hysterical chick. At the first sight of her, all the chicks ran like lemmings, frantically trying to hide under each other. Hope didn't like to think what Millie had done to them to cause this panic.

Hope took the wire cover off and put the first chick in a smaller box, which she then gave to Toby to hold. She had decided that it was more important that Toby get over his fear of countryside creatures than to be hypersensitive about germs. She went through loads of disinfectant hand wash as it was. 'Don't kiss her and don't put your hands near your face if you touch her,' she warned. Toby gazed at his squeaking chick with awe.

'Where's mine?' wailed Millie.

Hope handed her another box.

'What chick is that?' Millie asked, already sticking her hand into the box to grab her prey.

'Mopsy,' lied Hope. She was never totally sure which was which as they all looked pretty alike at this point. The grand naming ceremony had made for an enjoyable few days when Toby and Millie came up with all sorts of mad suggestions. Millie was keen on Beatrix Potter names and refused to believe that Mopsy and Flopsy were traditionally names for rabbits. Toby had come up with Bear (after his favourite teddy) and Thomas (after the Tank Engine). Hope named the smallest chick Fifi and had been considering a sixth and final name when Millie piped up that they could call the fattest chick Auntie Finula.

'You can't do that,' Hope said, desperately trying to keep a straight face.

'But I want to,' said Millie.

'Why do you want to call that chick Auntie Finula?' Hope knew she shouldn't go down this road but she couldn't resist.

'I don't like Auntie Finula. I don't like that one,' Millie said firmly, pointing her finger at the innocent chick in question, an enormous cuckoo of a bird who looked as though her skinny little legs shouldn't be capable of supporting her fat body.

Hope bit her lip. 'We can't call it Auntie Finula, it might upset the real Auntie Finula.'

Millie's impish dark eyes glinted. 'Don't care!'

Mary-Kate was having more success with persuading Virginia to come out. They'd got into the habit of talking on the phone quite a bit and had already had one night out at the cinema where Delphine had come along too and enchanted Virginia.

Now Mary-Kate had asked Virginia to go to the Widow Maguire's pub the following night.

'Just yourself, myself and Delphine,' Mary-Kate had said on the phone. 'A girls' night out before Christmas.'

Virginia didn't feel up to it and wondered how she could politely wriggle out of the invitation without upsetting her new friends.

They made an odd threesome, Virginia thought. The outwardly prim Mary-Kate, herself grief-stricken and Delphine, Mary-Kate's niece, with her wild Celtic beauty and mad clothes. Delphine's idea of normal clothes were pinstripe trouser suits with a low-cut T-shirt underneath when she was in a business-like mood or a long, purple velvet dress with huge costume jewellery when she was in party mode.

In Dublin, in her previous life, Virginia wouldn't have made friends with such a diverse group. Her friends had all been women of her own age, women with husbands and grown up families, and their conversations had always taken well-established, conservative lines. They grumbled happily about how their husbands were always late home for dinner and talked about unsuitable sons-in-law. Now Virginia couldn't bear to be around her old women friends: they reminded her too much of what she'd had and lost so suddenly. Her friends went red with guilt when they realized they were groaning about tardy husbands. They were kind and loved her, and did their best to change the subject, but Virginia was a realist. She knew that's what long-married people talked about: their partners and their families. It wasn't their fault that this topic sent shrapnel into Virginia's heart.

Her new friends were very different. Straight-talking Mary-Kate was forty-four, conservative on the outside and startlingly original on the inside. She may have looked sedate with her old-fashioned glasses and slightly prim manner, but she was wry and marvellously acute. Mary-Kate had some sadness inside her, Virginia felt, which was how they'd probably been drawn to each other. The man she'd loved and lost was obviously the secret but Virginia would never have dreamed of intruding by asking.

The exotic Delphine, another Redlion inhabitant, was a mere twenty-nine, lived with Eugene, a delightful teddy bear of a man, and worked in the beauty salon of the luxury hotel five miles away. Manoir Rouge Leon was practically six star it was so posh, Mary-Kate informed Virginia. And it was managed by a hunk who set every woman's heart aflame, Mary-Kate added, pointing out that for some strange reason, this hunk had never made it to the chemist to ask her out.

'Christy De Lacy's not your type,' Delphine laughed when her aunt said this. 'You've always told me that it's what's in a man's heart that matters – not his face.'

'If he's as gorgeous as everyone says he is, I could make an exception in his case,' protested her aunt.

Livelier than a firework, Delphine was Mary-Kate's niece and god-daughter. When Mary-Kate took Virginia to her heart, so did Delphine. They'd brought Virginia to the cinema already and now the three of them were due to go to the Widow's for a night of entertainment, food and wine. Virginia felt about as outgoing as a turkey at Christmas.

'I think I'm getting a bit of a headache,' she lied on the phone to Delphine, deciding that it was easier to lie to Delphine than to her aunt.

'If you've a headache going into the Widow's, you'll be ahead of the rest of us then,' Delphine laughed, 'because we'll all have a head-ache at the end. It's the Nashville Springtime Girls tonight and they're godawful.'

In spite of herself, Virginia laughed.

'I'm tired,' she tried.

'Forget it,' said Delphine in her lilting Kerry accent. 'You're coming and that's it.'

The Nashville Springtime Girls were setting up their equipment when the three of them took up position at the back of the Widow Maguire's, as far away from the speakers as possible. The Springtime Girls had obviously chosen their name in an ironic way, Virginia decided, seeing as how none of them appeared younger than her and looked like sexy grandmothers in their denim and cowboy boots.

'Coming in early has its advantages,' Mary-Kate said with relief, sitting back against the extra cushion she'd stolen off a nearby bench. 'My sciatica is killing me. But I've taken two of those muscle relaxants and soon I won't feel a thing.'

'You won't be able to feel a thing if you drink either,' Virginia scolded. 'They'll react with the whiskey and you'll be as high as a kite.'

'Don't nag,' said Mary-Kate equably. 'I lead a very dull life and I'm entitled to a bit of being high as a kite. Anyway, it's okay to have a drink with these ones, I promise. I'm a professional and I can tell.'

'If that's the case, can I have a supply of them for Christmas,' begged Delphine. 'I'll need some sort of drugs to help me get through the festive season.'

Virginia shuddered at the thought of Christmas. She wished it could be wiped off the calendar. Last Christmas she'd been in a miasma of tranquillizers; this year, she'd be going without.

'What are you and Eugene doing for the big day?' Virginia asked, trying to sound normal. Just because her idea of Christmas was hell on earth, that didn't mean it was the same for everyone else.

Delphine's pale Celtic skin paled even further and her misty dark-green eyes suddenly became liquid.

Mary-Kate patted Delphine's hand briskly.

'I'm sorry,' Virginia said anxiously, 'I didn't mean to say the wrong thing.' She must have missed some subtle hint about Delphine and Eugene's relationship. Delphine always spoke of him so lovingly that it was hard to imagine them having a row or anything.

'It's not your fault, Virginia,' Delphine said, snuffling a bit.

'Don't tell me, it's your business,' Virginia said, distraught at having upset her new friend.

'No, I'd like to tell you. *You'd* understand,' Delphine said. 'It's Eugene and Christmas, you see. He was married before and he's divorced and . . .' She gulped miserably.

Mary-Kate handed her niece her drink and finished the story. 'My dear sister Pauline is one of those high-minded people who think that married people have no business going off and attempting to get divorces and she believes that Delphine is ruining her immortal soul by living with Eugene. She refuses to talk about him, absolutely refuses to have him in the house and has only recently started talking to Delphine again. Mind you, the level of conversation never rises above the "when are you going to come to your senses and dump that immoral man or are you going to shame us all forever?" sort of thing.'

'Christmas is going to be just awful,' wailed Delphine.

Both Virginia and Mary-Kate leaned over to give her a hug.

'Last year, I hadn't told her about him and he had his own place but this year we're living together . . .' Delphine pulled a paper napkin from the table and wiped her eyes with it, 'and she keeps going on about how I have to come home for Christmas and how it's God's day and it's a sin what I'm doing and I'll never be able to get married now in the church. She'll kill me if I don't go home but I can't leave Eugene on his own on Christmas Day, I just can't.'

'And there's no way you can say anything to Pauline?' Virginia asked Mary-Kate, who looked at her with resigned eyes.

'You haven't met my sister,' Mary-Kate said glumly. 'She wasn't just behind the door when the Lord was doling out compassion and understanding – she was in another room entirely getting more than her supply of prejudice and signing up for the gossip-mongers' guild.'

'You got her supply of compassion,' Virginia joked gently, trying to lift the atmosphere. 'Delphine's lucky she's got you.'

Delphine grinned stoically. 'I'd go mad without Mary-Kate,' she said. 'I think I'll hit the loos and repair myself,' she added. 'It'd be bad for business for all the people in the pub to see the local beautician looking like she applied her mascara with a paintbrush.'

She hurried across the room, russet curls dancing as she went, causing many a man to look up from his pint. Even an over-sized tangerine man's jumper and a flowing silk skirt couldn't hide her Rubenesque figure.

'Poor Delphine,' Virginia said. 'I'm sorry I put my foot in it.'

'It's not your fault,' sighed Mary-Kate. 'It's bloody Pauline's.'

Virginia was startled. She'd never heard Mary-Kate swear.

'I do not know under God how we are sisters because she is a million miles away from me. She hasn't an understanding bone in her body,' Mary-Kate raged. 'She has put that poor girl through hell and all so that she can prance first in the queue up to communion on Sundays.'

'But so many people get divorced now, surely she can see it's common,' Virginia said. 'People have to live their lives differently, even the Church sees that. One of my friends in Dublin was on the church baptism committee and they were taught to treat all new parents the same whether they were married or not. That type of blinkered thinking is a thing of the past, surely.'

Mary-Kate laughed sourly. 'The Vatican will be announcing the election of the first female cardinal before Pauline changes her mind about marriage being for life. She's entitled to her views but she's not entitled to ram them down Delphine's throat.'

'What about Delphine's father? Does he think the same?'

They both spotted Delphine emerging from the ladies.

'My brother-in-law, Fonsie, gets on very well with Eugene but is too afraid of Pauline to say anything. His notion of independence is to secretly buy one of those gossipy Sunday newspapers as well as the one that Pauline considers suitable.'

Mary-Kate turned to her niece. 'Delphine, will you order us another round, we're parched. Tell us about your day,' she said cheerfully.

'Don't ask. I had to give a manicure to that bitch Miriam Concannon from the television show. She's staying in a huge suite in the hotel and in between flirting madly with Christy, who was flirting back, I can tell you, she bitched about everyone on the planet. Believe me, she may come across as sweet on that programme but she thinks she shits chocolate and pisses eau de cologne,' sniffed Delphine.

'Where do you hear these sayings?' demanded Mary-Kate. 'You've a mouth on you like a docker.'

'We get lots of interesting people into the salon,' said Delphine, unperturbed, 'and they've got these very colourful turns of phrase. That's a real Dublin saying, apparently. Listen to this one . . .'

'Delphine,' warned Mary-Kate. 'Virginia didn't come out tonight to listen to your depraved mind. How about you Virginia? How was your day?'

They ate, drank and listened to the Springtime Girls run through an entire Tammy Wynette/Patsy Cline catalogue about love, men and how they always let you down.

'I thought we came here to be cheered up?' Mary-Kate said after yet another sad song about a woman with a fatal tendency for the wrong sort of man. 'I'm going home to have more muscle relaxants if this doesn't get happier.'

Delphine, who couldn't hold her drink very well and was already deeply merry after four glasses of Guinness, burst into hysterical giggles.

'Can you send a bumper packet of those over to my mother? She really needs them,' she chuckled, before suddenly growing maudlin. 'I phoned home today and she would barely talk to me.'

'Ah sure, with Pauline, that's a blessing in disguise,' Mary-Kate tried to cheer her up. 'My sister would talk the hind legs off a donkey,' she added for Virginia's benefit. 'And you, my girl.' She patted Delphine's knee. 'You need more nights out with normal people so you can remember that not everyone is as narrow-minded as your mother. I think it's time we revived the Macramé Club?'

Delphine perked up. 'It's been out of commission since Aggie left Redlion but we could start up again.' She turned to Virginia, 'Aggie was one of the founder members,' she explained.

Virginia was mystified. 'Macramé? I wouldn't have put you two down for arts and crafts.'

Mary-Kate and Delphine exchanged looks. 'The major craft is learning how to make the perfect martini,' Mary-Kate said solemnly.

'Think *Witches of Eastwick*,' added Delphine.

'Only I get to be Cher and I want Jack Nicholson to myself,' interrupted her aunt. 'We've got to reconvene after Christmas. You will come, won't you, Virginia?'

'What should I bring?' Virginia asked, wondering if she could do crochet instead of macramé.

'Gin,' suggested Delphine. 'Vodka maybe. Handicrafts are the last thing that go on there. It's a letting your hair down sort of night.'

'And where did you come up with the name?'

Mary-Kate beamed. 'We didn't even have a name for it originally. It was just a group of us meeting up to relax and chat, you know. But when Finula Headley-Ryan moved to the village, she was desperate to get involved and none of us could stand her, so we told her it was a handicrafts night. I thought macramé sounded suitably off-putting. Finula wouldn't be interested in anything so pedestrian. And the name stuck. It came in handy for keeping my sister, Pauline, off the scent too. Pauline would have seen it as an opportunity to hear all sorts of dirt and personal stories, and that wasn't the point of the club at all. Oh look, it's Hope,' Mary-Kate added as the Parkers came into the pub by the side door. 'Matt is the latest convert to the Kerry school of creative scribbling and Hope is his wife,' she explained to Virginia and Delphine. 'She's lovely. I think she could do with a bit of macramé too.'

Virginia watched the newcomers with interest. It was nice not to be the newest person in the village any more, so she watched the people who'd taken her place. Hope and Matt did not fit the normal artistic community bill. For a start, Hope was dressed in very normal black jeans, chambray shirt and navy windbreaker instead of the sort of flamboyant flowy stuff that the awful Finula Headley-Ryan always wore. Virginia had met Finula in the chemist on one occasion and had not felt as if she'd met a kindred spirit. Hope was also pretty in a subdued, old-fashioned way, although she was cast into the shade by her marvellously handsome husband.

'He's a fine thing, isn't he?' Delphine said of Matt, admiring the tall, dark man with the chiselled jaw and soulful eyes. 'He can fill a pair of jeans. Is he the latest eejit to fall under Mrs HR's spell?'

'Afraid so,' said Mary-Kate sorrowfully. 'I don't think poor Hope knows what's hit her. She's very lonely, God love her, and embarrassed to admit it.'

'So you know her well?' Virginia asked Mary-Kate in surprise.

Delphine laughed. 'Know her well? If Watergate had happened in Redlion, Mary-Kate would have been Deep Throat.'

'Isn't this nice?' Hope said, looking around happily. She liked the pub. It was so pretty with its dark beams, cosy corners and all the bric-a-brac dangling from hooks everywhere. If you were tall you were in danger of being concussed by hanging lobster pots, storm lanterns and farmyard implements from another era. Matt was so tall he'd already narrowly missed being strangled by a bit of wayward fishing net.

'We could have gone to Finula's,' Matt pointed out. 'She was making boxty, which is some sort of traditional Irish dish.'

'Well, we can have traditional Irish food here,' said Hope, smiling in a forced manner. They'd had a mild argument earlier when Matt had tried to renege on his promise to take her for dinner in the pub by saying that Finula had just invited them to her place for dinner.

'That was nice of her but I hope you told her we'd arranged to go out,' Hope had said, gritting her teeth and thinking of the hassle she'd had getting a babysitter.

'Well, no . . .'

'Phone her then,' snapped Hope, sitting down heavily on their bed to do her minimal make-up.

'I will, I will. Keep your hair on.'

Matt was subdued when he came back from phoning Finula. 'I'm sorry about that, Hope,' he said. 'I should have told her no in the first place. Now, she's cross with me and you're cross with me . . .'

Immediately, Hope dropped her mascara wand and looked up from her hand mirror. 'I'm not cross, darling. I only wanted some time on our own, that's all.'

'You're right.' He dropped a kiss on the top of her head. 'I'm a selfish bastard. You need to see more of this village than Finula's house.'

Hope smiled privately. That was so exactly what she'd been thinking. He'd been so self-obsessed for the past few weeks that she'd forgotten how clever Matt was at getting inside her head when the mood took him.

'I'll get menus,' Matt said now.

They both ordered mussels and garlic bread, with red wine for Hope and Guinness for Matt.

'You'd should have some,' he said taking a deep draught of the inky black pint. 'You'd love it.'

'Give me a taste. Ugh, horrible,' she said, wishing she could spit it out.

They sat in companionable silence for a while, looking around and breathing in the atmosphere. People were settling themselves in for the night, buying lots of drink and looking as if they planned to be there till closing. It was an interesting mix of people. Two men with jumpers and wild beards were staring moodily into their pints in one corner, while a very glamorous blonde woman in a suit, whom Hope had noticed rushing in and out of the estate agent's, was beside them talking furiously to an abashed looking man who'd removed his suit jacket and had damp patches under his arms. Definitely a couple having a row, Hope decided. She could also see Mary-Kate with two other women, one young and exotic with flaming red hair, the other older and quietly elegant, with silver hair, sad eyes and a ladylike look about her. Hope would have liked to say hello but she didn't want to butt in.

'How did the writing go today?' she asked Matt tentatively instead. She hadn't asked him much about the novel, sensing that Matt didn't want to talk about it.

'OK,' said Matt guardedly.

'You're great at that sort of thing, you're so creative,' Hope said. 'Remember that terrible pension plan ad when the clients rejected eight different ideas and you still came up with a ninth.'

'Hell, yes,' laughed Matt. 'Those clients were a nightmare. But it's not quite the same. Ad campaigns and novels are very different things, or so I'm finding out.'

'Tell me,' said Hope. 'Tell me all about it.' She let the fingers of her right hand entwine with those of his left under the table. Matt gripped hers tightly in return.

'Let's not talk about work,' he said, tucking a wayward curl behind her ear. 'I know you didn't want to come here,' he added gently, 'but it's been good for us, hasn't it? This place has a good effect on us, it makes us better. If we were at home, I'd probably only be getting back to Maltings Lane now and you'd be worn out with working all day and having the dreaded quality time with the kids.'

She nodded ruefully. 'And I'd be angry with you for being so late home because the dinner would be burned to a crisp and I'd had nobody to have an adult conversation with all evening.'

'And then you'd go to bed because you were shattered and I'd stay up watching Sky Sports because I didn't want to get into bed and face the icy cold of your back turned towards me.' Matt grimaced at the memory.

'My icy back in my stay-away-from-me pyjamas, don't forget,' Hope laughed, thinking of the winceyette passion-killers she'd worn on purpose on those nights when Matt had annoyed her. That had been her idea of letting him know she was annoyed. Easier than saying anything outright, she'd hoped he realize why she was angry without her having to tell him.

The food arrived and Matt dug in, eagerly scooping out delicious garlic-flavoured mussels with one hand, still holding onto Hope with his other hand. He dunked a bit of bread into the mussel juice and held it to her mouth. Hope bit off half, leaving the rest for him. 'It *is* good for us here,' he said with his mouth full, 'isn't it?'

Hope nodded. 'It's just a bit hard to fit in because I feel as if I don't have a role here. Sorry,' she said apologetically. 'But I feel a bit lonely. I'd love to have a part-time job or something. I love being with the children every day but I never get to see anyone, it's terribly lonely . . .'

She broke off. She felt guilty even saying it. She'd spent so long dreaming of the fantasy world where she'd be able to be with the children all the time, but it was hard to be so isolated from other people during the day. In Bath, she'd have had friends nearby; lunch with Betsey, a night out with Yvonne and Denise from work, Sam coming down on the train for a long weekend; here, she had nobody.

Matt sighed deeply. He didn't need this hassle, really he didn't. He'd hard a hard day working on the damn book and no matter what he did with it, his main character remained resolutely wooden. 'I'm sorry, Hope,' he said, trying to be accommodating. 'I'm not trying to be selfish. I go off every day to work and it's a big stress trying to get the novel off the ground. It's not easy you know.'

Hope glared at him. He was unbelievable. Selfish wasn't the word.

'It's not easy for you?' she hissed. 'How easy is it for me? I love the children to bits but it's tough to be buried at home with them all day without any friends.'

'I know . . .' he interrupted.

'No you don't,' she said. 'If you did, you'd make a bit of an effort. Why can't you work from home a couple of days a week and give me a chance to get part time work?'

'Doing what?' he demanded. 'What are you going to do? Work in a shop? Get a job in the pub?'

'I don't know,' Hope retorted. 'It's not *what* the job is that's important, it's the fact that I've got one. I've worked all my life and it was hard to give it up for you. And I did give it up for you,' she reminded him. 'I just want a bit of independence again. There's at least another month before the day nursery can take the children, I don't know if I can cope with another month buried away all day feeling lonely while you write the great novel.'

Thinking of how badly the great novel was going, Matt scowled at her.

'I feel very isolated right now,' Hope added. 'Our social life round here is limited apart from dinner at Finula's' she grimaced. 'We need to meet more people and make friends. Me working would be part of that.'

'How am I supposed to work if I'm watching the kids?' Matt demanded.

Hope gave up. They ate their food and listened to the music in silence for the next hour. Hope brooded on her need to spend time with other adults, time when she was someone other than a wife and mother. Matt didn't understand this. He seemed to think it was a betrayal of him and the children if Hope wanted anything else. He didn't realize that Hope's job had given her confidence. Neither had she, to be honest. Until it was gone. Without the job, she felt her confidence slipping away until she was afraid she'd become a reclusive creature who viewed meeting people with fear. She couldn't let that happen.

Matt stared gloomily at the Nashville Girls and brooded on the novel. Did all great writers have this problem, this not-able-to-write-a-word problem?

'Hello Hope. Nice to see you.'

They both looked up from their brooding to see Mary-Kate and her two companions: the elegant silver-haired lady and the voluptuous redhead.

'We're going home before our eardrums give in,' Mary-Kate said pleasantly. 'I thought I'd introduce you to Delphine and Virginia.'

Introductions were exchanged and Matt roused himself from his gloom to be charming.

'You must come out with us some night, Hope,' Delphine said. 'We're thinking of having a girls' night soon.'

Hope felt her eyes stinging as she nodded gratefully at the three women. 'I'd like that,' she said.

'And you said you never meet anyone,' remarked Matt when they'd gone, waving goodbye and promising to phone Hope.

'She seemed lovely,' said Virginia as she, Mary-Kate and Delphine said their goodbyes outside the pub. 'But nervy, I think. You're right, May-Kate, she looks lonely.'

Delphine grinned. 'We'll soon sort that out.'

# CHAPTER EIGHT

Sam sat in the first marketing meeting of the new year and listened intently to the latest single from Hot Banana, a sexy all-girl band from Birmingham, Alabama. There were nine people around the long matt wood table, all with pages of densely typed marketing reports, A4 pads and biros in front of them and coffee in plastic cups – the office mugs were always being stolen, so disposable cups were the only option.

'Boy, don't do it to me, yet,' cooed the Hot Banana lead singer in a breathy voice to a background of pizzicato strings intercepted with a pulsating drum beat.

On the enormous flat screen TV mounted on the wall, Hot Banana danced with a troupe of black male dancers, five tiny tanned blondes writhing with the muscle-packed dancers, clinging to the dancers in a way that was just on the right side of decency. The lead singer, the girl with the longest blonde extensions and the shortest mini skirt, pouted with her inflatable pool lilo lips and breathed the last few words to the camera. She was nineteen, looked about seventeen and had jail bait written all over her.

'Good video,' said Sam, swinging her matt grey leather chair away from the screen and back to the table and her plastic cup of fizzing painkillers. She had a murderous pain in her belly, something between the pain of an agonizing period and another, unidentifiable ache. She picked up the cup and stirred the contents with her pen, watching the last bits of tablets dissolve. 'What's the story for *Top Of The Pops*? They're not bringing all those dancers with them, are they? The hotel bills would be horrendous.'

'No,' said Karen Storin, Sam's publicity director friend, who was masterminding the publicity and the arrangements for the tour. 'Their manager has them working with the choreographer who did last year's MTV awards and they've got an amazing routine together. They're very focussed girls, Sam. They want to crack Europe so badly, you wouldn't believe it.' She consulted her papers. 'The album is at number seven in the US album charts. If only we can get them some airplay on MTV, I think we've got a real chance of breaking them here.'

'Great,' said Sam, draining her painkillers with distaste. 'What are we going to do with them, then?'

For the next fifteen minutes, all nine people around the table discussed Hot Banana and the company's plans for launching their first album in the UK in April, just over three months' time. A round of media interviews was planned, Karen had managed to get them on the cover of *Smash Hits*, they were appearing on four TV shows and on a kids' Saturday morning programme 'in longer skirts,' added Karen, mindful of shocking parents with scantily-dressed singers appearing in front of their impressionable ten-year-olds. Promo T-shirts had been printed, along with expensive key-rings for when the first single would be sent out to radio stations.

There would also be a month of personal appearances and gigs in shopping centres around the country, along with five gigs supporting a boy band, El Mega, who were currently number two in the singles charts but belonged to another label. A Titus tour manager, along with publicity and marketing personnel were assigned to look after the Hot Banana girls.

'Just make sure you keep them away from the actual Megas,' Karen advised the tour manager. 'The word on the street is that two of the boys from the band are experimenting with heavy drugs.'

Everyone winced. There was nothing worse than seeing a band you'd worked your fingers to the bone for turn to the bad parts of the rock 'n' roll lifestyle. Bands like El Mega appealed to a very young female audience and their image had to be cleaner than clean. One hint of heroin addiction and the whole band would collapse like a house of cards.

'It drives me mad,' said Cheryl fiercely. One of the publicity assistants, Cheryl had become devoted to a Titus signing called the LLBoys, who were launched at the same time as El Mega and who'd failed where the Megas had succeeded. 'You wouldn't mind if they had any talent in the first place. They're just singing stuff someone else has written and trying to pretend to the fans that they wrote it themselves!'

Everyone laughed at this.

'Cheryl, if the only people with songs in the charts had actually written them themselves, there wouldn't be a *Music Week* Top Hundred, it would be *Music Week*'s Top Three!' joked another of the publicity team.

Cheryl went pink.

'Right, let's move onto Enchanting ,' said Sam, who had a budget meeting at five and who wanted to cover everything important in this meeting before she had to go.

Enchanting were another new act, one which had been signed by Sam's predecessor but who hadn't yet released an album. Two pretty London sisters who sang almost identical soprano, Steffi and Katya Ceci were just seventeen and their version of 'Jerusalem' would bring tears to anyone's eyes. Desperate to find their own Charlotte Church, the wunderkind Welsh girl with the angelic voice who'd sold millions of CDs, LGBK had signed the Cecis for a huge sum of money the previous year but, as Sam found out as soon as she took over, the two girls were totally unsuited to a life of fame.

Shy to the point of neurosis, both sisters were reduced to silence by interviewers and Karen had discovered that their mother – the original nightmare stage mother – gave them beta blockers before they went onstage to calm their nerves. Karen was also convinced that Steffi was anorexic and firmly believed neither girl would be able to cope with journalists breathing down their necks and writing articles about them being too fat, too thin, too dull or too wild. Becoming a hit act meant your private life became fair game and Sam wasn't sure if her newest protégées could cope with it.

They'd spent six months on and off recording their album and now that it was to be released, the girls were practically having breakdowns at the thought of doing publicity, while their mother was apparently spending all their advance money in the Versace shop buying herself a selection of highly provocative dresses for a launch party that hadn't even been finalized yet.

'Mrs Ceci was on the phone this morning because she knew we were having a marketing meeting,' Karen said wearily.

'How did she know about it?' demanded Sam.

'I don't know. She's like the FBI, that woman – she knows every-thing. I can't cope with her,' Karen said with a shudder. 'She wanted to come in for the meeting.'

Sam raised her eyebrows. 'She did?' Nobody but staff ever went to marketing meetings. Artists and their managers sometimes came in to marketing presentations for campaigns but that was generally only the really big stars.

'She's been phoning me all week saying she wants to be involved because she doesn't want us "screwing up her little girls' big chance" – and that's a direct quote,' Karen said.

'Perhaps I should talk to her and explain how we do things,' Sam said grimly.

The people round the table grinned at the thought of Sam Smith taking the obnoxious Mrs Ceci down a peg or two. Mrs Ceci thought she was a match for anyone – wait 'till she met Sam.

They eventually had to leave the troublesome Cecis and moved onto a handsome Latin American singer who'd sold millions of records so far and showed no sign of letting up. 'Thank God for Manolo,' Sam said, looking at the sales figures for his last two albums. Reliable, clever, utterly committed and entirely professional, Manolo was no trouble at all. And his ever-growing sales would make up for some of the chunk of money they'd spent buying up the so-far useless Cecis.

Sam looked at the album cover where Manolo smouldered inside a white shirt, his bronzed skin a startling contrast. For a moment, her mind rippled back to another man in a sexy white shirt, a man who had come to bed eyes and who could certainly give Manolo a run for his money charisma-wise.

'What a pro,' said Karen fondly after she'd reeled off the lengthy list of engagements Manolo had obligingly agreed to do. 'He's doing three entire days of press and TV interviews at the Dorchester and I know he won't complain once.'

'Great,' Sam said mechanically, trying to put the man next door out of her mind. She hadn't set eyes on him since the morning after the party, although the builders were working at full speed on his house, banging and hammering all day. Despite peering out her window occasionally, hidden behind the curtains of course, Sam hadn't noticed Him going in or out at all.

'Speaking of complaints,' interrupted one of the product managers, 'we've got a problem with Density.'

Sam felt her insides grind painfully. Maybe it was just stress: mention Density and something went pop. 'What is it this time?' she said.

Karen interrupted smoothly. 'We'll talk about it afterwards, Sam, if that's OK with you,' she said, shooting a fierce look at the product manager.

Sam nodded. More trouble ahead. Things had to be bad if Karen wanted to discuss it in private.

For another hour they ploughed through the list, discussing rock bands, a soul singer and a group of folk-singing grandmothers who'd been a huge hit on a talent show and who'd just been signed. Sam fidgeted in her seat, trying to get comfortable but unable to. Her belly ached and no matter which way she sat, it didn't help. Neither had the painkillers. She had more in her desk drawer, she remembered with relief, although if she felt this bad when her period was due, how awful would she feel when she got it?

Finally, the meeting was over.

'Thanks everyone,' Sam said, trying to sound upbeat and positive but unable to. She felt so ill.

'Are you OK? You look a little tired,' Karen said as everyone hurried out of the room.

'Late night,' lied Sam, grinning.

'Lucky you,' laughed Karen. 'I was in bed at ten watching *Ally McBeal*.'

You and me both, Sam thought silently.

Back in her office, she peered into her make-up compact mirror and winced. She didn't look tired: she looked grey in the face, grey with a film of sweat sheening on her forehead. She quickly slapped on another layer of Clinique base and brushed on cheekbones. Mascara and a slash of rich lipstick made her look slightly more presentable. As a finale, she popped another couple of painkillers in water, doing her best not to read the instructions about how many you were medically allowed to consume in a twenty-four hour period.

Enchanting loomed large and scary at the budget meeting with Steve and two guys from finance. Their album had cost a fortune to record and the video had been nearly as expensive having over-run by two days because the director had had to coax the two reluctant stars into smiling occasionally. As a marketing director, Sam had often faced the hard facts about artists not recouping money for the record company, but in her new job, she faced these facts from an entirely different perspective. Now that she was the managing director of the label, the buck stopped at her desk. The label had spent an arm and a leg on Enchanting and they still hadn't made so much as three pence profit from them.

Steve wanted to know why the album's release date had been put back. 'We're giving out the wrong signal to the trade by doing that,' he growled, lighting another nuclear cigar.

Sam was feeling too ill to bullshit him. 'Yeah, I know,' she said. 'But we should never have signed them in the first place. You know that, Steve.' She eyeballed him. 'My people and I are taking the flak for someone we didn't sign, so don't give me a hard time about putting the album back. If we work on the theory that selling 30,000 albums will be a miracle, at least we're being honest about it. I've been doing some figures and if we're lucky, we'll recoup half the costs. That would be doing brilliantly given the problems we're discovering with the girls.'

Steve stopped in the middle of lighting his cigar to stare at her, astonished by such candour.

'Don't sit on the fence about this one, Sam,' he joked. 'Tell us what you really think.'

Sam fixed him with her fierce blue gaze. 'Steve, we have one possibly anorexic and two definitely stressed-out kids on our hands. They've got the most pushy mother my team have ever encountered and when anybody they don't know enters the recording studio, they refuse to sing. They may have wonderful voices but they are not performers, it's that simple. Their mother wants this far more than they do. If she could sing, she'd have made millions by now because she apparently had the brass neck for anything. Her daughters don't. Breaking Enchanting as a successful act is going to be damn near impossible. If it works, fantastic, but at this point, our only option is releasing the album and letting it off on its own without sending the girls out with it. If you want an MD who lies through their teeth to you, then you better rehire. Capisce?'

The two other people in the room blinked. Steve let out a giant roar and started laughing so hard his belly rocked the table.

'You're something else, Smith, you know that? We lucked out the day we found you, that's for sure.'

Relieved that Steve hadn't blown a gasket, the two accounts guys laughed. Even Sam found the energy to raise a smile. They discussed the redundancies and Sam was grateful that Steve didn't question the people she'd chosen to lose.

He'd lose respect for her as a ball-breaking bitch if he discovered that she'd insisted that the pregnant woman kept her job, as had the young guy who'd just bought the big apartment. Sam had spent hours trying to find a solution to the problem and had finally come up with three members of staff who'd been actively looking for jobs elsewhere and who would be happy to take a lump sum, along with a glowing reference and a chance to move. Sam was now waiting for the last redundancy candidate to agree on their package.

It was nearly eight when she stepped out of the Titus building and into lashing rain. As if rain wasn't enough, it was freezing cold – the temperature had definitely dipped since Sam had left her flat that morning clad in her leather coat and no hat. Now she shivered like a whippet after the tropical heat of the office and wondered if she'd get a cab. The underground was miles quicker and the station was literally two minutes away but she couldn't face trekking miles down the escalators into the bowels of the earth to get one. She was too tired. She was always tired these days. Maybe it was just the January blues. Or maybe she'd make an appointment with the doctor.

Hope's e-mail was upbeat for the first time in ages.

*Hi Sam, how are you? You sounded tired on the phone on Sunday night. I hope you're looking after yourself. You need to visit us and I'll fill you full of good country food. A blast of Kerry air would be good for you. Listen to me! I even sound like a local now after two months! Seriously, though, you should have come to us for Christmas. I know you promised Catrina and the gang that you'd go to the cottage in Brighton as usual but Redlion is lovely at Christmas. Apart from the rain!*

*Matt's working hard and Millie and Toby are starting at a new playgroup next week. I can't wait and neither can they. Millie is finally tired of playing with the baby hens, who are all growing huge, by the way. I've ordered a book that tells you all about them because I can't keep asking other people when they're going to lay eggs or whatever. Apparently, you can tell when they've got an egg ready to lay by feeling their bums but I can't bring myself to do it!*

No mention of how Hope herself was doing, Sam thought critically as she scanned through her sister's chatter about their new friends and how she and Matt had started going out to dinner once a week.

*When are you going to take some holiday and come and see us? We'd love you to visit us. Please say yes soon. I miss you.*

Sam felt a lump in her throat. She missed Hope too. They'd been so close as children but when Matt had come along, some sort of barrier had grown up between them, a barrier Sam didn't feel strong enough to break down. It was only natural, of course. Sam didn't waste time getting jealous or feeling lonely about it. Siblings had to drift apart a little bit when they had their own families. Well, when one of them had her own family. But instead of getting used to being without Hope, Sam had found herself missing her sister even more lately. It was the sense of family she missed, she reflected.

She'd managed so well for years with her own family of friends. People to spend Christmas with, people to go to dinner with. Now, that didn't seem enough. She wanted more, yet she felt too proud to admit it. It would be too humiliating for strong, go-it-alone Sam Smith to admit that she really needed people, which was why she hadn't gone to Ireland for Christmas. She did feel terribly guilty about it. Hope had certainly asked her often enough. But in Sam's current state of mind, three days celebrating was as much as she could handle.

She'd gone to Brighton to the cottage that Hugh and Catrina had owned for years and had managed two days of smiling with the gang until she could take it no more and had used the excuse that she had to see an upcoming band who were playing on December 27th as an opportunity to escape. She'd hoped her dashing off sounded high-powered and not anti-social.

*Better fly, Sam. Matt's just finished putting the kids to bed. Talk soon and I mean it about coming to stay here soon. We'll only be here for a year and I want you to visit.*

*love*

*Hope*

Sam sat at the computer for a moment and tried to imagine Hope's life. What would it be like to live in a family unit, to have to constantly think of other people and worry about dinner or who was looking after the children? Would it be very strange? Having someone sleeping in your bed all the time, having two little people utterly dependent on you, demanding all your time and leaving you with nothing private? Not to be an individual any more but to be Mummy or somebody's partner. Weird.

She clicked onto the 'reply' button and composed her answer.

*Hi Sis, I'm feeling great,* she lied. *I've been very busy with the new job and it's getting busier. We've got some great new acts coming up in the next few months and I'm going to be up to my eyeballs with them. I know you love Manolo so I'll send you his new album. He's doing loads of publicity for us so I'll be able to tell you what he's like in the delectable Latin flesh. I've got to fly to Brussels next week for an international meeting which will be interesting. I've never been to one of the international meetings as an MD. They're usually exhausting but at least I'm getting a suite in the hotel. There have to be some perks. Karen Storin is going too. I've told you about her, she's great.*

The e-mail was entirely about work, Sam realized, rereading. Probably because it was easier to rattle on and on about international meetings and new acts instead of telling her sister that she felt low, miserable and lonely. Yes, that was it: lonely. Fifteen years of slogging her socks off for an office with a view and now that she'd got there, the view was increasingly desolate and her sense of job satisfaction was disappearing faster than the months to her fortieth birthday.

She tried again.

*Going to a dinner party tonight at Catrina and Hugh's. I'm going with Jay,* whom I haven't seen since Christmas, nearly a month ago, despite meaning to phone her every day, Sam reminded herself guiltily. *I must rush out and buy some flowers or wine to take, so I better go now. I'll talk soon,*

*Love Sam.*

She'd managed to avoid mentioning the suggested holiday in Kerry. In London, she could keep up the increasingly shaky façade of being in control of her life. With Hope's big grey eyes watching her anxiously, searching for answers, *knowing*, Sam knew the façade would disintegrate totally.

She left the carrier bag containing a bottle of champagne in the taxi and ran up to Jay's apartment block. She pressed the buzzer for Jay Raskin.

'Jay, it's Sam,' she said when Jay answered. 'I've got a cab waiting, will you be long?'

'Down in a minute,' said Jay in the soft Atlanta accent that hadn't changed despite twenty years in the UK.

Sam got back in the taxi and leaned tiredly against the seat. She half-wished she'd made more of an effort with her outfit instead of staying in her business-like black suit and mannish white shirt. With her hair tied back, it looked a bit butch. But she simply hadn't had the energy to put on anything else.

Catrina was infinitely stylish and always dressed as if a glossy magazine was just about to photograph her. She'd undoubtedly be wearing something divine from an unknown designer who, in a month's time, would be on the cover of *Vogue*. You'd think she was a designer herself instead of a recruitment consultant.

The only consolation was that, no matter how career-woman Sam's outfit was, Jay's would be equally un-partyish, albeit in a different way. Jay's style was a cross between the Merchant Ivory wardrobe department and Sixties hippie chick. Her favourite garments were trailing antique lace skirts worn with biker boots and little T-shirts with messages on them. It was a look a million miles away from Sam's career lady chic and Catrina's style queen image.

When the entire group of friends were out at dinner, Sam often noticed people looking at the disparate crowd and trying to figure out what they were doing together. Jay looked younger than the rest, Hugh looked older. Jay dressed like a student, Catrina dressed like a fashion editor and nobody would have worked out that they had all gone to the same university.

Jay's front door slammed and Sam looked up. She blinked in astonishment. Jay didn't look like Jay. Instead of the usual trailing outfit, Jay was unrecognizable in a slim little pistachio-coloured skirt that came to the knee and was finished off with sheer tights and high heels that looked like Jimmy Choos. She was without her famous astrakhan coat (Oxfam, £8) and sported a fitted winter white number that was definitely cashmere and could only have come from some expensive boutique. Jay normally avoided expensive boutiques like the plague.

Sam wished she could stop goggling.

'You look so different,' she gasped as Jay got into the taxi.

Jay blushed prettily and tucked a strand of poker-straight dark hair behind her ear. Another change. Jay's hair was normally curly and uncontrollable. 'You haven't met Greg, have you?' she said, sitting down to reveal a man climbing in behind her.

'Hello,' said Sam politely, as if she wasn't utterly astonished. Jay had vowed never to lay a hand on a man after her last boyfriend, a futures analyst named Stefan, had run off with his sister's best friend. It had taken a year and many vodka-fuelled nights with Sam for Jay to wash him out of her hair.

'Nice to meet you,' said Greg in a seductive Scottish burr.

Sam shook his big hand and tried to eye him up and down without looking as if she was eyeing him up and down. Not tall, he was lean with pale reddish hair and the blond eyelashes and striking blue eyes that often went with such colouring. His complexion was freckled and sported a healthy golden tan as if he'd just come back from somewhere very hot. With his big engaging grin and intelligent, laughing eyes, the whole effect was very attractive and Sam could see why Jay had that daft, besotted smile on her face. What she couldn't see was why Jay hadn't told her about this new amour.

He sat on the bucket seat of the taxi and grinned across at Jay, who was dimpling back at him. Sam couldn't have felt more like a gooseberry if she'd suddenly turned round, hairy and green.

'We met in Lanzarote,' Jay said to Sam, without taking her eyes off Greg.

'I didn't know you'd been to Lanzarote,' Sam said lightly. 'You must have gone right after we got back from Brighton.'

Jay patted her on the knee. 'You've been so busy with the new job and everything, we haven't talked since Christmas. I went on the spur of the moment – I needed a break. It was just a week in the sun.'

Greg, who appeared to know the area, directed the taxi driver to an off licence.

'We've got to get a gift for Catrina,' Jay explained.

'Won't be long,' Greg said, hopping out of the taxi athletically, his dark raincoat flapping around his legs.

'You're a dark horse,' Sam said as soon as he was gone. 'Why didn't you tell me?'

'I wanted to surprise you,' Jay smiled.

'I'm surprised. Now tell me *everything*!'

Jay ticked it off on her fingers: 'He's thirty-four, runs a landscape garden business, has never been married, comes from Fife and I'm crazy about him. It's only been three weeks but this is for real, Sam. This is the Big One.'

Sam gave her a hug. 'I'm so glad.' She thought for a moment. 'Does Catrina know he's coming tonight?'

Jay nodded but looked out the window so she didn't have to meet Sam's eyes. They could both see Greg coming, swinging an off licence bag. 'She's met him. We all went to an exhibition in Duke Street.'

Sam had the curious sensation of feeling like the child in the playground whom nobody wanted on their rounders team. She'd known Jay, Catrina and Hugh for years. They were part of the gang, seven people who'd shared student life together. Now, with one quick move, she'd been sidelined by coupledom, intellectual enjoyable coupledom at that.

When was the last time she'd seen an exhibition or gone anywhere that didn't involve work?

Hugh met them at the door, looking every inch the successful barrister in a striped shirt that didn't really disguise his girth. He would never win any Mr Universe awards but he had the kindest eyes of anyone Sam had ever known.

'Come in,' he said, grabbing Sam in a bear hug. 'Where have you been hiding out, Madam MD? We've missed you.'

Inexplicably, Sam's eyes welled up and she was glad that her face was buried in Hugh's well-padded shoulder.

'I haven't been anywhere,' she said with a creditable imitation of a laugh. She wriggled out of his embrace and hurried into the hall so nobody would see her glistening eyes. 'Where's Catrina?' she added.

'Slaving over a hot stove,' joked Hugh.

Sam dried her eyes as she made her way down the corridor. It was a beautiful house, not unlike Sam's flat in terms of decor as it was a vision of clutter-free loveliness with simple interior design. But while Sam's flat was decorated entirely in off-whites, Catrina had painted every room a different colour. The hall was a welcoming buttercup yellow with only yellow flowers ever allowed on the modern furniture, the small study was olive green, the big bathroom was purple and Catrina and Hugh's bedroom was shades of misty ocean blue. Sam reached the kitchen (turquoise), a room that would have made any Michelin chef feel right at home with its big steel appliances, professional copper-bottomed saucepans and coolly tiled splashbacks.

'Burnt to a crisp from standing over the hob stirring sauces?' inquired Sam from the door.

Catrina turned around, looking a far cry from the frazzle-faced cook. Beautifully groomed in a slinky salmon pink Ghost dress, she looked unconcerned at the thought of cooking up dinner for ten. Sam knew for a fact that Catrina bought her dinner party materials in containers from a catering company and the only effort involved was heating them up and chopping up the coriander to sprinkle on top of the soup. The caterers sent that too.

'Darling Sam, hello.' Catrina presented one Elizabeth Arden-scented cheek for a kiss and then the other.

'You look tired,' she said bluntly.

Sam smiled ruefully. Catrina may have looked like the perfect hostess, but she'd never lost that straight-talking charm that had earned her the nickname No Holds Barred in college. Being utterly honest had made her one of the City's most successful recruitment people.

'Busy day at work,' Sam said blithely. 'Shall I put this in the fridge and can I help?'

'You don't need to do a thing,' Catrina assured her. 'But you could open a bottle of white wine from the fridge. I know you like white. Everyone else is here. I suppose the young lovers are still helping each other off with their coats?'

Her head in the fridge looking for the wine, Sam smiled. 'You said it. I got such a shock when he appeared this evening.'

'He's good for her,' Catrina said. 'You should have seen them in Lanzarote. I've never seen Jay so happy. She spent ages . . .'

Sam didn't hear the rest because she was so shocked. They'd all gone to Lanzarote and nobody had thought to mention it to her. Her best friends, people she'd seen over Christmas, dammit, had been planning this and never said a word. Sam stared at the big bowl of rocket salad sitting in the fridge and felt betrayed. And why had Jay lied and said that Hugh and Catrina had met Greg at an exhibition? Probably because she knew Sam would feel left out if she heard about the holiday.

'You're not upset, are you?' Catrina asked shrewdly. 'The holiday really was a last minute thing. We were all sitting round freezing in Brighton after you'd gone back to London and Hugh suggested we take a week in the sun. You know you hate sun holidays, Sam. Ever since that week in Crete when you said you'd go insane if you had to lie on the beach for one more minute!'

Sam nodded, doing her best to look as if it didn't matter in the slightest that she hadn't been asked on the holiday. Not that she'd have wanted to go or anything but, oh, to have been asked.

In the dining room (Sahara colours) Andy was the only other one of the college gang there apart from Jay and Sam. He was thinner than ever since his divorce the year before; Sam could feel his ribs through his baggy jumper when he gave her a hug.

'That's some diet you're on, Andy,' she said reprovingly, looking at the slight frame and the serious eyes behind the tortoiseshell glasses that Andy had started wearing when he first became a teacher.

'Right back at you, Ms Smith,' he said. 'You've lost a few pounds yourself.'

'It's the Stress Diet,' Sam said bitterly.

Hugh introduced everyone. There were two other couples: Maya and Tom, who were Catrina's guests because she worked with Maya, and Dennis and Emily, who were Hugh's invitees because he worked in the same chambers as Dennis.

Sam was polite but couldn't summon up too much enthusiasm for the evening. For a start, she was still smarting from being left out of the Lanzarote holiday plan. Secondly, she wasn't in the mood for a business party where Hugh and Catrina had invited colleagues for duty meals. She'd expected a gang-only night where they could all let their hair down. Now she had to be charming to the boring Dennis who wanted to talk all evening about the music industry and was 'it true that you just manufacture bands these days?'

Luckily, Andy, who was sitting on her other side, came to Sam's rescue before she could stab Dennis in the eye with her soup spoon.

'Is it true that barristers make behind the scenes bets on who'll win the case?' he asked innocently.

Dennis choked. 'Rubbish,' he spluttered. 'That's an offensive suggestion and I might add . . .'

Andy grinned. 'Gotcha!' he said pleasantly. 'What you said to Sam was just as bad.'

Dennis got the point. 'Sorry,' he said weakly to Sam. 'Didn't mean to be offensive but you hear such stories . . .'

'Yeah, you do,' Sam said and turned to talk to Andy.

'Everything all right?' asked Catrina nervously, seeing her fabulous dinner party in danger of collapsing.

'Fine,' said Andy. 'Are you okay?' he asked Sam gently. 'You don't look in the best of form and normally, you relish the chance to put people like Dennis firmly in their place.'

'You mean I'm Queen Bitch and it's rare for me to pass up an opportunity to savage someone?' she said harshly.

'Hey, relax,' he said. 'It's me, your friend, remember? The one who held your hand on the Journey of Fear roller coaster.'

They both laughed.

'It was your bloody fault I went on it in the first place,' Sam pointed out, giving Andy a poke in the shoulder. 'I'm terrified of heights as a result.'

'Do you still avoid the glass lift in the office?' Andy asked slyly.

Sam shuddered. 'Now *that* was scary. No, that was my old office and I'm in a new job now.'

'Sorry, I forgot. It's hard to keep up, isn't it? You get so involved in your own problems.' Andy gazed down at his half-full soup bowl. Sam felt like a total bitch. Here she was getting all tantrum-ish over the fact that she hadn't gone to Lanzarote with the others, while Andy's problems were much more serious. His divorce had been acrimonious and still was, with vicious rows over access to his two children. The last time Sam had met him, he'd been living in a shabby bedsit – all he could afford on his teacher's salary after paying out maintenance – and his ex was insisting that she wouldn't let the kids visit him there. It was Catch-22 time.

'I can't manage to live anywhere better,' he'd told Sam then, looking for all the world like a broken man. At the age of thirty-nine, Andy looked fifty.

That had been six months ago, she realized guiltily. She hadn't been a very good friend to Andy, had she?

He could have done with someone to drag him out to the pub for a drink, someone to listen to his problems when he was in the depths of depression, someone to be a friendly voice on the other end of the phone. But she'd been too busy, right? At least Catrina and Hugh were kind and thoughtful and invited him to dinners and parties.

Sam took a deep gulp of mineral water – she wasn't really in the mood for wine, strangely enough, even though she knew it would be superb because Hugh was a bit of a wine buff.

She had to stop being selfish and try and enjoy herself for everyone else's sake.

The food was sublime and the music wasn't bad either. Sam didn't really go for the sort of middle of the road stuff that Catrina and Hugh adored but she wouldn't dream of saying so. For fun, she'd once given them a batch of garage rock CDs for Christmas but had never heard any of it played.

Tonight, the music was very much in the background as the ten people around the dinner table laughed, joked and discussed life, the universe and everything. Well, eight of them joked and laughed: Jay and Greg, seated beside each other, stared deep into each other's eyes most of the time and laughed at the jokes a good two minutes after everyone else. Sam was sure they were playing footsie under the table judging by their giggles.

She did her best not to stare but somehow couldn't help it. There was something so utterly tender about the way Greg fed Jay some of his chocolate pudding because she'd chosen Catrina's fruit salad instead. Sam watched under her lashes and wondered bleakly if anyone would ever feed her with such love ever again.

'Gosh, this Stilton is good,' said Dennis, hoovering up the contents of his plate.

Sam looked at the elaborate cheese board and remembered when the gang's idea of a dinner party had been something with minced beef and rice and when the wine had come in litre sized screw top bottles because they were all broke and couldn't afford the expensive stuff with corks.

Everything had changed so much for all of them.

She did her best to remember what she'd hoped for in those far off college days. Had she assumed she'd be utterly happy with a superb career or had she ever dreamed of anything else? She couldn't remember.

It was no good, she couldn't enjoy herself. She felt out of synch with everyone. Catrina and Hugh were exchanging loving glances down the table all the time, Jay and Greg were in lover land and everyone else, bar herself, was well on their way to being drunk.

At eleven, Sam decided it was time to go home. She finished her coffee and wondered how rude it would be if she were the first to leave. She'd hoped that she and Jay could have gone home together because she really wanted to discuss her bouts of exhaustion and illness with her friend, but she couldn't now. Getting Jay on her own would be impossible as she'd doubtless be glued to Greg in the taxi home too.

'We've got an announcement,' Catrina said suddenly, her eyes glittering with pride.

Hugh beamed up the table at her.

'You've been made partner!' gasped Sam delightedly. 'Oh Catrina, that's wonderful.'

Both Hugh and Catrina laughed.

'No Sam, you are such a workaholic!' said Hugh fondly. 'Catrina's pregnant. We're going to have a baby.'

Immediately, the table erupted with squeals of delight and congratulations. Everyone got up and hugged the happy couple.

'That's wonderful,' Sam said genuinely as she held Catrina tightly. 'I'm so happy for you.'

'Thank you,' Catrina said.

The more she looked at her, the more Sam was astonished she hadn't copped on earlier. Catrina was blooming, so it wasn't just a pregnancy myth. Her face glowed with joy and pride and her slim figure had the gentle swelling of the fourth month. Sam smiled wryly to herself. Trust her to come up with the career-orientated answer to Catrina's announcement that she had something to reveal. People with real lives would probably have worked out what the news was instantly. Only career spinsters thought exciting news meant a promotion.

After several bottles of champagne had been consumed to toast the baby, Sam finally said her goodbyes.

'I'm sorry to be such a party pooper but I've a half seven meeting in the morning,' she lied.

It didn't make her feel any better that nobody begged her to stay. She was now officially so boring that rooms lit up when she left rather than when she entered them.

At the front door, Catrina and Hugh kissed her goodbye.

'It's such wonderful news,' Sam said, standing on the front step and holding Catrina's hands. Her eyes misted over with the emotion of it all. 'I'm so happy for you.'

Misreading the signs, Catrina gave her hands a squeeze. 'Don't worry, Sam, it'll happen to you,' she said comfortingly. 'It's not too late. We thought *we'd* left it a bit late but we were wrong.'

Sam's heart missed a beat. Then it hit her: traumatized and divorced Andy wasn't the only person they all felt sorry for. They felt sorry for her too. Everyone else was doubled up, secure in happy partnership and she was the cautionary tale, the woman who'd been too busy for a man and family, the lonely working woman with nothing but a lifetime of meals for one and cosy nights in with the remote control to look forward to.

For pride's sake, she laughed heartily. 'Me?' she gasped. 'Oh Catrina, you'll be a wonderful mum but that particular path's not for me. Bye,' she said with added cheeriness. She waved exuberantly as she walked to the taxi, keeping up the bubbly façade. 'I'll phone soon. We must go shopping for maternity clothes!' And she was gone, into the taxi and finally able to wipe the rictus of a smile from her face.

The taxi driver pulled up outside the wrong house on Sam's road and, as he was a bit deaf and it had taken several goes to explain where she wanted to go in the first place, Sam didn't bother to correct him.

'Great, thanks,' she said tiredly, handing him the fare through the side window.

She walked slowly up her road, too weary to even look into the lit-up houses of her neighbours. Hearing footsteps behind her, Sam felt momentarily nervous. She whisked round but the person running behind her wasn't a mugger: it was a girl with long dark hair, wearing a big fleecy coat and high heeled sandals that weren't much use for running in. She fled past Sam and as she did so Sam realized that the girl was the doe-eyed beauty she'd seen with the man next door, leaving his house after the party. And that she was crying.

Honestly, Sam thought, it was like having a soap opera next door. One minute, stunning girls in silver dresses left the house, the next, they ran back in sobbing their hearts out. The girl was banging on the front door by now and Sam watched with interest as it opened and he appeared. At least he had his shirt on now, Sam noticed tartly, as she passed by and opened her own gate.

'Maggie?' he said as the girl collapsed into his arms. 'My poor girl, what happened?'

Sam banged the gate loudly. The neighbourhood was really going down. No other residents lived their lives in public.

At the sound of the gate banging, he glanced up and saw Sam. His brows narrowed at the disapproving expression on her face.

Sam sniffed, stuck her nose in the air and ignored him as she got her keys out of her handbag. As if she cared what age his girlfriends were.

She opened the door quietly.

'Stop making noise,' roared Mad Malcolm from the top floor.

'Oh shut up,' roared Sam back.

If he dared come out while she was going up to her apartment, she'd kill him!

At home, she slopped some soluble painkillers in a glass with water. What a crap evening. She'd discovered that her best friends had gone on holiday without even mentioning it to her. She'd had to witness love's young dream in Catrina's house and more love's young dream next door. Well, love's young dream and Mr Ageing Playboy. It was enough to make you sick and it was so unfair. Men could be lotharios at any age, dating women zillions of years younger than them if they wanted, but women were supposed never to get any older than thirty. It was all downhill afterwards.

Sam thought grimly about the articles she'd read claiming that women's sexual peak was in their thirties and forties. So bloody what if it was? There was no one who wanted to have sex with them then.

She knocked back her painkillers as if they were a shot of tequila, took a sleeping tablet for good measure and went to bed.

\* \* \*

The next morning was Saturday. Sam was up early and had her morning coffee sitting on the window seat that faced the street. Half-leafing through the paper, she spotted people walking down the next door path. Him. And the girl, although this time she was wearing baggy jeans that were way too big for her and had been turned up at the bottom. His jeans. How cute, Sam thought sourly. How bloody cute. She'd bet a tenner the girl had wandered round all morning in one of his shirts and nothing else, long tanned legs appearing endless under the shirt tails. If he owned a proper shirt, that was. Wasters like that didn't. They owned expensive T-shirts they bought with money from their trust funds and they never had shirts because shirts meant jobs and idle rich layabouts thought that jobs, like taxes, were for the little people.

Sam was pretty sure he was a waster. All the signs were there: wild parties, no visible means of support, girls coming out his ears. She hated people like that.

After breakfast, she unearthed her running shoes, her sweat pants and a double-layered fleece that was perfect for running in when the weather was cold. She hadn't had any exercise for so long, she was sure her legs would seize up before they'd even warmed up. Doing a bit of mental arithmetic, Sam figured it was nearly three months since she'd had a run, although at least she hadn't put on any weight.

Outside, the January air was icily fresh. The streets were filling up with people meandering off to leisurely Saturday lunches or doing their shopping. Sam breathed deeply and ran, trying to remember the rhythm she ran best at. It wouldn't come. Running felt wrong and her body felt tired, clumsy. She persisted for a mile, refusing to turn back because she just couldn't wimp out. But finally the weariness got the better of her. She began to weave her way back through the lush, expensive streets of Holland Park. And then she stopped suddenly. A wave of nausea hit her and she sank down onto the kerb, her legs so weak they weren't able to hold her up any more. Sam wasn't sure what was worse; the feeling of being so utterly feeble that she had to sit on the dirty kerb or the fact that she was no longer in control of her own body. Shaking, she put her head between her knees and tried to breathe deeply. Even that failed her. She could only draw in ragged, short breaths. Tears pooled in her eyes. What was happening to her? What was wrong? And how was she going to get home?

After a few minutes of feeling her legs and bum going numb with the cold of the kerb, she got shakily to her feet and leaned against a fat cherry tree for support. If only she'd brought her mobile phone she could phone someone for help. Only who could she ring? Sam thought bleakly. There was nobody she could think of. She'd let her friends drift away from her. She was truly alone.

Two women, in fresh new tracksuits, power walked past with the zeal of the January exerciser determined to shift the Christmas spare tyre. Leaning against her tree, Sam barely looked at them. But they noticed her. They walked briskly past and then stopped, before returning.

'Are you all right?' asked one tentatively.

Sam shook her head. 'I was jogging and I suddenly thought I was going to pass out.' She tried to laugh. 'I'll be fine in a moment, I just need to rest. I only live half a mile away.'

'You're as white as a sheet,' said the other woman. 'You don't look fit to walk another yard.'

'I'm fine, honestly,' protested Sam, still clinging onto the tree.

The women looked at each other. The first one produced a tiny mobile phone from a pocket. 'I'm phoning Michael to bring the car round,' she said firmly. 'We can't leave you here.'

Michael turned up in ten minutes in a gleaming new Range Rover and they all piled in. Sam was feeling too weak to protest too much and she sat in the back wondering what exactly was happening to her.

They stopped outside her house.

'I can't thank you enough,' she said, tearfully. 'Please give me your names so I can repay you in some way.'

'Nonsense,' said Michael's wife. 'This is our good deed for the day. Take care of yourself, my dear. You really should see a doctor.'

In the flat, Sam lay down on her bed with her track shoes still on, not caring that she'd leave marks on the creamy bedclothes.

They'd been so kind to her. If *she'd* seen a strange woman leaning against a tree, she'd have walked by as fast as she possibly could and thought 'drug addict.' Today, she'd learned that there were nice people out there, people who weren't riddled with cynicism like herself.

She'd definitely phone the doctor. On Monday.

On Monday, Sam was in her office by eight. She worked steadily through the paperwork on her desk, only stopping to drink a cup of coffee and to make a doctor's appointment for that lunchtime. She felt fine, really, she convinced herself. She was probably pre-menstrual or just run down. A tonic was what she needed. And no gin.

At half ten, Karen Storin came into her office for a meeting.

As usual, Karen looked marvellous, vibrant in a cream trouser suit that looked incredible against her black skin.

'I love that suit,' Sam said. 'It's Joseph, isn't it? You look wonderful.'

Karen stared back at her. 'I wish I could say the same for you, Sam.'

Sam felt herself tense.

'I don't want to overstep the boundaries but Sam, you look terrible. You've lost so much weight and you look . . . well, worn out.'

'Do I?' There was no need for pretence with Karen.

'Yes,' she answered bluntly. 'Do you want to talk about it?'

Sam shook her head and gave a tight little smile. 'I think I'm run down and I'm going to see the doctor today, OK? Can we keep this between us, though?'

Karen looked hurt. 'I wouldn't dream of saying a word to anyone.'

'Lydia,' Sam said via the intercom. 'Can we have a pot of coffee in here, please?' Anything to change the subject.

When Karen had gone, Sam got Lydia to cancel her appointments for the rest of the day.

'I have to go out,' she said, ignoring her assistant's startled face. Sam Smith never cancelled appointments, Lydia knew. She was an automaton and would work until nine at night every day if she could. Something was up, Lydia decided.

\*　　\*　　\*

Sam was rarely sick. She took vitamins, was addicted to the herbal immune booster Echinacea and was convinced she always did her best to look after herself. Which was why she'd never spent much time in the doctor's surgery. Today, she fidgeted in her seat, looked at her watch and glared at the surgery door crossly. She was a busy woman; she didn't have time to hang around while people had major conversations with the doctor. The woman who'd gone in before her had been in there ages. What was she doing? Having her tonsils out?

Finally, Sam gave up and rifled through the dog-eared magazines on the coffee table in front of her. As *Time* magazine was the only one not dedicated to telling her how to get a man, enchant a man or cook for a man, she picked it up and was engrossed in an article on internet piracy when her name was called.

The doctor was a brusque forty-something man with tired eyes. As briskly as if she was in a ten-minute meeting, Sam outlined her symptoms. The tiredness, the pains, the nausea.

'Heavy periods too?' he asked.

'Well, yeah . . .' she admitted.

'How long have you had these problems?' the doctor said, reading through her file.

'Six months,' Sam admitted, a bit ashamed. 'I've been busy . . .' she said, breaking her own management rule about never giving an explanation to someone who didn't need one.

'Should never be too busy to look after your health,' the doctor said, looking at her properly.

Sam stared at him stonily.

He asked a lot of questions, discussed her periods, how much menstrual blood she lost each time, and the exact position of the pain, talked about her diet and her bowel movements, and then said he'd better give her a pelvic exam.

Sam lay down on the examining table, feeling vulnerable and exposed with her naked lower half pale and ridiculous looking compared to her fully dressed upper half. With practised ease, the doctor appeared not even to look at her when he came behind the curtain. His hands were cold as he palpated her belly, fingers surprisingly nimble as they splayed over her pale skin. She winced in pain.

'Does that hurt?' he said unnecessarily.

'Mmm,' she said, biting her lip.

He prodded some more and she winced again.

After a few minutes more of this, he slipped on a rubber glove, spread jelly on it and slid it inside her. Sam felt as taut as elastic as his fingers probed painfully.

Ouch! God, what was he doing? Prospecting for gold? Looking for his car keys?

'Relax,' he said.

Relax! thought Sam grimly. You bloody well try and relax when a total stranger is sticking his enormous hand up inside you! She said nothing and tried to ignore the pain as he probed from the inside.

Finally, it was over.

Sam dressed quickly. Her clothes back on, Sam felt more like herself, more in control.

The doctor didn't waste any time.

'I'd say you've got fibroids and irritable bowel syndrome,' he said brusquely, writing as he spoke to her.

'What are fibroids?' Sam asked. She knew all about irritable bowel: every woman in the gym had it. No dinner party in London ended without some discussion on the latest cure and what herbal remedy worked best. Sam was bored rigid by those conversations.

'Fibroids are benign tumours of the uterus. They can make you anaemic, which is probably why you're so tired. They cause heavy, painful periods, abdominal and pelvic pain, fatigue and sometimes painful sex.'

Sam scowled. Not a problem she had.

'The other spasms you describe are most likely the bowel problem although you can get fibroids attached to the uterine wall and they twist, which is painful. You need an ultrasound to be sure. At your age . . .'

Sam winced but the doctor didn't notice.

'. . . there are several options, myomectomy, endometrial resection, endometrial ablation, but in my opinion, the only final way to deal with them is a hysterectomy. But that depends on whether you want to have children or not.'

Sam opened her mouth to say 'I don't,' and then shut it again. How many times had she said that? At parties and to people like Hope or Aunt Ruth? Aunt Ruth, when she'd been alive, had always nodded firmly and said 'good idea, Samantha, I don't see you as the children sort.' Hope always looked sad and told her sister that you never knew when you might change your mind. Hope had desperately wanted children. Sam knew she wanted to create the sort of loving, happy family atmosphere they'd been denied as children, which seemed a bit futile. You couldn't make up for the gaps in your own childhood by reinventing yourself as an earth mother complete with a huge adoring family. Then again, Sam reflected glumly, *she* was trying to make up for the gaps in her childhood by ensuring that she *didn't* have children, so there were no small beings to feel unloved and abandoned with an unmaternal, stern adult saddled with looking after them.

The doctor was scribbling again. Sam would normally have tried to see what he was writing: she was an expert at reading upside down and sideways, the result of years of office politics where being able to read memos on other people's desks was a vital survival skill. But today, she didn't bother. She fiddled with her watch strap aimlessly.

'If you come back tomorrow you can pick up a letter for the specialist about the fibroids,' the doctor said, still writing. 'I'll get my receptionist to make an appointment for you or you can make it yourself if you've a tight schedule. When that's sorted out, it may be sensible to have tests done to check your bowels too. Just to be on the safe side.'

'About the hysterectomy thing . . .' began Sam. 'I mean, the other things you mentioned are options?' She didn't know why she was saying this. It was a bit pointless.

'Yes there are but I haven't gone into them because it might be easier to let the specialist do that. Some women are totally against a hysterectomy but you didn't seem unduly worried about the prospects of having one. At your age, women either have children or don't have them. If you'd had any fertility treatments they'd be on your file so I assumed you weren't interested.'

'Rather a lot to assume,' Sam snapped.

How could he get away with it? He should have been struck off, fired, hung, drawn and quartered. How dare he assume that just because she didn't have children yet, she didn't want any? And did she look that over the hill? Obviously.

'Are you this rude to all of your patients?' she asked drily.

'I didn't mean to be insensitive,' he said, startled. 'We can discuss all the other options, drugs to shrink the size of the fibroids . . .'

He didn't get any further.

Sam walked out of the surgery. She'd see the specialist and if he was rude to her, she'd hit him. Men.

There was no point going back to work, so she went home, stripped off her suit and changed into slobbing around clothes which consisted of an old grey-T shirt, black gym leggings and a lambswool cardigan. Taking her crammed briefcase, she sat at the dining room table to work. But her brain refused to focus on marketing reports and budgets. She kept thinking of the doctor's words. *Fibroids. Hysterectomy. Tests. Just to be sure* . . . She wished she'd asked him more but she'd been too shocked and too angry. Still, she could look it up on the internet. Honestly, what was she turning into? Two months off her fortieth birthday and she was falling apart.

She made another cup of coffee and wandered over to the dining room window to look out. The garden belonging to their house was long and narrow, almost all patio except for a wild bit at the bottom. The couple with the ground floor flat had several lovely containers planted up and even in the bad weather, the shrubs flourished.

Sam opened the window to let some air in and looked into the garden next door. It had been a complete mess for years but since He'd moved in, He'd been clearing it and now the overgrown briars were gone and a plot of freshly turned earth stood in their place. Sam leaned forward nosily to see exactly what He'd been doing and then drew her breath in suddenly. He was there, carrying a huge paving slab from the side of the house. Making sure she was partially hidden behind the big brocade curtain, Sam watched him place the slab beside a carefully laid group of others. He was laying a patio, she realized in astonishment. Who'd have thought that Mr Trust

Fund Playboy could do anything so practical. He was obviously warm despite the cold day and was stripped down to just jeans and a white T-shirt. Sam cradled her cup of coffee and watched him work. It was interesting how he did it. Each slab took ages to hammer into place and then there was a whole palaver with bits of string and some measuring implement to see if they were level. A couple of times, Sam noticed him glancing up towards her window, but he couldn't see her, she was sure . . .

After a few minutes, he stopped, looked directly up at her window and yelled, 'Are you going to watch all day or are you going to help?'

Sam shrank back from the window as if she'd been scalded. Caught out. She hadn't thought he could see her. How embarrassing! Peering carefully from behind the curtain, she saw him put down the big hammer and lope towards the house. Boy, he could lope too, those muscles rippling through that white T-shirt and those legs striding in the jeans. Levis would pay him to advertise their product, she was sure of it, because he was a magnificent animal. That's all he was, of course, an animal. A party-mad animal who screwed around with girls miles younger than him. Sam sighed. Why was she even wasting her time looking at him? Just because he'd given her goose bumps when she'd seen him that first time at the party didn't mean anything.

When the doorbell rang a moment later, the blistering noise in the quiet of the apartment made her jump. Who would be looking for her at this time of day? She was never, ever at home during the week. It had to be someone ringing the wrong bell. Window cleaners or something.

'Yes,' she said into the intercom phone.

'Delivery of flowers,' said a voice.

Sam perked up. Flowers! Lovely. Karen Storin was so kind. She'd obviously been talking to Lydia and discovered that Sam wasn't going to be back at work that day.

Grabbing her front door keys with a smile on her face at the thought that *someone* cared, she hurried out of her apartment and down to the street door. She whisked it open and gasped. There, still in jeans and a smudged white T-shirt, with a small bouquet of wild narcissi in his hand, was Him. The Man From Next Door.

'I thought there was someone here with flowers,' Sam said, still in shock.

'There is.' He handed her the narcissi, and by instinct she buried her nose in them and breathed in the delicious smell.

She looked up cautiously, seeing the narrowed treacly eyes watching her like a bird of prey watched its victim. The bird of prey effect was heightened by the hooked nose. Very predatory. She didn't know why but he was very daunting or overwhelming or something. She felt herself prickle up with a fresh crop of goose bumps. What was it about this guy? Even her skin went into meltdown when he was near.

'What are you doing here?' she asked, doing her best to get her voice back to normal.

'Since you're obviously bored and you were watching me, I thought I'd ask you to help me with my patio,' he said, eyeing her old grey T-shirt and gym leggings lazily.

'I'm not bored,' she retorted. 'I'm studying reports.'

'Looking out of the window into my back garden?'

For a brief moment, Sam tried to think of a suitably cutting and derisory retort. Nothing came to mind. She leaned against the door and sighed.

'Yeah, you're right. My mind isn't on my work today,' she admitted. 'Murderous migraine,' she lied, 'although it's gone now, thankfully.'

His handsome face creased up into a big smile, which miraculously transformed him from predatory male to friendly neighbour, despite the dark stubble on his jaw. 'I figured you were sick because you're never at home in the daytime, so I thought why not invite you over.'

'How do you know I'm never home during the day?' she asked.

'I watch you striding off down the road every morning,' he said, still with that engaging grin.

'You *watch* me?' she said, eyebrows raised.

'There's something about this neighbourhood that makes you watch people,' he said without inflection.

Sam had to grin. 'How am I supposed to help with the patio?'

'You can supervise,' he said. 'You look like the sort of woman who's good at supervising. And now that you're migraine-free, you can make the tea,' he added cheekily. 'Shall I wait here for you?'

Why am I doing this? Sam muttered repeatedly as she scurried round the flat looking for her track shoes and something warm to throw on over her cardigan. I must be mad. I don't know this guy. He could be a serial killer and he's going to lure me into his house to bury *me* under the patio! But she still went downstairs. Well, she reasoned, she was bored and at least he was company, even if he was a playboy waster. It wasn't as if they were going on a date. It was a neighbourly thing.

She was way too old for him for a start. He didn't even look at a girl unless her age was lower than her waist measurement. And probably about the same as her IQ, Sam thought bitchily.

'Ready?' he asked pleasantly as she came to the door.

'Ready,' said Sam with her most innocent smile.

He led the way round to the back of his house where the patio slabs were piled high. He'd laid about half of them and Sam had to admit that it all looked very professional. She was impressed.

'Aren't you going to introduce yourself,' she said, to hide being impressed. He held up two dirty hands ruefully. 'Forgive me if I don't shake but I'm covered with dirt and cement. I'm Morgan Benson.'

'Sam Smith,' she said briskly.

'I know,' he said.

Startled, she said: 'You do?'

'I like to know all my neighbours.' He grinned again and Sam noticed the tiny feathering of lines around his eyes, endearing crinkles that gave his face character. 'Particularly ones who disrupt my parties.'

Her face flared bright pink. 'If you've brought me here to insult me . . .'

Morgan handed her a strange oblong metal implement with what looked like three glass bubbles in it. 'This is a spirit level and I need you to help me check if I've got the slabs straight, OK? I didn't bring you here to insult you. I brought you here to make friends.'

'I've enough friends, I don't need any more,' Sam said hotly.

'Ah don't be crabby,' he said, hunkering down to examine the last slab. 'Let me show you how this thing works. The trick is to have the patio draining in a particular direction so that rain doesn't gather on it . . .' he explained.

She couldn't be angry with him, Sam realized, because he just ignored it.

'Now when the air inside the spirit level is correctly aligned in each place, then the slab is flat . . .'

By the fourth slab, Sam was a dab hand at the spirit level and was keen to lay her own slab.

'Let me have a go,' she said.

'I'll just make sure the sand is level,' Morgan said from his kneeling position. He bent over the smoothed-down sand, making a minuscule adjustment.

'I can do that,' she protested. 'I've watched you do four.'

He sat back on his knees and wiped the sweat from his brow with one muscular forearm. 'Are you always this impatient?' he inquired.

'No,' lied Sam, kneeling beside him.

'Why don't you do this one totally on your own, then,' Morgan said, smiling at her. 'I'll take a break and watch.'

Sam's eyes gleamed with pleasure. A challenge. Just what she liked.

Morgan sat down on an upturned bucket, folded his arms, stretched out his long, cement-encrusted legs, and watched. It wasn't as easy as he made it look.

'Where did you learn to do this?' she asked. 'I wouldn't have you pegged as the handyman type.'

Morgan looked at her with his lips twitching.

'And what sort of guy did you have me pegged as? A party animal type of guy, perhaps?'

'You don't appear to go to work at normal office hours and you're obviously well off enough to buy this house, so I didn't see you as the sort of person who'd know how to lay his own patio . . .' Sam knew she was getting deeper and deeper into this ludicrous explanation but there was no turning back. 'You know, I thought you'd get someone in.'

'Ah.' Understanding dawned. 'You meant that you thought I was

217

too feckless to do anything like this myself when I could pay someone else to do it.'

He had an unerring knack of hitting the nail on the head. '*I'd* pay someone to do it,' stammered Sam.

'But then you couldn't lay a patio, until now anyway,' he said. 'I can so it would be a waste of money to get someone else to do what I can do. Besides, I like working with my hands.'

I bet you do, Sam thought, imagining those long fingers trailing all over the succession of women he had in the house.

'What line of work are you in?' she asked.

'I'm retired,' he said flatly.

Bingo, Sam thought triumphantly. He *was* a trust fund guy, either that or an internet millionaire. Who else could retire at forty and who else would go round wearing only jeans and scruffy old T-shirts with holes in the seams? Mind you, if he was an internet millionaire she'd have a lot more respect for him than if he was just a waster.

'You look frozen. Would you like tea?' he asked.

She nodded.

He led the way into the kitchen, which didn't look too different from the last time she'd been there, that never-to-be-forgotten occasion.

Sam sat down on one end of a workmen's bench that was decorated with paint splatters.

'I love what you've done with this place,' she said deadpan, looking around at the cans of paint on the floor and the half-finished kitchen cabinets.

'It's the latest look,' Morgan replied, busily making tea. 'I had the place feng shui-ed and they told me that wallpaper and paint were messing up my happiness corner and that if I didn't put doors on the cabinets, I'd experience inner peace. I need chaos, apparently. Milk and sugar?'

'Just milk. Seriously though, what are you going to do with this place?' Sam asked. The kitchen was pretty much a shell but it was so light and airy that she could see how wonderful it would look when it was finished.

'Maple everywhere in here,' Morgan said, putting two mugs and a pack of biscuits on the table and pulling up an elderly deckchair for himself. 'I once lived in a house where the whole place was awash with antique pine and I don't want a shred of it here.'

'Don't tell me: you had an Aga as well?' joked Sam.

'How did you know,' he groaned.

'I can just see you in a palatial pile with an Aga and a butler,' Sam added.

Morgan looked amused for a moment, then he shook his head. With a strange glint in his eyes he said, 'Yes to the Aga, no to the butler. What sort of house did you think I lived in?'

Sam shrugged. 'Somewhere big with family silver.'

'We had family silver, all right,' Morgan said, still with that strange glint in his eyes.

Sam smiled to herself. She knew it.

'Are you going to live here when you've got rid of all the antique pine?' she asked.

'I don't know,' he said.

'Don't tell me,' Sam remarked, 'you're going to sell it for ten times what you paid for it?'

'Do you disapprove?' He ripped the top off a packet of biscuits.

'No. There's nothing wrong with that . . .'

'You do disapprove, don't you? You're a very disapproving lady, Ms Smith,' Morgan said, handing her the packet of biscuits. 'Is it having a migraine or are you always like this? I'm only asking because I like an easy life and if we're going to be friends, you'll have to tell me when you're having one of your disapproving days.'

Sam dropped the biscuits as if they were poisoned.

'I'm sorry,' he said, sounding genuine. 'I didn't mean to upset you. I was trying to be funny.'

'I'm not in the mood for funny,' Sam said tightly. She felt like a little bomb packed full of emotional explosives and ready to go off any minute. It had been an awful day what with the doctor and everything, and now this man was being horrible instead of flirting gently with her and making her feel good.

'Please stay.' He held her hand tightly.

'No,' she said, wrenching it away. 'I have to go. I'm not well.'

'I know, I'm really sorry.' He sounded it too. 'Me and my big mouth. I'm not used to company.'

Sam's eyeballs swivelled upwards with disbelief. And after the trail of women she saw wandering in and out.

'Migraine back again?'

'Er yes,' she said, glad to be let off the hook.

He grinned.

On Tuesday, Sam phoned in sick and then went to the doctor's surgery to pick up her letter of referral. The receptionist told her she had an appointment with a consultant in three weeks.

'That long?' asked Sam, aghast.

'That's quick,' replied the receptionist. 'You're going to see the top consultant in London, she's very busy. We only got that appointment because the doctor wants you seen quickly and because they'd had a cancellation.'

*He wants you seen quickly.* Ominous. Sam tried to put it all out of her mind.

She bought a couple of fat glossy magazines on the way home, and then decided to get some groceries. Proper food was what she needed. She'd do chicken breasts or something nourishing.

A wire basket hanging from her arm, she was in the vegetable department of the local supermarket when she heard a voice behind her.

'Hi there.'

It was Morgan, looking his usual disreputable self with at least two days' worth of stubble on his jaw, wearing an open-necked shirt (ridiculously cold in this weather, Sam told herself, trying not to gape at the sliver of chest visible at the open neck) and that beige suede jacket he never left the house without. She'd seen him wear it countless times. Not that she'd been looking or anything, but from her front window seat she couldn't miss him.

'Hi,' she said brusquely and turned back to squeezing avocados.

'I think that even heart massage won't bring them back to life,' Morgan remarked.

'Ha ha,' she said tonelessly. 'Ever thought of being a comedian?'

She waited for him to begin to answer then interrupted. 'Well, don't.'

'Is it a migraine or just a common or garden headache you've got today?' he asked unperturbed.

'Neither,' she snapped. Honestly, would he ever get the hint that she wanted to shop in peace?

She looked into his trolley. As she'd suspected, a huge TV dinner sat on the top. Roast beef with Yorkshire pudding and gravy. Yeuch.

Noticing her glance, Morgan picked the package up and looked at it with distaste. 'I know, this stuff is awful for you but the guy doing the plastering with me insists on eating this sort of junk for lunch.' He put it back in the basket to one side so she could see the rest of his shopping: far more vegetables than Sam had in her basket, fresh fish and a packet of dill. 'I prefer proper cooking myself.'

Sam coloured. Her own basket contained three TV dinners and she never bothered buying fresh fish. It made the apartment stink and why kill yourself cooking something smelly when you could get your weekly dose of seafood in a restaurant instead?

Since she couldn't shake him, she'd embarrass him. Marching over to the feminine hygiene products, she positioned herself in front of the tampons and studied them carefully, as if she was planning to write a thesis on applicator versus non-applicator. To her chagrin, Morgan studied them too, head to one side before he picked up a pale blue pack and put it in his basket.

'What did you do that for?' she demanded.

'You never know when you might need them,' he said blandly.

He was insufferable!

Sam threw her usual brand into her basket and marched off to the cash register.

She banged the basket down on the conveyor belt and waited.

'Hi Morgan,' said the girl on the checkout. 'How are you doing?'

Naturally, he was standing behind her. Sam turned round to give him her hard stare but he ignored it.

'Fine Tanya,' he smiled back at the girl on the cash register, showing wolfish white teeth against that dark stubble. 'How about you?'

Sam watched in disbelief. Tanya actually batted her eyelashes. She was smiling fit to burst a gut and she'd missed scanning Sam's bag of avocados because she was too busy mooning at Morgan.

Sam barely knew the name of the supermarket, never mind the names of the staff. But why was she surprised? This was the Babe Magnet she was standing beside. His house was like a homing beacon for west London's young female population. He probably knew the name of every twenty-something in the whole metropolitan area, not to mention what her favourite sexual position was and what sort of tampons she liked best!

Tanya finished with Sam's groceries and Sam thrust her credit card into the girl's hand.

She signed the docket, whipped back her card, packed up her shopping and left without saying a word.

It was too close to the house to get a taxi, so Sam struggled along the road with her four carrier bags. They weren't heavy but she suddenly felt so tired, as if all her muscles had turned to jelly.

'Do you want a hand?' he asked. He must have sprinted from the shop.

'I can carry my bags myself,' Sam snapped, knowing she sounded like an ungrateful harpy but unable to stop herself.

Morgan gazed at her thoughtfully. 'You know, Sam, for a good looking woman, you're an awful bitch. I was only trying to help.'

'Yeah well, maybe I don't need help,' she snapped back. 'I'm a grown woman, not one of your child bride types who probably need help with their shoelaces and their maths homework, OK?'

To her utter aggravation, he leaned against the wall and began to laugh so loudly that a woman wheeling a pushchair nearby crossed the road in alarm.

Sam watched in taut fury as Morgan's face creased up in mirth, making him look even more attractive, the bastard. And there was no sign of him stopping. He kept laughing and even wiped his eyes, as if she'd just told him a spectacularly good joke and he couldn't control himself.

'Stop it,' she hissed after five minutes of belly laughing. 'You're making a fool of yourself!'

'You're a really something, do you know that?' he said. 'Or as my granny used to say, "you're a caution".'

Sam picked up her bags and stomped off. It was amazing how rage could give you a fresh burst of energy. When she got to the pedestrian crossing, she allowed herself a glance back to see if Morgan was following her. But he wasn't. He'd disappeared. Feeling strangely let down that he hadn't come after her, Sam walked home, her burst of energy gone.

After she'd shoved the groceries away, she didn't feel like cooking, so she went into her bedroom and lay down on the bed to relax and read her magazines.

She woke up at half seven that evening, feeling groggy and astonished that she'd fallen asleep in the first place. Rubbing her cheek to get rid of the creases from falling asleep on a magazine, she got up and automatically looked into Morgan's back garden. She'd been such a bitch to him and she didn't know why. Well, she amended, she did know why. She fancied him, was deeply attracted to him, whatever. And because it was clear that he wasn't interested in women of her vintage, she'd gone out of her way to be horrible to him. Queen Bitch strikes again, she thought miserably.

What was wrong with her and her life? She had a fantastic new job, she was one of the few women ever to reach the position of managing director of a record label, she was tipped for career stardom and yet she still felt empty and miserable inside. No, Sam corrected herself, not empty: she was full of despair, that was it. Despair. No matter which way she looked, she could see no bright future, only the draining loneliness of the rest of her life.

# CHAPTER NINE

Darius both loved and hated opening his post. As an artists and repertoire scout, or A & R man as they were commonly known, he got sackloads of the stuff every week: demo tapes and CDs from hopeful bands and even more hopeful band managers, each one convinced that their demo would be The One. To the hopefuls, The One meant a million-pound signing and a career of number one albums and singles, not to mention wall to wall groupies and a life-style of drinking champagne in the back of limos. To Darius, The One meant the kudos of having discovered them, and hopefully promotion and an assistant to go through the demos and sort out the chaff from the wheat.

When he was interviewed by hip music magazines about his job at Titus Records – 'the best job in the world!' as the interviewer normally described it jealously – Darius rarely mentioned the down side of trawling through hundreds of terrible demos looking for something good. Scrupulous about his work, Darius refused to do what some overworked A & R people did and listen only to the first song or two. He listened to the whole demo carefully, no matter how horrifically busy he was.

'These are people's dreams,' he'd explain, when asked about this, 'it's not fair to give them a cursory listen and then dismiss them.' This wasn't a media sound bite: Darius Good was serious. He knew just what it was like to long for musical stardom and the cover of

*Billboard*. Until he'd got this job, he'd been the singer in a college band. The Effervescent Bunnies were long disbanded but Darius never forgot what it was like to send a demo off to a record company. He remembered waiting two whole months for some sort of response and when it had come, it had been a blunt form letter which the whole band had gone into gloom over. Of course, they were a terrible band, he realized now. But that hadn't made the pain of being rejected any worse.

Consequently, he was always plugged into his Discman, listening to demos, and he went through a lot of headache tablets after enduring dire songs that sounded as if they'd been recorded in the sort of register that only bats and police dogs could hear.

On the last Thursday in January, he arrived at his desk with a mild hangover after a wild session with Density. The band had had an appearance on breakfast telly that morning and he hated to think what they had looked like after a three-nightclub crawl that had involved a shot-drinking game.

Those boys could sure party, Darius sighed, easing his lanky frame into his chair. His post was a smaller pile than usual but it was full of the same brown envelopes or yellow padded ones containing people's hopes and dreams.

Darius groaned and leaned his forehead on his desk. He couldn't cope with other people's bloody hopes and dreams today. He didn't want to be kind and scrupulous; he wanted to sweep the whole lot into the bin because chances were, there wasn't a single decent song, band or singer in the lot. He'd had it up to *here* with people who thought an adequate Oasis impersonation meant they were destined for stardom. Coffee. Coffee would help, he decided, and went off to find some.

Half an hour of gossip and two sugar-saturated lattes later, Darius felt marginally more human. Ripping open the first envelope, he stuck the minidisc it contained on the player, sat back in his chair and put his trendy trainered feet up on his desk.

Not another Whitney clone, he groaned silently, as the strains of the first song started and he recognized 'The Power of Love'. He closed his eyes and listened, wishing he wasn't quite as diligent about his work. But as the singer started, something strange happened. The hairs on the back of Darius's neck stood up. The woman's voice was the most sensual, husky thing he'd ever heard in his life. Utterly untrained, of course, but the magic was there. She could hold a note as pure as a piece of Waterford Crystal and then let it drop down into a velvety huskiness that would make a bishop blush.

Darius loved it. When he'd listened to the four songs on the demo once, he listened all over again. And again, with the volume up so loud that Moll, the marketing woman next door, came in briefly to ask him to turn it down but stayed to listen, just as rapt as Darius.

'Who *is* that?' she asked.

'I don't know but she's got an incredible voice, hasn't she?' said Darius excitedly. However, there needed to be more than a voice. He read the accompanying letter from one Nicole Turner which was brief and actually offered no information apart from her address and mobile phone number. There was no picture, sadly, which would really have helped. If Ms Turner was young and a looker, with a voice like that, and if they could get the right songs for her, there'd be no stopping her. The combination of a wonderful voice and hits from the top songwriters could make it all happen. Unfortunately, that huskily experienced voice made it sound as if she'd been around a bit. The wrong age and the wrong looks would all work against her and in an industry dominated by youthful talent, Nicole Turner could fail before she'd started, no matter how beautifully she could sing. There was only one thing to do: Darius had to meet her. Casually, not too hyped up, of course. Just in case she was a velvet-voiced fifty-year-old who'd have her hopes unfairly raised by meeting the guy from a record company who were unlikely to sign her.

He popped his head round the door of the marketing woman's office.

'You wouldn't do us a favour, Moll, and not mention that demo to anyone, would you? I don't want to get people interested in case she's not what she's looking for.'

Nicole was attacking her cod and chips with gusto in the office canteen when her mobile rang. She fished it out of her bag, her mouth full of chips.

'Hebbo?'

'Er hello,' said Darius, mildly disconcerted at this muffled reply.

'I'b eabing my dinner,' mumbled Nicole. 'Thorree.'

She swallowed. 'Sorry,' she repeated.

'Nicole Turner?' asked Darius.

'Yeah,' she replied, spearing a few more chips.

'This is Darius Good from Titus Records.'

Nicole's jaw clanked open and she dropped her fork.

'Wow.'

In his office, Darius grinned. She sounded young, that was definite. 'I liked your demo and I'd like to meet up. Would that be possible?'

'Tell me when and where,' Nicole said simply.

'You pick,' he said.

Nicole was thrown. Astonished by his phone call, she couldn't think of a venue for the life of her. 'Er . . .' she stammered, racking her brains, 'er . . . the Red Parrot.'

'Seven tonight?' Darius pressed.

'Sure.' She gave him brief directions. 'I'll see you there.'

Nicole pushed the 'end' button on her mobile and groaned. What sort of a moron was she? Suggesting the Red Parrot and agreeing to meet him tonight? For a start, the Parrot was a total dive and not the place to meet a cool record company bloke who probably only ever went for cocktails in trendy members-only bars. He sounded far too posh for the Parrot. And secondly, she should have played it cool and made a date for a few days. Talk about being too eager. Stupid, stupid, stupid.

'What's wrong, Nic?' asked Sharon, sitting down with her cottage cheese salad and eyeing Nicole's chips hungrily.

Nicole rolled her eyes but there was a slight uplift at the corner of her mouth. 'You'll never guess who I'm meeting tonight.'

Contrary to Nicole's expectations, Darius was perfectly happy in the Red Parrot. Used to visiting flea-ridden venues to check out upcoming bands, he didn't care that the red brocade banquettes were faintly sticky from years of having booze spilled on them or that the table in front of him still bore the empty glasses, torn crisp packets and half-full ashtray from the last people who'd sat there. He ordered a pint and waited, looking up eagerly at each new influx of people.

Strangely, he was sure he'd recognize Nicole. Lord knew why. One minute on the phone hardly gave him a clear concept of her physically and he hadn't asked what she looked like, but Darius somehow felt he'd know Nicole the moment she stepped into the bar. She'd look *special*, he knew it.

At ten past seven, Nicole, who'd been loitering outside with an anxious Sharon so they'd be fashionably late, strode into the Parrot and smiled at the landlord behind the bar. She didn't look around, fearful of appearing as nervous as she felt. Instead, she sashayed up to the bar and leaned against it, trying to look as nonchalant as she could.

From his seat, Darius watched the girl in the sharkskin jeans and fitted leather jacket. His eyes followed her eagerly as she joked with the barman, bought a drink for herself and her short, blonde friend, and then turned to cast a cool, speculative eye over the premises. He knew instantly that she was Nicole.

She was beautiful. Absolutely beautiful. Skin the colour of caramel with high cheekbones like Nefertiti and glittering, tigerish eyes. Not much more than twenty-one or two, he guessed, but she certainly looked streetwise. Wary, almost, in spite of that cool demeanour.

The hair was wrong, he thought instantly. There were quite a few beautiful dark girls with long straight hair on the circuit. They couldn't let his Nicole look like a clone. She was far too talented for that. He could just see her hair cropped short, clustering round that beautiful skull, feathering around her high cheekbones, hair soft enough to stroke . . .

'Darius?' She stood in front of him, tall, slim and self-possessed.

Hoping he hadn't been looking at her like a lovesick calf, Darius stood up and nodded solemnly before shaking her hand.

'I'm Nicole, this is Sharon.'

'Sit down, please,' Darius said formally and cursed himself for sounding as if he was at one of his mother's garden parties. 'Do you want a drink?'

'We've got one,' Nicole said shortly.

It was weird, Darius thought. He was the one who should have been in charge and she should have been nervous, but it was the other way round. He tried not to stare into the liquid dark eyes which were boring into him and looked down at his half-finished pint instead. What was happening to him? She was gorgeous but he'd met gorgeous women before. Famous ones too.

'Have any trouble finding this place?' asked Sharon, to be sociable.

'Not really,' he replied.

Two minutes more of idle chit chat was enough for Nicole, who was not known for her patience. She had to know why this guy wanted to meet her and now that he was here, he was burbling on in his posh voice about the perils of getting a cab driver these days who knew where he was going.

'What did you want to talk to me about?' she asked brusquely.

'Well, I like your demo,' he said, still not looking at Nicole. 'Really like it. Your voice is fantastic . . .'

He felt her hand on his arm, touching him lightly. He could smell her perfume now, something seductive with cinnamon in it. He gulped.

'You really like my voice?' she breathed.

Feeling as if he was drugged, Darius looked up to see that Nicole's coolness had melted away and that she was staring at him in delight. 'You like my voice,' she repeated, as if she'd just been given the winning lottery ticket.

'Yeah,' he said, gazing at her animated face and the small, perfect mouth curved up into the most kissable smile. 'I wouldn't have come otherwise. When I heard it, the hairs stood up on the back of my neck.'

Nicole shot a gleeful look at Sharon, who was too busy gazing at Darius to respond.

'So what happens now? Do you sign me up? Do I go into a studio and record an album? What do we do next?'

The warning signal went off in Darius's head too late. 'Er . . . well, it works a bit more slowly than that.'

Nicole whipped her hand away as if she'd been burned. 'What do you mean?' she asked anxiously. 'You liked my voice.' She looked at him suspiciously, waiting for him to say that liking her voice wasn't important and that he'd come here to let her down gently.

'I do,' Darius said earnestly. 'But I'm only one cog in the wheel. We need to get more people interested and we need to see how far you'll go.'

'Whaddya mean? How far she'll go.' This time Sharon was looking suspicious.

'I mean how serious you are about music as a career,' Darius explained quickly. 'It's not all fun and parties. It's very hard work and I mean seriously hard. I've been spending some time with Density and they work their asses off.'

'Never heard of them,' Nicole said, feeling hurt and wanting to hurt back.

'You will,' he assured her. 'The thing is, you don't suddenly become a star overnight. It can take up to two years to get an album off the ground and get the marketing set up.'

'Two years,' Sharon said, aghast.

Nicole said nothing, just stared at him.

'Please don't think I'm wasting your time, Nicole.' Even saying her name gave him a shiver. This girl had star quality and something else, but he daren't mess around with things by falling for her. She was too young for that, thought Darius with the wisdom of his twenty-seven years. And she was definitely vulnerable under that cool exterior. Although if she made it in the industry, she'd soon have an even cooler, harder exterior. 'I believe in you. I've simply got to convince other people at Titus to believe in you too. I'll phone you in a couple of days, OK?'

'Fine,' she smiled tightly and pulled Sharon's sleeve to signify they were going.

'Bye Darius,' cooed Sharon as Nicole dragged her out the door.

'Did you see him?' Sharon sighed lustfully as they trudged through the rain to the bus stop. 'Bloody gorgeous face and what a bod. What do they give to these posh blokes to make them grow up like that? It must be all that rugby playing in the snow at those posh schools. And his accent. And imagine having naturally blond hair . . .' She poked Nicole in the ribs playfully. 'D'you fancy him?'

'No way. These posh guys look right through the likes of you and me. He's only being nice to us because he sees us as useful opportunities,' Nicole said scathingly.

'I don't know,' Sharon grinned. 'He was looking at you in a very interested way, like he wouldn't mind if he got the opportunity.'

'Yeah right.'

'Really he was,' Sharon protested.

'You've been reading those bodice ripper books again, haven't you, Shazz,' Nicole teased her. 'Where the handsome duke ignores the toffee-nosed ladyship they've got lined up for him and marries the housemaid with the big tits.'

They both laughed.

'I've certainly got the big tits,' joked Sharon, 'but it was you Darius was looking at.'

'Well, he can keep looking,' Nicole said as they reached the bus shelter.

'Ah Nic,' Sharon pointed out. 'He was nice.'

'You think everyone is nice,' Nicole said sharply.

'Yeah, and you're suspicious of everyone,' her friend retorted. 'The whole world isn't out to get you.'

'It's better to think that way when it comes to guys like him,' Nicole insisted. 'He's probably screwed half the female singers he knows and he's not going to have me as another notch on his bedpost.'

Sharon eyed her. 'If you ever hear that he screws singer's best friends, can you put in a word for me, then?'

Nicole grinned. 'OK, but we'll wait until he actually comes up with a meeting with someone in his office before I give him the combination to your chastity belt, milady.'

There was a chain of command at Titus and Zak, the Titus A & R director, was the person to whom Darius reported directly. In theory, at least. In reality, Zak had done his brain cells too much damage in his distant drug-taking years to be capable of directing anything and only the fact that he was Steve Parris's best mate saved him from joining an exclusive dole queue which was full of washed-up record company execs who'd been too busy doing a line of coke in the loo to realize that the music industry was now a giant corporate business and vehemently anti-drugs. Steve and Zak went way back and if Zak wanted to sign up two tramps playing the harmonica outside Piccadilly tube station, Steve would hand him the company cheque book and let him add as many noughts as he liked. Which should have meant that Zak was exactly the right person to go to with the demo of Nicole Taylor's fabulous voice. *Should have* being the important words. Because Darius knew that Zak's music of choice was heavy, eardrum bursting rock. It was no accident that Zak had developed tinnitus, the constant ringing in the ears from years of over exposure to loud music. His idea of gentle, romantic music was Aerosmith so Nicole Taylor, with her rich, throaty voice, would not be his thing at all. He'd throw her demo in the bin and some other record company would end up signing her. Darius couldn't let that happen. He wanted Nicole for the LGBK label. And for himself, he admitted wistfully. There had to be a way around things. If he went over Zak's head, Zak would go mental. But what if somebody else heard Nicole's demo by mistake. . . somebody with power who didn't care who the hell Zak was and who'd stand up to Steve Parris? There was one person who fitted that description: Sam Smith. The new MD of the LGBK label, she was supposed to be a total bitch with steel caps in her toes for kicking people, or so they said. But Darius had met her at the Density gig and she'd seemed nice enough. Not a pushover or anything, but not the hard-edged *über*bitch she was made out to be. Rumour had it that she didn't take any crap from Steve. She was the person he needed to see.

Lydia, Sam's assistant, was chirpy and said that Sam was free after lunch. 'What shall I say it's about?' inquired Lydia, who, with an eye to being made permanent, was making an effort to be businesslike. Sam got really pissed off when she doled out appointments without finding out why the person wanted to see her.

'Just business,' muttered Darius.

'Lydia, what do you mean by writing "just business"?' Sam asked crossly an hour later when she looked at her appointments book and saw Darius's name in it. She had been anxious and bad-tempered these last few days and she knew it. 'What sort of business exactly?'

'Don't fly into a huff,' said Lydia, a bit huffy herself. 'I did ask him but that's what he said.'

Sam's eyes went heavenwards. 'Fine, Lydia. He can't have long whatever he wants. I've got the Ceci girls and their mother in at two forty-five. And remember, if Mrs Ceci comes in and demands champagne, do not get her any. This is an office, not the Met bar.'

'Wouldn't dream of it,' Lydia sniffed. 'Coffee's my limit. I'm not a bloody waitress.'

Darius was outside Sam's office at two-fifteen on the dot.

He'd been planning how to approach the situation and was still in two minds. He could go for honesty and tell Sam he was worried that if Zak got the demo, he'd bin it. Or, he could pretend he was there to discuss something entirely different, casually mention a new singer he was keen on, and then seem reluctant to let Sam listen to the demo. That would be sure to pique her interest. Yeah, that was probably the best bet.

But he hadn't reckoned on Sam. After one minute sitting in front of her desk, Darius found himself feeling uncomfortable. She was gazing at him with a clear, honest gaze and Darius felt that she wasn't the person to lie to. Even if he did lie, he reckoned that she'd chisel the truth out of him efficiently. Those candid tawny eyes may have been beautiful, but they were shrewd too. He knew that a woman didn't get to run a record label by being stupid.

'What do you want to talk about, Darius?' Sam asked pleasantly.

Darius's mind ran through his options and he gulped. 'Well . . . er, you see . . .' he stammered. He decided to go for the honest approach. Taking a big breath he started: 'I've found this girl with an amazing voice,' he said.

It was Friday evening and Nicole and Pammy were watching *Bob The Builder*. Or at least, Pammy was in her Barbie nightie watching it and Nicole was staring blindly at the screen and thinking about Titus Records. And Darius. It had been over a week since she'd met him and since then, she hadn't heard a thing. Not a phone call, nothing.

Even Sharon, the only other person who knew about Darius and the sort of woman who could remain upbeat in the most depressing circumstances, was beginning to suspect that Nicole's musical career might be over before it had begun.

'Come out with me and Elaine tonight,' she'd begged earlier. 'It's Friday after all, you need to go mad and get pissed to cheer yourself up.'

'Can't.' Nicole was looking after Pammy that night as her mother had a hot date with a fireman who'd been phoning her for months asking for a date before she'd given in. 'Mum's out tonight.'

'Oh.' Sharon said nothing else. She'd often thought it was wrong the way Nicole had to take on so much of the responsibility of looking after her little sister but then, Sharon's own family was big – there had always been an older brother or sister to baby-sit so Mum and Dad could go out. But with Nicole's family, there were really only the three of them.

'Shall I come round? We could watch a video and have a take away?' suggested Sharon. An evening in with Nicole compared favourably to an evening out with Elaine, who got drunk very easily and had to be looked after thereafter. Sharon spent more time minding Elaine's handbag than she did minding her own.

'Nah, I'm going to bed early,' lied Nicole. There was no need to mention that she hadn't slept all week with misery and going to bed early tonight wasn't going to help. 'Phone me tomorrow and tell me all about it.'

The *Bob the Builder* video ended and Pammy looked hopefully at her big sister, huge blue eyes pleading to be allowed to stay up later than usual.

'No silly billy,' said Nicole, ruffling Pammy's soft hair gently. 'It's ballet tomorrow and you'll be too tired if you go to bed any later. It's half seven as it is.'

Nicole strictly enforced Pammy's bedtimes even at weekends. She remembered when she was a kid, when they'd lived with Gran, and Gran had always insisted that early bed was important for kids. Nicole used to grumble about not being allowed to stay up late like other girls at school but Gran had been firm.

'Little girls need their sleep,' she used to say, packing Nicole off up the stairs after she'd had her hot milk and special bedtime biscuit.

When Sandra had got her own home and they'd moved out, Nicole had been allowed to stay up until God knows when. Sandra wasn't a rules person. It had been strange how Nicole had felt nostalgic for those nights when she'd been tucked up in her bed in Gran's house, looking at the gleam of the streetlights from beyond the flowery pale pink curtains and telling stories to send herself to sleep, knowing that she was safe with Gran firmly in charge.

Consequently, Pammy's bedtime routine was straight out of her grandmother's textbook: a hot milky drink and a biscuit as a treat followed by a story. Pammy was currently going through a princess phase and tonight she wanted to hear the story of the princess and the pea. Reluctantly, Nicole found the book and started to read. Not that she minded reading to Pammy: she'd have read *War and Peace* from cover to cover if her darling sister wanted it. But she couldn't help but feel that all the fairytale princess books were a bad influence on small girls. All that carry on about how the prince would appear on his white horse, save the swooning princess, and everything would work out – it was plain old dangerous, Nicole thought crossly. There were no princes and the only way an intelligent princess was going to get on in life was if she got a job and could afford to tell the prince where to stuff his proposal of marriage.

However, it was hard getting this message across to a five-year-old for whom Barbie in a sparkly wedding dress with a tiara on her head was the ultimate fantasy.

With Pammy settled down to sleep, Nicole made some coffee and plonked herself down in front of the fire to see what was on the box. She flicked through the channels rapidly, bored with everything until she came across a show on cable that featured a group of young women in what looked like a school hall singing an old chart hit as if their lives depended upon it. Nicole knew that the singers weren't the original band and she watched for a moment, interested to see who they were because they looked so young and inexperienced. The story was made clear a few minutes later. The show was about the search for a pop band. Five talent scouts were auditioning eager young people for a four-member female pop band and, via subtitles because the show was in French, she realized she'd tuned into the segment where the scouts were in Paris and had pared down the competition until only twenty girls were left.

Fascinated, she turned the sound up and watched, engrossed. Her fascination soon turned to horror, though, as she watched the contenders being put through their paces. It was like watching a beauty contest where it wasn't enough to be ravishingly beautiful: the girls had to be talented too, *and* conform to whatever notion of a superband the judges had in their minds.

Nicole winced at the comments from the scouts, comments that thankfully, the girls auditioning couldn't hear: 'Her hair's terrible. With short blonde hair, maybe, but we've got enough girls with long dark hair to fill a swimming pool.'

Nicole wanted to switch over there and then but she was hooked.

Three of the girls were fantastic singers, gorgeous looking and could dance into the bargain. All three were interviewed and spoke of a lifetime of stage schools and working towards this moment. Being in a band was their lifelong dream. Nicole felt sick just watching them. How could she have thought she had a career in the music industry when compared to these girls, she was a novice?

*They'd* tap danced their way through their teens, acting, singing and dancing in an attempt to make it. *She'd* spent her teens having fun, only ever dancing round her handbag in nightclubs and doing her best to avoid any kind of job that could be termed a career. She'd sort of fallen into the job at Copperplate Insurance and to be honest, it wouldn't bother her if she lost it tomorrow, apart from the difficulty that would create when it came to the Turner family finances. She hadn't been focussed on anything much, while these girls were determined to succeed in a way that bordered on the obsessive. She'd toyed with writing a few songs and she could play her acoustic guitar a bit, but she wasn't Eric Clapton by any means.

In the commercial break, Nicole miserably examined her hair for split ends. She was a fraud. That was why Darius from Titus hadn't phoned her. He'd seen right through her and realized she wasn't in it for the long haul. He'd been able to tell that being a singer wasn't her lifelong dream.

The show came back on and Nicole watched gloomily. She didn't even *look* like any of the would-be pop stars.

They all had funky hair styles. Blonde hair styles. She fiddled with her long jet black hair some more. She wanted to be a singer, honestly she did. Maybe she hadn't longed for it with all her heart when she was a kid but she'd grown up now and she'd changed her mind. She loved singing and she'd do anything to succeed. She could take dancing lessons, she could change her hair . . . That was it. She'd change her hair. That would show everyone how serious she was.

To give her some Dutch courage, she went to the cupboard where her mother kept the booze. Nobody in 12a Belton Gardens drank very much but there was always some bottle or other stashed behind the biscuits in case of emergency or guests. Nicole pulled out a bottle of whisky. She didn't like whisky much but that was all there was. She poured some out, mixed it with orange juice and took a sip. Ugh. Horrible but necessary.

Upstairs, Nicole drank some more whisky and rummaged through her mother's top drawer. Old lipsticks, tampons with the plastic unravelling and crumpled up scraps of paper mingled with empty deodorant bottles and odd earrings. She shoved that drawer closed and opened the next one. Hair removers and an ancient looking leg waxing kit lay abandoned alongside what Nicole was looking for: a home dying kit. Sandra Turner had been mousy haired until she'd discovered bleach at the age of fourteen, although Nicole had often wondered exactly how her mother had drummed up the courage to dye her hair seeing as how Gran thought dye was the first step on the path to eternal damnation.

Her mum got her highlights done in the hairdressers these days but there had been many cash-strapped times in the past when she'd dyed it herself. Nicole examined the instructions on how to turn herself into a Nordic blonde. It sounded simple enough, she thought, not for a moment considering that her luxuriant black hair might be harder to dye than her mother's mousy curls.

Three quarters of an hour later, she peered in the bathroom mirror at the froth on her head and wondered if she was cooked. She gingerly rubbed a strand of long hair. Still not Nordic blonde. It was a bit orangey, actually. She'd leave it on for another ten minutes just to be sure. Busily imagining herself looking like an exotic Amazon with dark skin and striking blonde hair, Nicole didn't notice the time rushing by.

When she did glance at her watch again, seventeen minutes had passed.

Shit! She bent over the bath and let the shower attachment wash all the foamy bleach away. The box had recommended shampooing twice to get rid of any last traces of colour, so with her eyes still closed, Nicole groped around for the shampoo, washed twice and then rinsed. It was odd but her hair felt different, coarser and stringy somehow. She groped for the small tub of expensive conditioner. That would help. Except that it didn't. The more she rubbed, the more her hair felt like the consistency of old rope. Finally, Nicole chanced opening her eyes a bit to see what her hair looked like and the sight made her drop to her knees like a stone. The lustrous black skeins had been replaced by hanks of straw-like hair that was the colour of gone off apricots. Nicole mopped up her dripping hair and looked at it in horror. Not even apricots, more the colour of oranges. Or those neon vans that advertised plumbing services. Or Bobo the Clown's outfits. Nicole started to cry.

When her mother came home with her fireman friend for a coffee, Nicole was sitting glumly in the sitting room with her third huge whisky. Her hair, which she had been unable to comb due to its extreme dryness, was sticking out like an electrocuted bush and looked for all the world like orange hay.

'Your hair!' said Sandra, startled out of her usual apathy by the sight of her daughter's strange coiffure.

Nicole burst into tears again. 'I know, it's terrible,' she sobbed. 'I used your dye and it didn't work. I think I left it on too long.'

'Reminds me of work,' said the fireman with a grin. 'It's fiery . . .'

'Shut up,' howled Nicole and Sandra simultaneously.

\* \* \*

On Saturday evening, after a day when Nicole hadn't so much as stepped outside the front door, Sandra's friend, Charlene, arrived with a metal make-up box full of hair dyes and her scissors. Thankfully, she didn't purse up her mouth like a prune and shake her head, which was what Gran had done. Gran was still muttering about the dangers of hair dye as Charlene checked the damage Nicole had done.

'It might have been OK if you'd gone to a salon but home dying with out-of-date stuff is a no no,' Charlene said. 'With your type of hair, dying is incredibly difficult anyway.'

'Mum's always dyed her hair,' Nicole said weepily.

'There's a big difference between Asian hair and your mother's hair,' Charlene said simply.

After a few minutes of examining Nicole's head, she looked grim.

'It's ruined,' she said sympathetically. 'I'll have to cut it off before I try and fix up the colour. You do know that if you'd had this done to you in a proper hairdresser's you'd be made up for life with the compensation.'

Nicole blinked miserably. It didn't make her feel any better to realize that she'd brought her misfortune on herself.

'Just cut,' she said between gritted teeth.

Charlene cut. Long wafts of orange straw fell to the floor as she wielded her scissors expertly.

'Charlene's the best,' Sandra promised, seeing the look on her daughter's face. 'You'll love it.'

'I don't even want to ever look at it again,' Nicole said. 'I'm buying a hat.'

'You won't need a hat,' Gran laughed. 'It's a wig you'll be needing.'

# CHAPTER TEN

Despite having been unable to sleep with excitement the night before because they were finally going to the Hunnybunnikins nursery, on the Monday morning in January in question, Millie threw a tantrum and decided she didn't want to go.

She petulantly stomped her tiny, pink-socked feet and refused to allow Hope to pull her purple dungarees on. 'Don't wanna go!!' she roared at the top of her voice, flailing out her arms like an angry windmill.

Toby, who was used to such tantrums, stood in the corner of the bedroom sucking his thumb and watching with interest.

'Millie, behave!' roared Hope. She knew this wasn't the way to deal with toddler rages but she was tired herself and beyond calm reasoning. Ignoring Millie and showing her that her attention-seeking wouldn't be tolerated was what all the child care books prescribed but it was easier said than done. None of those people could have ever been in the supermarket with a red-faced, sweet-obsessed toddler from the way they advised walking away and ignoring the child in question. Hope had tried this once and as soon as her back was turned, Millie had run off down the baking aisle, rampaging through the glacé cherries like a tornado and getting them stuck in her fringe before screaming blue murder when a kind shop assistant tried to help her.

'Not going to Bunny place!' Millie roared. She stomped a bit more and Hope gave up. It was only a playgroup after all, the playgroup she'd been dreaming of for the last month as a method of giving her a teeny bit of freedom. So what if they missed the first, longed-for day?

She sat on Millie's bed and looked out the window at the wilderness of the walled garden. The brambles were less demented in the icy January weather having had their plans for world domination thwarted by the frost. She really had to do something with the garden. The chicks were going to have to go outside soon. She couldn't keep them in the scullery forever and they'd get lost in the wilderness as it was.

Something moved in the garden. Hope's eyes swivelled to the moving bit and narrowed. Something brown and small. Rabbits maybe, she wondered? Or a cute hedgehog baby snuffling adorably for food. It moved again. Fat and sleek with a long tail and cunning rodent eyes. A rat.

'Aggh!' shrieked Hope in horror. Rats in the garden! Plague, pestilence, horrible creepy things that would attack them all and converge on the house at night!

Alarmed by her shriek, Millie's lip wobbled.

'Sorry Mummy,' she said tearfully.

They had a group hug while Hope looked fearfully over the children's heads into the infested bit of the garden. Perhaps it was a one-off. Perhaps the rat was on its own and had mistakenly wandered into the Parker garden like Peter Rabbit but wouldn't stay.

The rat reappeared with a friend, both scuttling in the same direction, from the big rhododendron past a scrap of bare ground, over to a rusted old barrel. They were definitely scuttling with intent. A smaller one followed. For the next ten minutes, Hope watched the rat cabaret gloomily.

She'd thought that rats were nocturnal animals, scared of humans. It was just her luck that her rats were brazen and had no problem running around by day as if they were eagerly auditioning for a nature programme.

How had she missed them before? And what was she going to do to get rid of them?

241

She phoned Matt, to be told he was out for a walk. Hope's eyes narrowed some more. It was only half nine in the morning. What the hell was Matt doing walking around when he was supposed to be working? If this was how he spent his time in the bloody centre, no wonder he was monosyllabic when asked about how the great novel was getting on.

'Mummy, are we going to the Bunny place?' asked Millie innocently. She'd put on her dungarees herself although the fasteners had defied her so she'd stuck the straps into the neck of her pansy-printed jersey.

'In a moment, poppet,' Hope replied, leafing through the local phone directory.

The pest-control man was very reassuring.

'Don't worry, the place is full of rats. It's just a matter of keeping them in check. We'll handle it. I'll be out at midday,' he said. 'How many of them have you seen?'

'Definitely three,' Hope replied, the phone jammed under her chin as she fixed Millie's dungarees properly, 'but there could be more. They all look the same to me and there could be loads of them but you only ever see three of them at a time.'

'Do you have children or domesticated animals?' he asked.

'Children and hens.'

Cue sharp intake of breath. 'Hens,' he intoned gravely. 'This could be more serious.'

The lady in charge of Hunnybunnikins was a softly-spoken German woman named Giselle who could have come straight from central casting as a fairy godmother. She had golden curls, kind eyes and a warm motherly expression that made Hope wish that *she* was going to spend time at Hunnybunnikins as well as the kids. When Hope had met her in December to get the feel of the playgroup, she'd been charming. She was just as nice now that Hope was an hour late, flustered and anxious about the invasion of the killer rats.

'I'm sorry we're late,' Hope began. 'I know when we spoke on the phone I said I'd have them here by half nine but . . .'

Giselle stopped her. 'That's perfectly fine,' she said in her faultless

English. 'First days can be difficult. Let's get Millie and Toby settled in and then you must try some of our homemade cookies.'

When Hope finally drove off an hour later, she was comfortably full of ginger nut cookies and confident that Hunnybunnikins was going to be great for the children. They were going twice a week, on Mondays and Thursdays for the moment with the possibility of more days should Hope get a part-time job.

'I don't know what work I could get,' Hope had told Giselle. 'I've always worked in a bank or building society and since the village doesn't have one, that's a problem.'

'The summer is better,' Giselle replied. 'The tourists bring lots of jobs but now, it's not so good. Still, you never know what will turn up. Don't worry about the rats. This is the country with lots of little beasts. Good thing we don't know what else is out there!'

Rats were bad enough, Hope thought darkly, not in the least cheered up by the notion that there could be other scuttling things in the undergrowth, eyeing up her hens and her ankles.

The pest-control man surveyed the area around the old rusted barrel and said 'mm' a lot, particularly when he saw the two old beech trees in the corner. He shuffled around in the beech nuts and looked glum.

'What do you think?' asked Hope, who was wearing her jeans tucked tightly into her Wellingtons to prevent rats leaping up her trouser legs. She was also carrying a big stick to beat them off. Naturally, there wasn't a rat to be seen.

'There are signs of a lot of rodent activity,' he said gravely. 'You've got all the major things rats need: a water supply in that small stream behind the garden, food in the form of last year's beech nuts. They love beech nuts,' he added, 'and you've got chicken feed in the shed.'

'But they can't get to that,' Hope protested.

'No, but they can smell it and they love it. Rats are omnivores – they'll eat anything.'

'Even hens?' she squawked.

'No, not hens but they'll eat any food you put out for the hens and if they soil it, the hens can pick up infections which could then get passed into the eggs.'

'Oh dear.'

'Don't worry. I'll put down poison in our special tamper proof bait boxes which are only big enough for rats and that should control the them for now, but unless you get this area cleared of all this junk, overgrown briars and beech trees, you're always going to have a problem. Particularly if you have your hens out.'

'That was the plan,' Hope sighed.

She wrote him a huge cheque before he started putting down poison boxes. Feeling doubly queasy at the thought of both the state of the bank balance as well as the rat invasion, Hope went inside, washed her hands as feverishly as if she'd been cuddling the rats, and phoned Mary-Kate.

'Have the children settled into the playgroup?' Mary-Kate asked.

'Yes, but that's the least of my worries,' Hope groaned. 'We've got rats and I've got to get the garden cleared before we can get completely rid of them, otherwise I'll never be able to let the hens out. Do you know anyone who could do a job like that? I can only afford to pay around fifty pence, that's the problem.'

She could feel Mary-Kate grinning at the other end of the phone.

'I don't think that'll be enough,' she laughed.

'I'll do anything to get this sorted out,' Hope said. 'I hate rats.'

'I know a man with a machine-hire business who has a baby JCB that would clear all the briars and junk in no time but he'd want some kind of payment and believe me, Hope, you wouldn't be so quick to say you'd do *anything* to get this sorted out once you see him.'

For the first time all morning, Hope laughed. 'Unless he needs some payment in kind like his finances sorting out or money changed from dollars into euros, I'm no good to him.'

'Something will turn up,' consoled Mary-Kate. 'I better go. I've a list of prescriptions as long as your arm to fill out. The whole town is sick. Talk to you soon.'

When the phone rang fifteen minutes later, Hope didn't expect it to be Mary-Kate again.

'You won't believe it but I just had the most amazing idea,' she said. 'You know Erwin, your man with the machine-hire business I mentioned to you, well, his wife handles the office business and he was in just now with a prescription for shingles for her, God love her. She's in bits and she won't be working for at least a month. Erwin says he'll be lost without her. I've told him about you. How would you like to fill in for her?'

Hope just gaped at the phone. 'I . . . I . . .' she floundered. 'I've never done anything like that,' she said.

'You could keep the office ticking over until she gets better and he'd pay you and probably do your back garden for free into the bargain. It'd be a couple of mornings a week and it'd be a start wouldn't it?'

Erwin had sounded pleased, if monosyllabic, when he'd phoned to ask her about Mary-Kate Donlan's suggestion.

'It'll only be for the month,' he'd pointed out. 'Nothing long term, mind. The wife will be better soon.'

'That suits me fine,' Hope said. 'I'll come on Thursday.'

By half six, Hope felt as if she'd survived a maelstrom: the children starting playgroup, hiring the pest-control man and getting a new job. Matt had only been gone since nine that morning and it felt like a month. So much had happened and she couldn't wait to tell him.

The children were worn out after their time at Hunnybunnikins and Millie was already asleep on the couch, clutching a book she insisted she'd only 'borrowed' from the playgroup library. Toby, who normally ate everything his mother put in front of him, was too tired to eat his dinner and his long eyelashes kept drooping onto his cheeks as he held his plastic fork tightly.

'Come on darlings, up to bed,' said Hope happily.

A succulent pork casserole was simmering on the range, scenting the air deliciously, and in honour of her new job she had a bottle of wine in the fridge. Just a quiet night in for her and Matt to celebrate new beginnings. He'd be so proud of her; Hope smiled as she ran the children's bath. He was always worried about money these days and her wages would pay for the playgroup. Yes, some people might think she was mad working purely to pay for playgroup, but Hope knew that she needed to get out a couple of days a week. And even though she wasn't going to have much left over from Erwin's wages, if he did the garden for free, that would be a huge advantage.

For once, she got away with reading the shortest of bedtime stories. Both children were sleeping soundly before she'd reached the final page. Kissing them softly on their foreheads, she slipped out of their room and into hers. She quickly swapped her usual uniform of jeans and sweatshirt for an olive cobwebby knitted skirt and a matching tunic top. She let her hair fall around her shoulders and sprayed herself with scent.

A crunch of brakes told her Matt had arrived but instead of him getting a lift with Ciaran Headley-Ryan, it was Finula herself who dropped Matt off, clearly determined to invite herself in.

'Just popped in for a minute to say hello,' she said gaily, settling herself down on the most comfy chair as if she was there for the night.

As usual, she was dressed for a fancy dress party in flowing florals with a huge knobbly crimson cardigan over the whole rig out. It was jumble sale chic as opposed to bohemian chic.

Matt gave Hope a perfunctory peck on the cheek and threw himself tiredly onto the couch. In his faded jeans, with an old grey fleece hugging his muscular body and a day's dark stubble on his chiselled jaw, he looked more like an off-duty rock star than a would-be-writer.

'You'll have a drink, won't you, Finula?' he said, his voice low.

He was not in a good mood, Hope figured.

'Well just the one . . .' Finula said with a great show of reluctance. She batted her eyelids at Matt, unable to stop herself flirting with him. That was the effect her husband had on women, Hope realized grimly: drawn in by the movie star dark good looks, they were doubly hooked when they realized that there was a sharp and incisive mind behind the gorgeous façade.

'I'll have a glass of wine too, Hope,' Matt added.

Hope's eyes narrowed. She was obviously cast as maid servant for the night.

Her nicely chilled bottle of wine didn't last long, so Matt opened some red. The wine had certainly livened him up but he wasn't any happier, Hope thought, as she took the casserole off the range and covered it with tinfoil. He was more animated than he'd been earlier but still as tense as a tightly coiled spring, long fingers drumming the arm of the couch. As if he was brooding on some inner problem and was trying to be chatty for Finula's benefit. Not that Finula would have noticed. Drink in hand, she was leaning as close to Matt as she could get without actually sitting on his lap, telling a story about some artist she'd admired ten years ago, who was now famous and successful.

'People tell me I have a good eye for art, you know,' she said mistily before she took another big gulp of wine. 'One does one's best but it can be difficult. So many of us artistic people are forced to live in the cultural wasteland.'

Hope was pretty sure that *she* was one of the cultural wasteland people, while Finula and Matt were the misunderstood artists.

'We mustn't bore Hope talking about art. How about literature? You do read, don't you?' Finula asked her, like a patronizing aunt making the effort to talk to a not-very-bright niece. 'What have you read recently that moved you?'

'*The DIY Guide to Getting Rid Of Rats*,' responded Hope. 'It made me nauseous.'

Finula laughed throatily and Matt stared at Hope.

'Rats?' he inquired.

'I'll tell you later,' she said.

'What do you think of Matt's work?' Finula inquired, not interested in domestic details. 'I'm fascinated by his ideas.'

It was Hope's turn to stare at her husband. *She* hadn't seen one word of the famous novel but obviously Finula had. Rage bubbled up like the casserole that now sat on the worktop.

'Now Finula, don't get me into trouble here,' Matt said, uneasily. 'I haven't shown anybody what I'm working on.'

'I know, you wretch.' Finula smiled coquettishly and hit him a playful thump on the arm. 'But from the way you've spoken about it, Ciaran and I can't wait to read it. With your intellect, it'll be a wonderful novel, of that I have no doubt. I bet you're proud as punch of your husband?' she addressed Hope again.

'Very proud,' Hope said with gritted teeth.

Finula didn't go until the second bottle of wine had been drunk, waving off Matt's offers to phone a taxi by saying she had only to drive down a small country lane and she'd be home. 'They were only teeny glasses of wine,' she said gaily as she clattered out to the car in high heels deeply unsuitable for country living.

'Stupid bitch will probably drive straight into the hedge,' Hope fumed as she dumped the two wine bottles in the bin. Finula was a boring, pretentious cow. She might have thought she was talking in deep intellectual terms about art and culture but in reality, she was just wittering on and on about this exhibition she'd seen and that book she'd read in an attempt to show off. The combination of hunger, two glasses of wine, and rage that Matt had ruined her cosy evening by bringing Finula home, fuelled Hope's temper. She slammed the dirty glasses into the sink.

Matt shut the door after waving Finula off and sat down again on the couch, long legs resting on the coffee table, staring moodily into the middle distance.

'Dinner is probably ruined,' Hope snarled. 'I mean, what a stupid bloody question: "what have you read recently that moved you?" Patronizing cow!' She ripped the tinfoil from the dish and stared into the dried remains of her lovely casserole. No matter how idiot-proof they were making jars of casserole mix these days, no concoction was up to two hours drying out in a cantankerous oven.

'Even better: "*do you read, Hope?*" Meaning, are you a stupid housewife schmuck or do you have a bit of a brain in there as well?' The casserole dish hit the kitchen table with a resounding bang.

'You'll wake the kids,' Matt warned.

It was like lighting a fuse. Hope's eyes blazed with rage. 'If they do wake up, it'll give them a chance to talk to their father for a change. They've had a long day, an interesting day, come to that. But you haven't bothered to ask about them, or about my day. Oh no.' She was warming to her theme and her voice went up an octave. 'When dear intellectual Finula is here, why bother asking stupid wifey how her day was? It's much more interesting to drag the neighbourhood gossip round and get her to patronize me *and* ruin our dinner!'

'She invited herself in!' hissed Matt.

Hope could see the warning signs. She could see the muscles in his jaw working rapidly, signs that the inner tension was uncurling and was about to erupt. But she couldn't stop. Her long-nurtured hatred of Finula started seeping out.

'And you tried to stop her, right! That stupid cow is obsessed with you and it's annoying the hell out of me . . .'

'It's great to think that *something* provokes a reaction from you, then,' Matt snarled. 'It's been like living with a bloody robot for the past month. I've had more interesting conversations with my laptop than with you.'

'And whose fault is that?' screeched Hope, stung. 'You spend more time talking to your laptop than you do to me.'

'Oh gimme a break,' snapped Matt.

'You're never here to help out with the kids,' she yelled. 'You've dumped us all in this backwater and I'm supposed to run around like Martha Stewart and keep the house perfect for you. Little wifey! And when you get home, you snap my head off if I ask you how your day went!'

'Just stop it!'

They faced each other across the steaming, dried-up casserole. Hope had never seen Matt look so angry. His lips were clamped together as if he was trying to stop himself saying something he'd really regret. And then, the anger left her in a sudden rush, flowing out of her body like a bubbling stream. Hope could never maintain anger: she was too scared to. People who got angry were bad people and got dumped. What had she said? She'd hurt him, she'd wounded him and now he'd go. Oh no. A sudden surge of memory meant she recalled exactly how terrified she'd been when she'd thought he was having an affair, the fear of thinking he'd leave her. Swamped by this fear, Hope knew she had to apologize.

She reached out to touch him and say sorry but Matt was way beyond that now.

'I'm sorry for bringing you to this backwater,' he said cruelly. 'If you want to go, I won't stop you. You can always run home to Sam if you don't want to stick by me. All I wanted was support for this dream I've always had.' He looked at her bleakly. 'We'll talk about it tomorrow. I'm sure there's enough money in the account for plane tickets for you and the kids.'

Hope gasped and her hands flew to her mouth.

'Don't wait up,' Matt added coldly. He pulled his big leather jacket off the rack, flung it on and slammed the front door behind him.

What had happened? It had all got so out of control; she'd started something she couldn't stop. Hope bit her lip but the tears had started flooding and nothing could stop them. Upstairs, a child wailed. Toby. He was a light sleeper and she'd never get him off to sleep again, not now, not with her in floods of tears. Matt hadn't been serious about her and the kids going home, had he? He couldn't have been. What had she done? She should have kept her mouth shut about Finula. She should have kept her mouth shut full stop.

Matt knew he shouldn't be driving, not after the wine, but he didn't care. He drove to the top of the lane, and only then guilt over drink driving hit him and he left the car and marched the last half a mile to the village. The Widows was crammed as usual, full of a combination of locals and tourists. People who stayed in the luxury hotel up the road sometimes dropped in for a taste of genuine Irish pub life and forgot to go home. The hotel was always having to send a minibus to the village to pick up lost residents who didn't realize that Irish alcohol measures were bigger than European or American ones and who'd lost the run of themselves after the Widow herself had poured them '. . . one more for the road'.

There was one unoccupied stool at the bar and Matt sank onto it.

'Double whiskey,' he said to the young girl behind the bar. 'Jameson. No ice.'

Hers were not the only eyes to widen appreciatively at the sight of the tall, dark man in the leather jacket who'd stormed into the pub. He looked angry with that fierce scowl, but that only heightened his handsomeness.

He was sort of dangerous looking with that stubble and the dark long-lashed eyes. A fine thing, definitely. She didn't recognize him but he didn't look like any of the rich people from the hotel. From under the bar, she retrieved her handbag, checked her lipstick in a hand mirror and applied another slash of hot, sexy pink.

Oblivious to the effect he was having, Matt drained his drink in a few gulps. The Jameson hit his system like a lava explosion and he took a sharp intake of breath.

He looked up to wave to the barmaid but she was in front of him immediately, lips glistening a hopeful pink. 'Can I have another,' he said. 'Please.'

'Of course,' she breathed hopefully, not realizing that even when he was in a bad mood, Matt Parker was oblivious to flirtation.

He nursed this one briefly, holding the glass in his hand and swirling the amber liquid gently. What the hell had happened with Hope? He'd been in a bad mood, sure, but that was no reason for her to go ballistic and take it out on him. She just couldn't bear Finula and she didn't know why. Finula was harmless and her flirtation was like a balm to his soul these days. At least Finula seemed to believe he was a talented writer. Nobody else did. Lively folk music rippled all around him and the pub was rowdy, but Matt ignored it all and sipped his drink contemplatively. What he missed, he realized, was the constant excitement of life at Judd's. If you were working on a bitch of a campaign, there were others with you to commiserate and help and drain a couple of bottles of decent wine in the evening as you moaned about the client. And if you'd come up with a campaign that would win awards, there were people to tell you how marvellous you were. He missed both. Sitting on your own and writing down your thoughts was a fantastic idea in theory but a terribly lonely one in practice. He desperately missed the buzz of the office, the quick-fire wit in the creative department, the bawdy humour and the in-house jokes. And perhaps that wasn't all. He shivered involuntarily, as if someone had walked over his grave. Instinctively, he drained his glass, anything to block out the thoughts in his head, the thoughts he didn't want to face.

The girl behind the bar smiled coyly at him. She wasn't bad looking, Matt thought. Dark hair and freckles with those blue Celtic eyes. Very Irish looking. He could just see her in a Guinness commercial, laughing as she held onto a pint of the black stuff. Mystical Irish music in the background. He grinned to himself. Once an adman, always an adman. He and Dan had spent many happy hours mentally casting total strangers in imaginary adverts.

'Tampon ad, definitely,' Dan would say in the pub as they watched a couple of lithe young girls in skin-tight jeans wiggling their tiny bums as they crossed the floor.

'Chocolate bar,' Matt would counter, when one of the girls looked their way, showing off the sort of plump, pillowy lips that would look best puckered up round some type of phallic chocolate bar. Matt never knew why more people didn't complain about those sexy ads.

'You win,' Dan would sigh. 'She's perfect. Or . . . perhaps lipstick?'

They never did it with people they knew: it would be too cruel. Privately, Matt thought that the newest copywriter would be perfect as the weedy guy who didn't get the girl in a soft-drink campaign and the accounts secretary would look great trying to get stains out of her son's football shirt in a washing powder ad. And Hope? Hope would look totally out of place in a modern commercial.

She'd only work if cast in a historical setting: perhaps a shy lady-in-waiting for an advert for historical tourist sites? But historical commercials were few and far between. Hope. How would he ever tell her what was wrong? He couldn't because if he did, Hope would realize that he'd uprooted them all for nothing. The great novel was going nowhere. Matt was furious with himself and needed Hope's support, but all he'd got was a shrewish wife who didn't seem to understand that. Was Hope blind? Couldn't she see what was going on inside him?

He smiled at the barmaid, a bitter little smile, and asked for another double. He wanted to get terribly, terribly drunk.

It felt very cold but Hope wasn't sure if it was frosty or not. She'd become more used to anticipating the weather these days; if it was going to be frosty, the night sky was icily clear and you could see every star in the sky. She'd never been aware of the weather or the sky so much before. In Bath, if it was cold, she'd merely turned the heating up a notch and she'd rarely peered out of the windows at night. But with the limited heating system in Curlew Cottage, she'd got into the habit of listening to forecasts and monitoring the weather herself. If it was frosty, she needed to put much more wood in the range so the house would remain warm all night.

Tonight, Hope thought the cold might not be due to the weather. It seemed to come from inside her very bones. She'd been cold for hours now, since Matt had stormed off into the night.

Once Toby had finally gone back to sleep, she'd tiptoed downstairs and sat beside the range, her toes resting on the ledge, trying to keep warm as she waited for Matt. But he didn't come back. Midnight came and went. The pubs closed at half eleven, she knew, so he'd be home soon. Only he wasn't.

At one, she turned off all the lights except the small lamp inside the front door and made her way up to bed. Her movements slow and almost painful, she undressed and climbed into the big bed. The cold embrace of the sheets was so icy it hurt. Her feet were freezing but she'd deliberately not put on her white fluffy bed socks. Matt hated them, even though without them her feet felt like two lumps of ice. She wanted to do something to please him, something to make up for earlier. If only he came home, she'd apologize and tell him it was all her fault. She'd been shrewish, horrible . . .

Her tears wet the pillow she clung to, trying to imagine it was Matt's warm body. She watched the luminous hands on the clock crawl round to two and then three before she fell into an uneasy sleep.

The peal of the alarm made her sit up in bed in shock. Half seven. The time Matt usually got up. She was shocked to realize that his side of the bed hadn't been slept in.

Normally, Hope managed another ten to fifteen minutes in bed before Toby and Millie launched themselves at her, grumpy or delighted, depending on the mood. But this morning, she could hear them downstairs, already tucking into their breakfasts she deduced, from the noise of spoons clattering into bowls.

She pulled on her candlewick dressing gown, the one that made her look like the Michelin Man's fatter sister, and dragged herself downstairs, prepared for the disaster of her two children making their own breakfast.

Instead, Matt was there, whisking up some eggs while the kids sat sedately at the table with cups of milk. He looked terrible, as if, whatever he'd been up to all night, sleep hadn't been on the agenda. Hope's heart hardened as she looked at him.

He hadn't phoned or anything, she'd been sick with worry, thinking he'd driven the car into the ditch or was lying in a pool of blood somewhere. And now here he was, blithely unaware of what he'd put her through, making the children's breakfast as if he did it every morning.

Saying nothing, she marched over to the kettle and switched it on.

'Mummy, Daddy's making Fwench toast,' announced Millie happily.

Is he now, thought Hope grimly. 'He better tidy up after himself,' she hissed.

Matt gave her a long, hard look which Hope ignored.

She made a cup of instant coffee and marched silently back upstairs. Let Matt look after the children for a change; she was going to go back to bed and read.

But this plan, which had always seemed such a nice one because she never got the chance to do it, wasn't as enjoyable as she'd thought. Instead of being able to relax with her detective novel, she sat and simmered, listening to every word from the kitchen, all the while wondering where the hell her husband had spent the night. She wouldn't ask him: no way. It was up to him to tell her. If he didn't tell her, she'd never ask. Never.

The cold war continued all week. Every morning, Matt was gone before Hope had got the children dressed and ready. Every evening, Matt was coolly polite to her, inquiring about the children's behaviour as if the pair of them were distant acquaintances meeting on the street. He'd just grunted when Hope told him about her job. She cooked dinner mechanically and they ate in silence, with the television on in the background. In bed, they lay like statues, each one at the farthest possible edge, determined not to let so much as a big toe mistakenly reach across the expanse and touch the other person.

Finula had obligingly told Hope that she'd been delighted to give dear Matt a bed for the night after the row.

'Artistic types can be hell to live with,' she'd said, clearly thrilled to have insider information on the Parkers' family life.

Hope had agreed with that.

Men were so good at war, Hope realized sadly on Wednesday afternoon as she peeled carrots for dinner. They could sustain it for much longer than women.

She longed for the battle to be over but for once, and possibly for the first time in her life, Hope resisted the temptation to rush up to her husband and beg forgiveness so that life could go back to normal. *He* was wrong this time after all; she couldn't plead for forgiveness when the fault was Matt's. She'd done that all her married life and for the first time, she realized that it was a mistake. The pattern had to break. Or something had to break.

But although Matt was the one in the wrong, he carried on as if he was furious with her for something.

On Thursday, she drove Matt to the artists' centre in the now customary stony silence and then took the children to Hunnybunni-kins. The eagerness with which they raced in to meet Giselle made Hope aware that the cold war was having an effect on them. How could it not? No matter how hard she tried to behave normally when the children were present, the atmosphere in the cottage was positively Siberian. It would have to stop tonight, she decided firmly. They'd have a frank discussion with no abject apologies on her part, and they'd sort it out. Feeling slightly more upbeat than she had all week, Hope drove on to her first morning's work.

Erwin Donald's machinery hire business was situated ten miles outside Redlion on the Killarney Road. The office was a cold looking concrete structure attached to the enormous, steel-doored garages where the machines were kept. Hay balers and harvesters cost hundreds of thousands of pounds and few farmers could afford them, which was why men like Erwin made money hiring out machinery.

But February was a quiet time on all fronts. The weather was generally too bad for even building work, which meant there wasn't much call for any of Donald Machinery's wares.

'We just need someone to keep the place ticking over until Moira gets well again,' said Erwin, a giant of a man in his fifties with a shock of red hair and an explosion of freckles on his face. 'It's really only answering the phones and that. Moira was going to get the files sorted out for the tax man before she got sick,' he added, as he switched on the light in the office.

Hope bit her tongue to stop herself gasping with the cold. The bare little room felt icier than outside. No wonder poor Moira had got sick. The only miracle was that she hadn't succumbed to double pneumonia before shingles. Shivering, Hope looked around at the forlorn white walls, the big steel filing cabinets and the old linoleum on the floor and hoped there was a heater behind one of the two elderly wooden desks.

'We can have the office phone switched through to the house, you see, so we didn't spend much time here,' Erwin said apologetically as if noticing the desolation of the office for the first time. 'There's a kettle and teabags and there's a toilet down the hall.' He dragged an old hot air heater out from under one of the two desks and switched it on. Hope half expected it to fuse the electricity system but after a few moments, it began to belch out warm, fusty air. When Erwin had explained how to deal with phone callers, and they'd arranged a time for him to come to Curlew Cottage with the JCB, he left. Hope stared at her little empire and shivered some more. The pale blue woollen polo neck and plain black trousers that had seemed business-like earlier weren't adequate protection against this place so she left her coat on.

Two cups of tea later, the phone hadn't rung once and Hope was bored out of her mind. Was this what she'd put her two beloved children into a playgroup for? To sit in a freezing office for two mornings a week and look at a silent phone? There wasn't even a radio to amuse herself. She looked at her watch. An hour had crawled by. Two more interminable ones to go. She toyed with the idea of phoning Mary-Kate to ask if Erwin had really needed help or if Mary-Kate had bullied him into it but perhaps that was a bit paranoid. As she couldn't face another cup of tea, Hope prowled around to keep warm and began opening filing cabinets. Erwin hadn't asked her to do anything other than answer the phone but she had to do something to earn her wages or she'd go mad with boredom.

The first filing cabinet drawer went back ten years and seemed neat and tidy with files labelled tax, accounts, outstanding, etc. Hope opened the second drawer which, according to the label, contained papers from nine years ago. The note was accurate: the papers were nine years old. They weren't filed however. They were just jumbled on top of each other. In disbelief, Hope lifted some out, little slivers of paper drifting out from the haphazard pile and fluttering to the floor as she did so. She flicked through the papers and realized that everything from bills and receipts to catalogues and price lists was jumbled up in the pile.

She checked the third drawer. Still the paperwork of nine years ago and still messy. She began to see why Moira had developed an illness rather than cope with the tax forms. Hope smiled. She now had a task. Rolling up her sleeves, she sat down and began to sort through the paperwork.

By half twelve, she'd dealt with four phone calls and had filed one drawer with ruthless efficiency. There was something very satisfying about sorting out such utter mess, she thought. If she was doing it every day, she knew she'd probably have a different view, but for now it had been enjoyable. Deep in the realms of technical details and uncomplicated pieces of paper, Hope had forgotten the war with Matt. Bits of paper didn't give you reproachful glances or make you feel guilty. They just lay there waiting to be assigned a proper place.

She left an explanatory note for Erwin with his phone messages adding that she'd done a bit of tidying up, then she switched off the heater and left, feeling strangely satisfied.

Mary-Kate's assistant, a shy young man with the most un-Irish name of Otis, was in the middle of serving a customer when Hope entered the chemist, so she sat on the chair beside the prescription counter and waited, feeling impatient and eager to tell someone about her morning.

'Mary-Kate said you're to go through to the back,' Otis said when she'd asked for Mary-Kate.

Surprised at this, Hope hurried through, expecting the aroma of her friend's favourite blend of coffee to be scenting the air. Instead, the coffee maker was off, the gas fire was off and Mary-Kate was just pulling her raincoat on.

'Sorry to barge in,' Hope said, immediately apologetic. 'I just wanted to tell you how I'd got on at Erwin's. I can see you're on your way out so I'll let you get ready.'

'What are you like?' said Mary-Kate fondly. 'It's you I'm going out with. We're going to the Widows for a sandwich to celebrate your new job.'

Hope felt absurdly pleased. It was so nice that somebody appreciated her. 'How did you know we'd be celebrating?' she asked.

Mary-Kate laughed. 'Stop with all the daft questions and tell me how you got on with Erwin.'


Buoyed up with new found energy, Hope took the children for a walk in the afternoon. When they got home again, they were so tired after the walk and their morning in the playgroup, that they were both happy to sit down and play quietly without murdering each other. Hope decided to tackle the ironing.

After an hour of ironing fiddly toddler clothes, all of which were rock hard having been washed in the lime-rich local water, she felt both virtuous and tired, yet she still had one more job to do: cook dinner.

She flicked through her *Queen of the Kitchen* book for something simple. Everything she liked the look of involved ingredients she didn't have and the recipe for stir fried pork – which she *did* have – required ginger, which she didn't have. Blast. Slamming the book shut, Hope decided that working women didn't have time for cooking and she opened one of her favourite jars of instant dinner mix. It was nice to be a working woman again. When the pork was bubbling away and seeing Millie, the main mischief maker, fast asleep on the big armchair while Toby was colouring in, Hope rushed upstairs to check her e-mail. She'd got into the habit of checking it every day to see if Sam or anybody else had been in touch. When she'd left Bath, she'd promised to keep in touch with her friends and had had quite a few e-mails wishing her good luck, Happy Christmas, or asking her how she was getting on. Now Betsey had written and Hope clicked on the message eagerly: Betsey's correspondence was always a howl.

*How are you doing in darkest Kerry, she wrote. God, it must be lovely having got out of the rat race. I'm up to my tonsils with a huge women-in-politics feature and haven't had a moment to write since Christmas. Dan's working on a beer campaign and he's driving me mad. You know what he and Matt get like when they're being creative. Total nightmare. Dan says he can't remember what it's like to have a family dinner at home because I'm either working late or he is.*

*And we've got the Bionic ad awards next Saturday night and I'm longing to hit London and Harvey Nicks to get something new. You know what the competition will be like and if I'm not dolled up to the eyebrows in Chloe or something, I'll be labelled an old hag forever. Remember last year when Erica turned up in that old pink velvet thing that looked like her granny knitted it? Dan will be mortified if I don't get glammed up but I don't have the time. Boo hoo.*

*How I envy you being able to slob around with the kids and not worry about award ceremonies, nannies, nurseries or having your eyeliner straight in the morning. What bliss. Have you met any other mums? I hope you're making friends. Are coffee mornings still a big thing for non-working women? I was thinking of doing a feature on them. They sound so seventies, don't they. Do tell us how you're getting on and if you two are planning a trip back to civilization anytime soon,*
   *Ciao,*
   *Betsey.*

Hope glared at the message. *Back to civilization?* Where the hell did Betsey think they were – the Congo four hundred years ago? And as for *'have you met any other mums'* and *'how I envy you able to slob around . . .'*

What sort of twilight zone was Hope supposed to be in now that she'd left work? Had giving in her notice meant she'd traded in her brain and her dressy clothes as well, turning into a zombie housewife from hell with nothing on her mind but cleaning out the fridge? Betsey had never stayed at home with her kids for more than the statutory maternity leave and obviously reckoned that anyone who did was insane or stupid. Or both.

Hope switched off the computer and stomped downstairs furiously. She was so cross that when Matt arrived home, she forgot the cold war and launched into an impassioned tirade about the e-mail.

'Honestly, who does she think she is?' Hope finished as she slopped pork onto plates. 'It's as if we've been marooned a zillion miles away from civilization and are running round in grass skirts while the natives beat drums around us. And how patronizing to assume that anyone who stays at home with the children has a lobotomy.'

'It can't be that bad,' Matt said placatingly, pleased that Hope was talking to him again. She'd made the first move, therefore he could now afford to be magnanimous and talk back. He still could barely believe she'd kept up the silence all week. Once, Hope would have been begging for forgiveness within minutes of a row. She was changing, subtly, but still changing. 'I'll have a look at her e-mail.'

He stomped downstairs a few minutes later. 'Stupid bitch,' he muttered.

'You see, I knew you'd think it was over the top,' Hope fumed.

But what had upset Matt wasn't the reference to coffee mornings or the implication that they were living in the middle of nowhere because they weren't in the UK any more. No. It was that casual reference to Dan's beer commercial and the excitement of the advertising awards. Matt longed to be in the thick of it all again with an intensity that shocked him. He craved the thrill of the awards, where everybody drank too much and pretended to be blasé about the Best Creative Team gong, even though they were desperate to win. He yearned to be in the middle of a brainstorming session on whatever damned beer it was, with ideas rippling around his head like aftershocks from an earthquake and everybody ad-libbing and joking around the table, brilliant minds honing ideas until they were as sharp as Sabatier knives.

Hope put her arms around him, suddenly realizing that she'd broken the ice despite her vow not to. Oh well, it was better this way and she was proud of the fact that she'd made her point by remaining angry with Matt for so long. 'I'm glad we're out of that particular rat race,' she lied. 'It's better here, isn't it?'

'Yes,' lied Matt in response, returning her hug. 'Much better.'

# CHAPTER ELEVEN

On Monday morning, Nicole stalked into work with her short feathery hair a glinting copper colour. The hideous orange had been replaced by subtle shades of dark burnt umber mixed with gleaming metallic tones, all of which looked absolutely stunning against Nicole's café au lait skin. Even better was the cut which clung to her perfectly shaped head and showed off cheekbones to die for. She looked utterly different from the girl who'd left the office the previous Friday. Always beautiful, she was now stunning, thanks in part to hair that would make heads turn.

'Holy shit,' said the receptionist in astonishment as Nicole walked past in tight black trousers, high boots and a teensy faded denim jacket clinging to her slender body.

'What happened to your hair?'

'I fancied a change,' said Nicole. She and Sharon has agreed that this was the best response because Nicole was far too embarrassed to admit that a home dyeing accident had actually been to blame. Except where the hell was Sharon? They'd been supposed to meet in the café across the road so Nicole would have some moral support when she braved the slagging from her workmates.

'You the new mascot?' demanded a guy from new business as she got into the lift. 'Copperplate, copper hair, geddit?'

'It's fashion,' said Sharon, panting as she just made it into the lift in time. 'Don't men have fashion too?' she added, then, staring disgustedly at the man's balding head, added: 'you'd give your eye teeth to have some hair so you could dye it!'

'Bitch,' he snapped.

Nicole gave him the finger as she and Sharon fell, giggling, out at their floor.

'What happened to your hair?' gasped every second person in shock when they spotted Nicole.

'It's lovely,' breathed the girls who sat nearest to Sharon and Nicole.

'I wish I was brave enough to do something with my hair,' said a pretty Indian girl named Shirin who had long black hair just like Nicole's. 'My father would kill me if I dyed it.'

Nicole's face burst into a big, rueful smile. 'That's about the only advantage of not knowing your father!' she joked.

'Sinclair at nine o'clock!' hissed Sharon, spying Miss Sinclair advancing on the cheerful little group.

Faster than mice who'd noticed a creeping cat, the gang scattered and flung themselves into their allotted seats. They needn't have worried. Nicole was Miss Sinclair's real quarry. What had the stupid girl done with her hair?

'Your hair,' said Miss Sinclair in disgust.

'Yes,' smiled Nicole, the smile not reaching her eyes, 'hair. I have hair. I got it cut.'

Grim in the face of such cheekiness, Miss Sinclair growled deep in her throat. 'It wasn't the cut I was talking about,' she said icily.

'Don't you like the colour?' Nicole asked innocently, knowing that there was nothing Sinclair would have liked more than to have her fired for breaking some stupid workplace appearance code. 'Lots of people dye their hair,' she said, looking pointedly at Miss Sinclair's hair where an inch of dandruff-riddled mouse showed through the dark brown. 'It's not a problem for women of Indian heritage to dye their hair, is it?' she added wickedly and had the satisfaction of seeing the bitch step back nervously. She knew that Sinclair picked on her because she didn't like her, but ostentatiously playing the race card would serve the old cow right.

Miss Sinclair's nostrils flared. 'Don't be ridiculous. I was commenting on your hair, that's all. But the denim jacket is not allowed. You know the Copperplate rules: no denim.'

Silently, Nicole shrugged off the jacket, revealing a white T-shirt, the thin fabric of which did absolutely nothing to hide the high, braless breasts with erect nipples underneath.

Miss Sinclair's eyes really did pop then, which made Nicole grin. There was no rule about not wearing a bra, now was there?

When Sinclair had stormed off to the top of the room to make someone else's life hell, Nicole phoned Sharon up.

'That cow,' she hissed. 'The sooner I get out of here the better, because I am going to end up in jail for murdering her one of these days.'

'Cheer up,' said Sharon kindly, 'when you're a big singing star, you can bitch about her to everyone you see and she won't be able to do a thing.'

'Yeah right,' Nicole said gloomily. 'Hell will have frozen over before I'm a big singing star.'

'You shouldn't have said anything about Indian women,' Shirin chided her later when they met in the ladies' at one minute past one. 'My father says it's wrong to claim special treatment on account of our race.'

'Well, Shirin, your dad sounds like a real old pet but although I have fifty per cent Indian blood in me,' Nicole pointed out breezily, 'I'm West London through and through. I never even met my dad. The only culture in my house is my gran's cultured pearls.'

'I am sorry for you,' Shirin said.

'What's she sorry for?' asked Sharon, coming in to put on some lipstick.

'Nothing,' muttered Nicole. What was Shirin on about? Just because she didn't know her dad and anything about his culture, didn't mean anything. She got plenty of culture from her gran, anyhow: she could sing the 'Old Claddagh Ring' and any number of Irish traditional songs thanks to Reenie's training. What else did she want?

It was a long, dull day. Nicole got bored by half three and began circling ads for other jobs in the evening paper. When Sinclair prowled around, she didn't even bother to hide the paper, half willing the supervisor to fly into a rage and fire her. Nicole was fed up to the teeth with Copperplate.

It was all Darius Good's fault, she thought crossly. If he hadn't come along and given her false hope about her singing career, she'd still be happily working away, joking with Shazz and the gang, playing tricks on Sinclair and not giving a damn about life except to hope Friday came around as fast as possible.

Now, she'd had a glimpse of another life, and she was hungry for it. She didn't want to be stuck in this office for the rest of her days.

At coffee break, she turned her mobile phone on – they were banned from having them on for personal calls during working hours – to check if there were any messages.

'You have no messages,' cooed the automated telephonist.

Nicole was so miserable that she didn't even bother turning the phone off again.

It was ten to five when the mobile began to bleat from the depths of her rucksack.

'Where is the damn thing?' hissed Nicole, poking around in the rucksack looking for it.

'Yes?' she snapped, pushing the 'yes' button.

'Hi Nicole, it's Darius Good from Titus.'

Nicole straightened up in her seat. Who cared if Sinclair saw her on a personal call.

'So, what's the story?' she said casually.

Darius couldn't hide the excitement in his voice: 'Can you come in tomorrow and meet the boss? I know you've had to wait a few weeks to hear from us but the boss, Sam Smith, has been really busy. She loves your voice, by the way.'

'She does?' Nicole beamed.

'What time tomorrow?'

'Ten?'

'Perfect. Give me the address, will you?'

When she'd written it down, she inquired: 'Will you be there?'

'You bet. You're mine,' Darius said. 'I mean,' he stammered, 'that I discovered you . . . that, I brought you in . . . you know what I mean.'

'I do,' said Nicole huskily. 'I'm looking forward to it.'

She hung up and grinned at Sharon.

'Get your coat, Shazz, we've got to hit the shops.'

'It's not half five for ages,' Sharon protested.

'We'll sneak out,' giggled Nicole.

'I can't.'

'Ok, I will and give me a buzz on the moby when you get out and we'll meet. I've got to buy a very special outfit.'

Nicole unbuttoned the top three buttons on the deep scarlet cling-ing shirt dress she'd bought in Next the previous day. The black leather knee-high boots she'd had to buy to go with them had been way out of her price range but, she'd thought as the assistant in Russell & Bromley scanned the price tag, what else were credit cards for?

Sharon had made the ultimate sacrifice and loaned her older sister's cherished Prada handbag, on the proviso that it was back in its place in the wardrobe by that night or Tina would kill her.

'You'll look a million dollars,' Sharon had sighed reverently when she saw Nicole wearing the whole outfit, including the handbag, which had been smuggled out of Tina's wardrobe in a high security operation.

Now Nicole sat in the chrome and smoked glass expanse that was the Titus reception area and tried not to look too awestruck as people, all trendily dressed, rushed to and fro, talking at the tops of their voices on mobiles or to each other. A particularly glamorous woman with a blunt platinum blonde bob, and distressed leather trousers that Nicole knew were D & G, sashayed past, clutching the latest electronic organizer in purple-tipped fingernails.

Nicole would have loved to have asked the receptionist who the woman was and what she did, but Darius appeared at that moment and Nicole didn't want to appear gauche.

'Hi,' she said calmly, as if she was quite used to sitting in record company lobbies waiting to find out if she was going to be offered a record contract or not.

'Hi,' he said back to her,

Nicole ran her eyes over Darius. He looked even better than he had the last time.

His fair hair was shorter and fashionably spiky and he was one of the few people she knew who suited casual shirts worn open over jeans. His welcoming face was warm and friendly and he looked like he was ready to find a sunny spot in Hyde Park and lie down on the grass with a bottle of wine and Nicole, with bees buzzing lazily around them as they stared deep into each other's eyes.

'I love your hair,' he said admiringly.

Her reverie interrupted, Nicole smiled, hoping that he never heard the true story of her haircut from hell.

She felt her cool façade wobble as Darius led her to the fifth floor where, he explained, Sam Smith, Sophie Lanson, Nadia Vieri and various other members of the team were waiting to meet her.

'Like a group of people?' Nicole said, wishing she could smoke.

'Yeah, well, everyone wants to meet you and afterwards we'll probably have a chat with Sam on her own. She's tough but she's cool, I promise. She loves your voice.'

'You said that before,' Nicole pointed out through chattering teeth. 'What does that mean precisely? What's going to happen next?'

'What it means is that if Sam agrees, we'll sign you for a deal where you go into a studio and work with songwriters and producers on songs and, if it's all good enough, we'll release singles and hopefully, an album.'

'I don't have many songs, that's the problem,' Nicole said. 'I've written a few but nothing incredible.' She might as well be honest. The night before, she'd gone through her entire catalogue of songs and realized that they were all terrible.

'We could look at your songs, but if they're not up to scratch, don't panic. Lots of artists don't write their own music,' Darius comforted her. 'That's fine. You've got the voice, that's what matters to us.' He didn't add that LGBK was so keen on Nicole because their last two young British female singers had failed dismally. They needed young blood and they needed a hit singer. If Nicole was what they were looking for and was successful, then they'd all be delirious but only time would tell.

'Why do you keep saying "artist"?'

He shrugged. 'That's what we call singers and musicians.'

'Oh, like piss-artists?' joked Nicole.

She stopped joking when she went into the big, modern board room which was ten times classier than any part of the Copperplate office block. Seated around a large table were more trendy people, looking at her intently. In one corner sat the platinum blonde she'd noticed in reception. Nicole gulped and then took a deep breath. This was her chance; she'd show them.

'She's fantastic,' Sam said to Karen Storin afterwards when Darius was showing Nicole where the ladies' loos were. 'She's a bright kid and she knows what she wants.'

'And she's utterly stunning looking,' sighed Karen. 'She could be a model. If the music works and if she's got what it takes, then we could go a long way with Nicole.'

'I hope so,' Sam said fervently, 'because we've spent a fortune on Density and I have a feeling that they're not going to go a long way. We need a sure-fire, no hassle hit act to make up for those boys.'

'Did they like me?' Nicole asked Darius anxiously as he escorted her to Sam Smith's office. She'd given up any pretence of being ultra cool with him. It was clear that he wanted her to succeed just as much as she did.

Darius beamed down at her. 'They loved you, I told you they would.'

'So we're going to work in the studio and record some songs and see, right?'

'Just a couple,' Darius said, 'and then Sam will see if she can offer you a deal.'

'I don't know if I can stand the waiting,' Nicole said impatiently.

'Look, if you can sing even half as well as you did on your demo, then you're a dead cert, I promise.'

Sam's office was a lot like her, Nicole thought: immaculate, businesslike and without any frills. There were no photos of kids clustered around her desk, no carefully tended pot plants hanging from filing cabinets, no watercolours on the walls: just a seating area with a table, a huge, clear desk and platinum singles on the walls. Sam was definitely a tough cookie, Nicole decided. Small, slim and elegant in what was obviously a dead expensive grey suit, Sam was very attractive looking but she gave off vibes that said she didn't take any bullshit. Nicole liked that, even if it was a bit daunting.

But Sam had been really nice to her all along, which was a good sign.

'What did you think of all that?' Sam asked her when the three of them were sitting down at the table.

'It made me a bit nervous to be honest, all that talk about voice coaches and choreography and stuff like that.'

'I'm delighted you were nervous,' Sam replied, to Nicole's astonishment. 'This is a serious business and we're going to be asking you to give up your job to work with singing coaches and producers to record songs, get an act together, work with a choreographer, all of which comes with a guarantee of exactly nothing.'

Nicole blinked.

'You'll get the advance for signing the contract, assuming we do sign you, but if it doesn't work, after that, it's goodbye. This is a tough business and I don't want you to go into it with your eyes closed, Nicole.'

'I'm not stupid,' Nicole said hotly.

'I didn't say that,' Sam was calm. 'I can tell you're anything but stupid. But you'd be surprised at how many people think they're going to be a huge star and when it doesn't work out – and there's a high failure rate in the music industry for your type of act – they're heartbroken and astonished. This isn't telling you that you're going to fail,' Sam was speaking very intently now, 'this is just to make sure you're aware of the possibility of failure.'

Nicole looked a bit shocked.

'Cheer up,' Sam said. 'I have every faith in you, and in the LGBK label. We've a great team here and if we can't make it work, Nicole, then nobody can. Nobody can break an act like LGBK, I promise you. Right, first things first, you need a manager. Darius, what's the story about management for Nicole?'

When Darius and Nicole went down to the lobby in the lift half an hour later, Nicole felt as if she'd been in the presence of a tornado.

'She's impressive,' Darius said, 'but I hope she didn't scare you?' He looked anxiously at Nicole, hating the idea that she might be upset.

But Nicole's feline little face was alive with exultation. 'No,' she said, 'it was wonderful. I'm even more determined than ever to make this work!'

Sam could feel the familiar nagging pain growing in intensity, gnawing at her insides, spilling out from the centre of her belly into a dull, ceaseless ache in her lower back and her entire pelvic area. If there was a time and a place for everything, this wasn't it. The Density album launch was being held in the hottest rock venue in town and the place was jam packed, although it was hard to tell if it was packed with the right sort of people. There were at least three hundred milling around, drinking free drinks and eating free canapés, but if they weren't the top media people, the correct rock show hosts and basically the *right* people, it was a waste of time.

Sam had to make a speech, a short one, luckily, before Steve's. Which was why it was not the time to feel utterly crippled with oncoming period pain. Another wave hit her and she was suddenly terrified the damn thing would start and she'd ruin her skin-tight beige trousers. Almost stumbling in her haste to get to the loos, she cannoned off Mrs Roberta Ceci, mother of Enchanting, and absolutely the last person Sam wanted to see right now.

'Sam,' said Roberta, holding up a talon. 'I need to talk to you . . .'

'Sorry, can't right now,' gasped Sam and fled, leaving Roberta Ceci looking angry, which wasn't unusual.

In the loos, Sam stayed in the cubicle for a long time, glad she'd learned to carry tampons with her all the time nowadays. She was certainly living the boy scout motto: be prepared. She dry swallowed a painkiller and sat down on the toilet lid, hoping the pain and the faintness would go away. These bloody fibroid things were killing her. Ever since she'd seen the GP, she'd began to trace backwards and remember all the other times when crippling period pains had made her life a misery.

There had been many occasions, she realized, thinking of the back ache and the dull gnawing in her pelvis that she'd tried not to notice at the time. Or had been too busy to notice. Her appointment was in nearly three weeks' time and, not for the first time, she began to wonder if she shouldn't have insisted on being seen by a consultant sooner. She knew there was a crisis in the National Health Service, but she was going privately and had enough health insurance to skip the queue, surely. Then again, it was probably nothing and she was worrying needlessly. She'd look like a neurotic woman if she rang up and frantically tried to change her appointment now. Her GP's secretary *had* insisted that this was the earliest one they could make for her.

After ten minutes, she felt marginally better and emerged from the loo. The sight of her ghostly white face in the mirror made her realize she needed to slap on a bit of blusher to disguise how she felt. Unfortunately, Sam was not the sort of woman who carried lots of make-up in her sleek handbags, so she had to make do with putting a few dots of pink lipstick on her cheekbones and rubbing it in. The repair job didn't really work but it was dark in the club, so hopefully nobody would notice.

Outside, the time for speeches had clearly arrived and Sam could see Steve standing at the backstage door, looking around furiously. Sam rushed over to him.

'Sorry, I was giving an interview to the *Mirror*,' she lied.

Placated, Steve pushed open the door and they went onto the stage. Density were waiting in the wings, ready to perform as soon as Steve had told the world they were the hottest band on the planet. It took all of Sam's professionalism to smile, shake hands with the band's troublesome manager, and tell the band how incredible they were. The problem was that she had a bad feeling about Density, a feeling which magnified every time she met them. For a band who'd never sold a record, they were too smug by half. And if they failed, they'd probably bring her down with them.

Her speech lasted two minutes, Steve's lasted five, and then the band were cranking up their guitars and roaring at the crowd.

'I love those boys,' yelled Steve to Sam over the noise.

'Me too,' she said cheerily as they left the backstage area.

Mrs Ceci appeared like a bad penny and collared Sam, her face purple under a heavy layer of Max Factor.

'Don't think you can just walk out on me like that!' she squealed. 'I need to talk to you and I won't be pushed aside . . .'

Sam had had enough. She moved slowly forward until her face was only inches away from Roberta Ceci's. 'This is an album launch and I'm working,' she breathed. 'I do not know what you're even doing here because I did not see your name on the guest list, but if you wish to speak to me, you can phone my assistant at the office and, *if*,' she emphasized this, '*if* you have anything valid to say, then I'll see you. Do you understand?'

Roberta Ceci's eyes widened. She understood all right.

'And by the way, you can stop phoning my staff and giving them hell,' Sam added. 'If you have something you want to say, say it to me because I won't take any crap from you.'

After another half an hour, Sam slipped out and hailed a taxi. Nobody would notice she had left, she hoped. As the taxi drove her home, she phoned Karen Storin on her mobile. Karen answered with the noise in the background making Sam realize that Density were still playing.

'Karen,' Sam shouted, 'I've had to step out for a moment, I got an urgent call on my mobile. If Steve's looking for me, tell them I'll be back in an hour.'

In an hour, Steve would be too far into the champagne to notice she hadn't returned while Density's manager would be too far into the Colombian marching powder to notice anything at all.

London's lights flashed past and Sam forgot about the hassle with Mrs Ceci. What she couldn't forget was the pain she was in and the anxious, upset feeling that wouldn't go away. What was wrong with her, was it really only fibroids? Should she have insisted on getting an immediate appointment with the specialist instead of settling for one in nearly a month's time?

At home, her feeling of anxiety got worse, so Sam booted up her computer and decided to research what was wrong with her. She loved surfing the internet and was an expert at zipping in and out of interesting sites. Medical sites were not ones she'd ever visited before, so it took a few gos before she found one on women's health.

It wasn't long before she was engrossed in illnesses she'd never heard of. And then she found it, a list of symptoms that mirrored hers exactly. The pains, the nausea, the period problems, the list described her perfectly. Only it wasn't a description of the symptoms of fibroids. The disease in question was ovarian cancer. The more Sam read, the more she realized that when a woman had symptoms like hers, the disease was at an advanced stage and was a killer. Symptomless until it was too late, she read, with an ever growing sense of horror.

Shocked, she clicked on a self-help group and the first thing she saw was a poem from a woman whose sister had died of the disease, a poem calling for more women to be aware of the silent killer.

*We had two months before you died, Juana,*
*Two months to fill with memories,*
*Two months to remember a lifetime.*
*It wasn't enough.*
*We all miss you so much;*
*We miss you more because it shouldn't have to be this way.*

The accompanying biography explained that Juana had been expected to live for at least six months from diagnosis, but had survived for only two. She left three teenage children and a husband behind her, along with a sister who vowed to stop other women dying needlessly and who'd set up a group to increase awareness of ovarian cancer.

Sam wrenched the internet connector from the wall and punched the off button on her computer. Numb, she stared at the darkened screen for a long time before the tears came. Now she knew what was happening to her, now she finally knew why she'd been ill and losing weight. She was dying. Time was running out for her. She didn't have three weeks to wait and see some specialist; she needed help now. But then, what was the point if she was dying anyway?

It was strange: her hands didn't shake and she didn't cry. Instead, she rocked herself back and forth in her favourite chair and thought about how she'd taken every day for granted.

Waking up was never a miracle for her, she'd never thanked anyone for her existence, she took it as her right and went on living, fully expecting that no matter what happened, she'd wake up the next day. And the next, and the next.

Except not any more. Time really was precious and hers was running out. It was such an enormous idea to get her head around. Like trying to imagine infinity, her brain couldn't imagine a time when she would cease to be.

What would it be like? Was there anything out there? Was there nothing? And who would mourn her, if she were truly honest?

An image of Hope came into her head, Hope with Millie and Toby, laughing. That's when the tears began to fall.

Sam didn't bother going to bed that night. Instead, she sat in her silent living room and drank glass after glass of white wine. Why bother with abstinence when you were dying? In the early hours of the morning, her face swollen with crying, Sam finally made up her mind. There was only one thing for it. She knew what she had to do.

# CHAPTER TWELVE

Matt had the car that afternoon meaning that Hope was stuck at home. It was too wet to think of walking into the village, so she decided to work on the chair she was attempting to revamp. It was a plain wooden kitchen chair but the fretwork at the back was pretty and Hope imagined it could be lovely if only it wasn't covered with layer upon layer of thick cow-dung brown paint. She'd taken a week to strip off the old paint, and had painted it with lemon yellow wood varnish. Now, she planned to stencil wild flowers all over it with the help of the Irish wild flower book she'd got from the library. Millie was very keen to help, so both she and Toby were wearing their old crèche painting smocks over their clothes in what Hope knew was a vain attempt to keep them paint-free. Hope was wearing an old shirt of Matt's over her T-shirt and jeans for the same reason.

'Mummy, give me a go,' Millie said imperiously, holding out one fat little hand for the tiny paintbrush.

Millie painted pictures like a novice decorator painted a huge wall: with sloppy, enormous strokes and little attention to detail. Hope smiled because she knew they'd all be covered in paint soon.

'Now you can do one bit here,' she said firmly, giving Millie a tiny brush with a tiny smidgen of paint on it, 'and Toby can do this bit.'

Millie's tongue poked out of her mouth as she concentrated.

They were all so engrossed in the chair that none of them heard the car and the sound of someone knocking on the door gave them all a huge shock.

Hope leaped to her feet and vowed to get a doorbell. She was used to doorbells, but the sound of knocking reminded her of films where the police knocked before they raided the place.

She opened the door and gasped, for there, shivering in her shearling coat and with her eyes huge in a thin, haunted face, stood Sam.

Hope was momentarily speechless but when her sister uncharacteristically burst into tears, Hope threw her arms around her and pulled Sam out of the doorway and into the house. At first, she couldn't get any sense out of what Sam was saying but she figured out that something awful had happened.

'I've made such a mess of everything,' Sam sobbed, her voice shaky. She felt so thin, Hope realized with horror. She used to be slim but now she was like a walking skeleton. 'I've got nothing, n . . . nobody,' stammered Sam. 'Who's going to give a damn when I'm gone? Nobody, that's who. I've turned so bitter and it's all eaten me up on the inside. That's why I'm sick. I'm even beginning to repel people who like me. Like him, I mean, he was only being nice and I haven't liked anyone so much for ages and I was horrible . . .' She broke off with howls of misery, like Millie when she scraped her knee and couldn't begin to tell her mother how awful it was.

'Is it the guy you told me about in Bath?' Hope asked. 'Have you split up, love?'

Sam's big eyes were stricken. 'There was no guy,' she whispered. 'No guy for a long time. Who'd come near me? And I've even frightened off my friends. Jay and Catrina . . .'

'Hush, hush,' crooned Hope as she held her sister tightly, trying to stop the shuddering.

Poor darling Sam.

'And now I'm sick I'm dying and nobody but you cares.'

Hope finally understood the phrase about your blood turning to ice. She felt every litre flood icily through her veins.

'You're sick. What? Tell me. Now.'

It took endless moments for Sam's shuddering to stop. Hope held her tightly and prayed like she'd never prayed before. Aunt Ruth hadn't been much of a one for religion but Hope made sure the children said their prayers every night. *Dear God, please, please let it not be true.*

Finally, Sam was able to speak.

'I read about it on the internet. It's ovarian cancer.'

'But a doctor hasn't told you, you haven't had tests or anything?'

'I can read, Hope! I've got all the symptoms. I've got an appointment with a specialist in three weeks but I know it without seeing her, don't you see?'

'But surely they wouldn't make you wait this long to see someone if it was serious . . .' began Hope, but stopped when Sam began to sob hysterically in a way Hope had never seen her cry ever before.

Hope sat her sister on the couch and instructed a wide-eyed Millie to sit beside her aunt while she got Sam some tea. Millie loved Sam but she was scared of this wild-eyed, sad person and she stood behind an armchair, twisting her pinafore in her hands and peering out nervously. Toby, however, climbed up on the couch and began to show Sam his new favourite toy, a big dumper truck with a yellow hydraulic trailer that actually went up and down.

'Up and down,' said Toby gravely, demonstrating this. 'Up and down.'

'That's very good,' Sam said, doing her best to sound normal because she could see how her behaviour had upset Millie. 'Do you let Millie play with it?'

'No,' said Millie indignantly from her position behind the chair.

'What new toys have you got, then?' Sam had herself under control now.

Millie came out of hiding and began to pile toys on the couch beside Sam. 'See, loads.'

Hope brought the cups of tea from the kitchen and laid them carefully on the low table away from small hands.

'Now Millie and Toby, Auntie Sam wants to have her tea. I'll put a video on for you, OK?' she said in a bright voice.

Sam smiled at her sister weakly. For the first time, she could see how mummy-dom meant having to subdue your real feelings and pretend nothing was wrong.

When the children were engrossed in the *Teletubbies*, Hope sat beside her sister. 'Tell me everything, from the very beginning,' she commanded.

'The consultant I'm to see has no appointments for over three weeks. She's supposed to be the best there is but I'm afraid to wait any longer. I thought if I was here, it would be easier.'

'Sam, why didn't you insist on seeing another consultant? You've got the health insurance, they could have managed it.'

'I know,' Sam said, 'I didn't think. I panicked at the thought of waiting three weeks. And what are they going to tell me, anyway? That it's spread all over me and that I can put myself through agonizing chemo just for a few more weeks. I've read all about it . . .'

'Sam, please, don't say that,' said Hope, distraught. 'Cancer is one of the most curable diseases now. Modern medicine is incredible and there's always hope.'

'Not with this when you have symptoms like mine,' sobbed Sam. 'By the time you notice, it's too late. You should have seen this site on the internet.'

Hope silently raged against scare-mongering sites where other people's terrible experiences made you fear the worst. 'Listen, there was something on the internet recently that said you could get cancer from using deodorant. How about that for rubbish?'

'I know but this is different.'

Afterwards, Hope put Sam to sleep in her and Matt's bedroom.

'I can't take your room,' Sam said wearily.

'I'll make a bed up for you later but for now you're exhausted and you need to sleep,' pointed out Hope. Sam hadn't slept for well over twenty-four hours, and on her emergency flight from London to Kerry via Dublin, she'd obviously been too distraught even to doze.

'I won't be able to sleep,' Sam said frantically. 'Will you sit with me?'

'Of course.'

With the children now playing in their bedroom under pain of death not to make a noise, Hope sat on the edge of the bed and stroked Sam's cold hand. Her sister's blonde hair fanned out on the dark blue pillow case and she looked frighteningly pale against the dark background.

'I'm scared, Hope, that's why I had to come to see you. You're the only one I've got,' Sam whispered. 'I don't want to be alone to face this.'

'You won't, I promise you. Now hush, Sam, get some sleep,' said Hope, as softly as she spoke when she soothed Toby after a bad dream.

She kept stroking Sam's hand and within minutes, her worn-out sister was asleep. When Sam's breathing was even and measured, Hope slipped out of the room and wondered what she should do.

The tables were certainly turned. After years of being the one whom Sam had looked after, Hope was suddenly the strong one. The one who had to take charge.

Like a swimmer gingerly testing the water temperature with one toe, Hope wondered what it would be like to be the coper. Then she realized that she had no choice: she had to do everything for Sam and, if she was dying, Hope would fight to the bitter end with her. Thinking of Sam's dying made her chest throb with a nameless ache, but she knew she didn't have time to get emotional. It was time for action. Medical action. Sam would never stand the strain of the three weeks until her appointment with the consultant and, if she was truly ill, it could be disastrous for her to wait that long. Hope was furious with the nonchalant doctor who hadn't rushed her sister into hospital immediately. What an incompetent moron.

Hope Parker, the one who had traditionally let other people take care of problems, swung into action.

She found Sam's diary and found the consultant's appointment marked in for nearly three weeks' time, with a telephone number.

It was nearly five, just in time to catch someone in the consultant's office. Hope phoned and got through to the consultant's receptionist, explaining the story very simply.

'I can't discuss this with you, Mrs Parker,' the receptionist said politely.

Hope grimaced. 'I'm not asking you to discuss it with me,' she said. 'Just find an earlier cancellation as soon as possible, please. She is having a breakdown. Or else recommend someone else for me. This is an emergency.'

The woman promised to phone back the next day. There was nothing else Hope could do. She hung up and thought she better start dinner.

'Who does the hire car belong to?' asked Matt, arriving home shortly after six. He threw his car keys down on the coffee table and strode into the kitchen, looking for the mystery guest.

'It's Sam's,' Hope said, shivering at the thought that Sam had actually driven from the airport in her state. It was a miracle she hadn't crashed.

'Sam,' he said, stunned. 'What's she doing here?'

'Daddy, Daddy,' squealed Millie, running down the wooden stairs and making a noise like a herd of elephants.

'Quiet,' hissed Hope. 'Sam's asleep upstairs in our bed, I don't want her to wake up yet.'

'She's in bed?' Matt repeated. 'Hope, what is going on?'

Hope pulled him towards the back door and told him, whispering in case Sam was awake upstairs and could hear.

'Jesus,' Matt said, visibly shaken at the news. 'That's terrible, Hope.' He put his arms around her and kissed the top of her head gently. 'Are you all right?'

In his embrace, feeling as if someone else was in charge at last, Hope let herself go and began to cry.

'It's all right, love, I'm here with you. You'll still have me and the kids if the worst comes to the worst,' he soothed.

'I know,' sobbed Hope into his denim shirt, 'but why can't I have Sam too?'

Rather than wake Sam, who slept the sleep of the truly exhausted, Hope made up the sofa bed in the spare room and she and Matt spent an uneasy night there.

In the morning, she was awake at dawn and lay on the uncomfortable sofa bed staring out at the lightening sky through the curtainless windows.

When the phone rang at five past nine, Hope leaped at it.

'Yes?'

It was the consultant's receptionist with an appointment for three days' time.

'Thank you, thank you,' said Hope gratefully. 'I'll see you then. I'll bring her.'

She woke her sister after eleven with a tray filled with coffee, fresh orange juice, one of her own hens' eggs boiled, local brown bread, and homemade butter and gooseberry jam from the Saturday morning farm market in the soccer club hall.

Hope had never tasted better food than the food she bought on Saturdays: just-dug-up vegetables with earth still clinging to them, nutty brown bread, butter that just begged to be spread fatly over everything, and jams and chutneys that she always meant to store but which were consumed greedily, so that she inevitably had to buy another consignment the next week.

'I can't believe I've slept so long,' Sam said in amazement, sitting up in bed with Hope's pink fluffy dressing gown wrapped around her shoulders.

Hope put the tray on the bed. 'You were exhausted,' she said.

She sat on the bed and drank a cup of coffee, watching Sam eat in the same way she anxiously watched Millie toying with cut up bits of chicken.

'Eat up,' she said, 'you need some proper food inside you.'

'Yes Mummy,' joked Sam.

Hope smiled. 'I know you're on the mend when you start teasing me.'

'That's because you're so pathetically easy to tease,' Sam laughed fondly, almost upsetting the tray in the process.

'Remember that time in school when some kid got nits in their hair and we had to bring a note home to Aunt Ruth telling her to watch out for them . . .'

'Oh yes,' Sam interrupted, 'and I told you that you'd got them and that the only way to get rid of them was to cover your head in Aunt Ruth's Yardley talcum powder and hang your head out of our bedroom window for an hour!'

'That was mean,' said Hope, laughing at the memory. 'I hung there for *ages* and Aunt Ruth went mad because I'd used all her powder up.'

'You were so innocent, then,' Sam said, spreading jam on her bread.

'And what am I now, then?' demanded her sister. 'What's the opposite of innocent?'

'You're still innocent,' Sam smiled, 'and kind. Thank you for looking after me.'

'I haven't finished yet,' Hope replied. 'I've made you a new appointment with your consultant for three days' time. She can fit you in and I'm coming with you.'

Sam could say nothing but she reached out and held her sister's hand, her eyes flooding with tears.

'Eat up,' said Hope briskly. 'When you finish that, we're going for a long, revitalizing walk.'

'We are?'

'We are,' Hope said firmly. 'You need some fresh air.'

'What about the children? Where are they, anyway?'

'Matt took them to the crèche this morning so you and I have the place to ourselves. Eat up, lazy bones.'

It was a glorious February day, with pale sunshine burnishing the bare branches of the trees. Hope and Sam walked up the laneway, enjoying the faint heat of the sun.

'I'm sorry, I should have stayed at home and not given you all this hassle. I should have changed the appointment myself,' Sam said, walking along with her hands firmly in the pockets of the light anorak she'd borrowed from Hope.

'Don't be ridiculous. You did the right thing. Where else could you have gone?'

Sam nodded miserably. 'Yeah, you're right. Where else could I have gone? Nowhere, that's where.'

Hope could have cursed herself for speaking. In the middle of Sam's tearful story the night before, she'd mentioned Morgan and it was obvious that Sam had feelings for him, but that nothing had happened. It was also obvious that there hadn't been a man in Sam's life for a long time. Hope felt ashamed that she'd believed Sam's vague stories about men friends. She should have known that her sister was lonely after all but just putting on a very successful façade to hide it.

They reached the main road and as they walked in the sun, Sam marvelled at the friendly drivers who raised a few fingers from the steering wheel in greeting at the sisters as they drove past.

'Funny, I'm totally used to that now,' Hope said. 'I thought it was strange at first, and not everyone waves, but most people do.'

Sam grinned. 'I can't imagine anyone doing that in London. If someone waves fingers at you, they're telling you to eff off.'

They walked in silence for a while, then Sam spoke suddenly: 'Mum and Dad were much younger than we are now when they died. She was twenty-nine. I can still remember her perfume although I've never known exactly what it was. I was in a perfume department in Paris one day and I spent ages sniffing everything but I never found one just like it. Do you remember it?'

Hope shook her head. 'No, I don't. I don't really remember them either,' she said. It was the first time she'd ever admitted it to anyone. She'd been three when their parents had been killed. Sam and Hope, three and six respectively and being cared for at home by babysitter Marina, knew nothing until the following day. Even now, Sam hated the name Marina. To her, it symbolized when everything had changed.

'You never told me before that you didn't remember them,' Sam said now.

Hope shrugged. 'When we were little and you asked me if I remembered Mum's perfume and the special song she sang to get us to sleep, I said yes, because I thought it was the right thing to say. I thought you'd be angry with me for forgetting.'

'I'm sorry,' Sam said, feeling the increasingly familiar flood of tears swell up in her eyes. She burst into tears at everything now. The slightest provocation and she was off. She hated that.

'I wanted us to remember everything because Aunt Ruth didn't want to talk about them at all. She used to interrupt and change the subject when I said anything about Mummy.'

'I don't think she meant it in a bad way,' Hope pointed out. 'She just wasn't used to either kids or death and she probably thought it was better for us if we forgot them, that we'd get over it all quicker if we never spoke of them or talked about them, which was totally wrong, of course.'

The sisters were silent, remembering the tall, quiet, old-fashioned house in Windsor where childhood giggles felt out of place in case they upset the bridge ladies in the parlour and where the mention of Camille or Sandy Parker made Aunt Ruth inhale swiftly and say, 'now girls, no looking back.'

'She wasn't bad at taking care of us,' Hope said.

'She wasn't. It must have been a nightmare for her. Two kids dumped on her while she was grieving for her kid brother.'

It had been years before Aunt Ruth had explained that she'd felt she had to take them on because both sets of grandparents were too old to take care of two small children. Both of their parents were the children of older parents themselves. That had to have been a bond between Camille and Sandy, Sam always thought. And because of their tragic death, their children ended up being brought up by someone much older too.

'Would things in our lives have been different if Mum and Dad hadn't died, do you think?' Sam asked.

Hope shrugged. 'We'd probably both still be bonkers,' she said lightly.

A shiny new red car stopped beside them.

'Halloo,' yelled Delphine, rolling down her window. 'Hiya Hope and you must be Sam,' she said enthusiastically. 'So nice to meet you. God,' she added, 'anybody would know you're sisters, you're the cutting image of each other.'

Sam and Hope looked at each other and laughed.

'Nobody's ever said that to us before,' Sam said, leaning across to shake Delphine's hand.

'It's my Celtic ancestry,' Delphine beamed. 'I'm part psychic and I just know things. Either that, or it's my new crystal necklace.' She waggled a couple of crystals that hung on a chain round her neck. 'They've got a whole new line of druidic jewellery up in the Mother Earth craft shop and this must be giving me vibes that told me you were sisters. Are you coming to the Macramé Club tonight?' she asked.

'Well, I was going to but with Sam here . . .' Hope broke off.

'Get away out of that,' said Delphine dismissively, 'Sam has to come too.'

'I don't want to intrude,' Sam said, horrified at the idea of crashing a party which had obviously been arranged ages ago.

Delphine raised her eyes to heaven. 'What are the pair of you like? Of course you're invited. The Macramé Club is for like-minded sisters, druidic jewellery not a requirement, and you both have to come. This is our first meeting for ages. It'll be a blast. Anyway, Mary-Kate has been stocking up on vodka and making her fabulous martinis, so if you don't come, myself and the others will have to drink it all and nobody in the whole town will be able to get a prescription tomorrow if herself has a raging hangover! Byee!'

And she drove off at high speed.

The sisters looked at each other and laughed.

'Isn't she amazing?' Sam said. 'What a place.'

'That's Redlion for you,' Hope said proudly. 'It doesn't so much embrace you, as swallow you whole and refuse to spit you out again.'

# CHAPTER THIRTEEN

Tonight was the first meeting of the Macramé Club. Virginia had bought a slab of locally made cheese and a bottle of white wine as her contribution to the evening's party, even though Mary-Kate kept insisting that she bring nothing.

'Bring yourself,' said her friend, 'that's all you need. Delphine and I are providing the goodies. Don't drive, whatever you do, and have some soluble painkillers ready for the morning.'

'Are you intimating that we'll have hangovers, oh health professional?' inquired Virginia.

'Not a bit,' said Mary-Kate briskly. 'I simply like to be prepared.'

Virginia glanced at her watch and decided that she needed to leave in half an hour so she'd be there in time, but beforehand, she decided to inspect the spare bedrooms at the front of the house. Jamie, Laurence and Laurence's new girlfriend, Barbara, were coming to stay in a couple of days' time and she wanted to be sure the bedrooms were in good shape. Virginia had wondered if Laurence and Barbara would prefer to share a bedroom but decided that she'd make up three rooms just in case and they could sort themselves out whatever way they wanted, with minimum embarrassment on all sides. The wallpaper was mildly tinged with damp in one outer corner but the second bedroom, a feminine boudoir pink, was perfect and would be lovely for Barbara. The blue and yellow room at the front of the house boasted a bright pink sink in one corner and another patch of damp but Virginia decided that Jamie would put up with it.

Old houses, Virginia sighed, were like middle-aged ladies like herself: every time she thought she'd banished some symptom of age, another sprung up just to remind her of the frailty of woman. Her arthritic hip had been twinge-free for a week, despite the freezing weather, but the painful shoulder spasm she hadn't experienced for years had reappeared, just when Virginia needed to be energetic. With the children coming to stay, it was important that she looked vital and capable, instead of feeble and in need of being looked after. Not that they were children, Virginia corrected herself. They were adults. Twenty-seven and twenty-five respectively. But somewhere in the depths of her mind, Laurence and Jamie would always be children. They had their own lives to lead, grown up lives where they worked all the hours God sent. Laurence was building up the dental practice he'd set up with two friends in Swords, while Jamie was a science teacher in a boys school. She was so proud of them, proud of all her three boys. Virginia just hoped she'd managed that parental cliché: to give them roots and wings. It had been hard to leave Jamie and Laurence in Dublin when she moved and she'd felt selfish for it. Dominic, in married bliss in London, had Sally and little Alison, while Laurence had been so caught up with the practice, he'd seemed utterly contented. But Jamie had always spent lots of time with his parents, even though he had left home at the age of twenty-two, and actually lived nearby in a house with three college pals. He'd been constantly dropping in for dinner or to borrow something or to get Virginia to bung his clothes in the washing machine as the one in the shared house had broken down yet again. Dear Jamie, her baby. But in her grief over Bill, Virginia hadn't been able to cope with looking after even herself, never mind Jamie.

Both Jamie and Laurence had seen Kilnagoshell House when she was first considering buying it, and when they'd realized there was no point convincing her not to up sticks and move to the country. But they hadn't been to stay since and she was strangely nervous about their visit.

Barbara and Laurence had been going out for four months and Virginia hadn't met her yet. Before Bill's death, Virginia knew Barbara would have been a guest in their house so often, that she'd be almost like family by now. That was Bill all over. Welcoming and generous, he'd wanted his sons to bring their girlfriends home right from the very beginning. Virginia sat on the dusty bed in the paisley bedroom and remembered Laurence's first girlfriend, a wild, hippie-ish girl who'd gone in for torn jeans, unwashed long hair ('After a month, it cleans itself,' she'd insisted) and automatic confrontation with anyone over the age of twenty. Even the besotted Laurence had blanched when she'd tried to start a row with Bill over having a lawnmower that used diesel instead of unleaded. Bill, smiling, had refused to be riled.

'She's not what I'd have picked for Laurence myself,' he'd whispered to Virginia in the kitchen later, 'but if she's his choice, we'll support him.'

'Does that mean we *all* have to get our belly buttons pierced?' said Virginia, smothering a laugh at the thought of her conservative husband trying to fit in with his son's new girlfriend.

Bill winced. 'It does look painful,' he admitted. 'But young people need to do different things. Remember how my father thought drainpipes and Elvis Presley were signs of the devil?'

'You know what I love about you?' Virginia asked, putting her arms around him. 'You're such a fair minded person.'

She was kissing him when Laurence, with his girlfriend in tow, had arrived in the kitchen.

Laurence, used to his parents' constant displays of affection, ignored the kiss and opened the fridge. His girlfriend stared at them in astonishment.

Virginia pulled away from Bill's lips and grinned at her. 'Strange though it may seem to you, my dear, people over the age of forty are allowed to have sex lives,' she said crisply. 'Why should you young people have all the fun?' Even if Bill hadn't minded the rude attack about the lawn mower, *she* had. Nobody was allowed to hurt darling Bill.

The girl blushed. She hadn't lasted long after that.

Lawrence had gone through many girlfriends since then but had rarely been as besotted as he sounded about Barbara.

'She's kind and wonderful and . . . just lovely,' Laurence had said in a dreamy voice on the phone.

'She's a bit annoying in a helpless sort of way,' Jamie had pointed out in a separate phone call. 'But she'd bossy at the same time. It's all very passive aggressive,' he added.

Virginia grinned. Jamie's dalliance with psychotherapy courses in university had meant he'd analysed them all to bits.

'You mean you don't like her?' Virginia asked.

'No,' he said with uncharacteristic firmness.

Virginia sighed and wished she had Bill with her to help referee the weekend. Thinking about Bill had the usual effect and she reached for her ever-present tissue and dabbed her eyes with it. Think of something else, she commanded herself. Now, what was she going to do about that damp patch?

Putting in a damp course would cost a fortune and she didn't have a fortune. Replastering. Would that work? Bill had known the answers to questions like that. Oh Virginia, stop it!

She went down to the kitchen and made herself a cup of tea she didn't want. Why was tea considered such a panacea? In times of emergency, people always insisted on making you tea, as if a few leaves swirling in boiling water could cure anything. Virginia had been brought up on the habit and, even now, she still went automatically to the kettle when a crisis loomed. Her insides were probably pickled with tannin as it was. Stupid tea. She emptied the cup down the sink and decided that she wouldn't drive to Mary-Kate's house that night. Virginia, currently unaccustomed to social gatherings, had planned to only stay for a short while and stick to mineral water, despite Delphine's constant reminiscing about the perfect martini and the remembered hangover from the last club. But why be a party pooper? She decided. If anybody could do with a few perfect martinis, it was her.

Mary-Kate opened her front door and welcomed Virginia in.

'I wasn't sure you'd turn up, you know,' she said as Virginia handed her the cheese and wine and the bunch of daffodils she'd picked from the swathe that flourished to the left of the mossy lawn at Kilnagoshell.

'I nearly didn't,' Virginia smiled, looking around Mary-Kate's house with fascination. She'd never been there before.

'You know the routine,' Mary-Kate said firmly, steering her into a room papered entirely in rich crimson. 'If you feel miserable tonight, just let it all out. No bottling stuff up at the Macramé Club.'

That was the wonderful thing about her new friend, Virginia thought: you didn't have to pretend with Mary-Kate.

'This room is incredible,' she breathed as she admired a room that looked as if it belonged in a Hollywood version of 1930s Shanghai. Two huge sofas covered with oriental brocade and fat, tapestried cushions sat opposite each other, with a big dark wooden low table between them covered in knick knacks, wooden animals and a chess-board made from carved jade. The walls were hung with oriental paintings, elegant silk curtains the colour of old roses draped the windows, while old tiffany lamps and richly coloured fringed shades kept the lighting to a dusky, amber glow. A bronze Buddha sat and gazed down at them from the mantelpiece where candles burned brightly scenting the air with a mixture of spice and cinnamon. All the room needed was Mary-Kate in a kimono and the scene would have been perfect.

'It's beautiful,' Virginia said again genuinely.

'It's probably a bit kitschy but I love it,' Mary-Kate said. 'In my mother's time, this room was the parlour, formal and never used. She had a small horse-hair chair you'd slide off if you sat on it, not that anyone ever sat on it, except for at weddings and funerals.' She stroked the black and white cat who'd prowled into the room and was now peering around to see what he'd play with first. 'I wanted something different and as I never really got to travel, this room is my escape where I listen to music.'

'Isn't it fabulous,' sighed Delphine, arriving in from the kitchen carrying a tray set with proper martini glasses, a cocktail shaker and all sorts of cocktail accoutrements. 'I want a room just like this in my house. Drink, Virginia?'

'Why not.'

Delphine sat on a big velvet cushion on the floor and stroked the cat, while Mary-Kate put on some music and Virginia sipped her martini.

'God, this is good,' she said as the liquid slipped down her throat like quicksilver.

'I told you she was great at martinis,' Delphine said. 'She's wasted as a pharmacist. The Plaza Hotel in New York would pay her a fortune but she insists on staying in Redlion mixing up cough mixture for the masses.'

Mary-Kate tweaked a strand of Delphine's hair. 'Did you get the crackers sorted out, madam?' she asked.

'Forgot. I'll get them now.'

'Let me do something,' Virginia said, getting up from her comfy seat. 'I feel terrible coming here and letting you do all the work.'

'Come and help, then,' Mary-Kate said, leading the way to a small, tidy kitchen. 'Mind you, there's no work for the Macramé Club. Whoever's hosting provides some drink and that's it. If you tidy up for the club, you get drummed out. The whole point is that it's a trouble-free night.'

She gave Virginia some unopened crackers to put on a plate. 'There's cheese in the fridge and get a few knives, little plates and the napkins under the cutlery drawer,' she said. It was very relaxed entertaining, Virginia decided. Refreshingly relaxed. Mary-Kate wasn't rushing around cutting up crudités for dips. Instead, she was giving her guests something to soak up the martini. Conversation, not catering, was the point of the night.

'Who's coming?' Virginia asked. 'You better tell me about everyone so I don't put my foot in it and say something awful.'

'Hope, for a start. You met her in the Widow's that night with her husband. She's bringing her sister, Sam, who's over from London.'

Virginia nodded, taking it all in. She remembered the pretty Hope Parker, with her big, anxious eyes and that good looking, confident husband.

'And Giselle. She's German and she runs the crèche, Hunny-bunnikins, near the hotel. She's been living here for years and was one of the original Macramé Club six. We always had six from the beginning.'

Virginia nibbled a bit of cheese. 'Sounds very coven-ish. How did it start?'

'It was Sheila's idea, at first. She and I had been at school together but we hadn't really kept in touch. I was in Dublin and she was here. Then her husband left her and ran off with the doctor. They were both lovely men, who'd have known?'

Virginia's eyes widened.

'Sheila and I met up round then because I was just back from working in Dublin and we wanted to have a night out away from all the gossips who wanted to know about Sheila's husband and why I'd come back to Redlion with my tail between my legs and no husband.'

Virginia said nothing. Personally, she was quite interested in the mystery of why Mary-Kate wasn't married.

'Giselle was so lovely to Sheila then. She never asked her a thing and took the children for a couple of weekends while Sheila tried to persuade himself to come back – he wouldn't by the way. Anyway, there were six of us who didn't feel we fitted in and after a great night in Sheila's, we decided to meet once a month and just bitch about everyone and everything. It's great therapy.'

'And you did study macramé in the beginning?'

Mary-Kate giggled. 'That was subterfuge. Both my sister Pauline and Finula Headley-Ryan were madly keen to come along, mostly so they could hear all the gory details about Sheila's husband, so to put them off, I said we were having macramé lessons. Finula thinks she's above such banal gatherings and Pauline had always hated anything except knitting so there was no excuse for either of them to come. I used to buy macramé pot holders occasionally so we could pretend we were actually making things but I've stopped bothering. You can't get them anywhere any more. Honestly, I've looked all over, although I think Pauline has figured out that we don't do much arts and crafts on these nights because she came into the chemist one morning after and I was dying of a hangover.' She sighed. 'Poor Pauline. She's her own worst enemy. You could say the same of Finula, mind you.'

'Sheila's not coming tonight, then?'

'No. She lives in the South of France with an electronics millionaire now. But when she comes back on holidays, we have a club night for old times' sake. She said it kept her sane all those years ago.' Mary-Kate smiled ruefully. 'It kept me sane too.'

They carried the goodies into the Shanghai room.

'There'll be us three, and Hope, her sister Sam, Giselle, and Mai Hondu, she's Japanese and her husband works in the computer factory.'

'There hasn't been a proper quorum for ages, since Sheila went,' Delphine said.

The doorbell rang and Delphine went to answer it.

'Giselle and Mai, welcome,' she said happily. 'Drink?'

Hope and Sam were late. Suspecting that her mother and her aunt were going out somewhere exciting without her, Millie had refused to get into her pyjamas and had played up until Hope had finally given up and asked Matt to put her to bed. At which point, Millie had suddenly started behaving sweetly, blinking her long eyelashes at her daddy and doing everything she was told. 'She's a little terror,' Matt had whispered to Hope fondly as Millie rummaged in the toy box for the longest story book she could find.

'Yes, and she's got her Daddy wrapped around her little finger,' Hope whispered back.

Now they walked up Mary-Kate's path, Sam clutching a bottle of wine. Hope, who'd normally have felt mildly nervous about meeting all these women who knew each other, wasn't even slightly nervous now. She had Sam with her and it was her job to take care of her beloved sister. For a change, Sam was the one who felt nervous. Her world was out of synch and everything had shifted, making her more unsettled than she'd ever been in her life. But as soon as she walked in the door and breathed in the relaxed atmosphere that came when everyone was one martini down and laughing at the cat playing with a toy mouse on the floor, Sam relaxed. She hadn't expected to. Unused to all-female gatherings, she was half-afraid they'd get all Stepford Wives at a coffee morning and start discussing the merits of washing powder.

But this wasn't that sort of night. Coffee mornings didn't usually involve strong vodka martinis, complete with olives, or hysterical conversations about their ideal men. The only men that women at coffee mornings were supposed to talk about were their husbands, while at this party, Giselle was delightedly giving a description of her first love, who was apparently very handsome but not a great intellectual genius.

'Claus is so different,' Giselle said, referring to her beloved husband. 'I prefer clever men to beautiful ones but that boy, he was so good looking, I didn't mind how stupid he was,' she sighed, once Sam and Hope had been given drinks and seats. 'He was a male bimbo, I suppose.'

'A himbo,' supplied Delphine.

'There's nothing wrong with that,' Mary-Kate said. 'I wouldn't mind a himbo myself. With one of those ten-packs.'

'Six packs,' chorused Sam and Delphine automatically and everyone laughed.

'I was kidding,' Mary-Kate insisted. 'Do you really think I don't know the difference between a six-pack and a ten-pack? Have you lot never heard of irony?'

The ice was broken and they all dug into the cheese and crackers, chatting wildly about anything and everything. Sam, who was not given to confidences, found herself sitting beside Mary-Kate and talking about herself and her distraught flight to see Hope.

'It sounds so stupid to be sure I'm seriously ill without any actual medical evidence,' she said finally, the hand holding her martini shaking with nerves.

'I don't think you're stupid to get upset,' Mary-Kate said in her warm, soothing voice, 'but don't plan the funeral until you know for sure.'

Sam smiled weakly. Hope had said that Mary-Kate had a very direct way of making you see sense.

'What I mean,' Mary-Kate continued firmly, 'is that you know nothing for definite. Doctors do sometimes make horrific mistakes, I know that, but from what you've told me, I'm not so sure he has. If he thought you were seriously ill, he wouldn't have let you off into the ether with an appointment a month down the road. At least you're going to see a consultant in a couple of days. When you've got it all sorted out, you'll feel better. So don't panic yet.' She grinned at Sam. 'I'm an ould wan and a pharmacist, so I know what I'm talking about.'

'I do hope I'm just overwrought, I really do,' said Sam earnestly. 'But I'm not the sort of person to get all worked up like this, really I'm not.'

'Well then, your body is trying to tell you something,' Mary-Kate pointed out. 'It's up to you to work out what it is and deal with it. You're used to looking at worst case scenarios, so that's what you did, mistakenly I hope.'

Sam realized that Mary-Kate had put her arm around her and was hugging her gently as she spoke, holding Sam's thin body against her own wiry one. Mary-Kate couldn't have been that much older than Sam but there was something comfortingly motherly about the embrace.

'I've never been much of a one for listening to my body,' Sam said wryly. 'I've spent years making it listen to me: *get out of bed; you don't have flu; so what if you're sick, keep going.* That sort of thing.'

'You might have to change, you might have no option. Imagine if you were seriously ill, you'd have to change your life. So why not change it now? You are going through a crisis, Sam. You must see that.'

Sam nodded. 'Racing over here to see Hope is definitely a sign of something. I've never done anything like that before. My colleagues would be astonished to see the Queen Bitch being vulnerable about anything.'

Mary-Kate tipped her head to one side and scrutinized Sam. 'Are you Queen Bitch in the office?'

Shrugging her shoulders, Sam said: 'Not all the time but I feel that I'm becoming it. And I don't want to be but . . .'

'Then change,' said the other woman bluntly.

'It's not that easy to change.'

'Why not? Hope sees another side to you, a warm, kind side, the sister she loves.'

'Yes, but we're all different with our families,' Sam protested.

'And you're trying to be something you're not because you think that's the way to remain strong and in control,' Mary-Kate said.

'Ouch,' laughed Sam. 'You're good at this but it hurts. I don't know if I can cope with much more analysis.'

'Yes you can. You're a strong woman and you need strong friends and strong words to help you.' Mary-Kate was silent for a minute, as if she was considering whether to mention something or not. 'In the old days at the Macramé Club we used to have a game, our own truth or dare, without the dare bit. When we had problems, we talked about them, said truthfully what we really wanted in life and – this is the hard bit –' she added, 'asked our friends to give their opinion.'

'We've never done that since I've been coming,' interrupted Delphine, tuning into their conversation.

'Done what?' asked Hope, looking over at Sam to check she was all right.

'Macramé Club Truth Drug,' said Mary-Kate.

Giselle laughed. 'My last baby was born as a result of one of those nights. Too much of Mary-Kate's truth drug and you forget to use your contraceptive cap!'

'What's the truth drug?' asked Sam.

Mai smiled. 'You're drinking it.'

'Oh let's do it,' begged Delphine. 'It'll be fun. I love girlie confessional nights.'

'It's not easy,' Giselle said. 'People may say things you don't like to hear. But the good point is that you can talk about anything and know that it's safe. Nobody refers to it again and not a word of it goes beyond this room.'

'Let's do it,' Delphine said again.

Mary-Kate, Mai and Giselle looked at each other and shared a smile.

'We need a vote,' Mai said. 'We can only do it if everyone agrees. All in favour put your hands up.'

'Only if you're gentle with me,' begged Sam.

'Deal,' said Mary-Kate.

Six hands were raised.

'Right, Delphine, you go first,' said Mary-Kate, 'but just let me make up some more martini first.'

'You have to pick one area of your life that you want to change and be truthful about it,' Giselle explained. 'Then, we can offer advice, if we think we can help.'

'Do I have to go first?' Delphine said.

'Yes,' said the others.

'Right, confession time,' she said, taking a deep breath.

'Hold out your glass first,' Mary-Kate said, returning with another jug of martini.

'This reminds me of this game we play in the beauty salon,' Delphine said, when her glass was full and she had three fat olives on a stick into the bargain. 'You have to pick three words to describe yourself. It's much more fun when other people have to do it to you. Last week, the new girl, Anna, did me and said I was sweet, sexy but couldn't stand up for myself.'

Everyone winced.

'That's was a bit cruel,' Sam said.

'Yes, I think she believed we had to be deeply honest when for the rest of us, it's a bit of fun,' Delphine admitted. 'You know, you say nice things about each other. The manageress is always worried about her figure, so I said she was voluptuous. The odd thing is, Anna was right. I've been thinking about it all week and she was right. I don't stand up for myself.'

'Neither do I,' Hope said, not wanting Delphine to feel exposed.

'It's terrible, isn't it?' Delphine said, twirling her olives. 'I want to stand up for myself but it's easier not to.'

'Is that what you'd like to change, then?' asked Giselle.

Delphine's chin stuck out firmly. 'Yes.'

'How can you do it?' persisted Giselle.

For once, Delphine was speechless.

'This is the bit where we interrupt,' Mary-Kate pointed out. 'Marry Eugene.'

Startled, Delphine looked up at her. 'You know why we haven't got married . . .' she said.

'I do know why and it's because you won't stand up to Pauline,' retorted her aunt.

'Fill us all in on this story,' Sam interrupted, sliding forward on the seat.

Delphine took a big slug of martini. 'My fiancé is divorced and my mother won't even meet him, never mind go to our wedding. We've been putting it off until Mum gives in and accepts him, but she still won't. My dad has met him, secretly, mind you, because she'd kill him if she knew. She thinks getting married to a divorced man will destroy my immortal soul. She wants a big church do and that's out of the question because he's divorced.'

'Poor you,' said Mai, patting Delphine's shoulder.

'That's what I would describe as a textbook example of not standing up for yourself,' Sam said. 'It's simple: you've got to arrange the wedding, invite your mother and, if she doesn't turn up, that's her loss. You've made your decision and how she reacts to it is out of your hands.'

Delphine looked at her. Sam was so self-possessed and confident. Hope had told them all about her fabulously bright sister and her incredible job. Even too thin and tired with dark circles under her eyes, she emanated forcefulness and drive.

'It's easy for someone like you,' Delphine fretted.

Sam laughed ruefully. 'Delphine, I make mistakes all the time but one of the few I don't make is not standing up for myself. Standing up for myself is practically my area of expertise. When I'm at work and a tough decision needs to be made, I think of it in simple terms to make sense of it. So, in your case, imagine say, you want to dye your hair pink, right?'

They all grinned.

'She's had it pink already,' Mary-Kate said.

'Punk is dead,' announced Delphine. 'I was only sixteen and it was not a good look for me. Continue, Sam.'

'OK, you want pink hair but you're afraid to do it in case your mother won't like it. What do you do? Dye it and let her deal with how she feels about it? Or don't dye it and spend ages feeling bitter and angry because you're letting *her* feelings prevent *you* from doing what you want?'

'You do have a great knack of reducing problems down to their most simple form,' said Mary-Kate admiringly.

'It's easier when it's someone else's problem,' Sam said with a wry smile.

'Let's see if I've got this,' Delphine said. 'I get married anyway, no matter what Mum says.'

'Well, Pauline isn't talking to you now,' Mary-Kate pointed out prosaically. 'What's the difference if she's not talking to you afterwards? Maybe she needs a kick up the backside to make her see that the world doesn't revolve around her.'

'Hear hear,' said Giselle.

Delphine's eyes blazed with righteous fervour. 'You're right. I'm going to do it. Go and buy hats girls, you're all invited to a wedding next month.'

'A toast,' said Mary-Kate delightedly. 'To Delphine, Eugene and the fabulous Truth Drug!'

More crackers and cheese had to be produced to soak up the drink.

'Sam,' said Mary-Kate meaningfully, 'do you want to go next?'

Sam winced. 'I'm not good at this kind of thing,' she confessed. 'Taking advice is like taking cough medicine: I try and avoid it.'

Hope leaned over and gave her a hug. 'Go on,' she said, 'we're with friends.'

It took five minutes for Sam to relate the story of her last few months, and this time she admitted that she had probably totally overreacted to the whole thing and now felt embarrassed at dropping everything to race to Redlion to see Hope.

'There's nothing wrong with that,' Delphine said. 'You wanted to be with your sister, that's perfectly normal.'

'I know, but I don't usually do things like that,' Sam said.

'Ah ha,' pounced Mai, 'then something is different. You are different. You might not be ill but you are suffering from a crisis. This is a sign to tell you that you must change things, rearrange the pieces.'

'What do I change?' Sam said helplessly. 'I have a job, a mortgage, responsibilities. What can I change? C'mon girls, this is the real world here, not Yoga-Land.'

'Ask yourself are you happy with what you do every day?' Giselle advised. 'Work is so fundamental to happiness and if you're not happy doing the same thing any more, you must change your job.'

'Make time for the people in your life: you feel left out of your friends' lives and yet you can't hope to have a life of your own if you work so hard and push yourself to the limit,' Virginia added.

'Take care of your body,' Hope said fiercely. 'I pray that you're going to be fine and when you are, I'll personally kill you if I hear you're burning the candle at both ends. You don't eat properly, you never rest, you don't relax. Why are you surprised when your body rebels.'

'Stop pushing people away,' said Delphine eagerly, keen to help the woman who'd made matters so clear to her. 'You've got all these barriers up. You liked that hunky guy next door but when he tried to make friends with you, you froze him out. That's crazy, Sam. You're beautiful, I'd kill to look like you, so why not get some benefit from it. I didn't know how happy I could be until I met Eugene. This guy might be your Eugene.'

'I never wanted a Eugene, you see,' Sam pointed out. 'I didn't not want him either, if you see what I mean, but it just happened that way. In the past few years I've been interviewed a couple of times and the journalists always want to know how I made the choice between career and family. But I didn't, and they don't understand that. Who plans their life?'

Nobody said anything but they all looked on sympathetically.

'I didn't have a great master plan where I said no to some things and yes to others,' she continued fiercely. 'It just happened that way. I'm fed up having to justify my life.' She looked as if she might cry.

Mary-Kate leaned forward earnestly. 'Nobody is asking you to justify your life, Sam. Your life is as valid as anyone else's here, whether they've got a scatter of children or not, or husbands or not or toyboys or whatever. But when *you're* so defensive about your own life, that's saying that you feel uncomfortable with it for some reason. Not us, you. There are lots of people round here who think I'm a dotty old bat because I had this great job, a fine premises, money and yet I never got married. But that was my choice and I wouldn't change it.'

Virginia shot a glance at her.

'Not that I'm saying I never had a man in my life,' Mary-Kate put in, with a wicked glint. It broke the tension and the women laughed.

'I think Sam may have had enough advice,' Virginia said softly, looking at Sam's shell-shocked face.

Sam shook her head. 'No, it's great,' she said. 'It's years since anybody told me what I should do in such blunt terms. I'm the person who normally lays down the law. The only problem is, where do I start?'

'Wait till you see the doctor and then decide what to do with the burden you're bearing. You're an intelligent woman, you'll know which seems right,' said Giselle.

'I can't change my job, though. Whatever about all the rest,' Sam added. 'I've only been doing this for a few months and I've got to make my mark . . .' Her voice trailed off. For the first time since she'd found out about ovarian cancer on the internet, she began to think she'd been over-reacting.

Had she merely panicked – the cool, calm Sam Smith flipping and panicking for the first time in her life? And if she had flipped rather than intuitively known something was wrong, what did that mean? Sam knew the answer, even though she'd have killed for it not to be true: that she really couldn't cope with her life any more for some reason. Perfectly content and emotionally secure people didn't have mini-breakdowns where they thought they were dying.

'I suppose it's my turn next,' Mary-Kate said, seeing that Sam was very tense about the whole discussion. 'We can't have Sam on the rack all night. What do I want?' she mused out loud.

'Other than a himbo with a six-pack?' inquired Delphine naughtily.

'Very funny. Actually, that would be nice,' her aunt joked. 'One with massage skills so he could do things for my bad back.'

'Would he be restricted to your back?' asked Mai with a glint.

'I won't say anything if you don't stop teasing me,' Mary-Kate said, picking up the cat and settling him on her lap. 'What I want . . .' she stopped. 'What I want is to stop looking back all the time,' she said wistfully. 'There, that's it. I don't want advice and I've decided that I'm too old to be psychoanalysing myself. Every time my sister, Pauline, turns up here, she does it for me for free. She tells me where I've gone wrong in my life, asks me why I couldn't be sensible and get married like her and, this is the best bit, adds what a joy marriage has been for her. No offence to your father, Delphine,' Mary-Kate

301

added, 'but I would never have put your parents' marriage up there on the great love stories of all time list.'

Delphine nodded grimly in agreement.

The evening began to wind down as Mai had to leave. Her husband was scheduled to pick her up at eleven and it was five to.

'Sorry, ladies,' she said, 'but I have to be up at six and if I wait any longer, I will not be able to move out of my bed in the morning. I'll have to tell you my truth at the next meeting.' She left after much hugging and the rest of the guests began searching for handbags and coats with a view to going too. Mary-Kate phoned taxis.

'You never said what you wanted, Hope,' Mary-Kate said when she came back into the room.

Hope blushed. 'Nothing really,' she said.

'Go on,' urged Sam, 'you must have something you want to change, something you need to get out of your system. It's amazing really to have everyone give you advice like this. I feel better already!'

And she did, thought Hope, looking at her sister's pale face which seemed to have miraculously had all the worry lines taken from it.

Hope dithered, not because she had nothing to say but because she had so much to say that if she started, she might not stop. She sat down again. Oh well, she might as well say something but what?

'I'd like to stop being afraid,' she said, and startled herself. 'I don't know where that came from!' she gasped, 'I've never thought that out loud before now.'

'Keep going,' Sam said warmly.

Hope did her best: 'Afraid of lots of things,' she said. 'I worry about the children all the time. When they were babies, I had this compulsive thing about checking them every few hours at night in case they stopped breathing.'

'That's perfectly normal,' Giselle pointed out.

'And before we came here from Bath, I was afraid that Matt was having an affair,' Hope revealed, feeling ashamed even to be saying it. 'He wasn't, but I was so sure he was seeing someone else, so sure that I wasn't good enough for him, that I'd convinced myself he was.'

Sam patted her sister's shoulder. 'That makes two of us who can convince ourselves of things without having actual facts.'

'You at least have been feeling ill,' Hope argued. 'I based my notion on absolutely no evidence apart from my own insecurity. You see, it's fear. I'm always afraid of the thing that's over the horizon.'

'It sounds as if you're afraid of people you love being taken from you,' Mary-Kate said wisely.

Hope nodded. 'That's part of it, too. You know that our parents died when Sam and I were young and I suppose I've never got over that feeling that people I love are going to leave.'

'We understand that,' Delphine said. 'It must have been incredibly traumatic.'

'Yes but because of that, I . . .' Hope paused. It was hard to find the words to describe it. Hope knew that she yielded to Matt's will purely because she was sure that if she didn't, he would be angry and leave. 'As a direct result of that, Matt and I hardly ever argue,' she said. 'I know that sounds crazy but we don't or we didn't. I thought that if we fought, he'd leave. That makes me sound like some dimwit with room temperature IQ but that's what's always going on in my head. As if I'll do something wrong and he'll go. So I avoid fighting with him. I sulk a bit, mind you.'

They all grinned.

Hope said. 'We never fought until we came to Redlion, to be honest. If I got angry, I hid it.'

'People who hide their anger have a big furnace of rage boiling away inside them,' Virginia pointed out. 'It has to go somewhere when you don't vent it on anyone else, so it eats you up. It's supposed to be much healthier to lose your temper occasionally instead of bottling it up forever.'

'I do get angry now,' Hope said. 'I do say what I want. But it's not a dramatic change, mind you. It's such a big step for me that it's happening very slowly. Matt wouldn't be able to cope if I turned from a yes-woman to a harridan in one fell swoop.'

'Slow but sure, like an ass eating thistles,' quoted Delphine.

'What does that mean?' laughed Sam.

'That it's happening slowly but that eventually, the donkey will eat all the thistles,' Delphine said. 'It's my dad's favourite saying.'

'But you do argue now?' Virginia asked. 'So you are already changing what needs to be changed. It's not easy changing the habits of a lifetime but you have to think that you are important and special, you need to think that Matt is lucky to have you and that maybe one day he'll be scared of you leaving him.'

'I doubt it,' laughed Hope. 'Why would Matt ever be worried that I'd leave him?'

Virginia shrugged. 'I'm not saying it's going to happen that you'll leave, just that you should start to see yourself as a valuable person.'

Hope smiled, pleased at this thought. 'This is a great idea, but it's exhausting.'

'Yes it is,' said Virginia. 'I'm sorry, girls.' She held her hands up in surrender. 'I'm exhausted, I don't know if I have the energy to bare my soul.'

'There's no need,' Mary-Kate said swiftly.

'You mean we only have to bare if we need to bare?' Virginia asked shrewdly.

'That's it.'

The doorbell rang, signalling the arrival of the taxis.

'Good,' said Giselle, getting stiffly to her feet. 'I'm also too tired to bare anything. Till the next time, yes?'

'Yes,' they all said, tipsy but happy.

'I feel healed, calm, wonderful,' announced Sam as she said goodbye to Mary-Kate at the door. 'And it's not just the martinis.'

'I know it's not,' Mary-Kate said. 'It's a first sight of what you're looking for, Sam. Most people think they have no option but to settle for what life has shown them. A few lucky ones know that they can change their lives and go searching for something better.'

Sam smiled beatifically. 'Tonight was great. Can I come again?'

'You can come any time,' replied Mary-Kate warmly.

After the Macramé Club, Teddy the taxi drove Virginia home at precisely fifteen miles an hour. Virginia sat beside him and wished he'd go a bit faster because she was so tired that she felt she might fall asleep and she didn't particularly want to drop off on his shoulder.

'The roads are terrible,' he muttered, eyes on the rain-swept road ahead of him. It was the fourth time he'd said it.

Virginia, incurably polite, had replied the first time that yes, the roads were terrible. Now, she realized that no response was necessary. She felt mildly drunk thanks to Mary-Kate's martinis but she'd eaten enough cheese and crackers to soak it up. At least she hoped she'd eaten enough. She was too old for raging hangovers and she simply had to tackle the guests' bedrooms in the morning. They were coming on Friday, which was only two days away, and the dust wouldn't disappear magically. But it had been a lovely evening, very intense when everyone had been talking about their hopes and dreams, but somehow very healing.

'Would you look at the size of that pothole,' demanded Teddy.

Virginia looked wearily out into the bleak, lashing night and saw, suddenly, not the pothole, but a small white dog huddled beside the verge. A terrier with white fur plastered to a shaking body, it cowered as the taxi's lights shone on it. Even from inside the car, Virginia could see the animal's heartbroken little face and knew that this wasn't the sort of dog that should be out on such a night.

'Stop the car,' she commanded in such a firm voice that Teddy put the brakes on immediately. He'd barely stopped before she'd jumped out into the lashing rain to run back to the shivering animal, which shrank down at she approached.

'Hello,' cooed Virginia crouching down. 'Hello you poor little pet.' She held out a hand but the dog still cowered. Virginia wasn't a country girl for nothing. And she loved dogs. This poor thing needed to be rescued and she was the one to do it. 'Come here, boy,' she crooned, reaching further until she could touch the soaking wet fur.

The little dog shivered but when Virginia's hand started petting the wet white head, it looked up anxiously and whimpered. 'It's OK,' repeated Virginia, oblivious to the lashing rain. She edged closer to the dog and reached for its neck, seeking a collar. There was none. Still petting, Virginia got close enough to pick the bedraggled creature up, wincing as she realized how thin the animal was under its covering of thick fur. She could feel delicate ribs and the poor dog's heart beating fiercely with fear. But it didn't growl or show its teeth. It lay frozen with terror in her arms.

'You poor little thing,' she said softly.

Teddy had reversed the taxi until he was beside Virginia, who, still carrying the dog and seemingly oblivious to how wet and dirty it was, motioned to him to roll down his window.

'I'm bringing the poor dog home. We can't leave it here,' she said.

Teddy gulped. He didn't want a small, scruffy wet dog in his immaculate taxi and if any other passenger had tried to rescue a roadside stray in the middle of a downpour, Teddy would have told them where they could get off. But he got the impression that Mrs Connell could be formidable when she wanted to, for all that she was so quiet and ladylike.

'Well . . . yes,' he said, looking at his clean seats.

'I'll wrap her in my coat and you won't got a bit of dirt or rain in the car,' Virginia said imperiously.

There was nothing you could say to that. Teddy meekly opened the passenger door and Mrs Connell got in, the dog bundled up in her expensive coat like a baby.

At the house, she grabbed the first banknote that she could find in her handbag and gave it to Teddy. It was twice the fare and Teddy stared at it for a moment as if contemplating whether he had change or not. 'Consider it a tip in case there's any dirt on the seat,' Virginia said graciously. Then she was gone, with the dog still bundled up in her coat. Teddy watched Mrs Connell walk gracefully up to her front door, coatless in the lashing rain. Women, he thought. What hope had a mere man of understanding them.

Once they were inside, Virginia unwrapped the little dog and quickly found a big towel to dry it off properly. The kitchen was always warm at night, so they went in there and Virginia rubbed the dog gently, talking nonsense to it all the time until the worst of the nervous shivering was over. It was a West Highland terrier, a sweet little white dog that should have been sitting in front of a warm fire instead of dumped by the side of the road on a wet night.

'I'm so sorry to have called you a boy when you're a little girl,' Virginia said, looking fondly down into the still anxious eyes. 'What's your name, pet?' The dog blinked up at her, as if disbelieving that somebody was being nice to it.

Virginia got some milk from the fridge and put a bowlful on the floor. The dog looked at the bowl mournfully and then back up at Virginia.

'Go on,' she urged.

With another mournful look, the little dog began to delicately lap up the milk with her little pink tongue. Even in her hunger, she lapped gently and without slopping a drop of milk.

'You're starved, you poor thing,' Virginia said. She found a left-over bit of chicken and gave the dog that too.

Finally fed, the dog seemed to relax a bit and slowly wandered round the kitchen, sniffing here and there. She stopped at the back door and looked up at Virginia anxiously.

'Somebody trained you well, darling,' Virginia smiled and let the dog out, standing in the doorway all the while in case she wandered off.

'I wonder who you belong to,' Virginia said when the dog came back, not quite as nervous now, and sat at her feet. 'We'll phone the police and the dog pounds in the morning to see if anyone's reported you missing but until then, we both need our rest.'

Virginia made up a bed beside the radiator in the kitchen, left a bowl of water beside it and then went to the kitchen door. She looked back at the little dog who was now looking at her with an expression of abandonment on its small white face. Virginia's heart melted. The poor little thing had obviously been abandoned often enough.

'Would you like to sleep upstairs with me?' she asked.

Was it her imagination or did the doggy face smile? Virginia picked up the make-shift bed made out of an old blanket and carried it upstairs, the dog stepping neatly behind her. 'I can't keep calling you dog,' Virginia said as she patted the blankets into shape in a neat nest beside her bedroom radiator. 'What name will we give you?'

The dog tilted her head to one side as if considering the matter.

Virginia cast her mind back to the dogs she'd known. Her mother had a lovely little terrier called Dinky, a family pet as distinct from

307

the sheep dogs that slept outside. Dinky had been sweet-natured and docile, like this little dog.

'How does Dinky sound to you, as a stop gap?' Virginia asked. 'Bed Dinky.'

Dinky licked Virginia's hand and trotted off to her bed, curling up in it snugly.

'Dinky it is,' smiled Virginia.

She got ready for bed, chatting all the time to Dinky who lay watchful in her bed, big eyes following Virginia's every move. It was nice to have someone to talk to again, even someone who couldn't talk back. Virginia climbed into bed and turned out the light. In the dark, she thought of the evening and the marvellous Truth Drug session. What a clever idea and Mary-Kate, in her inimitable way, had known that Virginia wasn't ready to talk about what she wanted from life just yet.

Peace, Virginia thought suddenly. That's what she wanted. The peace of feeling at ease and not having that tearing in her heart when Bill came into her head. And she thought she might slowly be getting peace. She could chat to Bill when she went about her everyday chores, telling her about her day, sharing the stories she'd read in the morning paper. She could think about him without bursting into tears and she could now remember the good times without feeling her heart clouding over because the good times were over. Being able to remember and be thankful for the good times was a huge step for her and she thanked God for it. That's what she could have said tonight. Still, there were more nights to talk about it. Virginia snuggled down on her pillow and slept better than she had in a long time.

In the morning, she was awakened by Dinky standing on her hind legs and tentatively sniffing the bedclothes.

Virginia patted the covers invitingly, and without hesitation Dinky jumped up and snuggled down beside her.

'Aren't you a little pet?' Virginia crooned.

Dinky licked her hand lovingly.

After breakfast, Virginia forced herself to phone the police station and told them she'd found a little white dog.

'No mention of it here, Mrs Connell,' said Sergeant O'Hara. 'But we'll keep your name and number in the book in case someone does come along looking for her.'

Next, she rang the animal rescue agency and the local animal protection organization.

Neither had any notice of a lost white terrier.

'I can't believe that someone hasn't missed her,' Virginia said. 'She's such a dear little thing.'

'You did say she was very nervous of you at first, wasn't she?' said the animal rescue woman. 'That doesn't sound like a dog that was well treated to me. She was probably dumped.'

'But how could anyone just dump her on the side of the road?' Virginia asked. 'It's cruel.'

'That's nothing to what some people do to dogs,' the woman said sadly. 'If nobody comes forward, do you want to keep her?'

'I'd like nothing more,' Virginia said genuinely. 'I already love her. I know it sounds awful, but I hope nobody comes forward because she's a beautiful little dog.'

'She was lucky you found her,' the woman said, 'or she could have been run over. Lots of lorries use that road and at night, sure they'd have her run over before they'd see her.'

Virginia reached down to pet Dinky who was sitting loyally at her feet. 'It was lucky for both of us,' she said fondly.

The morning after the Macramé Club, Sam was up earlier than anyone else and was making Rice Krispie buns with Toby and Millie when Hope wandered downstairs.

'You're up early,' she said, feeling decidedly woolly-headed after their late night.

'Yes and I feel wonderful. I hope you don't mind, but I've booked myself on the evening flight so I can be home tonight.'

Hope stared at her sister. 'I thought I was going with you.'

'No you're not. You're too busy here. I'm going to go home and go to the consultant myself. I'm not a baby, Hope.'

'But I wanted to . . .'

'I know.' Sam made the fatal mistake of leaving Millie alone with a big bowl of chocolate in order to hug her sister. 'I can manage on my own, you've calmed me down and made me feel normal again.'

They hugged until a squeal and a crash made it obvious that Millie had taken the catering into her own hands.

'It fell,' Millie said, wide-eyed when they both looked at her and at the broken bowl and the chocolatey mess covering the floor.

When both Sam and Hope started to laugh, Millie giggled happily. She'd never thought anyone would find that funny.

# CHAPTER FOURTEEN

Far from the chalk-stripe suited consultant Sam had imagined, Professor Olivieri was a tiny grey-haired woman of few words who was even smaller than Sam but who had warm, shrewd eyes in a pale face.

She read the letter from Sam's doctor silently, while Sam sat in the high-tech consulting room and shivered with a mixture of nerves and embarrassment. Now that she was here she felt hideously ashamed at the thought of being considered a deranged hypochondriac. Ever since she'd stopped panicking, she'd regained her appetite and the night before had managed to consume an enormous pizza with half a bottle of wine as she watched *Sense and Sensibility* on video.

'I'm really sorry about all this hassle,' Sam said. 'I was nervous and I didn't think I could wait so long . . .'

Professor Olivieri merely smiled. 'Do not worry,' she said. 'Now I am going to examine you for cysts in the abdomen, glands and in the neck of the uterus. Then we will give you a scan to be sure.'

Sam nodded weakly. 'Fire away,' she said in a whisper. She had talked herself into believing she was going to be fine, but what if she was wrong after all?

In Redlion, Hope sat in the kitchen and stared at the Little Mermaid clock that hung on the wall over the kitchen table. Five past three. Sam's appointment was for three. How long could it take? Hope

began to work it out: perhaps five minutes waiting to see the consultant. Then fifteen to talk about what was wrong, five or ten for an
examination. Then, what if the consultant had to send Sam off somewhere to get a scan? Would that mean a separate appointment somewhere else?

Curlew Cottage was quiet except for the gentle ticking of the Little
Mermaid and the distant lowing of a cow in the field nearby. Matt
had kindly taken the children out for the afternoon and contrarily,
now that they were gone, Hope wished they were there. Millie and
Toby would have kept her mind off worrying about Sam.

As she sat and waited in anguish, Hope raged with herself for not
flying to London with Sam. It would have been so simple: Matt could
have taken care of the children and she wouldn't have been sitting
in Kerry now, hoping for a phone call to tell her everything was fine.
She'd have been holding Sam's hand, being with her, helping.

Damn Sam for being so stubbornly independent. But even as she
thought it, Hope knew that being independent was what Sam had
needed at this time. She could be strong on her own; if Hope had
been with her, she might have crumbled.

Damn, cursed Hope. There was nothing for it: she might as well
do the ironing.

She'd ironed ten shirts with savage speed when the phone rang
and she left the iron perilously on the board, racing to the phone.

'Hello.'

'It's me,' said Sam.

Hope took a deep breath, praying she'd know what to say.

'I'm fine!' gasped Sam. 'Absolutely fine. The scan shows fibroids
but nothing else and they can whip them out no bother.'

'Oh Sam,' sobbed Hope, 'I was so afraid, so very afraid.'

'Me too,' sang Sam delightedly, comforting her sister, 'but it's
wonderful now. I'm free, free and well and healthy. She wants to
book me in for something called TCRE, transcervical resection and
it's easy. I could be in and out of the clinic in one day.'

She threw her head backwards as if she was greedy to breathe
in life now that she had it guaranteed, 'I'm so thrilled, what'll I
do now?'

'Have a party?' suggested Hope, who longed to be there at that moment to hug her sister.

'Great idea,' said Sam.

Hope felt a pang of loneliness but quashed it.

'Tell me who you're going to ask?' she said.

Catrina was all on for a last-minute dinner party on Friday night.

'I never go anywhere any more,' she wailed. 'I suddenly feel huge, you know.'

Jay and Greg were going somewhere else later, but agreed to drop in.

'No sloping off to the bedroom for a bonk,' warned Sam over the phone.

'What's the party for?' asked Jay suspiciously.

'For me being happy and alive,' said Sam, wiping away tears. 'I had a bit of a bad moment last week when I thought I was ill, but I'm fine.'

'What do you mean you thought you were ill?' demanded Jay.

'I'll tell you later. Now what shall I cook: take away Thai, take away Indian or take away Italian?'

'Why don't you go the whole hog and ask Delia Smith along? It'd be easier.'

Sam danced into the office on Friday, astonishing everyone who'd been told she was ill all week by Lydia.

'You sounded at death's door with that flu last Friday,' Lydia remarked, looking at her boss who was radiant if slightly too-thin in a cream fine wool trouser suit. 'You're sure you haven't been at a health farm?'

Sam grinned at her. 'If you want to leave, why don't you try the more conventional route of handing in your notice, rather than making me fire you,' she teased.

She left the office early in the afternoon, stopping off in a taxi to pick up several huge bouquets of flowers. The wine and food were being delivered later at great expense. As Sam had said gaily to Hope on the phone the previous night: 'Why earn all this money if I don't do anything with it?'

'Exactly,' said Hope, thrilled that Sam was in good form but still feeling a bit left out at not being there to share the celebrations.

At home, Sam gave the apartment a cursory tidy up – it didn't need much work due to her obsessive cleanliness – and arranged her flowers everywhere, a bowl of coral pink roses on the dining room table, blood red amaryllis surrounded by striking foliage in the cool white living room, and beautifully-scented stargazer lilies in the hall.

She was just putting a couple of rose buds in a crystal glass on the dining room windowsill when she glanced out into the next door garden and saw Morgan hauling a bay tree in a huge stone container along the patio. It clearly required more than one person to drag it along but that was so Morgan: one man taking on the world.

Sam smiled at the sight of him, then ducked back when he stood upright, rubbed his aching lower back and looked directly up at her window. He'd seen her.

Suddenly, she flushed with shame as she remembered the last time she'd met him and she'd been such a bitch. He'd been nice to her, not just nice, friendly and a bit flirty, and she'd behaved like a crocodile who'd just been to the dentist for root canal work. As the deep-seated shame spread through her body, she realized she had to make amends.

She was going to change her life after all, she decided firmly. Apologizing to Morgan would be first on the list. Racing out of the apartment before she could change her mind, she reached his front door and rang the bell forcefully. Several minutes elapsed before the door was wrenched open.

Morgan was clad in his trademark jeans and there were bits of leaf and dirt clinging to his jumper and to his rumpled tawny hair.

'Yes?' He looked at her warily, as if waiting for her to land a punch or something. Even when he was mad, he couldn't get the sex appeal out of those treacly eyes. Although they were narrowed and suspicious as they surveyed her arrogantly over his proud, hooked nose.

'I've come to apologize,' she said, launching into it before she could have second thoughts. 'I was so horrible to you and I apologize. I was being a bitch but if it's any excuse, I was going through a bit of a personal crisis. Not,' she amended, looking down at her shoes because she couldn't meet that wary expression any more, 'that having a crisis is any real excuse. I'm really sorry, Morgan. I understand if you'd never want to see me again but I'd like us to be friends. I'm having a dinner party tonight and I wonder if you'd like to come?'

She looked up, hopeful that her grovelling had worked.

It was worth it to see his face light up in a glorious smile.

'Can I bring ten bimbo girlfriends?' he asked evilly.

Sam bit her lip. 'If you want, you can bring one,' she said.

'Only kidding. I'll just bring myself,' Morgan said, looking very pleased.

'It's strictly cas . . .' began Sam and stopped herself. She'd been about to say 'strictly casual,' but then, what other clothes did Morgan Benson possess?

'Jeans are fine, then?' he asked, the corners of his mouth lifting.

'Fine,' Sam said gravely. 'Just not those ones.'

They both looked down at the frayed hems at the ends of his long legs.

'I'll go then,' Sam added. 'Cooking and so on, you know.'

'I know. Dinner parties can be hell,' he deadpanned. 'All that stirring risotto and hoping the butler's not getting stuck into the desert wine.'

Back at the apartment, Sam realized that the food and drink people would be rolling up any minute, so she had to dress. But instead of going for her usual casual uniform of a cotton shirt and tailored trousers, she dressed in a soy-sauce brown silk wrap dress, with a flattering V-neck and a skirt that showed off her slender legs. She'd bought it for a party and then never wore it, as it was too girly. And what was wrong with being girly anyway, she thought gaily, slipping on crazy stack heeled sandals that looked as if they'd been custom made for Carmen Miranda. There had to be a place for frivolity in her life, hadn't there?

By eight, all the gang were there: Jay and Greg still heartbreakingly in love; Catrina and Hugh proudly expectant and eager to discuss every scan and baby detail; Andy with a shy fellow teacher, named Vanessa, who looked as if she was getting him over his divorce.

Morgan astonished Sam by turning up looking devastating in a crisp charcoal shirt unbuttoned at the neck and grey trousers, all of which screamed expensive and classy. His lips brushed Sam's cheek as he handed over a bottle of wine. 'How lovely of you to invite me, Ms Smith,' he said formally. 'What a pleasure it is to have such nice neighbours. Will there be loud music later?'

Sam giggled and sat him next to Jay and Vanessa, before rushing into the kitchen to dish up the first course.

'He's gorgeous,' murmured Catrina to Sam when they were tucking into Thai chicken. 'Where have you been hiding him?'

'He's just a friend,' Sam protested, handing round the salad.

'With friends like that, who needs husbands?' replied Catrina with a salacious wink.

The evening raced by. Sam had never had such a successful dinner party and it was due in part to how relaxed she was, and, she was astonished to realize, to how happy she felt to have Morgan there. The rest of the gang clearly liked him too, with Hugh and Morgan hitting it off particularly well. They were talking intensely about people they both knew and Sam was desperate to overhear because she was still in the dark about Morgan in so many ways, like what he did for a living, for a start. He and Hugh seemed to know lots of the same people and Morgan had apparently worked in New York years before, where he knew Hugh's older brother, Christopher.

'What were you and Morgan talking about?' Sam asked Hugh idly when he was helping her make a second batch of coffee.

'Oh just work and that. He's a decent chap, Morgan. Seems glad to be out of the rat race, though.' At that moment, Morgan arrived to help so Sam had to stop probing.

It was nearly twelve when Catrina announced that it was time she and Hugh went home. 'I don't know what's going to happen when the baby comes and you lose your designated non-drinking driver,' she remarked as a tipsy Hugh kissed Sam goodbye.

'We're going to get the baby a driving licence,' declared Hugh.

'What else are we having children for if it's not to look after their dear old parents?'

Jay and Greg said they were too tired to bother going on to the party now and got a taxi with Andy and Vanessa, who were going in the same direction.

'I'll help you clear up,' said Morgan when everyone had been waved off.

Together, they stacked the dishwasher in companionable silence, with Macy Gray playing softly on the CD player. It was like being an old married couple, Sam thought sentimentally.

'You're very laid back tonight, Ms Smith,' Morgan said, filling the sink with hot water to rinse the glasses.

Her tongue loosened with a couple of glasses of wine, Sam let her defences down and told him about her frantic week.

'No wonder you were so upset,' Morgan said, drying his hands on a towel and, to her astonishment, pulling her into his arms. 'I'm so glad you're not ill. You must have been terrified.'

Sam was speechless in his embrace, loving the feeling of his arms wrapped protectively round her and the sensation of being safe against him. He felt even better than she thought he'd feel: solid and warm, his chest hard against her face. It was nice to be held by someone who wasn't Hope or Hugh or Andy, someone who wasn't hugging her in a sisterly or brotherly way.

Then, just as suddenly, Morgan moved away, leaving Sam reeling with excitement as she stood there limply.

'Sorry,' he said abruptly, 'I didn't mean to invade your space. Sometimes I forget the proprieties.'

'No, that's fine,' muttered Sam, feeling let down.

Too late she remembered the first time they'd met when she'd accused him of invading her personal space, just before she kicked him on the shin.

'I should go,' Morgan said. He wasn't looking at her, but at the last few glasses he'd gone back to rinsing.

'Of course,' she replied politely, staring at his solid charcoal-shirted back. 'Thanks for coming and for staying behind to wash up.'

'No trouble.'

He didn't kiss her on the cheek when he left but merely said thanks again. Sam stood at the door for a moment, waiting for him to turn back and smile, but he didn't. She shut the door, conscious of a sense of anti-climax. There had been a definite air of anticipation in the air until Morgan had pulled away from her. She wondered why, then stopped herself. If he was interested, he'd make a move, she decided firmly. If he wasn't, he wasn't. What was the point torturing herself over it. She'd made her peace with him and that was the main thing. The new, improved and deliriously happy to be alive Sam Smith was not going to get her knickers in a twist over what might have been. She was going to be happy, contented and change her life for the better. She was going to take up yoga, eat organic food, be kind to everyone and try to live her life filled with inner spiritual light. She would not worry about the hunk of manhood who brooded Byron-ically in the house next door, absolutely not.

# CHAPTER FIFTEEN

Virginia couldn't for the life of her see why Jamie thought Barbara bossy. She seemed very quiet, almost docile.

Tiny, in direct contrast to the three tall Connells, she had long strawberry blonde hair that trailed down her back in romantic ripples. A heart-shaped little face, demure rosebud mouth and big blue eyes all added up to the very picture of sweetness. It was easy to see how Laurence was crazy about her.

Beside Virginia's strapping sons, Barbara looked like a nymph between two linebackers.

'Would you like some tea? You must be exhausted after the drive,' Virginia said once the introductions had been made.

'If it wouldn't be too much bother,' said Barbara.

Virginia spotted Jamie raising his eyes to heaven.

'Not at all,' she said, shooting Jamie a glare.

Dinky trotted confidently after Virginia as she led the way into the kitchen. When nobody had come forward to claim the little dog, Virginia had bought her a lovely tartan collar and a dog licence. If anyone wanted to take Dinky away from her now, they were in for a fight.

'How are you Ma?' asked Jamie, immediately sinking onto the old armchair beside the big dresser and hanging his long denimed legs over the arm. He looked so like Bill, thought Virginia fondly, except that Bill had been a heavier build, while Jamie was tall and lanky, with chestnut hair falling into mischievous blue eyes. Even at twenty-five, he still looked boyish. Laurence, on the other hand, looked tired, she thought anxiously. From a distance, he and Jamie were like twins, but up close Laurence's blue eyes boasted new lines and his hair didn't really suit him in that new, going-to-see-the-bank-manager cut.

Virginia vowed to get Laurence on his own and ask him if the practice was going well. She wouldn't embarrass him by asking in front of Barbara.

Installed in the kitchen on a chair, Barbara seemed to perch like a bird and gazed around her with those big blue eyes.

Dinky, who had so far greeted even the postman with a happy bark, approached and sniffled round the hem of Barbara's long black skirt with the politeness of a duchess genteelly greeting a friend . . .

'Oh a dog, how nice,' said Barbara, drawing her skirt in closer to her as if Dinky had been a fierce wolfdog with fangs bared.

'Do you not like dogs?' asked Virginia, perfectly prepared to banish Dinky to her bed if necessary. Not everyone loved animals the way the Connell family did.

'I love dogs,' cooed Barbara, still holding her skirt in.

As if to say that the new guest was lying, Dinky shot Virginia a wry glance.

'Yes, she loves dogs,' interrupted Laurence anxiously as if scared that anyone might think his beloved girlfriend was anything less than a saint.

'Dinky, come here,' said Virginia. Perhaps Barbara was merely nervy, she deserved the benefit of the doubt.

Dinky, ever the lady, came and sat quietly at her mistress's feet. She stayed there while Barbara explained at great length why she loved the country. Virginia felt herself tuning out eventually and wondered why Barbara had drawn a very dark lip liner around her mouth that bore no relation to her actual lip line. Fashion, she assumed.

After twenty minutes of Barbara's version of country life, Virginia realized that her son's girlfriend's notion of the country was restricted to watching TV soaps about rural communities and occasionally going to the races, where she'd nearly won the best dressed lady competition twice.

'You looked a million dollars at Leopardstown,' Laurence said, reaching across the table to pat her tiny little hand with his big one.

'I've got the photos somewhere, they were taken by a professional photographer, you know,' Barbara added smugly.

She was probably just trying to impress, Virginia thought charitably, as they all heard about the hat with the handpainted flowers that the judges had so admired. Of course the woman who'd won owned a boutique so had unrivalled access to lots of clothes, which wasn't fair, as Barbara said.

'In that case, she definitely cheated,' Jamie said, straight-faced. 'Boutique-owners shouldn't be allowed to compete. You should have asked for a steward's inquiry.'

'Why don't you all have a walk or a bath or whatever and I'll start dinner,' Virginia suggested, shooting him a warning glance. It had been so long since she'd had to cook for more than one that she needed the kitchen to herself and wanted to scotch any notions Barbara might have about helping. Those beautifully painted nails couldn't have ever had much to do with peeling vegetables.

Everyone shot off, leaving Virginia and Dinky alone.

'What do you think of her?' Virginia asked Dinky, who laid her pink nose on her paws and looked gravely upwards. Not very much, was the answer.

Jamie asked the same question an hour and a half later in the dining room as Virginia got him to help her lay the table.

She hadn't had a chance to answer before Barbara's voice could be heard from the sitting room where she and Laurence had just arrived.

'Should that dog be allowed in the house?' said Barbara in much more carrying tones than the babydoll ones she'd used so far.

Virginia stiffened.

'Told you,' said naughty Jamie, appearing beside his mother. 'She may look and act like butter wouldn't melt but she's a direct descendant of Attila the Hun's nasty older sister.'

'You might have told me,' scolded his mother.

'I did. You didn't believe me,' Jamie snorted.

'She's a lovely little dog,' they heard Laurence say placatingly.

'Mmm. This entire house needs an overhaul,' continued Barbara in tones of disgust. 'I don't know how your mother can live here. I mean, the *damp* in our bedroom. It can't be good for my asthma. There's a huge damp spot on the wall . . .'

Virginia heard no more. Jamie propelled her back into the kitchen before she self-combusted.

'How dare she?' growled Virginia, 'how dare she?'

Jamie, irrepressible as ever, laughed. 'Why don't you send Dinky on a suicide mission to kill her?' he asked.

'I wouldn't let Dinky near her. She'd poison the poor dog.'

At dinner, Barbara was back to being Ms Butter Wouldn't Melt, even calling Dinky over to her to offer a bit of bread. But Dinky wasn't stupid. She stayed watchfully at Virginia's feet offering support to her mistress, who was no longer in the mood to put up with false politeness. When Barbara gushingly said she *adored* Kilnagoshell House and loved the faded curtains that Virginia hadn't got round to replacing, Virginia had to bite her tongue.

'Ouch!' was all she said, but that was because Jamie had kicked her under the table.

She glared at his innocent face but, for Laurence's sake, said nothing to Barbara. If he loved Barbara, it wasn't her place to upset things. And with luck, he'd soon realize that a woman who could be sweet in public and shrewish in private was not a good bet.

The next day, Barbara got up early and used up all the hot water having an enormous bath. Seeing as how Virginia had mentioned that the plumbing was sensitive and that she'd been meaning for ages to get someone to sort out the hot water situation, she was understandably cross to have to endure a freezing cold shower.

'Sorry,' Barbara said in her baby doll voice. 'As this place was a B & B before, I thought the plumbing would be wonderful.'

Virginia glared at her. Nobody looking at the faded, elegantly run down Kilnagoshell with its elderly bathrooms, could have imagined that it had decent plumbing. In fact, Virginia was always waiting for the hot water tank to come crashing down from the attic whenever she switched the heater on.

After breakfast, Barbara suggested accompanying Virginia on her daily walk with Dinky.

'What a lovely idea,' Laurence said, giving his mother an affectionate hug.

'Yes, lovely,' said naughty Jamie. 'The whole family together, lovely.'

Barbara was not cut out for walking. First, she had the wrong sort of shoes for muddy country lanes, then she wailed like a fishwife when she caught her trailing, pure white Macintosh on a bramble and a thread pulled out.

Finally, she said she'd love to see cute little animals like rabbits and wherever were they?

Shaking in their warrens frightened out of their skulls by your screaming, I dare say, Virginia muttered to herself.

Back home, she took Dinky and rushed out of the house saying she had errands to run, anything to get away before Barbara suggested another en masse trip.

Mary-Kate was quite happy to leave Otis in charge for ten minutes while she and Virginia went into her cosy office to share a coffee and some of the pastries Virginia had brought.

'I hate to think I'm turning into one of those awful women who loathe their daughters-in-law and their sons' girlfriends,' Virginia groaned. 'Mothers-in-law cause so much strife. Apparently, they even have classes in Italy where mothers-in-law can go to learn how to get their claws out of their sons and let the marriages run normally. Or is it India? Somewhere beginning with an I, anyhow.'

'But not Ireland,' Mary-Kate said mischievously. 'Only joking,' she added, seeing Virginia's stricken look. 'You get on brilliantly with your other son's wife, don't you?'

'Sally, you mean?' Virginia snuffled a bit until she found her handkerchief. 'Yes I do but that's different.'

'Exactly, that's different because she's nice and kind and you love her. This Barbara sounds like a total bitch and you don't like her. But you'll just have to put up with her, I'm afraid.'

Virginia looked distraught at this. 'All I want is for the boys to be happy, I want them to be married to wonderful, kind women I adore, then I know they'll be content.'

'Yes, and I want world peace and to win the lottery but neither wish is going to come true, so I'll have to live without them,' Mary-Kate pointed out pragmatically. 'You never know, Laurence could get tired of her and dump her. Men are always dumping women. He must have had loads of girlfriends in the past.'

'When he was younger, yes,' Virginia said gloomily. 'This is different. This is serious. Barbara's the sort of girl who won't rest until she's got the diamond solitaire on her finger and has the church booked.'

Mary-Kate looked thoughtful. 'That serious, huh. I wonder if Delphine could persuade any of her drop-dead gorgeous friends to lure Laurence away from Barbara for one night of passion. That'd put a stop to her wedding fantasy gallop.'

Virginia laughed. 'Only you would think of that. You're far too Machiavellian to be running a chemist's. You should be CEO of some giant corporation.'

'You could be horrible to her and tell Laurence you hate her.'

Even though Virginia knew her friend was only joking, she still shook her head. 'No, I refuse to pander to the wicked mother-in-law legend. I'm sick of hearing about bitter women who treat their daughters-in-law like bonded servants and their sons like spoiled pashas. I won't join the twisted sisterhood.'

'Practice a fixed smile, then,' Mary-Kate advised.

They finished their coffee and had said goodbye when Virginia thought of something else about Barbara that she hated.

'And you won't believe it,' she added grimly. 'Barbara doesn't like Dinky.'

Mary-Kate held a hand dramatically to her chest. 'That does it. I'll get the rifle out now. This woman must be stopped!'

'You're a big idiot, do you know that?' Virginia chuckled.

Her good humour was short-lived.

That night, Laurence took them all out to dinner in the Pigeon Club, a local five-star restaurant.

'The practice must be doing well, Laurie,' said Jamie, wincing as he looked at the prices. 'I should have become a dentist. I couldn't afford this place on a teacher's salary.'

'We wanted to come somewhere special,' Laurence said, smiling over at Barbara, who dimpled up at him, 'because we've got good news. Barbara and I are getting married.'

Virginia didn't know who was the most astonished: herself or Jamie. From somewhere, she summoned up the ability to smile, say congratulations and to kiss Laurence. Then, with supreme effort, she gave her first ever air kiss, to Barbara, because she couldn't bear to touch her.

Barbara didn't notice, she was too busy beaming with sheer delight.

As Virginia looked at her daughter-in-law-to-be, she realized that Barbara's big pale blue eyes were as cold as the winter sky before snow.

'Any news of the wedding of the year?' inquired Sally, a week later, when Virginia had just about got over the shock.

Virginia laughed heartily into the phone. At least she had one daughter-in-law she got on with.

'No, you brat. Don't remind me. You won't be so chirpy when you've had her for the weekend.'

Barbara and Laurence were due to visit Dominic and Sally in London soon.

'She'll insist on going to Harrods where Laurence will be made to buy her something expensive, and you won't be able to understand a word she says because she's got the weirdest, put-on accent I've ever heard in my life.'

'So Jamie says. He hates her.'

Virginia shook her head miserably. 'I'm not a huge fan, either. Oh, let's talk about something else. I've been spending far too long thinking about bloody Barbara. When I can't sleep, I find myself grinding my teeth and thinking of all the things I'd like to say to her. Anyway, Sally,' Virginia said proudly, 'I've made a phone call I've been meaning to make for ages. I've booked lessons with a pro in the local golf club and I start in a week.'

'Fantastic!' said Sally.

Virginia suspected Sally would have said 'fantastic' if she'd mentioned taking up the trapeze. Any sign that Virginia was coming out of her gloom was a positive sign, no matter what she decided to do.

'I'll probably be terrible at it and I'm a bit old to start,' Virginia said.

'Nonsense,' said Sally staunchly.

Her mother-in-law grinned. 'You're a terrible liar, do you know that?'

They both laughed.

'The pro asked had I played any other sport and I said camoige when I was a teenager and he said that was perfect. Mind you, I pointed out that it was forty years since I had a camoige stick in my hand and he said that was still perfect, I wouldn't have any bad habits to unlearn.'

'Camoige's that game that's a bit like hurling, is it?' inquired Sally, a born and bred Londoner who had never heard of such mad Irish games as hurling until she'd fallen for Dominic.

'Much more violent,' smiled Virginia. 'I'll probably be banned from the local course for belting the Lady Captain with my nine iron.'

'You've certainly got all the lingo,' Sally pointed out.

'Living with a besotted golfer all those years, you'd have to be deaf not to,' Virginia said. Living with Bill, she meant. Lucky she had a tissue up her sleeve to wipe the tears away.

The golf professional in St Cecilia's Golf Club was a gruff and grizzled man in his forties who was short on small talk and who had obviously got out of bed the wrong side.

'Why is the club called St Cecilia's?' Virginia asked politely as the pair of them walked from the clubhouse to the tiny driving range where she was to receive her first lesson.

'Don't be asking me,' snapped Fintan O'Riordain. 'I'm here to teach you how to play golf, not to give you a history lesson.'

Count to ten, Virginia told herself.

'My husband played and these are his clubs,' Virginia said, stroking one of them.

'Probably too big for you, Mrs Connell. Women need shorter clubs than men do.'

Virginia eyed him coolly. He was shorter than she was and no doubt used men's clubs, but she held back.

'Now watch me,' Fintan said and hit a few drives to impress her. Bill would have hit them further, Virginia thought proudly. He'd always said he was a long hitter.

'Your turn,' Fintan said.

After ten minutes when he showed her how to grip the golf club and managed to sigh heavily every few seconds at how stupid she was proving, Virginia had had enough of Fintan.

'Two knuckles, woman!' Fintan roared, wrenching the five iron from her grip and demonstrating.

'Tell me,' she said conversationally, 'do you get much repeat business, Fintan? Because you're the most bad-tempered pig I've ever had the misfortune to meet and if this is how you plan on teaching me to play golf, I'd rather chew off my own leg.'

'Nobody's ever complained before,' said Fintan, looking hurt.

'*I'm* complaining,' said Virginia, smiling. 'Now if all it took to learn was just to look and immediately know how it was done, we'd all be Tiger Woods, wouldn't we? Even you, Fintan and you wouldn't have to be teaching golf to stupid women.'

He blinked nervously.

'I'm not up on fancy ways of Dublin women,' grumbled Fintan.

'Fintan, I may have lived in Dublin for thirty years, but I was born and bred just outside Tralee and no Tralee woman would take that sort of abuse from a man she was paying for a lesson.'

'Well if you'd said *that,*' he said indignantly, 'I'd have been treating you like a local.'

'So locals get preferential treatment,' said Virginia, feeling the laughter creeping into her voice.

'Could be. But the price is the same,' he said firmly.

When the lesson was over, they walked back up to the club house, a grand old building with ivy growing over the door and a terrace on the first floor where people could sit outside on warm days and watch weary golfers playing the eighteenth.

'Do you want to come into the bar and be introduced to them all?' Fintan asked, obviously on his best behaviour now.

No, Virginia wanted to say. I don't want to meet anyone and have to explain that I'm a widow, that my husband is dead a year and a half and that I ran away because I couldn't face being in our old haunts without him. 'That would be nice, Fintan,' she said mildly.

St Cecilia's Golf Club was olde worlde on the outside and even olde worlde-ier on the inside. Virginia washed her hands in a pretty ladies' room decorated with rather dark mock Victorian paper and reapplied some lipstick in a gilt-edged mirror with decoupage cherubs on the surround. She combed her hair and tied it back again with the plum-coloured velvet ribbon. That would do. Her fine hazel eyes with the arched brows looked cool and collected and the cream polo shirt and darker cream trousers were suitable, she was sure. Just one drink, then she'd be free to retreat back to her lair and be alone again.

Fintan was at the bar when she climbed the steps to the club lounge, a darkly panelled room with an excess of burgundy swagged curtains.

'What'll you have?' Fintan asked.

'A mineral water, please,' Virginia answered, looking around. Apart from the young barmaid and a couple of men in one corner sipping whiskey and not talking to each other, the place was empty.

'The course was closed this morning,' Fintan said, seeing her looking. 'Maintenance.'

'Oh', said Virginia, realizing that she wasn't going to be introduced to many people if there was no one there. Good.

She sipped her mineral water and relaxed in her chair. Fintan wasn't the chatty type and that suited her fine. She had no need to talk to him if it wasn't necessary.

She was finishing her drink and was about to make another appointment with Fintan for a lesson when someone else entered the bar. A tall rangy man with collar-length greying hair, a healthy tan he hadn't got in Kerry in March, and the upright bearing of someone who'd once been in the military, he nodded at Fintan and smiled politely at Virginia, intelligent eyes flickering over her briefly. He was handsome, Virginia noticed, not gone to seed as so many men in their sixties did.

There was no beer-induced stomach here or whiskey-reddened cheeks. Just a lean man with a lined face, a Roman nose and warm, intelligent eyes.

'Kevin!' said Fintan, sounding as relieved as a man overboard who'd just spotted the lifebuoy. 'Come and meet Virginia.'

Kevin held out one hand but before he got to say hello, Fintan went on with his introduction.

'Sure, you'll have loads in common,' Fintan said. 'Virginia's learning golf and she's a widow from round here. Kevin's a widower. Isn't that a coincidence?'

Clearly delighted with himself for having got Virginia off his hands, Fintan grabbed his half-finished pint and made his way over to the two whiskey-drinkers in the corner.

Virginia's clear hazel eyes met Kevin Burton's warm grey ones, and instantly they both laughed.

She took his hand, still laughing: 'Virginia Connell, widow of this parish and would-be-golfer,' she smiled.

His hand was warm and the clasp strong. 'Kevin Burton at your service,' he said, also smiling. 'Widower and also would-be-golfer. I've been learning golf for a long time. The first thirty years are definitely the worst.'

Virginia giggled, a sound she hadn't heard emerge from herself for a long time. 'Fintan will tell you that the first lesson is definitely the worst. I don't think I impressed him very much.'

'Fintan is never impressed very much,' Kevin said. 'He has to be nice all summer to the visitors so during the rest of the year, he lets his normal cantankerousness loose to make up for his efforts. You can't expect him to be polite all the time.'

They both laughed again, and Virginia was struck by how relaxed she felt. Later on, she wondered what would have happened if Fintan hadn't introduced them with his usual lack of manners. Would they have laughed so companionably if not at his gauche behaviour? Would they have ever realized that they had so much in common? Probably not.

Virginia imagined that she and Kevin would have said hello occasionally across the bar and perhaps encountered each other on the driving range but that was all. Fintan's spectacular introduction had done them both a favour.

In the end, Virginia had another drink. 'A real one,' Kevin had said softly.

He was very softly spoken, as if he knew that people listened to what he said so there was absolutely no need to raise his voice.

'How did you find your first lesson?'

Virginia grimaced. 'I was pretty terrible,' she admitted. 'My husband, Bill, was an avid golfer and he was always on at me to play. I never bothered and now I know why! I'm awful at it.'

Kevin smiled encouragingly at her. 'We're all terrible when we start. It took me years to get down to a decent handicap.'

The conversation flowed easily.

He knew the people who'd owned Kilnagoshell House before her. He and his wife, Ursula, had been to dinner there a few times.

'Lovely place but I think running the B & B was a bit much for them when they got older.'

'Did your wife play golf?' Virginia asked.

'Yes, she was marvellous,' he said ruefully. 'We played together a lot.'

They laughed and talked for over an hour. Virginia had another glass of Chardonnay and felt herself grow enjoyably tipsy. Kevin and Ursula had been to the Far East too and they discovered that Virginia and Bill had stayed in the same hotel in Singapore, only on different years. Both couples had gone to St Andrews to play golf, although Virginia grinned and admitted that she'd spent the entire glorious weekend relaxing while Bill had joyously played the old course.

'Do you know what's lovely about talking to you?' Virginia blurted out suddenly. 'Talking about my husband and knowing that you understand. You haven't tried to change the subject as if I must be mad to mention him at all. You haven't muttered something about how we've all got to move on and frantically thought of something else to talk about. That's such a relief. My sons are nervous of mentioning their father in case it upsets me. Only my daughter-in-law understands and speaks about him naturally.'

She would never have said that at home in Dublin. There, she was buttoned up and kept her public face on show: Virginia Connell, ladylike, gracious and reserved. Here, it was as if she was allowed to speak her mind.

Kevin's face was sad for a moment as he considered what she'd said. 'People think it's for the best, you know,' he said. 'They don't mean to be insensitive but they think that you'll heal better if you *don't* talk about the person who's died. When you and I know that you desperately want to. Nobody wants to hear me talk about how Ursula and I always planned to go on a cruise when we were both retired. They think it's morbid and that I'll never forget if I keep talking about her.'

'I loved the idea of a cruise,' Virginia said quietly. 'That's what's so awful, you know. Thinking of all the things you'd planned to do but never did. I had cruise brochures in the kitchen and I used to look at them and think of how nice it would be when we could go, when Bill was retired. Nothing madly expensive, mind you. Just relaxing and fun, seeing the Mediterranean or the Adriatic.' She was misty-eyed at the memory. 'Then Bill died and that was it: plan over. You can't go for a cruise on your own.'

Kevin's hand came down over hers, comforting and kind, nothing more.

'But you can learn golf,' he said. 'I'll take you out and show you the ropes. Kerry isn't the Mediterranean, I know, but we can improvise. Two old friends helping each other out.'

'We're not old friends,' Virginia pointed out.

Kevin smiled, a lovely warm smile that lit up his face. 'After that conversation, I think we're damn good friends,' he said.

Sally had left a message on the answer phone when Virginia got home.

'Just phoning to see how the golf lesson went,' said her daughter-in-law's cheery voice on the tape. 'I'm in all day so phone back if you get a minute. Dominic is working late so I'd love to hear from you.'

Virginia stared at the phone as if it was remonstrating with her for abandoning her family. Dominic and Laurence and Jamie, her sons, Bill's sons. What had she been doing: talking and flirting, yes flirting, with a man when the man in her life was her beloved Bill and he was dead. She crumpled up the events listing she'd taken from the club, with its notices about a ladies' fourball for charity and details about the course's opening hours.

How could she have talked so openly and happily to a strange man? Bill was dead and there was no more happiness to be had in the world. To laugh and forget about him for even a moment was betrayal. To laugh with someone else for well over an hour, well, that was the most heinous betrayal.

Virginia sat on the bottom step of Kilnagoshell House's grand curving staircase, the sort of Victorian staircase that Bill had always liked the look of and had maintained they'd own one day. She buried her face in her hands and wept. For Bill and for herself.

The note arrived the next afternoon.

'Phone me if you want to play a nice relaxed nine holes of golf,' Kevin had written in a strong, decisive hand. He'd left his number and finished with the words 'no pressure. Phone if you feel like it.'

She did want to phone. And she didn't. After a frantic, dream-filled night where Bill had remained tantalizingly out of reach although she could see him in the distance, Virginia had woken feeling as if she'd ploughed the front garden. The guilt of having fun with Kevin weighed on her heart like a millstone. To recompense, she'd got up early and gone to eight o'clock Mass, hoping that the familiar words in the mouth of twinkly-eyed Father McTeague would penetrate her soul and make the world seem normal. But Mass had remained as horribly uncomforting as it had been since Bill had died. She murmured the familiar words mechanically, reams of prayers tripping off her tongue with ease, but none of it made any sense. It hadn't been able to comfort her then and it didn't help now, either.

Still desperate for absolution, she'd come home and attacked the shed at the back of the garden, making a huge heap of rubbish from old paint containers to bits of wood with nails stuck on. By lunch time, she was worn out but still miserable. There was nothing she could face but an evening at home on her own. However, she'd promised to go out with Delphine and Mary-Kate, for what Mary-Kate described as 'a feast of chicken wings and chips in the Widows and a few drinks before Teddy Taxi drives us home.'

There was no moping when Mary-Kate was around, so Virginia found herself having a glass of wine and the Widows famous fish pie, because she hated chicken wings.

'Fair play to you for learning golf,' Delphine said, attacking her chips with gusto.

'And you met Kevin Burton? He always strikes me as a nice man,' Mary-Kate said casually.

'Yes, he is,' replied Virginia, just as casually. She looked up and caught Mary-Kate smiling at her. Virginia flushed. 'What?'

'Nothing,' said Mary-Kate innocently.

Matt stared at the blank screen of his laptop. It flickered in the soft lights that were dotted all around the big attic room, the cursor winking at him cheekily. The room was silent, as ever. Talking wasn't permitted in the writing room. Only two of the seven desks were occupied this morning, one by an elderly lady writer who'd confided to Matt in the kitchen that she was filling out her tax return and needed somewhere quiet to do it; the other by Ciaran Headley-Ryan who was typing away briskly. He worked there every morning from nine to one and his fingers never stopped. He didn't appear ever to be struck by either writer's block or a crisis of confidence.

Matt gazed out the big window at the desolate, wind-swept landscape. It was a horrific morning, with gale-force winds buffeting the pine trees around the centre and lashing the rhododendrons beside the gate. You needed to be able to write *something* in the first place to have writer's block, Matt thought desperately. He'd been ploughing away for months now and it was all total rubbish.

The beautiful, lyrical book he'd dreamed of writing for so long, a novel that would have the world's literati queuing up to shake his hand, refused to take shape. Something had taken shape all right: a third rate TV movie of a novel that wouldn't interest anyone. His depressed hero was more like an escapee from a bad science fiction book than the main character in something Salman Rushdie would want to review. An avid reader, Matt knew the difference between rubbish and a decent book and, no matter how much it pained him to say it, his was definitely rubbish. He hadn't had the courage to tell Hope how awful it was to stare at the screen with so much intensity and still come up with only a few terrible sentences that looked even worse when he read them a day later.

He'd spent half an hour scrolling through the previous week's work and had felt his heart sink into his sturdy boots with each passing minute. Tip tap went Ciaran, his fingers flying. Matt had never read any of Ciaran's historical escapades although Finula had pressed three on him. He didn't want his own creativity to be tainted by reading anyone else's stuff. Well, that was the reason initially. Until he'd realized he couldn't write for toffee. Now, he couldn't bear to look at Ciaran's novels on the grounds that it would physically hurt to see someone else making a living out of doing what he couldn't.

Painful though it was, Matt had realized that he wasn't a writer: writing ad campaigns and writing a novel weren't the same thing. They were a million miles apart; like being able to play the piano and assuming that meant you could also play the violin. Similar, definitely, but still different enough to ensure that doing one did not necessarily mean you could do the other.

That hurt, hurt terribly. But even worse was the knowledge that his mistaken belief that he *could* write meant he'd uprooted the entire family to Kerry. He'd given up his job, their home and their life, for *nothing*.

'Coffee,' mouthed Ciaran, appearing suddenly beside him.

Matt nodded gratefully. Anything to get away from that malevolently winking laptop cursor.

Together they went downstairs, past the two big art studios where the sound of muffled laughter signalled that the morning art class was coming to an end. To make the centre profitable, the committee rented it out for two and three-day art courses and week-long writing courses during the year. Today's group had abandoned the idea of drawing outdoors and Matt had seen them dragging in branches of trees and mucky great lumps of rock for a still life session when he'd arrived. Luckily, he wouldn't have to exchange idle chit chat with the visiting painters.

The visitors always had their mid-morning coffee in what was called the library, a small room decorated with unsold paintings and books written by the centre's past and present writers. Ciaran had an entire shelf to himself. Matt miserably decided that the only way his work was going to ever be exhibited in the library was if he took up art. Making potato prints was probably his level, he thought bitterly.

'How's it going?' Ciaran said kindly. He would never betray for a second that he could recognize the signs of someone who was struggling. Ciaran had seen people come to write in the centre and discover that they had some glorious hidden talent buried inside them: their fingers flew over the keyboards with joy as they wrote, finally letting the creativity ring out like a triumphant piece of music. And he'd seen the people who'd spent years promising themselves that they'd write one day, people who'd saved up for a week at the famous Redlion Artistic Centre, only to discover when they sat in the big attic room, that it wasn't as easy as it looked, that the words didn't fly out but had to be dragged forth, kicking and screaming. Words that didn't work on any page and never would.

Matt didn't look like the former: he had the stunned, depressed look of the latter, the face of a man who'd made a big mistake and didn't know how to face up to it.

'OK,' said Matt guardedly, 'it's OK. I'm still thinking about the plot really.'

'Of course,' said Ciaran soberly. 'That's very important.' He went back to spooning coffee into his cup and reflected that he was never able to work on the plot without writing anything. Poor Matt. Ciaran felt sorry for the younger man, and sorry for his sweet, quiet wife. He just hoped that Matt realized writing wasn't for him before it affected their whole family. He'd seen Hope dragging those two little kids listlessly into the village a few times, all of them looking as bored and misplaced as a refugee family. Now she was working a few times a week so money was obviously a problem. It would be fairer if Matt upped sticks and went home. Fairer for Hope and much better for him too. Torturing oneself over not being able to write wasn't good for the soul, Ciaran knew, from having seen too many people like Matt.

'Finula asked me to invite you to ours next week, we're having a bit of a party,' he said casually.

'We'd love to go,' Matt said. Anything to break the monotony. Maybe he could get totally plastered and forget, for a few brief moments, that he was a failure.

A week later, Matt negotiated a bend in the road at what Hope considered to be a deadly speed.

There was no point saying 'slow down.' Such a remark would only make him drive faster and rely on his brakes even more. She wouldn't mind so much but the Metro was not built for hurtling over bumpy country roads.

Her knuckles white from clenching the side of the seat, Hope stared tight-lipped into the back of the car where Toby was asleep in his car seat. Millie was beaming from ear to ear. No speed was too fast for her. Like her father, she preferred the white-knuckle style of driving and had been known to squeal 'faster, Daddy', on occasion.

They were driving back from a shopping expedition in Killarney where new shoes had been purchased for both children. Millie was thrilled with her sky blue suede Mary-Janes. Hope was less thrilled on the grounds that Curlew Cottage and sky blue suede were not compatible. Exactly how did you get mud out of suede? Matt was what passed for happy these days because he'd bought a new thriller and a couple of expensive computer magazines, Toby was happy because, well, Toby was always happy. Hope was depressed and grumpy because she hadn't bought anything – apart from some groceries. Sadly, two-for-the-price-of-one for toilet cleaner could only thrill a woman so much. She'd planned to buy something cheap and stunning to wear to Finula's party that night but strangely enough, the shops were all out of garments that fitted the 'cheap and stunning' bill.

Hope tried to take her mind off Matt's Formula One driving and flitted over everything party-ish in her wardrobe, mentally discarding at least half of it.

There was a direct correlation between clothes and dislike, she decided. The more you disliked someone, the better dressed you wanted to be when you met them. On that basis, Hope knew her only sensible option would be to phone up Milan and ask Donatella Versace to send over a dress. If only there was some way out of going to the damn party, but there wasn't. Baby-sitting problems couldn't be blamed because Finula had insisted that the children be brought and put to bed in one of her spare rooms.

'They probably won't even wake up when it's time to bring them home,' Matt had said happily when he told Hope about this plan.

And if they did, Hope vowed, he could sit up with them. He'd been so bad tempered for the past month, so hellish to live with, that she'd had to do everything with the kids. Well, she hadn't wanted to go to this bloody party, he had, so he could deal with two crying, confused children who wouldn't appreciate being woken at midnight to go home.

The entire Parker family were dressed in their best when they parked outside the Headley-Ryans' at eight o' clock that night. Millie and Toby were in their best pyjamas, Millie wearing the new shoes which she refused to take off. Matt was looking particularly handsome in a Paul Smith suit he'd rarely worn before, complete with a grey shirt worn open without a tie. The effect was both casual and effortlessly classy. Hope felt she never managed to combine casual and classy, so she'd gone hell for leather towards classy and was shoehorned into a scoop-necked little black dress from Next that had clung a bit too tightly around the waist when she'd bought it and which hadn't got any looser with age. Pearl earrings, her hair up and sheer barely black tights with classic suede court shoes finished the look.

You couldn't go far wrong with a little black dress, screamed all the best fashion magazines. As she was also wearing the uncomfortable, constricting all-in-one underwear that was supposed to suck all your fat in, Hope prayed that the magazines were right. She felt like a piece of chicken breast in the supermarket: squashed up into an odd shape with her boobs bolstered across the front. It would be worth it, though, if she looked better than Finula.

'There are a lot of cars here,' Matt remarked.

Big, expensive cars, he added mentally. Their Metro looked lost among the BMWs and sporty Audis. Matt thought of the low slung sports car he'd driven until the move. A company car, it had gone back while he was on sabbatical and he hadn't thought he'd miss it until he was forced to drive Hope's elderly Metro. The Metro couldn't compare to the elegant lines of his old car, the powerful engine and the throaty roar it made when he put his foot to the floor. They couldn't afford a second car at the moment. Hope didn't seem to mind but Matt did. He was fed up being broke.

Ciaran greeted them at the door and led them off to the spare room to settle the children.

'Will I get Finula to drop in and say hello?' he asked before he bore Matt off to the party.

Hope smiled and shook her head. She'd recently decided that Ciaran was a nice man, after all. It was Finula she couldn't stand.

Naturally, Millie had no plans to go to sleep without having milk, water and several trips to the bathroom.

It was nearly nine, therefore, and the party was in full swing when Hope finally left the children asleep. She felt tired instead of party-ish.

'Darling, lovely to see you, are the kiddies asleep?' said a voice.

Finula's vowel sounds were even more strangulated than usual. No surprise, there, Hope thought. Finula was on impress-mode, which meant she'd be littering her conversation with French, mentioning distant artist acquaintances as if they were close friends, and carrying on as if she had champagne for supper every evening. It was very wearing. After ten minutes, Hope wanted to go and lie down. There was a great film on the telly that night, she remembered crossly.

Clearly, Finula was bored with Hope too. 'Now, you must meet my sister, Priscilla Headley-Clarke,' Finula said, as a woman approached.

Priscilla was a thinner, more conventionally dressed version of Finula, with the same fascination for red talons, too much jewellery and a *faux* posh accent.

'Priscilla Headley-Clarke,' Priscilla said, holding out her hand, as if Hope was deaf and hadn't heard the double-barrelled moniker moments before.

'Hope Parker,' Hope said, suppressing both a giggle and the desire to call herself Hope Smith-Parker.

She could just imagine Priscilla hearing that her elder sister was adopting a double-barrelled surname by linking hers with her new husband's.

'If she's having one, so am I!' Priscilla would scream, determined to be Headley-Clarke if Finula could be Headley-Ryan. Hope wondered if Priscilla had made her husband go double-barrelled, as Finula had with Ciaran.

And what happened if double-barrelled daughters got married, she wondered idly. Treble-barrelled last names or quadruples?

Released from having to listen to Finula drone on about how all the pictures in the house were painted by personal friends of theirs, Hope found Priscilla easier to talk to.

A Galway-based interior designer, Priscilla wasn't averse to mentioning the famous people she'd worked for but at least she didn't try and score intellectual point every few minutes, like her sister. And she actually listened to what Hope said, also unlike her sister.

'It must be difficult to up sticks and move,' Priscilla commented when they began talking about the Parkers' move to Kerry.

'I miss *friends*,' Hope said, 'although I've made some good ones here.'

'Finula, of course,' Priscilla said reverently.

Hope didn't correct her. 'We've only been here a few months and some of the time, I feel as if we've been here forever. This place does grow on you.'

'Don't you get bored?' Priscilla asked. 'I find the country a bit dull. I like city living, I must admit.'

Hope realized that she hadn't been bored lately. She worked two days a week for Erwin, although that would be coming to an end soon, as his wife was on the mend. However, she wouldn't be out of work for long. Delphine had told her that the accounts office in the hotel urgently needed some part-time help.

On the social side, Hope regularly met Mary-Kate or Delphine for coffee, she and Matt went to dinner with someone at least once a week, and now that she'd started walking with Delphine at lunchtimes twice a week as part of a get-thin-for-summer plan, she was busy. Plus there was the Macramé Club which was fun because they all let their hair down and talked about anything and everything. The only minus was the fact that Mary-Kate had a very heavy hand with the vodka. Every time they met, Hope promised herself she wouldn't have any martinis but then she fell by the wayside and ended up with a killer headache the next day. The only sad thing was that Sam was in London but they phoned each other every second day now, not caring about the phone bills but wanting to keep in touch. Hope knew Sam was taking one day at a time and trying to change her life, but she was still worried about her sister.

'It must be dull compared to Bath. Isn't that where you lived before?' inquired Priscilla.

'Actually no, I love it here,' Hope said, surprising herself. 'There's a great sense of, I don't know . . . community here. I like that, it's like having a very big extended family where you know everyone.'

Priscilla snorted. 'Finula's been here for ten years and she says she still feels like a stranger.'

Hope suppressed a smile, thinking of how Finula descended upon the village shops like Lady Bountiful condescending to the natives, talking loudly as if she were in Outer Mongolia and nobody could understand her or her desire for organic lentils. It was even worse if she bumped into anyone who was in Redlion to work at the artistic centre. Hope had witnessed Finula buttonholing some poor poet in the butcher's, telling him how she loved the rural simplicity and the simplistic wildness of both the people and the landscape. The butcher's wife, a highly educated, marvellously funny woman, had been apoplectic with rage behind the counter and had been in danger of slicing off the butcher's assistant's fingers with her boning knife as she overheard the conversation.

'Well,' Hope said, trying to be kind, 'not everyone fits in.'

'Oh Finula's fitted in,' Priscilla insisted. 'She just says the locals are very unfriendly.'

Eventually Hope escaped from Priscilla and got to talk to Mai, her fellow Macramé Club member. Neither Mai nor her husband, Chan, were artistic but had been invited on the grounds that Chan was something big in the computer factory. Finula liked the idea of mixing art and industry at her gatherings.

It was one before they left. 'Did you have a good time?' asked Matt, caressing her thigh through her silky sheers.

'Great,' said Hope. And it had been fun once she'd managed to escape the double barrelled sisters. 'How about you?'

'Yeah, I miss going out.'

'We get out here,' Hope said, stung.

'You know what I mean, that's just us. I mean going out to parties with Dan and Betsey. Talking to different people, networking, I suppose.'

They were both silent. Matt, realizing that he missed the social aspect of his old job, Hope upset at the idea that her conversation wasn't good enough.

They drove home slowly, trying to avoid potholes and miraculously, the children didn't wake when they were transferred from the car to their beds. Hope was taking off her murderously painful all-in-one underwear when Matt rushed into the bedroom, eyes glittering excitedly.

'There's a message on the answer phone from Dan. You won't believe it. Adam Judd's had a heart attack. He's all right,' Matt added, 'he's not in any danger, but he'd going to be off work for six weeks. He asked Dan to find out if I would come back and fill in for him until he's better.'

Hope stared at him blankly.

'It's an emergency,' he added, unable to stifle his joy. He was going back. He was still a player. Judds needed him, the company needed him. So what if he wasn't going to write the great novel. He was still the only man for the job of taking care of Judds.

He took Hope in his arms, holding her half-naked body close to his clothed one, letting her feel just how turned on he was. And somehow, Hope knew that it wasn't the sight of her that had made him want her: it was the thrill of the job. Hearing that he was needed had flicked a switch inside him, the switch that turned him on. Hope let him nuzzle her neck and caress her until they fell down on their bed and made love. But afterwards, when Matt fell asleep, half on her side of the bed, Hope lay there with her eyes open. Why was it that Matt was enough for her, but she wasn't quite enough for him? He needed something more from life and all she needed was his love.

The following day, Matt rushed around making phone calls, sending e-mails, booking his plane ticket. It was like old times, Hope realized. Buoyed up by the knowledge that he was needed, Matt was on a high and his enthusiasm was infectious. The children, not knowing that he was going to be away for six whole weeks, danced around him happily. Hope did her best to be cheery but she felt desolate that he was going and twice as desolate at how happy he was to be going.

They drove to the airport that afternoon, with Millie finally cross because the penny had dropped that her beloved daddy was going away. In the back of the car, she roared all the way to Killarney. It reminded Hope of her arrival in Kerry.

'Don't come in,' said Matt as they parked. Hope's pale, upset face was making him feel guilty enough. It would be worse for her to have to say goodbye in a teeming airport and then drag two screaming children back into the car. Far easier on them all to kiss goodbye now in the car.

He held her hand tightly, hoping she'd understand.

All Hope understood was that Matt was so eager to be away from her that he was denying her the chance to say goodbye properly.

When he bent to kiss her, she gave him the lightest peck. 'Bye,' she said in a small voice.

# CHAPTER SIXTEEN

*Hi Hope,*

*Sorry I couldn't talk yesterday. I was just running to a meeting and literally didn't have a second. This is a quickie early morning e-mail because I've lots of meetings in the office first thing and we've got a sales conference on afterwards and the whole building is decamping to Hertfordshire for three days. How are you getting on without Matt? I bet Millie's playing up as usual. She really is Daddy's girl.*

*I know today's the first day of your new job, so best of luck. You'll be fabulous, natch. That hotel sounds pretty amazing. Maybe next time I come, we'll book ourselves in for a night and spend a day in Delphine's salon getting beautified. I could do with it! My skin has gone to pot over the last few weeks – I am convinced it was the anaesthetic from getting my fibroids done. So much for 'you'll be out of the hospital within twenty-four hours and suffer no ill effects'! Only kidding. Dry skin isn't much of a price to pay and I'm feeling great. I've started doing this yoga video at home but I think I need to sign up to a class to do it properly. And I'm eating properly, drinking loads of water and*

*actually cooking dinner every night. You'd be proud of me.*
*I won't have time to phone today probably, but I'll*
*try and give you a ring tomorrow,*
*Love Sam.*

Hope smiled at the thought of her hopelessly undomesticated sister cooking every night. She clicked on reply.

*Hi Sis, it's all right. I understand you're madly busy. I keep getting your answering machine in the evening. This is just a quick note because I've got to leave the house in five minutes to get to the hotel for my first day and from the sounds downstairs, Millie is killing Toby. I am a bit nervous about the job to be honest because the only interview I did was simply over the phone with the accounts' office boss, Una Hutchinson, and she said they needed someone for a couple of days a week to cope with a backlog of filing.* Hope smiled to herself at the thought of her new job. She'd got it after the most unusual interview of her life. On the day of her interview at the hotel, Una had phoned first thing to say her husband was ill, consequently she was confined to home and could they do the interview over the phone?

'I'd love that,' Hope had laughed, thinking of when she'd gone for job interviews in her twenties and had suffered horrific nerve pangs as she sat, all dolled up in a neat little suit, waiting to be asked lots of difficult questions she was sure she'd never be able to answer. By comparison, talking with the companionable Una Hutchinson over the phone had been a doddle.

She quickly reread the e-mail and then continued. *The other job I've had since I got here was so laid-back that it felt like giving a neighbour a helping hand with the filing, and in contrast, this job is in a five-star hotel where they probably have a complex accounts system and I'm a bit nervous about that. But I'm going to do my best. If I can cope with the wiring in the house going haywire since Matt left, and with Millie acting up (you're dead right, she's been a minx since he left), then I can cope with a new job. Do you know, it's three weeks since he left? I almost can't believe it myself. I've been so busy that I don't miss him during the day, but it can be lonely here at night. Still, the girls are great at dragging me out of the house.*

This wasn't totally true. Hope missed Matt like crazy but didn't want to tell Sam or she'd doubtless phone him up and launch a tirade about neglecting her sister.

*Glad to hear that your skin is the only casualty of the operation. I'll ask Delphine for her recommendations. She probably knows some hideously expensive bottle of cream (the ninety quid for an ounce variety) that'll do the trick. Better still, you could visit Redlion and she'd administer it herself. All the girls at the Macramé Club are always asking about you and you know I'd love you to visit. By the way, Giselle is going to London in November and wants to know if you can meet up.*

*Matt's fine although he's harder to get hold of on the phone than you! Judd's is madly busy and he's doing Adam's work as well as some of his own.*

Hope didn't mention that Matt was the worst e-mail correspondent ever, believing that it was a mistake to get private e-mails at the office in case other people read them. Consequently, he made do with phoning Hope and the children, which wasn't satisfactory because he did it when he got in from work at nine, forgetting the children were in bed by half seven. Even more annoying, he hadn't phoned the night before or this morning to wish her luck in her new part time job at the Manoir Rouge Leon. Delphine, Mary-Kate, Virginia and Giselle had all remembered, but not Matt. Hope's pledge not to bitch about her husband was taking a rattling. She longed to let it all out and tell Sam how neglected she was feeling but she couldn't: couples owed it to each other to keep their differences private, Hope felt. And Sam would certainly try and fight Hope's battle, which was another no-no. She kept writing.

*Bet you're going to some lovely hotel for your conference, so have a good time. Talk soon and take care of yourself! It's only two weeks since your op, don't forget. You're not superwoman. OK, you are, but don't push yourself,*

*Love*

*Hope.*

Toby's voice sounded plaintive as he roared up the stairs: 'Mummy, Millie hit me with Thomas the Tank Engine.'

Hope hit send and rushed downstairs.

An hour later, Hope's jaw dropped a bit as she drove up the manicured driveway to Manoir Rouge Leon. She'd seen the brochure photos that Delphine had given her, she'd heard Mary-Kate saying the hotel was an oasis of utter luxury, and she'd even heard about the prices – the price of a suite for two weeks would buy you half a house in Redlion, apparently. But nothing had prepared her for the sight of the soaring castle that lay nestled in a splendid valley of beech trees and mighty oaks a mere six miles from the village. The hotel was enormous, with a huge tower on either side of a vast wooden door, plenty of gargoyles and crenellated bits in between, and a castle wall that stretched around the rambling, spreading building as if it was guarding a precious jewel.

'Wow,' she said, not daring to park the Metro in the visitors' car park alongside all the Mercedes and Bentleys. Since she'd banged it off the rusty gate on the lane, the car looked more disreputable than ever. She followed the signs for the staff car park and then dithered about taking the back entrance. Delphine had advised her to go in the front door 'or you'll get lost. The back of the castle is like a rabbit warren and we'd find you a month later locked in some back office,' she'd said.

But now Hope felt unsure about sauntering in as if she was a guest. She was only coming in to help because the accounts office were short staffed. Still, there was no choice. The front it was. A liveried doorman opened the big door to her and smiled 'Hello Madame.'

Hope smiled back, thrilled that her smart black suit made her look posh enough to pass as a Bentley-driving guest. She must make an effort with her hair and make up more often. For a moment, she stood and admired the lobby, a vast richly panelled room with tapestries on the walls, enormous arrangements of flowers on two marble tables, and a suit of armour lurking malevolently by the grand double staircase.

'Beautiful, isn't it?' said a soft, male voice.

'Lovely,' said Hope untruthfully. Suits of armour reminded her of horror movies for some reason.

'Can I help you?' The voice belonged to a man in a suit, a man with a mop of curly dark hair that refused to be subdued and that reminded Hope for all the world of a Tibetan terrier's coat. It was the only wild thing about him. From the tips of his perfectly white, double cuffs to his gleaming leather shoes, he had the style of someone from Blackwells Best Dressed Men list. He oozed gypsyish charm and Givenchy for Men from every pore and as Hope looked up into his shining black eyes and the saturnine face, she could do nothing but smile dumbly.

'I'm ... er ... looking for the accounts office,' she managed after what seemed like an age. 'I'm supposed to be working there.'

'You must be Mrs Parker,' he said.

'How did you know?' Hope said astonished.

'It's my job to know everything that goes on around here,' he said in that soft, caressing voice. 'I'm Christy De Lacy, the general manager.'

Before she was even aware of it, he'd taken her hand in his. 'Welcome and thank you.'

Hope wasn't sure what she was being thanked for but it was very nice to have this delectable specimen of manhood holding her hand and thanking her, so she wasn't about to break the moment.

'Which direction is the accounts office?' she asked.

He finally let go of her hand and Hope wondered if it would smell of his aftershave now.

'I'll show you,' he said gravely, 'and perhaps give you the grand tour as well.'

'Actually,' Hope pointed out, 'I'm supposed to be there at half nine and it's nearly that now.'

Christy shrugged in a Gallic manner. 'I'm the boss,' he said with pride.

Flustered, Hope began to protest. 'But I don't want to take up your time ...'

His voice, already low, dropped an octave. 'I'm never too busy to escort a beautiful lady,' he purred.

Hope's stomach did a little flip that wouldn't have earned her any points in an Olympic gymnastic display but which was still pretty good for a 37-year-old woman's stomach with limited experience of somersaults.

He guided her over to the lift and the tour started.

'This panelling was taken from a house in Malta,' he explained gravely and as the lift began its stately ascent, he told her about the work that had gone into refurbishing this section of the castle. He was very knowledgeable about it all but Hope decided that it was hard to say the correct things about wood panelling and the expense of maintaining antique furniture when all she wanted to do was hear Christy call her a 'beautiful lady' again. And there was something very sexy about being in the lift with such a man. Hadn't there been fabulously hedonistic goings on in a lift in some movie? Didn't modern hotels have cameras in the lifts? Would they be spotted if Christy flung her against the railing and kissed her?

'The first floor refurbishment is the best, I think,' Christy intoned as the door opened.

She did her best to ask intelligent questions and soon discovered why the castle wasn't called a castle and why Christy knew so much about it.

'I was here for all the refurbishment,' he said. 'It took two years and it was like watching a gracious old movie star turn back into a youthful goddess.'

Hope sighed. 'It's beautiful, but why is it called a manor hotel? Why not a castle?'

'You ask all the right questions.' Christy smiled benignly on his pupil who glowed as much as if she'd just been given a gold star on her copybook. 'It looks like a medieval castle in places but the oldest parts are only nineteenth century. A wealthy landowner built it for his young wife as a love token, because she said she'd always wanted to live in a castle, only she died before it was finished and in his grief, he insisted that nobody ever call it a castle again. It's more of a folly really than a castle.'

'How romantic.' Hope ran a hand over a silken tapestry on one wall.

As they waited for the lift again, Hope found herself gazing up at Christy with the shining eyes of the love struck. Stop it! What are you doing, she asked herself? It was like being a fifteen-year-old on a first ever date, desperate for compliments, smiling gauchely up at the object of her desire and waiting for him to say that her hair/jeans etc were nice.

On the top floor, he whisked her along to one of the unoccupied suites, which contained the biggest bed she'd ever seen.

'Wow,' she said, resisting the temptation to sit on it and bounce up and down.

'Sit, it's a waterbed,' he said, sitting down and bouncing. 'Fun, huh?' His eyebrows were distinctly devilish when raised in that provocative way.

Hope perched as far away from him as possible. This was crazy. There was something dangerous about this man.

As if reading her mind, Christy got to his feet.

'Forgive me,' he said earnestly, 'I get so carried away with my beautiful hotel that I forget it can be boring for other people. You see, I want the people who work for me to appreciate the beauty of the Manoir. It makes them proud to work here, that's why I gave you the tour. I hope it hasn't bored you. Now let's bring you to the accounts office and you can see the rest of the hotel later.'

Hope felt stupid for even imagining another motive for the tour. Of course, he was the manager and he wanted to impress upon new staff that this was a special place. As if someone as suave and sophisticated as Christy De Lacy would seriously be interested in her.

They went down the back stairs, Hope burning with embarrassment at how silly she must have looked as she simpered up at him like a schoolgirl. Obviously, a man so handsome must be used to women throwing themselves at him but she hadn't so much thrown herself as launched herself from a great height. How humiliating.

She could barely speak for embarrassment.

He delivered her at a plain door. 'I'll tell Mrs Hutchinson you're here,' he said, opening the door.

After a moment, he came out and told her that Mrs Hutchinson, head of the accounts office, was waiting for her.

'We shall meet again soon, I hope,' he said, giving her a formal handshake.

'Thank you, Mr De Lacy,' Hope said, trying to pull off the double whammy of being polite and apologetic all in one.

'It's Christy, not Mr De Lacy,' he smiled.

Hope watched him as he strode off down the corridor.

Had she imagined it or had that last searching look as they said goodbye been a look that couldn't possibly be construed as platonic? No. She must have imagined it.

Mrs Hutchinson turned out to be a jolly local woman of fifty who was just as friendly as she'd been during Hope's phone interview and immediately insisted that Hope call her Una. 'This office isn't the place for formality, as I've always said,' she smiled, introducing Hope to the other accounts person, an impish young woman called Janet.

'The way Mr De Lacy called you Mrs Hutchinson, I thought it was,' Hope said.

'What did you think of him?' inquired Una with great innocence.

'He's very nice, I found,' Hope said lightly.

She missed the glance between the two others.

'Such a pity he'll never have a girlfriend,' said Janet mournfully. 'Such a tragedy . . .'

'What tragedy?' asked Hope, jumping straight into the trap.

'Gotcha!' giggled Una. 'He's irresistible, Mr De Lacy, isn't he? Everyone falls for him.'

'I haven't fallen for him,' protested Hope hotly. 'I'm a married woman with children, I'll have you know . . .'

Una patted her on the arm. 'You're going to fit right in,' she said. 'Until they let us have a television in the staff room, lusting after Christy De Lacy is the only entertainment we get around here! And no, he's not married, before you ask.'

They giggled again. 'Bet you were putty in his hands,' sighed Janet.

'Don't be ridiculous,' Hope said firmly in her best Mummy tone. 'Now, I expect you've work you want me to do,' she added, trying to banish the image of herself putty-like in Christy De Lacy's firm hands; kneading her flesh, getting the knots out of her tense shoulders and then splaying further down . . .

\*     \*     \*

Mary-Kate and Delphine turned up at Curlew Cottage that night with several bottles of wine and a pot of Mary-Kate's legendary mushroom soup, 'so you don't have to worry about cooking,' she told Hope.

In the three weeks since Matt had gone, the three women often had dinner together and Hope had learned that Mary-Kate was the most incredible cook.

Delphine was greeted with delight by Toby and Millie, who considered her to be a bigger version of themselves with the added bonus that she was allowed to work the video recorder.

For a few moments, nobody could hear themselves think with the children trying to drown each other out in asking Delphine to play *their* game.

'Mine, mine!' yelled Millie, who could roar for Ireland.

'We'll play your game *and* Toby's,' Delphine announced diplomatically. 'But I have to talk to your mummy first. How did you get on?' she asked.

'Wonderful. Una's lovely.'

'Oh, she's an utter pet,' Delphine cried. 'She practically runs that place and she doesn't have a bossy bone in her body. It's only since her husband's been sick that she's had to take all those days off and there are so many bits of paper flying in and out of that office, that the place can't cope. And isn't Janet gas?'

'Great. Oh, and I met the manager,' Hope said idly. 'Christy De Lacy.' She couldn't help it: she liked saying his name, liked the way it rolled off her tongue.

From her position on the couch between Millie and Toby, Delphine shot a look at Hope. 'And you liked him?' she inquired.

Hope glowed. 'He was an angel, he gave me a tour of the hotel. Sorry, Manoir.'

'How come I've never set eyes on this man?' Mary-Kate demanded. 'I must be the only woman in a ten-mile radius who doesn't swoon at the mention of his name. Why does he never come into the chemist looking for spot cream or anything? I think I should write a letter of complaint to someone. What does the Minister for Justice do again? Would he be able to handle it?'

Hope laughed. 'You should book yourself in for a tour of the Manoir,' she said. 'Then you'd get to meet him.'

'Ah,' Mary-Kate said wisely, 'maybe he only gives those tours to gorgeous thirty-something women wearing fitted little suits.'

'There'll be no wine for you, madam,' Hope joked, 'if you keep up that line of thought. He's just a nice man, that's all. Nobody's swooning.'

Just talking about the hotel with him was hardly the first sign of a *grande affaire*, now was it, she thought to herself.

Delphine picked up Millie's story book with a sense of unease in her heart.

She didn't like to tell Hope that she'd seen Mr De Lacy being very not nice, being downright nasty in fact, when the Latin curl of his lip had turned into a sneer and his much admired eyes were as hard as nails. Most women seemed to love him; they fell hook, line and sinker for that suave business even though Delphine felt it was all an act. Even poor Una Hutchinson, God love her, who was besotted with her big lummox of a husband, had a soft spot for Christy.

A soft spot that wasn't the Bog of Allen, as Delphine's father might have said wryly.

Still, it wasn't up to her to warn Hope off him. Hope was married to the utterly gorgeous Matt, a man who'd knock spots off the smarmy Christy any day of the week. Why would Hope even look twice at Christy when she was married to Matt? It'd be like living in a cream bun factory and sneaking out to buy diet biscuits from the corner shop. No, there was no need to worry.

The children went to bed reluctantly although the fact that Delphine was going to tell them a bedtime story cheered them up.

'You're sure you don't mind?' Hope asked her, not wanting to take advantage.

'I love doing it,' Delphine said. 'I love kids and this pair are little dotes.'

Hope went downstairs to Mary-Kate.

'She's so good with children, she'll be a wonderful mother,' she said. 'Do you think she and Eugene will have kids?'

'I'm sure they'd love to but I think she's waiting for her mother to welcome Eugene into the bosom of the family first. Poor Delphine,' Mary-Kate sighed. 'I'm afraid she'll be waiting a long time. I don't know why she just doesn't get married and let my idiot of a sister like it or lump it.'

'People can be very cruel without knowing it, can't they?' Hope said. 'What right has anyone to tell Delphine how to live her life?'

Mary-Kate said nothing but just stared into the middle distance. She looked sad and fragile, Hope thought suddenly.

'Are you feeling all right?' she asked.

Her friend seemed to visibly shake herself back to reality. 'Old memories,' she said finally.

Hope felt as if she'd stumbled clumsily across someone else's pain and did her best to backtrack. 'Shall we have some of your wonderful soup?' she said brightly.

The older woman didn't appear to have heard her. Hope had never seen Mary-Kate look maudlin or sad. It was scary. Mary-Kate was the one who buoyed them all up and made them laugh. She was the one who helped the Macramé Club women laugh at life and see the funny side. To witness her looking so forlorn was a shock.

'I think they're asleep,' whispered Delphine, tiptoeing downstairs. 'They were tired. I only managed one story.'

'They're always tired on the days when they're at the crèche,' Hope replied. 'I don't know what Giselle does with them there but it's fantastic.'

'She probably has a special baby gym and she ties them to the walker for an hour every day and leaves them at it,' suggested Delphine mischievously.

'Now there's a thought,' Hope said. 'I'll have to invest in one of those myself.'

Even Mary-Kate laughed at that notion.

They were soon feasting on the delicious soup mopped up with chunks of soda bread, all washed down with wine. The talk turned to the sort of week they'd all had and Hope managed to talk about her morning in the accounts office without mentioning Christy again. Delphine made them scream with laughter with her story of an elderly film star who was staying in the hotel with his wife and who'd wanted his chest hair waxed that afternoon.

'Stronger sex indeed,' she laughed. 'I've given women Brazilian waxes that would bring tears to your eyes and they clench their teeth with pain and say nothing. But your man . . . he roared so much that I couldn't bear it from wanting to laugh and I had to get Antoinette to take over. And you wouldn't mind but when it was over, he came out all macho and asked me if I wanted to have a drink with him later! The nerve of him. His wife is a sweetheart, I did her nails earlier, and there he was asking me out!'

'Such excitement,' teased Mary-Kate. 'I hope you said yes.'

'I told him it was unethical to go out with clients,' Delphine grinned. 'I managed not to mention that I'd rather pull my own teeth out with a pliers first. Yeuch. He was creepy. Let's talk about something else.'

'I'm afraid I've had a very dull day compared to the pair of you,' Mary-Kate said. 'But I did meet the Merry Widow Maguire and I got to hear all about her new venture.'

'I didn't know there actually was a widow,' said Hope in surprise. 'I thought the pub was just called that because it sounded good. I've never seen her.'

'That's because she spends most of the winter in her villa in Portugal,' Mary-Kate explained. 'She's the quintessential merry widow, Belle Maguire is. And why not. It's a mystery to me why she didn't die of sheer suffering before her husband popped his clogs because he was the most miserable man ever walked on the earth. But he was rich.' She grinned. 'Virtue does have its rewards. When he died, Belle renamed the pub – it was plain old Maguire's until then – got herself a villa and doesn't come back to Ireland until March. Rumour has it that she's got a boyfriend half her age out there but she never brings him back here, more's the pity. I'd love to clap eyes on a toyboy.'

'She sounds fascinating and dead glamorous,' Hope said.

'She's glamorous in a perma-tan-and-gold-handbag sort of way,' Mary-Kate explained, 'but the only people she bothers to fascinate are men. She's not a woman's woman. I'd keep Matt clamped to your side when she sees him because he'll be just her type.'

'She'll have to fight off Finula then,' Hope said with a hint of bitterness. 'She's round here every second day asking how he is and what he's been up to. As if I'd know. I'm only his wife.'

'Ah now,' Delphine said comfortingly, 'you know he'll be missing you like mad. Men are hopeless at phoning.'

'He's probably guilty at having left you here on your own with the children,' added Mary-Kate.

He has a funny way of showing it, then, Hope thought to herself. He hadn't phoned since Tuesday evening. Two whole days ago. Hope wouldn't have lasted eight hours away from her family without phoning anxiously but it seemed that Matt didn't feel the same way. He'd walked out that door nearly three weeks ago and had forgotten about them. She'd been feeling lonely since he'd gone but it was apparent that he wasn't suffering at all. No doubt Betsey was squiring him all over town, triumphantly dragging him to parties and launches as a sought-after man on his own. The fact that he had a wife at home in her rural paradise wouldn't matter to the man-hungry predators who prowled the party scene. Without her and the kids to cramp his style, Matt would have a whale of a time, she thought glumly.

Both Delphine and Mary-Kate gave her an extra-tender hug when they went, as if they were physically telling her what they didn't want to say with words: that they knew she was lonely and that they were there for her.

Hope remembered her friends in Bath and wondered frankly if any of them would have been as good to her as her new friends here in Redlion. She tidied up, locked the doors, checked the windows and then went up to her lonely bed. But strangely, she didn't mind being on her own tonight. She curled the duvet snugly around herself. She could lie there and indulge in a fantasy where Christy De Lacy's shining black eyes loomed large. Matt had gone off to Bath, so she was entitled to have a little dream about Christy, wasn't she? It was harmless after all. Like Baileys and ice as a comforting night cap when you were on a diet. Slightly naughty but so, so nice.

On Sunday night, Hope found herself rifling through her wardrobe trying to work out what to wear. It had been years since she'd done that. She'd worn a uniform at Witherspoon's and since she'd been living in Redlion, her daily outfit was almost as predictable as the office skirt and blouse: jeans or one of her pairs of navy chinos and either a sweatshirt or fleecy top. For a total high fashion look, she sometimes added eyeliner and lipstick, but not all the time. She didn't want to frighten the hens with full make-up.

None of the above were suitable for a morning in the Manoir, of course and the bed was soon piled high with blouses, skirts and trousers she hadn't been able to get into for years.

The pile reminded her of being a teenager riddled with anxiety about what to wear. Sam, two and a half years older, had never seemed to be bothered about clothes. With her, it had been a simple matter of opening the colour coordinated wardrobe and instantly pulling out something suitable. Sam hadn't worried about what boys would think of her bum in those trousers or whether she had fat arms or not. Sam's attitude had been: 'Let the boys worry – why should I?'

At the time, Hope had longed for the effortless chic of her older sister. What was she thinking about – she *still* longed for Sam's effortless, uncaring chic.

Matt, who'd made up for his lack of phone calls with a long one on Friday, rang at ten past eight.

'Hello,' whispered Hope, half in and half out of a clingy polo neck and praying the children wouldn't wake up because of the phone ringing.

'Why are you talking like that?' asked Matt.

'So I won't wake Toby and Millie,' she said, pulling off the polo neck.

Matt groaned. 'I wanted to talk to them,' he said miserably.

His wife shook her head in disbelief at the male sense of timing. 'What time is it, Matt?' she inquired sarcastically. 'Do you not realize they're always in bed by now.'

'No they're not,' he replied. 'They stay up later sometimes.'

'Sometimes,' she agreed, 'but not often. You should have rung earlier. We were here.' *While you were having fun in Bath and forgetting all about us*, was the subtext.

'I thought you might be out,' Matt said.

Hope didn't bother to tell him that it had been raining buckets all day.

'What are you doing?' he asked.

'Tidying up the linen cupboard,' Hope said with a twinge of guilt as she looked at the debris of her Christy-attracting clothes hunt.

'Oh.' Pause. 'What did you do all day?'

Hope fingered a russet silken blouse speculatively. Now that could be nice with a black skirt. Left loose it would hide her waist. 'Er . . . nothing,' she said. 'Millie has a mild cold so we stayed in. And you?'

'Went for lunch at the Meadows' with Dan and Betsey. The au pair was looking after the children.'

'The au pair?' demanded Hope. 'Betsey and Dan have an au pair? Since when?'

'Since a week ago.'

'She always said she didn't believe in farming her children out to other people,' Hope raged. 'So I suppose this au pair is seventeen and looks like a Britney Spears clone?'

Matt laughed. 'Are you mad? You know what Betsey's like. She's far too jealous to have anyone like that in the house. This au pair is a twenty-three-year-old devout Christian girl from Strasbourg and she is a million miles away from Britney. She's very prim and shy and calls Betsey "Madame".'

Hope harrumphed. 'Betsey would love that. She'll have her in a maid's outfit next, curtseying and bowing and asking *if Madame would like tea in the drawing room*. What was the Meadows' like? Was it lunch or a party?'

'A party,' Matt said unwisely. 'It was their tenth anniversary and they wanted to renew their vows.'

Sitting on the bed in their cold little country cottage where nobody had called all day and where the main amusement had been watching *The Sound of Music* on the television in the afternoon with a box of chocolates on her lap, Hope simmered.

It didn't matter that she and Matt barely knew the Meadows and that, if Matt hadn't been staying with Dan and Betsey, he'd hardly have been invited. The fact of the matter was that he'd been enjoying himself without her and now he'd rung too late to speak to the children.

'Well, we were here listening to the rain drumming off the shed roof while you were out at the Meadows' having fun, and drinking cocktails,' Hope said, knowing she was nagging but, in her jealousy, not able to stop herself.

'It was dull as ditchwater,' Matt lied. 'You wouldn't have enjoyed it.'

'That's easy to say seeing as I wasn't asked!'

'Don't give me that,' snapped Matt. 'You're not a child, Hope. You're perfectly capable of going out and doing something for yourself. Stop the martyr act.'

She glared at the phone. Martyr! He'd dared to call her a martyr. While she was here looking after his children in a place he'd chosen, and he was off swanning around at vow-renewing parties. The cheek of it.

And then Hope did something she'd never done before. She hung up without saying another word. He was annoying her too much. Let him suffer. It wasn't as if he could come home in half an hour and be cross with her for hanging up. He wasn't going to be back for weeks. She took the phone off the hook so he couldn't ring back and then smiled at her reflection in the mirror. Bizarrely enough, she felt good.

She picked up a slinky black body that Sam had bought her once for Christmas and that she'd never had either the nerve or the correct bra to wear. Hope tried it on now without a bra and admired the effect of the gathered silky fabric coming down to a deep V below the point where most bras crossed the chest. She tried on her grey skirt suit with it and did a bit of model-type twisting in front of the mirror. It was all way too sexy for a morning doing the accounts in an office where the other two members of staff dressed in sedate business outfits.

Well, this *was* a business suit, Hope convinced herself. It all depended on what sort of business you intended doing.

\* \* \*

In the chintzy spare room in Dan and Betsey's house, Matt sat with his mobile in his hand and felt miserable. Great. Hope had hung up on him. She'd never done that before.

He hadn't meant to needle her but she'd driven him to it. He just hated the way she expected him to make everything all right in life, as if it was his duty to direct all their lives like some great ruler. Do this, Hope, do that, Hope. Don't take responsibility for anything.

He lay back on the flowery duvet gloomily. That wasn't totally true, he admitted. He'd wanted to be the great ruler. He'd liked being the one who told Hope what they'd do next, what video they'd watch, what sort of car they'd buy for her, where they'd go on holiday.

If he was utterly honest, he'd liked the fact that Hope waived her right to make the big decisions and let him do it. He liked being in charge, so he could hardly fault Hope for not wishing to be in charge when she was left on her own. Even when she got those jobs in Redlion, she'd rushed to tell him, wanting him to approve of them. Hope wasn't an independent type, not like her ball-breaking sister.

Only it hadn't been Sam who'd slammed the phone down on him and who had now left it off the hook in a gesture of defiance. It was Hope.

'Matt,' said a soft voice at the door. 'I am making coffee. Would you like some?'

He hadn't been entirely accurate in his description of the au pair, either. Chantal was prim, Christian and certainly not a hot babe. But he'd intentionally made her sound a bit plain. She was actually very pretty in a quiet way and she had undoubtedly got a massive crush on him, which was sweet. She wasn't that unlike Hope, really. All huge eyes, eager to please and absolutely no hassle. Correction: like Hope *used* to be. But she *wasn't* Hope. And Matt was definitely a one-woman man. No matter how many women batted long eyelashes at him, he wasn't interested.

'I'd love a coffee, Chantal,' he said warmly. 'I'll be right down.'

It was a miracle that Hope got out of the house the next morning without getting cereal, juice or some other bit of breakfast on her suit. With her deadly accurate radar sensing that Mummy was Up

To Something and in a rush, Millie was wildly uncooperative at
breakfast and managed to fire an entire bowl of Coco Pops across
the floor with remarkable strength.

Hope, keyed up and as nervous as a thoroughbred filly before a
big race, shouted at her, with the result that Toby was sucking his
thumb and Millie was sobbing as they finally piled into the car.

'I want Daddy!' wailed Millie, her cherubic little face bright pink
with misery.

'Daddy will be home soon,' soothed Hope, doing up Millie's car
seat straps expertly as Millie drummed on the seat with her heels.

'Now, now!' screamed Millie, bouncing Barbie off her mother's
skull.

'Ouch. That hurt. Behave, Millie,' said Hope crossly.

Cue more roars.

By the time they got to Hunnybunnikins, Hope had a headache
from the combination of Millie's roars and the *Singalonga Nursery
Rhymes* tape that both children normally loved.

'My poor Millie. Have you had a bad morning?' crooned Giselle
as she welcomed them into the playgroup and immediately spotted
Millie's red eyes and trembling lower lip.

Millie shot into Giselle's arms, giving a heavily reproachful look
at her mother, before leaning angelically against Giselle's shoulder
looking for all the world like a misunderstood flower fairy with her
dark curls tumbling around her face.

'Missing their father, I suppose,' Giselle said gently to Hope.

Hope nodded tight lipped. 'Men,' she said grimly.

'I know,' Giselle said, taking both children by the hands. 'Can't
live with them, can't kill them.'

'Don't you look nice,' said Una, admiring Hope's outfit as she brewed
them all a cup of coffee.

'Oh, this old thing,' said Hope, settling into her seat. 'Now what's
first?'

'Horrible job, I'm afraid,' Una said. 'We've got a problem with
the fishmonger's invoices. 'The filing here's gone to pot because I've
had to take so much time off and there's war over fish that's appar-

ently been delivered but was never signed for, so we haven't paid – we only pay if there's a signature from here – and they're going to stop delivering. Poor Christy is going demented about it, so we've got to get it sorted out this week. Only thing is,' she added, pointing to a big folder on the floor beside Hope's desk, 'there's a lot to go through.'

'No problem,' said Hope joyfully, imagining having lots of exciting meetings with Christy where he'd tell her what a pleasure it was working with someone so efficient.

'Nobody could have handled it the way you did,' he'd murmur as they stood with the haddock receipts between them.

Unfortunately, her morning didn't go as planned. Although the door from reception to the accounts office opened many times with the two receptionists looking for Una, there was no sign of Christy. Every time someone came in Hope looked up eagerly, fixing a smile on her face so she'd look welcoming as well as efficient. But it was always one of the two elegant French receptionists, Claude or Sophie, who both ignored Janet and Hope and spoke only to Una.

As the morning passed with nothing more exciting than elevenses and proper shortbread biscuits from the hotel kitchens to enliven things, Hope began to agree with Una: sorting out the fish dockets was a horrible job. She'd been meticulously entering all the payments and the numbers of the dockets relating to them into the computer all morning and she was still only ten per cent of the way there.

And to add to her sense of anti-climax at not setting eyes on the delectable manager, she'd discovered that the lovely silky body got very hot and un-sexily sweaty in the centrally-heated office, which Una kept at boiling point.

'My hands get so cold that I can't work,' Una had said apologetically. 'Bad circulation, so I like it very hot.'

'That's OK,' said Hope kindly, from behind a film of sweat. She hoped she had deodorant with her. Otherwise she couldn't dare raise her arms or she'd asphyxiate someone.

There wasn't much chit chat in the office. Not that Una and Janet weren't friendly, but they had the radio on all morning listening to talk shows and the conversation ranged from the odd comment on the various radio guests, to discussions on whose go it was to make coffee. And of course, during the commercial breaks, they talked about food. Hope had never worked in an office with women where they *didn't* talk about food. At Witherspoon's, they'd discussed diets. Yvonne had tried them all, from ones where you only ate carrots, to ones where you could eat anything you wanted as long as you only ate half of it. Hope had tried that one diligently but it hadn't worked. How did you define half a scoop of ice cream?

Here, they talked about gourmet food. Una was trying to tempt her husband's appetite because he was laid up with a broken hip and wasn't eating. She kept bringing home little morsels of delicious food from the hotel in the hope of getting him to eat properly.

'He loves duck à l'orange,' she said, 'but Luigi says it's unlikely to be on the menu again for a couple of days.'

'That thing they do with the angel hair pasta and the Pernod sauce,' drooled Janet. 'I could eat that till it came out of my ears.'

Hope, who had that morning started the must-lose-a-stone-for-Christy-De-Lacy diet, was nearly weak with hunger listening to them. She took another low-calorie mint from her handbag and crunched in desperation.

Claude marched in from reception, cross after an altercation with a guest who was demanding to see Christy.

'I have to see Mr De Lacy,' Claude said angrily, waving his arms in temper.

'Well, he's not here,' Una said tartly. 'You know this is his day off. Frederick's on instead.'

Both Claude and Hope's faces fell. Hope sighed. They could have bloody told her and she would have saved this outfit for another day.

By ten to one, Hope was squinting from keying numbers into the computer.

'You've been wonderful,' Una said gratefully. 'The last person we had here helping out didn't fit in at all but you do. I don't suppose you could do more than two mornings a week? It would be such a great help until my husband's better. In fact, it would be such a great help permanently. We really could do with another pair of hands, couldn't we, Janet?'

Hope was absurdly pleased. It was nice to be needed and appreciated.

'Shouldn't you check with Mr De Lacy first?' she asked. Giselle had already offered her another day for the children at Hunnybunnikins.

'No need, he thinks you're great,' Una said, thereby making Hope's stomach do one of its flips.

He thought she was great. In what way, exactly? Great in a good-for-the-accounts-office type of great, or great in a wildly-attracted-to sort of great?

'Do you want to come to lunch with us?' Una asked. 'One of the perks of the job is amazing food.'

'I better not,' Hope said, thinking of the long-term effects of angel hair pasta in Pernod sauce on her waistline. 'I have to do the shopping before I pick my children up from playgroup.'

'You must bring in photos on Thursday,' insisted Una. 'They sound like such little sweethearts.'

Hope's face softened and she felt utterly guilty about being cross with poor Millie that morning. 'They are,' she said.

She hurried out the back door to the staff car park, writing a shopping list in her head, totally oblivious to the world around her.

'Hello Hope,' said a familiar purring voice.

She whirled around to find Christy grinning wolfishly at her from the driver's seat of a silver sports car. His hair was wet and slicked back and he was wearing a cream sweater instead of his manager's suit. He looked even more attractive in casual clothes than he had in formal ones. His hair made him look vulnerable slicked back like that. It was like seeing him naked, she thought, then bit her lip at the very idea. He must live at the hotel, it came to her suddenly, and he'd just hopped out of the shower.

'Oh er, hello,' she said lamely. Trust her to meet him now, when she was flushed and un-lipsticked, and not earlier when she'd been looking her best waiting for him.

'Not staying for lunch?' he asked.

'No,' she said, hoping she wasn't blushing.

'Aren't you hungry?'

'Well, yes but I don't have time . . .' she began.

'Nonsense. You should always take time to eat. I'm going to have lunch myself in the Pigeon Club. Want to join me?'

The Pigeon Club was an elegant restaurant ten miles away and completely in the other direction to Redlion. Hope had never been there although she'd heard enough about it from Finula, who raved about the food and the decor and the fact that only the very best people – meaning herself – went there. Up till now, Hope had never had any desire to go there. But suddenly it sounded utterly alluring. And she was, after all, hungry.

'I've got to pick up the kids this afternoon,' Hope said anxiously. 'I said I'd be there by half three.'

'Loads of time. Why don't you bring your car and follow me. When you're ready to go, you can drive off to get your children,' Christy said, as if it was simple.

'OK.' She felt her face flush for definite this time. Lunch with Christy De Lacy. What was she doing?

He rolled up his window and Hope scurried off to her car. Christy wasted no time roaring down the drive, tyres scattering gravel like confetti. Hope did her best to roar after him, wondering how she was going to drive *and* apply a bit of make-up if he kept taking corners at this speed.

She'd managed to drench herself in White Linen, powder down the shiny bits of her nose and slick on some coral lipstick when Christy's silver bullet of a car took a sharp right and belted up a tree-lined drive. He was already out of the car when Hope pulled up beside him, got out and stared at the Pigeon Club. A long, secretive looking house with a thatched roof and small windows peering out, it looked as if it was made for assignations.

Inside, a man shook Christy's hand enthusiastically, introduced himself to Hope as Liam, the owner, and then found them a table in a window recess where they were practically hidden from the rest of the room. Hope was pleased at this on the grounds that nobody could see her having an illicit lunch while her husband was away. But when she realized that she and Christy could strip down to their underwear and begin to have sex on the linen tablecloth and nobody would see that either, she began to be nervous. This wasn't her scene.

Christy excused himself when he'd settled Hope in her seat. 'I've got to talk to Liam for a moment,' he said.

While he was gone, Hope panicked.

She loved Matt, she'd never had an affair in her life. She'd tried to be sophisticated with Christy and it had backfired. He couldn't just be bringing her to lunch for the good of his health. He had to be looking for something, something Hope couldn't give him. He probably thought she'd take him back to her cottage and bonk him senseless; that she was a bored housewife looking for cheap sex! Oh God, no.

But it's only lunch, said the little voice in her head, the voice that yearned for excitement. Matt's away having fun in Bath and not bothering to phone you, and all you're doing is going out with a handsome man, a colleague, in fact. Nothing wrong with that. Anyway, Matt and Christy would like each other and they could have dinner parties and invite Christy.

But then, Hope reminded herself honestly, there wasn't a chance in hell of having Christy and Matt in the same room. She was kidding herself with this dream of intellectual dinner parties. She felt herself quiver with excitement just being near Christy and it was a bit unlikely that Matt wouldn't notice this. A person with no perception whatsoever would notice it.

'Sorry about that.' Christy slid into his seat. 'I wanted to have a chat with Liam about something. That's why I was coming here today. I hope you didn't mind me asking you along.' His dark eyes were innocent. 'I thought it would be nice to have the company. I hate eating alone and Liam never has more than a moment to sit and talk to his guest.'

Hope felt some of the tension and guilt leave her – he made it sound so reasonable . . .

They examined the menu, and, after a bit of chat with Liam about his recommendations, ordered. Christy also ordered a bottle of red wine.

'I can't, I'm driving,' Hope said.

'Just a teeny glass,' Christy wheedled. 'It'll do you good after all your hard work this morning. Now, tell me what the situation is with the fishmonger crisis?'

365

Hope relaxed a bit more. He just wanted to talk about work. What was the harm in that? This was a business lunch, actually, now that she thought about it. She could tell Matt that she'd had a business lunch, if he asked. Not that he'd ask, but if he did, she'd be able to tell him it had all been above board. Utterly respectable. What could you get up to in a public place, for goodness sake?

She talked about the trail of fish receipts and Christy listened, filling her glass with wine occasionally. The starters were a long time coming and with nothing but bread rolls to fill her up, Hope began to get drunk. In Christy's skilled hands, the bottle was soon empty, most of it having gone into Hope's glass. Nerves always made her drink more.

He really was the sweetest man, she thought tipsily. He didn't want to talk about himself at all, he just wanted to hear about her.

'Your husband's writing a novel, I believe,' Christy said as they began their starters. A second bottle of wine appeared magically on the table. 'Tell me all about it. I'd love to meet him. I think I've got fantasies about writing a novel – don't we all, I suppose!'

Wine had removed ninety-nine per cent of the tension in Hope and this guileless statement removed the rest. Dear sweet Christy, he was interested in her family – he'd love to meet Matt. How nice. He was a friend, nothing more. A handsome, utterly sexy friend and it was so nice to be able to go out to lunch with him in a platonic way. That's what she needed: lots of sexy platonic friends with kind eyes.

Staring over at Christy with glazed eyes, admiring the way the chunky jumper clung to his broad shoulders, she thought he was very sexy indeed. Sam would like him too. If anyone asked, she could say she was finding a nice man for Sam.

They talked about life in Kerry and Hope was thrilled that she was clearly being so entertaining about adjusting to a totally new life. It was amazing that the stories of the rat invasion and her attempts to rear six chicks could sound amusing, but they did. Christy laughed uproariously and didn't interrupt at all.

At half three, the sound of a vacuum cleaner could be heard starting up in the distance. Hope, who was leaning on her hand and smiling at Christy as she mistily told him how she'd spent ages looking for something nice to wear that day in case she'd bumped into him, sat up at the sound. Through a drunken haze, she looked at her watch and gasped.

'The children! I've got to pick them up!' she said.

'Not yet, surely,' said Christy, looking a bit put out.

'Yes! I'm late!' wailed Hope getting clumsily to her feet. She knocked over her wine glass, mercifully empty, in her attempts to get out of the seat.

'You can't drive, darling,' Christy said. 'You're plastered. I'll drive you.'

'You're drunk too. I can't let you drive my children,' Hope said.

'I haven't had as much as you,' he replied truthfully, having poured much more wine into Hope's glass than into his.

'No,' insisted Hope. *She* was drunk, she was ashamed to admit, but she wouldn't let anyone else in that state drive her precious children. 'You can drive me to Hunnybunnikins and I'll phone Teddy Taxi to take us home.'

She passed a mirror in the hall on their way out and was shocked to see that she no longer looked as lovely as she felt she had an hour ago, when she'd admired herself in a happy drunken haze in the ladies' room mirror. Her face was flushed, her eyeliner was all gone and she'd rubbed her lipstick off with her wineglass.

Christy's car felt very low as she swung herself inelegantly into it. The interior was also very small and when Christy's hand settled on the gear stick, it was only inches away from her knee.

'Settled?' he asked.

'Yes,' she said, feeling trollopy and like a bad mother.

She began to feel slightly queasy as they raced along. Christy certainly didn't slow down in deference to the wine he'd drunk. Hope stared guiltily out the window and worried about being late for the children and about Christy driving after drinking. She was worrying so much, she didn't notice that between gear changes, Christy rested his hand on her knee. It was only when they reached Hunnybunnikins that she realized why her knee felt warmer than the rest of her.

Christy stopped the car on the other side of a big tree that shielded the playgroup from the road. It also shielded the car from anyone inside the building. The next house was a few hundred yards away. Nobody was looking.

'Bye darling,' said Christy softly. He moved like a big cat until his arms were around Hope and his dark, saturnine face was inches away from hers. He closed the distance between them and then his lips touched hers in a deep, open kiss. Hope felt her body melt automatically against his hard chest and she arched herself instinctively upwards, as if waiting for his hands to slip into the valley between her breasts and discover that she wasn't wearing a bra. Every nerve in her body tingled, waiting for his next move. Her nipples quivered with excitement, hard as bullets. Then, before she had a chance to say anything, he pulled away and brushed her lips with his thumb tenderly.

'I've wanted to do that from the moment I met you,' he said, staring at her with his deep, unfathomable eyes.

Hope breathed heavily.

'I'll see you soon,' he said and put both hands back on the steering wheel.

'T . . . thanks for lunch,' she stammered and clambered out of the car, catching her tights on the door and snagging them.

Christy drove off with a crunching of tyres and Hope was left standing beside the playgroup, feeling juddery from too much drink and too much excitement. How was she ever going to explain this to Giselle?

Giselle took one look at her, said nothing, and then led Hope into the adults' quarters where she made her a cup of coffee so strong a duck could trot across it.

'I had a couple of glasses of wine after work and I got a lift here and I knew I couldn't drive the children home . . .' Hope rattled on.

'And you got a lift?' Giselle inquired, her kind face concerned.

'From someone at work,' said Hope with a hiccup. 'May-Kate's always telling me to loosen up. I suppose this must be what she means! Can I use your phone to call Teddy Taxi?' she added.

At home and still tipsy, Hope skipped around the cottage, happily playing with the children and feeling wildly energetic.

'You smell funny,' Millie said, confused by this unusually giggly version of her mother who hadn't changed into her normal old clothes.

Hope picked her up and they danced around the room together. Toby wanted to join in, so Hope put on some music and the three of them twirled and danced for a while. Both children had been making things with glitter and gold stars in the playgroup, so as they danced, flecks of glitter fell.

'I'm shiny like a star!' sang Millie, twirling on her toes like a ballerina with glittery fragments dancing around her in shafts of pale sunlight.

'Lovely stars,' sang Hope happily as she twirled too.

But by half five, both Hope's hangover and a terminal dose of guilt began to kick in. What had she been doing having lunch with Christy? She must have been out of her mind. And that kiss outside the playgroup . . . Just thinking about it made her quiver somewhere deep in her solar plexus, but it had been wrong, absolutely wrong. It must never happen again. What if somebody had seen them and told Matt? Hope paled at the very thought. No, it must never happen again.

She woke up in the middle of the night in a panic, having just had a fevered dream where Matt had walked in on her and Christy making love in the hotel jacuzzi. Dreams were so weird: she didn't know if the hotel *had* a jacuzzi. Hope's pulse raced with shock as she remembered the look of devastation on Matt's dear face when he'd realized that his naked wife was straddling a total stranger, clinging to him like a sex-starved limpet. Devastation was the only word for it.

The guilt overwhelmed Hope. Why had nobody ever told her that cheating on your husband would be so awful? All those films and books had made it plain that the only risk was getting caught, nothing about the agony of guilt over hurting someone you loved. And this wasn't even proper cheating; it had only been a stolen kiss. She tried to convince herself that it wasn't so bad. It wasn't full-blown sex in the jacuzzi. It wasn't sexual at all, really.

Oh hell. Hope felt like crying. It was no use trying to convince herself that her afternoon with Christy had been innocent: it hadn't.

If his sports car had been any more like a double bed, she'd have been stripped down to her underwear in seconds, so great had been the electricity between the two of them. Flattery and excitement meant she'd almost shoved her boobs in his face and if he'd touched her any more, she'd have swooned in her eagerness to be made love to.

Tearfully, she got out of bed, wrapped herself in Matt's old dressing gown for comfort, and went downstairs. Sleep would be impossible now: she might as well turn on the TV and watch some mindless middle of the night television.

With a reviving cup of tea in her hand, Hope switched on the television and started to watch a repeat of an '80s American soap. She was just remembering a time when she'd worn jackets and jumpers with huge shoulder pads like the women on the show, when she realized that the heavily shoulder-padded actress screaming at her downcast husband was upset because he'd admitted to having an affair.

'Why did you have to betray me?' screamed the woman, doing her best to look devastated without ruining her inch-thick eye make-up.

Hope couldn't change the channel fast enough as another wave of shame surged in her soul. Would she ever forgive herself for almost cheating on Matt? Would she have to live with this guilt forever? She knew that magazine agony aunts urged people having affairs not to tell purely to purge themselves of guilt. Doing so only salved the guilty person's conscience and did nothing to help the relationship. But Hope longed to be able to admit all to Matt and be absolved. If only she could turn the clock back and do things differently.

# CHAPTER SEVENTEEN

Virginia and Dinky were gardening when the phone rang. Virginia pulled off her gardening gloves as she ran into the house, Dinky running ahead helpfully.

It was Laurence and he sounded upset.

'I don't know how to tell you this, Mum,' he said, 'but Barbara's not happy with the wedding plans.'

'What do you mean "not happy"?' asked Virginia.

Laurence sighed. 'She says she's always wanted a beach wedding, you know, with everyone barefoot on the sand and the waves in the background.'

Virginia counted to ten. It was a mistake to bitch to your son about your future daughter-in-law, she knew.

'Why didn't she say this in the beginning?' Virginia said mildly. 'You booked the church and the hotel last month. Perhaps it would have been easier to say what she wanted before everything was organized.'

The wedding was due to take place in four months and the reception was to be in one of Dublin's poshest hotels. So far, the only trauma had been the fact that the pretty church that Barbara had set her heart on had been booked already for another wedding. However, since Barbara and Laurence – or, should that be Laurence, Virginia thought – were paying for the wedding, Virginia had no intention of putting her oar in. 'I'm sure you'll lose your deposit from the hotel for cancelling,' she added gently, knowing damn well who'd be out of pocket due to Barbara's newest fantasy.

'I know,' Laurence groaned. 'She says she didn't want to make a fuss.'

There was no point in saying that changing her mind four months before the actual wedding would create far more fuss than being upfront about what she wanted in the first place.

'What do Barbara's parents say?'

'They just want her to be happy. And so do I. Mum, I know you were looking forward to it so much. Would you hate it if we went to the Caribbean instead?'

'Of course not, Laurence, love. It's your wedding, not mine. But lots of people probably won't be able to travel that far. It's a big expense,' she added delicately. 'Have you checked out dates and places yet?'

'I'm going to,' he promised. 'I've just been so busy at work, I haven't had a chance to make any phone calls yet.'

Virginia couldn't resist it: 'Why can't Barbara check it out?'

'She hates doing things like that,' Laurence said. 'She's very shy, you know, Mum. She's not organized, like you.'

Virginia privately thought that Barbara's problem was nothing to do with shyness. Over-indulged was more like it. Her poor parents would probably agree to a wedding on Mars if it pleased her. And now she had Laurence singing off the same hymn sheet. Pleasing Barbara was the name of the game.

'Well Laurence, when you've checked it out, phone me back. There's no point making a drama out of it.'

Jamie was much less reserved when he rang.

'That bloody bitch Barbara is doing my head in, Mum. She treats Laurence like dirt. Have you heard the latest about the wedding? Stupid cow wants to get married on a beach. If she's not careful, when she gets to the beach, I'll shove her into the water and hold her head down and she can glug "I do" with a mouthful of seawater.'

'Jamie,' chided his mother.

'Well, she deserves it. She's messing Laurence about big time. The poor guy's distraught. They're going to lose a fortune on the hotel deposit, not to mention the holiday deposit now that Madam wants to honeymoon in the Caribbean instead of Thailand.'

'We can't get involved, Jamie,' Virginia said. 'I refuse to be an interfering mother-in-law.'

'Mum, if Dad was alive, he wouldn't stand for it,' Jamie said angrily. 'He'd back Laurence up and show him he deserved better than that stupid Barbara.'

'He wouldn't interfere,' Virginia said weakly.

'He would if he thought Laurence was going to get hurt,' Jamie said.

Virginia had been standing by the phone in the sitting room, now she sat down heavily on the corner of the couch.

'Mum, you're not the only person messed up by Dad's death,' Jamie went on. 'Laurence took it hardest. He was so close to Dad. You know how sensitive he is. Just because he doesn't talk about it, doesn't mean he isn't miserable. He hasn't been the same since and Barbara is the first person he's fallen in love with. He's totally messed up and she's taking advantage of it. He needs us, he needs us to tell him to call the whole thing off. They're rushing into it. Oh, there's my mobile. I better go, Mum. I'll call soon.'

And he was gone. Jamie always was the high-speed one of her sons, rushing everywhere, living life at ninety miles an hour. And Laurence was the quiet, sensitive one; the one who bottled up his feelings and never told anybody how he really felt.

Dinky, knowing her mistress was upset, positioned herself beside Virginia's feet and raised her big eyes anxiously. For once, Virginia didn't even notice. She was too shattered. All she could think was that she'd been so busy taking care of herself when Bill died that she hadn't taken care of her sons.

As usual, talking it over with the pragmatic Mary-Kate helped.

'I don't know what to make of Barbara,' Virginia moaned as they drank coffee in Mary-Kate's cosy back office. 'She said she wanted a romantic proposal where Laurence produced the ring, and then, when he did, she wanted a different one because she didn't like the one he'd chosen.'

'Why not pick it together in the first place?' Mary-Kate asked. 'That's what most couples do nowadays.'

'Not Barbara. It's like the ten labours of Hercules,' Virginia said. 'Barbara likes making people exert themselves on her behalf. She needs to have Laurence running around after her all the time.'

'How many labours has Laurence clocked up so far?'

Virginia shrugged gloomily. 'Not enough, I daresay. Barbara probably has a list. I'm just terrified she's one of those awful women who never want to be responsible for anything, the sort who can't be satisfied but who never make an effort to satisfy themselves,' Virginia said.

Mary-Kate looked as if she knew exactly what her friend was talking about.

'You know,' Virginia continued, 'the sort of woman who never makes a decision about anything, who plays the victim card like as if it was the Ace of Hearts in poker, and then, when it all goes wrong, spends her life telling anyone who'll listen that *it's all his fault.*'

'Ah, I know what you mean.' Mary-Kate's face was grim. 'I knew a woman like that once. She should have had "poor me" tattooed on her forehead. She got married to this lovely man because he stood for all the things she wanted in life: money, stability, a big future. Marrying him was a career move for her, a career of being the lady of the manor. Then, when the marriage didn't work out according to her plan, she refused to acknowledge it. There was no way she was giving up her position in life, God help her. She wanted to hold onto all the material trappings and she spent years telling anyone who'd listen that it was his fault, that he was a terrible husband and she didn't know why she stuck with him. She'd never admit that they shouldn't have got married in the first place.'

Mary-Kate's eyes were filled with unshed tears.

It was obvious to Virginia that there was more to this story than met the eye. 'They were friends of yours?'

'I knew him at college, before he married her,' Mary-Kate said. 'The whole class went to the wedding and I think every single one of his friends knew he was making a big mistake. They were far too different to ever be happy together.'

Suddenly it all made sense. Mary-Kate was talking about the man in her life, the man she still mourned over. 'You loved him?' Virginia asked quietly.

Mary-Kate nodded. 'We lost touch and met up a few years after he got married and we fell in love. Timing is everything, right? If we'd fallen in love before he'd met her, who knows what would have happened. Anyway, we were together for six years. We were crazy about each other.'

'What happened?' Virginia's voice was gentle.

'She found out about us, had a breakdown and begged him not to leave.'

'And he didn't?'

'No.' Mary-Kate blinked back the tears, as if she'd shed quite enough for her lover already. 'I came down here to take over the chemist and they had another child.' She gave a little half-shrug. 'That's my sordid story. I don't look like the other woman type, do I?'

Virginia smiled softly. 'Well, the absence of fire engine red lipstick and black silk stockings did throw me. You're pretty good at keeping secrets, Mary-Kate.'

'When you live in a small village, some things need to be kept secret. Nobody knows about him although I think Giselle may have guessed – she's very intuitive. But I wouldn't want anyone else to know. It's better that they think I'm the spinsterish pharmacist rather than the harlot who was in love with a married man. I haven't shocked you, have I?' She was suddenly anxious. 'I felt as if I could tell you but I'd hate to lose your friendship . . .'

Virginia fixed her with a glare. 'If you think I'm the sort of uptight moral hypocrite who'd condemn you, then you don't know me very well. Aren't you talking to Redlion's second merry widow, who's scandalizing the ladies in the church by having a wild fling with poor innocent Kevin Burton?'

They both laughed. The gossipmongers of the village were already on full alert at the news that Virginia often had lunch at the golf clubhouse with Kevin.

'I'm afraid you have upset some of the local ladies who thought they might have a chance with dashing Kev,' Mary-Kate admitted. 'Miss Murphy who does the church flowers is particularly upset and thinks you're a brazen hussy. Her hopes of walking down the aisle for the first time at the age of sixty were scuttled when you appeared in your Dublin finery. But,' Mary-Kate smiled, 'rivalry over Kevin is having a good effect on my business. I'm doing a roaring trade in discreet silvery blonde hair dye since you moved in. There are plenty of women who've realized that if the elegant Mrs Connell can look like a film star, then there's no reason for them to have dull grey hair. They'll be coming to you for make-up tips soon.'

'You're priceless,' Virginia said grinning.

'You think I'm joking, don't you? I'm not,' her friend retorted.

'I'm not after Kevin, not in that way,' Virginia said. 'It's just nice to have someone to play golf with.'

'Tell that to Miss Murphy.'

Virginia fiddled with the card Kevin had sent her for so long that she creased one corner irretrievably. She'd never been a fidgeter. Neither had Bill. They'd both been calm people.

Virginia remembered when the children had been small and the little boy next door, Freddie, had stuffed four peas up his nose.

'Oh Christ, what'll we do?' roared his mother, who'd been having a companionable cup of coffee with Virginia while the children laid waste to the back garden.

Virginia had calmly dropped her boys off at her friend two doors down, had taken Freddie and his mother to the doctor's, and had them all back home in an hour, no fuss, no hysterics. Apart from a slight tantrum from Freddie when he set eyes on the instrument of torture the doctor produced to remove the peas.

Thereafter, Freddie's mother considered Virginia to be the greatest solver of disasters in the area. When her washing machine flooded, she rang Virginia. When Freddie's younger sister nearly electrocuted herself with the toaster and fused the entire house, she rang Virginia.

'I hope her husband doesn't leave,' Bill had teased. 'She'll be on the phone to you like a shot.'

But Virginia's legendary calmness had deserted her when she'd received Kevin's card asking her to the recital. As formal as an invitation to a royal garden party, Kevin's invitation was old-fashioned and absolutely unthreatening.

*Would you be my guest on Thursday evening for a recital in Kilmonbeckin? If you can go, I'll pick you up at seven.*

So why then was Virginia terrified at the idea of meeting him in the evening? Because, she thought, evening meant a date. That would really give the church flowers ladies something to gossip about.

Virginia deliberately wore a new dress the night of the recital. It would have been wrong to wear something she'd worn for Bill – the evening would have been doomed from the start. Virginia knew that if she'd sat fingering the material of her favourite rose-coloured woollen dress and thinking of the last time she'd worn it, a dinner with dear Antonia and Michael in Howth when she and Bill had to get a taxi home after Michael had insisted they all try some of his special Armagnac, then she'd have descended into tears of guilt and depression. Not the ideal way to spend an evening. It would also have been unfair to Kevin. He'd asked her out for the night, not her and the ghost of her husband.

So she'd taken a trip into Killarney and bought a simple pale amber dress in a soft knit fabric. She'd tried on a lovely black one, beautifully cut and very chic, but in the harsh light of the shop, Virginia realized she looked like a caricature of a widow in her weeds, so she went for the amber instead. Anyway, she thought, Bill had always hated her in black.

'I know you love shiny things,' he'd joke whenever she put on any of her black clothes, 'but you don't have to look like a magpie into the bargain.'

The combination of her silvery blonde hair and a black outfit *had* made her resemble a magpie, but she'd never let him away with saying it without a bit of retaliatory teasing.

'Talking of shiny things,' she'd say sweetly, 'I hope you're saving up for my Christmas pressie. Weirs have some lovely diamond chokers and they're only a couple of hundred thousand each.' Even if they could have afforded a diamond choker, Virginia wouldn't have wanted one. She was totally happy with the simple pearl necklace Bill had bought her for their silver wedding.

'Damn,' Bill would joke. 'I'd ordered that diamond thing for the other woman. I suppose you want one too, do you? Honestly, there's no pleasing some women. I'll have to ring up the Swiss bank again.'

Virginia would then throw a cushion or something at him. 'Just as well you're joking, my boyo,' she'd say. Then she'd wonder was it worth changing her clothes. 'Is black awful on me? Should I wear something else?'

'Nothing you wear would ever look awful,' Bill would reply. 'You're a stunner, Mrs Connell, do you know that?'

'You look charming,' Kevin said formally when he picked up her in his car at seven.

Virginia's smile was a little strained. 'Thank you,' she said. This was so strange. There was none of the relaxed camaraderie they'd shared on the golf course. It was easy to chat while you were doing something sporting in broad daylight with other people around, and not so easy at all when there was just two of you in a car in the evening going on a date.

A date. The very thought of it made Virginia's heart break. She shouldn't need to be dating, she should be tucked up at home with Bill, doing the crossword.

They drove along in deafening silence. After a few minutes of keeping his eyes firmly on the road, Kevin cleared his throat. 'Er, you're very good to come along tonight,' he said stiffly. 'It's nice to have a guest at these things.'

'Yes, it is,' said Virginia, just as stiffly. She looked out of the window into the inky night.

What are we like? she asked herself ruefully. Two ventriloquist's dummies sitting in the car, unable to speak. Neither Bill nor Ursula could have wanted that.

So Virginia decided to chat as normal, the way they did on the golf course.

'I've been practising my putting like mad,' she said brightly. 'My son, Jamie, sent me this carpet putter and it's great. Once you shoot the ball at it, it whizzes it back across the carpet to you. Dinky loves it. She thinks it's for her and keeps chasing the golf ball.'

Kevin smiled. 'Those things are addictive,' he said. 'Ursula bought me one once and I spent hours playing with it. It's probably stuck in the attic now. I bet Bill had one too?'

Virginia tried to remember. 'Not that I can recall, but he probably did although I don't know what became of it, if so. He had everything. If they made golf oven gloves, we'd have had them too.'

'You mean you *don't* have golf oven gloves?' Kevin said, doing his best to sound surprised. 'Mine are my most prized possession.'

And they were off, chatting and laughing, friends again instead of dummies.

Ursula had been a brilliant putter, Kevin said fondly. She'd won so many matches with marvellous puts.

'She sounds like she was a marvellous golfer,' Virginia said.

'Oh she was, she was.'

The big modern hall was buzzing with people when they got there, all clutching the glass of sickly mulled wine that the organizers thought would bring people out in droves on a cool April evening.

Virginia handed Kevin a glass. One mulled wine would be good for him. He needed to relax.

'Kevin,' called a voice from the throngs of Sunday best people waiting to be told to take their seats.

'Glenys, Richard, how nice to see you,' Kevin said, greeting a couple effusively.

Glenys, a matronly sixty-something resplendent in fur and a frosted hairdo, hugged Kevin before turning to cast a mauve-eyeshadowed stare over Virginia.

'Hello,' Virginia said warmly, 'I'm Virginia Connell, I'm a friend of Kevin's.'

'Glenys and Richard Smart,' Glenys said coolly. 'We're very old friends of Kevin's. And Ursula's,' she added with a determined lift to her chin.

Oh dear, thought Virginia, her smile never faltering. So that's the way the cookie crumbles. Loyal to the memory of our dear, dead friend, we don't want any mucky widow from Dublin getting her hands on the grieving widower.

'How nice to meet you both,' Virginia said. Bill had often teased her that she was an expert at being outwardly polite to people she didn't like.

Richard nodded hello.

Glenys turned away and took one of Kevin's hands in hers. 'Dear Kevin, how *are* you?'

It was a nightmarish evening. Glenys managed the seating plan so that Virginia and Kevin were separated, with Virginia sitting at the outside of their row beside a monosyllabic Richard. Hemmed in by Richard and Glenys, Kevin couldn't exactly reach over and speak to Virginia, which was probably Glenys's plan all along. At the interval, Glenys sighed loudly and said that the tragedy was that poor Ursula wasn't here to listen to the concert.

'She so loved recitals,' Glenys said wistfully, squeezing Kevin's hand. 'Do you remember that lovely night we all had in Dublin at the Concert Hall, when we stayed in the Westbury and had supper after the show?'

Kevin did remember, and soon the three old friends were laughing over the grand time they'd all had.

Virginia felt her fixed smile waver. How terribly, terribly rude.

She hoped that if her friends ever got to meet Kevin, they wouldn't stoop so low as to spend the entire time remembering Bill and all the lovely times they'd had when he was alive.

Rude and insensitive didn't even come close. Glenys was doing it on purpose too, because she clearly disapproved of Virginia. But why? What was she protecting Kevin from? Did she imagine that Virginia was some sort of evil hussy who'd left a trail of abandoned men behind her? Or was Virginia cast as the black widow, who mated, then killed? Whatever it was, Richard and Glenys Smart clearly believed there was some nasty intent in her friendship with Kevin.

After the recital, the four of them walked to the small pub nearby. Virginia let Glenys march alongside Kevin, one arm protectively through his, leaving Virginia and Richard to walk behind. Glenys kept up the train of babble about Ursula throughout.

During a five minute walk, they got through Ursula's love of classical music, her ability to recognize any piece from the first four bars and how she'd always wanted to learn to play the violin.

'Don't you think she'd have been wonderful at the violin?' Glenys said mistily to Kevin. 'She was so talented, wasn't she?'

Virginia, who'd previously felt that Ursula Burton was the sort of woman she'd have liked a lot, began to dislike her no end. How could any sane woman have been friends, no, *'best friends'* with the likes of the nauseating Glenys?

In the pub, Virginia took matters into her own hands by choosing a banquette with room for two and inviting Kevin to sit beside her. Glenys and Richard were forced to sit on two single chairs opposite from where Glenys glowered like Grumpy with migraine. For badness sake, Virginia put a hand on Kevin's arm. He started nervily and got to his feet.

'Drinks?' he said, obviously anxious to be away from his date. 'I'll get them.'

When he returned, he sat beside Virginia but kept as far away from her as was possible given the constraints of sharing a seat, and let Glenys carry on with the Ursula tribute concert. When Kevin did speak to Virginia, he was as formal as an archbishop, as if he didn't want to give his old friends the wrong idea.

Virginia's bullshit tolerance level bottomed out quite quickly. She finished her white wine quietly and then asked Kevin if he'd mind driving her home.

'You must come to dinner soon,' Glenys gushed to Kevin as they left.

Virginia knew that she most definitely wasn't included in the invitation.

The drive home was silent with the car radio the only distraction.

Virginia didn't see the point of talking to Kevin. If he was ashamed of his friendship with her, then she didn't want to see him again: it was that simple. Miss Murphy of the church flower arranging group could get her hopes up again.

At Kilnagoshell, she said a polite thank you for the recital and began to get out of the car.

'It was a pleasure,' Kevin said, sounding like his old self for the first time all evening. 'I'll phone you about golf?' It was a question rather than a statement.

Virginia gave him the benefit of her cool, clear gaze. 'Why?' she said.

He lowered his eyes first. 'I'm sorry,' he said. 'I know that was awful for you. Glenys and Ursula were such friends and Glenys can't cope with the idea of anyone replacing her.'

'You should have told Glenys that I have no intention of replacing Ursula,' Virginia said crisply. 'I went out with you tonight as a friend, nothing more. Friends do not sit idly by and let other friends be insulted.' She got out, slammed the car door shut and walked to the house, leaving Kevin with no option but to drive off.

'How was your evening?' asked Mary-Kate the next day, when they met by chance outside the post office. Virginia had discovered that it was impossible to go into Redlion without meeting someone you knew. In her current bad mood, she was grateful that it was Mary-Kate she'd bumped into and not Lucille from the fashion shop who spent many futile hours trying to get Virginia into the boutique to buy a little something.

Virginia filled her friend in on the grisly details.

'I don't know the Smarts but she sounds like a nightmare. Probably has fantasies about comforting the grieving widower herself,' Mary-Kate said prosaically. 'Having a handsome, unattached man around can do wonders for a marriage and Mrs Smart may have thought how nice it would be to have a spare man for her parties. You've ruined all that, you hussy.'

Virginia shrugged. 'I know, I'm just a heartbreaker, wilfully being nice to lonely men. There should be a law against it.'

'Don't give up, Virginia. Just because she's jealous of you, doesn't mean you can't see Kevin.'

Virginia looked down at the letters she intended to post. 'That's the thing, Mary-Kate,' she admitted, 'he *did* behave differently to me in her presence. I think he's already crippled with guilt for seeing me at all.'

'Guilt? But why? His wife's dead, she's been dead several years, he's not hurting her memory by seeing you.'

Virginia shrugged. 'Dead but most definitely not forgotten. It's obvious he feels disloyal for meeting me for the odd game of golf.'

Mary-Kate looked at her sadly.

'I think about Bill all the time, you know,' Virginia said softly. 'I loved him so much that there'll never be anybody for me but him, but that doesn't mean I can't enjoy the company of a man like Kevin. The very idea of having someone to go out for a meal with makes life sort of normal again. When Bill died, I didn't think there could ever be any normality in my life. But simple things, like buying a new dress or making new friends, help. They make me feel like I'm still alive, that I'm not just marking time until I die and join Bill.' Her beautiful, fine-boned face was earnest as she spoke and Mary-Kate thought that Kevin Burton was a fool if he walked away from lovely, gentle Virginia Connell because he and his so-called friends wouldn't let go of his dead wife.

'Do you understand what I'm saying, Mary-Kate? I can't give up on life, that would be wrong. I might as well take a razorblade into the bath and be done with it, if I do that. I've got to try to actually *live* for the rest of my life, rather than just exist. What's wrong with that?'

'Nothing. You're absolutely right. You shouldn't stop living just because there are people out there who feel threatened by a woman who doesn't throw herself on her husband's funeral pyre.' Mary-Kate was firm. 'Give Kevin a second chance, won't you?'

'Well, I might as well. I've been here a year now and he's the only handsome single man I've noticed, unless I try and wrench Richard Smart out of Glenys's tight little hands.'

They both grinned at the thought.

'Go on,' teased Mary-Kate, 'I dare you.'

Virginia shuddered. 'Even double daring wouldn't work. She's welcome to him. In fact, they deserve each other.'

# CHAPTER EIGHTEEN

'Mummy, phone!' said Millie indignantly the next morning, climbing onto her mother's bed and bouncing. 'Wake up, Mummy, it's Daddy on the phone.'

Mummy, head throbbing from a terrible night's sleep, dragged herself into a sitting position. Why hadn't they ever got a phone connection in the bedroom?

She stumbled downstairs and picked up the receiver, her voice croaky and tired.

'Hi darling, you sound as if you've just woken up,' said Matt cheerily.

Hope thanked God that video phones were an innovation yet to hit the Parker family. She was sure that Matt would be able to tell she'd been up to no good purely by looking at her guilty face.

'N . . . no,' she stammered. 'Just tired. I had a bad night.'

'You poor thing,' Matt answered. 'I'm afraid I've got something to talk to you about.'

Hope's eyes widened. How could he have heard? Who'd have phoned him? Nobody in the village had a clue where he was staying and it had only been the day before and surely nobody would be so cruel as to break up a marriage over a piece of vicious gossip . . .

'Things are so busy here, I'll be back as planned in about ten days but I'll have to go back to Bath for a couple of weeks, maybe longer,' Matt said. 'The office is so busy right now and Adam isn't back to

384

full strength. The heart attack has had a huge effect on him, he's changed, I must say. And since that new restaurant campaign's been nominated for the industry awards, Judds are the hottest agency around and everybody wants us working for them. The phones are hopping and Adam is loath to turn any work down, particularly since some of the people ringing are companies whose business we've been touting for for years.'

Hope sank onto an armchair with relief. He didn't know anything about her or Christy after all. Relief made her forgiving.

'It's all right, Matt,' she said warmly, 'there's nothing you can do. I understand.'

'That's great, love,' he replied. 'I was afraid you'd go ballistic. I know it's been tough for you coping with the kids on your own. I promise that when I get back, we'll ask Finula to babysit and we'll take ourselves off for a romantic weekend away somewhere, okay?'

The thought of a romantic weekend where she'd have to steel herself not to tell Matt what had happened made Hope's blood run cold.

Every part of her longed to blurt it all out. She'd kissed Christy De Lacy but honestly, it had been a mistake and she'd never meant to . . .

'What do you think, Hope? Would that be a good idea?'

'Lovely,' she said automatically. 'A weekend away would be lovely, but let's take the kids.' With Millie and Toby along, there'd be no time for either introspection or long talks about marriage.

Matt began discussing venues for the weekend away but Hope wasn't listening: she was crucifying herself. Except Matt got the wrong idea about her silence.

'Don't go all quiet on me,' he begged. 'I'm sorry I'm not going to be home this weekend. I know you think the kids will have forgotten me and you'll have got yourself a toyboy with the boredom of it all.' He laughed at the absurdity of the idea.

Hope joined in nervously. 'Funny, very funny,' she said.

She hadn't meant to dress up the next time she went to work at the hotel. She really hadn't. The night before, she'd chosen a boringly plain white cotton shirt to go with her tailored black trousers, an outfit that would probably make her a dead ringer for a waitress and which would kill any lust stone dead. She'd even practised what she'd say should she bump into Christy.

She'd spent forty-eight hours practising this; endlessly going over the whole prospective conversation in her head.

*I'm married, Christy. I love my husband. It was a mistake and I'd had too much to drink. I apologize for giving you the wrong impression. I am a happily married woman.*

She tried several variations on this theme, her skin burning with shame at the thought of having to actually say it to Christy. He'd probably be shocked to think that she hadn't meant it when she'd let him kiss her. Perhaps he'd thought she was some sort of wild, whorish woman who had affairs left, right and centre and trifled with men's affections. Oh no, please don't let him have thought that. In all her years married to Matt, she'd never even looked at another man, apart from the odd long-range crush on the likes of Mel Gibson, which was so far into the realms of fantasy, it didn't matter, did it?

What she really hoped was that Christy never came near her again, and that she could forget the whole sordid thing had ever happened. A sort of see-no-evil type of scenario where Christy was deaf, blind and dumb to the entire event.

In the end, it was Millie who made Hope change out of her waitress garb by getting strawberry jam all over both herself and her mother.

'Millie, careful!' said Hope, as Millie stuck a spoon deep into the jam pot, more for naughtiness than through any desire for jam.

But it was too late. Millie, and therefore, everyone around her, was instantly covered in jam. Small jammy fingerprints on Hope's sleeve rendered the severe white blouse unwearable. She rushed upstairs to change Millie's jam-splodged sweatshirt, before rushing into her room to find something for herself. The only other white blouse was squashed at the back of the wardrobe and she dragged it on at high speed, forgetting why she rarely wore it. Silky and outwardly demure, the blouse was a slave to static electricity and unless a tumble dryer freshening sheet was rubbed vigorously over it, the fabric stuck to the skin like a wet T-shirt.

Hope remembered this as she removed her coat in the accounts office, to find the blouse stuck to her body as firmly as if she'd rolled in superglue before getting dressed.

'Oooh static,' said Una sympathetically, staring at Hope, who was doing her best to pull the blouse away from her skin. 'I have a silky skirt just like that. If I don't put enough fabric conditioner in the wash, it sticks to me like mud. And with my legs, it's not a pretty sight.'

'This looks awful, doesn't it?' wailed Hope, looking down at her chest where the outline of her lacy white bra was as clear as daylight. 'I just need one of those tumble dryer sheets and it'll get rid of the static.'

'I'll ring laundry and ask them to send one up,' said Una cheerfully.

Janet was off that day, so it was just the two of them, working along to the sound of the radio, with occasional interruptions from reception.

Each time the door opened, Hope jumped guiltily, hoping it wasn't Christy because she was far too embarrassed to see him, particularly since she looked like a wet T-shirt contestant.

But the morning passed without any sign of the handsome hotel manager. He must be away, Hope reassured herself. There was no sign of anyone from laundry with the promised tumble dryer sheet either, but Hope began to stop worrying about her cling-on blouse. With luck, she thought, she'd be out the door long before Christy appeared and she wouldn't have to face him at all. She'd forget her impassioned apology, too, and hope that they next time they met, they could both be utterly professional and pretend it hadn't happened.

Like actors and actresses having lust-driven flings when they were on location making films. DCOL was the name of the game there, Hope had read: Doesn't Count On Location. All involved pretended afterwards that the affair hadn't happened, going chastely back to their partners as if they hadn't sinned at all. The hotel world must be the same, she decided.

At five to one, Hope turned off her computer and grabbed her coat.

'I know it's a teeny bit early,' she said, 'but I've got to rush.'

Christy had always appeared after one in the afternoon. If only she could leave early, she'd miss him.

'No problem,' Una said. 'Could you just drop this out to reception on your way?' She held out a document.

Hope took it and peered out at reception. The coast was clear: no sign of Christy. Thrilled, she handed Una's document to the receptionist and literally ran out the front door, her coat over her arm because she didn't have time to put it on. She rounded the topiary hedge and peered round a mossy statue of an Irish wolfhound to see if she could spot Christy in the car park. There was no sign of him. Walking as quickly as she could in her high heeled boots, she hurried to the staff car park but she'd only reached the gravelled entrance when Christy appeared in front of her.

Dressed in his beautifully tailored suit with his dark hair falling over those glinting, dangerous eyes, he looked incredible and disturbing. Much more disturbing even than when he had been naked and turned on in Hope's dreams, ravaging her furiously, telling her how much he wanted her in that deep, velvety voice.

'Hello,' he said warmly now, eyeing up her outfit. 'You're always rushing off somewhere, Mrs Parker.'

Hope was incapable of speech. Despite working out her spiel many times, she couldn't manage to deliver it now that Christy was standing beside her, making her heart beat double time.

'I have to pick up the children,' she said, then cursed because Christy would know she was lying. She hadn't picked them up until nearly four the other day.

'Pity,' he said lightly. 'We could have had lunch. I do like your shirt,' he added, one dark hand stroking the lapels of the traitorous blouse. 'You wear the most interesting clothes.' He was grinning at her, one hand still caressing the fabric of her blouse. He was so close that Hope could feel the heat of his breath on her face.

'This is a very disturbing outfit,' he said huskily. 'I can't imagine that I'd get any work done at all if I had to look at you all morning.'

'You don't have to look at me,' Hope said stupidly.

Christy smiled slowly. 'But I'd like to.' Those eyes roved all over her, taking in the swell of her breasts, the full curve of her hips and the soft coral mouth trembling in anticipation. His head came closer to hers, closer, until his full mouth hovered just over hers, the glimmer of a smile curving up the edges.

Hope didn't want to but she couldn't help it. Her 'I'm happily married' spiel fell apart in her mind and she let herself be swept along on the intoxicating sensation of being inches away from the sexiest man she'd ever met. When Christy's mouth plunged down on hers, she kissed him back. His hands joined together in the small of her back, pulling her close to him, moulding her to him. It was different from the kiss in the car. Then, they'd been constrained by space. Here, in a discreet corner half hidden by a tall hedge, there were no constraints. Christy held Hope's quivering body against his, letting her feel the lean hardness of his body jammed up against her. She responded fiercely, winding her arms around his neck, running her hands through the soft curls of his hair, pulling him closer to her as if she were a deep sea diver dying for lack of air and he was a spare scuba tank.

The kiss seemed endless, Hope was lost in Christy's deliciously probing mouth. Every inch of her body yearned for him, every inch leaned towards him like a flower reaching for the sun. Her hands rippled through his hair, sliding down to his shoulders, delighting in being able to touch him. His hands left the relative safety of her lower back and slid down to cradle her buttocks. Hope couldn't stop herself moaning as his fingers pulled her closer to him, leaving the most exquisite tingling sensation in her lower body. She wanted him, here and now. She wanted him to push her up against the wall and rip her clothes off, begging her to let him make love to her, crying out for her to say yes. Yes, yes . . .

'Yes,' moaned Hope dizzily as Christy's lips burned down past her neck into the buttoned up cleavage of her glued-on shirt.

'Yes?' he said hoarsely. 'You mean that?'

'Yes, I know it's wrong but I can't help it,' Hope wailed.

'It's not wrong.' Christy's expert fingers were rapidly undoing the buttons of her blouse and then his hands were inside, touching the fabric of her bra, one hand pulling it away to touch the sensitive skin of her breast itself. Hope moaned with lust as his fingers circled her nipple, tweaking and stroking until she was a volcano of excitement. She couldn't remember being so turned on in her life. Every part of her strained towards him, liquid with desire . . .

The shrill ringing tone of Christy's mobile phone made them both jump.

'Jesus!' gasped Christy, whipping a hand out from Hope's blouse and searching inside his jacket for his phone.

'Christy De Lacy,' he said smoothly, recovering his savoir faire while Hope stood there, both her mouth and her blouse gaping.

'Mr Wilson, of course we haven't forgotten you,' Christy was saying, switching into work mode at the drop of a hat. It was as if he hadn't practically been having sex with Hope a moment before.

The exquisite sensation of being wanted by Christy vanished, to be replaced by the hard, cold truth that when duty called, he had been quite capable of shoving her aside. And, like an animal on heat, she'd blindly forgotten her duty to her husband. What had they been doing? What had *she* been doing? Horrified, she buttoned up her blouse, picked up her coat from the ground where she'd dumped it in high passion, and ran to her car. So much for 'I love my husband very much', she told herself fiercely as she threw her belongings into the car.

You're nothing but a lying, cheating tramp, she cried, hurtling the car down the drive lest Christy race after her for a repeat performance. But there was no sign of him. No, she thought bitterly, he was back in character, playing the master of the Manoir universe to perfection, having no doubt forgotten his passionate snog with the stupid, wanton part-timer from the accounts office. The stupid *married* woman, with a cuckold for a husband. Now Christy would look down on Matt, smugly thinking *I had your wife, mate* and it was all her fault.

At that moment, Hope hated herself more than she ever had in her whole life. What had she done? At home, she stripped off her clothes and put on her oldest jeans and an elderly, deeply unflattering grey sweatshirt. She wanted to tell someone what had happened, to seek some sort of solace in the sisterhood of having someone say it was nothing, nothing had happened and, therefore, she had nothing to be guilty about.

But she couldn't reach Sam either in the office or on her mobile. In desperation, she tried Mary-Kate but the chemist phone was engaged. And Delphine knew Christy, which would make it harder to tell her. She sat at the computer and tried to compose a note to Sam but when she started explaining what had happened, the shame hit her again. Looking at those blank, cold little words describing what she'd done, *he kissed me and I let him, I kissed him back,* Hope knew she couldn't bear to tell Sam how low she'd sunk. Sam would be ashamed of her and with reason.

Miserably, Hope put on her Wellington boots and went outside to do the job she most hated: cleaning out the hen shed.

The hens didn't spend much time in their shed during the day, except when it was being cleaned out. Then, they abandoned their usual activity of pecking the ground for hours on end and arrived en masse to sit on their perches and look outraged at all the activity, clucking non-stop in disgust.

'Stop complaining,' growled Hope crossly, as she started shovelling out the floor which was a mass of straw and hen droppings. The smell was awful, but even worse were the maggots crawling from the eggs which flies laid in the midst of the droppings. Seeing those wriggling white bodies always made Hope feel nauseous. Well, she deserved to feel nauseous today. It was her punishment, her penance. Gritting her teeth, she shovelled fiercely.

When she finally got through to Sam late that evening, Hope decided against saying anything. Not that Sam was a prude or any-thing, but Hope knew that infidelity was not like any other sin in life. It was such a taboo topic, not the type of thing people discussed. People who condoned all sorts of mad behaviour could be shocked by the thought of cheating on a partner.

For all that Sam and Matt didn't get on, she might be utterly stunned to find out that Hope had even toyed with the idea of cheating on him. Worse still, she'd be so disappointed in her sister, so Hope said nothing and they chatted idly for ten minutes.

On Friday, Mary-Kate phoned to say she had the flu, so did Virginia, Delphine was getting it and that the Macramé Club on Saturday was therefore cancelled. Hope felt like crying. The weekend stretched dismally in front of her, with no adult company and no chance to blurt out her awful story.

'You sound a bit fluey yourself,' Mary-Kate said suspiciously.

'I'm fine,' lied Hope.

After she hung up, she stared miserably out the window where the children were happily making mud pies and were up to their eyes in dirt. They were utterly happy. She felt like hell but she had nobody else to blame but herself. There was only one option: she had to give up her job. She couldn't bear the embarrassment of ever seeing Christy again. But how would she ever face Matt?

# CHAPTER NINETEEN

'Where'll we go for dinner?' asked Morgan as he and Sam wandered out of the cinema into the cool night air of Leicester Square.

'Dinner?' she demanded. 'You've just eaten a mega bucket of popcorn. How can you be hungry? You must have a tape worm in there.' She pointed at his lean belly in mock horror.

'That's my secret,' he smiled. 'Us blokes have to suffer to be beautiful, you know. Leg waxing, tapeworms, the whole business . . .'

Sam laughed. 'I'd like to see your face if anyone waxed any bit of you. Like,' she grinned evilly, 'the bikini line.'

Morgan winced. 'OK, you win. Women have it really tough, blah, blah, blah. But it's not easy being a hunter gatherer.'

Beside him, Sam raised her eyes theatrically to heaven.

'Besides, we decided we'd go out for a movie and dinner,' Morgan added. 'We've only done half of it. I'm keen on doing the dinner part too. I'm a growing boy and I need my food.'

'Only if we split the bill,' Sam interjected because this wasn't a date precisely and she wanted to get the facts straight at the start. Morgan had phoned up the day before and said he fancied seeing the new Tom Hanks movie and asking if she wanted to come along too. Definitely not a romantic evening, Sam had decided, from his tone of voice. A casual tone of voice. Just a friend asking another friend for a night out. Which meant that the bill-splitting thing had to be sorted out.

'Whatever,' Morgan said. 'Anyway, I owe you for dinner at your place.'

They walked in companionable silence, Sam struggling to keep up with Morgan's long-legged lope. Normally, people had to hurry to catch up with her.

They wandered round Soho looking for somewhere to eat and ended up outside a suitably dimly lit Italian restaurant which promised lots of dishes 'like Mama used to make'.

'They've never tasted my mother's cooking, then,' Morgan joked as they went in. 'She's a highly talented woman but the kitchen is not her forte. My father has to do all the cooking because she can't boil water.'

Sam was surprised. 'You never usually talk about yourself.'

'Hello,' breathed a very un-Italian looking blonde waitress who smiled admiringly up at Morgan. 'Table for two? No problem at all.'

She found them a table then handed Morgan the menus, almost reverently. Sam watched, half-amused, half-angry. The only positive sign was that Morgan didn't appear to notice the waitress's wide-eyed admiration.

'I don't talk much about myself because there's not much to talk about,' Morgan shrugged when they were alone again. 'I'm very dull.'

'Our waitress doesn't think so,' Sam said impishly. 'Nor does Tanya in the shop near us, or any one of the trails of women I see smiling goofily at you all the time.'

'Jealous, Ms Smith?' Morgan had a piercing gaze when he wanted to use it: his face became more hawkish than usual, narrowed eyes staring at her curiously over that long nose.

For one crazy moment, Sam almost thought he wanted her to be jealous. That he wanted her to say 'yes, I'm jealous as sin of any woman who looks crossways at you.' But he couldn't, she was sure of it. Morgan, for all that she loved his company, wasn't interested in her, not in that way. She was most firmly a platonic friend, someone he liked but would never fancy, someone he could talk to when he was having a break from the Tanyas and Mirandas that waved to him when he stepped out his front door. Granted, he didn't pay them any attention. In fact, he was rarely more than friendly to them, really, even though they looked at him with undisguised lust as if they'd love to rip his suede jacket off his lanky frame and trail long nails over his muscles.

But best of all, there had been no sign lately of the youthful, doe-like Maggie, the girl who'd rushed into Morgan's arms that evening. Sam dared not ask about her but hoped that her absence meant she was out of Morgan's life for good.

She took a long, cool sip of water.

'It's hot in here,' she said, fanning herself with her hand.

Morgan grinned at her, eyes crinkling up in amusement.

'Stop grinning and start talking,' she said. 'You're far too secretive you know. You could be on the run from Interpol for all I know, or on the FBI's most wanted list.'

He nodded. 'There's a reward out for my arrest, obviously. Not much but enough to, say,' he considered it, 'redecorate your apartment and buy a nice car, I imagine.'

'A stand up comedian, I should have guessed,' Sam laughed. 'No, really, tell me about yourself.'

He rubbed his eyes with one hand, and then looked a bit blearily at her.

'Did it ever occur to you that when people don't talk about things, it's because they don't want to talk about them?'

'Yes,' Sam replied equably, 'but I still ask. I'm direct, you know.'

He laughed. 'There are chief inspectors in Scotland Yard who are less direct than you are. Right, get your notebook out, Inspector, what do you want to know?'

Sam felt herself go hot again. What she wanted to ask was about his relationship history, how many women he'd gone out with, if he had ever lived with anyone or been married. But she couldn't ask that sort of thing because then, he might realize she was interested in him. God forbid. How humiliating that would be. As if Mr Serial-Dater-of-Twenty-Something-Nubile-Blondes would be interested in a thirty-nine-and-eleven-months-year-old tough cookie. He hated tough cookies.

Sam did what she always did: when in a difficult situation, discuss work.

'You aren't an internet millionaire, I checked,' she said. 'So what do you do?' And how come you have the money to buy the house next door? was the unspoken question.

'You mean, how did I manage to buy the house next door to you?' Morgan said solemnly.

She bit her lip and burst out laughing. 'I confess, that was my real question.'

The waitress arrived with their meals.

'Can I get you anything else?' the waitress asked, gazing at Morgan.

He favoured her with a warm, engaging smile that made Sam go weak, as well as want to slap the waitress for impertinence. 'No thanks, everything's fine,' he said.

'Honestly, I've never seen anything like it,' Sam said crossly, digging her fork into her pasta. 'That woman was all over you like a cheap suit. They throw themselves at you. It's shameless.' She twisted her fork viciously.

'She was simply doing her job,' Morgan said in astonishment. 'She has to ask if everything's all right. What are you on about?'

Sam stared at him. Did he honestly not have a clue? Did he think that other men spent their lives with women giving them the sort of longing looks that chocoholics gave Snickers bars?

'Oh nothing,' she said. 'Go on, you were going to tell me about your job.'

'I was a venture capitalist,' Morgan said, mopping up sauce with his bread roll. 'I was a partner in a firm in the city and we found development money for companies starting out. It was high-risk but it's an addictive life.'

'Why did you give it up?' she asked unthinkingly. 'It sounds as if you loved it.'

She glanced up and caught sight of Morgan's face, which was mask-like.

Instinctively, she reached across the table and touched his hand, her slim fingers closing round his strong masculine ones. 'I'm sorry, I didn't mean to pry, Morgan. Forget I said that.'

The mask relaxed a little. 'It's all right. I've got to learn to be less uptight about it.' He smiled suddenly. 'That's what Charlie keeps telling me. Charlie's my stepson and he's very into psychology.'

'I didn't even know you had a stepson,' Sam said.

'You see, my man of mystery thing worked. Actually, I've three step children, two girls and Charlie. They live with my ex-wife but we're still very close. I've known them all since they were little.'

'Oh,' said Sam, sorry she'd been so intrusive. 'I really didn't mean to pry . . .'

'You're a woman, that's your job,' Morgan said through a mouthful of pasta.

'Well, you know all about me,' Sam began defensively.

'I'm teasing you,' he said softly. 'It's not so bad now I've started. I understand what you're like because that's what I was like: a workaholic. I lived for my job and at the end of the day, it broke up my marriage. We split up and now we're divorced, which is what spurred me to get out of the rat race. Too late for me and Val, mind you. That's it, that's my story.'

'I'm sorry,' Sam said.

He shrugged and pushed his plate away. 'It was my fault,' he said brusquely. 'The house was my project, something to take my mind off life until I worked out what I wanted to do next. When Val and I were married, I never changed a light bulb or hammered a nail. We got someone in to do it even though I could have done it, no problem. I was too busy.' His mouth twisted into that half-smile again. 'Too busy being a master of the universe to see that my family life was disintegrating.'

Sam was so sorry she'd started this. She hadn't meant to upset him or to make him remember things he'd rather forget.

'Will you go back into the City?' Sam asked to change the subject.

He shook his head. 'I don't want that sort of life any more. Index-linked pension funds aren't much compensation when you've got nothing else. The past year has given me time to see what I do want in life and I needed time to get over it all. That's why I'm not rushing into getting involved with anyone.' He stared deeply into her clear blue eyes. 'I wasn't rushing to getting involved,' he amended.

It was an electric moment, pregnant with meaning. Sam bit her lip nervously, wanting him to say more, to say he liked her, because *he* had to say it, she couldn't.

'Finished? Was everything all right?' The waitress swooped and cleared away their plates, gathering up side plates and the butter dish briskly, bestowing another beaming smile on Morgan. 'Do you want dessert?'

'No,' snapped Sam.

'Yes,' said Morgan. 'I've a sweet tooth,' he explained to Sam.

'I bet you do,' breathed the waitress with a naughty wink.

Sam glared at her but it was no good: the electric moment had vanished.

Morgan must have felt it too. He sat back in his chair, breaking the sense of intimacy that came from two people leaning closer to each other across a tiny bistro table.

'It's been sort of fun being a bum, never wearing a shirt with French cuffs, not having to leave the house at six in the morning for a meeting in Frankfurt.'

'And I thought you didn't have a decent shirt to your name,' Sam said lightly.

'What's wrong with this?' he demanded, looking down at the faded blue casual shirt he wore with his usual jeans with worn seams.

'Lovely,' she said kindly, intensely aware of the effect of Morgan sitting so close to her, his long, jean-clad legs occasionally touching hers under the table in a way that was both comfortingly familiar and utterly exciting.

They chatted idly over coffee and ice cream, and then got a taxi home. All the time, Sam was conscious of Morgan sitting closely by her, long jean-clad legs taking up lots of room as they talked and laughed. That was the great thing about him: he made her laugh all the time.

Outside their respective houses, Morgan handed the taxi driver money before Sam had even got her purse out. 'We're supposed to be splitting everything,' she said.

'Relax, will you?' he replied. 'I'm not going to demand payback of a carnal kind just because I've shelled out eight quid on a cab.'

Pity, thought Sam.

'How about having a cup of coffee at my place as a thank you, then?' she inquired, trying to make it sound casual.

'Sure.' He opened her gate. 'After you, Ms Smith.'

As they climbed the stairs, Sam felt her heart beating a tattoo in her chest. This was it: the chance to see if Morgan really did like her.

He prowled round the living room, running his fingers over her driftwood sculpture, hunching down to examine the silver Indian elephant, admiring the pictures on the walls.

'I forgot to say it to you the night of the dinner party but you really have a lovely place.'

'Thanks,' she said from the kitchen where she was looking around frantically for some fresh coffee. She couldn't be out of it, could she? Damn, double damn. She was. That was the fatal flaw in being a working woman with too little time to buy groceries: the cupboards were often bare.

'Will instant do?'

'Sure,' he said. 'Do you mind if I put a CD on?' he asked, adding wickedly, 'I promise not to turn it so loud that it annoys the neighbours and forces them to march in and pull the plug from the socket.'

'Very funny, Benson,' Sam replied. 'You turn that dial up over five and I'll kill you. The guy who lives above me bangs on the ceiling if he can hear the slightest noise from down here.'

'I'm sure you're a noisy neighbour' Morgan joked, 'all those wild girls' nights in with two-litre bottles of vodka and Gloria Gaynor on the CD player.'

'Don't even joke about it,' she begged with a shiver. 'Mad Malcolm upstairs has a dog that barks at all hours of the day and night, he's addicted to playing his music so loud that the people in the basement can hear it, and then, he hangs over the balcony at odd intervals telling us all to stop making noise.'

'Sorry, bad joke,' Morgan said. 'Can't you do anything about him?'

'Every resident in the house has reported him to everyone we can think of but nothing's happened. I'm waiting for him to go completely mad and get carried off to a mental hospital somewhere. Either that or I'll have to sell.'

'Let's forget about him,' Morgan said, as the strains of Nina Simone drifted gently out of the speakers.

'My favourite,' said Sam in delight. 'How ever did you know?'

Morgan settled himself comfortably on her big couch and grinned at her. 'You look like the sort of woman who likes good music.'

She was carrying the mugs of coffee over when the phone rang.

'Shit,' Sam said, dumping them down on the table. 'Who'd be phoning at . . .' she looked at her watch, 'a quarter to eleven.' She blanched. 'Something bad must have happened,' she said. 'Nobody phones me this late. Except Hope.'

She rushed to the phone and grabbed it from the cradle. 'Hello?'

'Sam,' said Hope. 'It's me. I needed to talk to you.'

'Sure, Hope, can I call you back?' said Sam, not aware of how her sister had psyched herself up to make this call.

There was a silence on the other end of the phone.

Morgan got up and waved at Sam. 'I'll go,' he mouthed.

Sam shook her head.

'It's OK,' said Hope on the other end, apologetically, 'you've obviously got someone there. I'll call some other time.'

She was clearly distressed about something.

'No, hold on, Hope,' said Sam as Morgan collected his jacket, waved goodbye and left, shutting the door quietly behind him.

'They've just gone,' Sam said, 'so tell me, what's wrong Hope?'

'Nothing,' Hope burst out. 'Nothing. I'll talk to you tomorrow. Bye.'

And she hung up. Sam sat looking at the coffee cups on the table and put down the phone with a sigh. She ought to give classes on how to end an evening on a high note.

# CHAPTER TWENTY

Nicole checked her make up for the nth time that morning.

'The mirror will crack if you look in it any more,' said her mother with her trademark giggle.

'Don't be daft,' said Gran. 'At least she looks in the mirror when she puts it on. You just close your eyes and plaster on the lipstick.'

Nicole's fingers tightened their grip on the cup of coffee. They'd been bickering ever since they'd left the house and got into the taxi.

First, Gran had muttered that a taxi was a waste of money when there was a perfectly good bus service and if it was good enough for her, it was good enough for the rest of them.

Sandra had countered this by saying that it was about time the Turner family lived with a bit of style and added that, talking of style, she had her eye on a very nice handbag she'd seen in a magazine that only cost £200 pounds in Harrods. With Nicole being very rich soon thanks to all that record company money, they'd be doing all their shopping in Harrods, wouldn't they?

'Harrods!' shrieked Gran, loud enough to give their laid-back Rastafarian taxi driver a shock. 'Far from Harrods you were reared, my girl. When I was a girl, we didn't have Harrods, I can tell you. Style, rubbish. When I was your age, madam, I wouldn't have *dreamed* of buying the sort of handbag that would keep the whole family in clothes for years.'

War had raged back and forth while Nicole stared out the window and wondered why she hadn't told the people at Titus that she was an orphan and would not be bringing anyone with her to meet the would-be managers.

Darius had insisted that she bring her family for moral support. 'It's highly unusual for a record company to be setting up this sort of interview in the first place,' he said. 'Most people have got a manager by the time we're going to sign them but Sam Smith really wants to make sure you've got the best representation. She's dead on, Sam is.'

'Yeah, she's nice,' Nicole said for want of something better to say. She'd been terrified of Sam that time they'd met. Calm, in control and silent for most of the meeting, Sam Smith had appeared to be icily cool. Not the sort of person who'd be putting herself out for a new singer by lining up a group of prospective managers for her. But Darius was very impressed by the whole thing and pointed out that by coming up with a list of people for Nicole to meet and choose between, Sam was actually making things slightly harder for herself.

'By getting you to meet the top management companies, she's putting you in touch with people who'll screw a better deal out of us,' he pointed out.

Nicole didn't know if she could trust Darius or not. She wasn't sure if she could trust any of them but this was her big chance and she had to plunge right in. The meeting with the first company was in the Titus boardroom at half ten and each meeting was to last half an hour, finishing up by lunchtime, when Sam and Darius would take the Turners out for something to eat.

Nicole prayed that her mother and grandmother would have stopped sparring by then. So far, they hadn't been much use in the moral support department. With half an hour to spare, they'd gone for a coffee in the chic little café across the road from the Titus office and, once Reenie Turner had complained loudly about the price of a cup of tea and why wasn't there proper sugar apart from those silly little paper tubes of sugar, the battle had recommenced.

They were now bickering over hair colour, a favourite topic for both of them. As Goldie Hawn's biggest fan, Sandra was a lifelong believer in the 'blondes have more fun' dictum while her mother's

Catholic upbringing had entrenched in her the notion that it was wrong to meddle with what God gave you.

'Look, you even have Nicole at it now,' grumbled Reenie Turner, whose greying dark hair had never seen a drop of hairdresser's colour.

'It suits her,' retorted Sandra. 'Better than going round with more grey streaks than an old English sheepdog.'

'Well, why don't you just insult me and be done with it,' snapped back Reenie.

With nerves eating away at her insides at the thought of the meetings to come, Nicole had had enough. Standing up abruptly, she shoved her metal chair across the floor with a resounding screech.

'I brought you both here to help me, to support me,' she lashed out at the pair of them. 'I thought that it might be nice for once to have support but all you both want to do is carry on your stupid arguments. If that's all you want to do, go home! I've enough to worry about without worrying about you two.'

Her grandmother and mother looked up at her shamefaced.

'Lord, you're right, Nicole love,' said her Gran apologetically. 'We're both sorry, love, really we are. We're just nervous for you.'

'And I'm not nervous?' demanded Nicole.

'You seem so cool about it all,' added Sandra helpfully.

Nicole sat down again and let her arms fall limply to her sides. She wanted to tell them the truth, that she wasn't cool about it at all, that she was scared stiff. But she couldn't. They relied on her too much. They needed to know she was ready for whatever life threw at the Turner clan.

'Don't be daft,' she said brusquely. 'There's nothing to be nervous about. This is all very straightforward. We'll meet five different managers and choose one. Simple. It'll be easier to concentrate if I'm not keeping you pair from killing each other, that's all.'

Her mother and grandmother stared at her with pride. Their Nicole: strong, clever and beautiful. Nothing fazed her and she was well able for those record company types. Wherever had they got her from?

Sandra was highly impressed with the smoked glass and chrome decor of the Titus headquarters. Her mother was less impressed with

403

the length of the mini skirt on the receptionist's long legs. But neither of them said anything. They were doing their best for Nicole. They were going to be decorum personified if it killed them.

However, Reenie couldn't help commenting on Darius when he left them alone in the board room in order to tell Sam that the Turners had arrived.

'He's a well brought up, boy, that one,' she said. 'Very grand and such nice manners. I thought all these record company people were mad into drugs and all that. Pity about the clothes, though.'

Despite her nerves, Nicole grinned. Personally, she thought Darius's distressed denim jacket, simple white T-shirt and black canvas trousers looked great on his long, lean body and she liked the way his fair hair was spiky with wax and stood up at mad angles to his skull. It was funky and yet somehow made his pale neck look vulnerable and young.

He liked her hair too.

'It suits you short,' he'd said admiringly, in the brief moment when they were alone while Sandra and Reenie were looking out the boardroom window admiring the view of London below.

Somehow, at that moment, Nicole began to trust him. There was something you could trust in that kind, open face. Something that said Darius Good was kind to animals, gave up his seat on the underground to old ladies and would never tell a girl he'd phone her if he didn't mean it.

She smiled up at him and the tough feline little face blossomed into the warm, beautiful, gentle one that Darius had known was there all along. 'Thanks,' she breathed.

'I mean it,' he said anxiously.

'I know,' she said softly.

As he sprinted along the corridor to Sam Smith's office, Darius felt ten feet tall.

Sam had five minutes before her next meeting.

'I'd love to say hello,' she told Darius. 'They must be nervous. Have you offered them coffee?'

'Er no but I will,' Darius said.

There was definitely something different about Sam Smith these days. He couldn't quite put his finger on it but she was changed. Softer, kinder, somehow. Or maybe he was imagining it. But Izzy, the A & R secretary, had said so too. Although she'd been slightly less charitable. 'Ms Smith must be getting it,' she'd said sagely over lunch one day. 'She's dumped the career bitch clothes and has gone all floaty and New Age on us. Did you see her with her hair in a pony tail with a flower on it the other day? Definitely a man. Those hard-as-nails types always lose the run of themselves when they've got more than a cat to go home to.'

Darius felt that Izzy was being a bit cruel but he had to admit that Sam had changed. She was chatty, warmer definitely, not the tough, no-nonsense woman he'd met initially. Still, he didn't care. Her new-found sweetness meant his darling Nicole was being wonderfully looked after and that was all that mattered. If a man was responsible for this change in the boss, he was happy for her. After all, he'd found Nicole, although she didn't exactly know it yet.

Sam strode along the corridor with her off-white John Rocha dress flowing elegantly behind her. She loved wearing it, adored the way it hung beautifully without clinging. Like a mini whirlwind, she swept into the boardroom.

Nicole got to her feet instantly, a slim, beautiful figure in black with a halo of bronze curls on her exquisitely shaped head.

'Hi Sam,' she said.

Sam found herself giving the girl a hug, not the sort of thing she'd have done before. Before The Illness, as she called it herself, in capital letters, had changed her life.

'Hello Nicole, lovely to see you.'

'This is my gran, Reenie Turner,' Nicole said, 'and my mum, Sandra.'

'Nice to meet you,' said Reenie formally, taking Sam's hand and giving it a strong shake. 'We're here to support Nicole in whatever way we can,' she announced firmly. Nicole had asked for support and she'd get it.

'It's so exciting,' trilled Sandra as she took Sam's hand in her own dainty one. 'You've got a lovely picture window here. How do you get any work done with the view?'

'You don't notice it after a while, I'm afraid,' Sam said regretfully.

She sized up the Turner women. At least the grandmother seemed like a sensible woman, not like Nicole's sweetly dizzy mother, who seemed to think that a cream leather jacket, floaty girlie skirt and pink high heeled sandals were becoming on a drizzly spring day. It was a look that could work well in the fashion pages of Sunday supplements when worn by a twenty-year-old model but it managed to look a bit too garden-partyish in the cold light of the normal world on a normal woman.

'I won't be sitting in on the meetings with you,' Sam explained, 'but I know Darius will if you'd like that and that he's told Nicole about the various people you'll be seeing.'

Nicole glanced shyly at Darius.

'You don't have to make any decisions today and don't let any of these people bully you. Their job would be to represent Nicole in her career and she has to feel comfortable with them. That's very important, Nicole,' Sam added. 'Your manager will work very closely with you, so you've got to get on with him or her and that's often an instinctive decision. Everyone coming here today is a professional and is damn good. So it's really up to you and how you feel about them all as individuals.'

Nicole and Reenie were watching her intently as she spoke. Sandra was admiring Sam's Gucci mules.

'Afterwards, if you have the time, I'd like to take you to lunch.'

Sandra lit up. 'Will there be champagne?' she asked.

'What did you think?' Darius asked at ten to one, when Nicole's head was spinning.

The highlight of the morning had undoubtedly been when her grandmother had sent a photo of one manager's top clients spinning across the shiny table with the words: 'if you think you're going to get my Nicole into an outfit like this . . . this . . . prostitute's costume, then you've got another think coming!'

'I don't think Gran liked the middle guy,' she remarked with a grin.

'Yeah.' Darius grimaced at the memory. 'Although hotpants aren't that unusual in this business.'

'I quite like hotpants,' Nicole laughed. 'It's just that Gran's never seen me in mine.'

Darius's eyes lit up. 'Do you think I might get to see you in them?'

She gave him an impish look. 'You never know your luck.'

'They're Gucci, those mules,' whispered Sandra to her daughter as they followed Sam and Reenie to the lift on their way to lunch. 'I've seen them in *New Woman* magazine on the fashion pages. I wouldn't like to tell you what they cost.'

Nicole linked arms with her mother. 'When we get this deal sorted out, Mum,' she whispered, 'I'll buy you a pair.'

'Promise!' breathed Sandra.

'I promise.' Nicole was pretty sure it was a promise she could keep. After meeting the various managers that morning, she'd been astonished at how much money they'd all insisted she could get from Titus. It had been more money than Nicole had ever dreamed of, and they'd all promised that this was only the start.

'If you really make it, you could become a very rich young lady,' the manager she'd disliked most had said.

Nicole hated being called a young lady. He was definitely out of the running. Those beady little eyes and eyebrows that met in the middle. Horrible. So was that tall bossy woman with the short haircut and the leather jeans. Her voice was so penetrating and she reminded Nicole of Sister Jerome who'd taught her geography for the three months she'd been at St Anne's before she was expelled. Nicole half-expected the bossy woman to demand to see her homework on the industries of the Ruhr valley. Definitely out too. The other two were OK, nice enough, but Nicole didn't have an opinion on them either way.

The best was a youngish guy who'd made her laugh and who hadn't attempted to talk himself up by telling her he could get her the best deal on the planet – unlike the other four. Casual in jeans and a wrecked looking leather coat, he'd told her about his other clients, an impressive list, Nicole noticed, explained what he did and added that he wasn't the sort of manager who believed in being a sycophant.

'A boot-licker,' Nicole whispered to her mother, who'd looked puzzled.

'I'm here because I think you're good and I think you'll go places. It's my job to help you go places. It's not my job to suck up to you and make you think you're Madonna. That's a mistake all round. If that's what you want, then I'm not your man.'

Nicole looked at his name on her sheet of paper: Bob Fellowes of DMF Management. A solid, straightforward name for a solid, straightforward guy.

'He's good,' Reenie said afterwards. 'I liked him best. At least he didn't have any pornographic photos of other people he looks after. I'm not having you dressed up like a fallen woman for anybody, Nicole.'

At lunch, Darius behaved like the well-brought-up young man he was and talked politely to Nicole's grandmother who was warning him off outlandish outfits for Nicole's future engagements. Sandra Turner, wildly happy to be having lunch in a posh restaurant with running hot and cold waiters, was busy watching the other guests and trying to work out where they'd bought their clothes and how much they'd cost.

Sam finally had a chance to talk to Nicole.

'How have you been?' she asked kindly.

With this new, friendlier Sam Smith smiling at her warmly and seeming really to want to know how she was coping, Nicole was honest. 'Freaked out,' she said. 'I never dreamed anything like this would happen. It's scary.' She looked down at her hands. 'I know that sounds stupid to someone like you, but this is scary to me.'

'It's not a bit stupid,' Sam insisted earnestly. 'There's nothing worse than being scared. Something happened to me recently that scared the hell out of me and made me change how I looked at everything. That's a hard thing to go through. I know how you're feeling.'

Nicole wanted to ask what had happened but she didn't feel she could.

'The secret is,' Sam continued, 'to be yourself and to trust yourself.

This is a wonderfully exciting time for you but of course it's scary, and that's why you need a good manager to make sense of it all. Hopefully, you'll have Darius and myself to help too. He's a good guy, Darius.'

Nicole nodded shyly.

Sam ploughed on. 'Some people change when they make an album and think it's important to behave in a certain way. They lose sight of who they really are – and they generally drive everyone else mad at the same time,' she laughed.

'You mean like asking for Jack Daniels in their dressing rooms and M & Ms with all the red ones picked out?' Nicole joked.

'Yeah, that sort of thing,' Sam admitted. 'But it's more than that. They begin to believe the hype and lose it. You're a lovely girl and you've got a fantastic voice. I want you to be successful but I want you to understand that this is a tough business and that you should hold onto your friends and onto who you are. Trying to turn yourself into something you're not is a big mistake.'

For a moment, the distant look on Sam's face made Nicole think Sam was really talking about herself. But she couldn't be.

They had a great lunch. Sandra was in flying form and Reenie, who firmly approved of Darius, thoroughly enjoyed herself. To keep things light, they talked about holidays and Sandra professed a life-long desire to go to Cannes.

'The South of France is so glamorous,' she said wistfully, picturing herself on the Croisette wearing head-to-toe Dior, possibly with a poodle or some such dog under her arm. Women in magazines often had small dogs with them although Sandra wasn't sure if dogs were let into restaurants and shops unless they were Labradors.

'You can't beat Eastbourne,' Reenie said. 'Although my best holiday ever was in Guernsey. We stayed in a little guesthouse outside St Peter Port and the weather was magic.'

'I saw a holiday programme about the Maldives and it looked wonderful,' Nicole sighed dreamily. 'Bounty bar beaches and incredible blue sea and nothing to do all day long.'

Darius's eyes met hers. 'I've always wanted to go there too,' he said eagerly.

Sam told them she'd had a lovely few days in Ireland with her sister.

'She lives in the most amazing place,' Sam recalled. 'It's so pretty and looks like a postcard with the most incredible landscape all around, all brooding melodramatic hills and valleys, and in the middle, this lovely village with these cute little houses, brightly coloured shops and the liveliest pub culture in the world. But it's a very healing place, if you know what I mean. It's friendly and there's a great sense of community, which is missing from everywhere else, isn't it?'

Reenie nodded sagely. 'Nobody knows their neighbours any more. You could be dead in your house and the only way anyone would know would be when the milk bottles piled up outside.'

Sam thought of the lovely kind people of Redlion who'd taken Hope into their hearts and who looked after her as if they were one big family. She thought too about the long walks she and Hope had enjoyed, letting the fresh country air fill her spirit, and she remembered the marvellous Macramé Club when she'd laughed so much, her ribs had ached, and where she'd begun to think about changing her life.

'It's peaceful too, although when you actually get to know the people there's more going on in Redlion than there is in central London, I swear! It's a hotbed of action.'

Reenie stiffened in her seat. 'Redlion, you say?'

Nicole looked at her grandmother curiously.

'Do you know someone from there, Gran?' she asked. 'Gran's originally from Ireland, from Kerry,' she explained to Sam. 'She left at sixteen and she's never gone back. I said that if I get a contract, we'll all go and see where she came from. I'd love to go.'

'Did you come from Redlion?' Sam said excitedly.

Reenie's pale eyes went opaque behind her thick glasses.

'No, from Killarney,' she said quickly.

At that moment the desserts arrived, so the subject was dropped. Sam wondered why Reenie Turner had reacted so strangely to the very mention of Redlion. The subject had certainly sparked something in her and she'd seemed interested in the whole notion of Ireland until then. But perhaps she hadn't good memories of her homeland. If Sam was accurate about Reenie's age, she would have left Ireland some fifty years ago.

Things were different then. Lots of people left and never returned for a variety of reasons. And Sam knew that some emigrants couldn't bear to return to their home country because of the bad memories of their life there, while some preferred to remember the auld sod in misty sepia rather than see it for what it actually was.

After lunch, Sam had to rush back to the office. She hugged Nicole goodbye and found herself on the receiving end of a double kiss from Sandra, who'd watched people doing it all lunchtime in the restaurant.

'Phone me any time if you want to talk it over,' Darius said to Nicole as he left with Sam.

'I will,' she said, gazing after him. 'I will.'

'What do you think?' Sam asked as she and Darius went up in the lift.

'She's incredible,' Darius said with a misty look on his face.

Sam grinned. Wasn't true love wonderful?

Karen Storin, who dropped in to see her at six on her way to an album launch, didn't think the whole thing was quite as wonderful. She loved Nicole's golden voice and was as keen as everybody else to sign her. But she saw problems in the future because Sam had been working so actively with Darius to get a hot manager for Nicole.

'Of course, the upshot could be that with a new manager, Nicole gets a better deal somewhere else and walks off leaving us with egg on our faces,' Karen warned.

Sam steepled her fingers and gazed up at Karen with a seraphic look on her face. 'If that happens, we'll have to live with it,' she said calmly. 'Worse things could happen.'

'Not much worse if Steve Parris gets to hear of it,' Karen pointed out.

The seraphic look vanished and Sam felt the familiar ache in her intestines, the ache she'd done her best to eradicate. The fibroids might be gone but the nervous tension was still there. Shit, Karen was right. If Steve Parris discovered that Sam's new-found sense of generosity meant the company had lost a prospective hit act, he'd

411

have her belongings in a bin bag and have her escorted out of the building by security in ten minutes flat.

Oh God, had she made a huge fatal error? Would she be out on her ear if he found out? Was the Pope a Catholic?

When Karen had gone, Sam sat in her office and reflected on how impossible it was to live her new, caring life and still do her job properly. How could her stress levels decrease and her spirit grow if she had to be the corporate raider every day of her life? It just wasn't possible. No matter how many cups of camomile tea she drank, she still had to make tough decisions that affected other people's lives, people who would no doubt wish all sorts of bad luck on her.

She left the office at seven and, as she walked to the underground, took out her mobile to phone Hope but there was no answer. In the days since Hope's strange late night phone call, Sam had done everything to find out what was wrong, but Hope now insisted that she was merely depressed over Matt being away.

'I'm fine,' she'd snapped the last time Sam had brought it up. 'Honestly, Sam, haven't you ever had a bad evening and wanted to moan to somebody?' Hope had demanded, too ashamed to say what was really wrong.

'Fine,' said Sam. 'Pardon me for being interested.'

But she was still worried about her sister.

She made it home by half seven to find a hand-written note stuck in the door for her: *Want to join me for an organic pizza?*

It was from Morgan. Since the night they'd gone to the movies together, he'd taken her out five times: once to the library for a talk on holistic lifestyles, three times for dinner and once to a juice bar where Sam had felt like spitting out the wheatgrass concoction that was supposed to do wonders for the system.

'The only wonder is that they don't give you a free roll of loo paper when you get one of these, because it goes straight through you,' Morgan had said, grimacing at the taste.

'You're just bringing me to these places to tease me,' she accused him, 'so you can laugh at my attempts to be healthy.'

'Not at all,' he said, desperately trying to be serious. 'Just because you've gone all holistic doesn't mean I can't help. I love New Age therapies. Imagine it, we could be like those Hollywood stars and fall out over our guru! When stars split up, they don't just fight over the house and the alimony, they fight about their guru too.'

'I don't have a guru,' she said, slapping him.

'You have me,' he said. 'I'm doing my best. My mantra is "enjoy life". Or is it my mission statement?'

'It's definitely your mission statement all right,' Sam remarked. 'I never met a man who tried to enjoy himself more.'

Tonight, she grinned at the thought of an organic pizza date. Up to now, her plans for the evening had involved doing her yoga practice and hand washing a basket full of delicate bits and pieces. Going out with Morgan was a distinct improvement on both of those options.

So, Morgan didn't look at her the way he probably looked at the twenty-something lovelies he fancied. But he was good company and they got on well. They were friends. Sam needed friends right now.

She phoned him. 'Organic pizza, Mr Benson. Is that the best you can do?'

She knew he was smiling now. 'The supermarket has run out of those yummy tofu burgers so I thought we'd have pizza instead. My place in half an hour?'

'We're not going out?'

'I can't face another health food restaurant,' Morgan admitted. 'But the topping is goat's cheese and wild mushrooms . . .'

'Sounds wonderful,' she sighed. 'I had a big lunch, though.'

'You've got to put a few pounds on,' he reproved. 'Don't want you falling down the cracks in the pavement. If you get any thinner, next thing we know, someone will have signed you up as a catwalk model and have you marching down the ramp in two square inches of lycra.'

'Dream on,' she retorted. 'I'll see you in half an hour.'

She was smiling as she raced around the apartment. There was no need to change out of her work clothes: her lovely John Rocha dress would be perfect.

She was still smiling when she skipped downstairs twenty-five minutes later.

Seeing Morgan was always such a relief after a day at the office.

What was most enjoyable about their relationship was that Morgan was so easy to get on with. Not that they had a relationship as such, she corrected herself. But the difference between him and most of the other men she knew was that Morgan was fun to be with. Undemanding. Laid back in the best possible way. She never felt she had to watch what she said with him or exhaust herself trying to look good when she wasn't in the mood to dress up. Morgan seemed as happy to be with her when she was wearing her scabby old jogging pants as he did when she was all glammed up in work clothes. He just accepted her exactly as she was. She'd never had that sort of friendship with any man before. Karl, who'd been her last big love affair, had required careful handling of the ego-boosting type. Karl liked being told how clever he was and how the company would be lost without him. He took great pride in that.

With Morgan, there was none of that 'how was your day, dear?' stuff before she could launch into what her day had been like. Perhaps it was different when you were actually going out with the person, she considered. Maybe Morgan wanted his girlfriends to mollycoddle him, to boost his ego and to tell him he was wonderful. Sam's favourite trick was to tell him he was making a hash out of the renovations. Being friends was definitely much better.

He answered the door in his usual uniform of paint and dust-splattered jeans and sweatshirt. His dark hair was dusted with white like an eighteenth century French aristocrat's and so was his face. Sam peered at the grimy Cape Cod sweatshirt he was wearing.

'You've been wearing that for three days on the trot,' she remarked as he let her in. 'I thought you'd plumbed in the washing machine.'

'I did but we're ripping up the ensuite bathroom and it's an awful mess, so I thought I'd keep wearing this until we were finished.'

'You're an environmental health hazard,' Sam pointed out. 'The council will be round any minute to fumigate you and I cannot have dinner with you if you insist on wearing that.'

Morgan leaned wearily against the front door. 'Don't nag,' he begged. 'I'm worn out.'

She regarded him sternly. 'Go up and take a shower. That's an order. And by the time you come down, I'll have dinner ready. Right?'

'Yes sir!' he barked, saluting.

'And throw down that disgusting sweatshirt, when you get it off,' she added as he started to climb the stairs. 'I'll put on a wash for you.'

'You're sure you weren't in the army in a previous life?' Morgan muttered, pulling the sweatshirt over his head.

Sam waited at the bottom of the stairs for the sweatshirt. Morgan threw it down and then ripped off his T-shirt, revealing lean muscles that rippled as he pulled it up and over his head. Sam felt as if she should look away. This was so intimate and private. And disturbing. Morgan's half-naked body sent a little excited shiver down her spine. He looked so damn good, from the powerful shoulders to the narrow hips. And he was so utterly unselfconscious as he stripped off, completely at home with his body. She wondered how many bench presses he'd needed to do to develop a physique like that and then realized that Morgan wasn't the sort of guy to sculpt himself in the gym. Laying patio slabs and breaking down dividing walls with a sledge hammer would be his preferred ways to keep in shape.

He threw down the T-shirt and carried on upstairs. Sam picked up the clothes, still warm from his body. They smelled of a male, musky scent, and of paint thinners, she realized. Eau de white spirit. He was out of sight when the jeans fell to the ground floor. He'd stripped them off when she couldn't see him. Damn.

His dirty clothes were boil washing when Morgan came down, clad in a pair of fresh jeans and a clean sweatshirt almost identical to the last one.

'Dressing for dinner?' she inquired with a grin.

'You wouldn't recognize me if I was in a suit,' Morgan pointed out, pulling up a chair.

'Oh yeah, and you've got a wardrobe full of suits,' Sam teased.

Morgan gave her a wry look. 'You'd be surprised if you saw me in a suit,' he said.

'I'd die of shock,' she remarked tartly. 'Now are you going to open a bottle of wine or do you expect me to bring my own?'

The talked so much over dinner that the last bit of Sam's pizza was cold by the time she got round to eating it. She loved spending time with Morgan, she thought happily, as he boiled the kettle for coffee. The only fly in the ointment was the fact that he still treated her like a good, but platonic friend, when Sam longed for more. Even tonight, when he'd been so charming, there was still something missing. Was he afraid to take that big step and ask her out? Or was he simply not interested? Sam didn't know if she could face the humiliation of asking. Far better to let their relationship continue the way it was. Good friends made the best lovers, didn't they? It was just a matter of waiting.

# CHAPTER TWENTY-ONE

Farranfore airport was manic when Hope and the children went to pick Matt up. He was going to be home for three weeks, three weeks which Hope simply didn't know how she'd face. If consummated affairs didn't ruin some marriages, how could an unconsummated one ruin hers? She wished the three weeks were up and that Matt was safely back in Bath, but he'd be home for good soon and how would she deal with life then?

When Matt appeared from amid the throngs of tourists weighed down with bulging suitcases, Millie and Toby launched themselves at him, shrieking 'Daddy, Daddy!'

He scooped a child up in each arm and somehow managed to shove the trolley along in front of him with his lean, jean-clad hips until he was beside Hope.

Still holding the children, he leaned forward and kissed his wife, who burned with guilt and wondered if he'd be able to tell that the last person she'd kissed on the lips hadn't been him.

'I've missed you,' Matt sighed. 'So much.'

'Us too,' said Hope brightly. Being ultra-bright was her only hope.

'Let's get Daddy into the car and you can tell him all the things you've been doing while he was away,' she said, still brightly.

The children needed no more encouragement and were soon trying to out shout each other with stories of glittery pictures successfully glued and how Millie had made a pie out of mud and even got mud on her knickers in the process.

'Mud on your knickers,' said Matt. 'That's amazing, how ever did you manage it?'

The children prattled excitedly and Matt listened happily as he drove, chattering back to them and occasionally patting Hope fondly on the thigh, giving her a quick smile. She managed to smile back. Things might be all right after all, she thought. If she kept her mouth shut and her upper lip suitably stiff, they might get through this.

In Redlion, Matt suggested having lunch in the Widow's as a treat.

'You deserve a break from cooking,' he said to Hope.

The Widows was busy for a Friday with plenty of tourists taking advantage of the balmy early May weather by touring the county. They found a table and agreed on sausage and chips for the kids, with fish pie (the Friday special) for themselves.

As Matt stood at the bar ordering, Hope watched him miserably, asking herself why she'd even been tempted by Christy. Okay, so Christy was good looking and that winsome puppy dog look could be charming, but there was no question that Matt was the more handsome. There was simply no comparison between Christy's saturnine face and Matt's lean, strong-featured one, no comparison between hot, sultry eyes and passionate, loving, caring ones. Matt was like a noble, proud lion to Christy's edgy, self-serving bobcat. Both beautiful creatures but with no similarities otherwise.

'Look who's here,' said Matt, smiling as he led Delphine over to say hello.

'Hi there,' said Delphine gaily, hugging Hope and dropping kisses on the foreheads of the delighted children. 'Eugene has a day off, so I took one too. We're being lazy and not bothering to cook lunch. Can we sit with you?'

Eugene ambled over, a cuddly bear of a man with a rumpled face to go with his rumpled clothes. No matter how carefully Delphine ironed his shirts, after one minute on Eugene's back, they looked as if they'd been dragged straight from the laundry basket by a herd of buffaloes.

'Pull up chairs,' said Matt.

They were soon all squashed into a table made for four, chatting about how lovely the weather had become and how the village was jam packed with visitors. Even Mrs Egan's de luxe B & B hadn't a room to spare, which was a miracle, they all agreed, given how unfriendly she was.

The hotel was full too, Delphine said, and she'd had to call in all sorts of favours to get her day off.

'They work you too hard,' said Eugene, a man not given to making idle statements. 'She hasn't had an extra day off since Christmas, you know,' he told Matt and Hope. 'That manager tries to run the place with a rod of iron.'

Hope started nervously at the mention of Christy.

Delphine grinned ruefully. 'It's not that bad,' she said. 'Mr I-Love-Myself De Lacy isn't a total despot. He might be a bit of a tyrant but I'm not going to be working there forever. I want to set up my own beauty salon.'

'Do you?' said Hope, keen to change the subject.

'Yes but you don't want to be burned out working for the Manoir,' Eugene insisted. 'I don't like that man,' he added. 'He's a shark and he uses people.'

Delphine laughed and patted Eugene's arm affectionately. 'Isn't it funny, Hope,' she said, 'how none of the men I know like Christy and practically all the women love him. Una up in the accounts office thinks the sun shines out of his rear end and Mary-Kate's raging that she's never met him.'

'Have you met him, Hope?' inquired Matt.

'Yes,' she said faintly.

'And?'

'And he's always been very nice to Hope,' said Delphine wickedly. 'I think he fancies her.'

Hope sat frozen while Matt and Delphine went off into peals of laughter.

'What a chancer,' said Matt, smiling at his wife. 'Should I challenge him to a duel?'

Eugene didn't laugh. 'That's what I don't like about that man,' he said in serious tones. 'He's unscrupulous, chatting up married women like a wolf looking for . . .'

'Hush,' said Delphine, putting a finger to her lips and gesturing to the children. 'Little pitchers have big ears.'

'What's a little pitcher?' asked Millie, bored with being ignored.

Delphine began to amuse the children, using their crayons to draw pictures on the paper placemats, and Eugene finished making his point, this time in a whisper.

'I don't trust any man who has so little respect for other people, that's all.'

Hope was grateful when their food arrived. She did not want to answer questions about how well she knew Christy De Lacy or hear anyone talking about his fatal fascination for married women. She merely wished someone had told her all this *before* she went to work for him.

Lunch arrived and as they tucked in, Matt made them all laugh telling them about the clients for his beer campaign, who couldn't agree on which beautiful girls should feature in the ad. 'They were only background actors after all, but arguing over which ones they wanted took longer than the decision about which campaign to go with.'

'You can't talk,' said Hope, 'you and Dan spend hours picking models for campaigns. You had more model cards than the fashion editor at *Vogue* when you were casting the insurance company advert. They have this game where they figure out who'll be suitable for which product,' she told Delphine and Eugene. 'It can get very rude at times. They decided that the sales assistant in the local chip shop, who had the glossiest lips and,' she whispered, 'a definite boob job, was perfect for marital aids.'

Delphine giggled.

'What are marital aids, Mummy?' inquired Millie, who had ears like a bat.

'Band aids for married people,' said Matt blandly, knowing that at the first sign of a word she shouldn't say, Millie would be roaring it at the top of her voice for days.

Delphine giggled some more. 'What should I advertise, then, Matt?' she asked.

He shook his head. 'We never do it on people we know,' he said. 'Oh go on,' urged Delphine.

'Shampoo,' suggested Eugene, running a hand through his girl-friend's rippling auburn hair.

'No, let Matt decide,' she said. 'He's the expert.'

'Shampoo would be great,' Matt said hurriedly.

'What's a boob job?' Millie asked loudly.

'Let's change the subject, please,' Hope said.

They ordered coffee and Matt and Eugene talked about football, while Delphine filled Hope in on the latest saga with her mother. She and Eugene were still plucking up the courage to announce their wedding plans.

'She rang me at work yesterday to tell me that my second cousin in Tipperary was getting married and that she'd heard that I'd been sent an invitation for two. Naturally, she was ringing to beg me not to bring Eugene.'

'That's terrible,' sympathized Hope with feeling. 'I just don't understand your mum. I know she's religious but that's no reason to be so unchristian.'

'When you love someone, you can cope with these things, can't you?' Matt said, holding Hope's hand in his firmly. 'Love will find a way.'

Feeling more like a charlatan than ever, Hope squeezed Matt's hand in return and tried to stop herself breaking into tears. She was a bad, bad person. She hated herself and she certainly didn't deserve him.

The Widow herself, Belle Maguire, arrived at their table in a cloud of Chanel No 5, gold bangles jangling on her tanned, skinny arms. Determinedly blonde and expertly made-up, she welcomed them all, smiling particularly at Matt, whom she hadn't met before. 'I hope you've all bought tickets to my charity night,' she said. 'It's for the guide dogs for the blind people and we run it every year. The more the merrier, I always say. We've got bands lined up and a buffet.'

'We're going,' Delphine told her. 'What about you, Hope?'

'Er yes,' said Hope.

'Good. I could do with another ticket seller.'

'I'm afraid I'll be away,' said Matt, on being told when it was.

The Widow's black-lashed eyes swept over him. 'Pity,' she said. 'But there'll be other times.'

It was after three when they all finally left, with Toby declaring that he felt sick because Millie had put so much pepper on his chips.

'Didn't,' she said truculently.

'Did!' said Toby, giving her a fierce glare that shut Millie up for once.

'Now kids, stop fighting,' said Hope mildly, but she was secretly pleased to see Toby standing up to his older sister. He was definitely getting more self-confident.

'Eugene's a sound bloke,' Matt said, fastening Millie into her car seat. 'Although he was coming over all Victorian about that De Lacy chap. Probably scared he'll start hitting on Delphine.' Matt smiled.

At Curlew Cottage, Matt was impressed with how big the hens were, how many eggs they were now laying (three to four eggs most days from the six hens) and how hard Hope must have worked to have cleared out the big briars at the front of the cottage.

'It's nothing,' said Hope of the enormous task that had taken her three whole, back-breaking days. More penance. Her hands, arms and legs were scraped with endless thorns and her shoulders ached from wielding the saw and the spade, but the bonus was that she'd finally got a nice clear space to plant flowers. There were some lovely bedding plants outside the supermarket that would look lovely there.

While Matt unpacked with Millie and Toby clinging to him, Hope went about her daily chores, tidying up the kitchen and pouring some home-made marinade over chicken breasts for dinner that night. Even more penance. She'd spent ages searching for the correct ingredients to make up the marinade from her *Queen of the Kitchen* book. Every time she bought fresh basil, it went limp and hopeless within days, so now she'd bought some fresh herbs in pots and was attempting to grow them in the shelter of the walled garden.

When Matt reappeared, he leaned over her shoulder and made impressed noises at the marinating chicken. 'You have been working hard,' he said, planting a kiss on the top of her head. 'Now, I know you want us to have time as a family but,' Matt looped his hands around her waist, 'I think we need time as a couple too. I asked Finula if the kids could stay with her for the weekend. You and I are driving to Kinsale tomorrow morning. It's going to be just you and me, with a big double bed and a town with some of the best gourmet restaurants in the country, so everyone says, anyhow.'

Hope gulped. There was no point saying anything. What could she say? Her thoughtful husband had organized a fantastic romantic weekend away for them and it was only her deceitfulness that rendered it agonizing. She thought of saying that Millie wasn't actually that keen on Auntie Finula but knew that as both children loved Ciaran, that excuse wouldn't really work.

Kinsale was even prettier than the guide book Finula had inevitably produced, with narrow winding streets, scores of restaurants tucked away in every corner, and a pretty harbour where all manner of yachts and crafts sat moored side by side while the owners sank pints of Guinness in the harbour bars. Under normal circumstances, Hope would have adored it.

Matt held her hand as they wandered the streets before choosing a pretty pub with a bright pink façade for their lunch. They sat in the snug, warmed by a blazing fire despite the heat outside, and Matt insisted that Hope have a glass of Guinness.

'It's medicinal, apparently,' he said, laughing as she screwed up her face at the first taste. 'You look so pale that you need a tonic.'

Afterwards, they took a brisk walk along the road out of town, before ending up on a sliver of beach where Hope happily collected shells for the children, ending up with a cache of the palest pink scallop shells and dolls' house sized mother-of-pearl cowries. Millie loved shells and would be raging to think that she hadn't had the chance to pick these ones, Hope thought fondly.

That night they ate fresh crab and dug out the flesh of a delicious lobster in a dimly-lit restaurant with lilting Irish music in the background and plenty of laughing and talking from the patrons in the foreground. People who came to Kinsale liked to enjoy themselves it seemed, soaking up the atmosphere and the fabulous food and drink.

'I love it here,' Matt sighed, sitting back in his chair, replete. 'There is a laid-back atmosphere in this country, for sure. I tried to explain what it was like to Betsey but I couldn't. She has this idea that if you're more than three hours away from London, you're on the far side of the moon.'

'Betsey wouldn't let herself enjoy Ireland. She secretly wants to live in Manhattan,' Hope pointed out. 'She thinks that if only she could off-load Dan and the kids, she'd be Carrie from *Sex And The City* and spend her life drinking cocktails, wearing vintage dresses and being chatted up by handsome men with houses in the Hamptons and trust funds.'

'She doesn't want that,' said Matt with a grin.

'She does.'

'You're very anti-Betsey these days,' Matt remarked. 'Back home in Bath, you seemed like best friends.'

Hope fiddled with her wine glass. 'We were, we are,' she said. 'But Betsey hasn't been exactly killing herself to keep in touch with me and when she does, she spends the entire time going on about what I'm missing in Bath. It's very annoying. And she thinks my having hens is hilarious,' she added crossly, 'as if they're living in the house with us, perching on the fridge and laying eggs on the couch. Honestly, she hasn't a clue about country life, for all the articles she says she's written about it.'

Matt roared with laughter. 'You're so funny when you're angry,' he said. 'You used to be in awe of Betsey, she bossed you round like nobody's business. You've changed, you know.'

Hope looked warily at him. She certainly had. In Bath, she wouldn't have looked twice at the likes of Christy De Lacy, never mind have two passionate encounters with him. 'I suppose I have,' she admitted.

'And remember when you complained that you didn't want to leave Bath and how you said you'd never fit in here?'

'I was wrong,' Hope replied. 'I love it.' She gazed at him frankly. 'It seems as if you're the one who hasn't fitted in.'

It was Matt's turn to look discomfited. Hope was getting very blunt in her old age. 'I have fitted in,' he said. 'My working in Bath is just a temporary thing. I haven't given up on the novel,' he added, crossing his fingers under the table and hoping that the novel hadn't given up on him.

His arm hung over her shoulder as they walked through the bustling town to their hotel. In their room, Hope undressed slowly, the guilt lying like lead in her heart. The previous night, Toby had had a bad dream just before Matt and Hope had gone to bed. By the time she'd calmed him and given him some soothing hot milk, Matt was asleep, sprawled in the middle of the bed, giving Hope a night's grace.

Tonight, she had no excuse. She unpinned her hair, letting it fall in soft curls to her neck, and took off her amethyst cardigan and matching camisole. As she unzipped the long black skirt that flared out over her hips, Matt put his arms around her and nuzzled into her neck.

'I've missed you,' he said, holding her close against him. He was stripped to the waist and his strong torso was warm and familiar. He smelled of the aftershave he'd been wearing for years and his skin was warm to the touch. They'd made love so many times before that they fitted together expertly, like much-loved old clothes that hung comfortingly even after many washes.

Tonight, Matt caressed her the way he always had, the way she loved, his recent absence adding extra passion. His hands unhooked her bra and held her heavy breasts, stroking and caressing, while his lips roamed over her soft neck and shoulders. Hope, who longed for him and couldn't bear his touch with equal measure, leaned her head back and felt the prickle of tears behind her eyelids.

How could she bear this when she felt so guilty?

They ended up on the bed, Matt finishing undressing her before undressing himself. Naked, he climbed on top of her, kissing passionately and touching hungrily, his voice hoarse as he told her how much he missed her and how many nights he'd lain in Betsey's spare room thinking of this moment.

'I love you, Hope,' he murmured, as his wife tried to caress him back with even a quarter of his passion, all the while trying to obliterate the nagging little voice in her head which told her she was a liar and a cheat.

She tried, oh how she tried. But it was so difficult to feel Matt's fingers on every part of her body, excitingly exploring those exact places which turned her on most, when she felt so bad about betraying him and when the image of Christy's glittering, dangerous face mocked her. Every endearment from Matt's lips made her want to cry out that she didn't deserve it or him.

'Hope, my love,' Matt said hoarsely when he finally slid into her, urgently, fiercely, desperate in his need of her. And in spite of her guilt, Hope's body answered his. Those many long nights when she'd yearned for him meant that when Matt cried out in orgasm, Hope reached a glittering climax too, holding him as tightly as she could, crying his name and then just crying, as great juddering sobs racked her body with the emotion of it all.

'Oh my love, are you all right?' gasped Matt, his mouth in her hair.

'I'm fine, I'm fine,' she cried. 'I missed you, that's all.' And then she sobbed harder because it wasn't exactly the truth.

They lay spooned together, with Hope's eyes tightly shut as if she could stop any more tears from falling. Normally, they cuddled and chatted after making love.

'What's wrong, Hope?' asked Matt, idly running his fingers up and down her arm.

Hope held her breath. 'Nothing,' she answered after a moment. 'I just feel a little emotional, that's all. I've missed you, I'm missing the children. And I'm a bit pre-menstrual.' With luck, Matt wouldn't think it odd that she was pre-menstrual two and a half weeks before her actual period. Infidelity was such hard work and required so many lies.

'Oh,' he cuddled her more closely. 'I've been thinking, Hope, now that Toby's nearly three, do you want another baby? I know you always said you'd like three children. You said yourself that you're so happy in Redlion, wouldn't this be the perfect time?'

Beside him, Hope bit her lip.

It was vital that she said the right thing, vital that she didn't give Matt the impression that she didn't want his baby, when she loved everything about him. In truth, she didn't know if she did want another child. She adored her children and loved being a mother but Millie and Toby took up so much of her energy, could she cope with a new baby? It had taken a year after Toby's birth for her to come to terms with having two children to care for instead of one. Yet the last thing she wanted to do was give Matt the impression that the idea of another child with him was one she couldn't bear.

'I haven't thought about it for a long time,' she said carefully. 'Our pair are such a handful, it's hard to imagine coping with another one. Toby sleeps so badly as it is . . .' She broke off.

'Has he been sleeping very badly while I've been away?' asked Matt.

'Not great,' said Hope, which was another lie. Toby had been a light sleeper since he was a baby, waking up at the slightest noise. But he had improved since they'd been in Redlion. The heavy country air made them all sleep more soundly.

'So you're not broody? I thought you were,' said Matt.

Hope wriggled round to face him and laid her face against his chest. 'Let's enjoy the pair we've got for the moment before we start planning any more, okay?' she said lightly.

Matt kissed the top of her head. 'Yeah, you're right.'

By the time Matt left for what Hope prayed was his final stint in Bath, she had almost convinced herself that nothing had happened between her and Christy. Life had slipped back to normal with surprising ease. Matt went off to the creative centre to write most days, although he got back earlier than he used to and wanted to spend more time playing with the children.

'When you're away from them, you realize that you're missing them growing up,' Matt told Finula one day when she dropped in unannounced for coffee and was put out to discover that Matt had a picnic planned with the children and wasn't cancelling it for anyone.

'I'm afraid you're stuck having coffee with me,' Hope said a touch vindictively to Finula, as Matt and the children set off down the lane with a bag of sandwiches made up by Hope and jam jars to collect tadpoles in the stream.

'Super,' said Finula, in a voice that made it plain the situation was anything but super.

While Matt had been away, Hope had managed to avoid seeing too much of Finula. She'd been forced to go to dinner with the Headley-Ryans once when Finula wouldn't take no for an answer and had spent the evening bored out of her skull. Luckily, without the lure of Matt, Finula wasn't too interested in spending time with Hope, so she'd been spared any other invitations.

This meant she'd almost forgotten how irritating she found the other woman. With her little finger crooked in what she fancied was a posh way, Finula drank her coffee and gobbled up half a plate of chocolate biscuits with astonishing speed for someone who claimed to have a wheat allergy. Typically, she couldn't resist showing off.

'We were in the Pigeon Club for dinner the other night,' she announced. 'It was wonderful, the food is superb. I had the most wonderful lamb.'

Hope, who knew just how good the food was in the Pigeon Club, nodded.

'Really.'

'The owner is a personal friend of ours. I'm sure you'd like it, Hope. I know Matt would,' Finula preened, as if she had the inside track on what Matt Parker did and didn't like.

It nearly killed Hope not to say that she'd met Liam, the owner, that she'd had the most fabulous lunch there with a genuine friend of Liam's and that Liam had given them the best table in the house. In fact, it was nearly a bed, never mind a table. She gritted her teeth and poured more coffee, resisting the impulse to pour it all over Finula's swollen head.

'Finula drives me mad,' snarled Hope later, when Matt returned with two mucky children, one with a big scrape on her knee, and no tadpoles.

'She's all right,' Matt placated her. 'She's just insecure at heart.'

'Insecure?' raged Hope. 'That woman is as insecure as Chairman Mao. She cannot stop boasting. Do you know she told me three times that she and Ciaran are getting a brand new Cherokee next January, and I lost count of the number of times she mentioned "*our holidays in Antigua*". I hope they get stopped by Antiguan customs for suspected dope smuggling and get locked up in jail for the entire three weeks!'

Matt further annoyed Hope by laughing. 'Hope, you're hilarious. Of course Finula's insecure. Why else would she keep telling you things like that – because she's jealous of you and the only way she can deal with that is to keep reminding both of you about her holidays and her jeep and her famous friends. She's sweet, I like her.'

Hope wondered how she and Matt could possibly be compatible when they had such wildly different views on people.

'Anyway,' she demanded, as an argument clincher, 'why would Finula be jealous of me? What do I have that she wants?'

Matt grinned wickedly. 'Me, darling.'

Although Hope worked in the Manoir for six mornings when Matt was home, she never once bumped into Christy. It was as if he sensed she was off his radar and he knew he had to leave her alone. Hope, who found her enjoyment of working with Una and Janet tinged with anxiety that Christy would walk in at any moment, was relieved that there was no sign of him.

By the sixth day, she had managed to almost convince herself that their passionate kisses had been like an episode of *Dallas* – and that she'd merely been dreaming.

'I'm going to be away for a week soon,' Una confided as they had their elevenses. 'I don't suppose you'd be able to come in for the whole week and help Janet out?'

'I'll have to check it out with the crèche but it shouldn't be a problem,' Hope said confidently. The whole Christy thing was over after all. She had nothing to worry about.

# CHAPTER TWENTY-TWO

Nicole sat on her bed and looked at her picture in the evening newspaper. It had been one thing to see the promotional photos in the comfort of a Titus office, dark and moody shots where her cheekbones stood out so that she looked like some sort of Indian princess, but seeing them in a genuine newspaper in the 'up and coming' slot was another thing entirely.

She was described as the latest LGBK signing, 'the hottest new singer in years,' according to Sam Smith, who was also quoted as saying there'd been a lot of competition to sign the golden-voiced Nicole. 'We're thrilled that she's signed with us because we discovered her and she's going to be a huge star,' Sam said.

Nicole's mum had been delirious when she saw the photo and had bought six copies of the paper, going round to all her friends in Belton Terrace to show them how well Nicole was doing. As always, when her mum went overboard, Nicole had compensated by going underboard, as it were.

'It's nothing, Mum,' she'd said when Sandra arrived home with her collection of papers. 'Only a picture in the paper. It doesn't mean anything.'

'It means you're famous,' Sandra said reverently.

'No it doesn't,' Nicole replied. 'Now, are you ready for your dinner or not? I've done egg and chips.'

Sharon had phoned half-way through dinner. 'Everyone at Copperplate has seen you in the paper!' she squealed delightedly. 'Even old iron knickers Sinclair! The whole place was talking about you in the canteen.'

Nicole briefly felt a moment of nostalgia for her old job. But it was only brief. It was only just over a month since she'd left the building for the final time and already it seemed a million years ago. Since then, she'd been working on her album – even *thinking* those words gave her goosebumps – and doing things like photoshoots, which sounded glamorous but were actually so boring that she couldn't imagine how models ever stuck it. Hours upon hours of posing woodenly, prefaced only by hours of getting plastered in make up. All a zillion miles away from sitting beside Sharon down the back of the motor department trying to think of ways to wind up Ms Sinclair or longing for her lunchbreak or for the weekend. These days, life seemed to be one long, weird weekend.

'Wow, Nic, you're famous.' Even Sharon sounded impressed.

Hearing her say it made Nicole sad. She and Shaz had been best pals for ages, ever since they'd joined Copperplate at the same time, as nervous eighteen-year-olds. Shaz knew what sort of person she really was. She should have known that Nicole was still going to be Nicole, no matter how many times her bloody picture was in the paper.

'What are you up to tonight?' Nicole asked to change the subject.

Sharon groaned. 'Going on a double date with Michelle, her fella and his best friend.'

'I thought you'd been saying no to that for ages,' Nicole protested, seeing the possibility of going out with Sharon disappearing. 'You think Michelle's fella is a plonker.'

'Yeah, well, it's something to do, isn't it?' Sharon said. 'How about you? Something dead cool, I suppose?'

Nicole looked at the kitchen table with the remains of her mother and Pammy's dinners congealing on their plates. Both had finished and left all the dishes and cutlery just lying there, the way they normally did. Sandra was not the sort of person who couldn't relax until the kitchen was tidy. She could quite happily leave the dishes to pile up for days, which meant that Nicole was the family's main washer-upper.

She knew from past experience that fried egg set solid on plates and needed a lot of effort to remove it. She wouldn't have minded clearing up if she'd thought she could go out with Sharon afterwards and celebrate having her picture in the paper. But it was obvious that Sharon had found a new best friend in her cousin Michelle and that she, Nicole, was assumed to have an exciting new social life for herself with her record company pals. She was off the radar to her old friends.

'Nothing,' she replied to Sharon. 'I'm not doing anything. It's been a mad week, I might go to bed early.'

When Sharon had hung up, Nicole threw the remains of her cooling dinner in the bin and began to wash up. The egg on all three plates was stuck solid, as she'd guessed. She scrubbed energetically and wondered if this was how other would-be singers spent their Friday nights. She *had* been invited to a party by Peta, one of the Titus publicity people, but she'd said no.

It was an album launch and Peta had said that it would be great for Nicole's profile if she went but Nicole couldn't really tell her that she was nervous of the idea of big, glam parties. Sharon would have loved the launch, Nicole reflected, since it was for one of her favourite bands. But it probably wouldn't be okay to bring a friend. Nicole knew that big stars often had an entourage of friends with them, but they were big stars and she was just a hopeful star that nobody had even heard of yet. Imagine how embarrassing it would be if she turned up with Sharon and nobody let them in?

When everything was tidy in the kitchen, Nicole went to her room and indulged in a few minutes looking at her photo in the paper. Incredibly, she looked beautiful. Like a stranger, almost. Anyone looking at that wide-eyed girl in the photo with the jewelled ethnic collar around her slender neck, would have thought that she'd be out partying every night. Not stuck at home.

Nicole threw the paper on the floor. She didn't have to be stuck at home, though, did she?

When she couldn't get through to Peta on the phone, Nicole phoned Bob Fellowes's assistant, Isya, because she didn't want to phone Bob himself with something so unimportant.

When she'd appointed him as her manager and they'd signed the deal with Titus and the LGBK label, he'd insisted that she phone him about anything. But Nicole was still shy around him and Isya was always utterly sweet to her and much more approachable. She couldn't talk to Bob about a party.

Isya listened to the problem gravely. 'Of course you don't need an invitation,' Isya said in her soft voice. 'Leave it to me. I'll get the stylist over to you and the limo will pick you up at nine. Lorelei, another DMF client, is going and you could go with her. You need to meet her anyway because you'll be doing the Teen Stars roadshow together.'

Nicole put down the phone in shock. Lorelei was a big star, she'd had two top ten singles. The limo, and a stylist to do Nicole up for the party, were coming. Nicole breathed out shakily. She was on the celebrity express train and there was no getting off.

The stylist dressed Nicole up in a minuscule leather skirt and a chiffon top that wouldn't have fitted Pammy's Barbie. Lorelei was wearing something even more daring. Needless to say, guys were drooling over them all evening. Not ordinary guys of the variety that Nicole knew how to deal with, but semi-famous ones, like the lead singer with Coral Fish, a dead-eyed giant named Zol who wore nothing but leather and had roving hands. He'd smoked a joint right beside her and asked her if she fancied coming back to his hotel room later. Nicole had laughed nervously at that.

Her habitual cool deserted her and she downed cocktail after cocktail to cope with it all. She hadn't said yes to Zol but he seemed to think she'd agreed to go back to his hotel room later anyway because he kept patting her bum in a proprietorial manner and fiddling with her hair.

'I'll look after you,' Lorelei had said when they'd met for the first time in the limo going to the party, but she'd more or less abandoned Nicole, which was why Nicole lunged delightedly at Darius when he arrived with the Density guys.

'Thank God you're here,' she'd hiccuped. 'It's mad here, they're all mad.'

'Nicole,' Darius said, as he held her hot swaying body in his arms. 'Are you all right? You seem a bit woozy.'

'Zombies,' she said, raising her half-empty cocktail glass to him. 'I've had loads. Four at least. It's scary here. Nobody seems normal.'

'That's because you've been with the abnormal people,' he said, putting down her glass and taking her to sit down in a quiet corner away from the dance floor and the bar. Nicole flopped into the big squashy sofa with the insouciance of the very drunk.

'I didn't think you were coming tonight,' Darius said gently, taking in the skimpy chiffon top that barely hid her small breasts and the leather skirt that revealed at least five inches of leg above the knee. Nicole's granny would have a fit if she saw her granddaughter in that outfit.

'I wasn't. I had to wash up the egg and chips plates and I was bored and lonely.' Her slender fingers curled themselves round Darius's collar and she gazed up at him hungrily, her shining black eyes liquid with desire. 'You're so nice, Dariush,' she slurred sweetly.

Darius gulped. He was crazy about Nicole but he had no intention of taking advantage of her when she was drunk out of her mind. He hated seeing her like this. She shouldn't have been there at all. Nicole was talented and just starting out. She didn't need to learn any lessons from dope-heads like the Coral Fish people or from cast iron little madams like Lorelei. Both would be on the way out in two years, he was sure of it, their limited talent squandered and their chances blown because of the way they messed people around. Even Density, whom he thought were hugely talented, were stretching his patience with their demands. But Nicole could be a huge star for a long time and it would ruin her to get caught up in the jaded lifestyle of the likes of Coral Fish.

He gently unhooked her hands. 'I really like you too, Nicole,' he said softly. 'But not here, not tonight.'

Suddenly, they were interrupted. 'Well hello,' purred a purposefully low voice. Lorelei, five foot six, seven stone and with a diamond-hard, truculent little face, appeared with a waiter in tow and three more cocktails on a tray. 'Who have we here? Don't keep all the beautiful ones for yourself, Nicole.'

Lorelei eased herself onto the sofa beside Darius like toothpaste oozing from a tube.

'Hello.' Her long manicured talons were a direct contrast to Nicole's short, clear-coated ones and she laid one hand on Darius's long, lean thigh. 'I'm Lorelei.'

Lorelei expected this intro, delivered in her trademark (and carefully worked upon) drawl, to work wonders. Some men had drooled when she'd delivered it, agog at the sight of her silicone breasts shoved up under her chin in a Wonderbra.

Unfortunately, it didn't have the desired effect this time.

'We've met,' Darius said shortly. 'At an awards ceremony last year.'

He turned back to Nicole and Lorelei, enraged to be ignored, stomped off in high dudgeon.

That was when, had Nicole but known it, it all went pearshaped. Lorelei was planning her revenge.

Nicole talked to Darius for ages, even when Zol from Coral Fish sent a message over that he was leaving and did she want to leave with him? Eventually, Nicole left Darius to go to the ladies. She was smiling as she swayed along on her new high-heeled sandals, then, before she knew what was happening, a blond giant picked her up in a bear hug and dragged her outside to where Lorelei was waiting with the limo.

'I have to get back to Darius,' slurred Nicole from the depths of the leather seat.

'Not tonight, dearie,' snapped Lorelei.

Lorelei made the limo driver take them all to another club and although Nicole spent ages tearfully trying to find Darius's mobile number in her phone's address book, she was too drunk to do it properly.

Depressed that he'd think she'd dumped him, she sank three tequila slammers to make up for it. And it was only thanks to the blond giant kindly putting her back into the limo at four in the morning that she got home at all.

\* \* \*

The following morning, when nobody answered the phone which had been ringing loudly for at least twenty minutes, Nicole dragged herself and her hangover out of bed, made it shakily down the stairs to the hall and picked up the receiver.

'Hello,' she croaked.

'How was the party?' Sharon asked sharply.

'What party?' Nicole's head was pounding.

'The one you were at last night? The one you went to after you'd told me you were doing nothing?'

Nicole sat on the bottom step and leaned against the wall with its yellow wood chip paper. She felt awful. Her stomach felt as if it was the epicentre of a force ten gale. If she could keep still for a few moments, maybe the nausea would pass.

'It was just a spur of the moment thing,' Nicole said weakly. 'I'd been asked to this party but didn't want to go really.'

'Well, you looked as if you were enjoying it in the *Globe* today,' Sharon snapped. 'Have you seen it yet? I'll read it to you: *New kid on the block, Nicole – latest megabuck signing at LGBK – hit the Coral Fish launch party in trendy club Shiva last night with wild child Lorelei, who says they're best friends and will be touring together on the Teen Stars roadshow. Sultry Nicole, whose first single is released in May, says she's a huge Coral Fish fan and loves their music.* I love their music too,' Sharon said, her voice wobbly. 'You know that. I've got their last two albums. But you never even mentioned you were going to their party. Just because you didn't want there to be any chance of your boring ordinary old friend coming along, you decided not to say anything. Fine.' There was no disguising the hurt in Sharon's voice. 'Be like that if you want.'

'Sharon,' protested Nicole feebly, 'I wasn't going to go to the party. When you phoned, I thought maybe you and I could do something but you were going out with Michelle . . .'

'Yeah, sure. Like you'd really prefer to go out with me and have a few slammers down the pub when you could be in some nightclub knocking back champagne with bloody Lorelei. Stupid bitch, she is. You always said you hated her.'

Now was not the time to explain that, having actually *met* Lorelei and found her to be a stuck-up little prima donna, Nicole hated her even more than she had when Lorelei was just another beautiful, distant face on MTV.

'Sharon, it wasn't like that.' Nicole didn't know which was worse: having a murderous hangover or having Sharon furious with her.

'I suppose the next time I see you, it'll be fifty years later on a documentary about your fabulous life and I'll be just one of a throng of boring old pals you haven't bothered to get in touch with!' Sharon hung up.

Utterly miserable, Nicole made it to the kitchen to get a pint glass of water, which she puked up ten minutes after drinking.

Darius phoned next. He didn't sound pleased, either.

'You got home all right, then?' he said, his clipped upper class tones sounding icy. 'I was worried when you disappeared and never came back. I searched for ages but the cloakroom girl said you'd gone.'

The vague memories of the night before hit her. Lorelei had had her kidnapped and Nicole swore Lorelei had done it as revenge because *she'd* liked the look of Darius but he hadn't given her a second glance. And now Darius was furious with her, which wasn't fair.

She did her best to explain what had happened but she felt so nauseous, she could barely speak.

'It was nothing to do with Zol,' she said finally. 'Lorelei had me kidnapped.'

Darius clearly didn't believe her.

'I wouldn't advise you to go off with Zol,' Darius said coldly. 'He's dangerous. He does every sort of drug under the sun. I thought I was going to take you home?'

'You were,' Nicole said sadly.

'I'll see you in a few weeks,' Darius said then, as if he was consulting his diary about a dentist's appointment. 'I'll be talking to Bob about the album, naturally, but that's all.'

'But aren't you coming with me on the Teen Stars roadshow?' Nicole asked. 'I thought you were going to be with me . . .'

It was a seven city tour and it was seen as an ideal way to let a novice performer learn the ropes, to polish their act before they had to hit the big time and to garner new, young fans. Some acts never made it any further than the Teen Stars roadshow, because they simply didn't have what it took. Nicole was absolutely terrified she'd be among the inevitable casualties. Because she was his discovery, Darius had planned to go along for the ride. But he'd changed his mind.

'You've already met Lorelei,' he said coolly. 'You'll be fine.'

Nicole felt as if she'd lost her only ally in the world.

Nicole knew her songs backwards, and she irritatedly told her mother so when Sandra flustered round her as Nicole packed for the tour, worrying about whether Nicole would be able to perform in front of all those people and what if she forgot the words . . .

'I hope you know them forwards as well,' cackled Reenie from her overseer's position at the end of Nicole's bed.

Nicole, miserable because she hadn't spoken to Darius for a week and nervous at the idea of performing live, snapped: 'That's a stupid thing to say!'

Instead of barking back, the way she did when she and Sandra rowed, Reenie Turner looked deeply hurt and said nothing. From the way her shoulders drooped as she left the cramped bedroom, Nicole knew her grandmother was upset.

Even Sandra gazed at her daughter with reproachful eyes but said nothing as she too left.

Nicole crammed her suitcase shut furiously.

What were they like? They spent their lives squabbling and now, the one time Nicole had said something smart, they were both behaving like outraged doves with ruffled feathers, cooing in shock and confusion. It *had* been a stupid thing to say.

Nicole stared fiercely at herself in the mirror, not really noticing the tiny little denim jacket she was wearing with the black cargo pants, an outfit that had thrilled her when she first got it. People said such stupid bloody things to her. Couldn't they see she was stressed?

But there had been no reason for her to be horrible back, she knew. She never was. In fact, she couldn't remember a time when she'd been so sharp with her poor gran. A wave of deep shame swept over Nicole.

Just then, the doorbell rang.

'Your car's here,' roared her mother from downstairs.

Nicole dragged the suitcase downstairs and said hello to the driver. She popped her head round the sitting room door.

'Well, bye,' she said brightly. There was no sign of her grand-mother.

'Where's Gran?' she asked her mother.

'Gone home. Have a good time.'

Sandra didn't even get up from her chair to say goodbye, which was most unusual. Sandra had been so excited about the Teen Stars roadshow that Nicole had half-expected a fanfare of neighbours and a bottle of sparkling wine. The grumpy, nervous Nicole would have felt irritated by such a display. But the ashamed Nicole felt her eyes go misty at the lack of the neighbours, the sparkling wine and the proud family farewell.

Only Pammy gave her big sister a huge hug. 'Say hello to Lorelei,' Pammy said in her breathy voice. 'I love her.'

You wouldn't if you knew her, Nicole thought grimly. She held her little sister tightly and said she would say hi to Lorelei. 'Go in to Mum, Pammy,' she ordered, and she shut the front door behind her. Nobody waved from the behind the curtains of 12a Belton Terrace.

Nicole climbed into the car and sat, red-eyed and silent, all the way to the airport. This pop star business wasn't all it was cracked up to be.

At Heathrow, the Teen Stars roadshow acts were congregated in one of the business class lounges and Nicole's first thought was that the entire group resembled a slightly older than usual school tour. The various record company and management staff were like the teachers, anxious at the thought of taking care of the singers, all of whom were carrying on as if they'd been let out of convents for the day and were determined to create as much havoc as possible.

Nicole could see four members of the supposedly sweet and innocent Carli Girls sitting in a corner smoking, knocking back glasses of red wine, and telling ribald jokes to a photographer, while Gregory, a fresh-faced young ex-soap star who was adored by teenage girls and their mums alike and who'd fronted a 'be nice to your parents' campaign, was smoking and screaming down the phone at someone, with every second word a profanity. Tina, a child prodigy who sang Nolan Sisters covers, was busily painting on Cleopatra-style eyeliner in a compact mirror and sneaking surreptitious gulps of the Carli Girls' wine while her mother wasn't looking.

Only Euston, a five-piece boy band with the squeakiest image in the world, were behaving. They were playing travel Monopoly. There was no sign of horrible Lorelei.

Maybe she'd cancelled, Nicole hoped. She didn't want to ever set eyes on Lorelei again.

Nicole was welcomed by both the LGBK and Teen Stars staff who were there to make sure that the paths of their young stars ran smoothly and without too many scandalous inches in the gossip columns. They'd have their hands full.

'We were worried about you,' said Andrea, the publicity woman from LGBK who was going to be travelling with Nicole. Andrea looked about twenty but as she was publicity manager, she had to be older, Nicole reckoned. Hopefully, she'd be fun and they could have a nice time. Nicole longed to be able to confide in someone and say she was as nervous as hell about the whole roadshow thing. But now was not the time.

'Traffic was terrible,' she said brightly, determined to be as professional as possible. 'So, what's the plan?'

'We need some photos for the Teen Stars magazine,' said Phyllis, the most senior Teen Stars tour person, who looked around three times Andrea's age and was obviously well used to ordering wild young bands around. 'Could we have the group together?' Phyllis called in an authoritative voice that brooked no argument.

In a flash, the Carli Girls stabbed out their fags and whipped out expensive compacts to re-do their make up. Phyllis swiftly removed the offending glasses and everyone tried to look like young, happy, squeaky clean pop stars. Gregory swore viciously one last time, hung up his phone and smiled the lovely, sweet smile that women of all ages adored.

'Hi babe,' he said, wriggling in beside Nicole and brushing back a swathe of naturally blond fringe. 'Haven't met you before. This tour could be fun.'

Nicole glowered at him. She wasn't dumb enough to fall for such a two-faced jerk.

'Hello,' said a familiar, hated voice. 'Stealing my boys again, Nicci. Very bad of you. I can see I'm going to have to watch you.'

It was Lorelei, dripping vitriol in skin-tight pink lace; an outfit that was extremely out of place in Heathrow at two in the afternoon. She looked as if she was ready to start dancing round the pole in a strip club.

Lorelei couldn't be only nineteen, Nicole decided. She was obviously one of the undead and had been walking the earth for centuries looking for people to torture. It would take a long time for anyone to become as twisted as Lorelei and nineteen years just wasn't long enough.

'Are we ready?' said the photographer.

Lorelei, scene stealing as ever, decided that she wanted to be in the middle of the group, so she clambered all over everyone else and plonked herself in the middle, managing to stab Nicole in the arm with one deadly fingernail.

'Ouch,' said Nicole.

'Sorry diddums,' said Lorelei. 'Me didn't mean to hurt you, diddums,' she added in babyspeak and hugged Nicole. 'We're bestest friends, you and me.'

And so it was that the first picture of Nicole's ground-breaking first tour was of her clutched in Lorelei's deadly grasp, with Lorelei looking angelic and Nicole looking grim as she realized that there were three more weeks of this to go.

Lorelei had messed things up for Nicole with Darius and Nicole was determined to pay her back if it was the last thing she did. Darius hadn't phoned since that morning after the Coral Fish launch and when she'd rung him in the hope that they could make things up, he'd been cool and businesslike, as if she was just another LGBK act instead of someone special.

Nicole had hung up and allowed herself to cry a few bitter tears. It astonished her how miserable she felt without his friendship.

The tour, despite everyone from Teen Stars saying the opposite, was surprisingly hard work. There were sixteen venues and two performances in each, often on the same day. Once the second gig was over, everybody was too tired to do anything except shuffle off to bed. Or at least, that was the plan. But Lorelei, Gregory and the Carli Girls generally found a burst of energy from somewhere and were determined to party. Nicole soon found that asking for a room on a different floor of the hotel and making sure that nobody but Andrea and Phyllis knew the number was the only answer. She discovered this after the first two nights in Manchester when Lorelei and Gregory set off a fire extinguisher outside her room door and then scarpered, leaving her peering confusedly into the hotel corridor just as security rounded the corner.

It had taken a lot of effort to explain that she'd just woken up and had nothing to do with the prank.

However, trying to avoid the vindictive Lorelei had one magical effect: Nicole's performing nerves disappeared.

At rehearsals, she was too busy waiting for Lorelei's next practical joke to be nervous and by the time the actual performances came round, she'd realized that she simply loved being onstage and could perform in her sleep.

As the *Edinburgh Clarion* music reporter wrote: *The Teen Stars roadshow may be manufactured pop, but you've got to applaud the organizers for bringing us the charismatic Nicole. With the voice of a husky angel and the looks of an Indian goddess, she's surely the star of this show. And from the screams she gets every time she's on stage, the fans think so too.*

This glowing review did not endear her to Lorelei, who broke two nails with rage when she read it and proceeded to spill nail varnish all over Nicole's prized D&G flower print jacket by way of revenge.

Nicole, fed up with being dignified and professional, put Lorelei's vast collection of make-up in the backstage microwave until it all melted into a Technicolor puddle. She then put it carefully back into the big steel make-up artist's box that Lorelei made other people haul around for her. This was Lorelei's pride and joy as she refused to use the make-up that everyone else did and insisted that the tour make-up artists use her own, expensive stuff.

Lorelei's un-amplified yells when she discovered what had happened were as loud as her miked-up performance.

'You bitch!' She stood at the door of Nicole's dressing room, looking for all the world like an enraged female velociraptor from *Jurassic Park*.

Nicole, who was talking to Phyllis at the time, gazed back at her innocently. 'What are you talking about, Lor?' she inquired sweetly.

'Yes, get a move on, Lorelei,' said Phyllis firmly, wanting to knock any arguments on the head. 'It's half an hour to the performance and you haven't let them start on your face yet.'

'My make-up is a mess, all drippy!' squealed Lorelei.

'You probably left it too close to the radiator,' Nicole said sympathetically. 'These rooms are very warm, for a change.'

The days raced by. Nicole found it strange being on her own. Not that she was alone or even lonely what with rehearsals, performances, flights and interviews. But it was simply that Nicole was so used to taking care of Pammy and Sandra that it was odd not to have to think about anyone else. At first, she felt adrift without other people to look after. But eventually she began to get used to it and to enjoy it.

On her time off, Nicole didn't want to rush into the shops like the other girls and go crazy buying clothes. Instead, she went for long walks around the cities they were staying in and saw the sights. The freedom was incredible. She wasn't responsible for anyone else; she didn't have to worry whether Pammy had taken her swimming things to school or if there was proper food in the house for dinner.

Nicole had felt like the person in charge for most of her life. When other girls she knew had moved out of home and into flats with their pals, Nicole had known that she could never do that. She could never leave her little sister and their mother alone. She wouldn't have been able to cope with the very idea of it. But now, living a carefree life for the first time, Nicole began to wonder what it would be like to have her own place, what it would be like to be without the responsibility of her family? It was a dizzying thought.

She talked to Pammy every day on the phone and missed her desperately.

Pammy was going to be a fairy in the school play and Nicole's heart swelled with pride when she heard the news.

'I've got wings,' announced Pammy importantly during one of their daily phone calls. 'Silver wings. Kylie's wings are blue and not pretty like mine.'

'Can I come and see you?' Nicole asked.

'You have to. Miss Vishnu knows that you're singing on the telly and then you're coming.'

Nicole smiled at her little sister's innocent explanation.

Sandra had supplied the silver wings. 'I got them in the market,' she told Nicole. 'I think Pammy's teacher wanted me to make them but honestly, can you see me sewing! This nice Italian lady down the market does stuff like that if you can't sew and they're beautiful. That poor little Kylie kid had to wear blue net ones. I said to Miss Vishnu, "my Pammy is the prettiest child and she's going to look like a pretty angel. No blue ones for her."'

Nicole was mildly astonished that her mother had even been talking to Miss Vishnu. Previously, Sandra had kept away from the school as much as she could, probably because she'd had so many unwilling conversations with teachers about Nicole's madcap ways, well, not conversations as such. The teacher in question would try to talk to Sandra, who'd sidle off and say she was in a rush, but they could catch up at the parent/teacher meetings. Except Sandra never went to the parent/teacher meetings. And here she was looking after Pammy and organizing her fairy wings.

It all went to prove that life could go on without her. Nicole couldn't help but feel strangely left out. Even her grandmother was different.

Reenie still hadn't thawed although Nicole had said sorry several times.

Their conversations were stilted, no matter how many times Nicole apologized.

'I don't want you turning into some stuck up little upstart,' Reenie said on one of the few occasions when she'd deigned to come to the phone.

'I'm not, Gran,' protested Nicole.

'Hmm,' was all Reenie would say, before passing the phone over to her daughter.

After ten days of touring, Darius phoned.

'I hear you're doing brilliantly,' he said.

Nicole, in her bathrobe and just about to dress for the evening gig, blushed with pleasure.

'I've missed you,' she said abruptly, then blushed even more at how that sounded. 'I mean . . . it would have been nice to have you here . . .' she added quickly, hoping to counteract what she'd said. God, he'd think she was some sort of *idiot*.

Darius interrupted her. 'I missed you too,' he said softly.

Nicole had been standing beside the phone. Now she sat down on the bed with a resounding thud. 'Oh.'

'Andrea says you've been fantastic. You're a real trouper, she says, and you've got one amazing review. In fact, we're sending up a group of people from some of the international Titus companies tomorrow evening. They're really keen to see you, they've heard you're going to be a big star. There's quite a buzz going round here about you.'

Nicole didn't care. They could be sending up the Emmy awards committee for all she cared. She sat on the bed, smiling with love. Darius had phoned. That was all that mattered.

'Are you coming?' she asked.

'Of course,' he replied. 'I'm sorry,' he added gruffly. 'You know, about the other week.'

'I didn't go off with Zol,' Nicole interrupted. 'Honestly. Lorelei was furious that you'd turned your back on her and she got this guy to drag me out to the limo with her. I didn't want to go, I wanted to stay with you. But when I tried to ring you, I couldn't. Too many Zombies,' she admitted guiltily.

'It's not your fault,' Darius said. 'You fell in with a bad crowd.'

'I don't want to be with people like that,' she said. 'I'm not like that. Lorelei drives me mad. She's a . . . cow.' She'd been about to say that Lorelei was a bitch, but somehow she didn't want to swear in front of Darius. 'Zol's worse. He kept touching my bum all night.' Nicole couldn't hide her outrage at this.

Darius was gratifyingly angry. 'Asshole,' he said furiously. 'I should never have let you out of my sight.'

Nicole, who'd have punched any previous boyfriend for implying that she required looking after, grew misty-eyed at this sign of protectiveness.

'I like the idea of you not letting me out of your sight,' she said.

As if she knew it was an important day for Nicole, Lorelei chose the following day to play up even more than usual. She delayed the bus leaving the hotel that morning by over an hour, claiming that she'd lost the lucky charm bracelet her father had given her.

Because they were so delayed, there was no time to check in at the hotel before the afternoon gig. Nicole, who was due to meet the Titus executives at the venue afterwards and had planned to doll herself up in the hotel before rehearsals, was furious. She was sharing a dressing room with two of the Carli girls and it would be impossible to smother herself in body lotion for Darius's benefit with them watching.

'You look upset, Nicci,' Lorelei said sweetly, when Nicole came offstage after having uncharacteristically botched her rehearsal.

Nicole shot her a vicious look but said nothing.

In the dressing room, the two Carli Girls were discussing Lorelei.

'I thought she was fun at first, but she's a nightmare,' said one.

'Jesus, yes. She's such a drama queen, she's doing my head in,' said the other.

'Tell me about it,' said Nicole.

With half an hour to go, they all changed into their stage clothes. The Carli Girls were going through a silver phase: they all dressed in sequinned silvery catsuits. Nicole's outfit for the day was a mixture of bronze and denim, a tight, sexy sleeveless top with a deep cleavage and customized Dolce & Gabbana jeans with bronze embroidery.

'See you later,' chorused the Carli Girls, as they left. They were on stage next, with Nicole coming on after them. Gregory was after her, then Lorelei, finally Euston ending the show. The running order was very important and the biggest act usually finished last. Lorelei was fighting viciously to be the last act but had failed so far.

Nicole knew she had fifteen minutes before she had to be onstage, which gave her a few minutes in the tiny dressing room bathroom.

Wearing just her jeans and a slinky see-through bra, she took her body lotion and perfume into the bathroom, shut the door and clicked the little bolt home.

She stripped off the bra and began to rub the musky lotion into her skin. Just in case Darius held her close, she wanted to smell and feel beautiful.

A sudden noise outside made her jump.

'Hello? Andrea? Who is it?'

There was no answer but Nicole stiffened as she heard somebody approaching the bathroom door. Suddenly there was a click as if someone was turning a key from the other side. Nicole unbolted the door and tried to open it but it didn't move.

'Who's there?' she demanded.

Nobody spoke but Nicole heard a smothered giggle she'd recognize anywhere: Lorelei.

'Let me out, Lorelei,' she roared furiously. But nobody answered.

Nicole used her entire weight to pull at the door but it wouldn't open. Lorelei had obviously found the key and now she was locked in with just fifteen minutes to show time. Nobody would notice her until the five minute call and then it would take a few minutes to find her and let her out, by which time she'd look deeply unprofessional to all the visiting record company execs. Nicole burned with fury at the very thought. When she got her hands on Lorelei, she'd kill her.

Five minutes went, then ten. Stuck in the bathroom in her bra and jeans, Nicole simmered and then panicked. She kept banging on the bathroom door, shouting and yelling all the time, but nobody appeared to have heard her.

'Help, help,' she screamed, scared of going hoarse from shouting but even more scared of missing her slot onstage. She'd worked so hard and now it was all going down the tubes thanks to that horrible, nasty cow.

You're not going to win, Lorelei, vowed Nicole. She looked around the bathroom for something heavy. The only possibility was a grimy old weighing scales that looked as if it had been around since Victorian times. It'd do. Picking it up, Nicole banged it against the door, splintering a big hole in it. Grimly, Nicole began banging the scales against the door handle, hoping to break it. She'd just landed a third, crushing blow when she heard her name being called.

'Nicole? Are you in there?'

'Yes,' shrieked Nicole joyously, dropping the scales to the floor. 'I'm locked in. Find the key.'

There was silence for a moment, then a voice said: 'I can't find it. Stand back, I'm going to break the door down.'

She darted to one side and waited until a mighty noise boomed, the door groaned and flew open and Darius stood at the other side, with his boot in the air.

'Darius,' breathed Nicole. She'd never been so pleased to see anyone in her life, for a variety of reasons. 'Lorelei locked me in, I'm sure of it.'

'That little cow,' he growled, his kind, easy-going face angry in a way Nicole would never have believed possible. 'You should never have been put on the same tour with her. It was like putting you in a pool with sharks and not giving you a cage to protect you. She's jealous of you.'

'Is she?' Nicole stood in front of him, not caring for how she was dressed. 'How did you know I was here?'

'I didn't,' Darius said, looking down at her longingly. 'I just knew you'd never be late and that something had happened to you.'

And because Nicole knew he was too polite to do anything to a woman dressed only in jeans and a bra, she stood on tiptoe and kissed him. In an instant, his arms were around her and they clung together fiercely, kissing, only breaking away when Darius came to his senses.

'You've got to get onstage,' he gasped, running a hand through his fair spiky hair, making it stick up more than ever.

'Afterwards,' said Nicole.

'Afterwards,' he promised.

'Where were you? We were so worried,' said an angelic Lorelei as Nicole raced backstage for her performance. Nicole didn't have time to say anything but after the show, she got her chance for revenge.

'Can you do a five minute interview?' begged Phyllis as they all trooped off stage after the finale. 'I know you've got record company people to go out with but you were so brilliant up there tonight that this girl from *Superb* magazine wants to do an interview with you.'

'No problem,' said Nicole, a wicked plan forming . . .

The interview took place in a small office backstage and when the inevitable question about co-star bitching appeared, Nicole was ready for it.

'I know what you're talking about,' she said, stifling a sniff. 'I know that Lorelei said terrible things about me. It's awful, this whole music industry is so cruel,' Nicole added mournfully. 'She's such a sweet girl at heart and I really like her but when your single fails, it's like you're a non person and that really has an effect on some people.'

The *Superb* reporter perked up at this fresh information. 'We didn't think her single bombed that badly,' the reporter said. 'It's been hard getting actual figures from the record companies,' she continued in a probing manner. 'Everyone denies it but I'm convinced they try and massage the figures to make it look better for some artists.'

Nicole bit her lip as if she'd made a huge mistake. 'Oh God, I shouldn't have said *anything*. Lorelei would be devastated if anyone knew . . . She's so proud. We were friends before this, you know, but . . .' meaningful pause, 'her second album dropped like a stone from the chart. She's so upset. I know she wouldn't have meant to bitch about me, we're friends, honestly.'

Nicole tried to look innocent. The reporter smiled, knowing now that Lorelei was hauling her ass round every small venue in the country because it was the only way her next single had a hope in hell. Suddenly her story had an angle. Lorelei had got on many people's nerves over her two-year career. It was payback time.

*    *    *

449

'How did the interview go?' Darius asked later, when they'd got a minute alone after the triumphant dinner with the European Titus people. They all adored Nicole and thought she had a fabulous career ahead of her, promising European appearances left, right and centre.

Nicole grinned. 'Wait till I tell you,' she said wickedly.

It was nearly two in the morning when Darius escorted her to her room. Nicole was exhausted after a long day, her voice was hoarse from talking and performing and her feet were tired, yet she still felt as if she could dance all night if only Darius asked.

He stopped outside her door and took her small hand in his big one. He was so gentle, Nicole thought. The kindest, politest man she'd ever met. What did he want with a tough little cookie like her?

'Well . . . goodnight,' stammered Darius, the boy who'd won debating contests at his public school and who'd never been at a loss for words before. He was speechless now. Nicole did that to him. Just one scorching look from those tigerish eyes and he was struck dumb.

'Yes . . . goodnight,' said Nicole, looking at her hand in his grasp. She couldn't talk. What was the matter with her? She wanted Darius to kiss her, she wanted more than kisses, but she'd made the first move once, she couldn't do it again. Not with someone like Darius. He was so upright and respectable, his voice made her think of the Queen's garden parties and regattas on the telly. His parents would probably drop dead with shock if he turned up at home with this half-Indian, half-Cockney brat . . .

'What are we like?' Darius suddenly took action. 'Where's your key?'

Dumbly, Nicole handed it over. He opened the door and dragged her inside. Then, he pulled her into his arms and kissed her until she thought she'd faint with lack of oxygen.

'Sorry,' he said, as she gasped for air.

'Sorry?' laughed Nicole. 'What for?' And she pulled his head down to hers again. 'You'll be sorry if you stop.'

Much later, they sat on the sofa, Nicole curled up on his lap, his big body cradling hers protectively. 'I've got something to tell you,' she said, not able to look him in the eye.

'You can tell me anything,' said Darius, his voice suffused with love.

'I'm . . . that is . . .' Nicole said haltingly. How was she ever going to do this?

'Tell me.' When Darius looked at her with that honest, blue gaze, she knew she could tell him anything.

'I'm a virgin. I've never . . . done it before.' She bit her lip anxiously. 'Everyone thinks I have. I mean, you can't say you're a virgin now-adays, can you?'

'Why not?' Darius said softly, tracing the outline of her lips with one finger. 'You're beautiful, Nicole. I'm crazy about you. I love you.'

'Me too,' she said quickly, 'that's why I wanted to tell you. It has to be special, you see or . . .' she paused. 'Or it can screw up your life.' She wanted to say more and Darius knew it.

'Tell me?' he asked.

'It wasn't my mum, you see,' Nicole said. 'It was Gran. Ever since I was a kid, she was always going on about mum getting pregnant when she was a teenager and how it ruined everything. I felt guilty, I was responsible.' Nicole's eyes glistened.

'You weren't, you were the innocent one,' protested Darius.

'Mum was innocent too,' Nicole said. 'You've met her. She's just the kindest person and she can't say no to anyone. She shouldn't be allowed out on her own, Gran always says. I love Gran, honest I do, but I love Mum more. I never wanted anyone to label my mum as some reckless mother with kids by different fathers. I hate that.' Nicole was vehement. 'That's why I tried so hard to keep things together at home.'

'Your mum is lovely,' said Darius truthfully. He knew exactly what Nicole meant about her mother, who was as naive and trusting as the day is long.

'Mum expects the best out of life and people,' Nicole said simply. 'There isn't a bad bone in her body. She's just a bit innocent, if that makes sense. She's always done her best for us but she was the sort of person who needed someone strong to lean on. I tried to be that person, and all the time, Gran was telling me that sex was bad and look what it had done to Mum.'

'Sex isn't bad.' Darius stroked Nicole's cheek softly. 'That's your gran's religious upbringing. You've got to understand that.'

'I know that,' Nicole smiled as if talking to a child. 'But I still wanted to wait for the right person.'

Darius couldn't speak.

'That's you, silly,' she said. 'You're the right person. But not here.'

She knew where she'd like to make love to him: in her own home, where she felt happy and independent, her own flat. 'I'd love to have my own place,' she said suddenly, 'but I can't,' she added.

'Why not?' asked Darius reasonably.

She stared at him. 'I can't leave Mum and Pammy, you know that.'

Darius was serious: 'You'll have to leave sometime, Nicole.'

# CHAPTER TWENTY-THREE

*Hi Sam,*

*How are you feeling? I hope you're not working too hard. It's a glorious day in Redlion with summer peeking round the corner. Toby and Millie are at my feet playing cards. Matt sent them this pack of animal cards from Bath and they spend hours playing snap. I was never so grateful to anyone in my life as I am to those cardmakers although Millie can get a bit stroppy when she loses. She's really Daddy's girl, I have to say. In the two weeks since Matt went back to Bath she's been so naughty and when I give out to her, she cries at the top of her voice and says she wants her Daddy!*

*But she's happy today because a new babysitter is coming tonight and Millie can't wait to get rid of me! I imagine she's hoping to get up to all sorts of tricks with a babysitter who doesn't know the rules.*

*I'm going out to this big charity do which was set up by the woman who owns the local pub, which is the hotbed of all sorts of excitement. Apparently it's amazing, everybody in the area comes. Tonight, we're raising money for guide dogs for the blind. Matt says that knowing the people who frequent the pub, it'll be guide dogs for the blind drunk. I have been roped in to*

*sell raffle tickets. It should be fun. As you know, I*
*haven't been out much since Matt went back to Bath*
*because both kids have had colds. Will tell you how it*
*went tomorrow,*
    *Love Hope.*

Geraldine, a nineteen-year-old Arts student whose parents ran the organic butchers, wasn't in the least bothered by missing the charity night to babysit.

'It'll all be old wrinklies tonight,' she told Hope dismissively. 'No talent whatsoever, just the usual clutch of ould fellas trying to drag me up to dance because they buy meat from my dad's shop, I'd hate it. It'll be like every charity night they've ever had in the town. Boring as hell.'

'Will all the ould fellows try and drag me up to dance?' inquired Hope, grinning.

Geraldine shook her head. 'No, they don't know you well enough. In my case, you see, they all look mistily into their pints and tell me they remember when I was a baby and all the times they changed my nappy. That's their grounds for hauling me round the dance floor. But they can't do that with you. You're still a visitor and you're safe. Besides,' she smiled in an awestruck way, 'they know you've got a gorgeous husband, so what would be the point.'

'My babysitter tells me the place will be full of old men desperate to drag young women up to dance,' Hope whispered to Delphine as they left their coats at the cloakroom.

'She's got that right,' Delphine whispered back. 'But there's bound to be a few nice ones too. I promise I'll rescue you if I see you being molested by anyone unsuitable.'

Hope had never been in the village hall before. On the outside, it was a barren looking breeze block building with zero charm that no amount of climbing ivy could hide. On the inside, however, Belle Maguire's group of charity ladies had transformed it with yellow crepe paper, plenty of trailing plants and a long table covered with a delicious looking buffet.

All the tables were covered in yellow table cloths and decorated with yellow roses, while the lights were all dim bulbs flattering to all ages and nicely atmospheric. It was obvious that a huge amount of effort had gone into everything.

By half seven, people started to arrive, the usual combination of people who were dressed to kill, along with people who'd come straight from work and hadn't had a chance to change out of suits and ties. Hope and Delphine were asked to roam the tables once people had piled their plates from the buffet. Hope, who hadn't had anything to eat since lunch, began to look longingly at the buffet with its beautifully laid out cold meats and the dressed salmon. By eight the place was full and the party raged on, with a few people not bothering with the buffet at all but getting stuck into the first hour of free drink.

'Do you think having a free bar for an hour is a good idea?' Hope asked Belle, when the queue to the bar was at least six deep with no sign of abating.

Belle smiled enigmatically. 'Wait till the auction,' she said. 'They're much more generous when they're plastered. When it's all balanced out, we'll have made a fortune.'

She was right. By ten, Hope had sold most of her tickets and the floor was heaving with happy partygoers dancing to a band playing disco music. Hope had been whirled around the floor several times and not with any of Geraldine's so-called ould fellas either. Eugene had brought along some friends, who been only too delighted to whisk off the pretty Mrs Parker who looked so sweetly sexy in a long flowered chiffon dress.

In fact, the gathering was pretty glamorous all round. Lots of gorgeous teenage girls drifted around affecting to look bored at being at a do with their parents, but secretly trying to attract the attention of one of the local rock stars, who'd turned up with his wife, an ex-*Vogue* model who was watching the teenage lovelies with a wary eye. The Oscar-winning actress who'd bought the crumbling Shanrock Castle was there with a party of guests from LA, one of whom was trying to Riverdance with the barmaid from the Widow's. Delphine's friends, a crowd of glamorous, French-manicured young things who looked as if they'd spent all day in a beauty salon, were being ogled by the LA guests and Eugene's friends. Meanwhile, two of the handsome Danish artists who'd been renting a house near the artists' centre since March had arrived on a Harley and were having a great time being indoctrinated into Irish cuisine by boutique-owner Lucille, who felt they ought to try crubeens before they went back to Denmark.

'What are crubeens?' inquired the younger guy innocently, taking a big bite.

'Pigs' feet,' Lucille announced pleasantly. 'The back ones to be precise because there's more meat on them. Anyone want some more?'

'How are you doing?' asked Belle, catching up with Hope in the ladies as she tried to tone down her flushed face.

'Brilliantly,' Hope said with delight. 'We're making a fortune.'

'Good. It's the auction next and I've a problem because one of my ladies has let me down.'

'Can I help?' Hope asked.

Belle smiled at her. 'I was hoping you'd say that.'

Which was how Hope found herself standing nervously onstage beside seven other locals, all of whom had good humouredly offered themselves up for the auction. Danny, a landscape gardener, was offering a day's work in someone's garden. Shona, a talented decorator, promised a consultation to help revamp someone's house, while Delphine was offering a home facial.

Hope wasn't sure what she was supposed to offer.

'Hen rearing skills,' suggested Mary-Kate wickedly from the safety of the dance floor.

'Why aren't you up here?' demanded Hope.

'You're prettier,' said Mary-Kate.

'No, it's because she refused,' Belle said. With her golden blonde hair piled on top of her head and wearing a very low cut pink suit out of which her magnificent bosom rose majestically, she looked like the madam of a successful brothel.

'What am I up here for?' Hope inquired.

'I keep hearing what a wonderful organizer you are – Una Hutchinson never stops singing your praises. You can offer two hours of sorting out people's business affairs.'

'I don't really do that sort of thing . . .' protested Hope.

'Nonsense,' said Belle. 'Don't sell yourself short. You're a very capable woman, remember that.'

The bidding was slow to start but by the time Shona's interior decoration services were up for grabs, the money was flowing.

'£300, can you imagine that,' said Shona delightedly as the bidding stopped.

'Oh God,' whispered Hope in embarrassment to Delphine. 'Nobody's going to bid for me. I'll die. Why did I let myself in for this?'

Belle, the perfect mistress of ceremonies, invited Hope to stand beside her, outlined her skills, and asked for the bids to start.

Hope smiled glazedly out at the audience, thinking that if only Matt were here, he'd bid for her, purely to save her from utter public humiliation.

'One hundred pounds,' cried Eugene loyally.

Hope smiled at him.

'One fifty,' offered Mary-Kate.

'One seventy-five,' said Paddy Slattery who'd sold her the hens. Hope sighed. If Paddy won the bidding, he'd probably have her cleaning out his henhouse for him.

'Two hundred,' said Erwin, whose machinery hire company she'd worked for. Hope smiled at him. She'd already sorted Erwin out.

'Two fifty,' said a man in a wheelchair. Standing beside him, giving her a thumbs up signal, was Una Hutchinson.

'Two seventy-five,' said the butcher's wife encouragingly.

'Three hundred,' said the rock star huskily, earning himself a fierce glare off his wife.

'Three hundred,' repeated Belle, gazing round at the audience.

There were no more bids and the only sounds in the hall were the noise of the CD player on low and the sound of glasses rattling down at the bar.

'Any more bids?' roared Belle.

'Three twenty-five,' said the butcher's assistant, no doubt primed by his boss.

'Three twenty-five it is,' said Belle, judging it to be the end of the bidding, 'going, going . . .'

'Four hundred pounds,' said a familiar voice.

There was a delighted roar from one of the charity ladies who was now semi-comatose from brandy. 'Fantasthic!' she slurred. 'Pray ish not my husband who's bidding.'

'Who bid?' whispered Shona, fascinated, peering down the back of the hall where the lights were dim and all the faces merged into one another.

Hope didn't need to see who'd bid for her. She knew. She'd recognize that honeyed voice anywhere. Christy De Lacy.

Her face burned.

'Four hundred pounds, any more bids?' said Belle, who knew a good thing when she saw it and who had no difficulty recognizing Christy's saturnine face from amid the throngs of guests. 'Going, going, gone. Sold to Mr De Lacy for four hundred pounds. Lucky you,' she added in an undertone to Hope. 'I wouldn't mind being sold to that boy for four hundred pounds. I'd let him have me for four pounds, never mind,' she added with a lascivious cackle. Hope wondered if she should write a cheque for four hundred pounds herself for the charity, seeing as how she had no intention of spending a moment in Christy's company ever again.

When the auction was over, Belle announced that the bar would be closing in ten minutes. There was a mad rush to the back of the hall. Some people began to gather up coats and bags to leave. At Belle's request, the bidders came up to claim their prizes and make arrangements to meet up. The hall lights were switched on to full and Hope watched as Christy, devastating in one of his signature Hugo Boss suits, strolled up to the stage.

'That was very good of you to bid so much,' Belle said, eyeing him up.

'It's for charity,' he purred.

'I wouldn't have had you down as the charitable type,' Hope said sharply.

Belle glanced at her but said nothing.

'When are you going to come up to the hotel and sort me out?' Christy said softly so that only Hope could hear. 'I've missed our little sessions.'

Hope said nothing. She was terrified that someone would hear. Delphine and Eugene were only feet away and Mary-Kate was chatting to Shona close by.

'Can I give you a lift home, Hope?' asked Christy loudly. 'It's on my way and I have to get back to the hotel by half eleven.'

'No,' said Hope abruptly. 'Eugene and Delphine are driving me home. My babysitter, Geraldine, lives near them and they're going to drive her home afterwards.'

'I can do that,' Christy said smoothly.

Hope shot Delphine a beseeching look but Delphine was busy getting her coat and didn't notice.

'Eugene, I'll drop Hope off,' Christy said to Eugene. 'It'll save you the drive.'

'I don't know ... if you're sure ...' said Eugene hesitantly, his dislike of Christy warring with his desire not to have to drive down the pot-holed lane to Curlew Cottage.

'Absolutely,' Christy said.

Unless she wanted a full-scale disagreement, there really was no option but for Hope to pull on her jacket, wave goodbye to everyone and go with Christy. She could have refused him point blank but that would only make Delphine and Eugene wonder why, and then Hope would have to explain that she was a stupid, flirtatious woman who'd made a fool of herself with Christy. Damn him! Couldn't he see she wasn't interested?

Christy, however, didn't appear to see anything.

'Mind your step,' he murmured, taking her arm as they walked out the path to the car park.

Hope pulled her arm away as if she'd been scalded. 'I'm fine,' she snapped.

He shot her a reproachful gaze with those puppy dog eyes. 'Tired?' he asked. 'Never mind. I'll get you sitting down in a minute and you can slip off your heels.' His gaze flickered over her, as if her high heels weren't the only things he envisaged her removing.

At his silver sports car, Christy flicked the alarm and then opened the passenger door with a flourish.

'Madame,' he purred, helping her in.

A blast of *déjà vu* hit Hope as Christy slammed the door and she shuddered at the memory of the last time she sat in the low-slung car. She primly smoothed down her skirt and folded her arms across her chest protectively. If her body language didn't give him the message, then she'd have to tell him straight up: she loved Matt and she didn't want to fool around. It had all been a big mistake.

'Comfy?' said Christy, sliding into his seat. The overpowering scent of Givenchy for Men flooded the car. He must use buckets of the stuff.

'Fine,' Hope replied. She must try to be civil after all. 'I'm tired, Christy. I've an early start in the morning.'

'Yes, Una's away from tomorrow. I know you'll manage, though. You're very capable, Mrs Parker.' He shot her a meaningful glance.

Ignore it, Hope told herself.

They sat in silence as Christy drove rapidly through Redlion, with scant regard for the thirty mile an hour speed limit in the village. As the car bumped down the lane to Curlew Cottage, Hope felt relief surge through her. She was home, Christy had said nothing and hadn't moved so much as a finger in her direction. He stopped the car quietly outside the cottage.

'Thanks,' said Hope abruptly, getting out.

To her surprise, he got out too. 'I'm driving Geraldine home, surely?' he said, noticing her surprise.

'Er ... yes, but I'll probably ask her to spend the night,' Hope stammered, having no intention of sending poor Geraldine off in the car with him.

'I'll come in.' He smiled that wicked smile.

Hope fiddled with her key, nerves making her clumsy. Surely he wouldn't try anything in the cottage, not with Geraldine sitting on the couch watching them?

But when Hope entered the house quietly, there was no sign of the babysitter perched on the couch with the television guide on her lap. Hope's face fell. She had told Geraldine that if she was tired, to leave a note and to go to bed in the spare room. But it was only half eleven, far too early for that, wasn't it?

'She must have gone to bed,' Christy said, silently closing the front door.

'Yes,' said Hope nervously. She took off her jacket and looked around for a note from Geraldine, her mind racing. Her chaperone was gone and she had to get rid of Christy quickly before he got any ideas. 'Well, Christy, thank you so much for dropping me home,' she whispered, trying to sound like a dinner party hostess getting rid of guests who'd overstayed their welcome and not like a woman alone with a man whom she had a history of kissing.

'My pleasure,' Christy purred. He gently laid his keys on the coffee table, shed his suit jacket like a snake shedding its skin, and was beside Hope in one smooth move.

'Hope,' he breathed, arms wrapping themselves around her. His glossy head bent and his mouth captured hers, stopping Hope from saying 'No!' as his tongue invaded her mouth.

'No,' she hissed seconds later, managing to move her mouth from under his. The pressure of his arms increased with one strong hand moulding her body closer to his, and the other crumpling the material of her chiffon dress, drawing it upwards so that he could stroke the softness of her bare legs.

Hope gasped with shock. The sense of unreality about the whole moment meant it was like watching a sexy movie rather than being in one: Christy's hand burrowed up under Hope's skirt and Hope felt as if she was watching in the distance as she tried valiantly to push him away. He was surprisingly strong and obviously deaf, because with his head buried in her neck, he didn't hear her saying 'Stop it, Christy,' in a fierce whisper. All she needed was for Geraldine to hear the commotion and arrive downstairs. It would be so embarrassing.

'Stop it,' she hissed again and had the satisfaction of seeing Christy straighten up and face her, eyes heavy with lust and with a smidgen of irritation.

'Oh Hope, stop resisting, you know you want me,' Christy murmured. 'You weren't saying no when we were up at the hotel. I've been thinking about you ever since, you are so sexy. Christ, I thought I'd go mad if I couldn't have you.'

She caught his groping hand with one of hers and pushed it away. There wasn't anything vaguely sexual about it for Hope. Any shred of passion she might have had for Christy had vanished once she'd realized that kissing him was betraying Matt. And now that he was pulling up her skirt and groping her against her will! How dare he? The sheer nerve of it.

'Did you hear me?' she hissed even more loudly. 'Stop it. I don't want this and I'll scream in one minute if you don't stop!'

She pushed him away and they stood facing each other, hair tousled, lips red and panting, clothes dishevelled from the encounter.

'That wasn't what you were saying last time,' Christy said in a loud, angry voice. 'You were hot enough for me then! You wouldn't have said no in the back of my car, that's for certain. Why have you come over all coy now? Back at the hotel, until my phone rang, you were all for it. Admit it, you were.'

'I think you should get out of my house, now,' said a low, angry voice, 'if you don't want me to call the police.'

Christy and Hope looked up in shock. Standing above them on the staircase, a face like thunder, was Matt. In an instant, Hope felt her legs go weak.

'Jesus!' said Christy, blanching at the sight of a tall, strong rival who had the law on his side and very possibly a baseball bat hidden somewhere. He grabbed his jacket and his keys and was out the front door faster than an Olympic runner out of the stocks. The door rattled as Christy started up his sports car and raced down the drive with a crunch of gravel.

There was silence in Curlew Cottage. Not a nice, peaceful silence either. Hope closed her eyes momentarily and wished she could turn back the clock, just a few minutes would be enough. What had Matt seen? What had he overheard? No matter that she'd been trying to get rid of Christy, the evidence was damning if you didn't know the facts.

'I'm so glad you were here,' she babbled, wishing she could get a bit of strength back in her legs. Her heart was racing after the encounter with Christy, and the shock of seeing Matt was making it race even more. 'He was all over me and he wouldn't take no for an answer,' she said anxiously. 'I told him to go but he wouldn't. You heard me telling him to go, didn't you?'

She stared up at Matt who was still motionless on the staircase. She'd never seen him look so angry in her life. His jaw was clamped in rage and his mouth was a thin line of hate. He looked perfectly capable of beating the hell out of Christy De Lacy. Which was the sort of thing that happened, she knew, when men found other men having sex with their wives. *Other men having sex with their wives.* Shit. Hope had to sit down. This was happening for real. This wasn't a TV soap episode. It was her life. She had to make things better immediately.

'Matt,' she said weakly, 'it wasn't what it looked like. He was coming on to me and he wouldn't stop, you saw that, didn't you? I wasn't interested.'

Matt's face might have been red with the heat of fury but his voice was at freezing point. 'I saw a lot of things and I heard a lot of things,' he said slowly, looking at her as if he was seeing her clearly for the first time in their marriage. 'What a pity I came back early as a surprise for you and the children. I'm sorry for interrupting your torrid little session.'

'It wasn't like that,' Hope replied, her voice rising with fear. Matt had never looked at her like that before, so coldly and so full of hurt. He wasn't even behaving the way he normally did in arguments. Then, he snapped and got angry. Now, even though his face was volcanic, his voice was low and pained. He looked devastated, she realized.

'It wasn't like that,' she repeated.

'Don't insult my intelligence,' he said. 'I heard you long before you saw me. I heard it all.'

Hope leaned against the couch feebly. Even her hands were shaking now.

Matt walked slowly down the stairs and Hope hurried over to him, wanting to wrap her arms around him, to tell him she loved him. He'd put his arms around her and it would all be okay. She got to within a foot of him and he recoiled. 'Don't touch me,' he whispered.

Hope flinched. She took a step back, not knowing what to do. She stared at her husband's stricken face.

463

She would have preferred it if he'd screamed at her, shouted that she was a whore for so much as looking at another man. But that pained, betrayed look on his face: she couldn't deal with that.

'Please Matt,' she begged hoarsely, 'please let me explain.'

'I don't want to hear your feeble explanations,' he shot back.

'You have to,' she insisted. 'Please, you never listen to me, you never want to hear what I have to say . . .'

'Oh, so that's it,' he said, eyes blazing. 'It's all my fault, is it?'

'No, but you don't listen to me,' Hope cried, 'you've always been like that. I just want to tell you what happened here. Please listen. It was nothing. He fancied me and didn't understand I was married, that I love you so much. I do, you know that.'

'That's what I can't forgive,' he said and his face was blank. 'I thought you loved me. I was never close to my family and you, you had only Sam and nobody else. We were supposed to be everything to each other, you were my whole family and I thought I was yours. And you've just destroyed that.'

'I haven't!' she cried. 'I haven't. It was nothing.'

His dark eyes regarded her with something close to loathing. 'That's even worse,' he replied. 'You've destroyed us for nothing. I thought that's what men were supposed to do.' For one brief moment, he looked as if he might cry. Hope had only seen him cry twice before, when the children were born. She couldn't imagine any other circumstance when Matt would cry. But as he gazed at her, she could see his face harden.

He turned away from her and climbed the stairs.

Hope burst into tears and sat on the couch, hugging her knees to her chest and letting the tears run down her cheeks. What had she done? It was all her fault, she couldn't even blame bloody Christy because all he'd done was flirt with her. It had been up to her to tell him she wasn't interested but she hadn't.

A noise from their bedroom made her look up. She recognized the sound of the bottom drawer opening: it was old and stiff, creaking madly when pulled open. There was nothing in there but the remainder of Matt's working shirts, the ones he wore in Bath but hadn't needed in Redlion. Hope's eyes widened in horror. He'd only open that drawer if he was packing.

She ran upstairs and tried to open their door but it wouldn't budge. It was locked.

'Matt,' she whispered, standing in anguish outside the door. 'Please let me in, please.'

He said nothing and the sound of drawers opening continued.

'Please,' whispered Hope, 'please.'

After a few minutes he unlocked the door and emerged, pale faced now and with the family's big suitcase in one hand. He was wearing his black suede jacket and carried his laptop case in the other hand.

Hope stepped backwards, ashen. 'Where are you going?' she whispered, barely able to get the words out.

'It doesn't matter,' Matt said bitterly, 'as long as it's away from you.'

'You can't do this,' she wailed. 'You've left me already, you dumped me here and forgot about me. You can't do it again.'

'I'm not abandoning you,' he snapped. 'I'm leaving you and lover boy together. But don't let him think he's getting his hands on my children, because he's not.'

'Matt! Stop and think, please,' she begged. 'We can work it out. We've got the children to think about. I was lonely, I felt depressed without you and when he flirted with me, I flirted back, that's all. I mean, you'd gone off and left me and you practically never phoned,' she said, knowing this was no excuse and that she shouldn't even be saying it.

'I left you to work, not to have it off with every woman who flirted with me.'

'I wasn't like that,' Hope insisted in vain. 'Please listen to me.'

'No, I won't listen to your pathetic excuse,' Matt said. 'When I think of you whining to me about Finula and how she fancied me, and you know I wouldn't so much as *look* at another woman. And then it's you who runs off with someone.'

'I didn't run off with anyone,' screeched Hope. 'Why don't you listen to me for once?'

'Listen to yourself,' Matt said coldly. 'You sound pathetic. You

465

wanted everything, well you can't have it. You can't have me and lover boy.'

He left the case and the laptop at the top of the stairs and went into the children's bedroom. Hope didn't follow him but she could hear him stoop to kiss Millie and then Toby, hear him whispering 'bye my little pets. I'll see you soon.' She could the rattle in his voice as it broke when he finished, saying 'I love you so much, don't forget that.'

She stopped trying to stem the flow of tears at that point. They ran unchecked down her face. What had she done?

Matt ignored her when he came out of the children's room. He hefted the big case down the stairs and Hope could only watch helplessly.

She tried to stop him at the front door. 'I flirted with him,' she sobbed, saying more than she intended to in her guilt and grief. 'Nothing more. He got the wrong idea and tried to take it further. I didn't want to, you know that, Matt. I love you, I love you.'

His dark, hurt eyes raked over her face. 'Do you?' he said.

'Please don't go,' she begged. 'Think of the children,' she added, as a last resort.

'You can reach me on my mobile if the children need me,' he said bluntly. 'Otherwise, don't bother phoning. I don't want to talk to you. When I'm settled, I'll give you a phone number and address. I don't live here anymore.'

Then he opened the front door, moved his belongings outside. 'There's a taxi coming. I'll wait outside.' And he slammed the door.

He stood outside until the taxi turned up.

The taxi driver obviously said nothing when Matt put the suitcase into the car, because Hope, who was leaning against the door listening and sobbing, could hear absolutely no conversation. She heard the taxi drive up the lane, bouncing over the potholes. Then she sank to the floor inside the front door and cried until she had no more tears left inside her.

Delphine was astonished to see the curtains still drawn when she parked outside Curlew Cottage the following morning at ten. She and Hope were bringing the children into Killarney for the morning and because it was unusual to see no signs of life, Delphine wondered if perhaps one of the children were ill.

The words 'is everything all right?' froze on her lips when Hope answered the door.

Delphine gulped. Clearly everything was not all right. Hope looked dreadful. No, dreadful didn't accurately describe it. She looked as if she'd just crawled from a car wreck where she was the only survivor. Her eyes were puffy and red-rimmed, her face was white and sunken and she was shaking like a sapling in a force ten gale.

'Oh Delphine,' she croaked. 'Delphine. Matt's gone, he's left me. He found Christy here and he jumped to the wrong conclusion.' Then Hope just leaned helplessly against her friend and shook as if she was crying, only there were no tears coming out.

Despite the jaw-dropping revelations that made her want to ask *what?*, Delphine hadn't grown up with her aunt as a role model for nothing. Mary-Kate was the epitome of cool in these situations and after years of watching her at work, Delphine sprang into expert, caring action, no questions asked.

She shut the door and helped Hope to the couch. Cartoons were blaring out of the television and Millie and Toby sat transfixed in front of it, with several packets of sweets scattered around them. Delphine knew that Hope was very keen on stopping the children from viewing sweets as the ultimate treat and gave them yoghurts and dried fruit instead as often as she could.

'I thought if they had some sweets they wouldn't notice anything was wrong,' Hope said wringing her hands. 'I don't want them to know what's going on.'

'It's all right, there's nothing wrong with sweets now and then. Sure where would us grown ups be without chocolate?' Delphine smiled but Hope didn't smile back. She genuinely looked too shattered to smile.

'When did this happen?' Delphine asked, taking one of Hope's quivering hands in her own and holding it tightly.

'Last night,' whispered Hope. 'Matt was here when Christy dropped me home. He'd got a taxi and sent Geraldine home in it

467

and then ... it was awful. He's gone and he's not coming back, ever.'

'And you haven't slept, right?'

Hope raised haunted eyes to her. 'Would you be able to?'

Delphine marched into the kitchen and made Hope a mug of strong coffee which she laced with a slug of brandy. She handed it to Hope and prayed that Hope would be able to hold the mug without spilling it.

'This has alcohol in it,' Hope said after a sip. 'I won't be able to drive or anything.'

'You can't drive in your state as it is,' Delphine said firmly. 'Drink it. Then you're going to go up and have a shower, fix your hair and your make-up and then we'll talk if you want to. But first you've got to look presentable for the children's sake. They can't see you like this and they're your first priority.'

'Yes, of course,' Hope's eyes filled with tears. 'I should be ashamed of myself. I'm not fit to be their mother ...'

'Now, now, hush,' Delphine said gently, hugging her. 'You're a great mum. You've had a shock, Hope. Of course you got upset, you're not a machine.'

Hope drank down the coffee like a child taking nasty medicine, then she went obediently upstairs. Somehow, by blanking out everything, she managed to shower, dry her hair and slick on lipstick to make herself look more human. Her hands shook when she pulled out the bright pink shirt that Millie loved and which Matt had told her suited her better than any other colour. No, she wouldn't think about Matt. She touched her mother's pill box, leaving her fingers on the painted surface as if she might feel some inspiration or strength travelling via her fingers into her heart. But she felt nothing, except guilt and shame. Her mother would be ashamed of her, Hope was sure of it.

'Hello Millie and Toby,' Delphine said brightly to the children. 'How are you?'

Toby was too enthralled watching the TV to answer but Millie looked at her solemnly. 'We're fine but Mummy has a pain in her head. She told me. That's why she's crying.'

'Poor Mummy,' Delphine agreed. 'Mummies sometimes get terrible pains in their heads and they need lots of love and kisses to get over it. Will you help?'

Millie nodded.

'Did you have your breakfast?' Delphine inquired.

Millie nodded again. Then whispered: 'I spilled all mine and she never noticed.'

'We might have some more later,' Delphine said decisively. Millie went back to watching the TV.

It was fifteen minutes before Hope came downstairs again, still looking pale but miles better than she had earlier. Millie and Toby threw themselves at her.

'Mummy, we had toast and chocolate spread and Toby got chocolate spread on his T-shirt,' giggled Millie.

'Did not,' said Toby hotly.

As they squabbled and cuddled up to their mother, she looked over their heads at Delphine and mouthed the word 'thanks'.

When the children stopped vying for their mother's attention, Delphine made more coffee – this time without the brandy – and sat with Hope at the kitchen table.

Hope told her everything, leaving nothing out, no matter how embarrassed she felt at the revelations.

'Confession is good for the soul, or so I hear,' Hope said miserably when she'd finished.

'That's what my mother's always telling me,' Delphine agreed. 'But she means it in a "confess and never make a mistake again" sort of way. I don't think humans are made like that. We keep making mistakes.'

'Not like mine, you don't.' Hope looked dismal.

'Don't be so hard on yourself,' Delphine advised. 'You didn't do this on your own. Christy's an expert at that sort of thing. Other people have hobbies: his is charming women. I've seen him flirting with female guests just for the hell of it. He can't help himself and because you were married, you were even more of a challenge.'

Hope looked unconvinced. 'I should have known better,' she said, staring into the depths of her coffee mug.

'Oh Hope, you were an innocent going like a lamb to the slaughter. Christy's trading point is excitement,' Delphine pointed out. 'He finds people who lack excitement in their lives and he provides it, in great big doses. Being whisked off to an exotic lunch with a handsome, attentive man is like something from a film and it doesn't happen to most of us in real life, which is why his victims are always so thrilled and convinced that they're the real thing.'

Hope shuddered at Delphine's choice of words. She had been a victim and she had thought, however briefly, that it was the real thing for Christy. He was so believable when he told her how he felt about her. And of course, she'd been nothing but a diversion for him. She had just ruined her marriage for nothing. That was the absolutely awful thing.

'Maybe he was a flirt or a playboy and I should have known better,' she said slowly, 'but that doesn't take away from the fact that I was interested in him. That's what makes me most ashamed. What sort of person can I be if I have a lovely husband and I'm capable of even thinking of cheating on him? You wouldn't do that to Eugene, how could I do it to poor Matt?' She was too worn out to cry but now she laid her head on her arms and sobbed dry, painful sobs.

'You didn't cheat on Matt,' Delphine protested. 'You got carried away and you kissed Christy. Big deal, that's all.'

'Matt doesn't agree with you,' Hope said.

'Matt doesn't know the entire story. You should have told him.'

'He wouldn't listen,' Hope said quietly.

That evening, Hope found the courage to phone Matt's mobile. Delphine had been urging her to do it all day but she was scared to: scared in case Matt told her their marriage was over. Not phoning was her version of the ostrich defence. The longer she kept her head buried in the sand, the longer she didn't have to face the truth.

The kids were drinking their bedtime milk and squabbling over which story they wanted read for bedtime when she picked up the phone and dialled. The answering service was on and, hearing Matt's steady, familiar voice telling her to leave a message, she chickened out and hung up, swallowing to deal with the huge lump in her throat. When the kids were finally in bed, she steeled herself and rang again, leaving a message this time.

*Hello Matt, it's Hope. We've got to talk. Please phone me, please. I love you. I'm so very, very sorry. You know I wouldn't hurt you for the world, please believe me. I love you.*

There really wasn't anything else she could say until he responded. Then, she phoned Betsey and Dan in Bath.

'Hello stranger,' said Dan chirpily when he answered. 'Long time no hear. How are you? Looking for Betsey, no doubt . . .'

'Er . . . no,' Hope said hesitantly. Matt couldn't be there. Dan would have instantly mentioned it if he had been. Unless Matt didn't want her to know where he was. 'Is Matt there?' she asked, knowing that if he wasn't there, she'd just told another person her tale of woe.

There was a moment's silence. 'No, Hope, he's not. He was going home to you for the weekend, it was a surprise . . . don't tell me he didn't get there?'

At the other end of the phone, Hope sighed. 'He got here, Dan. We had a row and he left again and now I can't get him on his mobile.'

'What are you like!' joked Dan. 'I never had you pair down for the tempestuous lovers. Betsey goes into a rage at least twice a week and flounces out of the house. She only comes back when she's done serious damage to the Visa card. Matt'll be back with a hangover, I guarantee it!'

If only it were that simple. 'I hope so,' she said.

She tried Matt's mobile again and left another message, telling him she was worried and to please phone. 'The kids miss you,' she added, knowing it was emotional blackmail but not able to help herself. She'd say she was dying if only it would make him phone her, because once they were actually speaking, she'd be able to convince him that she loved him, truly.

# CHAPTER TWENTY-FOUR

There was a certain type of nosy neighbour whom Virginia hated. The sort who adored other people's traumas because it gave them a cast iron excuse to arrive at the front door with a thrown-together pile of scones and a fake 'how *are* you?' refrain so they could peer around your house and see if you'd let the place go in the midst of your misery. Luckily, these neighbours were rare but Virginia remembered one particular example who'd arrived at her house the day after Bill had died, bearing a cake and dying to be asked in so she could see if Virginia was bearing up or if she'd been sitting in front of the television like a tranquillized zombie. Laurence had admitted Emily Dawson, blithely thinking she was a kind woman who truly wanted to sympathize, like the other people who'd been arriving at the house all day to hug Virginia and cry and say how sorry they were to hear about Bill. It was Jamie, who was much more observant and more worldly than his older brother and who knew Emily was on a mission to snoop, who whisked her out again before she could start compiling her list for the neighbourhood watch.

'Poor Virginia ... well, she just sits there, doesn't she? I saw the doctor's car outside the house earlier and she must be on something ... not a scrap of make-up on her, poor dear, and her always so well turned out normally ... those boys are very good to her ... wasn't the younger one a terror at school?' would be the report, delivered with saccharine sympathy.

Virginia knew the routine, having spent years trying to avoid Emily in case she got an update on whatever poor local person had just split up with their husband or lost their job or had a death in the family. *'I could have told you he'd up and leave her ... he had a roving eye, that one ... God love her and all them children ... the house looks like the local dump, not that I'm saying anything, mind you ...'*

Therefore, when Mary-Kate phoned and insisted that Virginia join her, Delphine and Hope on a girlie lunch in Killarney to cheer Hope up, Virginia refused.

'I'm sure she'd hate me to turn up at her house tomorrow,' Virginia had said, scandalized. 'The poor girl must be going through enough torment without thinking that the entire village knows her husband has left her.'

'The entire village won't know,' Mary-Kate said firmly. 'You'll know and you're not going to announce the news from the pulpit on Sunday. Hope needs a few people to bring her out and make her feel a bit normal. And she loves you, Virginia. She'd be delighted to see you. Let's face it, people are going to find out soon enough, so it might be easier on her if she has a few friends who know Matt's gone and can stop the worst of the gossip.'

'Why don't you ask her if she minds me knowing?' fretted Virginia. 'Say you haven't told me but that if she doesn't mind, you will and then I'll go with you.'

'Fine,' said Mary-Kate. 'You're a stickler for details.'

Virginia grimaced. 'I've had plenty of experience with nosy people who want to witness your misery. I'd hate to be one.'

Virginia couldn't get Hope Parker out of her mind all afternoon. She was a lovely, rather sweet woman, Virginia felt, who was one of life's givers and who'd be lost without that handsome husband of hers. Then again, Virginia thought sadly, she'd felt utterly lost without Bill and she'd still had to deal with the world. She'd had to face up to life no matter how devastated she felt. Hope would have to do the same.

Mary-Kate phoned that night. 'Get your party dress on, missus, you're coming to lunch with us tomorrow. The only problem with asking Hope would she like you to come was the fact that she got upset and thought you wouldn't want to meet her if you knew that she'd been carrying on with that bould lad up at the hotel. She thinks you're a very moral, decent person and was afraid you'd be disgusted with her.'

'God love her,' said Virginia, touched and saddened at the same time. 'I am glad you asked me along, Mary-Kate. I think we'll have to explain to poor Hope that the world isn't black and white and that her true friends know that.'

'Grey,' said Mary-Kate sagely. 'The world is grey, and talking of grey, I think I'll wear my grey dress tomorrow so I better go and iron it.'

'Mary-Kate!' reproved her friend. 'I am determined that one of these days I'll get you out of your greys and your muddy browns. Bright colours would look beautiful on you.'

'Mutton dressed as lamb more like,' laughed Mary-Kate. 'I don't have your style Mrs Connell to carry off clothes like a model.'

'Madam, are you insinuating that I'm mutton dressed as lamb?' demanded Virginia with mock indignation.

'Why would I do that and you an expert with a golf club? I'd be afraid you'd hit me with one of your irons.'

'As if I'd hit you,' Virginia said. 'No, poison would be best, something from your chemist, then the police would think it was suicide and I'd be off the hook.'

'You're reading too many of those detective novels,' Mary-Kate replied. 'I'll pick you up tomorrow at twelve.'

Millie was acting up, which cheered her mother up no end. For the past four days since Matt had left, both children had been subdued and clingy, reacting to Hope's palpable misery. No matter how hard she tried to be bright and breezy, the children sensed that something was wrong. Which was why Hope was so thrilled that on the morning of the girls' lunch in Killarney, Millie threw a major, class A tantrum.

She flew into a rage at breakfast when she heard her mother on the phone discussing going to Killarney. Toby and Millie were going to Hunnybunnikins and Millie decided that this wasn't fair. Killarney with Auntie Delphine meant treats, sweets and possibly ice creams with chocolate things stuck in them.

'Won't go! Won't go!' she shrieked at Hope. Her Barbie beaker of milk went flying along with Toby's cereal.

'Millie,' said Hope in a warning voice.

'Won't! Want to go to 'Larney!' shrieked Millie again, giving her cereal bowl a forceful shove that made it rattle to the edge of the table and whisk over it, adding to the cereal and milk disaster on the kitchen floor.

Thank God for slate floors, Hope thought calmly. She'd put lovely rugs all over the downstairs of the house to cover up the beautiful but cold slate floor. The only place without a rug was the kitchen, scene of many meal time disasters. It would only take a minute or so to clear away and Hope could deal with that. She could deal with simple, everyday matters without any problem, she'd realized over the past few days. If the range went out, she calmly lit it again. If Toby walked mud into the ochre and burnt sienna rug in the sitting room, she cleaned it up. The beauty of these things was that they could be fixed. Unlike her and Matt. So she was dealing with the whole situation by not thinking about it and by acting on super-calm auto pilot, serenely being a capable mother and trying not to give in to too many moments of despair. If she did that, she'd be a wreck.

'Toby,' she said now, 'you're a good boy and I'll give you more breakfast in a moment.'

She kissed the top of his head and began to clear away the mess.

Millie sat crossly on her seat and scowled at everyone. She wanted to be noticed. She wanted to be begged to be good, she wanted attention. Instead, she was getting none.

Speculatively, she bounced her spoon across the table and onto the floor.

Hope said nothing but picked Millie up and carried her into the living room where she sat her on the couch. 'Toby and I are having breakfast and if you don't want any, you can sit here,' Hope said firmly. Then she turned her back on her astonished daughter and went back to Toby.

After a full minute of sitting there crossly, Millie started peering into the kitchen. Hope was talking to Toby, telling him what sort of fun day he'd have in the crèche and how Giselle had said there was going to be finger painting and all sorts of other excitement. He'd have to go on his own, of course, because Millie wouldn't be going. Giselle didn't allow naughty girls in. Shocked, Millie glared at them both. After another minute, she wriggled off the couch and stomped into the kitchen. Her big dark eyes were sad and her full lower lip wobbled the way it did when she was upset or on the verge of a tantrum. Now, it was wobbling in an upset way.

'Can I go to the Bunny place, Mummy?' she said tearfully.

Hope pretended to consider this. 'I thought you didn't want to go,' she said, 'and you know that Giselle doesn't like naughty girls in the crèche. She'd be very cross if you spilled your milk.'

Millie's lower lip wobbled some more. Hope reached out and hugged her. 'All right, darling,' she said, kissing the top of Millie's head, 'you can go with Toby. And we don't want any more tantrums at breakfast, OK?'

Millie was instantly delighted, her cherubic face creased up into a big smile. 'No Mummy,' she said innocently.

With the children safely installed in Hunnybunnikins until half three, Hope went home, climbed into bed and started to cry. Rocking back and forth with the duvet around her, she sobbed and sobbed, letting all the tears she'd had to stifle come out. She cried for herself, for her marriage, for the children and, finally, for darling Matt.

Hope could barely manage to think about his anguished face without feeling like the most evil woman on the planet. He'd looked so devastated.

She could see his face and remember those words as if they were engraved on her heart; engraved without an anaesthetic: *We were supposed to be everything to each other, you were my whole family and I thought I was yours. And you've just destroyed that.*

She remembered in the early stages of their relationship, when she had fallen deeply in love with Matt and become hopelessly dependent on him, how she'd cried one night and told him that she'd always been scared of people she loved leaving her.

'I won't leave,' Matt had said gently, fixing back a strand of her hair that had come loose from its scrunchie. 'Don't be afraid, Hope. We're like the musketeers, always together. I love you.'

It was the first time he'd said it: in a quaint little pub in Oxford where they'd gone for Easter weekend. All around, people were chatting and laughing, tapping their feet to the background folk music, asking loudly for pints and demanding crisps and toasted sandwiches. Hope didn't notice the noise because she was so in love.

'I love you too,' she whispered joyfully, not having had the courage to say it until he did.

'My little musketeer,' Matt had said warmly.

He'd bought her an antique edition of the Dumas classic as a first wedding anniversary present.

'*The Three Musketeers*!' she'd exclaimed, thrilled and at the same time ashamed because her present to him was a boring briefcase.

'The first wedding anniversary is the paper one,' Matt had said proudly. 'What better paper than a book like this? I love it, it's one of my favourites.'

Now, sitting on their bed, Hope drew her knees into her chest and rocked some more, trying to comfort herself in her wild grief. She knew exactly where the book was now, sitting, still wrapped up carefully in tissue paper, in a box of belongings they'd never opened since leaving Bath. Curlew Cottage was smaller than the house in Maltings Lane and there were several boxes in the corner of the tiny spare room, stacked neatly on top of each other and waiting until the Parkers went back home. What was their home now? Hope wondered dismally. Would she get the Dumas book in the divorce or would Matt demand it back as an expensive love token he'd bought as an investment?

If only he'd get in touch, she could tell him how much she loved him and what a mistake it had all been. But after four days, she'd heard nothing. He could be dead in a ditch somewhere and it would be all her fault.

Eventually, the shaking stopped and she clambered out of bed and tried to repair the damage to her devastated face. Her skin was red, blotchy and she had an outbreak of spots considering whether to appear on her chin. In spite of her misery, Hope grinned weakly at her frazzled reflection in the bathroom mirror. In films, women with marriage breakdowns got thin, developed marvellous cheekbones and looked beautiful in a deeply haunted manner. In real life it seemed as if acne and a spare tyre from comfort eating toasted cheese sandwiches and Quality Street were the only things you developed.

On the off chance that Matt might have sent her an e-mail, she switched on the computer. There was nothing from him but Sam had written.

*Hope, my darling,*

*I am so, so sorry for you. How awful. When you told me last night, I have to admit I was stunned. That bastard Matt! I will kill him. How dare he leave you without giving you a chance to explain. Anybody who knows you, knows you would never dream of having an affair. Hell, we all flirt with people, even precious Matt flirts, I'm sure. So you are not to blame yourself for anything. You were simply being a normal woman and if Matt hasn't the loyalty or the sense to trust you, then he doesn't deserve you.*

*You leave it to me and I'll track him down and give him a piece of my mind. If he hadn't left you on your own with the kids, then you wouldn't have been prey to bloody predators like that De Lacy man. He's just as bad. How dare he try and assault you like that. Have you thought of phoning the police and pressing charges . . .*

Hope winced. Dear Sam was standing up for her as usual but raging against Matt, or even Christy for that matter, was a waste of time.

*I will fly over at the weekend. Don't panic. You can manage without Matt Parker and when he comes to his senses and tries to crawl back, he'll have me to contend with. You may be able to forgive him but I won't. Will phone later,*

*All my love, chin up,*

*Sam.*

Hope didn't have the energy to answer the missive. It had been difficult enough telling Sam what had happened, although Sam had been
loyalty personified. On the phone, she'd been so virulently angry with
her brother-in-law that if she'd been able to get her hands on him at
that moment, she'd have ended up in jail for murder.

'I'll kill him for doing this to you!' she'd raged furiously, leaving
Hope feeling guilty. Even if Matt hadn't listened to her side of the
story, she did have something to be ashamed of and there was no
escaping that brutal fact.

Delphine, Mary-Kate and Virginia arrived just before noon, bearing gifts.

Delphine had brought a sample of the new, hideously expensive
face mask they were using up at the hotel. 'It promises to rejuvenate
tired skin,' she said, reading the label, 'although the advert for it on
the television shows a fourteen-year-old girl without a line on her
face, so I don't know if we can trust them. Fourteen-year-old girls
don't need rejuvenation.'

'Do you not have a cream that does skin resurfacing?' demanded
Hope, trying to be light hearted. 'It's my only hope. I've come out
in spots. Probably from all the chocolates I've been munching.'

'Chocolate has nothing to do with your skin,' Delphine remarked
in her professional voice. 'Spots like those are probably hormonal.'

'A good bottle of wine will help cure them,' Mary-Kate said, adding
her gift to the pile: six bottles of home made wine. 'Frederich from
the craft shop makes the most beautiful elderberry and gooseberry
wine. It's not Chateauneuf de whatever, mind you, but it's very cheering to have a glass at night.'

'That's why you're so merry all the time?' Delphine teased her aunt.
'A glass of home made brew and one of your muscle relaxants . . .'

'I only use those for my back,' protested Mary-Kate.

'Yes,' agreed Virginia. 'She smokes hash if she wants to relax.'

'Jesus! Do you want to get me arrested?' exclaimed Mary-Kate. 'I
told you I only tried it that one time twenty-five years ago at a party
and it did nothing for me. I was a kid, I didn't know what they were
giving me . . .'

The other three broke off into howls of laughter.

'You should see your face, Mary-Kate,' Virginia said, putting one of her famous tea cakes on the table as her offering.

'You're a crowd of bitches,' Mary-Kate sighed. 'I don't know why I'm friends with any of you.'

Hope hugged her. 'You know we only tease you because we love you?' she said, feeling happy for the first time in days.

'Ah sure, I know, *a stór*,' said Mary-Kate, breaking into Irish as she always did when she was touched. 'Now come on. I've booked us a table at the best restaurant in town and I've told them to have the champagne cooling for us.'

'Champagne? What are we celebrating?' asked Hope in astonishment.

'Sisterhood,' said Mary-Kate firmly. 'Or maybe it was varicose veins. I forget. Never mind, let's go.'

After the champagne they moved on to wine and Mary-Kate pointed out that they'd have to leave the car and get a taxi home when they were finished.

'I hate getting Teddy Taxi,' Delphine said as she put her knife and fork together after some incredible scallops. 'He goes so slowly. He should be driving a hearse.'

'If he hadn't been going slowly, I'd never have seen Dinky looking bedraggled on the side of the road that night,' Virginia pointed out.

'She's a little pet,' Hope said fondly. 'Toby and Millie love playing with her. Maybe I should get a dog. Something to sleep on the bed at night . . .' she trailed off miserably.

'Now, let's not get maudlin,' Mary-Kate insisted. 'Everything's going to work out fine.'

'I don't know that it is,' Hope said. 'Matt hasn't been in touch since he left, I haven't worked for the last week and I am not going back up to the hotel anyway,' she added with a shudder at the thought of meeting Christy De Lacy again. 'The only thing going into the bank account is the rent for the house in Bath – which is going straight out again for the mortgage. Without my earnings and the money Matt got for his contract work for Judds, we're broke.'

Delphine put a hand on Hope's. 'We'll help out,' she said.

Hope smiled at her. 'That's so kind of you, Delphine, but I can't ask that of you.'

'You need to get more work,' Mary-Kate insisted. 'Next week, we'll start looking. Have you told Sam?'

Hope nodded. 'She's coming for the weekend.'

'She'll cheer you up.'

'I don't know,' Hope said gloomily. 'I feel incapable of being cheered up, not to mention incapable of working ever again. I feel so useless.'

'Nonsense, work is what you need.'

'Talking of Teddy Taxi and hearse drivers,' Virginia said, adroitly changing the subject, 'I was driving along the Killarney road the other day and this big black car overtook me at about eighty and guess what? It was a hearse.'

'Without a coffin, I presume?' Hope was wide-eyed at the thought of a high-speed funeral.

'Absolutely. But he was belting along, he must have been doing ninety.'

'Can you blame him?' Delphine asked. 'Imagine always having to drive at ten miles an hour, sure it must be torture.'

'So says the next would-be driver for the Jordan team,' teased her aunt. 'Since you got the new car, you're like a maniac.'

'Would you care for dessert?' inquired the waiter.

'No,' said Delphine, with a mischievous twitch of her mouth, 'but we'd like to have the thrill of looking at the dessert menu.'

Naturally, looking wasn't enough and the sight of something described as a Chocolate Orgasm made them all order it.

'What's in it?' Mary-Kate wondered.

'If you have to ask, you'll never find out,' Virginia said sliding her fork into the mound of dark chocolate.

It was nearly three when they left to pile, giggling, into Teddy Taxi's waiting vehicle.

'Afternoon ladies,' he said nervously. This lot of mad women scared him a little. When they were leaving those strange arts and crafts nights they had, they were always roaring with laughter and acting wild. He was only waiting for the night one of them would make some manner of improper suggestion. A man didn't feel safe with such women.

Virginia, who'd been given the honour of sitting in the front, was about to close her door when a pair of long legs in cream trousers ironed to a knife-edge appeared beside it.

'Virginia, how lovely to see you.'

Kevin Burton squatted down until he was at the same level as Virginia. He was tanned from the golf course and his grey, intelligent eyes were warm in the lean, dark face.

In the back seat, the other three began to giggle like naughty schoolgirls on a day trip who'd just caught sight of their first builder's bum.

Vowing to slap them later, Virginia graciously inclined her silvery head at Kevin and said hello. She hadn't seen him since the disastrous recital. She'd deliberately stayed away from golf club functions she thought he'd be attending and had played golf only with her lady friends.

'How are you?' he asked.

'Fine,' she said. 'We really must go, Kevin. Delphine is late for an appointment.'

Delphine, who, after a glass and a half of champagne and three glasses of wine was only fit for an appointment with the couch and the TV zapper, began to giggle uncontrollably.

'May I phone you?' asked Kevin, formal as ever.

Virginia felt one of the women in the back kick the back of the passenger seat in an unmistakable 'go for it, woman!' gesture.

'Yes, of course,' she said to Kevin.

'Thank you,' he said politely, then, 'goodbye ladies,' before shutting Virginia's door for her.

'Lovely man,' said Mary-Kate innocently, before Virginia shot her a warning glance that said 'not in front of Teddy.'

When the others had been dropped off, Hope and Teddy the Taxi drove by Hunnybunnikins to pick up Millie and Toby, who'd had a wonderful day of finger painting. Hope didn't know what sort of protective garments the children wore for this but they must have been like space suits: there wasn't a spot of paint anywhere on their clothes.

'We were very careful,' Giselle said as she waved them goodbye.

'I wish you'd teach me how to be so careful,' Hope laughed. 'When we paint at home, the only things that escape being covered in paint are the hens!'

When she got home, the green light on the answering machine was flickering, a sign that someone had left a message. Barely daring to hope it might be Matt, Hope pressed the button and listened.

'It's me,' said Matt.

Hope felt her heart lift with joy.

'I know you've been looking for me. I was talking to Dan and he told me you'd rung. I didn't want to stay with him and Betsey so I've been staying in a hotel in Bath.

'I just don't know if I can talk to you at all, Hope,' he continued bleakly. 'I can't cope with what's happened and I need time to sort it out in my head. Give the children my love, will you? We'll have to talk about access, obviously, and my mobile is on now so if there's anything wrong with either of them you can reach me. But don't phone to ask me to come home because I won't.' He hung up.

Hope's sliver of joy crashed into a thousand pieces. Access? What did he mean? Surely, the only people who needed access to their children were people in the middle of murderous divorces. Was that what Matt wanted?

That was when she began to get angry. Typical Matt, he'd made a unilateral decision without giving her a chance to make her point or put her side of the story. How often had he done that in their marriage? Scores of times, thousands of times. Matt made the decisions and she followed blindly. Well, not anymore. If he wanted a divorce, he could have one. Only *she'd* file first. That'd show him.

At Kilnagoshell House, Virginia stripped off her crimson silk shirt dress, threw on a pair of rust cords and a sweater and brought Dinky out for a second walk in order to clear her head after an unheard of three glasses of wine.

'Disgraceful to be drinking in the daytime, Dinky,' she said.

Dinky danced around her mistress's feet happily, grateful to the wine for this second walk. Most days they only had one long walk: two was a canine thrill.

Virginia walked briskly along the avenue down to the road, pausing only when Dinky scampered far into the woods. She knew the little white dog would know how to follow her but Virginia loved her new friend too much to want her to rush out onto the busy Blackglen road and possibly fall under the wheels of a juggernaut. Virginia paled at the thought that her beloved dog could easily have been killed that wet night she'd been abandoned on the side of the road.

'She's such a little pet,' Virginia had told Jamie on the phone the other day. 'I don't know what I did without her, although I feel a bit ridiculous to be so crazy about a dog. You're only supposed to love people that way.'

'Don't be silly,' Jamie said warmly. 'It's good for you to have Dinky,' he said. 'We all need someone in our lives, whether it's man or beast. Anyway,' he added wickedly, 'you're not the only member of the family to love a dog. Laurence does.'

'Jamie,' remonstrated his mother, scandalized. 'That's a terrible way to speak about Barbara. You're not too old for me to give you a slap on the ear,' she said.

Jamie, secure in the knowledge that his mother had *never* ever hit any of the children, merely laughed.

'Will you slap Laurie too, then? That'd bring him to his senses.'

She was so engrossed in thinking about her future daughter-in-law that she didn't notice Kevin's car approach until he was almost beside her.

He got out of the car and petted Dinky, who responded joyfully to his touch, even going so far as to lie down and roll over so he could stroke her belly.

'Good girl, Dinky,' crooned Kevin.

Oh well, Virginia reflected, a man who loved dogs couldn't be all bad.

'I came to apologize,' Kevin said, still petting Dinky.

'For what?' asked Virginia. She was determined not to let him away with this.

'For taking you out with the Smarts and letting Glenys away with being so rude to you the whole time.'

'Rude wasn't the word,' Virginia said shortly, remembering the hurt of that evening. 'What upset me, however, was that you wouldn't stand up for me. It's hard for old friends to see a widow or widower with someone else, so I understand her behaviour somewhat, although,' Virginia's voice was cold, 'I certainly don't condone it. But you let her treat me like that. That was unforgivable. I was your guest and it's not as if we're even dating each other, so to let her assume we were was appallingly thoughtless, not to mention presumptuous.'

Kevin got up stiffly. 'I know and I'm so sorry,' he said, taking one of her hands in his.

Virginia gently slid it away. She didn't want to be impolite but she didn't feel that Kevin had earned the right to hold her hand in that lover-like way.

'Please forgive me,' he said earnestly. 'There was no excuse except for the fact that I wish we *were* dating and that, somehow, made me guilty in front of Glenys's disapproval.'

Virginia's upright bearing became marginally more upright and seeing her face tauten, Kevin swept on.

'I would dearly like to go on a date with you, Virginia,' he said, 'both because I like you so much and also, to apologize. How does dinner in my house sound to you? That way, we're not meeting in public to let the gossips get started and it'll be very relaxed. I don't mean to insult you by asking you to my home,' he added anxiously, 'there's no catch, but I am quite a good cook.'

For the first time, Virginia smiled and it lit up her lovely face. 'If there was any catch, Kevin, you would find yourself in the deepest hot water imaginable,' she laughed.

'Then it's a date? Friday night, perhaps?'

'I shall have to consult my diary,' Virginia said. In her day, no woman leaped at the offer of a date without consulting her diary. They hadn't needed *The Rules* to tell them that.

'I'll phone you tomorrow to check,' he said eagerly. 'Till then.' When he took her hand to squeeze it, Virginia didn't pull away.

'You're a disloyal little wretch to quiver so delightedly when he petted you,' Virginia told Dinky on the walk home. But then, it wasn't fair to Dinky to say that. She was obviously a good judge of character in that she adored Mary-Kate, tolerated Teddy Taxi, and hated Barbara. 'What do you think of Kevin?' Virginia asked her.

Dinky, sensing that some reaction was required, wagged her tail.

'Dinner it is, then,' her mistress said.

As Hope stood in the arrivals hall in the airport waiting for Sam, she couldn't help but think of the last time she'd been there, waiting for Matt, full of guilt and angst. She'd been so terrified that he'd be able to see that she'd been up to something, as if her guilt was written in big letters across her face.

She thought of the interviews she'd read with marriage counsellors who, when asked if guilty spouses should admit their affairs to their partners, always said no. That last day at the airport, she'd longed to tell Matt everything so that he could hug her, forgive her and tell her he understood that it had been nothing.

If only she'd done that. Then she wouldn't be standing here today waiting for her sister, who was coming to offer tea and sympathy.

'Hope!'

Sam, looking radiantly healthy, threw her arms around her sister and they clung together, Sam in the role of comforter as Hope buried her head in her sister's shoulder and allowed herself the luxury of tears.

'How are you doing?' Sam asked as they stood there, oblivious to the crowds milling around them.

'OK,' snuffled Hope. She opened her eyes to see two small boys looking curiously up at them. 'Come on, let's go.'

On the drive back to Redlion, Hope told her sister the story, the entire story in all its grisly details.

'I feel so ashamed,' she said miserably as they negotiated the bend in the road just before the village bridge. 'I wanted to tell you all of this before but I thought you'd be disgusted with me.'

'Don't be silly,' said Sam, hurt at the notion that there was anything Hope couldn't tell her. 'You're my family, you're the closest person to me in the world, how could you even dream that I'd be disgusted by you?'

'Because I'm disgusted with myself,' Hope said, tearful at Sam's kindness. Kindness was her undoing. At any kind word, even if it was only the butcher smiling hello at her in a warm manner, she longed to burst into fresh tears. 'I know that Matt was wrong not to let me explain – he never lets me explain – but I was in the wrong too. It really is my fault, no matter how I try and pretend it isn't. You, Mary-Kate, *everyone* tells me he's at fault and should come back to give our marriage a go, but if it was me, if Matt had even thought about betraying me with anyone else, I don't know if I could ever forgive him.'

She'd thought about it so much and it was true: if Matt had become really intimate with another woman, Hope knew she wouldn't have been able to bear it.

'You don't mean that,' Sam said briskly.

'But I do,' insisted Hope. 'I thought I could forgive Matt anything because I need him so much, but I couldn't forgive him that. I can understand why he's gone,' she added, her voice bitter.

Sam was nonplussed. 'You've never felt like that in the past, you were perfectly happy to allow Matt to be in control.'

'You're right,' Hope replied. 'But the most fundamental part of our marriage was that we needed each other. I can see that now. He needed me just as much as I needed him. You know what his parents are like; they treated him like a second-class citizen. What he loved about me above all was that he was everything to me and that's why our marriage worked. To his family, he was a nuisance; to me, he was my life. Now, I've just ruined all that. He's very uncompromising, he can't go back if he thinks I don't adore him. Just like I couldn't go on if I didn't think he loved me absolutely.'

She parked outside Curlew Cottage and they sat in silence.

'The way he always had to be in charge, that was his way of loving me. I didn't see it then. But I do now and it's too late. He can't go back.'

As weekends went, it wasn't a fun-filled one. Sam felt as if she was walking on eggshells because she was so scared of upsetting Hope.

She quashed her instinctive desire to talk bluntly about alimony, access and arrangements for separated couples, and did her best to provide support rather than advice. Every time Millie or Toby prattled innocently about Daddy, Sam shot an anxious look at her sister, terrified she'd see utter despair on Hope's face. Yet somehow, Hope was coping.

She hadn't fallen apart as Sam had thought she would. She hadn't run to the doctor begging for Prozac and she wasn't sinking into the gin every night. Instead, she was trying to cope in a calm, strong way.

'I owe it to the children,' she said simply.

On Sunday afternoon they had lunch in Killarney before Sam's flight. While Millie and Toby coloured in the cartoon character paper mats that the restaurant had kindly provided for all small guests, Sam took the bull by the horns.

'What's next?' she said.

'I don't know,' Hope shrugged. 'Matt was the one who left, I don't want to close the door, you know that: I love him. But I can't make him come home.'

'Would you like me to talk to him . . .' began Sam.

'No.' Hope was vehement. 'If he comes back, it's got to be because he wants to and not because he's been pushed into it.'

Sam grinned. 'When has anyone ever pushed Matt Parker into doing one single thing he didn't want to?' she asked.

Hope's eyes brimmed and Sam cursed her thoughtlessness.

'Sorry.'

'I'm not a child, you know, Sam. I have to face the truth. He's left me and it might be for good.'

'It's your worst nightmare, isn't it?' Sam asked. 'Being left, being abandoned.'

Hope looked wry. 'Yes. What does it say about me when I manage to engineer the very thing I've spent my entire life worrying about? I've always been scared Matt would leave me, like Mum and Dad left us. And what do I do? Have a fling and ruin everything.'

'You didn't ruin everything,' Sam insisted. 'And it wasn't really a fling.'

Hope didn't reply.

Before she went through to the departure lounge, Sam hugged her sister warmly. Hope, who couldn't throw her arms around Sam because Millie and Toby were holding her hands, steeled herself not to blub.

'You could come to London, you know,' Sam said. 'We could get a nice house between us and you wouldn't be alone anymore.'

'Thank you, but no,' Hope said fondly. 'That's lovely of you, darling, but this is my home now.'

Hope and the children waved energetically until Sam was out of sight.

'When is Daddy coming home?' demanded Millie, looking around as if Matt might appear from nowhere.

'Soon, Millie, soon,' said her mother brightly.

The day of Virginia's dinner date with Kevin, she thought about Bill a lot. Sometimes, it was hard to imagine that it was over two years since his death. He was still with her in so many ways, his presence a palpable part of her life. And in other ways, it was as if he'd been gone longer because so much had changed. Or perhaps it was she who had changed. Her path through the mire of bereavement had been a winding one, when she'd taken one step forward, she'd found herself taking two back. It had been slow and painful. But life had gone on and she'd learned to live with it, because there was no option. For about six months after Bill's death, she'd eaten porridge for breakfast instead of her usual muesli. Making a bowlful with a dash of honey, the way Bill had every morning of his life, had somehow made him seem closer. Like wearing his shirts.

She remembered how when Bill's six month anniversary had come up, Laurence, thinking it was the right thing to do, had gently suggested a clear-out of his father's clothes.

But Virginia wouldn't hear of it.

'If you throw his clothes out, you might as well throw me out too,' she'd said fiercely.

She'd brought all of them to Kilnagoshell and hung them in one of the spare rooms. But the lingering scent of Bill had somehow left everything. When Virginia leaned against his favourite old tweedy jacket, a thing she'd spent years trying to get him to throw out, there was no evocative scent of him. Only the smell of an old wardrobe and clothes that no longer hung on a strong, much loved male body.

She'd cried the afternoon she'd packed them all away in suit carriers. But it had been the right decision. Bill would have wanted her to move on, she was sure of it. Even if it hurt her to do it, she had to. Otherwise she might as well have been buried with him that day. She made herself walk past the porridge oats in the supermarket, determined not to be a slave to memories.

Bill's old golf club jumper still sat in her bottom drawer, though. She took it out regularly and held it close to her face, tears misting in her eyes at the memories it evoked.

Bill, laughing as he packed his clubs in the car on a Saturday morning, kissing the top of Virginia's head and promising he wouldn't spend too long at the nineteenth hole, as golf club bars the world over were affectionately known.

'You better not,' she'd tease with a glint in her eyes, 'otherwise your dinner won't be in the oven when you come home, it'll be in the dog.'

After she'd dressed that evening to go to Kevin's, she sat on the bed and wrapped her arms around the jumper, as if she were cuddling a teddy bear. Dinky, sensing her mistress's melancholy, sat in her beanbag at the foot of the bed and gazed up soulfully, her little face between her front paws.

'You think I'm mad, don't you?' Virginia addressed Dinky. Then, she kissed the jumper and put it back in the drawer carefully. 'I won't be long, pet,' she told the dog.

Kevin lived in an old farmhouse that stood back from the road on the other side of Redlion. Virginia, who had a keen eye for gardens, would have imagined the best greenery for such an old house would have been rambling roses climbing over the door, large pots spilling over with tumbling flowers beside it and herbaceous borders dominated by fragrant night-scented stock and nicotiana. Instead, there were four beds of gladioli which looked as if they'd been planted with the aid of a slide rule and a T-square. Strangely formal, it all looked out of place.

'Admiring the flowers?' said Kevin from the front door.

'Er, yes,' lied Virginia, for gladioli were the only flowers she didn't like.

'Ursula was a wonderful gardener. She planted those beds herself and I try and keep them the way she'd have wanted,' Kevin said wistfully.

Inside, the farmhouse was just as formal, with a patterned Axminster over what Virginia assumed was a wooden floor. The walls were a lively dark red Laura Ashley which clashed violently with the carpet and the pale pink couch. Heavy oil paintings with gold frames hung on the walls, while occasional tables jostled for space with sideboards and plant stands. Every available surface was covered with silver photograph frames. It was all a bit overwhelming, like a Hollywood version of a cluttered Victorian house.

But one item dominated the room: hanging over the mantel piece was an oil of a woman in a blue dress. She was in her late forties and was smiling faintly in a Mona Lisa way, short dark hair cut tightly round her face, dark eyes glittering. It had to be Ursula.

'I had it painted for her fiftieth,' Kevin said in a proud voice.

'Goodness, she doesn't look fifty,' said Virginia.

He was pleased. 'She never looked her age. She was one of life's youthful women. Even at the end, she looked much younger that she really was. Everyone remarked upon it.' Kevin's voice was tinged with sadness and he seemed lost in reverie as he gazed up at the portrait.

'Do you need a hand in the kitchen?' Virginia said brightly.

He appeared to shake himself and said: 'No, goodness, it's all under control. I hope you like lamb.'

'Love it,' said Virginia.

She'd have liked to have gone into the kitchen to chat amiably while Kevin cooked, but he obviously preferred the more formal style of entertaining and, once he'd given her the glass of water she asked for, insisted she stay in the sitting room where a wistful piece by Chopin was playing softly.

Virginia knew it was bad manners to snoop, but couldn't resist peering at some of the myriad photos around the room. They were mainly of Ursula and Kevin with some single ones of Ursula. The portrait painter had flattered her, Virginia found herself thinking, as she stared at one close-up of Ursula at a wedding. Her dark eyes were much more slitty than the painter had portrayed and her heavy jaw was more defined. Virginia looked carefully and wondered if she and the dead woman would have been friends. It might be hard to be friends with such a paragon, particularly one who was so close to nightmares like Glenys Smart. And Virginia felt slightly uncomfortable in this house, for it was clearly Ursula's home. Her mark was everywhere, from the regimented flowers outside the door to the rather hectic decor which was at least ten years old and, therefore, dated from when Ursula was alive. Even if Kevin had changed the wallpaper and the carpets, it would still be very much Ursula's domain, because of all the photos of her. It was, Virginia thought, finishing her glass of water, a shrine.

Kevin had been right: he was a good cook. The lamb was tender as poached cod and they both ate hungrily, enjoying the tiny roast potatoes and the green beans dotted with butter. They chatted about friends and acquaintances, laughing over golfing stories and telling each other tales of their previous lives. Virginia found herself being careful about mentioning Bill too often as a reaction to how often Kevin mentioned Ursula. Her name came up in every second sentence and Virginia gave herself a mental check to see if she was guilty of this too. But she didn't think so. They both drank little and by coffee, the bottle of wine still had at least one glass remaining.

'More wine?' Kevin asked, proffering the bottle.

'No thanks, I've had enough and I'm driving,' Virginia said.

He put the cork in the bottle. 'For another day,' he said wryly, 'it's all too easy to sink into grief and drink too much. I'm sure many lonely widowers turn to the bottle to get over it all. When I sit here with my memories and Chopin, I know it would finish me off totally if I drank to numb the pain.'

Virginia glanced at him curiously. 'I know it's a cliché,' she said, 'but do you not find that time does help to heal?'

Kevin looked shocked. 'No, not at all. How could it? How could I forget Ursula?' His face was etched with pain as he spoke.

'I didn't say forget her,' Virginia said softly, 'I meant learn to deal with her loss. It's been two years since Bill died and you never forget, of course not. Bill was all of my life for so long, I could as easily forget to breathe as forget him but,' she paused, searching for the right words because she didn't want to offend Kevin, 'life goes on.' She laughed, 'another cliché, I'm afraid. You have to move on, though. Ursula sounds like such a lovely, vital woman: she wouldn't have wanted you to . . .' she was about to say *bury yourself alive for nearly five years*, but she stopped in time. 'She wouldn't have wanted you to stop living.'

'You're so right.' Kevin's face lightened magically. 'She was a lovely, vital woman. I'm glad I've been able to give you a picture of what she was like.'

He put one hand on Virginia's warmly. 'You'd have loved her, you know. The two of you would have been friends.'

'I agree,' Virginia said, 'and I'm sure you and Bill would have got on like a house on fire and spent hours on the golf course. But Kevin,' she continued earnestly, 'they're both gone. We have to move on. I moved out of our old house, probably more in grief to be honest, but it gave me the chance to start again without bursting into tears every time I looked at the bathroom sink and imagined Bill standing there shaving, or seeing the grass go wild in the garden and thinking of how he'd never have let it become so out of control. Change can help, it's not betraying the person who's gone.' She paused, wondering if she should delicately say it. Yes, she should. 'You could always, for example,' she said gently, 'redecorate to change things a little. That's just one idea to move on.'

He smiled at this. 'But I did redecorate. The paper was getting worn.'

Virginia smiled too. At least the hopeless coordination was his, probably Ursula had had a more matching colour scheme.

'You wouldn't believe the trouble I had getting the same wallpaper. That pattern had been discontinued. It took me two months to track down enough to do the whole room.'

He looked so proud at this industriousness that Virginia could say nothing. Well, there was nothing to say, was there?

Perhaps it was true that widows managed life better than widowers, who were so lost without their wives that they could barely face the world. How terribly sad. Sadder even was Kevin who wanted to recreate life with Ursula, right down to the same wallpaper she'd chosen. Virginia bet that every grocery in the house was the same as Ursula had bought, from the milk right up to the brand of kitchen cleanser. And she undoubtedly had taught Kevin to cook the most marvellous lamb, always served with tiny roasted potatoes and green beans with a precise amount of butter. Virginia shivered: it was like being watched over by a ghost. After a few minutes, she took a surreptitious look at her watch: a quarter to ten, late enough to leave without being rude.

'That was a lovely meal,' she said kindly.

'I'm glad you liked it. We'll have to do it again,' he said, smiling at her fondly. 'Maybe we should scandalize the whole town by going out for a meal the next time.'

Virginia nodded. 'They can hardly be scandalized by two old friends going out for dinner, now can they?' she said, deliberately misunderstanding.

She got to her feet and didn't ask if she could help Kevin tidy up. He'd probably refuse and besides, she had had enough of Ursula for the evening.

'Thank you, Kevin.'

She didn't wait for him to get her jacket, but went to the hall and took it off the peg, slipping it on quickly.

'Let me,' said Kevin, trying to help her.

'I'm very busy next week,' she said. 'I've several games of golf lined up. So perhaps the week after, we might play in a fourball.' Four people playing together meant less time for her and Kevin to be alone.

'Well, yes, of course if you're busy . . .' Kevin said.

She pecked him on the cheek and had the front door open in a flash.

'Byee,' she said gaily, rushing past the lurid pink gladioli to her car.

Safe in the car, she could wave at him until she was out the gate and able to relax. So much for a bit of sedate dating. The merry widow indeed.

Kevin had done his best to woo her, but it would never be a proper relationship. He liked Virginia with his mind but his heart was entirely reserved for Ursula. Which was a pity.

'I hope you're having some luck in heaven with a nice widow angel, Bill darling,' Virginia said as she drove home, 'because down here, I'm not having any romantic luck at all. Still,' she smiled, 'I've got the girls, so don't worry about me.'

# CHAPTER TWENTY-FIVE

On the morning of her fortieth birthday, Sam woke at dawn and sang the first few bars of 'Happy Birthday' to herself.

'This is a sure sign of insanity,' she told her reflection in the bathroom mirror, 'talking to yourself like this. You are now forty and mad. Congratulations.'

She stood under the shower and thought that maybe she should get a cat. The company would be nice, she liked animals, and it would give her an excuse for talking out loud when she was alone in the apartment. But then, perhaps people would start seeing her as 'a woman with a cat', which was shorthand for 'woman with a cat and no man'. Before forty, it was possible to have a cat and still be considered a fun, single woman who liked animals. After forty, she'd have to start styling her hair into a tight, spinsterish knot like Aunt Ruth's, take up bridge and become testy with shop assistants. She'd be so high up on the shelf, someone would need a step ladder to take her down.

As she made her face up, she thought of the statistics about single women. In the next thirty years, forty, or was it thirty per cent of women would live on their own. There was absolutely nothing wrong with living on your own, Sam knew. She liked it, or at least she had quite liked it. What was hurting now was the fact that all the other successful singles she knew were now coupling up like ticket holders for Noah's Ark. It was as if, after years of claiming they were happy on their own, they were now saying *actually, we were lying all along. We want love and another pair of slippers in front of the fire.* Sam felt more than a bit betrayed. Or did she feel lonely? She was afraid to be brutally honest with herself and ask which it was.

She checked the post but there was nothing except for an electricity bill. Sam refused to feel miserable because there was no birthday card from Morgan.

The radio blared out 'Walking On Sunshine' as she dressed in a rose coloured silk cashmere sweater with a rounded neck and a long, lean cream linen skirt suit. It was the sort of thing she would never have worn to the office before, it was more a summer wedding outfit, but she wanted to look feminine and pretty today, of all days. She had her fresh fruit for breakfast, took a bio yoghurt out of the fridge for eating later in the office, and rushed out of the house to the hairdressers.

'Can I have a manicure while I'm getting my blowdry?' she asked the receptionist.

'Of course Ms Smith,' said the receptionist in surprise. Ms Smith never had anything done but a speedy blowdry in the mornings.

'Going anywhere special tonight?' asked the manicurist as she settled down to work.

The stylist blowdrying Sam's hair raised her eyebrows in alarm. Sam Smith was not your average chatty client. She often read business reports while her hair was being dried or else she flicked through the newspaper, never glossy magazines.

To be honest, the stylist was a teeny bit intimidated by Sam who seemed to be the epitome of the successful, wealthy career woman: a woman with no time for small talk. But to her astonishment, Sam replied.

'No, more's the pity,' she said. 'I wish I was going somewhere. I'm just going home after work and if there's a good film on telly, that'll be the extent of the excitement.'

'I know what you mean, you're just too tired after work aren't you,' the manicurist sighed. 'I'm like that too. I have all these great plans and when I get home, I just collapse in front of the box. Now, do you want clear polish, French manicure or a colour?'

Sam considered this. 'Let's go for dusky pink, I never wear colours but, what the heck, it's my birthday.' As soon as she'd said it, she was sorry.

'Oh, happy birthday,' chorused the manicurist and the stylist.

Both women knew better than to ask her age.

'And you're not doing anything tonight?' the manicurist said sympathetically. 'I bet you've plans for the weekend, though, haven't you?'

Sam smiled weakly. 'Yes, of course.'

Hope was on the phone as soon as Sam left the salon and turned her mobile on.

'I missed you at home,' Hope said. 'You must have left early. Happy birthday, Sam love. Oh, I wish I was there with you. It's not right to have your fortieth birthday on your own.'

Sam's eyes filled up.

'I wish you were here too,' she said, fishing a tissue out of her coat pocket. 'Or better still, that I was there with you. Still,' she tried to sound bright, 'I'm going to have a lovely lunch with Jay.' Normally, she and Jay had dinner on their birthdays but this time, Jay appeared to have forgotten it was a special one, and anyway, she was permanently glued to Greg, so her dinnertimes were all tied up with him.

'Nothing tonight?' Hope sounded upset at the thought.

'I'm too tired to go out in the evenings,' Sam lied. 'I'm trying to get my energy back by catching up on sleep. Any word from Matt?' she asked.

'He's phoned every night this week to talk to the children,' Hope replied, 'although he can barely bear to speak to me when I answer the phone. He was in a hotel in Bath but he's moved into a rented apartment, which makes it sound as if he intends to stay. Millie keeps asking when he's coming home again. It breaks my heart.'

Sam winced at the thought of Millie's earnest little face as she asked after her daddy. Poor Hope. It was selfish to be feeling depressed about being forty when Hope was coping with single parenthood.

When they'd said goodbye, Sam walked along, enjoying the sun and the sensation of her silky hair flopping freshly washed on her shoulders. A girl with long dark blonde hair walked out of a shop onto the footpath ahead of Sam, carrying packages and bags. Her hair was fresh and bouncy too, but she looked no more than twenty-something in pedal pusher denims that tapered down to slim brown ankles. The girl's undulating walk took her past two suited guys talking animatedly beside a BMW. Both heads turned to watch her and then their eyes flicked over Sam with interest. Sam grinned. There was still something enjoyable about turning men's heads, even if you half despised them for turning.

In the office, a huge bouquet of flowers from Hope awaited her. Only her sister seemed to know that the stern and permanently in control Ms Smith adored the most romantic flowers going: Hope's birthday bouquet to her was a riot of pink Vendella roses, some full blooms, some exquisite little buds with tightly curled petals, all nestled in rich dark greenery that set off the luscious pink to perfection. Thrilled with her first, and so far only birthday gift, Sam hid the flowers behind a filing cabinet, not wanting anyone to see and ask her what she'd got them for. But the office network hadn't missed the delivery of pink roses to Ms Sam Smith.

Speculation on what they were for and who they were from was rife on the fifth floor all morning.

'A lover, it must be,' said the fifth floor receptionist.

'A married lover,' remarked the publicity assistant, who knew about such things.

'She probably sent them to herself,' said Izzy from A & R spitefully.

At eleven, Catrina phoned.

'Happy birthday Sam,' she said cheerfully. 'Had any nice pressies yet?'

'A few,' Sam said, not wanting to sound like Billy No Mates.

'Did you get ours yet?' inquired Catrina.

'No, sorry.'

'Oh, Hugh posted it several days ago. I'm sure it'll be there tomorrow. Or when you get home,' Catrina said. 'It's not very thrilling, I'm afraid. What are you up to tonight? Out for a mad party with your trendy record company pals, I suppose?'

Sam wondered if Catrina was taking any particular mind-altering drugs to help with her pregnancy. Sam had never been part of the trendy record company scene. Her friends were the gang. Or, at least, they *had* been.

'Well, there's so much on at the moment,' Sam said lightly. 'There's a party in the Sanderson tonight but I'm getting sick of drinking Cosmopolitans.' There, that sounded suitably hip and thrilling.

'Lucky you,' groaned Catrina. 'I haven't had a drink in so long, if I so much as smelled a cocktail, I'd pass out.'

There followed a lengthy discussion of Catrina's pregnancy. At nearly eight months pregnant, she was going through an exhausted phase where by the time she'd got into work in the morning, all she wanted to do was go back home to bed. Typically, being Catrina, she was determined to work practically up until her due date . . .

'You need to rest, Catrina,' Sam insisted. 'Stop trying to do everything and be superwoman. It's important for the baby. Why don't you and Hugh take a long weekend away somewhere nice? Forget about work for a bit.'

'You're right,' Catrina said, sounding like herself for the first time in the conversation. 'Everybody else is telling me I'm great for being so active and that I shouldn't stop doing all the normal things I do.'

'That's only if you feel like doing all the normal things,' Sam pointed out. 'You're only weeks away from giving birth, so be gentle with yourself.'

They said goodbye, with Catrina promising to phone Sam the following week.

Almost immediately, the phone rang again. It was Jay crying off lunch.

'I feel so terrible,' she said, 'doing this to you on your birthday but something's come up.'

Jay didn't say what that something was. In Sam's experience, people with genuine excuses gave them. When the excuse was *something* having come up, it was a fake.

The something was probably Greg at a loose end and begging Jay to get out of lunch with her dull, career-obsessed girlfriend. Sam hated women who let transitory men come between them and their friends. Men were just for Christmas; women friends were for ever. Hope's Macramé Club girlfriends would never dump her for a guy, Sam thought darkly.

'That's OK, Jay,' she coolly. 'I understand. Give me a ring next time you have a gap in your diary.'

'Oh Sam,' pleaded Jay. 'Don't be cross, please. You'll understand, I promise.'

Sam ground her pen so firmly into the yellow post-it pad on her desk that she made a deep dent in it. People were promising her a lot of things lately. She wanted to say that Jay had promised they'd have a lovely birthday lunch but she didn't.

'Just call me, Jay. I'm busy over the weekend.' That was a lie for a start. 'Maybe we could meet up next week.'

Sam could remember a time when she and Jay met up every second day.

'Bye Sam.' Jay sounded terribly subdued. 'And happy birth-day.'

'Yeah, thanks.'

Sam threw the defaced post-it pad in the bin. What a great day this was turning out to be.

There she was on her fortieth birthday and none of her close friends seemed to have remembered. Those that had, all had better things to do than spend the day with her.

At half twelve, Sam marched out of the building and went to Harvey Nichols, where she decided to investigate if retail therapy really did work. She started the investigation in the perfume department where she bought herself a giant bottle of Chanel No 5 and matching body lotion. If nobody else was going to buy her a birthday present, she might as well buy her own. Next stop was the lingerie section where she splashed out on two sets of exquisite La Perla underwear. Then she marched into the designer rooms and in twenty minutes flat bought a Richard Tyler black suit with a jacket so fitted it looked as if it had been sewn onto her, two delicious Fendi sweaters, and finally a wildly sexy iridescent Gucci dress that looked as if it was designed to fall off her body with one practised tug. The sort of tug that Morgan Benson was a specialist in, she thought gloomily as she signed the credit card slip. Why was she even buying this stuff? Who'd get to see the lilac uplift bra and where could she ever go where anyone would want to tug her dress off?

There were plenty of music award ceremonies where babes in Gucci dresses looked right at home but she was one of the music industry types who normally arrived in wall-to-wall Prada suits. Everyone would choke on their straight-up Stolis if she turned up in a sexy dress. Sex was for artistes. Suits wore suits.

Still, she'd be the best dressed bachelorette for miles around. She'd bought so much black that she'd better get a black cat so then the hairs wouldn't show up quite so much.

Her concession to lunch was a takeaway bagel with cottage cheese and slivers of avocado for protein.

It was just after two when she got into the lift at the office, big, expensive Harvey Nichols bags dangling. Retail therapy worked but only momentarily, she concluded. She'd felt good when she was trying everything on but now that she'd bought it all, she just felt as bad as ever. And with a diminished bank balance.

The lift doors were about to close when Steve Parris appeared at the gap and slammed the button. The doors, knowing what was good for them, opened obediently, and let him in.

Today, he was doing his laid-back look: white T-shirt, jeans, leather jacket. All designer, Sam knew. Steve was too paranoid about being five foot six and skinny to wear anything that didn't have a label hanging off it. The Titus staff often speculated that if Steve had been born taller, he'd have been much nicer on account of not having a chip on his shoulder about his height. Privately, Sam thought Steve was extremely well balanced seeing as how he had chips on both shoulders.

'Hiya Sam. Been shopping?' Steve said, small dark eyes whizzing over her. Sam knew that Steve could read a profit and loss account in three seconds. It was always disconcerting when he did the same with a person.

'Yes,' she said in her calm office voice, resisting the impulse to say no, she just liked carrying department store bags around with her.

'Anything nice?'

Sam blinked. This was very un-Steve-like behaviour. He never talked about anything but work.

'Er . . . a few things.'

'Anything drop-dead gorgeous?' he inquired chirpily.

Sam looked at him curiously. Mischief overcame politeness. 'Yes, a dress that's so hot, it comes with a Government health warning,' she breathed, then instantly regretted it.

God help her, the only fun she got these days was trying to shock the boss.

But he didn't look shocked. 'Great.' Steve's eyes, cold chips of ice which normally only ever lit up when the number one album and single were both Titus acts, gleamed with pleasure. 'Listen Sam, you know we've got the Lemon Awards coming up.' Of course Sam knew. Everybody in the industry with two brains cells did. These high-profile awards were a status symbol for both the artists and their record companies and Titus had several bands up for big awards this time round. Sam's biggest current problem was trying to limit the number of staff members getting the highly expensive and much-sought-after tickets.

'Well, I've got some of the Americans coming over for it – big players,' Steve waggled his eyebrows knowingly. 'You're going, obviously.'

'Obviously,' she said.

'Well, I'd like it if you could sit at my table.'

Sam looked at him warily. She had her own table organized for the LBGK label.

'And I'm having a very exclusive party afterwards in Shiva. I'd like you to come with me.' He touched her shoulder meaningfully. 'It would mean a lot to me.'

It had been a long time since Sam had been speechless. Was he hitting on her? Was Steve Megalomaniac Parris, the man with an Excel spreadsheet instead of a heart, actually chatting her up? No, he couldn't be.

'Of course I'll come, Steve,' Sam said carefully. 'I can hardly miss the Lemons, can I?'

Steve's eyes lit up.

'Thanks, Sam. It's important. And,' he smirked, 'wear the government health warning dress, won't you? It sounds incredible.'

The lift pinged at Sam's floor and she walked out in a daze.

Shit, shit, shit. He *had* been hitting on her. Why else would he want her to wear a drop-dead gorgeous dress? If only she hadn't been such a smart ass, she'd have been able to subtly steer him clear of being flirtatious. But she'd walked right into it.

Hoist by her own sarcastic petard.

She walked to her office, her mind racing. Apart from the obvious, that she didn't have the remotest interest in Steve, there was another reason for not getting romantically involved with him: the fact that inter-company dating was the worst career move since Marie Antoinette mentioned the possibility of letting the peasants eat cake.

At best, it would be deeply embarrassing if Steve actually thought anything was going to come from this date. At worst, he'd go ballistic when she slapped him down. And even worse, how bad could this look for her career in general? Would the all-powerful American people see Steve smiling at her and assume that here was woman who'd made it up the career ladder by lying back and thinking of the Empire? Sam cringed at the thought of it all.

Somehow, between now and the Lemon Awards (ten days away), Sam had to think of a way out of this disaster.

She managed to work through the rest of the afternoon, juggling meetings, phone calls and important e-mails without betraying for a moment that she was both miserable and frantic. She left the office at seven and got a taxi home, which was her penultimate birthday treat. The final one would be opening and drinking an entire bottle of wine before having a bath and smothering the body nobody ever saw in Chanel No 5 body lotion. The solace of the lonely career woman on her birthday.

She got home and saw that her answering machine light was lit up with four messages. But Sam only heard the first one, a terse-sounding Catrina: 'Sam, I know it's short notice, but Jay has just turned up and she's a bit upset. I don't suppose you could drop over?'

Even if Catrina's words were unemotional, Sam was convinced something serious must have happened. Some disaster to do with

Greg, Sam thought, forgetting that she'd been furious with Jay earlier in the day. Poor Jay. She and Greg must have split up, which was awful, because Jay was clearly smitten.

Sam grabbed her handbag and rushed out. It was impossible to find a taxi at this hour of the evening in such a residential street. Then she spotted Morgan all dressed up and getting into his battered jeep. It was a filthy vehicle and he never washed it but at that moment, it looked as beautiful to Sam as a Porsche Carrera.

'Morgan,' she yelled. 'Could I ask you a huge favour? Could you give me a lift? It's only ten minutes away by car and I'll never get a taxi at this hour?'

'Hop in.'

'It's my friend Jay,' explained Sam when she'd given him directions. 'Something's happened and she needs me. I'm really sorry to ask you but it must be serious or Catrina would never have rung.'

'No problem,' Morgan said. 'I hope it's nothing bad, she's a nice girl.'

'I hope so too.' Sam bit her lip with anxiety. 'Poor Jay has gone through hell with men, I hope Greg hasn't dumped her.'

'They looked totally in love when I met them at your dinner party; it's probably just a row.' He gave her hand a comforting squeeze.

The jeep rattled through London's streets with Morgan whizzing down back roads and sneaky short cuts until they finally pulled up outside Hugh and Catrina's house nine minutes later.

Sam leaped out almost before Morgan had put the handbrake on.

'I owe you,' she said as, long dark blonde hair flying, she rushed up the path.

Catrina opened the door looking calm and unflustered.

'What's wrong, where is she?' demanded Sam. 'Is it Greg? He didn't finish with her, did he?'

'You talk to her,' Catrina said. 'She's in the living room.'

Sam rushed into the room.

'Surprise!' chorused the group of people standing under the big Happy 40th Birthday Sam banner. There was Hugh, Jay, Adam and Greg, along with Sally and Danny, whom she hadn't seen in ages; all the gang smiling and raising their glasses at her.

Reeling with shock, Sam stepped back and collided with Morgan, who was standing behind her with an enormous grin on his face.

'I hope I didn't scare you,' Catrina said, rushing forward to embrace Sam. 'We couldn't think of any other way to get you here without making you suspicious and Jay came up with this idea. She just *knew* what conclusion you'd jump to.'

'Happy birthday,' squealed Jay, flinging her arms around both Catrina and Sam.

'As if I'd miss seeing you on your birthday,' she laughed. 'I had to cancel lunch today because the party was only half-organized. I thought we'd never get it all sorted. We've been getting ready for two weeks now and you've no idea the trouble we had setting it up without you guessing,' she added delightedly.

Sam thought of how cross she'd been with poor Jay earlier and how angry she'd felt because she'd assumed all her old friends had abandoned her. Emotion overcame her and she burst into tears.

'Don't cry,' said Hugh, adding his birthday kiss.

'Oh!' Sam sobbed.

'It's Sam's party and she can cry if she wants to,' paraphrased Greg, handing her a glass of champagne and planting a chaste kiss on her forehead. 'I'm just devastated that you'd believe I was a total bastard and had dumped my darling Jay!'

Everyone queued up to hug and kiss her.

'You're all so good to me,' Sam sobbed, looking at the balloons, the banner and the coffee table covered with gorgeously wrapped presents.

'You're our friend,' Hugh said affectionately. 'What did you expect, you big silly? You're not forty every day.'

After her second glass of champagne, Sam's tears had dried up and she was sitting on the big squashy armchair opening presents. Catrina sat on one the arm of the chair and Jay sat on the other one. Hugh was circulating with more drink, people were chatting and laughing, and Greg was helping Morgan to hand round plates of delicious nibbles.

'I love tapas,' sighed Jay as she accepted more goodies from Greg.

'Morgan told us you were on a health food kick but he said you'd still eat normal food.'

'Morgan was in on it all along?' Sam said, amazed.

'From the start. He and Catrina organized everything,' Jay said simply. 'I didn't do that much until today when Catrina had to work and I had to stay here and wait for the caterers, but Morgan chose the food in the first place and when Catrina and I worked out how to get you here, Morgan said he'd be ready with the jeep. I think he feels guilty that he was driving you, knowing there was nothing wrong and that you were upset. But he was the one who said that the ruse would certainly work because you were such a loyal person that if one of us needed you, you'd come immediately, no questions asked.'

'Ooh.' Sam felt the tears welling up again. Morgan thought she was a good loyal person, how lovely. And she wasn't, really. She'd been awful to Jay on the phone. She wasn't worthy of anyone thinking she was good and loyal . . .

'You can't cry for your whole birthday party,' Morgan said soothingly, appearing in front of her with a bottle.

'I can!' wailed Sam, feeling guilty.

'Open your presents, darling,' he said as gently as if he was talking to a child.

Sam sniffled. ' 'kay.'

She laughed at the furry hot water bottle cover in lurid leopardskin and sighed with pleasure over Catrina and Hugh's gift: a beautiful watercolour painting of an orchid.

Jay's present was an exquisite sculpture of an elephant, carved out of some exotic dark wood, while Greg gave her a wonderfully planted window box.

'It's full of treasures that will come up over the next few weeks,' he promised.

There was a gift wrapped bottle of her favourite Rioja, perfume, book tokens and pretty silver filigree earrings.

'Thank you all so much,' cried Sam, touched beyond words. She stared at her friends and they smiled back at her.

'I wasn't sure what to get you,' Morgan said. 'I did think of a few things but I mean, what would you do with a twenty-six-year-old Californian surfer . . .'

Everyone laughed.

'She'd think of something,' Hugh roared. 'Our Sammie is very inventive.'

'But,' Morgan continued, 'I thought of the one thing you'd love. I wasn't sure if it would be a good present, because they say you should never give things like this.'

Sam goggled at him. What on earth was he talking about and why was he so unaccountably nervous?

'If you don't want them, the lady will take them back, and don't worry about when you're away, because I'll look after them then.' He handed her a big cardboard box. Sam sat it on her knees and looked inside. There, wriggling and mewing furiously were two kittens, one marmalade and one tabby. Both looked insanely cross to be stuck in a box when they could be out testing their baby claws on the furniture.

'Oh,' she breathed, picking them up and cuddling them against her, 'they're beautiful. I adore them. It's a wonderful present.' And suddenly she laughed uproariously. 'Talk about ironic,' she added. 'I've become a lady with two cats!'

Her laughter was infectious but nobody was totally sure what she was talking about.

'Do you really want them?' Morgan's face was more anxious than she'd ever seen it before. 'I know animals aren't meant to be given as gifts,' he said, 'and if you change your mind, I'll understand. I thought that two would be company for each other when you're not at home and any time you're away on business, I'll look after them, I give you my word. I mean . . .'

'Stop,' she said, handing him the wriggling ball of marmalade fur. 'My aunt had cats and I know how to look after them. What's more, I love the idea of having cats.' She held the tabby up and kissed its pink nose. 'I've been thinking about getting one and these two are so beautiful. Aren't you, babies?'

The tabby nuzzled against her shoulder and began to purr loudly.

'Jay tells me you helped organize the party?' Sam said.

Morgan's kitten's claws were stuck in his white shirt as she tried to mountaineer up his chest. It took him a while to unhook her.

'Girls love getting their claws into you,' Sam teased gently.

Morgan smiled. 'I have a card for you too,' he said, fishing in his inside pocket.

He handed it to her and took the tabby kitten so she could open the envelope.

It was a simple card: a romantic oil painting with a frilly-dressed heroine sitting on a swing. Inside, there was Morgan's scrawl: *Happy Birthday Friend, to an exciting new year, I hope. Love Morgan.*

Jolted by how touched she felt at both his present and his tender card, Sam had to joke.

'Is this recyclable?' she demanded.

'Of course,' Morgan said. 'No trees were harmed to make it.'

Sam felt the corners of her mouth twitch upwards.

'Except four baby shrubs were battered to death to make the envelope. Only kidding,' he laughed. 'I like you all New Agey. It suits you.'

'Better than being a career bitch?' she said, her eyes hard for a second.

'Calm down,' he said gently. 'Conversation is not a contact sport.'

She grinned. He could always do that to her: defuse the situation until it was useless to get all hot and bothered.

'I liked you *before* you were New Agey, remember? Ouch.' The marmalade kitten had scratched his hand. 'Did your mummy tell you to do that? Thank Christ I didn't get tiger cubs instead.'

The kittens were adored by all and were soon flaked out in their box, sleeping off a bowl of milk and more exercise than they'd ever had in their short lives.

She enjoyed the party more than she'd enjoyed one for years. The reason was simple: everywhere she went, Morgan seemed to end up there too. It was as if they were a couple and no matter how far apart they were, some hidden magnetic force drew them back together again to exchange a joke or a few words.

'Are the kittens all right?' Morgan asked her as they met in the dining room.

'Peaceful and dreaming happily,' she replied, touching his arm softly. 'We'll have to think up names tomorrow.'

The tabby kitten had a sweet, trusting face, while the marmalade one was autocratic, with a disdainful sweep to her tail.

'She's very orange,' Morgan said the next day, examining her on the floor in Sam's apartment. 'We could call her Orange.' The kitten swiped him with a paw.

'She's far too classy for Orange,' Sam said. 'Anyway, she's apricoty not orange.'

'Apricot?' said Morgan. 'You could call her Apricot. I can just see you hanging your head out the window at night yelling "Apricot! Your dinner's poured out!" at the top of your voice.'

Sam grinned, busily making tea.

'Or maybe Marmalade?' he suggested.

'Too long,' Sam said. 'And it's not something you can shorten.'

'How about Spike,' said Morgan. 'She's definitely spiky.'

Sam didn't look convinced. 'It's a boy's name.'

'It suits her,' protested Morgan. He peered deep into the kitten's clear amber eyes. 'Spike. You like that name, don't you pet?'

Spike made her very distinctive husky mewing noise.

'She does!' crowed Morgan. 'Spike. Now you've got to name the other one.'

'She's a Tabitha,' Sam said fondly, abandoning the tea-making to cradle the sweet tabby kitten.

'Tabitha and Spike. What could be simpler.' Morgan looked delighted with himself. 'Are you cooking tonight or shall I? What do you fancy eating?'

Sam looked at him speculatively. She knew what she fancied and it wasn't eating. But Morgan didn't appear to feel the same. He liked her, she knew that for sure. Why else would he go to so much bother for her birthday? But when was he ever going to make a move?

# CHAPTER TWENTY-SIX

It took Sam ages to leave for her first yoga class a few days later. It was her own fault for leaving the leggings on the end of her bed where Spike could turn them into fringe-bottomed, eyelet-holed trousers after an hour's solid ripping. Spike was fatally drawn to clothes. She liked nothing better than to shred tights or tear great big holes in T-shirts.

All the towels in the apartment now sported big long loops where Spike had been scratching playfully and then pulled. Sometimes she got stuck and squealed piteously until Sam arrived to free her. Sam suspected that if she wasn't freed, she merely bit her way out, which accounted for the tiny holes near some of the biggest loops.

Tabitha was her sister's devoted slave and looked up to her. Sam hoped the marmalade terror wasn't going to teach Tabitha any naughty tricks.

'I can't wear these,' Sam said, holding up the leggings that had been in pristine condition a mere hour previously. 'Spike, you are a holy terror. I'll have to find something else now.'

Spike sat on the floor and continued grooming herself, utterly unconcerned. Tabitha, meanwhile, peered meekly from under the computer desk.

'Why didn't you come and tell me what your naughty big sister was up to?' Sam asked Tabitha, picking her up and cuddling her. Tabitha begged forgiveness by rubbing her tiny face against Sam's cheek.

'Oh you are a little pet, aren't you?' Sam said.

It amazed her how easily she'd got used to having the kittens around and how much a part of her life they now were after only a few days. They leaped onto the bed in the mornings, demanding love and breakfast. Sam hadn't been letting them out of the apartment because they were still too young. Until they'd had all their injections from the vet, they had to use their litter tray and content themselves with looking at the outdoors.

When she came home from work, they were thrilled, weaving excitedly around her ankles and purring loudly. Tabitha's favourite position was on the windowsill watching the world go by and gazing with huge, astonished eyes at the two robins who spent their lives in the birch tree outside the window. Spike's favourite position was wherever she could do most damage. No curtain was safe from her destructive, naughty paws and she was quite capable of leaping onto the coffee table and dipping one exploratory paw into whatever Sam was eating to see if she liked it.

'Stop it,' Sam would yell, making Tabitha whisk off under the sofa in terror, while Spike would blithely lick her paw clean as if she hadn't a care in the world and as if she had every right to be sitting on the table.

'I'm going to be late thanks to you, Spike,' Sam said, rifling through her drawers for something to wear.

The phone broke her concentration. It was Hope.

'I can't stop to talk,' Sam said apologetically, hating to not have time to talk to her sister who was, after all, going through so much. 'I'm late for my yoga class and bloody Spike has ruined my leggings.'

She was thrilled when Hope giggled. 'I'm sorry,' Hope said, sounding a lot more cheerful than she had for ages, 'but there's a certain sick humour in that. I have Millie laying waste to my wardrobe and you have Spike doing the same.'

'They should get a flat together,' Sam remarked. 'Can I call you back later?'

'Sure.'

'How was the yoga?' Hope asked that evening when Sam rang back.

'Marvellous,' replied Sam from her prone position on the couch. She felt absolutely wonderful, calm and serene as if she'd had a glass of wine but without the accompanying lack of sobriety. 'I feel as if I've just been in a flotation tank for an hour, it's incredible. And you have to try it, Hope. It would be so good for you.'

'Are you implying that I need relaxing?' asked Hope wryly.

'Well, you could probably do with a few months in a flotation tank,' Sam pointed out. 'And this is cheaper. I did get a book but you have to have lessons I think. There's no way I'd have figured out the breathing without it.'

'Oh, you mean like giving-birth-type of breathing?' Hope asked.

'Haven't a clue. But I did have to get into some weird positions today that made me *look* as if I was giving birth, so maybe that's the link. How are you, anyway?'

She could almost hear Hope grimacing. 'Okay, I suppose,' Hope said slowly. 'I still haven't made any huge, life changing decisions yet, which is just as well because everyone is telling me not to do anything but to "sit tight". I wish I knew what that meant.'

'It's what people say when they don't know what to say,' Sam said wisely. 'Nobody wants to offer any sort of opinion because it's only been a bit over two weeks and hopefully, it will all work out.'

'Two weeks and five days,' Hope interrupted.

'Whatever. Everyone's scared to give you proper advice because if they tell you it's good riddance and you and Matt subsequently make it up, they'll feel embarrassed forever. Likewise if they tell you to throw yourself on his mercy and you don't, then they'll feel like an even bigger idiot for having read the situation wrongly.'

'And what's your advice?'

Sam paused. In the period since Matt's departure, she'd wondered exactly what her sister should do. Her notion of Hope's reaction to Matt's leaving had been wrong. Sam imagined Hope would sob helplessly and do anything to get him back. But she'd been wrong. Instead, Hope had squared her shoulders and got on with life. During the weekend Sam had spent in Redlion, she'd been astonished to see her sister cope so well. But was it merely because she thought the separation was a short-term thing? If Matt filed for a divorce, how would she cope then?

'I don't have any advice, Hope,' she said candidly. 'I'm hardly an expert on relationships. Look, what do *you* want?'

'You know what I want. I want Matt to come back home but he won't even talk to me on the phone. He just says he wants to speak to the children and that he doesn't want to talk to me.'

It did not sound good, Sam decided. 'He's got to come to terms with it, I suppose,' she said.

'I know,' Hope said dismally. 'He won't let me explain anything. The only explanation he got was my frantic one the night he left, which was hardly coherent. I'd love the chance to say that I was wrong but that I adore him, that it was a mistake born out of stupidity and nothing else. If I'd been thinking, I'd never even have looked at Christy. But then,' Hope sounded bitter, 'thinking rationally has never been my strong point.'

'Shall I speak to Matt?' Sam asked tentatively.

'No.' Hope was firm. 'I want him to come back because he wants to, not because other people have made him do it. Maybe that's what "sitting tight" is. People do say the stupidest things.'

Sam attempted to cheer her up: 'Give it a month and I know exactly what people will be saying to you, and it'll have nothing to do with sitting tight. They'll be inviting you to dinner parties where they've got a spare man lined up for you. There'll be men crawling out of the woodwork for you, divorced husbands, men who've never had girlfriends, men who live with their mothers and don't buy their own underpants, you wait and see.'

'I hope not. I've had enough of men to last me for the rest of my life,' Hope said vehemently.

'They will, I promise,' her sister said. 'You never know,' she added, 'you might even find some absolute hunk.'

'I tried that,' Hope said drily, 'and look where it got me. Anyway, enough misery. How about you?'

'Not bad,' sighed Sam. 'I'm trying to find out why the hell the men I like refuse to make a move on me and men I wouldn't fancy if they were the last human beings on earth think I'm God's gift.' This last was inspired by Steve who had smiled goofily at her twice in the past two days. Morgan, on the other hand, appeared determined to keep their relationship strictly platonic.

'It's an anti-magnetic thing,' Hope offered.

'Aunty who?'

'Anti-magnetic. Some women have such magnetism they make men drop like flies at their feet. Some don't. You and I have obviously turned into the don't variety.'

'A cheerful thought,' Sam said.

'Well, we can turn mad and eccentric and never have to worry about anybody stealing all the duvet in the middle of the night again,' Hope said.

'I never *have* had to worry about that,' Sam pointed out. 'So, what have you been up to?'

On the other end of the phone, Hope thought about telling the truth. But she couldn't.

'Oh, you know, looking after small children, cleaning up hen shit and Mary-Kate's found me a job attempting to organize the Redlion Tourist Office which, apparently, hasn't been the same since the co-ordinator left last year to visit an ashram and never came back.'

'Busy, huh?' said Sam.

'Yes,' sighed Hope.

When she'd hung up, Hope went upstairs to check on the children, then came down and made herself a cup of camomile tea. Mary-Kate, who was a firm believer in medicine's advances in anti-depressants, had wanted Hope to see Dr McKevitt for a check-up. But Hope, knowing that she wasn't allowed anything on account of her pregnancy, said she'd stick to the odd glass of wine (which was a lie as she couldn't even have that) and camomile tea to help her sleep.

The tea made, she investigated the television guide to see what she could watch. This was her evening routine now; or at least, it had become her routine since the day she was tidying the bathroom and came upon a packet of tampons she hadn't used for at least two months. Only the anxiety of the past few weeks meant she had missed the unavoidable signs of pregnancy: feeling nauseous and a strange metallic taste in her mouth. She'd had exactly the same symptoms with Toby and Millie.

It was no little source of ironic amusement to her that she must have become pregnant on that fateful night in Kinsale when Matt had thought she'd wanted another baby; a night when she'd been consumed by guilt over her flirtation with Christy.

In the midst of all the shock, Hope knew one thing for certain: she wanted this new baby, and she didn't care how hard it would be to bring him or her up without a father.

She still felt devastated at the idea that her marriage was over. The thought of never laughing with Matt again, of not feeling his arms protectively around her, those thoughts were agony. But there was no point in dwelling on her misery. She had a duty to protect her children. Through her hubris, she'd already ruined their parents' marriage, now she had to stop feeling sorry for herself and take care of them properly. All three of them.

'I need to see the children, Hope. I'm coming to Ireland for the weekend and I'm going to stay in Killarney.'

Matt's voice was so cold and distant that Hope had to bite her lip to stop her voice shaking.

'That's fine,' she said bravely. She'd been dressing Millie for bed when he'd phoned and had prepared to hand the phone straight over to her daughter when Matt had said he wanted to speak to Hope.

'Yes?' she'd said eagerly, ever hopeful that he wanted a reunion, that everything was going to be fine.

'I'll phone you when I've booked a hotel and you can drop the children off on Saturday morning. I'm sure you won't mind them staying with me that night. It'll give you a chance to have some fun.' The bitter way he said the word 'fun' made it apparent that her husband thought she was still having fun with Christy De Lacy.

'You can have the kids on Saturday night,' Hope said. 'We should discuss what we're going to tell them.'

Matt had no bitter remark about that. 'I suppose we should,' he said heavily.

'I know they're small, but they know something's wrong and I haven't known what to say,' Hope confessed.

'How about "I've got a new daddy for you"?' rasped Matt.

Hope bit her lip again. This sort of stress could not be good for the baby. 'That type of remark doesn't help,' she said far more calmly than she was feeling. 'Should I get my lawyer to make the arrangements for you to see the children?' she asked. Two could play that game.

Matt sounded shocked. 'You have a lawyer?'

'If you can't be civil to me, it looks as if I'll need one,' she snapped. 'Phone me when you've booked the hotel.' She slammed the phone down and burst into tears.

'I didn't talk to Daddy,' said Millie tearfully. 'Did Daddy make you cry?'

'No,' wailed Hope. 'Daddy is the best daddy in the world and he would never hurt Mummy.'

Instantly, Toby began to cry too, until the entire family were sobbing, huddled together at the bottom of the stairs.

'I want Daddy!' cried Millie.

'I want a wee wee,' cried Toby.

'I want to turn the clock back,' Hope sobbed.

Thereafter, Matt was ultra civil on the phone, as if he was speaking to a new client for the first time.

'How are you?' he'd say formally.

'Very well,' Hope would reply, feeling like a Jane Austen character on her best behaviour at an assembly.

In this way, they organized the trip for Saturday. Matt was going to stay in the Hotel Europe on the other side of Killarney, a welcoming family hotel with a huge indoor swimming pool and a riding stables with beautiful golden ponies to amuse the children.

'Will you pack stuff for every eventuality?' he asked Hope, for one minute sounding like the old Matt, the one who could never tell the difference between the children's old dungarees for messing around in and good trousers that shouldn't be let out in the mud.

'Of course,' Hope said humbly. It wasn't his fault they were in this position. Maybe, a teeny bit his fault. But in the main, they were at a Mexican stand off because of her behaviour.

On Saturday, the children were ecstatic with excitement. Millie squealed a refrain of 'Daddy! Daddy! Daddy!' as Hope drove them and their baggage out to the Europe Hotel, feeling more and more tense with every mile.

This could be her big chance to make everything right. Perhaps Matt felt the same way. Perhaps he was waiting for her to apologize and he'd come home and it would all go back to being the same as before.

As she drove, Hope mentally practised what she'd say. 'I'm so sorry, Matt. Nothing happened. It was all my fault, I should have never let him drive me home and I can completely understand why you didn't believe me . . .'

But that was the one sticking point: she understood why Matt had stormed off, but she was still upset that their love wasn't strong enough for him to have given her the benefit of the doubt. The old pattern had repeated itself again when he hadn't waited for her explanation.

Hope turned into the long drive to the hotel and felt her heart bleed. She couldn't abase herself before Matt, because he'd been to blame too. He should have known that she wouldn't betray him. If she crawled on her hands and knees again, it would be like the old days. Him, in charge; her, the devoted, prostrate servant. And Hope knew she'd gone too far to go back to that. If they got back together, it had to be because they both wanted it and had both said sorry for what had gone before. The rules had to change.

Matt was waiting outside the hotel for them. She saw him standing with one long canvas-jeaned leg resting on the rails beside the ponies' paddock at the front of the hotel. He wore a white T-shirt that made his dark hair look even darker than usual and Hope's heart swooped at the sight of him.

'Daddy!' squealed the children in unison and Hope did her best to smile. She stopped the Metro, got out and smiled hello shyly.

Matt didn't move forward to kiss her or even touch her. Instead, he pulled open the car door and leaned in to hug the children in a flurry of squeals and cries and delighted giggles. Hope had to stand away from this touching tableau. When the children and their baggage had been removed, she waited briefly, longing for Matt to make the first move. All she needed was one 'would you like to come in and have a coffee?' and it would be fine. She could throw her arms around him and say *yes!*

'What time are you coming back tomorrow?'

It took a moment before Hope could drag herself back from dreams of joyous reconciliation to the harsh reality of life.

'Five?' she whispered.

'See you then,' Matt said politely. Then, he hoisted Toby onto his shoulders, picked up all the luggage in one strong arm, and taking Millie's eager little hand with the other, he walked off to the hotel.

Sadly, Hope got back into the Metro and drove home, with only one stop in order to find a tissue to wipe the tears from her streaming eyes. Until today, she'd had hope. Now she had none. How could she tell Matt about the baby now? He'd think she was trying to trap him. That was if he didn't assume it was Christy's.

# CHAPTER TWENTY-SEVEN

Nicole dumped her suitcase in the hall and wandered into the sitting room. She half-expected it to look like a bombsite because she'd been away for so long. Normally, unless *she* tidied up all the old papers and magazines, nobody else did. But the room was pristine, with no mugs left on the coffee table and no copies of *Hello* or *OK!* scattered across the couch. Weird. In the kitchen, it was the same story. The counters were spotless, there wasn't so much as a tea-spoon lying in the sink and the scent of lemon cleanser was in the air.

Gran, decided Nicole. Gran had been round scrubbing and clean-ing, probably as the result of an argument with Sandra about tidiness. Normally the 'honestly, Sandra, you're as untidy as a teenager!' com-ment produced a row and it was up to Nicole to restore order to the chaos. But Gran must have done it this time.

She dragged her case upstairs but didn't bother unpacking. She hated unpacking and despite being a tidy soul in most areas of her life, this wasn't one of them. The house was unusually quiet, it was strange, in fact. Nicole went into Pammy's pink room and sat on the bed, idly picking up a cuddly toy and stroking it. Even this room was tidy, with Pammy's collection of Disney characters lined up on a dust-free shelf.

Nicole's favourite was Tigger. She had an elderly Tigger of her own and had taken it with her on the tour, where it sat on her hotel bed and comforted her many nights. The night she and Darius had ended up cuddling for hours, talking and kissing, Tigger had stared disapprovingly at them from the dressing table.

'Tigger is shocked,' Darius had said the following morning, turning the cuddly toy away from them before they kissed goodbye.

'He shouldn't be shocked,' Nicole replied softly, 'nothing happened.'

But she wanted something to happen, all right. It was a matter of timing. She wanted the timing to be right. And the place.

She'd thought of nothing else since that night with Darius. During the final few days of the tour, she'd imagined finally having her own flat. Not one with Darius, no matter how much she liked him. No. A place of her own, a place he could visit but which would still belong to her, where she could keep the kitchen spotless and never see so much as a cup out of place anywhere.

The idea was so seductive that Nicole was constantly waking up after delicious daydreams where she'd been merrily shopping for duvet covers and lampshades, whizzing along with Pammy and her mum, picking out bits and pieces, laughing over silly shower curtains decorated with goldfishes. And then her eyes would open and reality would reassert itself, making her realize that she couldn't possibly leave them. For the first time in her life she had the financial security to have her own place to live, but her sense of responsibility meant she couldn't take advantage of it.

The sound of a key turning in the front door made Nicole race downstairs happily. She couldn't wait to see her mum and darling Pammy.

'Nicole!' roared Pammy, a small blonde princess in pink jeans and a tiny denim jacket.

'Oh love, I've missed you,' Nicole said, trying to bite back the tears as she held the small body to hers.

When she'd hugged her little sister, she turned her attention to Sandra.

'It's lovely to have you back,' Sandra said. 'We've missed you.'

'How've you been?' asked Nicole, immediately putting the kettle on for a pot of tea.

'We've been fine,' Sandra said, opening her shopping and extracting some chicken breasts, a couple of onions and a tin of tomatoes. 'Haven't we, Pammy?'

The little girl nodded proudly. 'We've had cooking every day, Mummy, haven't we? Not just egg and chips, Nicole. Mum said you'd say that was all we had.'

Both Sandra and Nicole grinned at this.

'I've learned how to do this lovely recipe with lamb and yoghurt,' Sandra said. 'It's very easy and Pammy loves it.'

Pammy nodded at this. 'Better than Barbie spaghetti,' she said, which was high praise indeed.

'And we had the boiled bacon that your Gran loves the other night. I did it all myself. Pammy wasn't so wild about that, though, were you pet?'

Pammy shook her head.

Nicole had to sit down on a kitchen chair. This was all too bizarre. Her mother cooking? Sandra never cooked. When Nicole had been small, they lived on eggs, chips, pizzas and anything else frozen that could be easily reheated. Now her mother was turning into Nigella Lawson.

'The place is looking good, Gran must have been spring cleaning,' she added.

'*I* was spring cleaning!' said her mother indignantly. 'Honestly, Nicole, you'd think I didn't know which end of the vacuum cleaner was up.'

Nicole bit back the comment that for years her mother hadn't taken much interest in being Mrs House Proud.

'So tell us everything,' Sandra said when all the shopping had been put away and chocolate biscuits had been produced to go with the tea. Pammy began colouring in at the kitchen table and Sandra started chopping onions for dinner. 'You look great. I saw the latest article on you in the evening paper. They called you "very talented". I got six copies.'

Nicole grinned. 'If the single flops, everyone will soon be saying I was talentless and they knew from the start that I'd fail.'

'That's newspapers for you,' Sandra said, browning the onion in what looked suspiciously like a new skillet. 'Paper won't refuse ink, as I always say. We're all proud of you, whatever they print.'

'I've been thinking, Mum,' Nicole began. She paused, got up and got another biscuit from the pack on the counter.

'You've given up smoking, haven't you?' demanded her mother suddenly. 'You never eat biscuits.'

Nicole blushed. 'I'm doing my best,' she said. 'Dar . . .' she corrected herself, 'the company told me it was bad for my voice.'

'Oh, did they?' teased her mother. 'Or was it that lovely Darius . . . ? Come on, tell me.'

Nicole couldn't stop the silly, sentimental grin that crossed her face every time she thought of Darius.

'Are you going out with him?' asked Sandra, abandoning the onions to start work on some mushrooms.

'Well . . . yes . . . well, that's part of what I wanted to talk about,' Nicole said anxiously. She got up to stand at the cooker and give the onions a stir. She didn't want Pammy to hear what she had to say next.

'I'm thinking of . . .'

'. . . moving out,' finished her mother. 'Don't look so shocked, love. I knew it'd happen. It makes more sense for you to have your own place, now that you'll be working in town all the time. You've got a career now, you need your own space.'

Nicole stared at her mother, astonished and hurt. 'But what will you do without me?' she blurted out.

Sandra's blue eyes crinkled up when she smiled warmly at her daughter. 'Carry on, Nicole. You were going to have to go sometime, weren't you? I knew I'd have to let you go. You're my daughter, not my prisoner.'

'But how will you cope?'

This time, her mother really did look surprised. 'Cope? Well, we won't have you running round after us, taking care of everything, Nicole, but we'll manage. I'm not useless, you know. How did I cope when you were a baby? I just had to, didn't I?'

'Yes, but Gran said she had to take over,' interrupted Nicole.

'Your gran is just like you, Nicole: she needs to be needed. She was the one who insisted I stay with her. I wanted my own place but you know your Gran, bossy boots from hell that she is,' Sandra added fondly.

Nicole wished she still smoked because she desperately needed a cigarette to help her cope.

'You were such a funny little girl when you were small,' Sandra went on. 'Always wanting everything to be perfect, just like your gran. The two of you were like peas in a pod, but even your gran isn't as much of a perfectionist as you, Nicole. She's never been able to get the taps in the bathroom cleaned up the way you do. I did worry about you, you know,' Sandra confided. 'I talked to the doctor about getting you help because you were so obsessed with things being right. But she put my mind at rest. Said that was your way of coping with life. She said you obviously missed having a dad, although it would kill you to let on to me, and you wanted everything ship shape on the surface. Said I should let you get on with it, that it was what you needed.'

'But . . .' Nicole didn't know where to start. This wasn't how she remembered things at all. 'But Gran said I had to look after you . . . and I felt responsible for everything . . .'

'I know.' Sandra's soft eyes hardened briefly. 'You were never responsible, my love. You and Pammy are the most precious gifts I've ever been given, you do know that, don't you? I don't regret a single moment of my life because I've got my two wonderful daughters. Your gran has her regrets and that's her business, that's why she's so anti sex before marriage. Not for moral reasons but because she never wanted you to be stuck with a child and no way of earning your living, like her and me.'

Too late, Sandra stopped stirring and stared horror-struck at her daughter. 'Oh Lord, Nicole, forget I said that.'

'*Like her?*' repeated Nicole parrot-fashion.

'Please, Nicole, don't say a word. Your gran would kill me. She never wanted you to know, she was sure you'd be ashamed of her. Just forget I said it.'

'I can't,' Nicole gasped. 'I'm not ashamed of Gran, how could I be? But tell me the truth.'

524

'The truth about what?' demanded Reenie Turner, appearing at the door with her keys in her hand.

The entire story took two more pots of tea and Nicole decided she'd have to pick another day to give up smoking. Once her grandmother started telling the story, the words flooded out, as if she'd longed to tell Nicole the truth despite everything. Reenie Turner had indeed been sixteen, going on seventeen, when she'd left Ireland for London. Except the bit of information Nicole had never been given included the fact that Reenie had fled her home after getting pregnant by a local lad, who had no intention in hell of marrying her. She'd lived in a small farm near Redlion, which Nicole remembered was the town where Sam Smith's sister lived. Not that it surprised her: this entire tale was so unbelievable that one more startling coincidence wasn't noticeable.

'It wasn't like now,' Reenie recounted. 'Being pregnant in those days was a mortal sin and a shame like nothing you can imagine, Nicole. My family didn't know. Sure, I barely knew myself. There was no sex education or the like, we'd all grown up on a farm so we knew what was what, but as for people having babies, that was like another, mysterious world. If I'd been a heifer, I'd have had a better idea of what was going on than I did as a young woman.'

The three Turner women, sitting around the table, smiled. Even telling a sad story, Reenie couldn't resist a bit of a joke.

'My sister, Heather, God rest her, was going to London to train as a nurse. She was three years older than me and I told her one night. I knew I had to get away or the family would have been destroyed with the shame of it all.'

Nicole's heart ached at the thought of a lonely young girl having to leave her family and her home all because she lived in an era where unmarried pregnancy was the ultimate taboo.

'It was either leave or get sent to the nuns,' Reenie said mistily. 'They had homes then for fallen women or magdalens as they called the likes of me. Those places were nothing but workhouses for pregnant women and I say a prayer to Our Lord every day that I missed that. Your aunt Heather took me with her to London and took care of me.' Sandra reached over and squeezed her mother's hand softly.

'When your mother was born, Heather and I got a place of our own and she told everyone I was widowed, that my husband had died in an accident on a building site. There were so many Irish builders, nobody thought much about it, or if they did, they said nothing. And when I met your grandfather, Charlie Turner, and he *was* your grandfather,' she added fiercely, 'because he loved Sandra like his own, we were a proper family.'

Nicole had only vague memories of a sweet, white-haired grandfather, who'd died when she was a small child.

'Why did you never tell me, Gran?' she asked now. 'As if I'd disapprove of you!'

'I didn't want to be washing our dirty linen in public,' Reenie said firmly. 'I did want to tell you, so many times, but it was never the right moment.'

'Nicole's got her own bits of news, Mum,' said Sandra, grinning. 'She's in love with that Darius Good. And she's going to move out and get her own place.'

'Not with Darius, I hope?' demanded Reenie fiercely.

'No,' said Nicole, stung. 'I thought you liked him, anyway.'

Her grandmother smiled. 'I do,' she insisted, 'I think he's a real gent and he'll be good for you. I just don't want you rushing into anything. You've got your career to think about now, Nicole. You don't want to be tied down to any man. Your mother and I want to see you making it before you start thinking about settling down. I've been watching that *Top of the Pops* programme and there's nobody on it near as good a singer as you,' she said loyally.

Nicole laughed. 'Ah Gran, you're biased.' She kissed both her grandmother and her mother. 'I'm just going upstairs to use the phone,' she said. 'I want to phone Darius.'

'Are you going to be telling him about me?' asked her grandmother suspiciously.

'No, why would I? I just want to tell him that I am going to get a flat after all,' Nicole replied. 'I didn't want to do it for sure until I felt it was the right decision, and now I'm sure it is.'

'You have to move on,' Sandra said matter-of-factly. 'Will you be having your dinner here? I'm making a casserole.'

'You bet,' said Nicole. 'Since I'll be racketing around soon in my own place, I might as well get as much home cooking as I can here.'

'Home cooking!' said Reenie, raising her eyes to heaven. 'I better check if I have my stomach pills. You know I can't eat onions . . .'

'Mum, you are a right pain, you know that,' interrupted Sandra.

Grinning, Nicole danced upstairs to phone Darius. Everything in the Turner household was back to comforting normality.

# CHAPTER TWENTY-EIGHT

Sam tried on her drop-dead gorgeous shimmery dress. Against her olive skin and with her poker straight dark blonde hair hanging like a sleek fall of silk, the dress looked stunning. Tiny spaghetti straps, iridescent fabric that clung voluptuously to her figure and a low cut back that scooped down dangerously, made it the sort of thing Hollywood divas wore to the Oscars.

Hanging on the wardrobe door was her other possible outfit for the Lemons: a black Prada suit that looked wickedly expensive and very classy. Chic but not overtly sexy, especially when she wore it with the white agnés b T-shirt which instantly transformed the suit into cool but casual.

The dress, on the other hand, screamed blatant sexuality and might not be the wisest thing to wear to an awards ceremony where you were going with your boss: a boss who'd made it plain he fancied you.

But Sam was fed up with looking coolly casual and she was sure she'd figured out how to deal with Steve. She could handle him, she knew it, and besides, she wanted Morgan to see her looking all glammed up for once.

She might not be in his target age group, but she cleaned up pretty nicely, she felt, and before she went to the awards, she was going to drop in on Morgan to say hi.

'Hi,' she practised it in front of the mirror as she kohled her big hazel eyes.

'I just dropped in for a moment to return your video,' she tried. Sounded a bit lame, she knew.

Oh what the hell. Why couldn't she just march in there and say, *hello, just wanted to drop in and see you before I went out. What do you think of the dress?*

She knew what she wanted him to think. She wanted those narrowed caramel eyes to lengthen with appreciation as he took in her glowing shoulders covered with a dusting of sparkling bronzer, then she wanted them to slide down to the exciting hollow of her cleavage, just about covered by the dress. She wanted him to be consumed with sheer lust.

That's what she wanted. And when he saw her in this dress, it would happen.

Triumphantly, Sam looked at her dazzling reflection in the mirror. She was crazy about Morgan; she was sure he was crazy about her, although he'd never made a move. He was waiting for her to say something first, Sam had convinced herself. He knew she was a strong woman and didn't like men presuming anything. He respected her. Now the time had come for Sam to let him know that love and respect could work very well together.

The limo was coming to pick her up at six, the kittens were fed and had had their daily ration of adoration, and Sam was ready by five, a time when she knew Morgan's workmen began winding down for the day. Hopefully, she'd be able to slip in without meeting anyone but Morgan because in this dress, the builders would give her quite a ribbing.

Just in case, she wrapped herself in a big plum velvet evening coat before she went next door. The front door was open, as usual, and Sam could hear the inevitable hammering noises.

The builders would be gone soon, they'd been renovating the house for months and it must have cost a fortune. Morgan hadn't talked about selling it for ages. In her dreams, Sam sometimes had a delicious fantasy where she and Morgan lived there together. She imagined telling guests how she'd helped with the patio, imagined Morgan smiling, putting his arms round her and telling everyone how he'd fallen in love with her independent streak when she'd insisted on laying part of it herself after watching him for only half an hour.

'Hello?' she called lightly, peering into the big airy drawing room. No sign of him. The builders were in the kitchen having the last cigarette of the working day.

'Hiya Sam,' they said, eyeing up the big coat and the dainty ankles in pink strappy evening sandals appearing underneath.

'Hi guys,' she replied. 'Any sign of the boss man?'

'In the conservatory,' said one.

Sam walked quickly through to the conservatory, which had been almost totally rebuilt. It looked great now and she could picture it beautifully decorated. Cane furniture maybe, she liked cane furniture. It signified holidays in the sun and would look lovely with plenty of plants and perhaps paintings like her watercolour orchid one.

Deep in these happy thoughts, she said 'Hello,' in a breezy, I've-just-dropped-in-for-a-moment voice. Her next words died on her lips. There, with Morgan's arms wrapped around her as if she was precious china, was the young girl with the big doe eyes. The same girl that Sam had first seen leaving Morgan's house after the party, having stayed the night. The girl who'd come out another morning clad in his jeans, her pert little twenty-something body cuddled up in one of his sweatshirts, looking for all the world as if she'd just been cuddling Morgan himself.

Sam had fondly hoped that this nymphet was a fling of the past. Recently, there had been no sign of women drifting in and out of Morgan's house with their lips glossed up ready to have the lipstick kissed off by him.

Sam had been so very sure that this was no coincidence and that, once Morgan had fallen for her, he'd dropped the bimbos. But from the way Little Miss Muffet was clinging to Morgan like a limpet, nestled against his old white T-shirt as if she belonged there, it was obvious their affair was very much in the present.

Sam felt like someone had struck her in the chest. The breath seemed to leave her body and she stepped backwards in shock. All of this took just a few seconds: from recognition to realization, only a moment had passed. Morgan stared at her dumbly, but without waiting for him to offer lame explanations, Sam whirled around at high speed and ran out of the conservatory.

'Love the dress,' roared one of the builders as she ran past him in the hall, velvet coat flying out open behind her.

Once inside her own apartment, she sat down on her window seat, still wearing the coat, too stunned to think of taking it off. Morgan didn't love her at all, she'd been stupid to think he did. He hadn't cared; she'd been fooling herself or had he been fooling her? Who knew. All she knew was that she'd run to see him with childlike enthusiasm and had made an enormous fool of herself. It had all been in her mind. How pathetic she must have seemed.

She didn't know how long she sat there, immobile and stunned. One half of her wanted Morgan to storm into the apartment and apologize, to tell her it was all a huge mistake and she'd got the wrong idea. That he loved her.

But the other half of her raged at her own stupidity at ever believing in a man. There was nothing for it but to cut Morgan Benson completely out of her life, because she couldn't stand the strain any more. He was gone, in the past, like some band whose next option she'd refused to exercise. People often wondered how it felt to work in an industry where tough decisions had to be made but Sam always explained simply that it was business. There was nothing personal in it, but no record company could carry passengers. Everybody knew that. You walked away and tried to remember that.

Now all she had to do was adopt a similar attitude in her own life. Morgan was like a band she'd invested so much time and money in, and now he'd failed her. Time to dice and slice. He was gone, history, finito. If she said it often enough, maybe she'd believe it.

In the limo on the way to Earl's Court, Sam didn't bother checking her make up. What was the point, she thought, staring blindly out the darkened windows at the streets whizzing by.

Thousands of fans, gathered outside the main entrance, screamed delightedly when Sam's car pulled up, thinking she was someone famous. When she got out, fiercely glamorous in her shimmering designer gown, they screamed some more.

'Probably think you're Jennifer Lopez,' smirked the limo driver.

'Give or take ten years, six inches of leg, and ten million bucks,' said Sam sourly.

She marched past the screaming kids and the frantically snapping paparazzi, knowing that the photographers were wasting film taking her picture just in case she was someone they should have recognized.

''Oo are you, luv?' yelled one guy with a telephoto lens like an elephant's trunk.

'Nobody,' hissed Sam menacingly.

The photographers got the hint.

Inside was organized chaos as thousands of dressed up to the nines people surged around, trying to figure out where the hell they were supposed to meet up with their friends and jealously checking to see if their table was in a less advantageous position than their rivals. Table positioning was almost a professional sport at these bashes, with lots of internal company anger when one group were right at the stage and another of their fellow execs were in the Siberia of the back of the room. Karen Storin joked that she could tell whose career was on the up and whose was going down purely by where they ended up sitting at award ceremonies.

Sam had laughed at the time and said that the two of them were going to have great fun at the Lemons betting on career prospects. Now, Sam didn't think she'd ever have fun again. She couldn't imagine even smiling again, and the thought of putting on a brave face nearly killed her. But she had to for her career's sake. And let's face it, she reflected bitterly as she looked over the wasteland of her life, her damn career was the only thing she had left.

'Love the dress,' Steve Parris said enthusiastically as Sam arrived at the Titus table – right at the front, naturally, because Steve wouldn't have stood for anything else. Everybody was there; twelve people crammed into a round table built for ten. The next table held international Titus head honchos, and Karen Storin, who, resplendent in a red leather trouser suit, was holding court. She waved across at Sam.

'You look fantastic!' she called.

Sam did her best to smile back. The one person she'd wanted to admire the dress hadn't.

Sam sat down three places away from Steve, who was already well stuck into neat vodkas. He should have been sitting with the international people but he'd obviously made a conscious decision to get drunk instead.

'You should wear clothes like this more often,' he said loudly, eyes darting over her outfit.

'Yeah,' said Sam, not really caring either way.

The meal was the type of thing where bowls were placed in the centre of each table and people could help themselves, which was a mistake as everybody was affecting to be far too cool to eat. Sam couldn't really be bothered with leaning in to take spoonfuls of Caesar salad or slivers of chicken breast, so she nibbled her bread roll and didn't argue when Steve leaned perilously across the table to fill up her wine glass.

'Thanks,' she muttered, her mind elsewhere; in the conservatory of Morgan Benson's home to be exact.

'My pleasure,' Steve said, admiring her with hot eyes.

It was a relief when the show started and the small talk could stop. Sam was fed up with listening to everyone at the table bitching about other record companies.

First to perform was an artist who'd been signed to the record company Sam had worked with until she'd joined Titus. Tula-Faye, a crossover country and western artist who had sold millions of records and got scores of record company people's backs up in the process because she was such a demanding diva, swayed onstage in a few strategically placed bits of chiffon.

'I thank the Lord for the chance to be here with you good people tonight,' she drawled.

Sam raised her eyes to heaven. She admired people with genuine religious sentiment but she knew damn well that the only God Tula-Faye worshipped was the one who looked after her dollars – all of which were tied up in investment funds that no hopeful future husband could ever hope to infiltrate unless he had one hell of a lawyer. Anyway, surely God preferred his chosen ones to wear more clothes? One good breeze and Tula-Faye's outfit would fall to the floor.

Tula-Faye was followed by the winner of the Best Female Act

category, and then, after another litany of awards, a hip young boy band came on, gyrating around six limber female dancers as they lip-synched their new song. The fans who were let in to create some atmosphere screamed themselves hoarse.

A Titus act won Best Album, and Steve went demented, yelling loudly in triumph. Not that it was a surprise to him, Sam knew. The record companies all knew exactly which band was going to win which award in advance. Otherwise, they'd never be able to coax their performers into turning up in the first place. Sam couldn't imagine the hell of getting a top act to an awards ceremony where they had to endure the humiliation of not winning the award they'd been nominated for.

Titus's fiercest rival record company won the next two awards and from the corner of her eye, Sam watched Steve sink another straight vodka. Trouble ahead, she thought idly.

Next came the nominations for Best Newcomer. Everyone at the Titus table perked up. Density were up for this award. Unlike the other awards, the winner of this was a fiercely-guarded secret because it was decided by the television company which broadcast the awards.

Sam watched Steve Parris sit up stiffly in his seat and shove away his empty vodka glass. He had a lot riding on this. Massive sums of money had been spent on the band and their first album had sold a disappointingly low number of units. The critics had loved it, which augured well for the future, implying that a band as talented as Density needed a couple of albums to hit the mega time with the fickle public. But if they failed to win such an important award as Best Newcomer, it would look very bad. And looking bad in the music industry was to be avoided at all costs.

Personally, she couldn't give a damn. Her life was in tatters. What did it matter if Density won? Morgan would still be bedding that brunette child bride type. If only he'd had the balls to tell her the truth; that they were friends, nothing more. Why put her through all that pain of *thinking* he liked her when she was clearly wrong. He was gutless, that was why. A gutless, dishonourable coward and she hoped she'd never see him again in her life.

The Earl's Court crowd, deeply blasé and not inclined to clap anyone except perhaps U2, gave a smattering of desultory applause as a handsome male soap star who played a womanizer in the show arrived with a female pop show presenter to present the award.

After the requisite giggling and flirting, which was even more hilarious because everyone knew the pair disliked each other, they read out the nominees. The Titus table practically moved a foot forward thanks to all the people on it shifting in their seats and leaning hopefully towards the stage, urging Density to win.

'. . . and the winners are . . .'

The Titus staff held their breath.

'. . . El Pirador!'

A roar went up at a rival record company table at the news that their band, made up of second-generation Italian girls with fantastic voices and the looks of four Miss World contestants, had won. The Titus people sighed heavily.

Steve's eyes went blank and he signalled a passing waiter, on hand to cope with both the vagaries of the pop world and depressed record company bosses who needed solace.

'Four bottles of Krug,' Steve demanded. 'No, make it five.'

Sam sat back in her seat with a sigh and engaged in some surface commiserations over the band. Thankfully, Density's manager wasn't around or it would have been a complete nightmare. She knew he'd blame her for the band's failure to win and there was no point telling him that if his charges were more media-friendly they'd have a better chance of success. The fact that the band had called one interviewer 'an ugly cretinous cow' hadn't helped their standing with the press for a start.

The champagne arrived and Steve stood to toast Density, loudly proclaiming that they were stars and didn't need any fucking awards anyway, and then proceeding to down most of the first bottle himself.

By the time the Lifetime Achievement award was announced – going to a band of rockers so walnut-like and wrinkly that they looked like they'd just been plugged into the mains to revive them after being dug up – Steve was at that stage of depressed drunkenness which is the most dangerous. His hard little black eyes were like two holes in the snow and his mouth was a flat line of anger. As mechanically as if someone in the mother ship was beaming down instructions to a micro chip in his head, he shuffled out of his seat and plonked down beside Sam, clutching her arm with one hand, holding his second precious bottle of Krug with the other. It was only a quarter full.

'D'ya know what I hate about this fucking award ceremony shit?' he hissed.

Sam swallowed. Steve sober she could just about manage. Steve plastered out of his mind was another thing entirely.

'I hate the fact that they could tell us who was going to win but they don't. Make us look like fucking idiots tonight.' He scowled in the direction of El Pirador's record company's table where a celebration party was raging, and where three waitresses were working at full speed to keep the drink flowing.

'Well, we do have a bit of a clue about the Best Newcomer when they ask us to make certain bands available,' Sam pointed out. The fact that Density were touring the Far East meant they'd had to say they couldn't be at the awards after their nomination had been announced. If they'd been around and had been bluntly told not to come, even a lettuce leaf would have figured out that they weren't going to win anything. As it was, they'd been told nothing, which was a sure sign, in Sam's eyes.

Steve's face screwed up. 'That's not f . . .' He broke off as the New York VP, a handsome German guy named Helmut who didn't drink, pulled up a chair beside both of them and patted Steve on the back.

'Never mind about Density,' Helmut said, his flawless English faintly accented with New York after ten years in Manhattan.

Steve put down his glass and took a sip of someone else's water in an attempt to impress Helmut. There was a lot of untouched water on the table.

'You win some, you lose some,' Helmut continued. 'We need to talk about the future of the band, I don't know if they're going to get a deal from us. I can't see them working in the US.'

Ouch, Sam thought. If the American office weren't interested in signing Density, that was a slap in the face for Steve. The muscles in his jaw worked a bit.

'Helmut, you must tell me about your new signings. I've heard some great things about them and I want to get my hands on them. Anything to harden that bottom line,' Sam said brightly.

After half an hour schmoozing Helmut, trying to distract him from Steve's constant drinking, Sam was wrecked. The party was winding down and everyone was leaving, phoning limos on their mobile phones and arranging to go to the all-important after-show parties.

'Are you coming to the party at Shiva?' Sam asked Helmut hopefully. It would be nice to have someone sober and senior along to keep Steve in line.

He shook his head ruefully. 'I have to catch the morning flight to LA but some of my other colleagues from New York are going.'

Damn, thought Sam, still smiling. That meant there was no way she could escape from Steve. She didn't know why she was bothering anyway. He was too plastered to appreciate her kindness in looking after him and wouldn't know how to say thank you.

Steve's limo was a triple stretch which looked as if it should come complete with a pimp and a couple of hookers in hotpants, and Sam had no idea how it was ever going to go round corners.

'Cool, huh?' smirked Steve, settling himself into the leather back-seat.

Four more execs, including the new Spanish MD, an Antonio Banderas lookalike called Jorge, and Karen Storin all piled into the limo.

Despite her misery, Sam was able to appreciate Jorge's sleek beauty and she smiled her first genuine smile of the evening as he wriggled his lean hips into the space between her and Karen.

Only it wasn't Sam he was interested in: instantly, he turned away from her and began chatting up Karen. Feeling about a hundred and utterly unlovable, Sam stared down at her strappy sandals where her shimmery pink toenails winked up at her. She remembered how happy she'd been the night before when she painted them, thinking all the time of the effect she'd have on Morgan when she nonchalantly visited him. Stupid cow.

Shiva was packed with Titus staff and their top artists. Sam hated being squashed in clubs and wasn't tall enough to appreciate standing all night while looking up at other people, clutching a glass and her handbag. Everybody seemed content to stand, but not Steve who clearly realized that if he didn't sit down soon, he'd fall down. Lurching into people left, right and centre, he dragged his group to the reserved area at the back of the club where endless squashy leather armchairs were grouped around a low table laid with olives and yet more champagne. When Sam sat down, she sank uncomfortably into her seat like a small child in an adult's chair. Her heart also sank when Steve dragged his armchair close to hers so they could talk.

'I really like you,' he slurred. 'I know you don't think I do but I do. You don't really know me but if you did, you'd like me too. You do, a little bit, don't you?' he said.

'Yeah,' said Sam absently. She wasn't interested and knew that Steve was so drunk he wouldn't remember a word of this in the morning.

'But you do like me a weeny, weeny bit?' he insisted drunkenly.

He was so close that she could smell the acid boozy reek of his breath.

'Yes,' Sam said, the same way she'd say yes to Millie or Toby.

'You see, people think I'm gay,' Steve revealed.

Sam breathed a sigh of relief. If he was gay, it meant two things: one, that he clearly didn't fancy her and two, that he was hopefully hiding a much kinder personality because he'd assumed he needed to be tough to succeed in the macho music world. If Steve were gay, perhaps they could actually become friends, united in the job of presenting a tough front.

She put a kind hand on his knee in what she hoped was a supportive gesture.

'I'm not, you know,' hiccuped Steve. 'I wish I was, it'd be bloody easier. I wouldn't have to deal with bitches like my ex-wife. But I hate gays.'

Sam removed her hand, her hopes dashed.

'And the bitch got the dogs,' he said miserably.

Sam hadn't thought Steve was a dog person. Perhaps there was hope for him.

'Just as well, I hated that bloody schnauzer. She got the Cure albums as well, bitch! She said I was no good in bed, which is a damn lie. I hate her. Not all women are like that, are they?'

Every fresh confidence made Sam gulp. Drunken confidences were deadly things. Steve *was* interested in her but her opportunity of telling him she didn't feel the same way diminished as he got drunker. Even worse, Steve was confiding in her like she was his dearest friend. He would, therefore, be gutted when she told him she wasn't interested. Then again, in the morning he might have forgotten he'd told her all this stuff . . .

Blearily, he smiled up at her from the depths of his squashy chair. Sam smiled weakly back at him.

In the distance, she could see Jorge's sleek otter head bent over Karen Storin's. They were laughing at something, Karen's full lipsticked mouth roaring with delight. Having fun, Sam realized. What was that?

Karen was on the phone first thing on Saturday morning, sounding anxious and with her voice resonating with that up-all-night hoarseness.

'Sam, please tell me that nobody noticed me going off with Jorge last night, please tell me. Steve would disapprove so much.'

Sam laughed mirthlessly. 'Karen, if you had danced the Dance of the Seven Veils with Jorge lying on the floor underneath you with his shirt off and his mouth open, Steve wouldn't have noticed. He was off his head drunk. If I hadn't half-carried him to his limo, he'd still be passed out at Shiva.'

'Thank you for that, I was so worried,' Karen said. 'It was great last night but this morning, I began to worry . . .'

'Stop worrying. You're entitled to have a life, you know. Anyway, tell me about gorgeous Jorge. Why is he wasting his life in this business – he should be starring in the new Steven Spielberg movie.'

Karen giggled. 'I know. He is gorgeous, isn't he?'

'Totally, you cow. I'm very jealous.'

'Oh get outta here,' Karen said, sounding pleased. 'Anyway, what was Parris bending your ear about all night? I thought he was going to fall down your cleavage he was so close.'

Sam shuddered. 'I suppose everybody noticed that?' she said drily.

'No. Well, yeah. But everyone knows you're not interested in him, Sam. He's just a total asshole.'

Thinking of the total asshole's declaration of lust the night before, Sam sighed. She really hoped he'd forgotten it all in the miasma of alcohol, otherwise her life was going to be a lot more complicated from now on.

Three o'clock in the morning is not a good time to go to bed, Sam reflected at lunchtime as she collected her purse to go grocery shopping. Despite having only had a couple of glasses of wine, she hadn't slept well and had woken up feeling groggy and tired.

Her eyes were dull and lined and her face was pale but she didn't bother with make-up. Who was going to be looking at her? Throwing a zip-up jacket on over her T-shirt and sweat pants, she left the apartment.

On the street she came face to face with Morgan. If it was any consolation, he looked just as hollow-eyed as she did, his unshaven face grey under his normal tan.

'Sam,' he said softly, 'I need to talk to you.'

'About what?' she hissed. 'About your harem? I am such a fool, I really thought you were over the pre-schoolers but I must have been wrong.'

'Sam,' he insisted, 'it wasn't what you thought . . .'

The rage that had been percolating in her system since the previous evening, exploded like a volcano. 'Not what I thought?' she hissed, sounding like somebody possessed in a horror movie. 'How do you know what I thought? You don't know the first thing about me. I know all about you, though. You can't keep your hands off women, can you? You're just disgusting.'

He moved closer, his narrowed eyes pleading with her. 'Sam, don't be upset. You've got it all wrong, I promise. I can explain . . .'

She glared at him furiously, wanting to scream at him so that everyone within a fifty mile radius could hear, but also wanting to retain some shred of her dignity. 'I don't want to hear your pathetic explanation,' she said, raising her chin regally. 'Why don't you just leave me alone.'

'Please, don't be like that,' Morgan begged.

'I'll be whatever I wish. You're nothing to me, I don't even want to talk to you ever again.'

'So you're not going to give me a chance to explain because you've already got it all worked out in your mind, is that right?' Morgan asked, his eyes strange, his voice cold.

For a millisecond, Sam hesitated. Then rushed on. She *knew* what it had been all right and he wasn't going to make a fool out of her a second time.

'I asked you to leave me alone,' she said fiercely, wanting him to go before she broke down. She'd never be able to keep up this dignified act if he didn't leave soon and she didn't want to break down in front of him. That would be too humiliating.

'Pardon me,' Morgan said flatly, again sounding very strange. 'You're saying our friendship means nothing to you? You don't trust me?'

'You don't have to explain to me. *Never explain, never apologize,*' Sam quoted bitterly. 'That's probably your mantra.'

'No,' he said in a voice that would freeze Hell. 'But I don't explain when I'm not trusted.' With that, he walked off. Sam would have loved to have walked after him but she couldn't, could she?

The following Monday morning, Lydia was at her desk drinking a Starbucks latte, nibbling a muffin and chatting on the phone to her best friend when Sam marched into the LGBK office, hideously late after the tube had decided to stop for half an hour in the tunnel. Clad in her sharpest black trouser suit, wearing boots with heels like dagger points and with her hair tied back severely, she looked like she'd looked six months before, Lydia thought idly: the tough career bitch.

'Is this lunchtime or is my watch wrong?' snapped Sam, glaring pointedly at Lydia's muffin. 'And the office is not the place for personal calls,' she added, stalking into her office and slamming the door so hard that the framed platinum discs hanging on the walls rattled.

Oh shit, sighed Lydia gloomily, the bitch is back. It wasn't just the clothes. The whole persona had returned.

She had to admit, though, that Sam in a black mood made for staggering efficiency. By one, they'd got through masses of correspondence, huge numbers of phone calls and Sam had had three meetings. She'd also had seven cups of strong, black coffee and had sent a junior out for cigarettes.

'I didn't know you smoked,' Lydia blurted out before she realized that the career bitch boss didn't like personal comments, unlike the recent touchy-feely version.

Sam, deeply ashamed of herself for giving in to the desire to smoke, ripped the cellophane off the cigarettes with unnecessary force. 'Nobody knows anyone really,' she said enigmatically. 'Can you get me an ashtray.' It wasn't a request.

Lydia rushed off to get one from somewhere, deciding that she wasn't going to be the one to point out to Sam that the entire Titus building was, officially, a no-smoking zone. Of course, Steve Parris smoked anywhere he liked, but he was the Big Boss. Mind you, the office gossip of the morning was the fact that Stevie had been draped all over Ms Smith at the Lemon Awards the previous Friday, so perhaps that was the reason for her bad temper. Having anything even vaguely sexual to do with Steve would certainly put Lydia in a bad mood.

The first cigarette made Sam nauseous but the second was better and by the third, she felt like a smoker again. She certainly wasn't hungry but unfortunately she had a lunch to go to. Even worse, it was with Density's manager, the hated Glenn Howard. The only good point was that the LGBK marketing director, Sophie, and Nadia, the product manager in charge of Density, were going too, so Sam wouldn't be forced to make conversation all on her own.

'I'll be back by half two at the latest,' Sam told Lydia, who was astonished because lunches with managers invariably lasted two hours and it was already five past one.

In the car taking the three LGBK staff to the restaurant, conversation was limited. Sophie, as befitting a marketing manager, was permanently on her mobile phone, so the other two were silent.

'Sorry,' apologized Sophie as the car pulled up outside Half A Cow, the latest hip and trendy restaurant which specialized in giant steaks, tripe, steak-and-kidney pie and sausage and mash.

'A man's restaurant,' Sam muttered as they entered.

'You can say that again,' sighed Sophie, who was vegetarian.

Glenn was already at the table, had ordered a bottle of red (without asking us if we want red or white, Sam growled to herself) and was full of bonhomie.

'Great to see you, Sam,' he roared, jumping to his feet and giving her a bear hug. 'How's the record industry doing? Have my boys made you another million today?' he added loudly.

Loudly enough for everyone nearby to look around and realize they were in the presence of a top manager, Sam knew.

'Sophie babe, how are you?' Glenn said to Sophie, this time without the hug. Hugs were for MDs in Glenn's book.

Ever professional, Sophie was ultra-polite in return, not betraying for a moment the fact that this man bawled her out on the phone on a regular basis.

'Hi,' Glenn said brusquely to Nadia, who was not even on the scale as far as he was concerned.

That irritated the hell out of Sam. People like Nadia had the hardest jobs in the industry and worked their bums off for the likes of Density. Nadia was responsible for the band's endless posters and sales presenters, she set up radio campaigns, worked hard on every nitty-gritty detail of the band's marketing, making sure that every i was dotted and every t crossed. It was a huge job that encompassed a huge area of responsibility. On those rare occasions when Density gave interviews, it was hard-working Nadia who got landed with co-ordinating the actual logistics of it all, sorting out venues for the band and supplying their increasingly bizarre demands, not to mention making arrangements for foreign press to turn up.

Sam still remembered the days she'd worked with Tula-Faye in her previous job. She'd been a marketing director and had borne the brunt of Tula-Faye's rudeness on many occasions despite the fact that it was Sam and her team who'd worked endless hours breaking Tula-Faye in the UK market. Sweetness and light when she'd met Sam's boss, the singer had been a cast-iron bitch to everybody lower down on the scale. Sometimes, the job could be so thankless. Sam was determined to change that.

'Still working twenty-four seven?' Glenn asked Sam.

'Yes,' she said grimly. She signalled to a waiter. 'A glass of white wine, please,' she said pointedly.

They studied the menus and Glenn chattered on and on about how well the band were doing on their tour and how they couldn't wait to get back to London to work on the new album. 'They're keen to work with Bruce Kaminska,' said Glenn.

Sam looked up from her menu and gave him a searing look. Kaminska was one of the world's top record producers. He was also one of the most expensive. His involvement in any album could mean the difference between a top twenty album and a number one album. However it added millions to the cost and, because he invariably wrote songs for the bands too, he demanded a cut of the profits. He was certainly a hit-maker but deciding to use him was an enormous decision to make. Sam didn't know if she wanted to blow such a huge chunk of her budget on a band who'd failed to make any waves so far.

Not to mention the fact that they were well on their way to becoming the Tula-Faye of Titus: hated.

'We'll have to think about that one,' she said shortly.

'Hey,' Glenn said in a menacing tone, 'Steve Parris wouldn't want you to just think about it.'

Sam put down her glass and stared coldly at Glenn, thinking that his band hadn't a hope in hell with such a manager. Perhaps it was time to tell him that the tables had turned. She was sure that Steve was no longer in love with his precious new find. The Americans were definitely not in love with them, and the press, though writing that Density were very talented, were fed up with rock star tantrums.

'Glenn, I'm a busy woman. I'm here to eat lunch. If you want to put me off my lunch, then I'll leave. Your choice.'

Glenn gulped and made his choice. 'Hey, what the heck!' he said in a false jovial voice. 'Let's eat.'

Back in the office, Sam worked on till half eight, ignoring her headache from the two glasses of wine at lunch and the dull ache in her stomach from eating beef. She finished the entire packet of cigarettes and vowed that she wouldn't buy any more. Lydia went at seven and Sam was conscious of a twinge of guilt because she'd been very sharp with the poor girl all day. It wasn't Lydia's fault that Sam's life was a disaster. It wasn't fair to make her suffer. Sighing, Sam put out her last cigarette and promised herself she'd be nicer to Lydia the next day. It was still light when she left the office, carrying her briefcase so she could look over some papers at home.

As she walked through Covent Garden, Sam watched the crowds of people enjoying the lovely evening and having an out of doors drink. Happy groups clustered round outdoor pub tables, drinking Pimms and beers, laughing and chatting, making plans to go for dinner and flirting. Light music drifted out from inside the pubs as she passed, along with laughter and the hum of voices. Girls in skinny little tops and low-slung jeans revealed slender limbs tanned by the last few weeks of blistering sun. Sam remembered sitting on her tiny back balcony in her bikini top a couple of weekends ago, letting the sun warm her body, turning her olive skin an even caramel colour. At the time, she'd indulged in a fantasy of being on holiday with Morgan, letting him rub sun lotion into her skin, imagining his breath quickening as his fingers stroked the cream over her body. Stupid cow. Fourteen-year-old girls were allowed to indulge in fantasy land, not forty-year-old women. Next thing she knew, she'd be buying frothy romantic novels and dreaming of dashing dukes on white horses rescuing damsels from danger. There were no dashing dukes in real life. Only lying, cheating scum.

Ignoring the voice in her head that said 'No', Sam ducked into a shop and bought another packet of cigarettes.

At home, she couldn't be bothered with cooking. Instead, she sat on her balcony with a glass of wine, her packet of cigarettes and the *Financial Times* and watched the daylight fade into twilight. Spike and Tabitha, finally allowed out, weaved around, investigating her glass, the wine bottle and the ashtray, screwing up their eyes in disgust at the unaccustomed smoke. Tabitha refused to sit on Sam's lap because of it.

'Suit yourself,' Sam said.

Her glance occasionally flicked into Morgan's silent garden but she did her best not to think about what he was doing. There was no light streaming from the kitchen window. When she went round for dinner, they usually sat in the kitchen for hours, eating off the iron table Morgan had finally bought when she'd nagged him about having nothing to eat dinner off. If the light in the kitchen wasn't on, Morgan wasn't home. Sam fiercely rubbed her eyes to get rid of the stinging sensation. She didn't care what he did or who he did it with.

The Friday after the Lemon Awards dawned gloriously sunny and as Sam walked briskly towards Holland Park tube station, she could hear the birds chattering madly to each other from the tree-lined road. It was a shame to be working on such a day, she thought, then reprimanded herself for being negative.

At half six in the morning, the morning rush on the Underground hadn't yet begun so Sam's carriage was only half full. On a seat beside her lay a women's magazine that someone had forgotten. Having nothing to read except a sheaf of papers in her briefcase, Sam began to leaf through it in a desultory manner. She flicked speedily through the fashion spread, which featured lots of flirty summer stuff that would look stupid on her and bypassed an interview with a self-obsessed actress who was claiming that she didn't need to diet to maintain her size six body. *I eat like a horse, honestly, and I love chips.* Yeah right, laughed Sam.

She stopped flicking pages when she came to an eight-page relationship special.

Normally, Sam viewed women's magazine articles on relationships with the same disdain with which she viewed women who thought that having a man was the be all and end all of their existence. But today, the headlines caught her eye.

'Too Proud To Say Sorry', 'Is Your Career Damaging Your Life?', 'Seven Relationship Secrets Every Woman Should Know'.

Sam settled down to read, expecting to scoff at it all. Career damaging your life – as if! But she found that she couldn't scoff. The piece about careers could have been written with her in mind: it described women who'd taken on men at the executive coal face but who hadn't understood that having a life outside work was as important as the life in work.

*Men have always understood the need to have other interests,* explained the psychologist consulted by the journalist who'd written the piece. *They have sports and hobbies, and, luckily for them, usually a female partner to do the chores so they have time for sports and hobbies.*

*But women, who can do four things at once, don't. They give their jobs their all and that's ultimately a problem. Very few careers are worth everything in the world.*

A man who'd got on the train at Notting Hill Gate and plonked himself beside Sam, leaned nearer as if reading the magazine and Sam abruptly pulled it closer to her chest. She'd hate anyone to realize that she was reading about herself: a sad and lonely career woman.

Even worse, the photo illustrating the career woman article could have been based on Sam that very day. Both were slim, grave-looking blondes in sleek dark suits with a simple white T-shirt underneath. Mr Armani's expensive uniform for women executives, Sam thought, feeling strangely jumpy.

She shouldn't be reading this junk. But she kept reading, holding onto the magazine when she changed trains at Holborn.

'Too Proud To Say Sorry' was painfully close to the bone and she had to stop reading when she got to a bit about how pride and a desire to have the blame for everything laid at somebody's door meant that couples forgot basic communicating skills. *Surely the most important thing is communicating so that the relationship starts working again. Does it really matter who apologizes first? Is that so important?*

No, realized Sam mournfully. She'd never given Morgan a chance to explain why he'd been holding a cute young brunette so tightly, but perhaps if she had, he'd have had a proper explanation. Even if he hadn't had an explanation, what business was it of hers? Instead, her pride and temper had made her lash out without giving him a chance. She'd tried to apply the principles that worked so well in the office: as a boss, Sam hated staff who couldn't own up to their own mistakes. That was ducking responsibility, in her opinion. If she made an error, she was the first to admit it. Then, they could move forward. But Morgan wasn't her employee, he didn't have to come up with a craven apology instantly so that she could deign to forgive him.

The lightness of step she'd had earlier had gone, now Sam trudged slowly to the office, picking up a caffe latte on the way. The office was empty apart from the security guard in reception.

'Morning Miss Smith,' he said to Sam.

'Morning,' she replied. 'It's quiet this morning.'

'Nobody's keen to be in by seven,' he said, 'except for yourself and Mr Parris.'

Sam might have guessed. Steve didn't get where he was today by wandering into the office with the first edition of the evening paper.

She might drop up to his office and talk to him about Density. The figures on their album were not good and she wanted to discuss the marketing spend. Their manager had been phoning her daily, insisting on a souped-up marketing campaign which would eat into her budget. Sam was loath to spend the money because she had a bad gut feeling about the band, especially after their losing out on the important Best Newcomer award. However, they were Steve's protégés so it would be wise to discuss it with him and gauge whether he was going off them too or whether they were still his golden boys.

The only problem was that they hadn't been alone together since the Lemon Awards a week ago. She'd seen him at the directors' meeting on Tuesday but there had been twelve other people in the room. Hopefully, he'd forgotten all about his drunken confessions.

Sam dropped her briefcase and her coffee off in her office and, carrying some of the latest sales figures on Density, got the lift up to Steve's office on the seventh floor.

Her shoes made no noise on the thick piled steel grey carpet. She entered the ante-office where Steve's assistant usually sat. Opposite was a smaller desk where the assistant's assistant sat. They weren't in yet, poor dears. Steve worked them so hard, they needed all the time off they could get. In fact, she was surprised that Steve hadn't made them come in when he was going to be in early. He liked having his acolytes present at all times.

The door to Steve's inner sanctum was ajar.

'Steve, are you there?' she said, knocking loudly on the door.

There was no answer so she peered in. Steve's office was a huge corner one, complete with a comfy seating area with giant sofas and a modern leather armchair, which was higher than the other furniture and was where Steve sat when he was playing hardball. Victims there for an earbashing had to sit on the squashy sofas which swallowed up all but the longest-legged people. Steve sat above them on his chair, looking down like a grand inquisitor.

The other side of the room held Steve's desk, a vast steel construction made specially for him by a rising young furniture designer. It looked more like an autopsy table than a desk. Beyond that, was Steve's personal bathroom with its own shower. Sam had never seen it but it was the subject of some back-biting among Titus executives who wanted their own shower rooms, too.

There was some noise coming from the shower room and Sam instantly turned to leave.

'Sam!'

She looked around to see Steve coming out of the shower room naked from the waist up, his hair damp from the shower, a towel in one hand. It was impossible to look at his skinny torso without contrasting it with Morgan's strong, powerful one. Sam wondered briefly how Steve had the confidence to stand there in his trousers and socks with no shirt on. But then, he clearly thought he was a hunk.

'Sorry for barging in,' she said, backing steadily towards the door. 'If you have a moment later, I wanted to talk to you about Density.'

'No, don't go,' urged Steve, advancing towards her. 'Sit down, I've got some coffee on.' And he went out the door to the anteroom where the coffee machine was.

There was no way she could leave now, so she sat on one of the squashy couches and picked up the copy of *Music Week* carelessly thrown on it. She'd already read the magazine from cover to cover but she wanted to give Steve time to put some clothes on.

He came back in with coffee, mugs, sugar and milk, put them on the table, then proceeded to sit down in his high chair and pour. He hadn't bothered to go back into the shower room and dress properly.

Sam was disgusted. There were very few men in the world she

wanted to have to stare at half-naked over coffee. Actually, there was only one and she'd already ruined her chances with him.

'Milk?' he said cheerfully.

Sam shook her head and snatched the coffee from him, eager to be out of there as soon as possible. 'The figures aren't good, Steve,' she said shortly. 'The album just isn't selling and the word is out, I'm afraid. You know what the scent of failure does in this business. For example, they were scheduled to have a big interview with one of the top music mags next month and the magazine has cancelled.' In Sam's eyes, that was ominous but Steve shrugged, not looking too worried, so Sam continued.

'The video shoot for the next single ran two days over because the band had hangovers every morning and refused to work until the afternoon.' That had particularly annoyed Sam. Just before they were heading off on their tour, the band had been booked to make the video but had decided it was more important to party every night to say goodbye to all their pals. The extra days of shooting had cost Titus thousands of pounds.

'And I've had Glenn Howard on the phone every day this week looking for a bigger marketing spend. He wants more money spent than was agreed in the contract. He's also being particularly vicious to Sophie, the marketing director.'

Steve still didn't look perturbed. He was smiling, Sam realized, smiling goofily and those dark little currant eyes were happy. And excited. A faint frisson of unease flickered over her.

'Don't you worry about Density,' he said smoothly. 'Let me worry about them.'

'That's nice of you, Steve,' she said facetiously, 'but they're eating into my bottom line.'

'Show me the figures,' Steve said, suddenly jumping off his seat and plonking down beside her. Sam's sense of unease went on to red alert. She handed him the spreadsheets and then moved away from him.

'There's no need to be shy,' Steve said, dropping the papers unread to the table. 'I've wanted to talk to you all week but I didn't know how to. This is perfect. Fate,' he smiled.

Not so much fate as an impending sense of doom, shuddered Sam.

'I won't beat around the bush but you know I like you and,' Steve's eyes grew as warm as Sam had ever seen them, 'I'm sure I'm not mistaken in thinking that you feel the same way.' With that, he lunged at her, pressing his scrawny naked torso against her, one sneaky hand snaking up to grab her neck and pull her face close to his. She could smell the acid reek of his breath and feel droplets of water from his wet hair dripping onto her face. Sam was shocked at the sensation of creepy Steve Parris's bare flesh anywhere near her body but she wasn't so shocked that she couldn't wriggle out before his slimy mouth got anywhere near hers. She wrenched herself away from him, got to her feet and stared at him in fury, breathing heavily with the shock.

'What do you think you're doing?'

Steve wasn't the boss of a multi-billion pound company for nothing. He made all the connections instantly, worked out that Sam was genuinely sickened, and sat up, red in the face.

'Sorry,' he muttered.

'Sorry?' demanded Sam, as she realized with disgust that he was covering his groin with his hands. She didn't even want to speculate why. 'What the hell did you think you were doing? How dare you force yourself on me?' He must still be pissed from the night before. Why else would he make such an error of judgement?

Steve's colour began to fade. 'I thought we'd got on so well the other night . . .' he started.

'The other night, you were pissed out of your mind and I had to manhandle you to your limo,' she hissed. 'If that's your idea of getting on well, then you're way off beam, Steve.'

'Look, it was a misunderstanding,' he said, recovering his poise in super quick time. 'We all make mistakes. I wasn't forcing myself on you, really.'

Sam looked at him coldly.

'You weren't?' she asked. 'What were you doing, then?'

'Making a big mistake, honestly, Sam, please accept my apologies for that. I completely misread the situation.'

He certainly looked contrite although whether it was because of what he'd done or fear of her slapping him with a sexual harassment suit, Sam couldn't tell. She could feel her own pulse slowing down and she began to think logically about what had happened. Her initial reaction had been instinctive. Now she needed to be politic.

The worst had happened and she needed to smooth it all out. There was no manual on how to pleasantly rebuff your boss without causing maximum grief. There should be, Sam reflected bitterly.

'Please forgive me, Sam and let's forget this happened,' Steve said, the big boss again, being magnanimous even half-dressed. He got up and held out a hand.

Sam had to admit, he had balls.

'How can we forget this?' she said evenly. 'Are you trying to tell me that this little incident won't affect our working relationship?'

'Hey, Sam,' Steve got up as he talked, went into his bathroom and came out pulling on a shirt, 'haven't you ever acted stupidly with a colleague after a gig when you've all been drinking, or at one of the conferences? C'mon, nobody's that much of a professional. Let's just pretend this happened late one night when we all should have known better and forget about it. Peace?'

Sam stared woodenly at him. If she did nothing, would it go away or would Steve make her suffer for humiliating him? Maybe, just maybe, they could manage to forget it all.

'I'll forget it if you promise me that you never mention this to anybody,' she said.

Steve winced. 'You think I'm going to be talking about this?' he asked incredulously.

'I mean it,' she insisted. 'No drunken gossip about the time you tried it on with me, OK? And this had better not affect our relationship here or my career, do you understand that?' Her voice was hard as nails.

'Sure,' he said.

'I'll make you suffer, Steve, if it does,' she warned.

'Get with the programme, Smith,' he snapped. 'This is the big boys' club you're in now.'

She glared at him.

'OK, OK, sorry I said that,' he said holding his hands up in apology.

'But we're grown ups, Sam, and we've got a company to run. There's no time for games here.'

'I sincerely hope not,' she said finally.

She turned to leave, but not before she saw his face hardening with humiliation and anger. As she walked to the lift, Sam sighed heavily and wondered if she'd just made a terrible mistake.

An hour later, Hugh phoned.

'Catrina had a baby girl this morning at six o'clock!' he announced joyfully.

'Oh Hugh,' said Sam, 'I'm so happy for you both. Is Catrina OK? Was it a difficult labour?'

'You'll have to ask Catrina about that for an accurate assessment,' he laughed, 'but I brought her to the hospital at midnight, she had the baby at six and she never said anything about us not making love ever again! The baby's beautiful, six pounds four ounces and the image of her mother.'

Sam felt her eyes flood with tears at the thought of a fragile miniature Catrina. 'I'm so pleased,' she said again. 'When can I come and see her?'

'We're leaving it to just family tonight, so how about tomorrow?'

'Perfect, I'll see you there.'

Sam ordered flowers for Catrina and made a mental note to buy her some of her favourite Chanel No 19 perfume. Sam knew that the baby would get lots of presents but she felt that Catrina had done the hard work.

Sam left early that afternoon, exhausted from her early start and worn out with the upset of the day. It was still glorious outside and at half four, the sun was still bright and warm. Sam walked through the streets, enjoying the feeling of sun on her face and thinking about the events of the day.

She wasn't upset by Steve's overture. Shocked and disgusted, yes, but not upset. Because Sam didn't feel scared or threatened by Steve Parris. If she had, then his assault would have been truly terrifying.

But she wasn't terrified: just angry and worried about the consequences. It would be so much easier if she could just tell someone and charge him with sexual harassment. But then, women at the top slid to the bottom faster than a player landing on a ladder in snakes and ladders if they made the mistake of filing harassment charges. Only the very brave went that route. Sam's career couldn't survive that sort of bravery.

She thought too about Hugh, Catrina and their new baby. All her friends had their lives in order, all except her.

She went into a delicatessen she liked and bought some goat's cheese, olives drenched in garlicky oil, ciabatta bread and slivers of smoked chicken as a treat. Then she hopped in a cab for home. In the apartment, she made a salad of the chicken and put some of the goat's cheese on ciabatta under the grill for a starter, then opened a bottle of wine. As she waited for the goat's cheese to toast, she flicked through the last pages of her magazine.

The back few pages were dedicated to women who'd changed their lives, according to the strap line, and this month the person featured was a woman Sam recognized.

She'd been a high-profile London banker who'd given it all up to buy a rundown property in the Dordogne. And she was happier than ever, she said, pictured beside a wooden-beamed barn with a field of misty lavender in the background and a smiling, barefoot toddler on her hip.

It looked heavenly, Sam thought wistfully. How much longer would she be able to stand it at Titus?

# CHAPTER TWENTY-NINE

Hope knew she'd made an irreversible decision the day she put Millie's name down to start in September at the Redlion National School. Putting Millie's name down meant she was officially staying in Kerry. There was No Going Back. The reasoning behind the move was simple: she loved Redlion and, if she had to be anywhere without Matt, it might as well be where she felt loved and happy with close friends around her, instead of in Bath where she'd remember their past life together every time she opened a cupboard in the house in Maltings Lane. It was as easy for jet-setting Sam to visit Kerry as it was for her to visit Bath, so there really was no reason to go back.

She hadn't mentioned the school to Matt. What would have been the point? There was no point getting maudlin, Hope told herself, as she drove into Killarney with the kids in the back of the car, to buy new clothes for the kids – and a pair of stretchy trousers for herself to cope with her suddenly exploding pregnant belly.

She'd told nobody about her pregnancy yet, not even Sam, which was hard. Initially, Hope had wanted to be well past the first three months of staring nauseated into the toilet bowl every morning before she actually said anything to anyone. However, at over four months, she was still sick every morning and she still hadn't told anybody. Telling people would make it real, that she was now a separated mother of two with a baby on the way. She could give lectures on how not to live your life, she reflected in her lighter moments. The only (slim) consolation was that at least she knew the baby was Matt's. Imagine the sheer heartbreak of not knowing who the father was.

Dr McKevitt had referred her on to Mr Murray, a charming, deb-onair gynaecologist in the local hospital and Hope had wondered did he have a terrible time with besotted female patients falling in love with him because he was so kind to them when they were vulnerable. He'd been very kind to her too but there was no danger of her falling for him. She'd had enough of that kind of thing.

His pale grey eyes had swept over the bit of the form she'd filled out with the words 'separated' on it, although there was still no formal separation, and he'd said nothing, which was a relief. If he'd looked at her with a smidgen of pity, Hope was prepared to give him a steely glance and tell him it was none of his business. But Mr Murray had merely told her she was very healthy and explained about the team of lovely midwives in the hospital.

Hope had felt as if she was coping until the day of her ultrasound scan. Sitting in the waiting room, she couldn't help but remember the other times she'd had scans. For Millie's first scan, Matt had sat holding her hand tightly as if something dreadful was going to happen.

'I want to be with you through all of this,' he'd said earnestly, gripping her hand so firmly that Hope had felt as if the circulation was going to be cut off.

And he had been with her through it all. Millie had taken hours to emerge, so long, in fact, that the epidural had worn off and giving birth to her was like giving birth to an indignant baby elephant who objected to being dragged out of a nice warm womb.

Toby's birth had been a foretaste of him as a child: no trouble at all. The epidural was still in effect when Matt brought in a snipe of champagne to toast his son and heir and when Hope had taken one tiny, forbidden sip, with baby Toby lying in her arms, she'd felt plastered.

Now she thought about this little baby, the one Matt didn't know about. This baby wouldn't feel left out and forgotten, she was deter-mined about that. This baby would be loved and adored.

But what about its father, said the little voice in Hope's head. Doesn't he have the right to know about his child? Doesn't he have the right to love this baby as much as you?

No, said the other voice stubbornly. He doesn't. He gave up that right when he walked out without giving you a chance to explain.

Hope knew she'd have to tell him some time, but she wanted to postpone it for as long as possible. She simply couldn't face the fighting and the recriminations when she did.

Still thinking about Matt, Hope parked the car in the big car park in Killarney and checked her shopping list: pregnancy trousers, new dungarees for Toby and more new shoes for Millie. She was just leaving the car park, with Toby in his pushchair and Millie stomping along in the red wellington boots she refused to take off despite the heat of the day, when a loud, faux posh voice assailed her: 'Hope, helloo.'

It could only be Finula. Fixing a rigid smile on her face, Hope turned to see Finula rushing across the road from the beautician's, flamboyant purple layers of clothes flying. From the way she was holding her hands ahead of her like a person feeling their way round a house in the dark, it was clear that a manicure had been on the cards. Sure enough, Finula's talons were blood red and beautifully painted, and the scent of nail varnish would have knocked a horse out.

'How have you been?' said Finula, with heavy emphasis on the word 'been'. 'Ciaran and I have been so worried about you.'

At any sign of pity, Hope felt a deep guttural growl emanate from within her. She knew she was due for lots of local pity. It was clear that the locals had worked out that Matt hadn't been around for a long time. Hope was sure they reckoned that his earlier absences had been trial separations and that now, he was gone for good. Miss Murphy who did the church flowers had thrown her arms round Hope the day before and said she was 'so sorry you poor dear, and I'm saying a novena that Mr Parker comes back to you.'

It had been kindly meant, but Hope wasn't in the mood for pity. Still, she could cope with sweet Miss Murphy better than with Finula Headley-Ryan, who had no doubt been running a book on how long

Matt and Hope's marriage would last from the first moment they arrived in the village.

'I'm wonderful,' gushed Hope, giving Finula a dazzling smile.

'You're so brave,' Finula said, shaking her head sorrowfully. 'I don't know what went on and I don't want to,' she said.

I bet, Hope thought to herself.

'But,' Finula went on, 'if I get my hands on Matt, I'll kill him for leaving you here all on your own. He should be shot with a shovel for thinking it's right to go off and leave you. All couples fight, it's not breaking up that's the trick.'

Hope's mouth was a perfect oval. This was not what she'd expected from Matt's most loyal fan club.

'Come on,' said Finula cosily, 'have you time for a quick cup of coffee? You'll have to take my purse out of my handbag to pay for it, though. I dare not smudge my nails.'

Hope was still reeling from the unexpectedness of it all when the four of them were seated with cappuccinos for the adults and ice creams covered in sprinkles for the children. Millie proceeded to slobber her ice cream all over the place. Hope ignored her.

'Don't tell me anything,' Finula insisted, 'but are you doing all right? Ciaran and I aren't the filthy rich or anything, but we're comfortable and if you need anything . . . I've been meaning to drop by for a week and ask if you wanted me to take the little ones some night but to be honest, I wasn't sure if you'd welcome me or run me.'

Hope had to grin. 'I would have thought you'd be on Matt's side in this one,' she said wryly.

'I adore Matt,' Finula said throatily, sounding more like her old self, 'but he's artistic and artists are often not in touch with the real world. And us girls have to stick together in times of need. I mean it about the money.'

Hope was touched. 'I'm fine,' she assured Finula. 'We're not on the breadline yet. Matt's boss in Bath is still off work, so he's still running the agency. I've been working three days a week at the tourist office and to be honest, I could work there full time because of the state of the place.'

'Tell me about it,' said Finula dramatically. 'I have been onto them for years to get them to have something on their website about the artistic centre. I might as well be talking to the wall for all the good it does me. They don't even have the centre on their maps!'

'There are a lot of improvements that could be made,' Hope agreed diplomatically, not wanting to be disloyal to the tourist officer, a nervy man named Ronan, who would visibly perspire when he spotted a phalanx of tourists bearing down on the tiny office. Since Hope had arrived to give him a hand part-time, Ronan had been giving her more and more responsibilities to the point that Hope could no longer get her work done in just three half-days.

'It was his novel, wasn't it?' Finula asked suddenly. 'The reason Matt left. I knew it, Ciaran told me that he could see Matt having problems every day and knew the novel was going very badly. Men are sensitive and when their work doesn't go well, it kills them. Their masculinity is threatened.'

Not half as much as when their wives play around, Hope thought grimly, but she was surprised at the revelation. 'Ciaran thought Matt's novel wasn't going well?' she asked.

Finula nodded. 'He said Matt spent hours typing and then he'd delete it all. Ciaran had another friend it happened to: it destroyed him not being able to write when he was sure so he had a book in him.'

Hope was silent. She hadn't known. Suddenly more of Matt's behaviour made sense. She'd had no idea that Matt's novel wasn't working out. He hated talking about it and she, blindly, had assumed it was because he was caught up in the creative process. When, in fact, he'd been stumbling around in pain and she hadn't noticed his anguish. To think she'd blamed him for not noticing her loneliness and depression, when all along she hadn't noticed his either.

'It was that, wasn't it?' asked Finula, eyes shiny with inquisitiveness.

Hope had to grin. That was much more like the Finula she knew: sensitive as a bull in the Waterford Crystal factory.

'I can't say, Finula,' she replied. 'Thanks for the coffee – and the offer of help, which I'll refuse gratefully. I may take you up on the babysitting someday, though.'

The other woman beamed. 'Never say I don't do my bit for the community.'

That evening, Matt phoned at his specified time of six. He phoned every night to speak to the children and nowadays, Hope merely said hello and passed him on to Millie.

Tonight, however, he asked Hope to stay on the line.

'I'd like the children to come and stay with me,' he said. 'I haven't seen them for so long.'

'They can't travel on their own,' Hope said sharply. 'I'm not sticking them on a plane with a "please look after this child" sign around each of their necks.'

'I'll come and get them. I want them for a week. I'm sure your lawyer would think that's acceptable,' Matt retorted irritably.

'I don't have a lawyer,' Hope said quietly.

'Well, let's hope you don't need one.'

She'd been on the verge of telling Mary-Kate, Delphine and Virginia so many times. Her three friends were so kind to her, dropping by endlessly, babysitting in turns so the others could take Hope out, arriving on lonely Friday nights with videos, food and homemade wine from the craft shop, which Hope had to pretend to drink and then empty her glass into the nearest plant pot in case they worked out she wasn't drinking alcohol and came to the inevitable conclusions. Her weeping fig plant would never be the same after having glass upon glass of wine thrown into it.

The only good news was that Delphine and Eugene had set a date for the wedding. They were getting married in two weeks' time.

'We had a long engagement, so we thought we'd have a shot-gun wedding,' joked Delphine.

Pauline would have to like it or lump it, as Mary-Kate said gleefully.

To save funds, Delphine and Virginia were making the dress, Mary-Kate's help having been dispensed with in the matter of fashion.

'I'd be getting married in a grey serge pinafore with a good pair of sensible black shoes on my feet if you had a hand with the dress,' said Delphine one evening as the four of them sat in Hope's kitchen and pored over bride's magazines.

'No, no,' laughed Virginia, 'dark grey wool,' she corrected Delphine, 'and those lace up boots.'

'Dark grey wool just happens to suit me,' retorted Mary-Kate, pretending to be hurt as the other three went off into peals of laughter. 'I suppose I'm wedding co-ordinator, then? Seeing as how I have no sense of style but am ruthlessly efficient.'

'Don't you know I love you, you big eejit,' said Delphine fondly, throwing her arms around her aunt.

'Stop messing,' said Mary-Kate, pleased. 'Now, let's get on with this list. Will we assume your mother is coming, Delphine?'

'Yes,' said Delphine firmly. 'I am going to deliver the invitation myself and if she decides she won't come, then that's her choice.'

'Sam will be so proud of you,' Hope said with a grin.

'How is she?' asked Virginia.

'Not bad. She's off to America for a conference soon and well . . . she's a bit miserable really. Remember Morgan, that lovely man she liked?'

'Yes,' breathed Delphine.

'She saw him with someone else, another woman, I mean.'

'The rat!' spat Delphine.

'Some young woman, too, which hasn't exactly cheered Sam up,' Hope sighed. 'Since she hit forty, she's feeling very vulnerable. I think her confidence has taken a bit of a dive.'

'Make her come here for the wedding,' begged Delphine. 'We'll soon cheer her up.'

'She says she's coming for a visit soon and she'd be thrilled to be invited. But won't that put your numbers up too much?' Hope said.

Mary-Kate looked up from her list and smiled. 'The more the merrier.'

They chatted about satin versus raw silk, weighed up the options for where the wedding reception could be held and ended up discussing Hope's job in the tourist office and how much more sensible it would be if she was working there full time instead of part time.

'I don't know why you don't apply for Ronan's job as tourist officer,' Mary-Kate said as she made the wedding list in her neat hand-writing. 'You'd be perfect for it, Hope.'

'But how can I apply for his job when he's got it?' asked Hope, confused.

'Oh no, here goes Deep Throat again,' giggled Delphine, deep in the realms of medieval satin-trimmed ball gowns with shove-'em-up corset detail.

Mary-Kate sighed. 'Just because I know what goes on around here, there's no need to be sarcastic. I was just saying that I believe Ronan's house is going to be up for sale soon. I met Lara, the estate agent, the other day and she told me.'

They all stared at her.

'And he's not looking for anything else round here which implies that he's moving out of the area.'

'Mary-Kate and the estate agent are in cahoots,' Delphine revealed.

'We are not,' said Mary-Kate equably. 'I just like to know what's going on. Anyway, Hope, you'd be perfect for that job. You have a newcomer's eye for the place and you can see what needs to be done, along with having a real love for Redlion.'

Hope was touched. 'You're right, you know. I do love it here. But could I be a good tourist officer?'

'You'd be better than Ronan,' said Delphine without thinking. 'Ooh,' she said as they all stared at her, 'I didn't mean it that way.'

Hope considered this. 'I actually enjoy working there and it drives me mad when I see how little Ronan does. It's only because Redlion is such a pretty village and is on the main road that it does so well at all. But if we worked hard at it, we could have hordes more visitors coming and not just ones who come in coachloads and leave later that afternoon, but people who rent houses in the area and stay in the small B & Bs. Finula's right, you know, she said that the artistic centre is an important focal point for the area. Imagine if we marketed the town in a cultural way and looked at the important artists, poets and writers who've worked here.'

'Like Matt's uncle Gearóid?' deadpanned Mary-Kate, 'the scratch and sniff artist himself.'

Hope laughed. 'That's not quite what I had in mind. I still haven't seen any of his poetry. I daresay he probably limited himself to writing haiku on Spam, which is a big thing on the internet, I hear.'

'That's a brilliant idea, Hope,' Virginia said enthusiastically. 'Not the Spam, but the artistic links to drum up tourism. There's an artist from around here who's exhibited all over the world. Kevin Burton's got one of his pictures. And it's not the one of Ursula, either,' she added wryly.

They'd all heard the sad story of the room redecorated in exactly the same way as Ursula Burton had decorated it, with her portrait staring down from the wall as if warning all interlopers off.

'At least Sam is fighting a live woman for her man,' Virginia said sorrowfully to Hope. 'I'm competing with a dead one.'

'How is Kevin?' asked Mary-Kate delicately.

'He keeps phoning me, asking me out to play golf,' Virginia said. 'I don't mind playing golf with him but then he thinks we should go out to dinner and I can't cope with that broken record of "Ursula said this, Ursula did that." Do I go on like that about Bill?'

'No,' they all said at the same time.

'Thank God for that.' Virginia was relieved. 'It's like competing with a saint. No matter what I do, I'll never measure up to Ursula and frankly, I don't want to. Sorry, I'm sounding bitter. I don't mean to.'

'You're not bitter,' Delphine said. 'Stupid Kevin needs his head examined.'

'Lots of people round here need their heads examined,' Virginia remarked. 'We should apply for a grant for a resident psychiatrist.'

'Can I have the first session?' begged Hope.

'You're doing fine, aren't you?' said Delphine with an anxious look in Hope's direction.

'Fine, yes, fine,' said Hope faintly. She couldn't tell them that she was going to have a baby in a few months and that she had no idea how she was going to cope as a single mother with three small children. She spent hours at night working out her finances and worrying about how much money she and Matt would get if they sold the house in Bath. How would the divorce courts view their circumstances? Would she get to stay in Curlew Cottage? Hope's list of worries was endless.

# CHAPTER THIRTY

'You're going to love Vegas,' Karen Storin sighed. 'It's a crazy place but there's such a buzz about it and after British weather, it'll be bliss to feel some real heat.'

Both she and Sam looked out the office window where a rainbow straddled the sky. There had been a lot of showers recently, which Karen clearly felt was outrageous behaviour from Mother Nature seeing as it was August.

'You get used to this sort of weather,' Sam said.

'I don't think I ever will,' Karen replied with a shudder. 'I know Chicago has the most awful winters on this planet, but at least it's hot and dry in the summer. The only negative is that Vegas is going to be very hot. I don't know if I'd have picked it myself as a conference venue. Sure, they have big hotels, which is what we need, but August can be very hot in Nevada. It'll be like an oven.'

'As long as the hotel has top-notch air-conditioning, we'll be all right,' Sam pointed out. Unlike Karen, she'd been at world wide company conferences before. In her experience, when four hundred of a record company's top executives gathered every couple of years for an intensive, five-day conference, nobody ever got to leave the hotel. The meetings started at eight in the morning, lasted till dinner, and with artists performing until the wee small hours showcasing their new albums, the chances of some free time alone to explore were non-existent. The participants could have been on Mars for all they got to see of the place they were visiting. At the last conference she'd been to in Zurich three years previously, all Sam had seen of the famous city was the hotel, the view from her bedroom window, and the view from the front seat of the people carrier which brought her back to the airport after four exhausting days. She'd bought some Swiss chocolate in the airport as if to prove to herself that she'd actually been there.

'I'm kind of looking forward to it,' Karen said.

'I'm not,' Sam said grimly. 'It's survival of the fittest at these things. I know there's a bit of that at ordinary UK conferences, with everyone determined to prove that they can work hard and party hard too, but at the big world wide gigs, it's worse. The meetings and presentations are so tiring, but nobody dares leave early at night to catch up on sleep in case it looks as if they're not up to the job. You'll be wrecked when you get home.'

'Yeah, but I guess we'll get a bit of personal time,' Karen said confidently. 'I'm going to take my training stuff with me so I can work out in the gym too but I won't go near the slot machines. They're lethal. The first time I was in Vegas was with my room mate from college and she blew a fortune.'

'I'm not much of a slot machine person,' Sam said, 'and it's years since I played Blackjack.' Just in case they did get any free time, she decided it wouldn't hurt to pack her swimsuit and a few casual outfits.

The rain showers had thankfully finished that evening as Sam walked up her road. In the past month, since the argument with Morgan, she'd taken to walking home a different way so she didn't have to pass his gate. This way, she rounded the corner, past the big cherry tree whose roots were slowly and steadily ripping up the footpath, then reached her gate, all in about one minute.

Even if Morgan had spotted her, he'd never be able to rush out and accost her in time. And if he rang her doorbell, which he hadn't, she'd have ignored it.

Contradictorily, she did want him to rush out and accost her, mainly because she longed for the chance to apologize for all the things she'd said to him, and because she wanted to hear his excuse.

She'd replayed that scene so many times in her mind, mostly in the heat of the night when she lay awake listening to the sound of traffic in the distance. In those replays, she'd been regal and hurt, making Morgan almost beg her to forgive him.

And she would forgive him.

Well, that was immaterial now. She unlocked the apartment door and, when the kittens didn't arrive to greet her, she shrugged off her light jacket and played her phone messages. There was only one. Billy No Mates strikes again.

Catrina had rung ten minutes previously. 'It's eight fifteen, Sam, I hope you're out and about and not still at bloody work. Even masters of the universe take breaks. I'm phoning to see if you and Morgan can come out to dinner with us next Saturday. I thought it would be nice if the gang could have a special dinner together to celebrate little Amber's birth. My mother's going to babysit her – she's the only person I trust. In fact, Amber behaves better for my mother than she does for me! Give me a buzz, byeee.'

Saturday week, Sam knew she'd be flying to Vegas for five days of pure exhaustion. She was almost glad not to have to face dinner with her oldest friends. She'd visited Catrina and baby Amber three times since the baby was born but, luckily, there had been so many other visitors that she and Catrina had never been alone. If they had been, Catrina would have asked meaningfully about Morgan and Sam couldn't bear having to tell her that it – whatever *it* had been – was over.

She'd phone Catrina from the office the next day and make her excuses. But Catrina wasn't giving up. At ten, when Sam was about to watch a documentary about stalkers, the phone went again.

'Got you at last,' said Catrina. 'You weren't at work until this time, were you?'

'No,' lied Sam, feeling guilty for lying, 'I was at an album launch and I only just got in. I didn't want to phone you so late at night.'

They chatted briefly, with Catrina making Sam laugh about how little Amber had changed her life.

'I am exhausted because she sleeps in bursts of two hours but I adore her,' sighed Catrina. 'Hugh is determined to be a new man and changes as many nappies as possible, but he's also exhausted because he wakes up when she cries and then can't go back to sleep. Now tell me, what about dinner next Saturday?'

'Can't, sorry. I've got to go to an international conference in the US.'

'Where?'

'Vegas.'

'How exciting,' sighed Catrina.

'Not really,' Sam pointed out. 'It'll be all work, I'm afraid. The only way to have fun at these things is to stay a few days after the conference and have a bit of a holiday.'

'Are you doing that?'

'No, I've too much to do here.'

'And who's looking after the kittens?'

Sam hesitated, thinking of how Morgan had publicly offered to take care of them on the night of her birthday.

'Er, Jay's taking them for me,' she said.

'Right.' Catrina paused and then asked artlessly, too artlessly, Sam should have realized: 'How's Morgan?'

It was Sam's turn to pause. What was the point of lying? 'I don't know,' she said candidly. 'We had a bit of a falling out and I haven't seen him since.'

'I know,' confessed Catrina. 'Hugh and I brought Amber out the other day and we met him on the King's Road. When I asked him how you were, he told me he hadn't seen you for weeks. You didn't need to be a nuclear physicist to work out you'd had an argument of some sort.'

Sam nibbled her index finger. 'He didn't say anything else?' she asked.

'No, just held Amber and said she was adorable, as if we didn't know. Oh yes, he had his step-daughter with him. She's very beautiful and knows it, mind you. And she's a bit flirty. I think Hugh was impressed in spite of himself, and you know he's not into twenty-five-year-olds. Well,' she laughed, 'I *hope* he's not into twenty-five-year-olds! With me still the size of a whale, you couldn't blame him for looking at skinny little brunettes with no stretch marks. I keep waiting to get miraculously thin with all the breast feeding but it hasn't happened yet.'

'But,' said Sam confused, 'that couldn't be his step-daughter. She's only fourteen or fifteen. I've never met her but she's only a teenager. Fifteen at the most.'

'This was definitely his step-daughter,' Catrina insisted. 'Maggie her name was. Quite the daddy's girl. The way she hooked her arm around his and proudly told us he was buying her a present to cheer her up, it reminded me of my sister when she was ten and wanted to marry our dad. That sort of carry on is all right when you're ten but it's a bit much for a twenty-something. Talk about a handful. She's been at college in London so I'm surprised you never met her.'

Sam bit her lip as the last bit of the jigsaw puzzle fell into place. 'Actually, I think I have met her, except I didn't know who she was.'

It took ages to write the letter. After four drafts, Sam finally thought she'd got it right. But when she re-read it, all the complicated explanations about how she'd thought the girl in his arms was a girlfriend and then Catrina had made it clear she wasn't, simply sounded stupid and trite. She ripped the fourth draft up and started again with a short note that would, hopefully, make Morgan understand that she'd wanted to see him again long before she realized that she'd wrongly accused him.

> *Morgan,*
>    *I'm sorry about everything. I was wrong and I'm so*
> *sorry. Please forgive me for all the horrible things I said.*
> *I miss you and our friendship. Please call me.*
>    *Sam.*

The next morning, she planned to deliver the letter on her way to work but as she was leaving she saw a taxi cruising down the road with its light on, so she raced out the gate and hailed it, thinking she'd drop the letter off that night.

The For Sale sign was enormous, a double-sided one in elegant Roman script telling all and sundry that Jefferson, Power and Dowden were the agents for the house sale. Sam stopped in her tracks when she saw it as she emerged from the taxi that evening.

'I can't wait to see what he gets for it,' said the voice of one of the neighbours, an elderly lady who was giving her two Yorkshire Terriers their evening walk. Both she and Sam contemplated Morgan's house. 'The builders have been there for months, so it must be lovely inside,' the elderly lady continued. 'I do hope somebody nice buys it. The road has gone quite downhill since that rock star chappy bought number 77. My friend at number 76 said they have sex in the garden at those all-night parties. Disgraceful, I call it. She saw them at it with her binoculars.'

Sam didn't have the heart to smile at this innocent remark. When she'd said goodnight to the lady and the panting terriers, Sam walked up to Morgan's door and slipped her envelope in the letter box. She wasn't to know that the house was vacant and that the estate agent scooped the mail up the next day, shoving it all into a drawer in the hall table so as not to make the place look messy for the first viewing on Saturday. He meant to take it all out and leave it for Morgan, but he forgot. Sam's fifth draft lay unnoticed between a flier about window cleaners and a bank statement.

# CHAPTER THIRTY-ONE

Nicole stared out of the car window and watched a little old lady with a shopping trolley walk briskly past while the car sat wedged in a traffic jam which had seen them inch forward about three yards in the past ten minutes.

'This is ridiculous,' she said. 'I don't know why we didn't get the underground.' It didn't seem very sensible to her to spend an hour in early morning traffic getting to the studio when they could have been there in twenty minutes on the tube.

Ollie, LGBK's new press officer, looked at her reprovingly. 'Artists don't get trains,' she said. 'You don't see Celine Dion on the train, do you?'

'You would if she was in a rush,' Nicole grumbled impatiently.

They were on their way to a magazine shoot for *Teen Babe*, the *cover*, as Ollie kept saying reverently. The cover was the Holy Grail for interviews and as far as the industry was concerned, getting the cover of *Teen Babe* was on a par with getting an audience with the Pope. The only downside, as far as Nicole could see, was that she had to spend the entire day in a studio with the *Teen Babe* people answering inane questions about her favourite colour, was she utterly thrilled about having a single out in two weeks, who she fancied most in the whole world and had she ever snogged anyone famous? Or at least these were the main questions the previous *Teen Babe* cover-star had answered and Nicole was not looking forward to an entire day of this sort of stuff. If she was really honest, she was nervous about the whole thing. Giving a ten-minute interview over the phone was one thing, but spending the whole day with a team of photographers, make-up artists and stylists was another entirely. But Nicole had discovered that since her single, 'Honey (Don't You Know) I Need You?' had been getting so much airplay on the radio, her career had moved up a notch. The single would be out in two weeks and everyone at Titus was crossing fingers, legs and anything else they could find in the hopes that it got into the top five. Top ten would be doing fine but to really make an impact, the single needed to hit the top five.

The record company had certainly pulled out all the stops. Nicole's smoky tones were heard blaring out of radios everywhere, which was great. But she'd had to spend the past week being whizzed around the country doing appearances and interviews, for radio, print and television, which wasn't great. Although she'd never admit it to anyone, Nicole was feeling shy for the first time in her life.

She'd enjoyed the touring because she was with a gang. It had been a bit like being down the back at Copperplate, only with Lorelei to tease instead of Miss Sinclair. Now, Nicole was on her own. She was simply Nicole, a star, expected to have opinions on everything and a fantastic life where she wouldn't dream of being home at night to watch her soaps and eat beans on toast.

The car pulled up outside the photographic studio and they all clambered out. As they did, Nicole's mobile rang.

'Hello,' she said softly, recognizing Darius's number.

'How are you?' he asked.

'We just got here,' Nicole said. 'We've been in traffic for ages. I should have walked.'

Darius laughed. 'Hugely successful, gorgeous sexy stars don't walk.'

Nicole sighed with pleasure.

'Good news on two fronts. One, I was talking to a girl from that estate agent's and they have another flat in the complex you like. It's got a smaller balcony but it's two bedroomed, which will be perfect if you ask Sharon to share with you.'

'Great,' Nicole said happily. 'When can we see it?'

'Tonight at six. I'll pick you up from the studio. And the second bit of good news is that Sam Smith is back from the US this weekend and her assistant has pencilled you in for lunch on Tuesday.'

'Thanks for organizing that,' said Nicole. 'I've something important to ask her.'

She blew a kiss down the phone to Darius and went into the studio, determined to be professional. And she was, right down to the moment when the journalist asked her what her favourite colour was.

Unable to help herself, Nicole convulsed helplessly, as the journalist, who couldn't have been much older than she was, looked on in amusement.

'I'm sorry,' the journalist smiled. 'That was last week's interview, the Bimbo Questionnaire. You suit the questions to the subject. If you get someone with a room-temperature IQ, what are you going to ask them? Explain Einstein's Theory of Relativity?'

Nicole laughed heartily. 'I'd like to pass on the favourite colour question but I don't think I want the Einstein one either.'

'You can never tell until you meet someone,' the journalist said. 'I think you might like the intelligent questions better. So, what do you think of this whole music star thing?'

Thinking of the enormous changes in her life and the stresses of her new job, Nicole grinned. 'It has its moments,' she said.


After the heat of Vegas, London felt deliciously cool. Sam breathed in the air as she emerged from the Heathrow Express at Paddington and thought that it was nice to be home, although she was sorry she hadn't got even a hint of a tan.

Originally, she'd planned to go straight home, have a long shower and unpack before going over to Jay's flat and picking up the kittens. But in the taxi from Paddington, she began to think about how lonely the apartment would be without Spike and Tabitha and she changed her mind. She'd get the cab to wait while she dropped off her luggage and then go immediately to Jay's.

'Sure, that'll be fine,' Jay said when Sam phoned her to check if that was all right. 'We're having a lazy Friday evening in. Greg's about to go and get a Chinese takeaway. Do you want to join us?'

'No,' said Sam, not wanting to impose. 'I've eaten.'

'I'll just be a moment,' Sam told the cab driver, as he pulled up outside her house.

She hauled her suitcase from the cab and rushed up the path. Pausing only to swap her light suit jacket for the worn denim one that hung on the cast iron coat stand inside the door, she rushed back down the stairs to the waiting cab.

Jay's apartment had been redecorated, which made Sam realize just how long it had been since she'd been there. The big living room had been a sunflower yellow for ages but now the walls were covered in a warm apricot shade that matched the tapestry throw flung across Jay's threadbare old couch.

'I like the new look,' Sam said enthusiastically.

'Sam, it's been like that for ages,' Jay laughed. 'I'm almost bored with it already.'

'Oh,' Sam said stiffly, sitting on the couch. Tabitha appeared from under the coffee table and climbed onto her lap joyously, purring deeply.

'Tabby, baby, how have you been?' Sam crooned delightedly. 'Where's Spike?'

'Probably sulking,' Jay said with a smile. 'She missed you terribly, although she'd hate you to find out.'

'Was she off her food?' Sam said anxiously, feeling like a bad pet owner.

'Off *her* food, yes. Off *our* food, no. Do you know that she puts her paw in anything she fancies and if it's on your plate, tough.'

Sam had to stifle a grin. 'Sorry, Jay. I didn't think she'd do it with anyone but me. She loves human food and thinks that cat food isn't suitable for creatures like herself.'

The door opened and Greg arrived with both a brown paper bag and an overpowering scent of Chinese food.

Sam felt her taste buds spring into action because she hadn't actually eaten.

'Hi Sam.' Greg gave her a peck on the cheek and then turned to Jay, whom he kissed gently on the mouth as if he hadn't seen her for months. They were still in that stage of love that meant being apart for five minutes made them weak with desire. Sam remembered being like that about a zillion years ago.

'Did you get chicken balls?' asked Jay, when she and Greg finally unlocked lips.

'Yes, love. As if I'd forget anything you asked me for.' They kissed again, slowly and languorously. Sam busied herself tickling Tabitha's chin. In any other circumstances, she'd say 'go rent a room' but she was in their home, after all, so she should be the one to go in order to let them eat their Chinese in post-coital bliss. There was no way they'd last until after eating to make love.

'I should go,' she said, getting up.

'No, don't,' said Greg half-heartedly.

'Stay and eat with us,' pleaded Jay, one arm still round Greg's neck, her fingers stroking gently, while his hand trailed up and down her back. *Last Tango in Shepherd's Bush*, Sam smiled to herself.

'I've got loads to do,' she said, and she wasn't lying. She had to unpack, put the washing on, dust the apartment because it was bound to be musty after a week, oh, loads of things had to be done.

'Well if you're sure . . .' Jay's voice trailed off.

'Very sure,' Sam said firmly and brightly.

The taxi driver wasn't keen on having two cats in his cab, even if they were in their cat boxes.

Jet-lagged and miserable, Sam fixed him with a venomous glare. 'I told the guy I booked the cab with that I was transporting two cats in their boxes,' she hissed, 'so if you've a problem with that, take it up with him.'

'Keep your hair on,' said the driver in alarm.

At Sam's house, he didn't get out of his seat and let her move the boxes and the big bag with their beds and toys in it out without any help. When everything was piled on the pavement, Sam paid him.

'What about a tip?' he said, outraged, because she'd paid the exact fare.

'Never leave the house without an umbrella,' said Sam evilly. 'That's the only tip you're getting from me.'

He was still mouthing furiously when he drove off. Sam moved her cargo into the front garden and then brought the two cat boxes up first. If somebody stole anything, they'd only get the bag of toys and their sleeping cushions, not her beloved kittens. Once the cat boxes were safely in the apartment, she ran down for the other bag and, for the first time, allowed herself to look at Morgan's house. The For Sale sign was still there, only now another board was glued on top of that: Sold.

Sam was so lost in thought when she climbed the stairs to her apartment, that she never even noticed Mad Malcolm's CD player blaring out 'The Girl From Ipanema' at top volume. Noisy neighbours were the least of her problems.

When the kittens were fed and played with, Sam realized she had to buy some groceries. She'd given them the last tin of cat food and they were not keen on long-life milk, which was all she had left in the fridge. Shrugging on her faded denim jacket, she walked briskly down the road to the local shop, passing her favourite local restaurant as she did so. The Greenwich Emporium served organic food with the emphasis on healthy eating, 'apart from the enormous carafes of wine,' as Morgan always joked when they ate there. The owners, George and Felicity, were constantly urging people not to bother having a mere glass of house wine when they'd be sure to have more and therefore a carafe would be better value. This wasn't the hard-sell: it was common sense. Nobody in the Greenwich Emporium ever had just one glass of wine.

All of which undid the goodness of eating organic food, Morgan would say politely to Felicity, who would blush frantically, touch her hair in a self-conscious way and have to rush away to see to another customer.

'You only like coming here because Felicity fancies you,' Sam had said once, only half-teasing.

'If you'd learn how to cook, we wouldn't have to come here at all,' he'd said in an indignant voice. 'This is only paying me back for the four meals,' he emphasized the word *four*, 'I've homecooked for you.'

'Home burned, you mean.'

'That's *well done* in restaurant parlance,' Morgan said gravely.

'Vegetables aren't supposed to be well done.'

'Whatever.'

Sam looked sadly in at the candle-lit interior of the Greenwich and thought of the many happy evenings they'd spent there. It all came back to Morgan. She'd never get over him, she was sure of it.

On the way back from the grocery shop, she had to pass the restaurant again. George was at the door, welcoming in a group of diners.

'Sam,' he roared as he spotted her weighed down with grocery bags. 'How are you?'

She had no chance to rush across the road and yell that she was late for something, so she had to stop, let George hug her and demand to know why he hadn't seen her or Morgan for ages.

'Felicity thinks you've gone off her chicken and aubergine special, but I said that was rubbish, you loved it and you were just busy.'

'Very busy,' Sam agreed and changed the subject. 'How about you? Is the restaurant busy?'

George grimaced. 'Yes and no,' he said. 'Jammed on Fridays and Saturdays and only ticking over for the rest of the time. Sorry, shouldn't be bothering you with this.'

'I'm sorry to hear that,' Sam said genuinely. 'I hope you're not considering closing down. It would be a huge loss to the area.'

George shrugged. 'I hope it won't come to that, but things are tight. If it wasn't for Felicity's organic jams and chutneys, we'd be out of business. She sells a tonne of that stuff in her friend's deli in Richmond.'

They said goodbye and Sam walked the rest of the way home, pondering George's business worries. Tabitha was delighted to see her and so was Spike, who'd regally decided to forgive her mistress for going away for a week on the grounds that she'd been grocery shopping and there might be cat treats hidden among the boring packets. Tabitha weaved around Sam's ankles, while Spike poked her perfectly shaped little head into the bags looking for something she'd like.

'I got cat treats, so you can stop looking,' Sam said, scooping Spike up and cuddling her.

After showering, Sam padded into the kitchen in her bare feet and contemplated the fridge. The chicken breasts she'd bought for her dinner looked palely unappetising and she suddenly longed for one of Felicity's delicious meals: succulent organic roasted chicken served with parsnip and carrot purée flavoured with nutmeg, tiny potatoes crusted with sea salt and aubergine cooked beautifully to Felicity's special recipe, so soft that it melted deliciously in the mouth. Sam was almost drooling thinking of it. Her own attempts at cooking the chicken would be workmanlike at best. And then it hit her: why didn't George and Felicity start up a gourmet takeaway for the days the restaurant wasn't busy? Individual portions of their beautiful meals for the affluent people in the surrounding area, many of whom liked the idea of organic food but didn't have the time or the inclination to cook it. Sam knew plenty of people who'd be delighted to come home and do nothing more domestic than stick one of the Greenwich Emporium's dinners in the oven.

She vowed to mention it to them. They might not be interested, but it couldn't hurt, could it? It might give them a new focus in business . . . And then it struck her: What if she completely changed *her* focus by advising people like George and Felicity? What if she left Titus and set up a company where she advised businesses in trouble? Solving problems was her forte. Faced with a seemingly insurmountable problem, Sam knew there was nobody better at looking at it from every angle until she came up with a solution. She adored problem solving, and, with her business acumen, what better job could she do? All she had to do was decide if she had the courage to go it alone and set up her own business. Sam smiled to herself. She'd been going it alone for most of her life. It would come naturally to her.

# CHAPTER THIRTY-TWO

Matt hated his apartment. 'Fully furnished modern one-bed available for a short let' the advert had said. And it was fully furnished – by someone who clearly thought the original series of *Star Trek* was the last word in style. The bedroom was purple complete with a lava lamp, the living-room-cum-dining room had one wall wallpapered in a design even Austin Powers couldn't have lived with, and there was simply no way you could get comfortable on the big square leather furniture. None of the canary yellow cupboards in the kitchen had handles on them and it had taken five minutes for Matt to figure out how to open any of them.

The letting agent thought the apartment was the last word in modern design, said it was owned by a dot.com genius and pointed out that the neo-sixties and seventies look was really hot.

But then, he was about twenty-four, Matt thought sourly, and didn't remember lava lamps from the first time round.

'I'll take it,' Matt had said miserably, as it was the last short let available and he'd hated all the others.

The only plus was the dot.com genius's enormous computer desk in the dining room, which was where Matt spent most of his time in the evenings, writing. He wasn't working on the great novel, though. He was having fun.

It had started out as the sort of witty e-mail he'd send to Hope if only they were still on speaking terms, a sort of of comfort e-mail where he'd tell her about his day. Of course, Matt was painfully aware that if he'd been sending this type of daily message to her in the first place, he might have realized she was falling for that greasy bastard up at the hotel and put a stop to it before the said bastard ruined his marriage. But he put that out of his mind. Thinking about Hope upset him too much.

He thought about her all the time these days, feeling guilty and sad at the thought of what had happened between them. He knew that Hope would blame herself but Matt knew that his behaviour had certainly driven her to it. If only he'd been able to share the mental torture he'd gone through in Redlion, the depression he'd sunk into when he'd realized he'd made such a huge mistake and was a failure. If he could have shared that with her, then perhaps he wouldn't have been so eager to run away back to Bath. And it had been running away. Faced with a sense of black depression and sheer failure, Matt had run like a small child running from danger.

It had taken him weeks to get over it. His black moods meant he knew he couldn't stay with Dan or Betsey; the only solution was to live on his own and sort himself out. Being a failure was Matt's greatest nightmare, but, as he'd discovered, once you face your greatest nightmare, you can tame it. It had been tough, but he'd done it. The proud, slightly arrogant Matt Parker had gone and in his place was a wiser man, the arrogance replaced by a rueful knowledge of what he was really capable of. He was a husband, a father and an advertising man, not a Booker prize winner. And he was good at being an adman. Adam's heart attack had been more severe than any of them had realized and he'd been ordered to recuperate for several months, which gave Matt the chance to do something he was good at.

Working on his amusing e-mail diary at night had helped too. It was his way of relaxing: being witty as he told Hope or an imaginary someone about how the beer commercial people had gone to lunch with Dan ('we'll be back in an hour, we've got lots of meetings on,' they'd said gravely) and come back four hours later utterly plastered and demanding to go to a strip club, or how the computer technician had said in shocked tones that he'd never seen anything so filthy as the pornographic pictures the graphics department had been sent via e-mail, and had then spent ages trying to print them off on the department colour printer.

Hope would have laughed at that, Matt thought. But he wasn't telling her, she wouldn't care. So he told his imaginary someone, his diary.

Diaries were for teenage girls, he knew, but it was cathartic to spill the beans about the day, so he got into the habit of doing this every evening. Until one evening he'd gone a bit mad and made some stuff up. The sedate receptionist at Judds *hadn't* enticed a motorbike courier into the ladies, desperate for a bonk because it was her thirtieth birthday and she hadn't had sex in a year, but it made a funny story and before long, Matt was giving his imagination full rein with the stories of life in Bath Ad Attack, his fictional advertising company. In Bath Ad Attack, it was a miracle that anyone got any work done at all, what with all the inter-company affairs and the fact that the CEO was trying to take as much time off work as possible to deal with his gender reassignment counselling.

At Bath Ad Attack, entire campaigns were lost on dodgy computer systems because people had been making love across desks and pressed important buttons on keyboards at the moment of orgasm; hard-working people were fired with great regularity for silly mistakes, while others (usually ones with great boobs) were promoted despite botching up even the photocopying; and the whole office rocked with bitchery, indiscretion and genuine mayhem. If only proper novels were as much fun to write, Matt thought one evening, as he reread the words he'd written in an adrenaline-fuelled two hours and found himself laughing like a drain at them. His much-vaunted literary novel was buried in a folder named TOXIC just in case he forgot what was in it and had to look at all those tortured words. Re-reading that novel had never elicited much emotion, apart from the usual grimace as he realized that writing miserably about misery in long, convoluted sentences did not a novel make.

He was never going to be published, never mind be up for the Booker or the Pulitzer or anything else. It was time to face facts. But he might win more awards as the hottest adman on the planet and if ever there was a market for scandalous, libellous farcical novels about life in an ad agency, he was the man for the job.

Matt switched off the laptop and switched on Sky Sport. Mind you, the chances of his becoming the hottest adman ever were going to be hindered when Adam Judd came back to work and took over the helm again. And where would Matt be then?

The following morning, Matt ran up the steps to the front door of Judds, feeling fit, healthy and ready to take on the world. He had two important meetings that morning and lunch in one of the city's top restaurants with a prospective client who'd keep the entire company in Mercedes sports cars for the rest of their lives if only the client signed on the dotted line.

'Morning Matt,' breathed Celeste, one of the work-experience students they'd taken on, arriving at the door at the same time as him.

'She fancies you rotten,' Dan had teased Matt the day before. 'Every time she opens her mouth it's "Matt says this" or "Matt says that" like she was talking about the Almighty.'

'Get out of it,' Matt had retorted, giving his old friend a slap on the arm with a copy of *Campaign*. 'You're just jealous because I won the squash last night.'

'The truth hurts,' Dan continued. 'Mr Advertising Guru, tell me how you make all the women wet their knickers? Is it your dark good looks or the size of your bonus?'

Matt had grinned to himself. Dan could never resist smiling at a pretty girl and didn't understand that Matt had no interest in girls like Celeste or even Betsey's sweet au pair.

Dan obviously felt that Matt deserved a fling to cheer him up but Matt's heart wasn't in it. He and Dan had blazed a pub and nightclub trail in Bristol the previous month but no matter how many lean-thighed babes had danced in front of him in the nightclub, shaking their booty in cowgirl fringed skirts, he'd only been able to think of Hope. At the London awards ceremony, the only thing he'd undressed was a bottle of mineral water which sat in front of him at the table and which he'd painstakingly de-labelled while all around him flirted and drank uproariously. Matt didn't need anyone to tell him he was turning into a bore.

'Morning Celeste,' Matt said, trying to sound professional. He didn't want to be rude or anything but he wanted her to get the message that she was a junior colleague and that was it.

He pushed the button for the lift, with Celeste eagerly beside him, having rushed to keep up with his long-legged stride. She was keen to explain to the handsome Mr Parker exactly what she'd been doing.

'I've been working with Ricky on the health club adverts and we're going to be finished today,' she said, batting her long eyelashes for all she was worth. He really was so dishy and somehow tortured with that lean dark jaw with a five o'clock shadow even though it was still first thing in the morning. There was something hideously *hot* about men who needed to shave twice a day.

'Great. Show it to Dan, will you?' Matt said absently as he pushed the third floor button, 'I've got a lot on this morning.'

Celeste's shoulders slumped. Honestly, what was the point? She'd worn her best leather jeans and had got in really early in the hopes of bumping into Matt Parker, who was always first in, and where had it got her? Nowhere.

He was obsessed with work, like all bloody men.

Jasmine Judd arrived just as Matt was leaving his second meeting. He was loosening his tie and popping the top button of his grey shirt when he saw her.

'Hello Matt,' she said, tearfully, looking for all the world like Jessica Rabbit in skin tight leather with zips everywhere.

'Jasmine, what a surprise,' Matt said, mentally saying 'shit'. Every time Jasmine arrived, she was there on a mission from Adam to see how things were going. Even though Adam had promised his cardiologist that he wouldn't set foot inside Judds or phone in for two months, he'd been cheating slightly by getting updates from Jasmine. Now she stood on the threshold of her husband's old office, currently taken over by Matt, and looked as if she was about to flood the entire building with tears.

'Oh Matt,' she sobbed, heaving herself into his arms.

Over her shoulder, Matt could see Dan giving him an enthusiastic thumbs up sign as if to say 'Result!' Matt scowled back. Five foot ten of blonde, beautiful boss's wife in tears was not his idea of a result.

'Sit down, Jasmine, you poor thing,' Matt said, thinking that Hope was always so much better at comforting people than he was. She was so good when there was any sort of emotional crisis: she'd have known exactly how to comfort Jasmine, he thought sadly. She was so kind and affectionate to everyone, hugging the kids all the time and telling them that she loved them. A longing for Hope and the children swept over him.

'Matt, I can't stop Adam. He wants to come back to work!' Jasmine's anguished tones broke into his reverie and she leaned against him tearfully.

Matt knew it had to happen. From the first day he'd taken over from Adam and had realized that he enjoyed being the big boss, Matt had told himself that Adam was ill, not dead. He'd be back and then the fun would stop and Matt would be demoted back to being an employee. A trusted, valuable employee, yes. But still an employee. One of the people who said 'how high?' when Adam said 'jump'.

'Would you like a cup of tea?' Matt heard himself asking in a perfectly normal voice. He waved at his assistant and made a drinking motion, then turned his attention back to Jasmine, who was sobbing and heaving all at the same time, her zips rattling and her leather outfit creaking. She smelt of some heavy perfume he didn't recognize and didn't like. Hope was more of a floral perfume person. Roses and lilies and stuff like that. Nice, girlie stuff.

'What has the doctor said?' he asked Jasmine, half-hoping that the doctor would have acted like one in a Victorian melodrama and said something along the lines of 'if Adam ever picks up a biro again, the strain will kill him!'

'He says it's about time Adam went back to work,' Jasmine sobbed, 'but I know it's too early. He could *die* and where would I be then?' Cue another bout of heaving sobs on his shoulder.

Matt hoped she wasn't ruining his charcoal Italian suit.

'Well, the doctor probably knows best,' Matt said, thinking to himself that the doctor should be struck off. 'Is Adam eager to get back to work?' Stupid question. Adam believed holidays were for people who'd been either fired or made redundant.

'Yes, and I don't understand why because I thought he'd been so happy at home with me,' she wailed.

The door opened tentatively and his assistant arrived with a tray of coffee and biscuits, which Matt knew were a waste of time. As if Jasmine was going to eat biscuits. You didn't fit into that sort of leather outfit by losing the run of yourself with the chocolate digestives.

It took ten minutes, two cups of coffee and a certain amount of patting Jasmine's knee for her to be satisfactorily cheered up. Matt knew it was in his interests to tell Jasmine that Adam should buy a yacht and sail off into the sunset with her, only stopping at sun-drenched islands with relaxed tax laws to stash away his regular income from Judd's, which would become wildly successful with Matt Parker at the helm. But he couldn't say that. Instead, he told Jasmine the truth: that her husband was the sort of man who'd die if he wasn't allowed to come in and run his empire and that after another month of enforced recuperation time, she'd be begging Adam to go back to work because he'd be driving her mad.

'He lives and breathes this place,' Matt pointed out.

Jasmine stifled a sob. 'Yes, but so did you and you gave it up. And now you have a lovely life in Ireland writing and you're not going to get a heart attack, are you? Hope's very lucky. She's got everything! She's got a lovely place to live and no stress and no work and every-thing! Not like me. I'm under so much pressure with all of this.'

Jasmine sobbed again and Matt, fearing for the state of his suit which was now sodden, sighed and put his arms around her again. The only person in the agency who knew about his separation was Dan, and Matt was grateful for small mercies. If Jasmine knew that Matt was separated, she'd doubtless be setting him up on blind dates with her bimbo-ish friends.

'Adam would never move anywhere nice to be with me,' Jasmine said shakily. 'He won't even take me to the Bahamas for our wedding anniversary.'

'He probably can't imagine needing a holiday because he's been away from the office for so long, but he will,' Matt said gently. 'Give him a month back here and he'll be thrilled at the sight of a holiday brochure, I promise you. And don't think Adam doesn't love you, you know he does. Remember,' he added ruefully, 'other people's marriages aren't always what they seem.'

'What do you mean?' she asked, dabbing at her eyes with a tissue.

'Well, Hope and I have had a falling out,' he said slowly. 'We're not talking and I haven't seen her for a while.'

'But you love each other, this is terrible,' wailed Jasmine. 'You've got to make it up, now! As soon as Adam is back, fly to see Hope and tell her you love her. Take flowers,' Jasmine added. 'And perfume. Women love perfume.'

It was like getting marriage guidance counselling from Barbie, Matt thought.

When Jasmine had finally been borne off by Sadie from the art department to a cheering-up girlie lunch, Matt sat at his, correction *Adam's*, desk and looked around miserably. It was all over: his delusion of power. Adam Judd would come back and after his brush with death, would undoubtedly be tougher and narkier than ever.

Adam had never made it any secret as to who was the boss at Judd's, the company he'd built up by sweating blood and guts, as he liked to tell anyone who'd listen. He would probably see Matt as a threat now; the man who'd taken over when he was sick and the man who could take over at any time. It wouldn't matter that Matt wasn't the sort of man to start a mutiny. Adam would want him out because every day he looked at Matt, he'd be reminded of his heart attack and his very mortality. Getting rid of Matt would become his mission.

What was worse was that Matt had given him the ammunition to do it. Matt's sabbatical had another few months to run, time enough for Adam to find another adman who'd undermine Matt and make it impossible for him to come back. And it wasn't as if he even had anything thrilling to go back to. One hopeless novel and a wife who didn't want him. Yah-bleedin'-hoo.

'Fancy a drink?' said Dan at six, when most of Judds had sloped off quietly to the bar next door which was having a tequila promotion. The office was silent except for the faint sound of the cleaning lady's vacuum. 'Betsey is on a girls' night out in London with her mates from the magazine and as she's due to arrive home at half one, pissed and screaming that all men are bastards, I reckon I'm due a night out in lieu.'

Matt, miserable though he was, had to laugh. 'You mean she's on a night out which will include the radical lesbian feminist columnist who writes those incisive interviews on the contents of celebrities' fridges?'

'Yeah, that's the one. Ms I'm-a-serious-journalist-but-just-let-me-file-this-copy-about-The-Spice-Girls-and-I'll-tell-you-my-views-on-Marxism-and-the-male. After an hour in her company, even the mildest mannered woman starts to think about Bobbiting her husband. You wouldn't mind, but Betsey's hardly the oppressed little woman. I do more ironing than she does, *she* controls the cheque book and if one of us had to give up work to mind the kids, it'd definitely be me.'

'My heart bleeds for you. Tell me, how many radical lesbian feminists does it take to change a light bulb?' asked Matt.

'Man, the old jokes sure are the best,' laughed Dan. 'Ten, one to change the light bulb and the other nine to hold a workshop about the oppressed role of the socket. You need to download some new jokes, my lad. Let's go and get plastered.'

On their third pint, Matt told Dan about his novel: both of them.

'The literary one was crap, that's the only word for it,' Matt said dolefully.

He was mildly offended that Dan didn't bother to console him and say 'no, mate, I'm sure it's great,' or anything like that.

'I tried that once,' Dan confessed, 'the big novel. Mine was crap too.'

'Oh,' said Matt, slightly mollified. 'It's not that easy, is it? But, you know, the second one is easier to write and it's more fun.'

'What second one?' Dan asked, waving at the barman for another pint and simultaneously eyeing up a spectacular female customer who was wearing a T-shirt that must have been originally made for a ten-year-old. On a grown woman, it stretched in all sorts of interesting places.

'I've been messing around at night and I've written about twenty thousand words of a . . .' Matt struggled to find the right word, 'sort of farce of a novel. It's about advertising.'

'That'd account for the farcical bit, then,' Dan said. 'It's not an autobiographical farce, is it?'

'The hero is stunningly handsome in a dark way and women are always throwing themselves at him, if that's what you mean,' Matt joked.

'So it's fantasy, right?'

'Ha ha. No, seriously, it's a bit of fun.'

The beer arrived.

'Are you going to send it to an agent?' Dan asked, fishing in his pocket for change to pay the barman.

'Forget it,' Matt said.

'Why ever not? It could be the answer to all your prayers. You could make us all sick by getting paid a mega-buck advance to sit at home all day and take the mickey out of the world of advertising.'

'Out of people like you, you mean?'

'Yeah, like me. Go on, what have you got to lose?'

# CHAPTER THIRTY-THREE

Dinky heard the doorbell first and began barking.

'You're a great early warning system,' Virginia smiled at her little dog. She slowly got to her feet, wiped the earth off the knees of her old gardening trousers and walked up past the gnarled old crab apple trees, stripping off her gardening gloves as she did so. Weeding was very therapeutic. Virginia loved working in the pale evening sunlight, clearing the flower beds slowly and methodically. Her baby sedum plants were almost smothered by some perfidious bindweed and a crop of particularly virulent nettles. Too much golf was bad for the garden, she decided. She'd been playing at least three times a week recently, once with Kevin and the other times with three very nice local lady golfers who were delighted to have someone else to make up a fourball. Of course, she was still very much a beginner but she no longer hit the ball sideways and her putting had improved beyond all recognition. And her three new golf partners were so encouraging. They were so full of stories about how hopeless they'd been in the beginning and how one of them had once hit a ball backwards straight into her husband's foot, that Virginia's confidence was growing. If only she could improve her bunker shots.

Thinking of this, she opened the front door and found an elderly couple complete with two suitcases standing on the step. The woman was leaning heavily on a walking stick and her frail face was pale with tiredness.

'Thank goodness you're open,' the man said delightedly. 'When we couldn't reach you on the phone, we were afraid you'd gone out of business.'

Virginia stared at both of them and at the man's hand which was holding a three-year-old copy of the bed and breakfast guide which listed Kilnagoshell as a charming, olde worlde retreat where guests could escape the rat race and enjoy Margaret Delahunty's famous cooked breakfasts and her husband Jasper's wonderful dinners.

'I'm terribly sorry,' Virginia said, meaning it, 'but this is a private home now. It's not a B & B anymore.'

Both faces fell and the woman looked as if she might faint.

'Oh no,' said the man. 'We should have phoned, I'm sorry. Monica, are you all right?' he added in alarm as Monica wobbled a bit.

'Come in,' Virginia said firmly. 'Leave the cases there. Nobody's going to steal them. Maybe a cup of tea will help you and I'll phone the nearest B & B – that's Mrs Egan's down the road – and see if they have any vacancies.'

'Thank you so much,' said Monica gratefully as her husband helped her in.

Virginia led them into the drawing room, which was high-ceilinged and faded in a shabby genteel way, almost exactly the same as it had been before except that Virginia's furniture now stood on the old flowered carpet which must have been there since the thirties. The curtains were beautifully made eggshell blue damask, with velvet fringing that was nearly all worn away with age.

'It's just the same,' cried Monica, looking around her.

'A bit different, probably,' Virginia said. 'I haven't changed much since I've been here, though. I'm Virginia Connell, by the way.'

'Edmund and Monica Harris,' said the man. 'Thank you so much for this. Monica hasn't been well recently and I couldn't imagine making her drive off again without a rest.'

Introductions over, Virginia got up to make tea.

She was back in ten minutes with tea and a plate of the cookies she'd made for a charity cake sale in town.

To her relief, Monica was looking healthier, although she was now embarrassed to have made such a nuisance of herself and to have interrupted Virginia's day.

'That's perfectly all right,' Virginia said kindly, handing her visitors their tea. 'The only thing you interrupted was a bit of weeding and I can do that anytime.'

'Monica loved weeding,' Edmund said fondly, putting sugar in his wife's tea. 'She's a talented gardener but since her hips went, she can't bend.'

'I did get one of those long-handled weeder things but I'm so slow at it, that it annoys me,' Monica added. 'The gardens here are beautiful, but they must be so much work.'

'So you have been here before?' Virginia asked.

'We came here for our honeymoon and I've never forgotten it.'

It was Virginia's turn to look surprised. 'Did you get married recently?'

'Oh no, fifty years ago. All we could manage was a week away and we came here, it was wonderful.'

'But that's incredible ,' Virginia said in amazement. 'I had no idea Kilnagoshell was a B & B that long ago. When I bought it, I was led to believe that it was turned into one only twenty years ago or thereabouts.'

'You see, the O'Neills, the family who owned it since the twenties, went through a bad time financially and the only way out was to take in guests. It wasn't like a B & B, really,' Edmund said. 'More like staying with friends in a house in the country and paying your way. There were no locks on the doors or anything and we'd all sit in here before dinner and have a little drink with Major O'Neill.'

'And dinner was whatever had been shot or caught that day. It was like a dinner party, you didn't have a choice but the food was delicious,' added Monica wistfully. 'We've stayed in the top hotels round the world, and there was none of them could beat Kilnagoshell.'

'It's the atmosphere,' Edmund added. 'You can't buy atmosphere, no matter how much money you put into a place.'

For a moment, Virginia thought of Mrs Egan's de luxe B & B with its dead plain façade, chipped front gate and the few withered looking geraniums that sat in plastic pots outside the gate.

Whenever Virginia allowed herself to peer in as she passed, she could see net curtains hanging stiffly as though starched and she had once noticed a cat-frightener device in the front garden to deter any unwary felines from doing their business in Mrs Egan's sliver of mossy lawn. The only atmosphere Virginia could imagine in such a house was an atmosphere of uncomfortableness.

On an impulse, she turned to Monica and Edmund: 'I'm not precisely equipped for it, but would you like to stay here tonight? On a no-pay basis because I have no insurance for paying guests and anyway,' she smiled warmly, 'no B & B inspector has been past these doors for years.'

It was worth it so see their faces light up. 'That would be wonderful,' said Monica, tears in her eyes.

'I've some news for you,' Virginia said the following evening when she phoned Jamie to say hello.

'Ditto,' he said joyfully. 'You first, Mum.'

'No,' insisted Virginia in alarm. 'I'm a mother and I worry. You first or I'll spend the next ten minutes thinking that your news is bad and that you're going to travel round the world as a male strippergram or something.'

'Mum!' Jamie was scandalized.

'They say the money's very good,' teased his mother. 'Go on, spill the beans.'

'Laurie will probably be phoning you later to tell you that it's off with him and Sergeant Major Barbara.'

'Off?' Virginia was astonished.

'Off. The engagement is off and I can't say I'm not pleased. In fact, I've just rung Dominic and Sally to tell them the good news too, but you've got to pretend that you know nothing. Promise? I only know 'cos I dropped into Laurie earlier to return a video and he told me.'

'Oh, the poor boy.' Virginia was devastated at the thought of her beloved Laurence being upset.

'Poor boy my backside! He's had a lucky escape.'

The fact that Virginia agreed with Jamie didn't stop her remonstrating with him: 'He's upset,' she said. 'Having someone break off an engagement with you is a huge thing, it's going to be very traumatic,' she said.

'Mum, you've got the wrong end of the stick,' Jamie said. '*She* didn't break it off; *he* did.'

This time, Virginia did gasp.

'He probably wants to tell you himself, Mum, but I couldn't resist,' Jamie said. 'It's totally possible that Barbara will phone you in floods of tears asking you to intervene. She's such a little madam.'

'I'd hate to see her try and get me on her side,' Virginia said, her mouth in a grim line. 'That's the best thing Laurence has done in years.'

'Mum,' said Jamie.

'Yes?'

'Please tell him that, won't you?'

'Not in so many words, Jamie. We have to be gentle with him. No matter who broke the engagement, it's a big shock.'

'And what's your big news?'

'I'm going to turn Kilnagoshell House back into a B & B.'

'Great, Mum,' said Jamie. 'You'll be a wonderful landlady. Look, I must fly. I'm going out with the lads tonight. Talk soon, byee.'

Virginia couldn't stop herself smiling as she hung up. Jamie was hilarious. Nothing fazed him. She could have said she was starting a brothel and his reaction would have been the same. To hear him blithely say it was a great idea made Virginia laugh to think that she'd spent a near-sleepless night thinking of the very possibility. Dinky and she had sat up until half one, considering every angle of the plan, until Virginia had got annoyed with herself and marched off to bed, informing Dinky that her mistress was an idiot who couldn't run a game of Scrabble, never mind a bed and breakfast. But when she'd woken that morning and still felt full of vigour and enthusiasm, she'd changed her mind.

Kilnagoshell was made to be lived in, made to be full of people. Turning it back into a B & B was a wonderful idea and she was determined to go through with it.

She longed to phone Mary-Kate to discuss it but didn't want the phone engaged in case Laurence tried to phone. She refused to phone him first and act like the over-protective mama. Let him tell her in his own good time.

He phoned after nine.

'Hi Laurence,' she said warmly.

'Jamie's told you, hasn't he?' said Laurence instantly.

'Can I have no secrets from you?' asked Virginia guiltily.

'You sounded so sympathetic,' Laurence explained, 'I just knew.'

'Do you want to talk about it?'

'Not really. Just that she was driving me mad. She wasn't marrying me, Mum, she was marrying the dentist. She fancied herself as the dentist's wife, that was it.'

Virginia knew it was time to say nothing.

'How are you, Mum? Still playing golf with the handsome widower?'

'Snap,' said Virginia. 'We are not an item any more, if we ever were, for that matter.'

'What happened?'

'He was still in love with his wife,' she said simply.

'Oh Mum, I'm sorry. He sounded great. He was good for you.'

'Not good enough,' Virginia attempted to joke.

'Don't worry, some gorgeous bloke will come along who *is* good enough for you.'

'I think I've finished dipping my feet in the dating pool,' she said.

'Don't be defeatist,' said Laurence. 'I'm not giving up and neither should you.'

Virginia's heart missed a beat. 'Would you mind me finding a gorgeous bloke?' she asked gently. 'Would that be all right? You wouldn't feel I was betraying your dad?'

Laurence laughed heartily. 'If any of us gave you the slightest bit of hassle over seeing another man, Dad would come straight down from heaven and beat us black and blue!'

Virginia relaxed. 'He would, wouldn't he? He was a special man, your father,' she added wistfully. 'I'll never find anyone like him again. He was a one-off.'

'Cheer up, Mum. There's no harm in looking.'

Once Laurence was off the phone, she rang Mary-Kate, who was so pleased at the idea of turning Kilnagoshell back into a B & B that you'd have thought she'd come up with it herself.

'I knew you'd do it!' she crowed delightedly. 'It's perfect, it's just what you need and it's just what Redlion needs: a classy, atmospheric country house hotel.'

'I didn't say hotel,' said Virginia in alarm.

'Country house hotel,' insisted Mary-Kate. 'That's different. Beautiful, elegant and atmospheric – and you don't need a jacuzzi either. Tell me,' she said thoughtfully, 'when were you thinking of opening?'

'I hadn't got that far . . .' Virginia said. 'Why?'

'Because we still can't find the right venue for Delphine's wedding and we could have it in Kilnagoshell. Think of it, Virginia, we could get all hands on deck to do your place up and the money for the wedding would help pay for renovations. Isn't it a wonderful idea?'

'God Mary-Kate,' Virginia shook her head ruefully. 'You're not a woman: you're a force of nature.'

From the way Lydia shuffled into Sam's office on the Monday morning after the conference, Sam knew something was wrong. Normally, Lydia was bright and breezy, ready to chat to Sam as she brought in the mail and the coffee, filling Sam in on her love life even though Sam had never asked for an update on Jake/Phil/whoever. But today, there was no spring in Lydia's step. Perhaps she wasn't well, Sam reflected, flicking expertly through her post. She drank some coffee, made some notes for letters to be replied to, then called Lydia into the office.

'Yes,' Lydia said.

She was white in the face, Sam realized.

'Everything OK?' Sam asked.

Lydia nodded her head tautly. 'Yes,' she said.

She was lying, Sam was sure of it. But Sam had other things on her mind, like Steve Parris and how he'd behave to her now they were back in London, in Steve's domain. In Vegas, they'd never been alone thanks to the chaperonage of other conference delegate and the company bigwigs that Steve loved hanging out with.

The morning passed with painful slowness. Lydia's misery wrapped itself round the office like a fog. Finally, Sam had had enough. She could barely concentrate.

'I'm going to the Italian for a bit to eat. Will you come with me?' she asked.

The startled expression on Lydia's face made her resemble a duck who'd been asked to go on an all-expenses paid trip to à l'orange.

'All right,' she stammered.

In the tiny Italian café, Sam ordered a pesto dish she didn't really want. She wasn't hungry but she liked Lydia and if there was any chance of getting her once-super-efficient assistant back on the rails, a private little lunch was it. If she was gentle, perhaps Lydia would spill the beans and things could go back to normal. But she didn't need to prod. Lydia started the ball rolling herself.

'I feel so guilty,' Lydia said, hanging her head over her half-nibbled breadstick.

'Why?' asked Sam conversationally.

'Because I've asked personnel to move me to another department and now I wish I hadn't.'

Sam gaped at her in shock. 'You asked to be moved? But why?'

Lydia hung her head. 'Because you've been so hard to work with lately and I can't cope. I've been having a rough time at home; my dad's sick, and I don't need hassle at work too. You used to be so lovely to work for, you were nice,' she added accusingly.

Sam still said nothing; she couldn't. Shock had made her speechless.

'Lately, you've turned into a bitch,' Lydia said, determined to get it all out now she'd started. Be honest in life, her favourite self-help book had said. So she was going to be honest.

'Everyone said you were tough and a bit of a bitch but I never found you like that,' Lydia went on. 'You had to work hard but I knew that was because women have to work harder to be recognized. I understood that and I admired you.'

The waiter laid their lunch in front of them but neither woman noticed.

'But lately I can't do anything right. For the last month, you've just snapped at me like I'm some sort of skivvy. There's no need for it. And now you're being nice to me and I feel so awful . . .'

Two large tears plopped onto Lydia's untouched carbonara.

Guilt and shame fought for supremacy in Sam's heart and shame won.

There she was accusing her boss of harassment, when she'd been guilty of harassment herself. So, she hadn't tried to flirt with poor Lydia, but she may as well have. Her bad temper had had the effect of making her impossible to work with. How could she have been so awful?

She reached over and patted Lydia's hand. 'I am so, so sorry, Lydia,' she said earnestly. 'I had no idea you felt this way and I feel so ashamed of myself. I . . .' she stopped, 'I want to excuse myself by saying that things have been pretty awful in my life recently but that's no excuse.' She stared down at her plate. 'You're a great assistant, you make me laugh and you never seem to be in a bad mood about anything, and I repaid you by taking my misery out on you.'

She'd never felt more ashamed in her life. 'I can't say how sorry I am and I'll talk to personnel and explain that your leaving was absolutely my fault.'

Lydia shook her head. 'But why didn't you tell me you were going through a bad time?' she demanded, red-eyed. 'I'm on your side, we're a team. I could have helped.'

'I know. I'm sorry,' Sam said. 'I did what I always do when I'm down: pull up the drawbridge like an embattled fortress and settle in for a long siege. I never want anyone to help me, I won't let them.'

'That's stupid,' said Lydia forcefully. 'We all need friends, nobody can do it all on their own.' She squeezed her boss's hand.

'I really am sorry, Lydia, and I mean it about talking to personnel. It's my fault you're leaving and I owe it to you to make sure personnel know too.'

Lydia dug her fork into her carbonara. 'Ah, forget about it. I'll tell them I was having a bad day and don't want to move after all.'

Sam looked down at her lunch but knew she couldn't touch it now. 'No, Lydia, don't, please. I don't know if I can do this job anymore. I'm tired of having to be tough, I'm tired of working all hours and having no life.' There, she'd finally said it. 'It's turning me into someone I don't like.' She laughed mirthlessly. 'It's turning me into someone that *nobody* likes.'

'Now that's plain daft, if you don't mind me saying it,' Lydia said firmly. 'I like you lots – of people at Titus like you. You're straight as a die, you don't expect people to suck up to you and you're fair.'

'That's very kind of you, Lydia, especially since I've been the bitch from hell for the last month, but I mean it. I think I've got to move on. Please don't say that to anyone in the office.'

'Of course I wouldn't,' Lydia said indignantly. 'But I think you're mad. You've got such a great career.'

'A great career and no friends because I'm turning into a fortress,' Sam said ruefully. 'Ms Smith locked in her office on the fifth floor. There's got to be more to life than a big salary and a pension plan, Lydia. By the time I'm ready to collect the pension, all the life will have been squeezed out of me and I won't have the energy to spend it. I really think I need to get out of the rat race.'

'Downshifting, they call it. Less money for less work and more life. Can't see the attraction myself,' Lydia commented.

'Yes, but you're twenty-three, Lydia. I'm forty. I've been working like an indentured slave most of my life and I have nothing to show for it except my own office stationery and a personal assistant who wants to be moved because I'm such a cow to work with.'

'Sorry,' Lydia said.

'You're not the one who has to be sorry,' Sam said firmly. 'That's my fault and I'll apologize again. Thank you for having the guts to tell me.'

Lydia laughed. 'It wasn't easy,' she admitted. 'You're no pushover.'

'Tell me about it,' Sam groaned. 'Anyway, enough of this. Tell me about your poor dad. What's wrong with him?'

They got back to the office at half two, Lydia cheered up by both the talk and two glasses of wine. Sam was cheerful on the surface but underneath, she felt numb. She was repelling people left, right and centre.

She left work early and phoned Hope, who was making fairy cakes with the children helping with the icing.

'Don't eat it all, Millie,' Hope could be heard saying. 'You'll be sick.'

'Won't,' said Millie defiantly.

'Pink icing is more enticing than cabbage, there's no doubt about it,' Hope groaned.

The sisters chatted idly for a few moments.

'Can I ask you a question, Hope?' Sam said.

'Sure.'

'How do you define yourself?'

'That's not a question, that's an essay,' laughed her sister. 'Yourself: define and discuss. I can see Miss Marsh giving us an essay like that in English.'

Sam chuckled. 'Miss Marsh wasn't an English teacher, she was a frustrated psychiatrist. The hidden meanings she got out of *Hamlet* ... No wonder I refused to do an arts degree, I couldn't have coped with all the analysis. That wasn't what I meant, Hope, about defining yourself.'

'What did you mean?'

'Well ...' Sam hesitated, trying to find the right words. 'I've always defined myself by my job. When I was in marketing, that was me: Marketing Executive.'

Hope interrupted. 'That was what you did, not what you were. Millie, stop, put that spoon down. You'll be sick.'

'Actually, no. That's what I was. It was the same thing for me, you see. What I did was what I was.'

'You're turning into Miss Marsh,' said Hope jokily, sensing the conversation was getting deep and intense.

'Exactly. Miss Marsh was a teacher, it was her whole life and didn't you always feel that she had no other life outside the classroom? That being a teacher was everything for her?'

'Sort of,' Hope replied. 'What are you getting at, Sam?'

'You're a mother and a wife ...'

'Er ... there's a bit of doubt about the latter description,' Hope said lightly.

'OK, so you're a mother, and a friend, you're doing sterling work in the tourist office, and you meet people and go to the Macramé Club for fun, and renovate old kitchen chairs and rear hens who produce real eggs, and you make fairy cakes,' Sam paused. 'You've lots of different sides to you. Whereas me, I'm a businesswoman and I'm nothing else. I've spent my life defining myself by my job and it's not enough. When I retire, there'll be nothing left. Like a balloon with no air inside.'

'You're hardly going to retire just yet?'

'No, but I can't keep doing this the rest of my life, I'll burn out. And what then? Burnt out exec in chichi flat with two cats, lots of office clothes and an ulcer.'

'Cheer up, it's not that bad, is it?'

Sam sighed and said nothing.

'It's Morgan, isn't it?' Hope asked. 'I though you were getting over him. You've got over guys before.'

'This is different,' Sam said sadly. 'I never saw a future with any of the other men. Even Karl. We had fun but I never looked further forward than the next few dates or the next weekend away. Planning a month ahead seemed like a big deal. I mean, who knew what you were going to be doing in a month. Morgan was different.' Even saying his name hurt. 'I never thought I wanted that togetherness thing but after meeting Morgan, I know I do. And I screwed it all up. Go on, tell me it's my fault,' she said gloomily.

Hope sighed. 'As if *I'm* going to give you romantic advice. Me, the woman on her own with two small children, six hens and a family of rats at the back of the yard and . . .' She stopped, wondering if this was the moment to mention that she was pregnant.

'You still have rats?' asked Sam.

'Either that, or aliens keep landing down by the beech tree frightening the hens every night. Those bloody rodents actually seem to *like* rat poison. I've a good mind to get a gun and shoot them.'

'When you're finished with it, will you lend it to me so I can shoot myself in the foot properly.'

'Sam!' chided Hope.

'Well, I spend my life shooting myself in the foot.'

'Stop being so negative. It's not like you, Sam.'

'I'm having a "not like me" sort of day,' Sam pointed out. 'I think I'm going to leave my job.'

'Good,' said Hope.

'Good? I thought you'd be shocked!'

'Why would I be shocked? If you didn't work all the hours, maybe I'd see more of you. That bloody job is killing you.'

'Oh,' said Sam, utterly taken aback. She'd imagined that Hope was so proud of her sister's fabulous job, like a satisfied mother who loved seeing her offspring in such a position of power. She could hardly say this, though, because she now realized that the only person who was deeply proud of her job was herself. As if reading her thoughts, Hope spoke again.

'I'd be proud of you no matter what you did, Sam. You don't have to prove anything to me. I know you're clever and talented and oh, loads of other things. You've proved it, now you can stop proving it and try another sort of life.'

Sam had to fumble blindly for a tissue.

'I do want another sort of life,' she gulped. 'But I couldn't tell anyone.'

'I know,' Hope said comfortingly. 'It's like spending ages driving on a winding road and finally managing to overtake the car that's been crawling along at thirty miles an hour and then almost immediately, you realize you have to stop for petrol or something and *you don't want to*. 'It's like you'll have to give up all the ground you gained and you can't bear to do it. But who's watching, who cares? Nobody but you.'

'You're very wise, you know that?'

Hope laughed heartily. 'Thank you. I spent years thinking I was an idiot and couldn't do anything without asking advice or getting the go-ahead from someone else, but you know, over the past few months, I've begun to realize that I'm not an idiot. Just lacking in self-belief. Delphine jokes that the two of us should set ourselves up as a telephone agony aunt service: problems-r-us.'

'I'd owe you a fortune, then,' said Sam with a grin.

'Don't write the cheque just yet. I don't think it's very professional to go into a counselling business advising other people when your own life is totally messed up,' Hope said ruefully.

'Why can't you and Matt sort it out? You know you're both crazy about each other, just tell him and stop playing Ms Ice Queen on the phone with him.'

'I'm not playing Ice Queen,' Hope pointed out. '*He* is or Jack Frost, anyway. I tried to tell him the truth in the beginning and he wouldn't listen to me.'

'That was his pride speaking. He was hurt,' protested Sam. 'Sorry,' she added. 'Talk about the pot calling the kettle black.'

'We're a right pair, aren't we?' Hope agreed. 'Anyway, he's coming over here in a fortnight to take the children back to Bath for a week. I hate the thought of them being away from me for so long. He's bringing them back on a Saturday morning, which is the day of Delphine's wedding, by the way, and you're invited. Millie's being a flower girl. I'm worried she may hit the other flower girl over the head with her posy.'

'Delphine's sweet to invite me,' Sam said, touched. 'Should I come?'

'Of course, I'd love to see you. It would be nice . . .' Hope's voice trailed off. It was now or never. 'Sam, you're going to kill me but I've something to tell you.'

'What?'

'I'm pregnant.'

There was a long silence.

'It's Matt's baby, Sam,' said Hope in exasperation. 'Honestly, I told you nothing happened between Christy and me.'

'Sorry, love. That's wonderful but does Matt know?'

'No.'

'Hope, you've *got* to tell him. He's a right to know, no matter what's been happening.'

'I'll tell him,' Hope said. 'In my own time.'

Nicole looked around the Titus Records reception area and marvelled at the change; not in the reception, but in her. The first time she'd come here, only months ago, she'd been nervous and shy, feeling out of place amongst all the movers and shakers. Now, she was one of them. She was Nicole, an artist in her own right with a single just about to be released and plenty of excellent reviews for her work on tour.

'Hi Nicole,' said Lydia, Sam's assistant, who appeared to take Nicole upstairs to join Sam before lunch.

'Hi Lydia,' Nicole replied.

As they walked off, Nicole noticed the receptionist look at her enviously. It wasn't Lydia she was looking at, it was Nicole. Clad in designer clothes, with her coppery hair styled beautifully, Nicole was indeed someone to stare after enviously. The feline face with the high cheekbones now graced billboards around the city.

'You're really famous now,' Sharon had said to her the other night as they trekked around looking at apartments. They'd both been astonished to see a huge poster of Nicole in the underground station.

'Does this mean you won't share a flat with me, then?' Nicole had demanded.

Sharon gaped at her and then burst into tears.

'I thought you were a bit fed up at home,' Nicole said.

'I am,' Sharon sobbed. 'It's just that I never thought we'd actually do it, now that you're a big star and everything.'

Nicole hugged her. 'I'm not a big star yet, for the record,' she said, 'and ever since we joined Copperplate, we've talked about getting a place of our own. This is finally it.'

'What about Darius?' asked Sharon anxiously.

'He might stay over sometimes,' Nicole said with a mischievous smile. 'When we feel like letting him, that is.'

In the lift at Titus, Nicole wondered if she'd bump into Darius. He wasn't going to lunch with them: it was just Sam and Nicole because Nicole wanted to ask Sam's advice.

'Sam will be with you in two minutes,' Lydia said, leaving Nicole alone in Sam's office. Sam swept in a few minutes later, looking coolly elegant.

'Hi Nicole,' she said, kissing her new star's cheek. 'Are you ready to go?'

They walked to a small local restaurant and Nicole was delighted to see Sam order fish and chips.

'Make that two,' she smiled at the waiter, who swooned at the sight of her. 'It's nice to eat normal food,' she confided to Sam. 'At lunch interviews in posh restaurants, everyone's always trying to order these weird things I've never heard of.'

'That's menu one-upmanship,' Sam smiled. 'It's a form of social climbing whereby the more bizarre your order, like asking if the fish comes from one particular bit of the sea or which grove the olive oil in the dressing came from, the more cool and trendy you are proven to be.'

'And ordering fish and chips makes the two of us dead common,' laughed Nicole, instantly getting it.

'We're so cool, we don't have to try,' agreed Sam. 'I know this amazingly rich and successful singer who orders prawn cocktail, steak and chips and a bloody Mary wherever she is. She likes it and she doesn't care what anybody else thinks.'

They enjoyed the meal and Nicole got to the point.

'Remember when you met my gran, Reenie, and we talked about the place in Ireland where your sister lives?'

Sam nodded.

'Well, it seems that Gran left there and never went back, for lots of reasons,' Nicole added discreetly. 'I think it would be lovely for her to go there and I wanted to arrange it as a surprise, for her and Mum. I can't go what with the single and all, but I'd love them to go. All-expenses paid, my treat. Could you help me arrange it?'

Hope tried to look astonished when Ronan told her he was resigning from his job as Redlion's tourism officer.

'That's a terrible shame,' she said, thinking that she could finally post the CV that Eugene had expertly printed up for her. As long as the tourism chiefs didn't mind her taking a teeny bit of time off to have her baby, she was flying. The way Eugene made it sound in the CV, they'd be lucky to have her.

'I'm going to recommend you for the job,' Ronan said, his big sorrowful face more sorrowful than usual.

'Thanks, Ronan, that's lovely of you.'

'Not really,' he said gloomily, 'you'd be perfect for the job. I'm only telling the truth.'

Delphine was mentally tied up with the menus for the wedding but still managed to rouse herself from the salad buffet versus hot food debate to be delighted for Hope.

'You could do that job with your eyes shut,' she said. 'You'll have the tourism industry doubled in no time at all.'

'Well, yeah . . .' muttered Hope, thinking that there was only the small matter of the baby to consider and then, yes, she'd be perfect for the job. In her application letter, she'd pointed out that she would like to work part time rather than full time. Who knew if the powers that be would go along with that.

'How are the children?' asked Delphine. 'Does Millie still want to be a flower girl?'

'Just try and stop her,' Hope said. 'She's been practising like mad with a paper tiara and her nurse's uniform. She's making Toby be the bride, so she gets to trail along behind him, picking up his train, which is my velvet dressing gown, by the way. The only thing is, I keep having panic attacks that Matt's plane will be delayed on Saturday and they won't get back in time.'

She knew that Delphine and Eugene were actually getting married on the Friday because it was the only day the registrar could fit them in for the civil ceremony. The wedding party was, therefore, not dependent on the usual split-second timing. An ex-priest friend was providing a blessing on Saturday in Virginia's rose garden. 'The holy bit,' Eugene had said ruefully.

'Stop fretting,' Delphine said cheerily now. 'We're not Brad Pitt and Jennifer Aniston. It's Eugene and me who are getting married. The official bit is the day before so this is a laid-back wedding.'

'Have you told Virginia that?' inquired Hope.

Virginia was busy supervising a team of decorators who were tweaking Kilnagoshell at lightning speed into a vision of country house loveliness in readiness for both the wedding and the inspection by tourist guide people who were keen to get her in their booklet for the January edition. The two upstairs bathrooms had been totally renovated to make them suitable for paying guests and Virginia was having ensuite shower rooms installed in three of the bedrooms. Downstairs, her kitchens had to be revamped to suit health regulations, while the cloakroom was also in need of an overhaul.

Delphine laughed. 'Poor PJ who did up Curlew Cottage for you is in shock, I can tell you. He's not used to working for a perfectionist like Virginia. I met him last night and he looked weak. He said "It's not that Mrs Connell ever loses her temper, it's just that calm way she looks at you that makes you sweat."'

'Someone should make PJ sweat,' Hope commented. 'My plumbing still isn't fixed.'

'Get Virginia to oversee it,' Delphine suggested. 'That way, he'll have it fixed in no time.'


'Ooh, it's lovely.' There were tears in Sandra Turner's eyes when she looked around the modern apartment that Nicole had just bought. With one big window looking out over Tower Bridge, the entire living room was bright and airy, a fact emphasized by the lack of furniture.

'It'll be nicer when the furniture's delivered,' Nicole said anxiously, desperately wanting her mother and gran to like it.

Reenie Turner said nothing. She walked around tight-lipped, looking out onto the small balcony, peering into the compact kitchen with its gleaming stainless steel oven, and scrutinizing the en-suite bathroom off the master bedroom.

Pammy was the only member of the Turner family behaving as normal and she was playing with the intercom, pretending she was phoning up her friends from school.

'No Pammy,' said Nicole automatically. 'You can't play with that.'

Pammy clutched Barbie in one hand and took her big sister's hand in the other.

'Now when you stay, you can sleep in here with me,' Nicole said, leading Pammy into the master bedroom, which had a wall of built-in wardrobes.

'Where's our bed?' asked Pammy.

'I haven't bought one yet,' Nicole admitted.

'Will it be as big as Mummy's?'

Nicole grinned. 'Bigger,' she whispered.

Back in the living room, Reenie had perched herself on one of the few bits of furniture in the apartment, a rather battered old couch. The apartment had been let for the two years since it had been built and the previous owners had left a few items behind, all things that looked as if two years of renting had been detrimental to their health.

'You'll have to paint the whole place,' Reenie said, looking around at the grubby mushroom coloured walls.

'I know,' Nicole said. 'But do you like it, Gran? You've got to imagine it when it's all done up and it is a good investment, too,' she rushed on, anxious that her grandmother say something positive. 'What do you think?'

Reenie looked at her grand-daughter in amazement. 'It's wonderful, pet. I'm as proud as punch of you. I don't have to tell you that, now, do I?'

Nicole's smile split her face in two. 'I thought you didn't like it,' she said.

'It needs work, mind you, and I'm going to have to ask George next door for advice on who to get because you don't want to get stuck with cowboys who don't know one end of a paintbrush from another but of course I like it.' Reenie marched into the kitchen and examined the oven. 'I don't like the look of this thing at all, though,' she announced. 'Could you not get them to take it with them and you can get a nice one like the one I have?'

Nicole and Sandra burst out laughing.

'What are you like, Mum?' demanded Sandra. 'I've never seen such a gorgeous flat and there are you, telling her what's wrong with it.'

'I'm family,' Reenie said indignantly. 'I'm allowed to be honest. Mind you, if anyone else dared to criticize our Nicole, that would be a different story. They'd feel the sharp end of my tongue and no mistake.' She sniffed.

Nicole felt sorry for anyone who dared to criticize her in Reenie's presence. She could vouch for the sharpness of Reenie's tongue, all right. 'You're great, Gran,' she said, throwing her arms around the older woman. 'What would I do without you?'

'Get ripped off by bad decorators probably,' Reenie said firmly.

They discussed colour schemes and it was an hour later before they left the apartment to go back to Reenie's where they were having dinner.

Reenie and Sandra went into the kitchen to cook and Nicole took

Pammy out to the park for a go on the adventure play ground. After half an hour pushing Pammy, '*higher, Nicole, higher!*' on the swings, they walked tiredly back to their grandmother's house.

Nicole let them both in quietly. Pammy immediately rushed up to the spare bedroom where her grandmother kept a supply of toys and books for when she stayed over. Nicole hung her coat in the under-stairs cupboard beside the kitchen and couldn't help overhearing the conversation between her mother and grandmother.

'Don't cry, Sandra,' Reenie was saying. 'You know it's the right thing to do.'

'I know,' sobbed Sandra. 'I've tried so hard. I told her I wanted her to go, but I don't want her to think I've pushed her out. I'll miss her so much . . .'

Eyes glittering suspiciously, Nicole opened the door.

'Mum,' she wailed, before throwing herself into Sandra's arms.

Clinging together, they sobbed until down-to-earth Reenie broke it all up with a comforting pat for each of them and three mugs of hot sweet tea so strong that it was the colour of toffee.

'A good cry is what you both needed, now cheer up. This is a day for celebrating.'

'I know,' said Sandra, wiping her eyes with her fingers. 'I'm sorry Nicole, I didn't mean for you to hear me.'

Nicole ripped some kitchen towel off the roll and handed some to her mother. With the rest, she scrubbed at her eyes. 'You didn't push me, Mum,' she said, when she was recovered enough to speak. 'I won't go . . .'

'You will,' said Reenie and Sandra in unison.

'Your mother isn't an idiot who can't cope on her own,' Reenie added, 'it's my fault for making it look like that. I couldn't help it,' she admitted with regret. 'I wanted to protect her from life and I've ended up over-protecting her. And so have you.'

Nicole squeezed Sandra's hand.

'Between the pair of us, Nicole, we've carried on as if Sandra can't manage on her own. That's just because we wanted to be indispensable. But we're not and she's not.'

Reenie looked intently at her grand-daughter. 'You need to spread your wings, love,' she said, 'and so does your mother. Nobody's saying we won't miss you, but you've got your own life now and you've got to live it.'

'You've still got your keys,' Sandra said, her voice wobbling, 'I expect you back at least once a week for your tea, right?'

They were all still tearful and snuffly when Pammy came downstairs, trailing a giant furry panda bear that was nearly bigger than she was.

'You poor little mite,' said Nicole, hoisting her sister onto her lap. 'You must be hungry. Are you?'

Pammy nodded. 'So is Panda,' she announced. 'I said we'd have milk.'

The air of tension was totally gone and the family laughed and joked over dinner, with Reenie back on form teasing Nicole about Darius.

'I'll lend you my white gloves when you go to visit his mum and dad,' she joked.

Nicole winced. 'That's something I wanted to talk to you about, Mum,' she said. 'Not about Darius's dad, but about mine. It's the newspapers, you see. You know I've been doing interviews and everything, but if the single works, there'll be more publicity than ever, or so everyone at Titus keeps telling me. What I'm worried about is the papers bringing up my dad,' she said. 'I've side-stepped it up to now but you know the papers: they want to know all about you . . .' she looked anxiously at her mother.

It was something Nicole had thought a lot about lately. Ever since Shirin in Copperplate had remarked that Nicole was losing out on one part of herself, Nicole had been thinking about her father. Sandra had never made a secret out of the circumstances of Nicole's birth. She'd been seventeen, naive, and had a huge crush on the handsome Nikhil, a stunning looking Indian boy from school. In turn, he'd been crazy about the lovely blonde girl with the sweet face and the irresistible giggle. It had never been a great love affair and when Sandra became pregnant, she hadn't told him. Nicole had never quite understood that but she'd assumed that a lifetime hearing about Reenie's run-in with a feckless man who didn't want anything to do with his child had something to do with it. But Sandra said no, it wasn't that. Nikhil's family wanted a traditional marriage for him. Sandra didn't want to ruin that over what was, she knew, a teenage flirtation that had gone too far. So she'd said nothing, and gave his baby a name that sounded not a million miles away from his.

'I never wanted him to know because he'd have tried to do the right thing,' Sandra said now. 'He didn't deserve that. He had his life mapped out for him.'

'He made you pregnant,' Nicole shot back, angry at her father. He should have known, he should have somehow worked it all out. 'He should have been made responsible.'

'Nicole, it's water under the bridge,' Sandra insisted.

'Not if the papers want to know where my dad is,' Nicole sighed. 'Look,' she added, 'I'll talk to Darius about it. He'll know what to do.'

Reenie cackled. 'It must be love . . .'

Nicole blushed. 'If you're not nice to me, I won't give you your sixtieth birthday present.'

'Don't remind me,' Reenie groaned. 'I can't believe I'm about to be sixty. Anyway, it's not for two weeks,' she added suspiciously.

'You need to know about this present in advance,' Nicole said mischievously. She dug deep in her handbag and found a travel folder, which she handed to her grandmother.

Reenie opened it, unfolded the first page, which was the itinerary, and gasped.

'It's a trip to Ireland. Three flights to Dublin, then on to Kerry, then seven nights at the Manoir Rouge Leon in . . .' Her voice failed her.

'In Redlion,' supplied Nicole, watching her grandmother anxiously. 'I thought it would be nice for you to go back. I know your family are long gone, but wouldn't it be nice to go back and get all the bad things out of your system?'

For what seemed like an age, Reenie said nothing, she merely held the itinerary in her hand, staring at the words as though in a daze.

'I'm sorry, I didn't mean to upset you,' Nicole said quickly, terrified that her plan had backfired hideously and that, in her haste to do something lovely for her grandmother, she'd done the one thing guaranteed to devastate her. 'Let me take it back,' she said, trying to grab the folder out of Reenie's hands.

But her grandmother held on tightly. 'Oh Nicole,' she said weakly, 'did you see into my heart or something? Your great great grandmother could see things, you know. She had the Sight, although she had to keep it quiet because the parish priest would have had something to say about that. Do you have it too because I've thought about this for years.'

'No, I've no special sight: I'm blind as a bat, Gran,' joked Nicole, shaking with relief. 'I just thought that if it was me, I'd want to go back, to lay the ghosts to rest.'

Both Nicole and Sandra watched Reenie carefully.

'These tickets are for me, your mum and Pammy,' Reenie said, reading carefully. 'What about you, Nicole?'

'I can't go,' Nicole explained. 'My single's being released in the next two weeks and I'll be like a blue-tailed fly rushing round promoting it.' She'd blanched when she'd first set eyes on the promotion schedule. It involved a ten-day tour and there were so many flights on it that Nicole was determined to sign up for air miles. The promotion tour was in preparation for the release of 'Honey, (Don't You Know) I Need You?' a rhythm and blues ballad which Nicole adored. Time would tell if the rest of the country adored it too.

'But you should come too,' her mother said. 'We can't do it without you.'

'I'll come next time,' Nicole promised. 'I can't this time. But you'll be okay without me. Sam Smith from Titus is going there for a wedding and she's going to be travelling with you. She helped me organize it all, actually.'

'Would you really like to go back, Mum?' asked Sandra.

At that moment, Reenie's face was miraculously softened by memories, with the lines of a tough life miraculously erased. 'I'd love to go home,' she said.

Sam didn't need anybody to tell her that the numbers for Density's album were bad. As she sat at her desk one gloriously sunny morning,

610

still plucking up the courage to resign, she knew the band were in trouble without even looking at her computer. When she dropped into record stores to keep an eye on the LGBK label displays, she saw piles of Density albums on the carousels, with the band's angst-ridden faces staring gloomily at her from the cover. Their current single had been dropped from all but the most rock-driven radio station playlists and the video, shot at great expense, was probably mouldering away in some dark cupboard in the MTV headquarters, never to be seen again except in a 'where are they now?' slot. The initial shipment of albums were steadily returning to the Titus warehouse while the album itself sat like a millstone in the number eighty-seven position in the album chart.

Eighty-seven was a fine position for an album that had stormed into the charts, spent ages in the top twenty, and then slid slowly and triumphantly out, after months of success and lots of hit singles. Density's album had been in the chart for eight weeks and had never risen higher than seventy-one. Their two singles had made as much impact as two flea bites on an elephant.

With a practised eye, Sam ran through the sales analysis on her computer. Even though the Titus sales team had told their customers that the band were hotter than hell, they'd still had to offer sale or return on the album. If unsold, the shops could send the copies back and now the thousands of unsold albums were returning like homing pigeons.

It wasn't as if the band had performed reasonably and could, therefore, hope for better luck next time. The album simply hadn't sold at all. Despite Titus pulling out all the stops marketing and publicity wise, Density were still dead as dodos. The combination of costs looked horrifying when compared to the dismal bottom line. Sam looked at the figures which detailed the cost of signing the band, recording their album, making the video and finally, the costs of the huge marketing campaign. There wasn't a hope in hell of making back any of that money.

'If only they weren't such stupid, arrogant fools, they could have a hope,' Karen Storin had raged to Sam the previous week when the band refused to appear on a TV chat show because they weren't the top act on the show. 'They told me no way they were going to play warm-up for some country and western singer from Abilene. That woman has sold ten million records! They've barely sold ten records.'

'They've got a big star complex without actually being big stars,' remarked Sam bleakly.

'You said it. Most of the press hate them. I practically hate them myself,' Karen admitted, 'although you're the only person I'd say that to. They're so rude to everyone and that manager of theirs is a giant pain in the rear end.'

'He may change his tune soon,' Sam pointed out. 'At this rate, we won't be able to risk making a second album with his precious boys. Let's see how sweet he'll become when he realizes there's a good chance the band could be dropped.'

'That bad?'

Sam nodded. 'That bad.'

Now Sam scrolled through the figures on her computer and knew that a big decision was going to have to be made soon. LGBK couldn't afford Density but if she dropped them, it would look as if she'd made a huge mistake that had cost the company millions. She'd been running the company for nearly nine months. Nobody, least of all the bosses on Madison Avenue, would remember that it was actually her predecessor and Steve Parris who'd signed the deal with Density. She wondered whether it was worth discussing it all with her champion, Julian Ruben, the European president who'd hired her in the first place.

'You look like you could do with a cup of coffee,' remarked Lydia, arriving into the office with a pile of opened mail.

'Do you have any coffee flavoured with Valium?' asked Sam.

Lydia grinned. 'No, just ordinary. If you're feeling down, a gang of us are going out to dinner tonight if you fancy coming along. It's me and a few others from the fifth floor.'

'Thanks,' said Sam, deeply touched. 'But tonight's off, I'm afraid.'

'Some other time, huh?' said Lydia.

'Yes,' Sam said slowly, hating herself because she was lying. She had nothing on that night, except for a date with her television remote control. But managing directors didn't go out for dinner with the staff. Why not? thought Sam savagely. Because it might erode their precious status if they were seen to be enjoying themselves with lesser mortals.

And all of a sudden, Sam was sick of it. She was sick of being the boss, sick of running a company where she sat at the top in an ivory tower, so far removed from everyone else that she had no colleagues any more, just people who worked for her, and probably hated her. In the time she'd spent at Titus, only Karen Storin had become a friend. Despite her so-called new life where she planned to concentrate on enjoying life and making new friends, nothing much had actually changed.

Karen was still her only true work friend. Sam was never going to change her life if she stayed in this job. She had to get out and now.

She phoned Lydia. 'Lydia, can you get me Julian Ruben's office on the phone? I'd like a meeting with him if possible. And by the way, if that offer of dinner is still on, I think I'll change my other plans and come along, if that's all right?'

'Cool,' said Lydia, pleased.

Hope was miserably packing a suitcase for Millie and Toby's trip to Bath when Sam phoned late that night.

'I hope I didn't wake you,' Sam said, sounding giggly after a couple of glasses of wine at dinner.

'No,' said Hope, 'the baby is having one of his or her footballing nights. I don't remember being kicked so much with the others. How are you?'

'Fantastic,' announced Sam. 'I've done it.'

'Done what?'

'Resigned. I did it today. I spoke to Julian Ruben and told him I couldn't do it any more.'

'Wow,' was all Hope could say.

'He was lovely, actually, begged me to reconsider, which was flattering, but I told him it wasn't the company's fault but that I needed a change.'

'Sam, we've big plans for you, you've got to believe that,' Julian had actually said. 'I want you to reconsider this, for all our sakes. I know you're having a rough time with Parris, but that won't last, believe me,' Julian had added ominously.

'I just said that it didn't matter what the plans were,' Sam recalled. 'I need a change, Hope. I need to downshift. And I've got just the idea. I'm going to run a management consultancy firm. Just a small operation. I got the idea from these people I know who've got a fabulous restaurant but are finding it tough to break even. I had an idea about how to change that, and I just thought, hey, I'd be good at that, telling people where their company is going wrong. I think there's a big market for it.'

'Problem solving,' said Hope, 'that's what you're brilliant at.'

'Yes, problem solving.' Sam sounded so happy and excited. 'I know there's a risk in any business venture but hey, I'm used to risk. It's like this big burden has been lifted,' she said joyously. 'You know, Hope, I don't think I knew how much I wanted to change my life until I actually did it.'

'What about money?' asked Hope, ever practical.

'It's not as if I haven't got savings and investments. I may sell the Holland Park apartment and buy something smaller if I need to realize some cash. But I don't care, Hope,' she said. 'That's the point. It's not about money or being able to eat out seven nights a week with an expense account, putting money into Terence Conran's coffers. I just wasn't happy.'

'What about Morgan?' asked Hope suddenly. 'I thought he was part of your long-term plan for happiness?'

Sam felt her bubble burst. Hope had hit the nail on the head. Without Morgan, she didn't know if she could be truly happy, but then, she'd just have to get over him. She'd heard nothing from him since that awful day after the Lemon Awards when they'd fought so horribly. He'd made his decision and there was nothing she could do to change that.

'Morgan's in the past,' Sam said.

'Are you OK with that?'

'No, but I have no choice in the matter. He's made the decision, not me. And look who's talking. You could have made the first move with Matt and you haven't.'

'That's different,' Hope retorted.

'Why?'

'It just is.'

'You mean that you still haven't told him about the baby? Why, Hope? He's going to find out eventually. Are you going to hide behind the sofa when he comes to pick up the children on Saturday so he doesn't see the bump?'

'No,' said Hope. 'I'm not going to see him at all. I'm asking Delphine to deliver them to the airport. I don't want to have to face Matt, not yet.'

'Because you're visibly pregnant and you don't know how to tell him or because you genuinely don't want him back?' Sam asked gently.

'I know you're going to become this mega problem solver,' Hope said a touch irritably, 'but don't start on me. Oh all right, of course I want him back but I don't feel very forgiving or apologetic right now,' she said.

She was pregnant and hormonal, dammit, she needed someone looking after her, never mind worrying herself about Matt thinking the wrong thing about her and Christy.

'Sorry, Hope, I didn't mean to hassle you,' Sam said.

'I'm just hormonal,' Hope said.

'You weren't with Millie and Toby.'

'Yes I was, I just didn't let it all out,' said Hope. 'But this is the new, improved me, the one who lets everyone know when she's grumpy!'

'Do you want me to talk to Matt . . .' began Sam.

Hope's yell startled her.

'No! Don't you dare. This is my life and I'll sort it out.'

'I was only trying to help,' Sam said, helplessly.

'Phone Morgan then. That'll help.'

'I can't.'

'Yes you can,' Hope said firmly. 'Stop worrying about me and go and sort out your own life, right?'

Virginia was very pleased with herself when she came out of the soft furnishing shop in Killarney. Those buttery yellow tie backs would look perfect on the dining room curtains and would finish the entire room off beautifully. It had been a frantic few weeks but Kilnagoshell was finally getting there and would look beautiful for Delphine's wedding reception. The six spare bedrooms had been restored to their former glory, thanks to PJ's careful decoration and also to Shona's skill as an interior designer. She'd been fantastic at sourcing beautiful fabrics and wallpaper at good prices, which was vital as Virginia couldn't afford to plough all her money into the redecorating. All that remained to be done was a bit of work in the garden and although Virginia had been promising herself that she'd tackle it, Mary-Kate had pointed out that she'd done enough.

'The rose garden looks wonderful and the lawn is in perfect condition. What else would anyone want?' she demanded.

She was such a dear friend, Virginia thought fondly, as she walked leisurely along, enjoying the sunshine and the hustle and bustle of the main street. If she'd been paying attention instead of just strolling along happily, she might have seen Glenys and Richard Smart storming up the street, arguing volubly.

As it was, she almost collided with them outside the book shop.

'I'm sorry, oh, hello Glenys and Richard,' Virginia said.

'Well, well,' said Glenys, her eyes glittering with malice. 'If it isn't Kevin's little friend.'

As she towered over Glenys, Virginia thought this was amusing.

'Charmed as ever to see you,' she said, managing to stop the corners of her mouth lifting.

'I'll just drop into the book shop . . .' began Richard.

'Don't be long,' snapped Glenys.

'Seen Kevin lately?' inquired Glenys, eyes travelling over Virginia's tall, slim figure, elegant in an ivory linen suit that wouldn't have looked out of place on the *Out Of Africa* film set.

Glenys, on the other hand, was sweating in a serviceable red blazer, the buttons of which were under severe strain.

'Kevin and I played a lovely round of golf at the club last week, actually,' Virginia said. She was almost enjoying this. It was clear that Glenys wanted to rage at her about Kevin and, because she no longer viewed Kevin as anything other than a friend, Virginia was no longer sensitive about him. Let Glenys rage all she wanted to.

'How can you stand there and smile at me like that?' demanded Glenys.

Virginia's kept smiling. She'd bet herself that it would take at least one minute before Glenys went in for the kill: instead, it had taken only thirty seconds.

She said nothing and waited.

'Poor Ursula is just a few years dead and you've no shame, Mrs Connell, dallying with her poor widower husband, a man who's still in shock after her death. Call yourself a grieving widow? Hah, that's a laugh.' She would have spat if she could.

Virginia might have let her ramble on in vitriolic style except Glenys added another comment: 'And you can't have loved your husband if you're so ready to hop into bed with another man and your poor husband not yet cold in his grave.'

Mentioning Bill was her big mistake. Virginia's eyes flashed fire. She drew herself up and glared stonily at the other woman.

'Have you ever heard of the phrase: don't condemn a man until you've walked a mile in his shoes?' she asked, her voice cultured and low. 'You haven't been widowed, Glenys. Lucky you. You don't know what you're talking about. You treat Richard with contempt.' Glenys went to interrupt, but Virginia held up a hand to stop her.

'You've had your say, now it's my turn. I loved my husband very much and I appreciated him when he was alive, unlike you,' she said scathingly. 'Now he is gone and my carrying on with my life doesn't mean I didn't love him. Bad-mouthing and bitter people like you make it hard for anyone who's lost a loved one to move on, because you prefer us in grief. You don't want bereaved people to have happiness because it'll show up the lack of happiness in your own sad, twisted lives. Kevin Burton is my friend, that's all. And may God pity you if anything ever happens to your Richard, because you won't know what's hit you.'

Leaving Glenys furiously mouthing, Virginia swept along the street regally and into the café where Mary-Kate was waiting for her.

'You'll never guess who I bumped into,' Virginia said, sitting down calmly and putting her purchases on the empty chair beside her. 'Glenys Smart and poor Richard.'

'Did she try and kill you with a knock out punch on the main street?' joked Mary-Kate, waving at the waitress for another pot of tea.

'She did her best,' Virginia said, 'all things considered. She wasn't physical but she was very nasty.'

Mary-Kate's eyes widened. 'I was only joking. Are you all right? Was she awful? What did she say?'

'Calm down,' said Virginia. 'She told me I was a hussy for daring to look at Kevin Burton and that I couldn't have loved Bill at all.'

Mary-Kate's gasp of shock was so loud that people at neighbouring tables looked around in surprise. Virginia must have been devastated, she had to be in shock, Mary-Kate thought furiously.

'It's fine, I promise. I gave her a lesson in widowhood and she's gone off with her tail between her legs. I admit, I've been dying to tell that woman a few home truths and it was very satisfying to actually do it.'

'You're amazing,' said Mary-Kate admiringly. 'I'd be in bits if someone attacked me on the street, but you're as cool as a cucumber. You're a strong woman, Virginia.'

'I was always strong,' Virginia said in surprise. 'Losing Bill took that strength away from me but over the past year, thanks to people like you and my new life, I've got it back again.' Virginia's lovely face was calm and happy. 'I don't know what I'd have done without you, Mary-Kate. You've been my saviour.'

'Nonsense, you've saved yourself.' Mary-Kate laughed suddenly. 'Can I set you on Pauline, please? She's received Delphine's wedding invitation and she rang me up and left a message on my machine to say there wasn't a hope in hell of her going.'

'Ouch,' said Virginia. 'I can only assume she phoned when she knew you'd be out so she wouldn't have to suffer your wrath.'

'You betcha,' Mary-Kate said grimly. 'If she doesn't turn up, Delphine will be devastated. I know she keeps going on about how it's her mother's choice and how it won't affect the joy of the day if she doesn't come, but of course it will. Delphine is so vulnerable.

Her father's delighted to come, though. He loves Eugene, although he wouldn't dare tell Pauline.'

Fresh tea arrived and they drank it, both deep in thought. Virginia began formulating a plan. 'Pauline is very religious, you say.'

'First in the queue at Mass every Sunday.'

'How about if we ask all the devout people along, like Miss Murphy who does the flowers, and so on? If they come, she'll be shamed into coming. Oh,' Virginia had a brainstorm. 'And let's ask Father McTeague. He's a sweetie and I know for a fact that he deplores the fact that poor Delphine can't get married in church.'

'You're evil, do you know that?'

They both laughed.

'Pauline won't know what's hit her. Wait till everyone in the village is telling her they'll see her on Saturday, she'll be shamed into turning up.'


Nicole, Darius, Sam, Reenie, Sandra and Pammy stood in a little group in Heathrow's Terminal One, with much hugging and kissing going on.

Pammy had taken a huge shine to Darius and was now half-crying because she wanted to stay with him and Nicole.

'You'll have a lovely time in Ireland with your mummy,' Darius told her, his gangly frame crouched down beside Pammy as he tried to cheer her up.

'And we're going to have adventures,' added Sam enigmatically. Thanks to Millie, she had enough experience of little girls to know that the promise of excitement to come helped cheer them up.

Pammy sucked her lollipop thoughtfully. 'What sort of adventures?' she asked finally, looking up at Sam with her innocent gaze.

'You're definitely related to Nicole,' Sam laughed, 'your big sister asks all the right questions too.'

'I wish you weren't leaving Titus,' Nicole said wistfully to Sam.

'I know.' Sam shrugged. 'I had to do it, but whoever takes over will look after you, Nicole. You've got a brilliant manager in Bob Fellowes and you've got the voice – and the professionalism.'

Nicole smiled. 'You forgot to mention Darius,' she said, sliding her arm through his.

'That would be stating the obvious,' Sam replied. 'I know he's going to look after you. And I expect that single to go to number one, Mr Good,' she commanded good-humouredly.

'It will, don't you worry,' he said confidently, squeezing Nicole's small hand.

'Do look after her, won't you?' Reenie said to him. 'She should be coming with us.'

'I'll be fine, Gran,' Nicole assured her. 'I just want you to enjoy yourself.'

'I will,' Reenie said, her voice breaking.

'We better go through,' Sam announced, not wanting everyone to get upset. 'Quick goodbyes and we're off.'

Leading the way, she took her group through security until they could no longer see Darius and Nicole, hand in hand, waving goodbye.

'I hope they'll be all right,' Nicole said tearfully.

Darius pulled her to him and gave her such a passionate kiss that a group of male golfers going home to Ireland after a week in Portugal gave them a round of applause.

Nicole giggled.

'Sam Smith is looking after them,' Darius said, as they walked away from their guffawing audience. 'They could put Sam in charge of the space programme and she'd have it running like clockwork in half an hour. Don't worry about a thing, love.'

Nicole beamed up at him. 'I'm not,' she said.

On the journey back to the flat, they were both almost too excited to speak. The sense of delicious anticipation made them both grin inanely and hold hands tightly. Darius had originally suggested they went out to lunch after leaving the family at the airport, but Nicole had taken a deep breath and suggested lunch at her place.

'A special lunch,' she'd said, gazing at him with those miraculous tiger eyes until Darius had felt his heart leap with love.

Once she'd made the decision, she'd had a wonderful time planning everything. Darius was a Thai food junkie, so Nicole had found a

Thai takeaway and ordered everything for half twelve. She'd run round the flat first thing that morning, tidying and polishing, arranging the bright yellow gerberas she loved everywhere and making the bed up with the virginal white bedclothes she'd bought but never used. She shivered excitedly as she thought of curling up in them with Darius's body moulded to hers. She'd deliberately left alcohol off her shopping list. There was no way that Nicole wanted this momentous occasion dulled by booze: she wanted to remember every incredible moment of it.

Thanks to frenzied traffic, it was nearly half twelve when they reached the front door, still holding hands tightly. Nicole was conscious of a certain sense of unease. Darius no longer looked deliriously happy; he looked nervous.

'Come on,' she said enthusiastically as she led him into the hall, 'you haven't seen my new bathroom stuff. I got a toilet seat cover that's clear and has coloured fishes embedded in the plastic!'

Nicole dragged Darius into the small, modern bathroom where she had let her sense of colour go wild. The walls were raspberry pink, the tiles were tiny aquamarine mosaics, the fluffy towels were the colour of sunflowers, and above the hand basin a giant Dali-esque mirror was surrounded by movie-star light bulbs for making up Nicole's face.

'I always wanted one of these mirrors,' she admitted, looking at their reflections. She, so small, dark and exquisite; Darius, tall and lanky, his fair hair and faintly tanned skin a total contrast to Nicole's café au lait perfection. She leaned back against him, letting him support her and watched as the anxiety left his face. Darius put his arms around her, letting his hands rest on her slender waist.

'Are you sure?' he asked tenderly.

She nodded at his reflection in reply.

Darius gently swung her round so that she was facing him and, as tenderly as if he was leaving a butterfly kiss on a baby's cheek, kissed her on her upturned little face. At first, his mouth was soft and then, as Nicole wound her arms around his neck, moulding her taut body to his, their kiss deepened into fierce passion. Their bodies leaned hungrily against each other as their hands ran greedily over arms and waists and hips. Darius inexpertly opened the buttons on Nicole's fitted denim shirt and then buried his head in the softness of her breasts. Nicole leaned her head back as his mouth burned a trail along the fine lace of the sexy little pink bra she'd bought specially.

She moaned with excitement as he kissed and nuzzled endlessly. She'd never felt anything like this before. Those few unpleasant late-night fumbles she'd had with other boys, encounters she'd felt uncomfortable about, had never been like this, this gloriously exquisite sensation that was sending ripples of pleasure straight down into her toes.

'That's wonderful,' she sighed, 'but you can't do all the work, love.'

She pulled at Darius's shirt, hearing buttons ping onto her tiled floor and wriggled until she was stroking and kissing his lean chest instead, making him moan with desire. The last thing Nicole wanted was to be made love to; she wanted to be making love, making Darius gasp with pleasure the same way he made her gasp with pleasure when his lips fastened on her nipples. She wanted to tear both their clothes off and . . .

Ding dong!

In their shock at the intrusion of the door bell, Nicole and Darius both jumped and he banged his shin on the edge of the bathtub.

'Ouch!'

Nicole dissolved into giggles and she hugged him. 'I bet that's lunch. I ordered Thai food for a treat!'

Still giggling, with Darius laughing as he hobbled along behind her, she went to the front door and hastily buttoned her shirt up.

'Don't make me laugh,' she warned him.

'Hello?' She opened the door to find a young, bored-looking guy with a big paper bag in his hand.

'Thai To Die For?' the guy said, looking at Nicole's shirt which was all buttoned up wrong. Both Nicole and Darius noticed it too.

'Yes,' said Nicole sedately while behind her, Darius had to stuff his hand into his mouth to stop himself corpsing.

'Er money?' said the guy at the door, still holding firmly onto the paper bag.

'Oh, yes, money. Darius, have you got money?'

Finally, they managed to pay the guy and Nicole shut the door, at which point they both burst into hysterical laughter.

'I thought I'd die when he started looking at my shirt,' squealed Nicole.

'Oh I don't know,' said Darius, taking the bag of take out from her and putting it firmly on the floor, 'I could understand him wanting to look at you, specially when you're wearing this.' He unbuttoned the shirt for the second time and took it off. Nicole stood still, enjoying the sheer sensuous pleasure, and let him continue. 'I love this bra,' he added, regretfully, 'but I think it has to come off too.'

Then his lips were on her breasts again, this time unhindered by her bra. Nicole clung to him, feeling the heady excitement growing. They never made it to the bedroom and her white sheets. Instead, they fell, entwined, onto Nicole's brand new couch, where they ripped off the remainder of their clothes. It seemed like hours of touching and caressing, fingers stroking and playing, but it was really only minutes because both Nicole and Darius were frantic for each other. When Darius gently pulled her matching pink lacy panties off, Nicole wound her legs round him like a little acrobat and pulled him closer to her, desperate to feel him inside her.

'Nicole,' he groaned, 'let's take our time.'

And he did. Nicole may have read about love making and how a man could give his partner exquisite pleasure, but reading about it and having it happen were two very different things. Just when she thought she could take no more without exploding, Darius's body melted into hers.

There was no pain, only the exquisite sensation of pleasure flooding through her body as Nicole's orgasm screamed through her body like an express train. They were clinging together fiercely and she couldn't stop yelling in passion until her orgasm died and she felt Darius finally let himself go.

She'd never felt more love or tenderness in her life as she held his spasming body in her arms, clasping him to her until they both sank back onto the cushions, weak from love, their skin wet with sweat, their breathing ragged.

The Thai food lay cooling in its bag but neither of them was hungry. Sated by love, they lay on the couch, limbs tangled, dozing lazily. Darius couldn't stop touching Nicole; his fingers stroked her hair gently and tenderly caressed her smooth shoulders.

'I'm glad I waited for you,' she said, playing with his watch strap.

'Me too,' he said, kissing her collar bone.

Nicole smiled serenely as she lay there. This was what it was all about; what those endless articles about love and sex had meant. Perfect, wonderful love making. She was passionately grateful that she'd waited for someone like Darius. For the first time, Nicole was glad of having been ingrained with her grandmother's beliefs.

'Did you think I was a prude because I was a virgin?' she asked Darius suddenly.

'Nobody who knows you would ever call you a prude,' he said. 'I admire you, Nicole. You're the sort of person who knows what she wants and doesn't want to settle for anything else.'

Nicole smiled a cat-like little smile. 'That's it exactly,' she said.

Eventually, thirst made them get up and head for the fridge and suddenly, the now cold lunch smelt tempting.

'Could we heat it up, do you think?' Nicole said, standing stark naked in the kitchen and looking curiously into the take away bag.

'Cold would be nice,' Darius said.

So they sat on the sitting room floor with their lunch spread out in front of them and drank vast gulps of icy lemonade.

'Have a piece of lemongrass chicken,' Darius said, leaning over and placing a dripping yellow sliver of food onto Nicole's thigh. Nicole laughed delightedly as he knelt and gobbled it up from her thigh, licking her skin languorously to get rid of all traces.

'Would you like some of my stir fried mushrooms?' Nicole asked, leaving a trail on his chest. 'Lie back there, how else can I lick it off?'

Suddenly they were licking bits of food off each other and the exhaustion had mysteriously vanished.

'How about we wash up and go to bed?' Nicole suggested.

Darius grinned. 'The way we're going, we're going to christen every room in the flat, so the bathroom is next.'

In the bathroom, Nicole lovingly sponged the lemon chicken from Darius and then said, 'It's no good. We need a shower.'

'Ooh!' she cried in astonishment as Darius swept her easily up in his arms and carried her into the bedroom.

'I'll lick you clean,' he promised, holding her over the bed as though he was going to drop her. 'I thought we might try a traditional venue this time.'

'I bought those sheets specially,' Nicole said, looking at the still-virginal whiteness.

'We can't waste the sheets,' he laughed, then rolled them both onto the bed in one giggly heap, legs and arms tangled. 'Mmm,' he added, licking his way up Nicole's thigh, 'this is definitely Thai to die for. Yum yum . . . or Tom Yum for spicy lemon grass soup.'

'Bad pun alert,' groaned Nicole. 'If I didn't love you, I'd have to throw you out for making remarks like that.'

Darius stopped licking. 'Do you mean that?' he asked anxiously.

'Do I love you?' Nicole repeated. She stroked his cheek. 'Yes. Do you love me?'

'Oh God, Nicole, so much!' he said, burying his face in her shoulder and hugging her tightly.

'Good,' she said and exhaled slowly. They lay there together, wrapped in each other's arms. This was perfect, Nicole thought. Just perfect. She had everything she ever wanted.

By the time the weary party of travellers clambered into a people-carrier at Kerry's airport at six that evening, they were all exhausted. Reenie and Sandra weren't talking to each other after a tiff about the suitability of the pink chiffon dress Sandra had worn for travelling, and Pammy had lost the Barbie she liked best out of the four she'd brought in her hand luggage.

While Sandra and Reenie sulked with each other, Sam was left looking after Pammy, and began to appreciate why Nicole was so mature. If she had to referee fights between the other volatile pair all the time, *and* take care of her little sister during the ensuing sulking session, no wonder she was the oldest twenty-three-year-old Sam had ever met.

'Is Barbie sad because she's lost?' said Pammy, lower lip quivering, as she sat on Sam's lap. She really was the most beautiful little girl, Sam thought, with those crystal clear blue eyes and shimmering blonde hair. The record company executive in Sam idly wondered if she'd have a voice like her sister's in fifteen years' time. If so, she'd give any star out there a run for their money.

'Barbies have a special Barbie island they go to,' Sam explained gravely. 'It has all the ponies they like, and the Barbie hair salon and a place for Barbie to go swimming. Sometimes Barbies need a holiday, but don't worry, we'll get a new replacement Barbie for you.'

'Oh,' said Pammy, fascinated. 'Is there a story about the Barbie place?'

'Well, there might be,' Sam said. 'Would you like a story?'

Pammy nodded.

Even the driver of the people-carrier listened as Sam wove a story about Barbieland for Pammy. Sandra and Reenie stopped sulking and smiled, slowly forgetting their row as they drove through the gloriously verdant countryside, still lit by the golden evening sun. Finally, they came to Redlion.

'I didn't think it was going to be so pretty,' said Sandra as the people-carrier drove down a gently curving street where pastel-painted houses and shops shone red gold in the dusk. Reenie and Sandra stared at the window boxes and hanging baskets overflowing with riotous summer flowers; they looked at the people sitting at the wooden trestle tables outside the Widow Maguire's pub, laughing and joking as Christy Moore's mellifluous voice drifted out from inside the bar.

'I wouldn't have recognized the place,' Reenie said finally. 'It was poor, a little old town in the middle of nowhere when I left and now it's . . . it's lovely and prosperous.' Her eyes were wet as her gaze roamed over the elegance of the carefully restored premises on the main street. The Victorian courthouse that had been half falling down in her day was now a restaurant with stars outside it; the battered post office had been done up and was now a refined looking estate agent's with no less than two posh sports cars parked outside it and a well-dressed woman in a suit closing up, talking on her mobile phone as she locked the door.

The old cottages by the bridge were unrecognizable. When Reenie had been young, the row had been run-down and disreputable, a place where slates regularly fell off the roofs when you walked past, a place where the worst drunk in the village lived in state, screaming and roaring until the wee small hours. Now, the cottages were charming little homes, with window boxes, carefully painted doors and windows, and fine cars parked outside.

'That's Mary-Kate's place,' said Sam, pointing out the well-appointed chemist shop with its stylish Lancôme display in the window. 'You're going to love her, girls. She's great fun. And we'll have to have a night in the Widow's, if we can get a seat with all the tourists here. Apparently, since Belle Maguire got this delectable young Californian barman, the place is totally jammed at night. Half of the tour bus guides are women and they keep dragging their bus-loads here for dinner, just so they can ogle Elliot.'

'Put Sandra down for a night of ogling,' remarked Reenie.

Sam gulped at the thought of hostilities resuming but Sandra just giggled and stuck her tongue out at her mother. 'I don't ogle young men,' she said happily, 'only ones my own age.'

'Well, put *me* down for a session ogling Elliot, then,' Reenie shot back, going off into peals of laughter. 'There's life in the old dear yet.'

Sam raised her eyes to heaven. She'd never understand the pair of them. Maybe that was how mothers and daughters got on. Who knew?

They drove to the hotel and Reenie went off into fresh sighs of astonishment about how such a place would never have been able to make a living in her day. The hotel was nice, Sam thought approvingly, as a liveried doorman helped them in with their luggage. She just hoped she got to make the acquaintance of one Mr Christy De Lacy. He would not enjoy the encounter, she thought grimly.

'Is Mr De Lacy around tonight?' she inquired idly as they checked in.

The receptionist squirmed. 'Er . . . no, not tonight,' she said, clearly uncomfortable. 'He is indisposed.'

Sam did her best to look nonchalant but vowed to get to the bottom of it. There was a story there, to be sure. Hopefully, one which involved pain and ignominy for Christy.

She dumped her bags in her room, went to see that the others were fine, then left to drop in on Hope. On the phone the day before, she had thoughtlessly suggested dinner at the hotel but Hope had pointed out that she'd die of hunger rather than eat there.

'Sorry,' Sam had winced. 'The Widows then?'

'I'll round up the troops,' Hope said, feeling brighter than she had all week. She missed Toby and Millie so much that it physically hurt.

The sisters were late getting to the Widow's. They'd both cried when they met, Sam at the sight of her beloved sister's gently rounded belly. 'Oh Hope, love, you have to tell Matt. He loves you, this will all blow over. You've got to sort it out for the sake of the baby.'

'You can't glue a marriage together with a baby,' said Hope, wiping away the tears. 'Band-Aid babies don't work. It's not fair on the baby or the parents.'

'I give up,' said Sam. 'C'mon. The poor driver thinks he'll never get home for his dinner.'

'Send him home now,' Hope said. 'I'll drive. That'll give me an excuse for the rest of them as to why I won't have a drink.'

'As if they don't know you're pregnant,' Sam said wryly.

'They don't,' insisted Hope. 'I'm very careful what I wear.'

Sam gave up. 'And you say *I'm* stubborn?'

'Sam, you made it!' squealed Delphine at the top of her voice when Hope and Sam finally made it to the pub.

Virginia, Mary-Kate, Delphine, Giselle and Mai had annexed a big table near the bar – 'and near Elliot,' Hope whispered.

'Is this your hen night?' demanded Sam when everyone had been hugged and kissed.

'Yes,' sighed Delphine. 'I can't wait till Saturday.'

'Only a day and a half to wait,' said Mai, brandishing a bottle of champagne sent over by Belle.

'Can Elliot pour it?' said Mary-Kate, batting non-existent eyelashes.

'Trollop,' squealed Delphine, with several cocktails under her belt. 'It's my hen night. I get to behave like a mad woman with any attractive available men.'

'You're both out of luck, I'm afraid,' Virginia pointed out. 'Since Sam came in, Elliot hasn't been able to take his eyes off her. His eyes are out on stalks looking at her.'

'Stop taking the mickey,' said Sam, embarrassed.

'This is no joke,' Virginia insisted. 'He's just given Emmet Slattery a pint of Guinness with no head on it, all from gazing over here at you, Sam. That's serious infatuation. Emmet will murder him. He's very particular about his pint.'

It was a fabulous evening. Delphine got hilariously tipsy, eventually ending up on a bar stool with her cardigan falling provocatively off one freckled shoulder, telling a group of exhausted Italian hill walkers who'd been hiking the Ring of Kerry that she was deeply in love with Eugene who was 'de bestest man in de whole whorld. You don't need to go to any campsite,' she slurred. 'Youz can schtay in my house tonight. Eugene won't mind. He ish lovely.'

Sam rescued her, smiling at Elliot, who beamed back at her. Lord, thought Sam, he was only about twenty-five and a thing of beauty, a bronzed Californian love god. Maybe she wasn't such a crabby old spinster after all.

It was after twelve when Hope dropped her back up at the hotel and Sam felt exhausted, even though she'd drunk very little. 'I'll bring my visitors to see you tomorrow,' she promised Hope.

'We can have lunch in the garden,' Hope said. 'It's lovely now. The hens have their own bit so you won't be stepping carefully to avoid the chicken shit.'

Sam laughed. 'I never thought I'd hear you being so blasé about chicken shit.'

'I'm a country woman now,' Hope grinned. 'Mind you, I've failed utterly to grow basil. My lettuce is lovely and the cabbage is rampant, but when it comes to herbs, I'm useless.'

Sam kissed her on the cheek. 'Never, ever let me hear you say

629

you're useless again. You're survived on your own. Not just survived,' she corrected herself, 'but flourished. We're survivors, us Smith girls.'

'You said it,' Hope said.

She drove down the Manoir drive, deep in thought. She hadn't been there for months. After the disastrous encounter with Christy, she'd never come back. As she negotiated the bends and crunched over the gravel, she thought of how foolish she'd been to risk a wonderful marriage for something so insubstantial with Christy. Yes, she'd been bored and Matt had been so vague, so distant, that she'd felt neglected. But that had been no reason to throw so much away. She simply hadn't thought it through, Hope knew. It was like Millie jumping in a puddle: fun for a moment, Millie never thought about the consequences. Which was fine for a child of nearly five, but not so intelligent for a woman who was about to turn thirty-eight.

Hope gritted her teeth to stop herself crying. She couldn't cry, she didn't have that luxury. She had to be strong.

Matt had never realized just how tough it was looking after two small children until he had Millie and Toby on their own in his rented apartment in Bath for an entire week. It was one thing to look after them for a few hours, safe in the knowledge that Hope would be back from the shops or wherever soon, ready to take over expertly. It was quite another to take care of, feed and entertain them all by yourself for days at a time, with nobody else to take the strain. For the first time, Matt began to have a new respect for his wife. No wonder Hope had wanted some time to herself when they'd moved to Redlion. After being a working mother for years, suddenly becoming a stay-at-home one in a rural area where she didn't know anyone, and, he admitted guiltily, where her husband was caught up with his own problems, must have been very difficult and frustrating. Small children were enchanting but damn hard work.

Even more irritating was Millie's habit of criticizing everything he did with her unblinking dark gaze. Used to thinking of Millie as 'his' little girl, Matt was disconcerted by her habit of telling him 'Mummy doesn't do it that way' ten times a day.

So far, he'd discovered that he didn't put on socks the way Mummy did, he didn't pour milk into cereal the way Mummy did, and he definitely didn't know how to wash hair without getting water in the eyes the way Mummy did.

After four days of this, he was nearly incandescent with joy when Betsey invited the kids over to her place for the afternoon to play with Ruby and Opal.

'Give you a chance to tidy things up in the office,' Betsey said.

'Give me a chance to lie down and sleep,' said an exhausted Matt.

That morning, the children were even more energetic than ever. Millie decided she felt sick. She rushed into the bathroom every five minutes to hang her head over the toilet bowl and pretended to retch, which had Matt hysterical with nerves in case she really was sick. The morning paper and the post all sat unread on the kitchen table while Millie ran back and forth to the bathroom.

When no vomit was forthcoming, Matt was thrilled, but Millie wasn't, so she opened a tub of pickle from the fridge and got most of that all over herself. Then she spilled the rest into the toilet bowl and was looking into it happily when her father appeared at the bathroom door with a world-weary expression on his face.

'Sick,' she announced cheerfully, pointing at the mess. 'I'm a big girl now like Mummy.'

Matt's face was a picture as he realized what she was saying.

Sam knew that Hope would kill her. *'Don't interfere,'* she'd warned on several occasions. But sometimes, Sam reflected, you had to go with your gut instinct. Hope loved Matt and needed him. At the same time, Sam was sure, in spite of her reservations about him, that her bull-headed brother-in-law adored his wife, but between the pair of them, they were behaving like two immovable objects, both unyielding.

Well, Sam decided the morning before the wedding, the time had come for action.

First, she phoned Dan at Judd's in Bath. He was delighted to give her Matt's phone number.

'I've told him not to be a fool and to make it up with her because

I can tell he's not happy without Hope,' Dan said, 'but then, when has anybody been able to tell Matt anything?'

'There's a first time for everything,' Sam said firmly.

Matt's phone nearly rang out before he picked it up, sounding out of breath.

'Yes,' he gasped.

'I thought you weren't in,' Sam said.

'I was dressing Toby and Millie got at the shoe polish,' Matt said. 'Her blue suede shoes are now blue and black, and the kitchen floor is not much better.'

'She is a handful,' agreed Sam. 'I'm sure you know why I'm phoning you, Matt,' she added, getting straight to the point as usual. 'This has gone on too long and there's something you should know . . .'

'Hope's pregnant,' interrupted Matt.

For once, Sam was speechless. 'How do you know? She hasn't told anybody.'

'Millie's new game is pretending to get morning sickness,' Matt explained.

'Oh. So what are you going to do about it?' demanded Sam.

'Don't get on your high horse with me,' began Matt hotly. 'I don't have to listen to your bossing me around . . .' He stopped abruptly. 'Sorry. You and I are like a broken record, aren't we? Fighting is all we're good for.'

'Yeah, you're right, sorry,' Sam said. What was she fighting with him for, anyway? The whole point of the conversation was to sort things out for Hope.

'I love her, you know.'

Matt's simple declaration touched Sam's heart.

'I know,' she said. 'I do too, that's probably why you and I fight so much. We have trouble sharing her.' She paused. 'Nothing happened with Christy. He flirted with her and she was flattered, that was all. If she wasn't so naive and trusting, she'd have told him to get lost.'

'I know that,' admitted Matt.

'And you're to blame too,' Sam went on. 'You pretty much abandoned her in Kerry. She's made a life for herself there but it was no thanks to you.'

'I know that too,' he said ruefully. 'I got so tied up in my own problems that I neglected her. I thought she'd always be waiting there for me, I took her for granted. That's no excuse, I know, but I was going through a difficult time in my life.'

'And now?'

'I'm going back,' Matt said simply. 'I need her, more than she knows, to be honest.'

Sam felt tears prickling her eyes.

'What about your job, though? Hope loves Kerry, she'd hate to leave, so how can you combine it all?'

That was when Matt told her his plan.

'Why did you pick a dress with thirty silk-covered buttons?' joked Hope on the Saturday of Delphine's wedding, as her fingers fumbled to fasten the tiny silk loops over the tiny buttons.

'I wanted Eugene to suffer tonight when he unbuttons me,' replied Delphine, her long red curls falling down her back onto the buttons, adding to the difficulty. 'He has to suffer to win me, you see, like the brave Celtic knights suffering to get their hands on the lovely maidens, or whatever. I can never remember the exact details of those old stories.'

'He'll fall asleep before he's half-way down your back,' remarked Mary-Kate, arriving into the pink bedroom in Kilnagoshell, scene of the pre-wedding party. 'Virginia is bringing up some nibbles for us all to keep us going because it's going to be hours before we're eating.'

'I can't eat or I'll burst out of the dress,' Delphine said. 'I want to be slim and virginal looking when Eddie says "I bless the marriage of Delphine Eustacia Lavinia Margaret Ryan and Eugene O'Neill . . ."'

'Delphine *Eustacia Lavinia* Margaret?' said Hope, awestruck.

'My sister read a lot of romantic novels when she was expecting Delphine,' revealed Mary-Kate. 'Delphine has no idea that if it wasn't for me putting my foot down, Pauline would have called her Marilyn Scarlett.'

Hope giggled so much she had to stop buttoning.

'Delphine is bad enough,' Delphine pointed out. 'Even the registrar

633

sniggered yesterday. You want to try being a ten-year-old in a class of boys and girls with a name like that. I wouldn't like to tell you the horrible rhymes they came up with. Delphine rhymes with lots of things. When Eugene and I have children, they're all going to be called Mary and Tom, nice simple names.'

'I don't know,' Hope said dreamily, 'I like Rosalie these days. And Rory. I like R names.'

Delphine and Virginia looked meaningfully at each other.

'For the baby?' asked Delphine.

Hope stared at them and realized they knew.

'Honestly, nothing's secret round here!' she said.

'Pouring all that wine into your weeping fig plant is not keeping a secret,' said Delphine.

'Not having even one glass of champagne on Delphine's hen night was an even bigger giveaway,' Mary-Kate added. 'And although I know you like chocolate, I didn't think you liked it enough to make your midriff swell quite so much.'

Hope made a noise that was half sob, half laugh with relief.

'How long have you known?'

'For ages,' said Delphine. 'Don't cry. I spent half an hour making up your eyes, you'll ruin them.'

'Does Matt know?' inquired Mary-Kate gently.

'You're as bad as Sam,' said Hope exasperated. 'She never stops going on about it.'

'You have to tell him. He's flying over with the children later. Will you tell him at the airport?' asked Delphine.

'Sam is going to the airport to pick them up,' Hope said, avoiding their eyes.

'Fine,' said Mary-Kate. 'Delphine, you know how much you hate people who interfere,' she warned. 'We can't interfere.'

'I hate people who interfere in *my* life,' grumbled Delphine. 'This is different.'

'Baby sandwiches,' announced Virginia, appearing at the door with Dinky at her heels and a plate of tiny cucumber sandwiches in one hand.

'Is this a conspiracy?' demanded Hope. '*Baby* sandwiches?'

Virginia bit her lip. 'I meant that I cut the crusts off,' she said. 'I take it the news is now out in the open?'

'There's going to be an advert in the local paper,' Hope said wryly. 'Yes, I'm pregnant. No, Matt doesn't know. No, I don't want to tell him but Yes I will. Eventually.'

'Fine,' said Virginia. 'Tea anyone?'

'You hold her,' said Sally, thrusting a wriggling Alison into Jamie's arms. 'You're her godfather after all.'

'I thought that meant I gave her money on her birthday, I didn't know I had to actually do anything,' Jamie grumbled, clutching inexpertly onto his niece who immediately stopped sobbing and smiled, happy now that she was causing the maximum difficulty. She pulled her uncle's hair joyously, causing him to yelp.

Everyone else ignored him, too busy watching the carousel for their luggage.

'Is that your case, Dom?' asked Laurence, as a battered old leather case appeared in front of them.

'Er no,' said Dominic. 'Er, yes, *yes*, grab it!'

After ten minutes, the entire Connell family had collected their belongings and had hired a taxi to take them to Redlion.

'Kilnagoshell House,' said Sally, who had realized that once the three Connell brothers got together, they reverted to childhood and were incapable of looking after themselves. No wonder poor Virginia was so capable. 'I don't have precise directions but . . .'

'No bother,' said the taxi driver, waving a laid-back hand. 'I have a vague idea of where it is.'

'Well, if that's all right with you,' said Sally, used to taxi drivers who wanted a postcode before they even started the engine.

Sam saw Millie before she saw her brother-in-law. Millie was running, pigtails flying, eagerly looking for her mother, eyes scanning the waiting crowds at the airport.

'Millie, hello,' yelled Sam.

Millie ran at her like a little hurricane and threw herself into Sam's arms. 'Where's Mummy?' she gasped.

'Mummy's waiting for you,' Sam whispered into Millie's dark hair. 'She's helping Auntie Delphine get married.'

'I'm going to be a bridesmaid,' crowed Millie. 'I've got my outfit. Daddy's got it in my case.'

'Hello Sam.'

It was Daddy.

Hoisting Millie up into her arms, Sam greeted Matt. Normally, they gave each other cool smiles, the smiles of people who were wary of each other. But today, Matt beamed at her and kissed her warmly on the cheek.

'Hiya Sam, lovely to see you.'

'You look pretty smooth, Mr Parker,' Sam grinned at him. 'New suit?'

Matt grinned wickedly. 'It's a special day, I have to look my best.'

'Auntie Ham,' said Toby from low down.

Matt hoisted him up so he could be kissed.

Sam lifted her nephew high in the air. 'We better rush or we'll be late. Do you want to drive, Toby?'

'No me, me, me drive!' yelled Millie.

'Sam's taking a long time to come from the airport,' said Hope, staring at her watch.

'Don't panic,' said Virginia. 'The blessing ceremony doesn't start until two, it's only a quarter to now.'

'I know, but Millie will never forgive me if she doesn't get to be a flower girl,' said Millie's mother ruefully. She looked out the drawing-room window for her Metro, which Sam was driving from the airport.

'Looks like more guests have turned up,' she said, as a taxi disgorged a group of people, complete with suitcases. Three tall, chestnut-haired young men, a dark-haired woman and a small child with bright red curls stood on the drive looking around. 'I didn't think any of them were staying here, though,' she added.

Virginia crossed the room to look out. 'Oh gosh!' she shrieked. 'It's my family. I can't believe it. They never told me they were coming.' And she shot out the front door to welcome Sally, Dominic, Jamie, Laurence and little Alison.

'You never told me you were coming!' she yelled.

'It was a surprise to celebrate your new career as the landlady of a five-star B & B,' said Sally.

'The inspectors haven't been in yet,' said Virginia, delightedly hugging her family.

'But you'll get the top rating, we know it,' Dominic told his mother confidently.

'What's going on here?' asked Laurence, looking around at the people in finery who were milling round excitedly.

'It's a wedding, my friend Delphine's getting married,' Virginia said. 'It will be lovely to have you here. Oh, Eugene's here with Eddie. It's time for the blessing. I do so wish Sam was here. Millie's meant to be a flower girl and she'll kill us all if she doesn't get to be one.'

'This little poppet could be a flower girl,' Mary-Kate said emerging from the house with a tray of glasses full of champagne.

Alison beamed adorably up at all the adults and momentarily stopped pulling her Uncle Jamie's hair.

'We don't want to gate-crash,' Sally said, 'I didn't know the wedding was on today. I thought that was yesterday.'

'Only the civil ceremony,' yelled Delphine, sticking her head out of an upstairs window. 'The more the merrier, I say. So nice to meet you. I'm the bride,' she added unnecessarily, as she was the only one with a wreath of white flowers on her head.

Pauline Ryan checked her reflection in the passenger seat mirror once again. Her lipstick was on fine and there was none on her teeth, but she was conscious of a sense that something wasn't quite right. Looking down at her pale blue lap, Pauline suddenly recognized the culprit: her second-best suit, the blue one she'd bought for a distant relative's wedding five years ago. Despite her best efforts to subdue her guilty feelings, a big wave of guilt kept bobbing up in her mind, like a buoy floating in the harbour. She should have bought a new outfit after all, she thought crossly.

This blue thing had been perfectly suitable until last week, which was when people began to stop her in the street and say how thrilled they were to get an invite to Delphine's wedding, and wasn't Eugene a lovely man and what a great idea to have the reception in Kilnagoshell House. Pauline, who *had* been planning to grace the wedding with her presence after all, was taken aback. In her eyes, this tawdry hole in the corner affair was one which would undoubtedly be shunned by everyone. Her second best outfit would be more than good enough. And now everyone from Miss Murphy to Belle Maguire was gaily telling her she must be proud of Delphine and how they were all in a dither over what to wear because you could never rely on the weather not to turn nasty.

Suddenly, the second best suit wasn't good enough, but when this really hit Pauline, on Friday, it was too late to do anything about it.

She couldn't shame herself by nipping slyly into Lucille's for an outfit. The whole town would find out and she'd be humiliated if they realized that the mother of the bride hadn't bothered to get herself a new suit.

'It's a fine house, isn't it?' said her husband, Fonsie, nervously as he drove up the winding, tree-lined drive to Kilnagoshell. He hated all this fighting. If only he was able to stand up to Pauline. He'd have loved to have told her to stop her nonsense and that he was going to his beloved daughter's wedding, church or no church. But Fonsie was a mild man who stood in awe of his wife.

'It's nice enough,' said Pauline grudgingly, looking at the gracious façade where a rambling rose blossomed sweetly over the portico.

Fonsie parked the car and got out, suddenly eager to see Delphine and hug her. He loved her to bits and thought Eugene was a fine fellow. Of course, Pauline didn't know he'd met Eugene. She'd flip her lid if she did. Fonsie slammed the car door. He was fed up with his wife, and that was the truth.

'I'm going in to Delphine,' he announced.

If the car had spoken to her, Pauline couldn't have been more surprised. Fonsie always did what she wanted and right now, she wanted to mingle and see who'd turned up.

But he was gone, striding into the big house as if he was the squire himself.

Pauline walked around the side of the house to the rose garden and was astonished. There, enjoying one of the most beautiful days of the whole year, was half of Redlion, laughing and chattering and having a whale of a time.

And there, she realized with shock, was Father McTeague, laughing his head off with his flock. Pauline's chest inflated like an angry bullfrog, then deflated just as suddenly. What could she say? He was a man of God, he knew the rules, surely he wouldn't be there if he thought Delphine would suffer eternal damnation for marrying a divorced man?

'Pauline,' he roared, spotting her. 'Come on over here. We thought the mother of the bride would be too busy to spend time with us mere guests.'

Half-smiling weakly, Pauline allowed herself to be led into the group, who all congratulated her on the whole event.

'I can't wait to see her dress,' Miss Murphy sighed romantically. 'Mrs Connell tells me she looks like a fairy princess, isn't that so? You must be so pleased?'

All eyes were on Pauline and for one uncomfortable moment, she wondered did they know that she'd opposed this Godless wedding. No, they couldn't possibly. Giving an airy wave she'd copied from watching Queen Elizabeth on television, Pauline sighed. 'Lovely isn't the word,' she said. 'We're delighted, of course.'

Father McTeague let his breath out and smiled. 'I knew you would be thrilled,' he said, his eyes twinkling. 'Now, I don't think you've met our visitors from London: Sandra, Reenie and Pammy Turner.'

'You look beautiful, Delphine,' said Fonsie, staring at the vision of loveliness that was his only child. Her dress flowed out into a full skirt from a tight bodice. Pale cream with hints of gold thread embroidered in the bodice and bottom of the skirt, it was a glorious dress and Delphine, her hair flowing in luxuriant curls around her shoulders, looked indeed like a fairy princess.

'I'm so sorry about your mother but she's here. I'm sorry I didn't stand up to her,' he said, looking down miserably.

'Nonsense, Dad,' said Delphine kissing him softly on the cheek.

'You're here now and that's all that matters. Will you give me away?'

'Mummy!' yelled Millie, running into the hall in Kilnagoshell House with her flower girl dress on but only half-buttoned. Auntie Sam couldn't do them properly in the back of the car because it was so bumpy.

'Darling Millie!' Hope swept her daughter up joyously. 'I was scared you wouldn't make it. Auntie Delphine is just ready now.'

She spun Millie around and did up her buttons. Then, she picked up the coronet of creamy roses that she'd had waiting for Millie, fixed it on with hair clips, and handed Millie her posy of flowers. 'Ready?'

Millie nodded excitedly.

Hope peered into the hall mirror to see if she looked terrible in her amethyst jacket and trousers. The trousers were too tight and Hope had had to leave the top button undone. She just hoped they didn't fall to the ground at some vital moment, leaving everyone staring at her big knickers and pop socks, a dazzlingly elegant combination. 'Where's Toby?' she asked Millie.

'He's with Daddy.'

'Daddy! What's Daddy doing here?' Hope gasped.

'Coming to the wedding. I was invited, wasn't I?' said Matt. He stood at the door, a tall dark figure with the sun behind him. He'd had his hair cropped too short and he looked tired, but even that couldn't disguise his fierce glamour. And he was all dressed up, in his best suit and the tie Hope had searched Bath for on the occasion of his fortieth birthday. He looked so dear to her that all she wanted to do was rush into his arms and never let go.

'Matt!' squealed Delphine delightedly, coming down the stairs with her father by her side and Mary-Kate bringing up the rear. 'Right. Are we all ready?'

There was no time to say anything. Millie was stationed behind Auntie Delphine and Mary-Kate and Matt and Hope had to rush outside to take their places in the rose garden.

The traditional musicians who played in the Widows struck up the wedding march, which sounded odd on fiddle, accordion and bodhran, but no sound had ever sounded sweeter to Delphine or to Hope.

Delphine stared at her dear Eugene, standing proudly there in his rumpled suit, waiting for her.

Hope stood beside Matt, feeling his hand clutching hers in a vice-like grip. Beside them stood Sam and Toby, who was tired and was leaning against Auntie Ham's knees.

Matt leaned over to Hope. 'I love you,' he whispered.

Hope squeezed his hand even more tightly. All the worry, all the anger seemed to have melted away as she held his hand. 'Please,' was all she could say for fear of floods of tears bursting out.

Virginia stood with her family, little Alison asleep in her arms.

'How do you do that?' asked Jamie in astonishment. 'She's a little terror with everyone else.'

'She knows she's with her granny.' Virginia smiled down at the little girl and stroked her russet curls.

There wasn't a dry eye in the house when Eugene finally leaned down and kissed his bride firmly on the mouth. Even Pauline could be seen to poke around in her handbag for a tissue.

'Have one of mine,' said Mary-Kate, handing one of a travel pack to her sister.

'Glad you came, Pauline?'

Pauline sniffed yes.

'And there'll be no more arguments, right?'

Pauline nodded again.

'Great. Now come into the house with me: as mother of the bride you get to help supervise the catering. We don't want to ruin your reputation, do we?'

'It's a pity Nicole wasn't here,' Reenie said, patting her eyes with a tissue. 'She'd have loved it.'

'She would have,' Sandra agreed, fanning herself with her handbag. 'You are having a nice time, Mum, aren't you?'

'Nice time?' said Reenie. 'That doesn't even describe it. I'm having a grand time. By the way, I had a chat with that nice priest and I told him that my family are long gone but I'd love to trace any other relatives. He's going to give me a hand on Monday. You never know what we might find.'

'Nicole would love that,' Sandra said. 'But what she'd really love is to find her dad.' Reenie patted her daughter's hand. 'There's a time for everything, Sandra, it'll all work out, don't worry. And you did a great job rearing her on your own, anyway, father or no father.'

'Really?' Sandra looked astonished.

'Really.'

While Delphine and Eugene were hugging and kissing everyone, Matt pulled Hope away onto the lawn at the front of the house. Sam, watching and hoping, took Millie and Toby by the hands and suggested finding Dinky for a game.

'Why did you come back today?' Hope asked, still holding Matt's hand tightly.

'Because I've been so stupid,' Matt said. 'I missed you so much, you wouldn't believe it.'

She thought of the sleepless nights and the painful weeks when she thought she'd never be happy again. 'Yes I would. I've missed you too. I thought you'd never come back to me. And I couldn't beg, you understand that.'

'I couldn't understand that for a long time,' he admitted slowly. 'I thought of the old Hope who'd never even *start* an argument and who'd be first to apologize even when it wasn't her fault rather than have a fight lurking in the air. To be honest, I thought you *did* love him, I was sure that was why you didn't phone me every hour, begging me to come back.'

'Oh Matt,' she turned to face him. 'Nothing happened with Christy. I flirted with him, that was all, and I was too stupid to let him know it was just flirting. I didn't love him, I didn't care one iota about him.'

'You're an innocent,' Matt said, stroking her face gently.

He sat her down on the lichen-covered stone seat. 'I knew it all along, really, but I was hurt, my pride was hurt. I couldn't understand how you'd do that to me and I couldn't understand why you didn't beg me to come back.'

'I've changed,' she interrupted. 'If I'd begged you to come back, I would have hated myself for begging and you would have hated me for what you thought went on. You had to forgive me because you'd worked it out for yourself,' she said earnestly.

'When I began to think about it, I did understand a bit,' Matt replied. 'I was pretty shitty to you. I'd left you to cope with everything when we moved here and then I was surprised when having to cope changed you.'

'For the better, I hope,' she said. 'I relied on you too much, now I've learned to rely on myself. Which reminds me, you never even told me the book wasn't working. If you had, I'd have understood why you were so . . .'

'Hard to live with?' Matt supplied, wincing. 'I didn't want to tell anyone that. After all these years of thinking I could do anything, it was a humbling experience to find that I couldn't. I'm sorry. It turned me into a total bastard. It wasn't fair on you. I neglected you and the kids.' His eyes were pained. 'What was killing me was that I was a failure and that you'd soon see I was a failure. I couldn't bear that. I brought you all this way to a strange place, left you alone to deal with it all and I failed at my part of the bargain.'

'You're anything but a failure, Matt,' Hope said, eyes shining. 'You're the man I love, you're not perfect but you're no failure. I'm not perfect myself, you know,' she laughed.

'I know. But I still neglected you and I promise I won't do it again. Especially not now.' He put one hand gently on Hope's swelling belly.

'It's your baby,' she blurted out.

'I know,' he said. 'I know you wouldn't have gone off with another man, I should have given you the benefit of the doubt. Seeing you with him made me freak out and made me feel more like a failure than ever. I wanted to roar off in a rage and get away from everything. I was running away from life not working out here as much as running away from you.' He hung his head. 'If I'd acted sensibly, none of this would have happened.'

'But . . .' Hope was puzzled. 'How did you know I was pregnant?'

'My first inkling was due to Millie thinking that morning sickness is a sign of being a grown up,' he said wryly.

He told her all about the pickle jar contents in the toilet bowl. 'And,' Matt added, 'don't go mad, but Sam phoned me yesterday to tell me to cop on and the pregnancy was discussed.'

Hope rolled her eyes. 'I've spent months telling her not to get involved,' she said. 'I'm amazed.'

'Sam loves you.'

'That's not why I'm amazed. I'm stunned that the pair of you could bury your differences for long enough to talk on the phone.'

'We managed it. She's great with the kids, isn't she? They went mad when they saw her at the airport. It's no joke looking after them. I don't know how you do it,' he said. 'I think we'll have to get a nanny so that when we're off travelling, the kids can be looked after.'

Hope just looked at him. 'What do you mean *get a nanny*? We're broke. We can barely afford a babysitter. Have you got your job back at Judd's?'

'It's a long story,' he said. 'Adam is back and to be honest, I'd find it hard to go back to working for him after so long running the show. So I won't be going back. The only option, under normal circumstances, would be to set up my own agency.'

Hope looked anxious, missing the reference to *under normal circumstances*. That would cost a fortune. How would they cope? 'What do you want to do?'

Matt could barely contain himself. 'My great novel was a bit of a disaster but when I was in Bath, missing you, I started writing this comic novel for fun. It's not literary or anything, but I enjoyed doing it.'

Hope was still staring at him, not sure where this was all going.

'Dan persuaded me to send it off to an agent. I thought he was mad,' Matt commented, 'but I did it, expecting to hear nothing back, to be honest. The day that Millie played morning sickness, I dropped the kids off at Betsey's and went back to the flat to open the post and there it was. A letter from my agent.' He grinned. 'I love saying those words: "my agent". Anyway, a letter from my agent begging me to phone because I had forgotten to put my phone number on the original letter. I phoned up and you won't believe it, he loved the book and he was so excited that he'd already asked a publisher to have a look at it.'

Matt took both Hope's hands in his and looked at her gravely. 'They've offered me a quarter of a million pounds for three books,' he said. 'I've done it, Hope. I'm a writer. It's worked!'

'Oh Matt,' wailed Hope. 'That's so wonderful, I'm so proud of you.' She threw her arms round him and kissed him madly.

'We've got two productions on the go,' whooped Matt, patting her belly.

'Just one thing,' Hope said, suddenly anxious. This was a vital point, but they had to discuss it. 'I'd like to stay in Redlion. It's very important to me. Do you think we can manage that?'

'Leave this oasis of creativity?' said Matt. 'Not likely.'

The first moment Nicole realized that her life had changed inexorably, was when she stepped out of the apartment building on Wednesday afternoon to see a crowd of at least fifteen photographers hoisting their cameras in the air and start clicking madly. Her mobile held to her ear as she spoke to her mother, Nicole looked blindly around to see who the photographers were so keen to photograph. But there was nobody behind her, no superstar in dark glasses attempting to be anonymous. This frantic activity was for her, Nicole Turner.

'Nicole, how does it feel to be tipped to reach number one with your first single?' yelled a female reporter, balancing a tape recorder in one hand and an enormous handbag in the other. 'Will you be phoning Lorelei to tell her or are you still feuding?'

Several more tape recorders were shoved under Nicole's nose.

Nicole blinked in shock and was relieved to feel Isya from Bob Fellowes's office grab her by the arm and haul her off for a quiet word.

'Nicole will be back in a moment,' announced Talia, the tall, commanding publicity woman from LGBK who'd virtually been Nicole's shadow for the previous two weeks of non-stop interviews and performances. 'We've been trying to reach you all morning to tell you,' she said to Nicole.

'We've left so many messages on your mobile,' pointed out Isya.

'I didn't turn it on until just now,' Nicole said, who'd spent her longed-for morning off in bed sleeping off a hectic two weeks of travelling. It had been her first time off in weeks. 'I got such a shock when I came out and saw all of these people . . .'

'We only just got here and we didn't think there'd be any press activity here,' Talia admitted. 'I don't know how they got your home address. We have a photocall set up for tomorrow morning's breakfast television show, I thought that would generate the most interest.'

'But why are they here anyway?' asked Nicole, still in shock. 'The single was only just released on Monday. It's not even in the chart, how can they be talking about the number one slot already.'

Talia allowed herself to smile with pride that all her hard work had paid off. 'The sales have been incredible,' she said. 'We've got the mid-weeks and "Honey, (Don't You Know) I Need You?" has had 50,000 over the counter sales in just two days. That's fantastic. If the single keeps selling this way, you'll definitely be number one and with one of the biggest sales figures ever.'

Nicole could barely take it in.

'Now,' said Talia, glancing at the waiting press, 'I want you to smile, pose and tell them how thrilled you are.'

'Don't mention Lorelei,' begged Isya. 'She *is* with the same management company as you.'

'And she's a right bitch,' Nicole said quietly.

'It's time to be magnanimous in triumph,' advised Talia. 'Lorelei's single was released on Monday too and according to the mid-weeks, the only place it sold well was round the corner from where her mother lives.'

Nicole allowed herself to grin. Served bloody Lorelei right.

She posed for the photographers and Talia said they had time to answer four or five questions. Nicole smiled and told everyone how thrilled she was when asked. Suddenly the question from hell arrived.

'You're half Indian but you never discuss your heritage. Do you think you're copping out of half your heritage by making yourself white?' demanded one journalist.

Talia and Isya both gulped but Nicole was ready for him.

'I've never met my dad,' she said simply, 'that's why I don't know anything about Indian culture, but I'd love to change that. I'm willing to learn, I'm proud of what I am – a little bit of everything.' She smiled that hundred watt smile at them all.

'Interview over,' snapped Talia, whisking Nicole away to the waiting limo.

'You handled that well,' she said admiringly.

Nicole shrugged. 'It was going to come up some time, so let's see what they make of that. I talked it over with Darius, my mum and my gran. We've nothing to be ashamed of and who knows, maybe I'll find my dad after all. I'd like that.'

Talia stared at her. There was no doubt about it, Nicole Turner was very different from the usual girl-with-a-fabulous-voice. Refreshingly different.

'Right,' she said. 'Next,' she consulted her list, 'we've got two press interviews, four radio drive-time interviews, and you've got to get all dolled up like a dog's dinner for the movie premiere tonight. The stylist has a load of great dresses for you to try on, so let's get moving, OK?'

'Yeah,' said Nicole, suddenly not able to stop grinning. Her single was selling brilliantly. How wonderful was that? Even if she didn't get to the unbelievable number one slot, she'd never forget the thrill of this day.


Backstage at *Top Of The Pops*, Nicole looked around her simple dressing room.

'Are you sure there's nothing you want?' asked a beautiful girl whose job it was to make sure that artists had everything their demanding little hearts desired.

Nicole, thinking of the horror stories of singers who insisted on making everyone's life a nightmare with their demands, smiled warmly at the girl.

'The only thing would be some lemon tea and honey for my throat, if that wouldn't be too much trouble,' she said politely.

The beautiful girl sighed with pleasure. If only they were all this easy. When that cow Lorelei had been in, she'd insisted on taking over four dressing rooms for her entourage, wanted six bottles of Krug in each room and had demanded that a top restaurant send over an organic fish dinner at great expense, which she had then only used to stub her cigarettes out in. Nobody had been too upset that Lorelei's single had flopped so spectacularly.

Darius, lounging at the door unnoticed by either of them, looked at Nicole proudly. She was incredible. The stunning looks, the voice of a seductive angel, and she was so sweet to people. Underneath that tough veneer she tried to keep up, she was as soft as butter. And she was going to be a huge star, he was sure of it.

Nicole understood that she wouldn't make it to the top by playing the prima donna. She knew, unlike lots of other people he'd worked with, that carving a career out as a successful star meant hard work, utter commitment and professionalism. So many of the people he met on the scene seemed to think that the only way to the top was to behave appallingly, assuming that rudeness, impossible demands and an ever-growing entourage made them more star-like. In Darius's experience, the bigger the entourage, the bigger the ego.

'Isn't she lovely?' said the *Top of The Pops* girl, coming out of the dressing room.

'She is,' Darius agreed, making Nicole look up in delight.

'You're here!' she said, springing lightly to her feet. She pulled him into the room, shut the door and locked it. 'I've missed you.'

He'd been in Sweden with a new band who were working on their album with the top Swedish producers, so he and Nicole hadn't seen each other all week.

They clung together, moulding their bodies into one. Darius's mouth fastened onto Nicole's eagerly.

'I've missed you so much,' he said hoarsely, holding her tightly to him as if he was afraid to let her out of his arms.

'Oh me too,' Nicole said, resting her head against his chest. It felt so nice there. She'd had such an incredible week, what with the single breaking all records for a debut, but in the midst of all the interviews and performances and signing sessions, Nicole had longed for a quiet evening with Darius where they could cuddle up on her new couch and talk and end up in her big bed to make love.

'Bob Fellowes is waiting outside and Sam's coming later,' Darius said. 'She's so proud of you. So am I,' he added gently. 'You're going to be a big star, darling.'

'Just promise me one thing,' Nicole said.

'Anything.'

'You'll be there for me?'

'I promise.'

It was amazing how much junk one person could accumulate in just a few months, Sam thought as she hoisted the cardboard archive box upstairs to her apartment. She'd cleared her desk at Titus that afternoon and she was sure she'd rupture something from the weight of the junk she'd had to bring home.

'All that minimalist, clean desk policy has to have a down side,' laughed Lydia when she saw Sam going through the overflowing drawers in her desk.

'Yeah, it does,' Sam groaned. 'You shove junk in the desk instead of leaving it on top.'

'See you tomorrow,' Lydia said as she left. 'And don't forget to dress up.'

Lydia was organizing a leaving party for her the next evening. Sam couldn't remember the last time she'd had a leaving party.

In the apartment, she checked her e-mail and was delighted to get a chatty one from Hope.

> Hi Sam,
>
> Hope you're well. We're all wonderful here. Matt is in fabulous form and he's going to be in London next week to sign contracts with the publishers. I hope you can meet up. Virginia and Mary-Kate are driving to Dublin with him. They've decided to fly to Germany and travel round B & Bs to see what standards Virginia should be aiming for. Mary-Kate says she can't wait. She hasn't had a holiday in years. Virginia keeps saying it's because Mary-Kate won't leave Redlion in case the whole place falls apart without her!
>
> We're minding Dinky while Virginia is away, which has Millie in utter delight. She's mad to get a dog and I'm not sure if that's a good idea until the baby's born.

*Dogs can get jealous of babies, they say. Mind you, Matt's keen on a dog too. He says we should get a male dog to balance out the sexes thing. My latest scan shows that the baby's a girl (we like Rosalie as a name, what do you think?) and he says that there'll be two males as opposed to three females unless we get a male dog to balance things! Honestly, what is he like?*

*We're going out to dinner with Eugene and Delphine tonight. They're back from honeymoon and Delphine is mad to show off her tan. My other bit of good news comes courtesy of Delphine, who says that slimy Christy has left the hotel for good. He carried on like he owned the hotel but even managers are expendable. On the phone, Delphine said it was something to do with a nasty scene with a guest's girlfriend round about the time you were over. There was some talk of a law suit and the owners fired him. I'm not surprised. I'll have to drag her into the restaurant loo tonight to get the full story from her.*

*How are Reenie, Sandra and Pammy? Everyone here loved them and says they have to come back again. And we'd all love to meet Nicole. Isn't it wonderful the way her single is still number one? It's never off the radio here, so her only problem if she came here is that she'd be mobbed walking down the street.*

*Do phone soon, I haven't spoken to you in ages,*
*Love Hope.*

Sam smiled as she turned the computer off. It was wonderful that everything had worked out for dear Hope. Sam couldn't help wishing that things had worked out for her too. Still, she scooped up Tabitha from the floor and kissed her, she had the cats and her new company. She'd keep herself busy, that was the trick. When the cats were fed, she decided to drop across the road to see Felicity and George in the Greenwich Emporium. They'd loved her ideas for making their business profitable and were her first clients in Spike Solutions. She'd spent ages trying to think up a name for the new company and it was only when Spike had climbed onto the table and lain down on the paperwork that Sam had given in.

She picked up her notes, put them in her briefcase, and left the apartment. It was a warm evening and as Sam opened the front gate, she looked automatically at Morgan's house. The sign was down now. It was sold. She wondered where he was.

George and Felicity were run off their feet as it was Thursday evening. After fifteen minutes discussing her plan, they said they'd have to run because they were nearly fully booked.

'Stay and eat,' insisted George.

'No,' said Sam. 'I won't be very cost effective if I keep eating into your profits.'

'Sit,' commanded George. 'A carafe of red?'

Sam forked up rocket salad and read her notes, stopping only to put down the fork and take another sip of wine. The restaurant was buzzing, mainly couples gazing deep into each other's eyes. Felicity and George waved at her whenever they passed, which somehow made her feel even more alone.

Her notes began to blur as she thought back over the past few weeks. So much had happened in her professional life. She'd undergone a total revolution work-wise, yet her private life was as unchanged as ever. She didn't know how she'd have coped without Spike and Tabitha to go home to. Their feline adoration made life bearable and when she felt down, she gathered Tabitha up in her arms and stroked the tabby cat until Spike appeared, outraged at being unloved.

'Oh my goodness,' gasped Felicity, rushing past with wine and a bottle opener.

Sam looked up to see Felicity blushing as pink as the bottle of rosé she was carrying. Sam knew only one person who had that effect on Felicity.

Morgan stood behind her. Large as life and instantly making people look up in the crowded restaurant.

In shock, Sam spilled her wine. It dripped ruby red all over the tablecloth, looking like a bullet wound in a bad movie. She could only stare at it, feeling her pulse rocketing up to marathon-running level in an instant.

'I'll get a cloth,' said Felicity and whisked off.

Sam looked up at Morgan. He was tanned and healthy looking, as if he'd just stepped off a plane from somewhere hot. He was wearing his wrecked old jeans and a soft grey shirt that revealed some of the strong chest that Sam sometimes dreamed about. His hair was shorter, though still a million miles away from a short back and sides. But his face was the same: the hawk nose giving him the look of some medieval conquistador, the narrowed treacly eyes surveying her. If he'd turned up on a crusader horse with a broadsword in one hand, Sam wouldn't have been at all surprised.

'May I sit down?'

She waved at him to do so. She wasn't being rude: it was just that she couldn't find words. Finally, her voice came back to her.

'How have you been?' she said, knowing she sounded incredibly distant but not able to help herself. She was too stunned by his appearance to say anything intelligent.

'I've been miserable,' he announced. 'Miserable as hell and it's all your fault.' A couple of people looked round.

Sam was still mute.

'That's why I'm here: to take it out on you, Ms Smith.' He got to his feet, and then sank to his knees. Everyone was now looking. People didn't get on their knees in front of other people much these days, certainly not in restaurants.

Sam stared at him, shocked.

'It's all her fault, you see,' Morgan announced even more loudly, for the benefit of the audience, who had now all stopped pretending to eat and were watching happily.

'You're prickly, you boss me around, you think my taste in clothes is execrable.'

Sam flushed with each remark.

'But despite all that, and despite the fact that you seem to think I'm the least discriminating lover since Casanova, I'm crazy about you.'

Sam wasn't sure she could have heard him right.

'Did you get that?' Morgan asked the couple next door who were listening so shamelessly that they'd moved their chairs to get a better view.

'Oh yes,' said the woman, admiringly. 'She bosses you around but you like it?'

'Not like it so much,' said Morgan in considering tones, 'but I love her, so you see I can cope with it.'

'Aaah,' went up the cry around the restaurant.

'Not too much bossing around,' insisted the male half of the couple.

'Not too much,' agreed Morgan. 'Just a little bit because then, we can fight. I can show her that I am in charge, naturally, being a man, and then,' he gazed at Sam with a look so hot it could have scorched all the linen in the restaurant, 'we can make up. Which is the best bit,' he breathed.

Sam was glad he could breathe: she couldn't.

'Making up is the best bit, isn't it?' he said, moving closer to her. 'I'm getting too old for this,' he said as his knees creaked. 'My joints aren't up to it.'

'Cod liver oil is great for that,' volunteered a woman at the table on the other side.

'Do you want to make up?' said Morgan. He was so close, she could smell the sweet mintiness of his breath and it reminded her of the first time they met.

'I'm sorry I got the wrong idea about Maggie,' she gasped.

'Maggie is wonderful but she thinks it's acceptable to have a crush on her stepfather – it's very embarrassing, not to mention inappropriate in this day and age seeing as I'm her stepdad,' Morgan said. 'She does it to play Val and me off against each other, and you walked in at the wrong time.'

'I'm so sorry,' Sam said again.

'Stop saying sorry,' Morgan commanded. 'I'm not used to hearing you say it.'

She laughed and slapped him playfully on the arm.

'Oh, hit me again, I like it,' he growled.

Then he leaned forward and kissed her so hard that Sam could feel every inch of her body quivering with lust.

Only the sound of applause made them draw apart.

'Show's over,' said Morgan, getting creakily to his feet. He pulled Sam up from her seat. 'We're going home to make up.'

'George, Felicity, I owe you for dinner . . .' began Sam helplessly.

'It's fine,' said George, looking like a cat who'd got the cream.

'But I want to . . .'

'Shoo,' beamed Felicity.

'Don't come back until you're married,' yelled an elderly man near the restaurant door.

Morgan shoved the door open and they were on the street, the sounds of everyone clapping and whooping behind them.

'What did you do that for?' gasped Sam, feeling her heartbeat get back to normal.

Morgan took her hand in his and Sam's heartbeat raced again.

'To shock you into realizing how I feel about you. If I'd met you on the street, you would have gone all formal and behaved like the perfectly in control MD.'

'I wouldn't,' she protested.

'You would,' he insisted. He took a deep breath. 'It's taken me a long time to tell you but I've been attracted to you ever since I met you. You came into my life like this raging fury, a small blonde dynamo who wrenched my stereo plug out and gave me a bruise the size of a melon on my shin.' He pulled up his jeans to show her the spot.

'Big baby,' she retorted, 'I was only wearing espadrilles. It hurt me much more than it hurt you.'

'Possibly.'

This time, his arm went round her shoulders and it felt only natural for Sam to slip her free arm around his waist as they walked.

'You are totally different from any other woman I've ever met,' Morgan continued.

'Is that good or bad?' she asked.

'Good,' he replied.

They crossed the road and ended up standing outside Sam's apartment building, right beside Morgan's old house.

'I couldn't believe you'd sold it,' she said, gazing up at the beautifully restored house.

'I haven't. The sale fell through. I've decided to live here. If I can find the right person to live in with me.'

Sam felt a quiver of excitement run down her spine.

'And I found your apology,' he added. 'It had been shoved in a drawer. I think I'll have it framed. And enlarged.'

Sam laughed.

'You know, for a woman who's supposed to be cool and make calm decisions, you're very hot-headed, Ms Smith,' he continued. 'You jumped to all sorts of conclusions when you came in that night of Maggie's party. You thought I was some ageing lothario when all I was doing was giving up my home to my stepdaughter for the night. And you thought that Maggie was my girlfriend.'

'You never told me the truth,' objected Sam. 'If you'd given me all the facts, it would have been different.'

'At first, I'd just got divorced and had spent months giving people the facts,' Morgan said with a shrug. 'I wanted to be Mr Anonymous and steer a wide berth away from women. Until this fiery next-door neighbour came into my life and refused to let go, totally screwing up my plan to have a female-free existence.'

Sam felt the wild grin going out of control on her face. She was beaming, she just knew it.

'But Maggie – how could you get that wrong, Sam? When you saw me with Maggie, I couldn't believe you'd really think we were going out. She's just a kid.'

'I know,' mumbled Sam, 'but I was beginning to think you'd never make a move and I was depressed about being forty and . . .' her voice tailed off. She realized that she'd never normally make an admission like that to anyone but, with Morgan, it felt right.

Morgan led her up the path to his house. 'I daresay that I'm the only person in the entire world who knows that behind that sleek exterior is a total pussycat with a soft centre.'

'I'm not a pussycat,' Sam said.

Morgan smiled as he opened the door. 'OK, a wild cat, then. Soft and fluffy looking but with deadly claws.'

'You ever call me fluffy again, and you'll be sorry,' she warned, deadpan.

Morgan raised both hands in resignation. 'What can I call you? Darling, perhaps?'

He stood in front of her and Sam gazed up at him expectantly.

'No,' said Morgan firmly. 'Something's wrong.'

'What?' Sam said, puzzled.

Morgan led her through into the dining room which was free of furniture except for a stereo in one corner. Sam burst into laughter as soon as she saw it.

'Now,' said Morgan happily, 'this is where it all began.' He lowered his head to hers and finally kissed her, deeply. It was every bit as wonderful as Sam had dreamed it would be and she held onto him tightly, loving the sensation of being able to run her fingers through his tousled hair. Her eyes closed, she gave herself up to the feeling of Morgan's body close to hers and the sensation of his beautiful mouth kissing her fiercely as though she might vanish at any moment.

'I'm sorry,' he sighed when he pulled his mouth away from hers, 'sorry it's taken us this long. We were both stupid. I should have been honest with you at first and not kept you in the dark about everything. I was so angry you couldn't trust me and I wanted to forget you but I couldn't, I've got you under my skin . . .'

'Shush,' Sam put a finger over his mouth. 'Let's not look back, let's look forward,' she said, and this time she kissed him, covering his face with kisses until he groaned and pulled her so tightly against him that she was standing on her tiptoes.

'Promise me one thing?' he murmured into the cloud of her hair.

'Yes.'

'Don't kick me.'